Sov

BROTHERS

CHAYYM ZELDIS

RANDOM HOUSE   NEW YORK

Library of Congress Cataloging in Publication Data
Zeldis, Chayym, 1927-
Brothers.
I. Title.
PZ4.Z46Br   [PS3576.E44]   813'.5'4   75-40555
ISBN 0-394-40331-2

Manufactured in the United States of America
2 4 6 8 9 7 5 3
First Edition

To my wife, Nina, who flowered where only nettles grew . . .

In the beginning was the deed . . .

PART

I

My village lay halfway up the eastern flank of a mountain. Approaching it from the valley at dawn, you saw a cluster of houses emerging from the mist like wraiths, and your heart trembled until you realized what they were. No matter how many times you had been to the village, you were always afraid until you knew the shapes you saw were houses and not dead men opening their arms to you.

As you walked up the hoof-worn path that twisted right and left around the boulders and clefts, the rude stone dwellings and mud animal sheds turned slowly white. On foot, you reached the village by noon, when it shimmered with heat. You went by dogs curled in the dust, their tongues swollen purple with thirst and exhaustion, and donkeys in dirty flakes of straw, their flanks ceaselessly twitching with the flies that crawled over them. None of the villagers was to be seen: it was as if the earth had swallowed them alive.

My house was highest of all. None was above it and no other on its flanks. Like a fortress, it sat with its back to a sheer rise of cliff in which eagles had built their nests. A wide courtyard fronted the house, with fig, pomegranate and loquat trees planted along its low rock walls. To one side was a shed where we kept the livestock, and to the other a grape arbor and a run for fowl. Over the door, chiseled in stone, was my father's name: Evenezer.

I remember that he had chiseled his name with his own hands, and I remember the day that he did it. He had had the stone for the house brought up from the quarry in the valley instead of using mountain rock as they did in the poorer homes, and he'd had the stones hewn by swarthy cutters who worked from sunrise to sunset with scarcely a stop. The pale blue mosaic tiles for the floors had been brought in oxcarts from Jerusalem and been laid by a squat hunchbacked recluse who lived in a cave some distance from the village and worked for no man but my father. The day the house was finished, all of the villagers stood in the courtyard and out in the terraces below, watching my father with hammer and chisel in his big, earth-stained hands. I was a mere child then and stood close by as, standing on the shoulders of two servants, he drove the letters of his name into the lintel. He hammered with short, vicious strokes, and his long, hollow-cheeked, gray face was tense. Several times he cursed the servants for moving. Only once did he laugh: when rock dust tumbled down into my upturned open mouth and choked me.

As a child, I adored my mother. She was ten years younger than my father—a volatile, strapping woman, full of energy and bustle, with dark, thick hair that fell almost to her waist. She had large, warm hands, small but well-shaped, and very radiant eyes, and a loud hearty laugh that could be heard from one end of the house to the other. I followed her everywhere, missed her when I was away from her, and devoured her with my eyes when she was in sight. I was never able to understand how she tolerated a man like my father. Often, at night, when she sang to me in her throaty voice before I slept, I asked her why she did not run away from him and take me with her. Though she smiled and squeezed my shoulder, I could feel her body grow tense.

When I was seven, a brother was born. I knew what her swelling belly meant and watched it suspiciously, with an anger I could scarcely suppress. Slowly but surely I began to withdraw from my mother, who failed, in her own burgeoning happiness, to understand or oftentimes even to notice that I was sullen and vexed. As an overwhelming act of revenge, I turned to my father, though at a distance. Through the months of my mother's pregnancy I followed him on his rounds. I trailed after him to our vineyard on the lower slope of the mountain, and to our rye and barley fields in the valley. I stood in the nettles at the fringe of the rows and watched him as he oversaw the work.

When he beat servants and laborers who malingered or were insolent, my heart beat so that my whole chest pained, and I clenched my fists with secret anguish and pleasure. I watched his sinewy brown forearms and callused knuckles as they pumped through the air, flailing the bent heads and backs beneath them with the same fierce motions he had used to drive the characters of his name into the stone above our door. Sometimes he drew blood, and I moved closer to see how the flesh had opened or what look there was in the eyes of the victim. Crows sped over the ripening grain, and their hoarse cries mingled with those of the broken man.

Once a week I rode along after him to the market in the next village, which was much larger than ours. I jabbed my donkey's hindquarters with a short stick I had whittled from a branch to dagger sharpness so that I could keep the jiggling gray rump of Father's mule always in view. The ride was long, the sun a blazing inferno, the flies a scourge, and I invariably arrived dust-covered, parched and weary. But I felt it was all worth it because it expressed my hatred for Mother. I hated her the more because, ecstatic with the new fruit she was bearing, she was not even aware of my hatred.

Now when she entered my room at night to wish me pleasant dreams, I feigned sleep. She left without knowing I was really awake, and I tossed in agitation for what seemed an eternity. One night about a month before she gave birth, when exhaustion at last overcame me and I slept, I dreamed that she stood naked before me and I held a chisel to her belly, swollen like an enormous cake of yeast, about to cut my name into her flesh. I awoke in a cold sweat, moaning. By my bed stood a dark form with an upraised arm.

"I thought I heard a thief in your room," my father said through clenched teeth. And he sheathed his knife and left.

The day she gave birth, Mother's screams ran through the house as before her laughter had. Servants rushed from the kitchen to the bedchamber and back again. An old woman with hair the color of cobwebbing made her appearance. I ran

5

out and down the slope to a spot in a terrace wall where dislodged stones formed a niche. I crawled under the long yellow needles of a cactus, brushed out the spider webs and squeezed into my shelter. I covered my ears with my hands, but still Mother's screams reached me. After a time I twisted out of the hole and peered over the wall. Avner, the most trusted servant, rushed from the house to the shed, his cloak flying, and rode out on Father's mule at a gallop.

Then Mother's voice called my name. She repeated it time after time. Father came out of the house, his face the color of wet clay. I slid back, hunched into the niche, and held my breath until I grew faint. Mother's screams grew softer and finally faded away. I did not leave my hiding place until evening. The sky was deep blue, turning black. There was a pale gold crescent moon cast over our house. I gazed up at it and thought of my mother's belly.

As the moon waxed, my newborn brother—red, squalling, with a chin that resembled my father's—grew while my mother wasted away. Avner had finally come back from Bethlehem, the nearest town, with a doctor. That was near midnight. He had delivered the baby as Caesar himself had been delivered, but it was too late. My mother had already crossed some invisible, fatal point beyond which there was no turning back. I saw her several times during the days that followed. She was extremely weak and did not at all resemble the woman I had known all my life. Her eyes had lost their luster, and her skin, almost transparent, was drawn tautly over the bones of her face like a hide on the rack for curing. Her cracked, shriveled lips faltered when she tried to smile, and tears wet her sunken cheeks. Beside her the infant cried faintly until the wet nurse took him in her fleshy red arms.

I went to my mother only when ordered to do so by my father. Otherwise, I absented myself. I took myself every place that I could think of: to the vineyard on the slope and the fields in the valley, to the well and to a wadi across the valley. Once I went alone to the next village and wandered its dusty streets aimlessly, rousing the dogs, but I found no peace. My mother had gone into labor on Monday. On Friday, for the first time in my life, I disobeyed an express command of my father: I ventured up the mountain above our house, which I had been forbidden to do under pain of the most severe punishment. I made certain that I was unobserved and started up by a path I had seen shepherds occasionally use. The going was rough, and I needed all the breath and dexterity I could muster. It was clear that at this height and beyond, the mountain was no longer hospitable to man. The rocks were split and jagged and sometimes they moved, making the footing treacherous. I held to clumps of grass and infrequent bushes, sweating as I climbed, for the path was steep and there were sheer drops, often unexpected, of hundreds of feet. I kept on, never looking back, feeling that here you needed wings or claws to survive.

I was determined to get to the peak, but of course I was to get nowhere near it. Behind a giant boulder which lightning had rent almost in two, a chasm blocked my way, and I could go no further. The great, yawning abyss fell dizzily almost to the height of the roof of my house, and I dared to approach it only by inching forward on my stomach. I reached the edge, carefully thrust my head out and peered down. Far below, on rocks black and sharp as canine teeth, I saw two or three complete skeletons, human bones, and a number of human skulls severed from their trunks.

This grisly sight, far from dismaying me, was fascinating and aroused my curiosity. The bones strewn over the bottom of the pit had long ago been picked clean by vultures. I stared at them almost greedily, wondering who the dead men had been and whether they had been slain by thieves or assassins or Romans and hurled down, or whether they had fallen accidentally to their deaths. In my mind I rearranged the bones to form corpses, bloody and torn as the men and women my father whipped. Then I reconstructed living men from the dead bodies and imagined how they had been tortured and finally slaughtered. And finally, gasping with excitement, I did the killing with my own hands.

Hours passed and I did not stir from my reveries. Over me, eagles screamed. From the valley I heard the sound of the cattle returning from pasture. Slowly the light of day failed and the skeletons began to lose their shapes. I gazed downward. The skulls looked like babies cradled in rock. A slight breeze stirred the heavy air. I rubbed my eyes, rose stiffly and with great caution picked my way down the path I had ascended hours ago. When I arrived home, I found that my mother was dead.

A tiny oil lamp flickered in the corner of the room where her shrouded body lay. My father, his clothes rent, stared fixedly at her form as if by the severity and steadfastness of

7

his gaze he could raise her to life. The servants crowded just outside the door, weeping hoarsely. It was unbearably hard to sit where I was and not stir, but I dared not move from my place. My father's face froze my blood: I saw that he had crossed into a territory of which I knew nothing.

The village elders were admitted to the house, and my father rose from his post when they entered the room, the oldest at their head. Two or three of them glanced over at me, and I did not turn away my eyes but met their gaze head on. Behind the anxiety I felt, there was a satisfaction so keen that it was almost painful to me. My mother, I felt, had deserted me long ago for her baby, so this further desertion was of no real account. I looked at her in the unsteady light, which sent monstrous shadows over the walls. She had a gross shape, like that of a fish. The winding sheet was wrapped around a belly that had gone flat again. Inside me, there was a sound that came near to laughter.

I thought I would never sleep—never again as long as I lived. I lay stiffly on my back, as *she* lay, in an unremitting agony of expectancy, for what I could not fathom. After a time I found myself to be in a strange, disturbing state between sleep and waking, perhaps between life and death. From the chamber where *she* slowly hardened in her linen shroud I heard the voices of the living, and at the same time I listened to soft mutterings from a world beyond this one. The darkness stirred—a muddy chaos out of which the shapes of my fear would emerge. I could not stop myself from blinking, and then found that my eyes were somehow drawn to a far corner of the room in which I became ever more certain someone or something was standing. I felt no terror, only an uneasy curiosity.

How much time passed I did not know. At length, from the corner I had been watching, my mother came forth. Wrapped in the cerements of the grave, she stood by my bed. She was rigid and silent. But I knew that she would speak if I spoke to her first. I knew that only my tongue could free hers. I sat up and looked at her coldly. She stretched out her hands to me and I moved back: I did not want to be touched. She motioned, imploring me without words to say something to her. When I finally did, it was not because she desired it but because I was curious.

"What is it you want, Mother?"

"For you to come with me," she said, sighing with relief.

"To come where?"

"I cannot tell you. You must follow me blindly—without asking, without knowing."

"Why?"

"I cannot say that either. It isn't permitted. But you must decide what you want to do. For I must leave shortly."

We stared at each other, once again in silence, and then she turned abruptly and made for the door of the room. I could not remain. I jumped out of bed and followed her as I was. Most of the servants were asleep in the hall. A few were still awake, weeping. As we passed the open door of the death chamber, I looked in. The elders had all gone away. Only the professional mourners were there, tirelessly intoning psalms. My father sat immobily in his place, his hands on his lap, his face alternately lit and shadowed by the erratic flame of the oil lamp. The bier was empty of my mother's body, but no one seemed to take notice of it.

Outside, the night air was pleasingly cool. My mother led the way, never once looking behind her, and I followed as if linked to her. Our feet cracked twigs on the earth. When we went past the animal shed, the dog leashed to a metal ring there shrank back in horror with a howl that died stillborn in its throat, its eyes rolling up into its skull. My mother walked very swiftly, and I had almost to run in order to keep up with her. We had not gone far when I realized exactly where we were heading: the very mountain path I had taken that afternoon in defiance of my father's orders.

One after the other, we climbed. Our feet dislodged pebbles and small rocks. My mother did not diminish her pace in the least; she seemed absolutely certain of her direction and her footing. I had no choice but to trust in her sureness. The sweat started from my forehead and trickled down from my neck and shoulders into the hollow of my back; my calves began to ache, and my straining lungs felt as if they were going to burst, but I was determined to keep the dim white curve of her spine in my view. Thus we reached the boulder and then the chasm directly behind it. My mother neither halted nor hesitated for an instant. Instead, she strode to the very edge and stepped off. Terrified by what I knew was out there, I hung back.

"Don't be afraid—you won't fall," my mother said without looking back at me.

I stared unbelievingly and watched her form float forward over the void.

"Come," her voice called thinly. "Come after me."

"I can't."

"Come after me—you need not fear."

Drifting as if the earth had no claim to her, she was by now half-way across the abyss. Her shroud, which had become partially un-raveled about the ankles, caught the luminescence of the moon. Inside me, a voice mocked my fear: the nagging voice of my curiosity. I wanted to scream with rage as I saw that she was disappearing; instead, trembling in all of my limbs, I flung myself headlong over the lip of the chasm. I expected the worst, but I too floated, rushing after her as if I were a feather on a current of air. Below me as I went, the bones and skulls of murdered men glittered among the rocks at the bottom of the pit; over me, they were mirrored in the sky as its stars.

My feet touched down on the rocky face of the other side. Far ahead of me my mother's form was fading into the dark. I exerted all of my strength to catch up with her and succeeded in narrowing the gap between us. My legs were cut and bleeding. A pack of jackals fled wildly by me as I climbed, rushing downward in panic and leaving their ghostly cries to hang in the chill air of the heights.

When she reached the peak, my mother stopped and stood quite still. I remained at a distance from her. Above our heads, arching over us, the sky flowed like a river whose depths could not be plumbed. To the east, huddling atop the hills, were banks of clouds. The moon had gone down and the stars glittered more fitfully than ever, as if they had devoured its brightness among their host. I could make out the houses of the next village nestling in the valley, and far beyond it just perceive the place where Bethlehem lay slumbering in shadow.

"Can you hear me?" my mother said.

"I hear you."

"Obey me."

I said nothing.

"Stay where you are. You mustn't move."

"And if I disobey?"

"Stay in your place," said my mother, her voice falling to a whisper. "As I tell you." She sank to her knees.

Something in me wanted to laugh, but a chill came over me. I felt pressure at the base of my skull, as if a cruel strong hand such as my father's had grasped the back of my neck and was slowly squeezing. Tears stung my eyes; I felt my cheeks wet with them and I was ashamed. I struggled to control my voice as I spoke: "Why did you marry my father?"

"You have no right to question me."

"Why did you bear his child?"

"What are you saying? You are his son as well."

"Liar! I am not his son. You know I'm not his son!"

My mother groaned and fell forward on her face. My anger blazed. I wanted to say more to her, but the words stuck in my throat. I shivered with sudden cold, and unwillingly, as if invisible hands forced me down, dropped to my knees. The vast canopy of sky flickered and turned pale: in its watery reaches, the stars floated like jellyfish. My scalp crawled as a hideous creature flew down from it and alighted before my mother. He was stooped and bowlegged and his skin was covered with reptile scales. Under his feet the earth was black, as if scorched by fire. His face was that of a very old man; he seemed weary as he bent over.

"Your time has come," he said to my mother.

"I know, I know," she answered softly.

"You must quit this world never to return again, depart from this earth never to see it again."

"I know that."

"You are sorry?"

My mother tried to raise herself up from the ground but did not have the strength. "I am sorry to leave my sons," she gasped. "They are the fruit of my loins."

I wanted to protest but my mouth was unable to form the words.

"You will forget your sorrow," the creature said. "You will forget there was such a thing as sorrow. Nor need you worry about your sons. They will forget you."

My mother moaned softly.

"This is your son who has followed you here?"

"Yes."

"Why have you brought him to this place, into my presence?"

"That he may behold the angel of death and fear for his life every moment he lives it. That he may purge his young soul of hate and honor his life and that of others."

"I see," said the creature. "Then I will give him a good look."

And the sky brightened yet more and he lifted his countenance unto me so that I could view it clearly: I saw before me the face of a corpse writhing with maggots that had eaten it half away, and I saw that from the vacant eye sockets a black fluid ran and did not cease from running. Then, with the bray of a jackass, the creature split in twain and I beheld the naked forms of man and woman confronting each other. The man was short and squat, with bald head and barrel chest, and the woman tall and thin, with pendulous breasts and wasted thighs. The two regarded each other in silence and suspicion; then each took a step toward the other. Instantly a serpent sprang from the man's crotch and struck at the woman. Again and again it lashed out at the woman, who seemed to be paralyzed with the poison it injected. She tried to retreat but instead fell to the ground. And the man dropped heavily upon her, a dagger now protruding in place of the snake. The woman screamed as his blade bit into her soft place. And then I heard the creature's laugh and saw the woman's body swell and engulf the man's, and then all burst and there was nothing before my eyes but barren rock. I was alone on the mountaintop. I rose and went to the spot where my mother had conversed with the angel of death. Only gray-white ash remained. And a dark wind brushed through the new darkness of the heavens from the east, from the direction of Bethlehem, and whirled it straight up into the air. I watched it mount and saw the last traces of it disappear among the failing stars.

Startled, a flock of sparrows flew from the roof of the animal shed and wheeled sharply over the house and went down toward the valley. First came the mourners, chanting as if their voices were rafts on which they had flung their lives. My father and five elders carried the bier. My father walked stiffly, his head held back, looking neither right nor left. Behind came the rest of the elders, in a tight group; the villagers, men first and women after; and finally the servants and hired hands. I walked by my father, conscious of the many eyes on me and setting my face into a mask.

The cemetery was beyond the last house of the town, surrounded by tamarisks and cypresses. A starling called raucously as we approached and took off from his perch with an insolent flapping of his wings. Avner and three other servants had been digging in the soft red earth for several hours, and they stood impassively by the heaps of soil, waiting. The body went swiftly into the grave; a loud cry went up from the crowd. Several of the women pressed forward. The prayers were spoken, and the oldest man in the village, soon to keep the same appointment, signaled for the hole to be covered. My father grimaced as clods rained down upon the winding sheet. But I made no sound. I looked coldly at the faces of the villagers, each stamped with its own particular mark of grief, fear or indifference, and then raised my eyes to the peak of the mountain. It was calm, commanding and untouch-able—as one day I would be. Then, lowering my eyes, I caught sight of movement on the grassy ground. A small brown-and-gray toad hopped close to my foot. I stepped on it and kept my foot there until the grave was covered.

On a warm day in May shortly after my eighth birthday, my father announced that he was journeying to Jerusalem and that he would return in three days. Though I knew by his mien that I should keep silent, that it would in no way avail, I asked my father to take me along. He was sitting at the table, finishing his noon meal. A half-empty carafe of wine was in one hand and a goblet in the other. He set the goblet down, sighed and called me over to him. His voice was steady and level, his face grave. When I stepped within reach, he slapped me so hard across the cheek I nearly fell to the floor. Then he filled his goblet.

The new tendrils of the grapevines, piteously green, twisted through the lattices of the arbor. A bee droned among the crossbeams, sailing away and then returning. I stood and watched as my father, Avner and a second servant rode out on the road going northward toward Jeru-salem, the dust from their mounts' hooves rising thick and yellow in the air. I watched until I could discern no mark of their passing, until not a single mote of dust remained, and then, relieved, I sauntered slowly through the streets of the village.

By an open field, I halted. A month ago I had killed a cat there. The cat had come out of the weeds suddenly, and on an impulse I had coaxed it to me. I stroked its head and back, intending no harm until the urge to kill it came over me. I made certain beforehand that no one was about. Then, still petting the animal with one hand, I reached out and picked up a sharp stone with the other. How strange it was! The cat had stared calmly at the hand with the rock in it, ready for the blow that seconds later would smash its skull in. It mewed and gazed up trustingly at the instrument of death without fear, without realization. Like men, I thought.

I had brought the rock down and made sure the job was well done. The flies were immediately attracted by the blood and buzzed around the wound. I had risen smartly and left, thinking that later the ants would come and then the maggots: a host of insects to share the remains. Like men. And I had wanted to tell someone about what I had done. But there was no one I could trust, no one.

Now, just past the last house on this edge of the village, a miserable hovel that housed animals and people alike, I caught sight of the crooked little man whom my father had hired to hew the stones for our house. He appeared suddenly out of nowhere, seeming to hobble along, though in truth he walked as straight as any man. I feared lest he slay me as I had slain the cat. Who would know? And what would it avail me if someone did know, if I were already dead? I pictured myself with a rent skull, covered with green-bellied flies and lying in my own sticky blood. How sharp the hunchback's tools were; they jangled in a worn sack slung over his shoulder. But then I ceased fearing: if he came at me, I would retreat. And if he ran I would certainly escape him, as I was the swiftest of runners. He passed silently, smiling toothlessly at me, his open mouth gaping at me like the hole I had opened in the cat's head. There was an odd look of complicity in his eyes which I did not like at all. I did not acknowledge him but turned quickly away, averting my eyes, and went down another path. I did not trust any man who had been hired by my father.

The way led to the cemetery, and without realizing it, I found myself alone among the graves. I stopped. Brilliant orange-and-black and pale-white butterflies cut through the air. Cicadas sang in a chorus. I had not been here since the day my mother was buried. I began to walk about. I found her grave at once and bent to touch the earth: it was soft from a recent rain and crumbled easily in my hands. I trembled. I knew the passing seasons of the living world would in turn dissolve and harden the crust of the grave in which my mother lodged; and that the passing days of time would wear the face of the tombstone of memory in the hearts and minds of those who had known her and whose lives were touched in one way or another by her life. She would be paler than when she died. She would be deader than before. But still she would hear the weeping of human children, still her unsleeping womb would contract with pain. Something inside me wanted to talk to my mother, to speak harshly to her, to accuse her. But I remained without speaking. I recalled that when I returned home from killing the cat my father pointed to my tunic near the right shoulder and asked me what the spot was there. It was blood, and I knew better than to deny it to my father. I told him I had struck my nose.

Then my mood changed. I felt that I was rooted to the spot, that I would not be able to get up and leave when I wished it. I was terrified. A feeling of great longing for my mother welled up in me, and I hated it. I felt as if I would be destroyed by the longing, as if it would choke or crush me to death. I felt that I would not survive if the longing were to get any stronger. I'd had such longing as a very small child, when I was close to my mother, when I adored her and believed that she would never deceive me. I loathed the feeling because it caused me to be soft and weak. I trembled; I fought the longing with all of my strength, and yet a part of me wanted to succumb to it, to allow myself to be annihilated. I looked down at the earth of the grave and thought that I would like to bury my hatred there. But I thought that to lose my hatred would be to lose myself. I struggled harder and vanquished the weakness. The longing left me and I was myself again, stronger than ever.

To the other side of the windrow on the northern fringe of the cemetery I saw something moving. My curiosity was aroused, so I rose quickly to investigate. Crouching low, I made my way noiselessly to the line of trees. Long ago I had learned to keep hidden whenever possible: it gave me options on the future I should not otherwise have had. I parted two branches carefully and peered through. There were two men I recognized at once: one a shepherd from the next village and the other a servant from my own. The former received a small, bleating lamb from the latter and hurried on his way. The lout from my village slunk away. I laughed to myself. What I had witnessed would be very useful.

I had also recognized the marking on the lamb. That very evening I went to see the man from whom the animal had been stolen. He was a short, fat man, with small greedy eyes and a hanging lower lip, whom my father thoroughly disliked. He was very surprised to see me in his home, and he eyed me with great suspicion as I entered the room. He had hastily covered something on the table before him; I knew instinctively that he had been counting money and wished to conceal the fact from me. The thought of the heaps of coins under the cloth took away my breath for the moment.

"Well, what the devil do you want?" he asked brusquely. "What is so urgent?"

"I want . . . to see you, Shimon," I stammered.

"To see me about what? Is this some sort of a poor joke that you come and stand before me gaping like a scarecrow? If you have a purpose, then speak to the point, you little fool!"

I muted both my confusion and my anger. "It's about your lamb," I said slowly, in order to control myself. "The one that was stolen today."

His face grew a deep red and his nostrils dilated. "How did you know a lamb was stolen from me? No one steals from Shimon—no one!"

I shrugged. "Well, then, Shimon, if no one steals lambs with your markings on them, then I have nothing to tell you."

He rose unsteadily from his seat, half dragging the cloth from the table; I could see the neat round edges of several stacks of coins. Shimon breathed hoarsely. His stubby fingers, each one of them beringed, clutched his coarse tunic. When I saw him that way—scarcely taller than I even though he had drawn himself up to his full height, with his blubbery lower lip hanging down and his tiny eyes almost lost in the loose fat of his face—I felt a contempt for him greater than that I had had before; and I gained full possession of myself, so that my voice became calm and icy cold. He had put up a hand to stop me from leaving.

"Wait," he croaked. "Don't go. Tell me . . . tell me who it is. I've been losing lambs and sheep for nearly six months—and I can't find out how." He took a step toward me. "Tell me—"

"Keep your distance and your manners," I said. "Or I won't tell you anything at all."

He stared at me, rubbing his shaven chin. "See here, boy," he said. "I had no wish to be gruff with you when you came in. It's just that— well, your father and I don't exactly see eye to eye on many things. But this isn't a matter in which your father is involved, not at all. It's simply between you and me—man to man. Actually, I'm very grateful to you that you decided to come, to visit me. I'm thankful that you have information which you want to share with me. I hope you realize how much this means to me. Feel free to speak. No one will disturb you. Perhaps you'd like something to drink? A cup of wine?"

I shook my head. "No, thank you."

"Don't be shy, lad. Say what you have to."

I smiled and stared silently past him to the table and the partially uncovered coins.

His eyes followed my gaze and he paled. "What is it? What are you staring at?"

I remained silent, not moving an inch. The smile locked into place on my face.

He scowled. "How much?" he whispered.

"How much is it worth to you?"

"A silver piece," he said hoarsely.

"Then I'll take twice that."

That night my mother visited me in a dream. I did not actually see her in the dream, but felt her presence and heard her voice. She said that since I had come to her grave and told her my innermost feelings, she was free to come and see me. She said that she loved me dearly, had always loved me, in spite of what I told myself to the contrary, and that she would cherish me as her first-born forever. That I had been at her burial place and told her of my longing gave her the strength needed to cross between the worlds.

My mother said that I should do well to relinquish my hatred; that if I were to build my life on foundations of hatred, my life would certainly crumble and I was certain to come to grief. She warned me that hatred did not and could not nourish, but that it cheated and destroyed: that it destroyed the man who thought he could live on it and not the object of that man's hatred. I listened to every word my mother spoke to me. Something deep inside me cried out that I should pay heed to her, that I should acknowledge the tender feelings welling up as spring water from my deepest parts. But I would not answer her, nor would I accept my tenderness. I stepped on what was soft inside me as I had stepped on the little toad in the cemetery. I killed the tenderness as I had killed the cat in the village: the cat that had trusted me. Stupid toad! Foolish cat!

My mother's words grew fainter in the din of my anger. How could she say that hate did not sustain? Did she have any idea of what I felt when the toad was beneath my foot? Why, I was the one who controlled its life, who decided its death! I held absolute sway over another existence: I could prolong it or extinguish it as I wished! No one could stop me! And the same held true for the cat, except that the existence was larger and more complicated in its case. My own existence completely encompassed the cat's: able to grant it grace or snuff it out at my whim! It licked my hand at the very instant that my mind plotted its death. What a thrilling power that was: I could spin its fate within myself and conceal what that fate was from it! How could my mother say that hatred and cruelty had not a reward? How could she say such a thing when she had lived with my father?

Thus my mother vanished from my dream, and in my sleep I was glad, I was glad! The bleating of the marked lamb took the place of her voice, and through a curtain of blue-green cypress needles I seemed to see the animal as it was passed like a bundle from the hand of a thief into the hand of a thief. Its eyes peered into mine as it bleated thinly, and I sought to understand what I saw there, as I had tried to fathom what flickered in the eyes of those men and women my father dealt with harshly. But I could see nothing except terror. The thief from the next village tucked the lamb under an arm and hurried off; the thief from my village looked furtively about him and ran up the opposite path. A hidden witness, I knew again the sweet heady taste of power. Two men's fates were given over to me. They were sleeping peacefully tonight, these two fine fellows, when they should have tossed fitfully. Their dreams were undisturbed where they lay this night, the two of them, when they should have suffered nightmares. I had lifted the skeins of their lives and was about to tear them, to rip them asunder! They had not the slightest inkling of what was in store for them, while I knew it for fact! And I had done it, I had wrought it, I had made it come to pass: a mere stripling, not even come to the ceremony of manhood!

I wakened from my sleep. The room was pitch-black, but outside I heard a cock crow with the false dawn and the stirring of the hens. The dog at the animal shed growled. A sudden fear possessed me. I sat

up with a jerk and felt under the pillow for my money. I closed my
fist over the two silver pieces, drew them from their covert, sighed and
felt calm and certain again.

The ox who had stolen the lamb
and the other animals from Shimon's fold was to be flogged on the
evening of the very next day. I had not hoped for so swift a retribution;
all of my senses were heightened when I overheard two servants talking in the kitchen and learned that punishment would be so soon in
coming. It turned out that the thief was Shimon's cousin, a poor relative who had used his family connection to gain unsuspected access to
the rich man's flock.

Floggings took place in the village square, on the lower slope of
the mountain. I was there among the earliest arrivals, before the condemned man had been brought into view, and I watched with curiosity
as a detachment of Roman cavalrymen that had been traveling the
road through the valley southward turned from their way and rode into
the village from the northeast. Perhaps they had spotted the gathering
crowd in the square and come to investigate, or perhaps they were here
for another reason. Perhaps there was a murderer among the inhabitants, or perhaps the leader of a rebel cell lived here. Breathing rapidly
with excitement, I paid the strictest attention to the Romans as, trotting
at a brisk clip, they came closer.

I was fascinated by these soldiers of Rome. There were five of
them: one who rode out in advance and four who followed in two pairs.
All of them had fine, sleek mounts with bobbed tails, the imperial colors
woven into their manes and ornate silverwork medallions on their
bridles, gleaming almost whitely against the well-groomed hides of
their foreheads. The riders were powerful, muscular men who carried
small circular shields with the profile of the emperor emblazoned on
them and wore broadswords in scabbards that slapped the flanks of
their horses as they moved forward. I could not decide where to feast
my eyes first: on the imperturbable masklike faces of the cavalrymen in
their close-fitting, plumed helmets; on their wide chests, hard-fleshed
forearms and thick calves; on their mirror-bright spurs; or on their
wonderful swords, leashed now but at any given instant ready to bite.

So moved with admiration for them was I that inadvertently I got too close to the lead horse, a coal-black stallion with a single white streak on its muzzle. Its rider, a tall, fair-skinned officer who spoke pidgin Hebrew and seemed to mock the guttural sounds of the language out of sheer boredom, warned me away. The men who rode behind him, all of them swarthy Romans, were amused and laughed as I jumped back in obedience to the command, showing their strong, even, white teeth. The detachment halted and the officer surveyed the square. His mount was edgy and stepped this way and that, at times striking the sun-baked earth with a foreleg.

"What's going on around here?" the officer said in broken Hebrew. "Who's got a lively tongue in his head and can tell me?"

He looked directly at me as he spoke. His blue eyes stared straight into mine and I felt their gaze almost hypnotize me. I was so confused I could think of nothing to say and stared back stupidly, flushing. A lot of the other children of the village had gathered around, heard the officer's question, and one after the other, shouted out answers. But the Roman ignored all of them. He kept his stallion tightly reined with one hand and with the other held idly to the hilt of his broadsword. He sat erectly but easily in the saddle, his sensual lips curled half in a smile, half in a sneer.

"Well, boy, I put a question to you. What great event will take place in this square?"

I struggled with the shame and envy I felt and managed to speak: "Someone is to be flogged here tonight, sir."

It was the first time in my entire life that I had ever addressed a Roman soldier, let alone an officer of the empire. And it was the first time I had ever called anyone "sir." My knees were weak and I was giddy, but I did not feel at all weak. Rather, the opposite was true: I felt that an immense strength flowed into me. That strength derived from the officer on horseback: it was as if he were filled with all of the power and the glory of Rome and as if he fed it to me in his look as a mother feeds milk to a nursing child. He nodded, pulled sharply on the reins and winced with pleasure as the horse's head jerked back and yellow-white spittle from its open mouth flew into the air all about. His irises seemed more blue than ever; they reminded me of the sea at Jaffa, which I had seen on a trip with my parents when I was three or four. Those eyes not only had the sea's color, but also seemed to carry its awful majesty and limitless power. Now the other children were silent, and they even moved back a little.

"What manner of crime is the condemned man charged with? Is it a wrongdoing against the emperor of Rome?"

When he pronounced the word "emperor," a thrill ran through me. He said it with reverence, as if it were too much for his tongue to bear, as if it were too much for any human tongue to bear. Yet there was a certain tone of intimacy in his voice when he used the word, as if he knew that the emperor was a god but knew as well that he was an approachable god, a kind of god-man whom one could importune and flatter and cajole—and even on occasion corrupt with a wink.

My knees knocked as I spoke; I was afraid that everyone would see. For the weakness in myself I would have killed myself at that moment! "No, sir," I said, gaining strength and confidence as I went along. "It is for no crime against His Imperial Majesty that this man is being punished, for there is no man, woman or child in this village who would as much as dream of committing an infraction against the government of Rome: to this I can attest under oath. The man who will be whipped before his neighbors this evening is a greedy fool who stooped so low as to steal from a blood relative; he is not worthy of the centurion's notice . . ."

A grave look came over the officer's features as I spoke; it did not escape me. He nodded slowly and said in a stern but softened tone, "So you know my rank, do you?"

My legs no longer trembled. "I know all the Roman ranks," I said proudly.

The men in the centurion's escort laughed again, but their officer retained his sober silence. He inclined his head slightly, and immediately the laughter ceased; he had indicated his will in a most subtle manner and they had responded perfectly, instantly, so keenly were these men attuned to his will. The officer leaned forward in his saddle, cleared his throat and said, "All right, name the Roman ranks as you boasted that you can. If you succeed, you shall indeed have a reward from the generous hand of Rome. But if you should fail, my Jewish child, then expect that you shall have a rebuke from the iron hand of Rome, from which you will learn not to make every idle boast that tempts your lips."

A crowd had collected now, adults as well as children. At its fringe

I caught sight of a familiar elder, the white-haired old man who was entrusted with keeping the peace with the Romans. His face was dark and contorted; it was clear that he feared I would somehow bring Roman wrath down upon the village. I was certain that had he been able to do so, he would have erased me from the earth without a qualm. Inwardly I rejoiced that I could bring anxiety to the elder and the village, though I knew they had nothing to be afraid of. I could recite the ranks of the Roman army backwards and forwards in my sleep. I had long admired and studied Roman military organization and had done as I boasted a thousand times over.

Bathed in the glory of the centurion and his contingent of cavalrymen, my voice rang out into the winy eventide air. Not only did I name the ranks of the army and navy in Hebrew, but I spoke them in the Latin tongue as well; and for good measure I added the names of all of the units of combat of both army and navy, beginning from the smallest and reaching even to the greatest, and also gave the Latin names for them. I beheld that the Roman officer and his men were astonished. When I finished, there was utter stillness, almost disbelief, and the centurion stared hard at me without saying a word for a very long time. I did not flinch from his gaze, nor did I move a muscle of face or body. In the last remaining light of the day, the horses and men looked like statues.

At length the officer smiled, his hard blue eyes gleaming fiercely, reached down into his saddlebag, drew something out of it, and with a flourish tossed down a small object. I caught it neatly in one hand, snapping it to myself as a ravenous dog snatches a scrap of meat which is thrown its way. "Here's a little something for you, my Jewish child, forever to remind you of this day. Continue to love Rome well, and you will prosper!"

He made the Roman salute and I returned it, drawn to my full height, with tears in my eyes. Then he touched his mount's flank with a knee and rode off, followed by his escort, their warriors' gear jangling to the trot of the horses. The dust they stirred rolled back over the crowd and over me. I saw that people coughed and swallowed hard and covered their faces, but I tasted that dust gladly and would have eaten it with joy! My fist closed over what the centurion had given me; my ears echoed with the words he had spoken. I scarcely heard the voice of the village crier announce that the flogging was about to begin.

The white-haired elder pushed his way through the milling crowd. "Well," he said, coming up to me, "what did he give you?"

"Nothing," I said, closing my fist yet more tightly. "Nothing at all."

I heard the village watchman cry out and knew that it was midnight. The house was silent, and except for the occasional braying of an ass, it was silent outside as well. A short time before, my brother had called out and the nurse had gone into his tiny room to attend him—I had heard her footsteps go by my door; she limped and I could not mistake her—but now he was still. I climbed out of bed, lit the oil lamp and set it down on the cool tile of the floor. On the wall my shadow was a giant one, and I enjoyed it: I was yet a child but there would come a day when I would be as large as that shadow, and then the shadow I sent forth would cover the earth! Something inside me whispered very calmly of this truth to come, and I trusted the voice that spoke; I did not believe it would lie.

Squatting by the lamp, my head swam with visions of the flogging. Over and over again I saw the scene. I saw the dense crowd of villagers, heard their muttering and sighing, tasted the dust, smelled the sweat mixed faintly with the smell of animal excrement that the westerly wind blew over the square from nearby cowsheds and sheep pens. I saw the dusky faces ranged around the whipping pole in a ragged circle, the faces of my neighbors that twisted with lust, hate, cruelty, pleasure, pain, horror, amusement, grief, pity, bewilderment, fear and envy as if they were masks of molten lead cast by some devilish hand. I saw the bunched, rippling back and arm muscles of Shabtai the whipper as, stripped to the waist and running with sweat that stained the earth about his bare feet, he wielded his whip in a slow, precise rhythm that both tantalized the crowd and satisfied it in the tantalizing. I saw the flesh of the thief as it uncurled under the lash like the bark of a tree, blood oozing slowly into each welt as it was opened. Over and over I heard the screams that seemed to issue from the parched lips of the culprit even after he had passed out and his limp body sagged from the wrist-ropes that bound it like a sack to the post. I saw Shimon's round, rabid face, with its bloated lip and beady eyes, as he hung on each blow of the whip, his short frame shuddering greedily every time a new path

23

of scarlet appeared. Four young men from the village were standing with pitch torches held high over their heads so the eyes of all of the inhabitants would have the scene painted for them in the redness of hell.

Shimon felt satisfied, and so did I. But my satisfaction was infinitely greater than was Shimon's, for it was I who had created this morality play. Yes, I was the author, and the actors followed my script to the letter! My will imposed on the wills of others, even my elders, even the entire village: when I thought of the matter in this fashion, the very essence of my being burst into flame as did the oil in the lamp when I ignited it. I saw that if I exerted myself I could be above life itself, pulling the strings that made other people dance or faint, weep or rejoice, sing or mourn. Indeed, I was doing exactly what God was supposed to do, for according to the belief of my people God sat on high and from His exalted throne oversaw the affairs of men on earth. But from what I had seen and learned of life, even in my few years of existence, it seemed clear to me that a handful of men held sway over vast multitudes and did with them as they pleased. I recalled the profile of the emperor of Rome emblazoned on the shields of his warriors as they sat on their mighty steeds: to me, these shields, with their symbol of authority graven for all eyes to behold, were the real coin of the earthly realm! And once more I recalled the quiet, certain, reverential tone of the centurion when he used the word "emperor." I said it now to myself in Hebrew and then in Latin and then in Hebrew again. There was a human who had in his own two hands the power and the glory of a god!

I squatted by the lamp. Again I glanced around the room and then listened. All was still. I leaned forward and pulled a small bit of folded cloth from beneath the mattress of my bed. Carefully I unwound the cloth and bent far over what it contained. Taking even greater care, I lifted the object from its wrapping, tossed the cloth onto the bed, and set my treasure on my naked open palm so that nothing separated me from it. Soft candlelight fell in one even stroke upon the hard image of the Roman Caesar implanted in the surface of a tiny gold coin.

My father came back from the town of Bethlehem with a bride!

We, the members of his household, stood in the doorway under the name "Evenezer" chiseled in stone: I, my infant brother, his nurse, the housekeeper and all of the other servants. Shielding our eyes from the blazing sun, we stood and watched the bridal party swing into view as it came up the mountain slope through the village. My father rode first. He sat astride a magnificent bay mare, and his bride rode behind on the same horse, so that only her hands locked about his waist were visible. Avner and the second servant followed, and they were succeeded in turn by several donkeys laden with goods. We had known they were coming for some time, for a man who lived at the northern edge of the village had been at work in his vineyard and seen them on the main road; he had told his neighbor, and word had spread rapidly from mouth to mouth.

All were astir with the unexpected turn of events, for my father had told no one of his intentions. My father did not believe in confidences. He was a man who was close to no other living soul; he was a man who felt that for him to reveal himself to another human being was to expose his weaknesses to a potential enemy. He was suspicious of most people and wary of all; he hated many and was indifferent to the others; and he tolerated animals, but no more. He gave nothing, anticipated less, and held tightly to his thoughts and his money. No man flattered him into friendship, and no man crossed him with impunity.

He had only one trusted servant, Avner, his chief steward. And that trust was based on a single tie: Avner had once saved my father's life. One spring before I was born and not too long after he had married my mother, my father and Avner had made a journey to Hebron. The way led through desolate, uninhabited terrain: rugged hills and deep wadis in which bandits often sought refuge. My father was impulsive and reckless. Spurring his mount, he had ridden far ahead of Avner and rounded a bend in the road so that each of the travelers lost sight of the other. Leaping out suddenly from behind a clump of cacti where they had concealed themselves, two cutthroats had fallen upon him. When Avner came around the bend he saw that my father, though defending himself fiercely, was trapped against a boulder wedged into the cleft between two hills. The servant could have escaped unseen, but chose instead to risk his own life in coming to my father's aid. Screaming at the top of his lungs and drawing his weapon, he charged the outlaws; at the same time he called over his shoulder, as if to a large number of men who would follow him. The bandits fled. Recovered, my father had a chance to retrieve his fallen bow, draw it, and sink an arrow into the neck of one of his attackers. Deserted by his companion, the wounded man was sprawled on his belly halfway up the slope, moaning softly. My father stooped and pulled the arrow out; the wound was not a serious one, and the man suffered from shock more than from anything else. My father prodded him with a toe in his ribs. "Get up," he said.

The man groaned weakly and turned himself on one side. He was middle-aged and blind in the left eye; a long purple scar split his chin almost in its center. He winced and with the hand he was not resting on touched his sparse, filthy hair.

"Who are you and where do you come from?" asked my father.

The man told him he was from Schechem, that he was called Ze'evi, that he was alone in the world, and then he blurted out his history, weeping as he spoke. He was the illegitimate child of a deserter from a Roman legion and a Jewish whore. He had grown up in Beersheba, run away from home when he was ten, and soon fallen in with thieves. Sobbing, he said that he had always known that this sort of life would end badly, that he had always wanted a better life, but that he had never been able to muster the strength to break away from banditry and find it. My father nodded slowly and said, "I understand that you never had the strength."

He stood thinking for a time and then turned to Avner and said, "Hand me my spear." He received it, balanced it in his right hand and continued: "Tell me, Ze'evi, what will be mine if I agree to set you free?"

The other shivered and hesitantly slid his fingers to the wound at the side of his neck. When he removed them, he saw they were covered with blood, and he went pale. "How can you free me from death?" he whispered hoarsely.

My father laughed. "No, you won't die from your wound, my friend. It's superficial. The blood's clotting already. So you may tell me: what will be mine if I bind your hurt and set you at liberty?"

Wiping the blood from his hand on his tunic, the man said, "My treasure."

"Your treasure?"

"Yes. All the wealth that is mine. The gold and silver and precious objects I have hidden away. I will lead you to the cache."

My father guffawed. "You really expect me to believe you?" he said. "A ragamuffin, a vagabond, a mangy cur like you owns treasure? Why, you live from hand to mouth, you jackal, barely able to survive!

How would you have wealth when you scarcely possess your own miserable skin?"

Covered with a paste of grime and sweat, the man stared up at him. He lifted his hand beseechingly. "Spare me, I implore you. In the name of mercy, spare my life—"

"And so what will be mine, scum?"

"My gratitude. My lifelong gratitude . . ."

My father raised the spear high above his head.

"In the name of your God, the Holy One of Israel—let me redeem my life on earth—"

My father sent the spear down with all of his strength; it shot through the prostrate man's open mouth and out the back of his skull.

So had the tale been related to me, word for word, by his eyewitness and companion, Avner. With pride.

My stepmother was a tall, heavy-boned woman with red hair, a sallow complexion, and eyes that clung to you like two leeches once they had fixed on you. She was hot-tempered, quick to lash out with her tongue and ready to deal a blow upon the slightest provocation. Her big, well-proportioned body could be upon you almost before you knew it, without warning, and her arms had a long and deadly reach. My father and his bride seemed a very well matched pair of daggers.

I avoided both of them as much as I could. My father was away for a good part of the day, and I managed fairly well to keep out of his way for the rest. But my stepmother took immediate charge of the household and wasted no time in assigning me chores. I had to discharge my obligations because she reported without fail to my father every night, but I lost no opportunity to deceive her when I could by pretending that the work had been done or by laying the blame for my negligence on someone else. It wasn't easy, though. She was a harsh taskmaster and missed little, and in addition she soon won the favor and enlisted the aid of Avner, who began to serve her faithfully, like a dog that knows no better.

One night when both my father and Avner were absent, I passed the room my father shared with his new wife. The door was half open; idly I glanced in. By the bed my stepmother stood naked. Her head was inclined a little to one side as she grimaced into a small hand mirror she held out before her. I had seen women without clothes on several occasions before this, but it had had little meaning for me. Once when I was very young, I had wakened and gone silently into my parents' room, where in the light of a lamp I had glimpsed them coupling; but my mother's body had been bathed in shadow and covered over by my father's. And two or three times, on journeys, I had seen women or maidens bathing by streams. But this time the sight of a naked female body had a powerful and magnetic effect on me. I halted where I was and gazed at her.

She was a strapping woman. Her back was beautifully curved, and she had large, milk-white breasts with swollen nipples almost the color of ripe purple grapes. Her buttocks and belly were flat; her thick, dark growth of pubic hair seemed to me to glow like a ruby. Over the skin of her shoulders, neck and arms rust-colored freckles were sprinkled, but the rest of her body was free of them. She had a tic, and every few seconds would toss her head in a circular motion to the left, though it was apparent that she was unaware of the spasms. I watched her standing so, touching her red hair and turning the mirror this way and that.

I felt myself a prisoner. There was something cruel, wanton and desperate about her nakedness, something that drew me to it. I could not tear my eyes away from her flesh; I wanted to devour it over and over again; I felt as if I could never get enough of it. I hated my step-mother, I would have gladly seen her dead, but the sight of her naked body made me ecstatic. A dreamlike stupor had settled over me: my limbs were weak, my mind was drowsy. Fortunately, the voice within me spoke to me, wakened me. I realized that I was in peril, that I would meet with a dire punishment if I were caught. She would tell my father I had pushed the door ajar or had entered the room in stealth. I broke the spell and moved from the doorway.

"Who's there?" her voice called out in alarm.

Barefoot, I ran down the hall at top speed.

"Who's out there in the hall?" her voice shrieked after me.

I dashed into my room, closing the door behind me. But I did not stop at that. I knew her well, though she had been in the house no more than five or six weeks. I undressed, slipped into my bed and feigned sleep, a skill I had often used to extricate myself from difficulty and was particularly adept at. I had learned quickly, as you must do in life if you are to live. Moments later, as soon as she had covered her nakedness, I heard my stepmother come into the hall. Her shouts and imprecations brought several of the servants; the noise came closer and closer to my room. My back was to the door, but I heard it burst open. My stepmother entered, muttering. I heard her approach my bed and kept my breathing even. There was no witness and nothing to justify whatever suspicions she had about me. Still snorting and mumbling, she left. I smiled.

I smiled because I had tricked her. I smiled because I had her naked body in my mind and there was nothing she could do about it. Whenever I wanted to see her naked, I could; whenever I wanted to think lewd thoughts about her, I could. In a way she had become my property, she was at my mercy, and there was nothing she could do to reverse things. She had betrayed herself and was beside herself with the betrayal. She was like the virgin who gives herself too easily and regrets it, but can in no way regain her virginity. I had good reason to smile.

But I did not gloat too long. I never wasted time gloating. It served no purpose, and too much of it lowered the defenses and made you lax. New thoughts entered my mind. How did my stepmother come to be naked? Why had the door been left ajar? Had she been expecting someone? I sat bolt upright in bed and stared into the darkness. I knew that out of darkness would come the shape of the future.

When he was married three months, my father held a feast—the first in all my life I had ever known him to hold. He had invited fifty or sixty guests to the gathering. They would sit in the open air beneath the heavy leaves of the grapevines on the arbor where the day before carpenters, under Avner's watchful eye, had constructed tables and benches especially for the occasion. In the yard, a wide-open pit had been dug, and at dawn on the day of the feast a roaring fire was kindled in it and a calf spitted over it. In the kitchen, fruits, nuts and herbs were heaped in mounds, and the blazing stoves held lamb, mutton and fowl of every description. My father had brought in a dozen extra servants to help get things ready.

I watched the preparations without understanding the purpose. Everything had to have some purpose, and I could not fathom what the purpose for this was. To celebrate for the sake of celebration was not a part of my father's nature. Pleasure was certainly no excuse for relaxing one's guard: to my father's way of thinking, life had to be lived with constant and unremitting vigilance. I observed him the day long. His mien was dark; his brow was often furrowed; he kept his lips pressed together. He toyed with a rawhide riding whip he kept with him. His red-haired wife rushed to and fro at a dizzy speed—bustling, imperious, shrill. She was all over the house and the yard but never seemed to complete anything. My father walked with a slow, deliberate step and encompassed all. He never once raised his voice; he never had to. He pointed a finger at whatever task he wanted done, and it was done without delay and without fuss or argument. I was perplexed. I knew that festivity was as alien to his soul as generosity. Then why the feast?

I kept my eyes open. I wanted the mystery solved: for my own satisfaction and for the benefits I might be able to obtain. It was always easier to make plans when one knew the plans of others. Something was in the wind and I had to know exactly what it was. By late afternoon almost all was ready for the guests. My stepmother went to her bedroom to dress, and her servants went to their quarters. The house was fairly quiet. A man whom I had never seen before, tall and badly scarred, rode up to our house. He was received by my father in his private chamber, where he did his accounts. The man stayed alone with my father for half an hour and then left, his horse clattering rapidly down the slope. He disappeared as the sun set, ominously flooding the cloudless sky with crimson.

As evening fell, my father sought out Avner. He found his servant in the yard, standing before the carcass of the calf, which, glistening with fat, rotated slowly on the spit over dancing flames. The two of them spoke in front of the fire, which hissed and spat whenever grease dropped into it. Avner nodded. My father reached out and put a hand on his shoulder, a gesture I could not remember ever having seen. When my father touched another man, it was to strike him. But I understood by the sign that whatever the pact between them was, it was sealed.

When Avner left, I stealthily followed him because my nose told me his was the scent to follow. I wasn't wrong. I saw him gather four of his stalwarts behind the animal shed and there distribute weapons to them: short-bladed swords and daggers which they concealed beneath their tunics.

A nightingale trilled, cicadas sang, musicians played. A great, ripe August moon hung low in the sky: perfectly circular, it was spun of the purest gold, and the lambent, unearthly light it gave off stained the heavens about it with an enormous halo. Beneath it, the mountain slope and the village took on a golden sheen, mottled everywhere with shadow that had the texture of velvet. The valley was lit, and the hills beyond it to the east; the next village over was visible, bathed in spectral yet comforting luminescence; and even the position of the town of Bethlehem could be discerned, its highest rooftops marking it as a phantom place. The night was a miracle of beauty, but the guests at my father's feast had neither eyes nor ears for it.

They were the elders of our village, their wives and concubines; the richest men of the village, their wives and mistresses; the notables and merchants of the next; and even a number of visitors from Bethlehem. Men's raucous laughter and the gay, seductive tittering of the women echoed against the steep rocky face of the mountain. A dozen torches on high poles combined with the moon, which shrank as it climbed into the arch of the sky but retained the melony splendor of form and color, to light the compound in which the arbor was set—the guests at table; the calf being carved now over whispering coals; the frenetic bustle of servants bearing platters of game and fowl, fruit and salad, and great flasks of wine. At the head of it all sat my father, his face deceptively softened by the reddish light, his eyes untouched by any of it. Though he was surrounded by jollity and carousing, he was as unmoved by the laughter of men and women as he was by their tears. Next to him, upright and open-mouthed, clad in a silver tunic and wearing jewels that I had never suspected the existence of in her hair and at her throat, sat his wife.

When Avner appeared out of nowhere, my father rose from his place and strode rapidly from the arbor to the front of the house. From the street below, there was the clattering of horses' hooves and the shouts of their riders. A torch blazed pinkly in the eerie moonlight. Six Roman soldiers rode behind its bearer. Then came a standard bearer on

31

a roan stallion. A litter borne by eight slaves swung into view. Bringing up the rear was an additional troop of eight soldiers, carrying lances at their hips. The litter was set down at our doorstep and two slaves rushed to its portal, out of which they helped a tiny, emaciated man with a long, quivering nose and sharp chin. The torchlight caught the ring on his right hand, and I saw before my eyes the signet of Roman authority. As slight, barren of flesh and ugly as he was, this man held the destinies of thousands and even tens of thousands in his hands. At the nod of that sunken yellow skull, the lightning of lances would be unquestionably released. At his command, doves would fly or heads would roll—however he chose it to be. He stepped lightly forward, as if disdaining the earth of mortals, his chin tilted upward, his thin lips pursed as if sewn together. His slaves bowed, his bearer dipped the standard, his soldiers saluted. He extended the hand of a skeleton, and my father went down on one knee to kiss its ringed finger.

Now at last the matter was clear to me. The man who had been closeted with my father in his sanctum and then had ridden away was a part of the Roman security system; he had come to transmit instructions to my father in advance of the official's arrival. Thus had Avner been charged with arming the best of our servants, for nothing untoward must occur while the official was our guest. The servants would supplement the protection of the military bodyguard. I understood it all: my father had made a connection with the empire which he desired to be open to the scrutiny of all. For his own reasons, he was placing the might of Rome on display for all who would to see: the news of this feast would spread far and wide. I tried to guess who the little man with the ring might be, and whether he was from Bethlehem or Jerusalem.

Proudly, accompanied by spurred warriors, my father led his guest to the place of honor. The others stood and saluted. It was as it should be: the men and women at feast, the servants in the yard and in the house, the village itself—all seemed to me to revolve about this august presence. Beyond him, physically free but tethered by his iron will, the soldiers of his escort wheeled slowly, surely around him in the night, like heavenly bodies around the central planet of their system: their weapons were ready against any harm. For his sake, the calf had been butchered, the lambs and fowl slaughtered, the fish snared, the herbs gathered, the tables and benches built, my red-haired stepmother clothed in silver raiment and bedecked in jewels. Every man and woman in his sight, no matter how rich and how influential, was under his sway—even his host. I watched this man, his every facial expression, his subtlest gesture, his shrewd, unwavering glances, and a strange feeling came over me: he was my father, I had sprung from his loins. I closed my eyes and the knowledge became yet more certain: he was flame, I was moth.

Someone had given me wine and I had stumbled away from the feast. When my head cleared, I found myself in a strange room, sprawled on the floor, reeking of my own vomit and urine. My temples throbbed, my mouth was dry; I felt as if I had been lethally drugged. "Mother," I whispered, and then my mouth twisted in rage, as if it wanted to tear itself away from the rest of my face. I sat up and touched my throat; I was relieved to find that no one was choking me. I rubbed my burning eyes: I had to know where I was. Then I heard a sound and stiffened.

But when I heard the next sound, my fear dissipated. It was a gentle sighing, almost a cooing. I got unsteadily to one knee, and then slowly, crouched as I was, began to move forward; I was almost certain of my whereabouts, but not quite. I peered ahead of me in the direction from which the noise had come and was just able to make out a half-known shape; above it was a pale strip of light. As I moved, the sound came again, soft, sibilant, melting almost instantaneously into silence; I relaxed. Where the sliver of light showed, I reached up and found a shutter; I freed the latch and it swung open with a creak. The light of the moon, like finely spun wool, fell into the room. I clearly saw my little brother asleep in his crib.

Nausea stirred thickly in my throat, so I rose and put my head out of the window, drawing in deep breaths of fresh air. From the arbor came blurred sounds of the feast, with now and again the shrill laughter of a woman pretending to be amused or frightened rising above all else. In brief intervals of silence, the musicians could be heard: their playing seemed pathetic and futile to me. Leaning on the sill, I turned my head to the right and spotted two of the escort soldiers on patrol, hands clasping the hilts of their swords. I followed them with my eyes as they walked erectly with the assured footsteps and natural precision of beasts of prey. I kept breathing in air, lulled by the patient rhythm of the Romans and comforted by their surveillance. When they disappeared from view, I left the window.

In his wooden crib, my brother slept the sound sleep of infancy. His face was round and pink in the moonlight; his look was tranquil. His features strongly resembled my mother's; only his knobby chin, with its small cleft, belonged to my father. His breathing was even and soft; if it had not been for the dovelike noises he had made before, I should never have known he was in the room. I drew closer. My brother lay on his back, with arms outstretched and legs apart. His hands were clenched loosely to make tiny fists; a drop of spittle glistened at one corner of his lips. I stood over him, holding to the side of the crib tightly. I remembered the toad I had crushed with my foot, the cat I had brained with a rock, the laborers my father had felled in the fields, the thief Shabtai had flogged into unconsciousness. I saw my mother's face, and it was dead, so dead; I saw my stepmother's ungarbed body and it was naked, so naked. When I looked down at my baby brother, it seemed to me that in the moonlight the flesh of his face and limbs had taken on the pallor of a corpse.

I bent forward. The pulse in his neck beat regularly, delicately: it looked as if a butterfly were moving beneath his skin. I reached down with one hand and lightly moved my fingers over the neck. Such a thin membrane separated this living child from death—just moments of filling his lungs with air. That was all. I put the other hand down and made a collar of fingers for his neck. He stirred but did not waken. His lips smiled. Perhaps he dreamed of pleasant things, for certainly he did not dream of the angel of death at his windpipe. Once again I felt the thrill of power I had experienced when first I had spied the thieves from my place of vantage in the cemetery. I held a human being's life in my two hands, and he did not know; more than that, it would not have helped him if he did. All I had to do was close my fingers, close them hard and bear down with my strength. There would be no telltale blood, no broken limbs, nothing to describe the relentless pressure that would shatter his lungs.

"What are you doing in here?" The nurse's voice shocked me and I spun around. "What are you standing over the crib for?" she stammered hoarsely.

"Shut your mouth, you bitch!" I snarled, jumping back out of reach.

34

But she ignored me and rushed to the crib. "The child—what in the name of God have you done to him?"

She lifted my brother into her fat arms, and he cried. Trembling, I left the room.

My father sat at the table, scowling. Abruptly, he pushed his supper plate from him with the food only half eaten and then drained the cup of wine he had begun at the start of the meal. His rawhide riding whip had fallen to the floor, and he bent to retrieve it. "Come here," he said to me, facing around.

I did not wait to be invited again. My stepmother, biting her lower lip, stared at me in silence as I rose from my place and went over to stand by my father. He had crossed his legs and was tapping the quirt gently on the upper knee.

"Tell me, my son," he said. "Do you love your brother?"

I hesitated.

"Do you love him?" my father repeated, raising the whip and looking at its tip with one eye, as if he were using it to sight by.

"I do," I said.

"Very much? Do you love him very much? Answer me when I speak to you!"

"Yes, I love him very much."

"How much?"

Out of the corner of my eye I saw my stepmother regarding me intently, her protuberant forehead severed in almost equal parts by a large, throbbing blood vessel which stood out darkly against her pale skin. She brushed her red hair, which had not been cut since she arrived, back from her face and sipped her wine. A servant offered her a bowl of nuts into which she thrust a hand with the predatory motion of a claw, waving the bearer immediately away as if she could stand to be near no one. She seemed as anxious for my answer as was my father.

"Well, I'm waiting patiently, my son. How much do you love your brother?"

"Very much," I said in a voice just above a whisper.

My father laughed. "Yes! So you love him very much! I'm sure you do, quite sure! I'm certain that you'd risk your life and limbs for him without bothering to think twice about it. Except that, for his sake, I hope he never needs your protection. At any rate, the problem is entirely theoretical, since most probably you will never set eyes upon him again."

My father saw the look of puzzlement mingled with expectation on my face and smiled broadly. His teeth were large and strong but yellowed and much stained; they were cruel teeth, the teeth of a man who passes the sentence of death through them without qualms.

"Don't get your hopes up," he said. "I'm not going to sacrifice him, if that's what you're thinking." He brought the rawhide quirt sharply into the open palm of his hand. "I'm going to send him away, that's the pith of it." He gazed directly into my face, as if he wanted to pry it open to see what secrets lay behind it. "How does the idea strike you?"

"As you command, Father, so be it."

"Spoken like the truly charming son you are! I congratulate you!" My father yawned and tossed his whip onto the table. "He leaves tomorrow."

My stepmother rose. I glanced over at her and discovered that her belly had begun to swell.

The day was overcast. Patches of mist rose from the floor of the valley and blew through the air. The mountain peak was buried in fog. You could hear the cows lowing down below, but you could not see them. At noon, the day was scarcely clearer than it had been at dawn, though a brisk wind pushed heavy gray clouds over the sky.

My father's brother, Yosef, arrived on muleback to take my little brother away. He was a slight, round-shouldered man two years older than my father. He had large, moist eyes; his sandy hair was thinning, and he walked with a perceptible limp. Yosef was a carpenter by trade and carried his tools in his saddlebag; he never made a journey without them. His worn, leather-skinned face seemed pained and his body cringed when my father talked to him; he was obviously very uncomfortable and kept looking away as if he wanted to escape. My father rarely, if ever, visited Yosef, and I knew he had sent Avner to Bethlehem, where Yosef lived with his childless wife Mara, to make all of the arrangements. I was certain that Yosef had received payment for taking the child.

In the doorway stood my stepmother, looking on morosely as the two brothers talked together, probably for the first time in many years; her lips were pressed firmly together and her heavy-lidded eyes showed venom in their look.

My father's brother Yosef did not cross the threshold; he stood in the yard, faint tendrils of mist blowing about him, and waited with the resignation of a beggar who is used to waiting. Behind him, tethered to a tree, his work-worn mule snorted and rapped the hard earth fitfully. After a time the nurse came out, carrying my brother and a small bundle in her arms. Her face was swollen and reddened with weeping. She hesitated and halted, as if she had forgotten what she was about. My father glared at her and then watched impassively as she went forward and, stifling her sobs, handed the child over to Yosef, who received him gently, muttering an inaudible thanks. Oddly enough, my brother did not cry or protest in any way; he seemed dazed, his eyes rolling dully in their sockets and his body inert, like a lump of dough. He passed in silence from the thick, sausage-fingered hands of his nurse to the bony hands of Yosef the carpenter. That seemed all there would be to it. But when the mule moved away from the house, he opened his mouth suddenly and vomited all over himself, Yosef and the beast. Yosef stopped the mule. My father and his wife had disappeared: I was the only one in the yard as the nurse had also left. The sight of my brother covered with his own filth sickened me. I left without looking back.

The child my stepmother had conceived did not live to enjoy the light of this world: it died at birth. The dead baby, a little girl who seemed no bigger than a doll when I chanced to see her, was buried in the village cemetery not far from my mother's grave. This time as I stood among the crowd of mourners I felt as if I had my stepmother underfoot. It was like killing two birds with a single shot: I had revenge on mother and child in one stroke. That night I dreamed that all of the children in the world were dead, that no more might be born, and that I was the sole hope of the human race. It was a glad dream and I exulted in it.

My stepmother was distraught and I was triumphant. I realized then that life gives the dead a power to punish the living in events that follow a death. I knew my stepmother for a harsh woman, yet I saw clearly that she could not remain so when life's harshness burned her own skin. There are those in the world of living men who are granite against wax, but become wax when they are opposed by granite. She was that kind of soul. But my father, whom she wedded, was granite in the face of granite: the crueler the blow against him, the harder and crueler he became.

I was surprised at the intensity with which my stepmother mourned her loss. She tore her garments and her red hair, wandered about the house and the yard distractedly, barely tasted food at mealtimes, spoke aloud when no one was near her and neglected her appearance. Busy with his affairs, which had prospered and become far more complex since the time of the feast, my father had little time or patience for his wife's despondent moods. Several times, when angered by her behavior, he had struck her in front of the servants. These developments could not have afforded me greater satisfaction. With gleeful impatience, I waited for what would happen next.

On a bright, windswept September day, when the first billowing swarms of swallows wheeled into silvery skies, two Roman couriers arrived. My father had been expecting them for more than a week. His bay mare was saddled, his saddlebags packed, and he strode into the front yard eagerly. My stepmother followed him, wept uncontrollably, and clung to him with such tenacious force that he had to thrust her away from him roughly. The couriers, who had not dismounted from their sleek horses, watched the scene with strict attention; I was quite certain that I detected contempt in the glances they exchanged. My father left with them, and I breathed a sigh of relief. A part of me felt that I was master of the house.

With my father gone and my stepmother distraught, I enjoyed a freedom I had never tasted. I rose when I pleased, ate whenever the mood seized me, ignored my chores, abused the servants, hid from Avner and roamed the mountain and valley just as it suited me, like an animal. Some months ago, my father had arranged for me to be instructed in reading and in religious practice, and I had been compelled to visit the home of my teacher, a slow-spoken, bearded man who was known throughout the district for his scholarship and probity. I avoided the lessons and when he called at the house did not appear; nor could anyone say where I had gone. Religion meant nothing to me: I found it nothing but a diversion from what was real in life. And reading, which I had already mastered, I considered to be simply a useful tool, like the tool a burglar might employ to break into a dwelling or storehouse or to pry open a strongbox.

One morning I succeeded in a remarkable feat: I managed to steal weapons from the room where they were kept under lock and key. Avner had been in the chamber and was called urgently away for several moments; never dreaming that I was in concealment nearby, he had not bothered to latch the door, and I had entered swiftly, taken what I'd wanted, and departed undetected. Actually I had planned the theft artfully, even down to the disturbance that had drawn Avner from the room for just the required length of time. I took not only a fine strongbow, one of my father's best, but also a dozen arrows, and best of all, a small dagger with an inlaid pearl handle and razor-sharp blade that I could easily hide on my person without being suspected.

All that day, far from the house and sheltered from prying eyes, I practiced with the bow and soon attained to a remarkable proficiency; I had every right to be proud of the speed with which I had mastered the weapon and of the strength, well beyond my years, I displayed in using it. At night I dreamed of my prowess and of the terror I inspired in numerous enemies who fled before the rain of arrows I showered upon them. The next morning I rose with the sun and made my way down the mountainside and across the fields and meadows. The bow burned in my hands. I shot at several quail and a hare and missed them. The next hare I saw was slow in starting away; I sighted carefully, held my breath and let fly. The arrow was true: it struck the hare in mid-bound and sent it tumbling head over heels into the grass. I rushed forward, almost falling in my eagerness. The hare lay on its side, run full through, its hind legs thrashing, its head twitching as with palsy, its large liquid eyes glassy with oncoming death. I squatted and waited while it ran the course of its final agony: I did not wish to finish it off quickly with a blow or a slash of my knife but preferred to watch it die slowly so that I could observe everything it went through. How could the studies my father had arranged for me compare with what I learned moment by moment from the creature expiring at my feet?

At length, the end came. I yawned, picked up the limp carcass and made my secret way back to the mountain and up its slope to the chasm, which I often visited. I built a small fire in an oven I made of rocks.

Then I skinned the hare, spitted it on a long stick and roasted it brown. My teeth ripped into the crisp skin and succulent flesh; juice dribbled down my chin and I gorged myself with the forbidden food. When I finished I tossed the bones down into the pit to bleach in the company of their human companions. I stood up and ran my greasy hands over my bloated stomach: it was as swollen as a pregnant woman's. I laughed out loud at the idea. But of course I would never give birth. I was glad of that: there were enough bastards in the world already.

The following day I went out again. Nothing seemed to satisfy my hunger for the kill. But try as I would, I was able to hit nothing. I stumbled into briar patches and cut my legs; I slipped once and grazed my knee on a rock; I was bitten by mosquitoes in a marshy tract; I lost an arrow and broke a second. By late afternoon I had a blinding head-ache and suffered a maddening sense of frustration. Then, in the last dying red rays of the sun, I caught sight of a doe, but she raced off before I could raise the bow. The single shot I let go pierced her rump, but not deeply, and she escaped, leaving a trail of excrement and then blood which grew fainter and which I followed until I was utterly exhausted. The stars were out. Bone-weary, I started back. I killed the first creature I met up with: a stray mongrel that approached trustingly. I taught it the meaning of trust with an arrow that reached its brain through an eye socket. I kicked the corpse and left it for the buzzards and jackals: carcass and scavengers deserved each other. On the way home I hid the bow and remaining arrows in the hollow of a tree.

By the time I got to the house the moon was up. In the kitchen, the cook was finishing up. She frowned when she saw me and began a protest when I demanded food. But I silenced her with a look: I had caught her stealing some weeks back and threatened to inform my father if she crossed me. Muttering, she set a platter out for me and left. I ate at the rough table where the servants took their meals and lingered long over my food. I was in no hurry. The kitchen was dark; only a small flame burned in the oven; it was so still I could hear the mice scurrying about. My food was well-cooked but it had not the taste of food I had stalked and slain. In the far distance, I heard the cry of a wolf and wished that I could kill it. I shoved my plate away as I had seen my father do.

When I came to the chamber where my father and stepmother slept, I stopped. Strange sounds came from the room. I listened closely. My stepmother moaned, but it was not the now familiar sound of her grief.

My stepmother repeated the sound: it was low, throaty and urgent; and yet it seemed like a sigh of relief. Though I heard no other voice, something inside me told me that another person was with her. I crept forward and put my head to the door. My stepmother whimpered. I stepped back, and acting on a strong impulse, left. It would not do at all to be discovered near her room. She had spies everywhere and the wherewithal to keep them eating out of her hand.

I got into bed without removing my clothes; I just pulled the cover over my head. Though I had spent an arduous day at hunt I could not sleep. Every time I shut my eyes my stepmother appeared. She was naked, as I had seen her that night, and she was running through a forest. I saw her flash whitely in among the trees. Now I could see her flat buttocks, now her dark-nippled breasts. I had my bow and a single arrow, and I was stalking her. She ran with great speed, but I was in no hurry. I was confident and nothing could shake my certainty. She reached a clearing and turned to look this way and that. At length she relaxed: it was clear that she thought she had eluded me. She bent low to drink from a brook. Her hair, long and knotted, hung down like red straw; her large breasts were like udders. I was quite near to her, though she did not suspect it. I took my time. I knelt, fitted my metal-tipped arrow precisely, raised the bow, drew back the bowstring and sighted carefully. She had finished drinking and stood erect. Her body was exactly as I had viewed it: breasts, belly, loins, thighs. I called out a single word: "Whore!"

Terror came across her face. She covered her chest and genital area as best she could with her arms. She strained wildly to see who it was that cried out, but she could not move: she was paralyzed with fright. Enough! I released the arrow and watched it slam into her exposed belly. She sank to her knees on the soft earth, bending slowly forward and moaning as I had heard her moan earlier. I rejoiced. I felt as if I had been the arrow.

I opened my eyes, immensely pleased with the fantasy, feeling in a sense that what I had invented had in fact really taken place. So engrossed was I in the workings of my imagination that the night had all but worn itself away. The house was very still, so quiet that I could catch every sound. When I heard the noise I was awaiting—my stepmother's door swinging open—I leaped out of bed. Footsteps went past my room, and when I judged the moment right I opened my door and peered out—but only for an instant, only for the fraction of a second necessary to see. I saw a familiar back, round, ugly shoulders, one slightly higher than the other, and long, dangling arms. The man I watched turned toward the kitchen, unaware that he had been seen. He had an unmistakable profile though I had already identified him from behind and by his uneven, shuffling gait: it was Shabtai the whipper. I closed my door and latched it.

I pulled my clothes from me and climbed into bed. I lay on my back, staring up at the ceiling and thinking. My stepmother's abandoned nakedness had baffled me the night I had seen her; now I understood it very well. I understood also that the mystery we call time so very often contains the missing pieces with which it alone is possible to put a puzzle together. I tossed and turned, more than ever unable to sleep. For vast new power had come into my hands, more power than I dreamed could be mine at this stage of my life. I decided that I would not use this power at present: it had to be kept for the propitious hour. Instead, I would seal what I had learned this night away as one hides money under a rock or beneath the tile of a floor, or as I had cached the weapons I had stolen. It did not pay to wound your prey; no, it was far better to wait for the right moment and ensure a kill.

There was talk that my father was coming home. I discounted the talk of the servants, for it was generally gossip, but when I heard Avner say it, I knew there was truth to the talk. Avner had neither the inclination nor the time for idle talk: my father seemed to take up Avner's life, as if the chief steward's innermost desires found expression in his master's affairs, or as if he could escape his own existence by making himself a part of someone else's. I never knew which. When I learned of my father's imminent return, something happened to me that I have not been able to explain to myself to this day. A wild and irrepressible feeling came over me, a feeling that I wanted to leave—more than that, a feeling that I had to go, that I must get out. I had no idea whatsoever of where I would go or how I would get on, but I knew I could not stay. The decision was made without thought, the compulsion instantaneous and irreversible. I always thought through my moves; I always planned my actions: why did I now yield to this fierce impulse? It was a question I could not answer and have never been able to answer.

From the time I was a very young child, one of my favorite pastimes was watching the men of the village, many of them the older men, play *schachmat,* or chess. They would pore over their boards in the village square on spring and summer afternoons until darkness made it impossible to go on. Though I myself had never played the game, I understood more of it than any of the participants guessed. They often wondered what held my attention, but I remained mute to their amused and sometimes mocking queries. Actually, I was fascinated by the play. I liked the power each player had over his pieces, I studied the strategies as far as I was able to grasp them, and I got a certain satisfaction from the symmetry of play and from the inflexibility of the rules. I liked most of all that the game's object was to trap the opponent's king, stripping him of all power and rendering him utterly helpless.

So I wanted to live my life. Each situation had to be judged within its own confines. All extraneous details had to be cut out. Emotions were superfluous. Each situation that arose had its opponent, its enemy, and the solution was ridding oneself of the antagonist. One assessed one's own forces and one's own position and then calculated the enemy's strength and disposition. Then, when all was thought through and when one's options were carefully measured against those of the opponent, one made the proper move.

There was no time to be lost. I made immediate preparations. I put whatever clothing I considered necessary into a sack I would sling over a shoulder; on my way out I would add whatever food I could comfortably carry and was sure would not spoil. I made slits in the soles of my sandals, inserted the two silver coins I had received as payment from Shimon into them, one to a sandal, and closed them cleverly so that no one could know. The tiny medallion given me by the centurion I sewed neatly into my undershirt. My knife went into a sheath which fastened to my belt. I had a small pouch which was closed with a drawstring and which went around my neck on a thong; into it I put a silver bracelet I had taken from my stepmother's chamber when the opportunity had presented itself. A maidservant who was often in trouble because of her insolence was blamed for the theft, whipped half to death by Shabtai—who as I well knew had his own private score to settle with the girl—and turned out of the house to starve or become a prostitute. I felt that the trinket might buy my way out of great difficulty and was glad to have come by it so easily and cleanly. There are few satisfactions greater than that of watching someone else pay for one's own wrongdoing.

I fixed the time for my departure. My mind was clear, completely untroubled. Nothing weighed on it, nothing disturbed it, nothing profaned its serenity. I felt strong and confident. All of my senses tingled with excitement; I seemed to see and hear more sharply and to touch with greater sensitivity. I was keen and certain, like an eaglet about to wing forth from the eyrie. I felt no fear, only a violent eagerness to be on my path. Everything was in readiness, even to the provisions of food I had arranged for myself in the kitchen. On the appointed day, I rose before dawn, slung my sack into place, patted my dagger to make sure it was in place, gathered my victuals and stole noiselessly out of the house.

I went first to my cache, retrieved my bow and supply of arrows, which I had managed by expert maneuvering to increase, and slipped through the streets so familiar to me out of the village. I had decided to head northeast, in the direction of Bethlehem and then perhaps to make my way to Jerusalem. I chose my path and struck a brisk pace. A fine mist blew gently against my face; the darkness, which would soon begin to dissipate, seemed to embrace me. I walked steadily for more than an hour, and then heard the distant barking of the dogs of the next village; as I approached the outlying houses, the din grew, and I gave them a wide berth. It began to grow light; I heard the cocks crowing. Then the village was well behind me. I continued down the road to Bethlehem, and the sun rose. It came from behind the mountains to the east; they turned a deep blue stained with violet as it ascended. The sky was like an open hearth; the clouds were long furrows of gold plowed into the brightening heavens. My heart throbbed, my mind exulted. The day was mine, the world was mine!

In an open field, among rocks, thistles and dying wildflowers, I killed a pheasant with a fine shot. I squatted, unsheathed my knife, and after I had plucked the pheasant, disemboweled and quartered it. I scooped out a shallow pit in the hardening earth, roasted the bird and ate of its flesh. Blood smeared my fingers and face, bits of feather stuck in my teeth, and my lips were covered with grease. My belly was full, my lust for slaughter was appeased; I belched and let wind. My knife lay in my lap, its handle glowing, its blade glittering; it was my companion, my true friend, for it too had steeped itself in gore. A slight wind blew; the fire died out to ash; the nettles and flowers of the field nodded. I was fetterless, without ties, without responsibility. I felt no loyalty, no restraint. My past had no claims on me; the dead were dead and could send no ghosts against me. They said there was a world beyond this one, but if there was, it had no meaning for me—did not exist for me, no matter what tales were told about it. And as for this world, the only one that was real as far as I was concerned, I would subdue it by gaining power over it: never would I allow it to achieve supremacy over me. My father was a person who had finally noticed Rome: I was a person who would compel Rome to take notice of me.

It was my belief that the Jews who were brazen enough to fight against Rome were vain in their struggle, and that they struggled in vain. They were foolish enough to oppose the certain visible might of the empire, which was as tangible and demonstrable as the detachments of Roman warriors who scoured the country from end to end rooting out all resistance, with their preposterous superstitions about an invisible, intangible undemonstrable being who was at once everywhere and nowhere! How could what they imagined about a nebulous ruler on high matter, when everyone clearly knew who ruled down below? And I felt myself well on my way to being a part of the world's sovereign force; and I felt that no one and nothing could impede my progress. So buoyant was I on my first morning of liberation that I did not bother to distinguish in the least between wish and fulfillment.

The sun passed its zenith, the hours went by, and the afternoon shadows lengthened. To the east, the mountains were gray and turning slowly darker as if they contained light within themselves, like vessels, and it was steadily draining out. Only their spurs and folds still glared whitely, as if the slopes had been raked by giant talons. The road grew rougher, the terrain more desolate. Volcanic rock littered the hills; the stray carobs and tamarisks were stunted; the earth was a hard rind, as there had been no rain in many months. I saw no sign of human habitation and no mark of animal life except for an occasional buzzard drifting high and then dwindling to a speck.

Then, ahead of me in the distance, I sighted a faint cloud of dust. I knew immediately that it came from the mounts of travelers. Though the riders were moving by daylight, I took no chances. I found a large cactus, hid myself well among its spines, and waited. At length, a group of four priests came by on mules. Their vestments were new, though covered over with dust, and their saddlebags stuffed to bursting. They were all four of them tall and lean, with glum-looking visages and carefully curled beards that were also whitened with the dust of their journey. They rode at a slow, steady pace in total silence, preoccupied perhaps with the God they could not see or touch but in Whom they believed nonetheless—or so at least they claimed. They looked, all four of them, as human as any other man, despite their sober garments, holy ornaments and somber hats. One had cheeks and forehead badly scarred by the pox; another showed an empty eye socket; a third had lost two fingers of his right hand; and the fourth coughed without stop, casting forth blood when he spat. I could not understand how their unseeable God helped them any or gave them any special power. It was true enough that they bowed to Him in their holy temple in Jerusalem and in their houses of worship throughout the land, but everywhere outside of these sanctuaries they bowed to the emperor. It might well be, as they said, that the kingdom of their God was forever and ever, but the emperor's kingdom was now: if they were able to ride the road they traveled along without fear of bodily harm it seemed to me that it was not because of the power of Him Who sat on high but because of the ironclad laws of the emperor who was enthroned in Rome. To me it seemed clear that the Eternal City far outshadowed the Kingdom of Eternity. Dour-faced, stoop-shouldered, looking bilious and weary and far more concerned with life in death than with the death in life that was so obviously theirs, they journeyed southward, to Beit Guvrin or perhaps even to the desert city of Beersheba far to the south. I watched them trundle along and spat with relief to have them out of sight. I had not yet reached a man's estate and yet I knew who made the world what it was and who kept it that way.

Late afternoon came; I had not covered half the distance to Bethlehem. A snake slid suddenly across the road in front of me. It was long and very black and shone like one of the whips Shabtai kept on his walls. I was pleased: snakes always gave me a sense of well-being. I admired the way they hugged to the earth, trusting it alone as worthy of their weight; and I admired the way they moved: never straightforward, but always oblique, always devious, always deceptive. Snakes were great favorites of mine: their venom, their armorlike scales, their veiled eyes, their forked tongues, their icy blood. They were truly kin of mine and I had no compunctions about killing them, just as they had no compunctions about killing me!

Evening fell. A hush came over the land. The birds and insects ceased singing. I scouted the area for a place in which I could shelter. After a while I found the perfect spot: a small cave high in the side of a hill. It was not too much larger than my body but large enough to hold me. That was enough. An animal had lodged in it not too long ago, and its odor was still strong. That was good. I sat hunched over in it and ate of the provisions I had brought with me: black bread, cheese, olives and scallions. I had also taken wine in a skin, and I drank freely of it. It was strong and good and rose to my head. My mind danced with visions that were intermingled, that I could not disentangle from each other: waking dreams whose meanings I could not even hope to decipher. I was highly amused by it all, and I was as detached from it as I would have been had players performed what I thought in the village square for the entertainment of all. I smiled and then gave such a great yawn that tears came to my eyes. Then I was overcome by drowsiness.

I curled up in my cave and fell instantly asleep. My slumber was deep: it was the slumber of innocence, of bliss, of utter primordial purity. My mother's entreaties and pleas, my father's injunctions and reprisals—these could not touch me at all, they had no influence on me, no power over me. My sleep flowed on like a swift river that could not be stopped: it was bottomless, forceful, uncontrollable and directionless. Neither dream nor nightmare reared itself like a rock to disturb the dark current. Only once during the night did I waken. It was very black and cold; a wind that seemed to come all the way from the distant, malevolent stars blew shrilly. Shivering, I peered out of the cave. The moon was up, a sharp half-moon sailing alone, isolated from the lesser orbs. I was fascinated by its aloofness, by its hauteur, and by its inviolate self-sufficiency. It seemed to me, in my drowsy state, to command the very night itself, to be sole and unchallenged majesty. As I gazed up at it, it flung down at me a quill of its frozen fire; and I in turn cast my javelin of cold scorn in response. We understood each other well: the dead body in the sky and the dead heart on earth.

I wakened with the sun, bade my cave farewell, and was on my way. The morning was uneventful; my pace was steady; and I was fortunate enough to find wild berries, carobs and even a few figs to breakfast on. I drank from a clear brook that crossed my path. Toward noon, a hill on my right caught my attention. It was higher than the others in the area and had atop it four crucifixes, each of them occupied by a body. In traveling with my father I had come across crucified criminals before, as I had seen naked women and girls; but now, as with the sight of my naked stepmother, the sight of these crosses struck me in a way I had never before experienced. Something inside me drew me to them.

I left the road, making a considerable detour. The hill was so high that the crucifixions could be seen for miles in all directions. I walked rapidly, my head bent forward, as if I had made an appointment I could not afford to miss. The sun beat down fiercely, I ran with sweat, and as I neared the crest, the stench became unbearable. Still, I pressed on. These four men, living or dead, had something to say to me, something I had to hear. When I was close enough to observe clearly, I stopped and wiped my brow. I had to shout to frighten away a flock of ravens which had been foraging, but even my loudest voice and vilest threats did not get rid of them all. Two of the men, on crosses slightly lower than the other pair, were dead: that I could make out right away. The birds had cleaned their eyes from their sockets and almost totally ravaged the rest of their faces; in spots only ragged threads of flesh clung to the facial bone. I hurled stones at the three or four birds who were brazen enough to remain and was glad when one struck its mark, bringing the raven to the ground, where I crushed its head with my foot. These two corpses had been bound to the crucifixes at the wrists and ankles, and there the flesh was black and running with fluid. One wore a soiled loincloth only, and the other a robe in tatters. I left them and went some yards further up.

The man on the cross to the left was a heavy fellow with a bald skull, puffed jowls and a thick yellowed nose that had been split open, perhaps by a whip. His big head was sunk on his chest, and but for the fact that he neither moved nor breathed, he looked as if he were napping. He, too, had been roped to his crucifix, and the ropes strained with his corpulence, cutting deeply into his skin. This man could not have been dead very long: it seemed to me that he was not yet used to his death, as if his earthly remains somehow nursed the hope that they would waken again. I wondered idly what crime he had been charged with and convicted of; he appeared too much the sluggard to have done anything worth bothering about. Of course, one never really knew: the body hid many sins and covered boundless evil. I had a single stone left in my hand, and on impulse, flung it at him. The stone struck him squarely on the top of his head and lacerated the scalp. I shrugged; let him shout at me for my action if he cared to.

That left the fourth and final man. He was much older than the other three, perhaps seventy or more, and I wondered idly why the Romans had bothered killing him rather than letting him die off of old age, for he was so thin and emaciated that he looked as if he had not long to go in any case. His head was shaven, in convict's fashion, and the arms and legs protruding from his ragged garment were so thin that they seemed almost the limbs of a child. Into the palms and feet of this man long iron spikes had been driven, nailing him firmly to his cross, as if his captors had somehow feared he might make good an escape. I looked up at him and saw that he still breathed but was surprised when he spoke; I had reckoned him far too weak for speech. His voice was remarkably clear.

"What are you doing here?" he said.

I felt him to be arrogant and stood with my hands on my hips. "I do not consider you in a position to interrogate me," I said loudly.

The little old man answered gently, "Have no fear, nor be you offended. I meant no harm with my question; I spoke to you as I did only for your welfare."

"For my welfare? No, you speak for your own. Each person speaks for his own sake, no matter how he may cover it over with interest in another."

"I am called Elimelech, and I mean only for your good. Tell me why you wander by yourself in this desolate spot. Why have you come to this hill of death? Did you run away from your home? Does your father know where you are? You may answer me in truth, for as I live, I intend you no harm."

I laughed. "Old man, you speak the words of a fool; indeed, you are much too old to talk as you do." I laughed again. "Tell me," I mocked, "does your father know where *you* are?"

The man called Elimelech was silent, as if in thought. His purple lips were parched and had burst and split so that they were all but unrecognizable as lips; over the cracks blood had dried in black gouts. Because he could not use his arms and because he had lost the strength to shake his head his mouth crawled with flies that did not even stir from him when he talked. He had been beaten savagely, that I saw, for his face was one great mass of bruises and lacerations. One eye had been shut completely by a blow, probably with a club or the butt of a whip, and his chin, matted with filthy stubble, had been laid open to the bone. When he finally spoke, his voice was even more soft than it had been before but it lost none of its unusual clarity. "Yes," he said deliberately. "Yes, my father does know where I am. Exactly where I am."

"So you make jest at my expense, do you, old man? You laugh at me, do you, you filth, you carrion, you vermin! You are an old man and your father is long dead and rotted in his miserable grave: how do you say to me that he knows where you are?"

"My father," replied Elimelech, "is alive, very much alive. Have no doubts about that. For my father is such a one as cannot die, one who has lived always and who will live to all eternity. But you, you, a mere child—how much poison there is in one so very young, in one who has hardly begun his life's journey. I am about to face death within the next few hours, and I do not fear what I shall see; but when I look into your eyes and hear your voice and stumble against the stone of your heart, then I am truly afraid, my child. How do you come to speak with such hatred?"

"I speak to you as I see fit. And soon, old man, there will be no more of you with whom to speak! You speak to me of my life while you are half a carcass yourself, nothing but bone and stink for the birds and the flies. And when you are black and gushing with pus and they need the crucifix for another one like you, they'll come and fling your dirty hide to the jackals! Your father, indeed! Your father is as dead as death, and so will you be before the day ends; then you can join your father in *Geheinom* and make sport with him as you fancy you do with me."

"My father," said Elimelech almost in a whisper, "dwells in heaven: his abode is on high but his spirit is with me, with me always. His spirit is everywhere, for there is no life without it. It whispers in the grass, it murmurs in the waves, it breathes in the trees, it sings with the breeze of evening, it shines forth from the eyes of dumb beasts—and if they but permit it, it speaks in the hearts of men. I know I am not mistaken when I say that it has spoken within you, and you have heard it plainly. It cannot be that one so young as you has already silenced it."

I guffawed. "If your God," I said, "or your father, or however you want to put it, is so powerful and has such dominion over the many forms of life, both great and small, how does it come about that a mere mortal man, and even a stripling, may cause Him to be silent?"

"Because," answered Elimelech, "God has chosen that man should choose Him. Man must decide for himself that he can hear the voice of God within him. Man must elect to recognize and know His spirit. Though God created the world in the beginning—and in truth there was no beginning as there will be no end—the world must be created anew each day, just as the sun must rise. Each man on this earth has a share in the world: he can create or destroy it, call forth order to it or call down chaos upon it." The old man's blasted lips trembled; his single seeing eye glistened. "But why do you stare at me with such contempt?"

"Do not exaggerate the importance of our conversation," I said coldly. "You and your old fool's words are not worthy of my contempt. You speak nobly of your God, who you say is everywhere; and yet, my corpse-to-be, your God has altogether deserted you. You tell me that your God's voice can reach the ear and the heart of every living man, and for all I know the dead as well, and yet the Roman warriors who marched you here to this hill and spiked you neatly as an insect to this cross did not hear so much as a peep from your God. And if your God allows a man to shut out the sound of His voice, what power does He have over a man? Do you really expect me to believe that if your God truly had the power to make a man behave as He wished him to, He would refrain from using that power? Does the emperor of Rome, who does not claim to dwell in heaven nor claim that he created the world in the beginning or will reign on high forever, does this emperor of men allow his subjects to cast his name and his wishes down? Has the emperor of Rome permitted you to drown out his voice? You say to me that a man can pretend that your God does not exist, but can you pretend that the emperor of Rome does not exist? Can you deny his nails or his cross or the cur's death that will be yours at sunset?"

Elimelech had listened in silence. But to what had he listened? Was it to my voice or another's, to my words or those of someone else? His good eye was luminous and the light in it soft, like the light that drops onto the petal of a flower in the early morning before the dew has vanished. He tried to smile, but his mangled lips and broken tooth stumps could not manage it: all that registered was the ghost of a smile. I did not know whether to laugh or cry, so incongruous was the attempt

in that wretched hulk of dying flesh. It seemed to me that I was looking at a jewel in a dung heap.

"I am far beyond the nails and far beyond the cross," said
Elimelech at length. "And I am far above the lowly, pathetic authority
of the emperor of Rome. There is nothing that this weak, vain, foolish
man or his myrmidons or his legions can do to me, no way that they can
touch my essence, no manner in which they can violate or mar my mind
or besmirch my soul or desecrate my heart. I am free of the emperor of
Rome and his hosts, nor can I ever be enslaved."

"You have a tongue in your head still, but it wags. When the
ravens get it, they'll make sense with it!"

Elimelech opened his mouth several times, as if he wished to say
something but could not bring himself to do it. After a considerable
time, he said softly: "I'm terribly thirsty. Can you give me a few drops
to drink? I don't need much, just a few drops."

"I've nothing to give you," I lied.

"Nothing at all?"

"Nothing."

The old man nodded. "It doesn't really matter. It was just a passing
whim, I've no need of it. Save whatever you have in your sack for yourself; there is no water in these parts."

Elimelech seemed to be staring past me, and wary of a sudden
attack, I turned and looked around. There was nothing to see except
parched, vacant hills from whose slopes the heat rose in a glassy curtain. Here and there a cactus grew: that was all. I faced the man on
the crucifix once again. Perhaps he had been looking at me or at least
thinking of me because he said, speaking with great difficulty, "You
should not be here."

"I can be wherever I like."

"Despise me as you may, I tell you this for your own good. The
Romans do not like anyone hanging around their crosses: they don't
want their handiwork disturbed. It's all right for people to see us from
afar—we're a good lesson to others, the Romans believe—but they
don't want anyone up close. You see, the Zealots have been cutting live
men down and freeing them; and when they find corpses on the crosses
they often remove them and substitute Roman soldiers or officials.
They may take you for a Zealot spy or scout if they should find you
up here. It won't make any difference to them that you are not yet a

grown man, they'll employ all of the devices they have to make you talk—even if you have nothing to tell them. It amuses their troops, keeps them from getting bored. Do you follow what I'm saying to you?"

"But I am no Zealot spy. And I have the means to prove it. If you were not already a crazy man and could appreciate it, I would show what I possess to you."

Elimelech ignored me. "And there are others whom you must fear as well: those who prey on the dead and dying, who take what the Romans leave and who sometimes even attack the Romans for what they have. You would not fare well with these scavengers."

"I can fend for myself, old man."

The lips, writhing like two crushed worms, trembled now. "Water," rasped Elimelech. "Just a drop. One drop."

I shook my head. "I have none. I have nothing at all to drink."

Moist with pain, the eye stared strangely at me, as if seeing me for the first time. "Why do you stay here?"

"I'm waiting."

"Waiting for what?"

"For you to die, old man."

"Of what use can my death be to you?"

"I want to see it. To be close to it. To watch it crawl toward you inch by inch; and to watch you crawl toward it. Perhaps there will be a miracle. Perhaps your God will stay the angel of death at the last instant. I want to see your face when you discover there is no miracle."

"You will see nothing that you can understand. Even if there is a miracle, you won't know it. You cannot see the life of a man; you will not be able to witness the death of a man."

"I will judge for myself, old man."

So saying, I seated myself at the foot of the cross. My companions were three cadavers and a pain-wracked body soon to be one. They were, all four of them, harmless. Like the quartet of priests I had seen earlier, they were pinioned to faith. But faith in what? I brushed away the flies that buzzed near to me: let them frolic on the meat above. I no longer smelled the putrescence, nor did the fierce heat of the day bother me. I yawned and gazed up at the cloudless sky; high in its glittering arch a swarm of buzzards circled, so tiny that they looked likes motes of dust. My stomach rumbled. Soon it would be time to eat.

53

Then I returned my attention to Elimelech's face, keeping a careful watch to see the stages it underwent on its journey from living man to dead soul. The old man's arms and legs were skeletal and at times seemed translucent, as if his flesh were about to give up its secret; every once in a while his lips twitched and I thought he would say something, but not a sound left them. I wondered if the God of whom he spoke could hear his silence. I scrutinized him exactingly, but there was little change. The flies swarmed over his lips and into his mouth, scarcely bothering to tumble out when he swallowed; they stuck at his good eye and clotted on the wounds of his skull. His battered face, if anything, softened and grew calmer, as if it had reached a point where pain could no longer twist it out of shape. The light in his glance did not diminish; once I even thought I caught a gleam in the slit that was the closed eye. I wondered what the old man thought about, wondered if he remembered his life: his woman or women, his children if he had any, his animals and fowl and properties, his riches, friends he had made, enemies he had hated, gains he had fought for, things he had hoped to accomplish. Or I wondered if he thought about the Romans, about his capture, the trial, the sentence that had been passed, the final hours before punishment. I wondered how he felt now that it had all—all of his life from the moment of his birth—narrowed down to this. Did he weigh or measure his life by some standard? Did he find the way he had lived worthwhile? Why had he allowed himself to come to this bitter end?

The afternoon wore on; the flaming sun slipped from its pinnacle, drawn down by a power greater than its own. In the same way the old man Elimelech was being pulled down into the pit of death by a power greater than he—a power which he claimed to recognize and accept. I fastened my eyes to his battered features, but there wasn't much to see. Whatever happened took place within him, away from the external world and perhaps far away from anything that had ever happened in his life. I took out my knife, turned it this way and that, blew on the point of the blade. I pulled out a half loaf of my bread and cut a thick slice of it; I chewed it into a paste before swallowing, and then ate a fistful of raisins one by one, savoring the sweetness of each, quite as if I were a miser. I washed the food down with several swigs of wine. The wine did not make me giddy; it seemed rather to have the opposite effect—to make me thoughtful, lucid.

Elimelech's voice drifted down; in a sudden flash of humor I fancied him a parrot on a perch. "You're not a child at all," he said. "You're a devil. I never believed in devils, no matter what I was told. But now I do. You are one."

"I am neither devil nor child: I am myself."

"You are not the age you look. Someone within you speaks, someone far beyond your age."

"I have no age. I was born without one, I will die without one."

"Yes, I see it. You make the devil possible. You make him actual. I understand it now."

In good humor, I opened my sack and returned the uneaten bread and the wineskin to it. "Well," I said, "why don't you get on with your dying? You're taking long enough."

Elimelech said, "You had wine with which you could have eased my thirst—I knew that you had it, or that you had water. But you gave me nothing."

"The drink was mine."

"And the terrible thirst?"

"That was yours."

"But if the situation were reversed?"

"It isn't."

"But if it were?"

"It could never be!"

"Still, if it happened so, what then?"

"I would expect nothing from you, fool!"

Elimelech's one good eye looked down at me. It had filled with a peculiar brilliance difficult to describe. The look was tender yet somehow strong, as if the strength came precisely from his compassion. Hard as I strained to find it, I could discover no malice in the old man's look, none at all. It seemed Elimelech had no need of malice, did not find it useful. But what I saw gave me no peace; as a matter of fact, it infuriated me, robbed me of my cheerful mood. I was filled with anger and wanted to strike Elimelech, but knew that it would have given me no pleasure whatsoever, since this man's flesh was beyond hurt. Instinctively, though, I knew I could wound his spirit. I rummaged in my sack and drew forth the wineskin once again.

"Did you really want a drink, then?"

"It's not the wine," said Elimelech softly. "It's that I wanted you to share it with me."

"So," I cried out, "so you shall have your wish!" I yanked the

55

stopper from the wineskin and waved it about, sloshing the liquid to the ground and laughing loudly as I did so. When I looked up again I saw that the old man had shut his seeing eye. I wondered if now he wished to die. I hoped so.

Sitting at the foot of the cross with the empty wineskin on my lap I remembered that Elimelech had said he was not afraid of death. But I wondered if he had been telling the truth. I wondered what it felt like to be nailed, hand and foot, to a wooden crucifix. Did one feel a part of the cross: immobile, almost inanimate, already lost to the world of the living? How was it to feel the life draining, bit by bit, out of the body one had inhabited for so many years; how was it to know that life was running, drop by drop, like water from a cracked vessel, and that nothing in the world could stop the flow? And what would death look like when it finally came? Would it be visible from afar on some distant inner horizon? Would its approach be gentle or terrifying? Would it grant a moment of respite in which one could harbor a last living thought, or would it press its claim with the swiftness of the executioner's axe? Would thought die slowly like a candle guttering, or would it snap suddenly like a thread a tailor breaks off between his teeth? Would the fear of dying kill before death arrived? Was not that fear of death itself death?

Elimelech's voice broke my thoughts. "Well," he said, "have you seen anything in my face?"

"Nothing," I answered.

"Am I transfigured?"

"No."

"I am tired," sighed Elimelech. "Very tired."

I glared up at him. "Perhaps your God will descend from the heavens in a chariot of fire and save you?"

"I have already been saved, my child. I have been spared a life like yours. I am grateful for that."

"You die like a mongrel and your God is of no help!"

"I die," said Elimelech, "like a man. A man who resisted death with all his might until it was no longer possible to do so. My choice was to live a slave or die a man: you can see how I've chosen. But you cannot understand what I accomplished, what I gained. Your eyes are blind, your heart is stone."

"I'm tired too, old man. Tired of you. Tired of your yapping. Tired of your cross. And tired of your God."

Elimelech ignored my words. "Are you Jewish?" he asked in an odd, melancholy tone. "Were you born in this land of Judea of Jewish parents?"

I shrugged. "I was born here," I said, "but who can say for sure what I am? Time will tell."

"No," whispered Elimelech, "you will tell."

And with that utterance he fell silent. His open eye seemed to dim and little by little the light went out of it. The hollows in his cheeks deepened, and his flesh took on a bluish-gray tone. I wondered if now he were in some no man's land between life and death, caught in a cross fire of entreaties from both sides. He was still alive: I could tell from his breathing. I was growing bored and restless: I began to feel it was not worth watching him die. He clung to life with such stubborn tenacity; I could not understand why. Perhaps Elimelech himself did not understand.

Evening came on. The first star strode boldly into the sky, confident that its chill blue light would burn a thousand thousand years, long after the men who gazed up at it now and for generations to come were dust of the field. Elimelech was quiet; I was quiet. It appeared that the two of us had finished our conversation: the old man was busy now learning a new language, the language of the void. The sky grew darker; the curves of the hills around me melted slowly one into the other. I had a last look at the crucified men —four shriveled crows against a lowering background—and then night folded them into its wrap. Perhaps I nodded, only for a matter of moments, but I came awake with a sudden start. Something had changed. I knew it was not Elimelech: his spirit had not left its shell. It was something -else, someone else. Kicking the bones of dead men aside, I inched my way back to the old man's cross. Its wood was rough, solid, almost large enough for me to hide behind. I crouched as near to the earth as I could and slowly drew out my dagger.

Now I heard footsteps clearly: they came from the direction of the two lowest crosses. A dark shape, gliding over the earth like a shadow, appeared on my left. If I were attacked, I would defend myself to the death. I shrank back against the crucifix and stiffened.

"Are you there?" a voice called out softly.

I didn't answer. The shadow stopped. It was difficult to make it out now, but I knew exactly where it was. I was not one to let a shadow evade me. When the voice spoke again, I realized it was a woman's.

"I know you're there. I saw you come this morning, and I watched you this afternoon. Answer me, please. I come in peace."

Still I said nothing.

"I won't harm you." The shadow moved forward. "You have nothing to fear, you can trust me."

To me it didn't matter, man or woman: an enemy was an enemy. I tightened my grip on the knife.

"Believe me, I'm here for the same reason you are. Don't be afraid of me." The woman moved ahead until she stood within scant feet of where I was, though I was certain she still did not see me. "My name is Zipporah. I was born in Safed. I'm a friend."

I uttered no word.

"There! I see you crouching by the cross! If I meant you harm, I should have done it already. Come here—come here, I say!"

There was no choice now. I rose slowly, holding my knife flat along my thigh. "Who are you?" I asked.

"A sufferer in Zion," said Zipporah. "A mourner. Like yourself."

I did not answer. I saw the woman more clearly. She was wrapped in a long cloak and wore a shawl over her head. Her voice had sounded young. I watched her hands for some sudden movement, but they were clasped before her, as if by pressing together they should somehow comfort each other. I could not make out her face, but kept close watch on her head, lest she signal with it. She stood quietly and talked to me.

"I saw you from my place of concealment when you first came to this hill. But I did not show myself; I don't dare to show myself by day. I have to be very careful. The Roman patrols come by here quite often to check and it would not do for me to be found out. You see, my husband was a Zealot with a large price on his head. They spent nearly two years hunting him down. They never would have located him—he was far too clever for them—except that someone informed. Even then it was no simple matter. He kept them in pursuit over a week, and then they had a very difficult time taking him. He was determined not to be captured alive. But they managed to surround him and break through in a massive attack. He tried to kill himself, but unfortunately did not succeed." She unclasped her hands and drew her cloak more tightly around her body. "The trial was immensely important for them. It created quite a stir in Jerusalem, and I have heard tell that word of it even reached back to Rome. The Romans wanted to make an example of him that would be remembered; Pilate himself attended the final session. They tortured him, of course. They had a lot to gain if they could get him to talk. And they were certain that their methods would bring results. But they were wrong. While in prison, he managed to have a razor smuggled in and cut off his tongue."

She leaned closer. In starlight, her face looked very white and cold, almost as if it was itself fashioned of the light of stars. Her eyes were large and luminous, swimming with mad light; her nose was aquiline, and her cheekbones high and prominent. Her thin lips were twisted into a grimace and twitched continuously, even when she was silent, as if they carried on a conversation to which she herself was not privy. "The dragnet was out for me. I had to run and hide like an animal, like a beast of the field. Friends in Nazareth hid me for a time, and then a Zealot family in Acre took me in. But it became very dangerous. The searches were sweeping and frequent. Though the family protested, I felt that my presence endangered them and that I had to go. One night I just slipped away. Since then, I've been living from pillar to post." Her cowled face contracted with pain: "Then in Jaffa I learned that he had been sentenced to crucifixion. That was merely an after-thought: during his imprisonment they had reduced him to a thing, a creature, a babbling hulk." She wept. "Now I'm here. It doesn't make sense. It's beyond all logic and reason. He was gone before they ever put him on the cross, and now he's a corpse. I can't do him any good. I can only do myself harm. If they catch me, I'll meet the same fate, or worse. They think I have information they can use; and even if they don't get anything, they'll feel that what they will do with me will deter others who might want to join the Zealots."

She left off. In the silence, I heard a strange sound. It came from above. It came from the cross, the cross with its rigid arms outstretched neither in pity, despair, helplessness, nor in supplication: it came from the cross with its stubborn arms of inflexible cruelty, of unrelenting

59

torture. The sound was soft, gentle, almost a bubble in the dark: it was the sound of the human broken on the inhuman. At that instant, what an affinity I felt for the crucifix! And for the whip and the bludgeon and the sword and spear and dagger and mace—and for all the instruments of violence that gave one man domination over another, that established a hierarchy of brute power! I realized that only a few feet above my head Elimelech's ghost was spurting forth from his feeble, fading flesh out to the furthermost stars and beyond. At last the old man would stumble into the mirage of his God in the black desert of eternity! A chill ran up and down my spine, and I turned my head to look up.

"Who is it?" whispered Zipporah. "Your father? An uncle? A friend of someone you love?"

I tried to catch sight of Elimelech's face but could not. Then, like the surge of a bird's wings, I heard his final sigh. It seemed to frame a word, but one which belonged to another realm. There was the wordless word and then a black space. The crucifix loomed against the vast pendulum of the constellations. It was over. Elimelech was dead. And he had cheated me. He had left in the dark, like a petty thief.

"Was he your father?" said Zipporah.

"My father is in heaven," I said.

"Was he a Zealot? A friend of your father's?"

I said nothing.

"I know . . . I know how you feel. I feel the same way."

I did not answer.

"Can I do anything? Can I help you? Do you want something to eat—I have a little, it's in a shelter I made for myself. I . . . I decided to keep him company. Until . . . until they take him down. And then I want to bury him. Somehow, some way, I want to bury him with his fathers. If I can, if only I can! At least I'll feel I've done something."

I remained silent.

"But come along with me. You can spend the night in my shelter. In the morning you can go. It isn't wise for you to stay here. Come with me."

"All right. I'll get my belongings."

I picked up my sack, my bow and arrows, and went with Zipporah. She had made for herself an excellent shelter: it was situated in a cleft between two large boulders. You had to push your way through a thick bramble bush to get into it, and the brambles hid the entrance completely. You could have passed it a thousand times and never known it was there. Inside, there was enough room for three or even four people. Zipporah squatted and gave me food: a piece of dried meat, dates and bread. I ate ravenously. She had water in a clay jar and gave me to drink as well. My belly was full and I leaned back against one of the rocks; my knife lay in my lap.

"Tell me about yourself," said Zipporah.

"I'm an orphan," I said. "My mother died when I was an infant, and my father was slain by a drunken Roman officer in a tavern. I lived with my grandparents in Jericho, but a month ago they were carried off by the plague. This man is an uncle, my father's eldest brother. I had hoped to stay with him but . . . well, you see for yourself what has happened."

"I see," said Zipporah. "Yes, I see." She handed me a carob. "What will you do now?"

"I don't know."

"Well," she said softly, "we'll see. Perhaps we can work something out. Perhaps we can help each other. We'll see . . ."

"All right," I said. "We'll see."

I saw her staring at me, squatting still, crouched like an animal in grief that seemed almost beyond her strength. She said nothing, but continued looking at me so for a long time, and then without a word curled up on the ground. "Rest," she whispered. "You'll need it." And then I heard the sound of her deep, regular breathing. She was asleep, far away from the death of her husband which awaited her on the hilltop when the sun rose; or perhaps her husband followed her into her dreams to possess her there. I watched her carefully for a time and then let my body and mind relax. The night was very still. There was no wind; the stars glittered feverishly. I returned my knife to its sheath, closed my eyes, and dozed.

I stretched my limbs and yawned. Zipporah was still asleep on the ground; one of her hands was flung out and the other clutched at her throat, as if a dark spirit within her slumber commanded her to choke herself. She was exhausted, and I knew it would be long before she would awaken. I stirred from my place and crept toward her on hands and knees. Expertly, with fingers that moved lightly as spiders, I went through her clothing. I found but a single coin, and it was not of the realm. I turned it over on my palm and reckoned it to be money minted by the Zealots. I decided to keep it; it might come in handy some time, one never knew. Then I searched her provisions. I took whatever dried meat there was, and the lentils, nuts and olives. There were two good-sized loaves of bread and I stowed them away in my sack. Of the water in her jar I took only enough to fill my wineskin and did not spill the rest. Then I parted the bramble bush, made my way through its branches, and crept silently away from the shelter.

To the east, the sky was turning gray. I stood and took a last look at the four crosses with the four men pinned to them: against the background of the coming day they looked like figures in a painting with the signature of Rome affixed boldly to it. I walked leisurely over to the crucifix with Elimelech on it and gazed up at his corpse's face. The single eye was glass—the eye of a jackass; and the mouth was wide open, frozen on the wordless word. It was the face of a defeated man.

The squad was camped in the shade of a clump of date trees, escaping the heat of the sun and eating its noonday meal. The soldiers, seven or eight of them, were sitting and squatting, chewing their food and swapping stories. Their shields and spears were stacked and they had thrown their helmets off in disorder. Apart from them, seated on a rock and swigging thirstily from a goatskin, was their leader, a noncommissioned officer of minor rank. He rinsed his mouth with a final gulp and spat it to the ground.

"Sir, I'd like to speak to your senior officer."

The squad leader put his goatskin down and belched. If he had seen me approach him, he had given no sign of it; perhaps he felt I was a tumbleweed or some other scrap of vegetation that had blown in from the hills. He was a heavy-set man, with a large, raw-boned, horsy face marked by severe bushy brows. His thick legs were spread out before him, and the broadsword buckled to his wide leather belt had dug its knobbed scabbard point into the sandy earth. He wiped his lips with the back of a hand and turned two small, crafty eyes on me.

"Where the devil did you come from?" he asked in a tone that still seemed to deny that I was present.

"From the road, sir."

"And what the hell do you want—a handout?"

"I don't want anything like that at all, sir—"

"Then what is it?"

"I want to talk to your senior officer."

The two watery little eyes grew still smaller: "And what is it exactly that you want to tell the senior officer? He's a very busy man, you know, and he can't go talking to just anybody. What's on your mind, you little Jewish bastard? Speak up."

"I have information to report, sir."

"Information? What sort of information?" The squad leader passed a hand over the sweat-clogged bristle of his closely shaven skull. I could sense that his mind was working, but it was working slowly, laboriously, struggling to keep up with events that it did not know how to analyze properly. The lips opened in a crude, forced parody of a smile; and the voice, under obvious control, softened. He rubbed his chin and looked me over carefully.

"So you have information to report, eh? You want to say some things to the senior officer, do you? Well, supposing you were to tell me and I were to pass the information along? Wouldn't that be even better? It would save you the trouble of going all the way over to see the senior officer."

"Well, sir, I don't know—"

"What's there to know, little Jewboy? As sure as your little asparagus is circumcised, I'm a Roman soldier, a noncommissioned officer. And anything you have to say you can just as well say to me."

Our conversation had attracted the interest of the other members of the squad. They had left off with their meal and were looking over at us. The nearest, a tall, gangling pimply-faced fellow who, supporting himself with one arm against the trunk of a tree, was urinating a heavy yellow stream, laughed loudly and called out, "If he's looking for something, there's some of us here who can give it to him!" His comrades laughed too, and several made obscene gestures. I glanced around at them. I was filled with disgust and apprehension. These soldiers were not the escort men, battle troops or cavalrymen with whom I was familiar. They had none of the bearing or the majesty of the soldiers whom the centurion had led, none of the regal hauteur and combat sharpness of the men who had guarded the official at my father's feast. They were men who had no idea of what it meant to serve the emperor and the empire. They were petty, mean creatures—gnats; and I surmised that they were for the most part conscripts or freed slaves or riffraff who had put on the Roman uniform to fill their bellies.

The squad leader picked up his helmet and toyed with its dirty plume. "Well," he said, "am I going to get an answer out of that ugly Jewish face of yours or not? To tell the truth," he continued—glancing over at the soldier who had spoken and who was now shaking the last drops of urine from his member, grinning foolishly—"to tell you the honest truth, the boys haven't been near women in a very long time, and you might possibly give them some amusement. Of course, it all depends on you, on whether you're going to be a stubborn Jewish brat or not. So make up your mind in a hurry. I don't have all day. Rome isn't Jerusalem, you know!"

It was quite clear to me. Behind the thick bone of that greasy forehead was the brain of an ape. It had to be satisfied somehow. He would have seized any real information about Zipporah for himself, and that would have been the end of me. There was no senior officer in the vicinity: that had been to gain my confidence and dupe me. It was too late to retreat now. The beady eyes, the flat nose, the tumorlike chin: they composed the face of a pygmy tyrant who had to be appeased. I was learning a lesson that I would not easily forget: that brutality cannot be safely entrusted to the brutish. I stirred my feet in the sand and stared down at them. "You see, sir," I mumbled, "the information I have to tell is about a man—"

"Louder! I can't hear a damn thing you're saying! Speak up clearly: Jews know how to talk loud enough when they want to!"

"It's this man, sir."

"What man?"

"I saw a man—"

"So you saw a man! What did he do?"

"He was one of those men who . . . one of those men who defy the emperor . . . who defy Rome . . ."

"You mean a rebel?"

"Yes, sir."

"A Zealot?"

"I think so, sir."

"When did you see this man?"

"Yesterday, sir."

"And where did you see him?"

"In the village next over to mine. As I was on the way, I stopped at the house of a friend of my father's. You see, sir, my father went to Jerusalem more than a month ago; he was supposed to have come back after a week's time. But he never returned. We have a farm, and there are six more children—small ones, your honor. And my mother bade me go to the Holy City to find out why my father did not come home, to discover what became of him—"

"Enough!" shouted the squad leader. "Enough of this imbecile's tale! Either you Jews have no tongues at all or your tongues work like mill wheels! Tell me, what was the name of your father's friend?"

"Ze'evi, sir. He is a cobbler by trade. He makes all of our shoes—"

"And you saw this man, this rebel, at Ze'evi's house?"

"In his animal shed, sir."

The squad leader slipped a long-bladed dagger from its sheath. He had long, hairy-knuckled, cruel fingers—the kind that are adept at tearing meat—and they grasped the knife's bronze handle and maneuvered it expertly as he picked bits of food from between his teeth with the point. With his free hand, he motioned me closer and spoke in a lowered voice. "And just how did you come to see the rebel?"

"It was this way, sir. I was on my way to the well to fetch water for myself and as I passed the shed I caught sight of a man inside it: someone I had never before seen . . . never in all my life. I had just a glimpse of him, your honor, but I knew that he was hiding—"

"But how do you know that the man was a rebel, a Zealot?"

"Because there has been so much talk of rebels in our villages, sir. We hear about them all the time. Sometimes they hide in ditches, sometimes in caves and sometimes in houses. This one was hiding in the shed."

The squad leader swallowed a sliver of food he had dislodged, made a wry face, and tapped the blade of his dagger on a knee. "Perhaps the man was a thief," he said. "Or a traveler who lodged the night in the shed. Could that have been?"

I dug the toes of one foot into the sand. "But he looked like a rebel . . ."

"And how does a rebel look?"

I was silent.

"Well, I'm waiting. A Roman soldier is waiting for a Jewish answer. What does a Zealot look like?"

"There was a woman," I blurted out suddenly. "There was a woman with him too, your honor. She was half undressed: I saw her naked breasts! There was a woman with him in the shed and he was a rebel and she was his helper, and it must have been so because everyone in our village knows about the rebels. My mother said if I disobeyed her one might carry me off, and I should not be heard from again!"

The squad leader hurled his knife at the earth: it buried itself almost to the handle an inch from my foot. I stared at it and then looked up at the squad leader. He rose slowly from the rock on which he had been sitting, letting prolonged deliberate wind as he did so. "So this"—he laughed bitterly—"so this was the information you had to impart to the senior officer, is it? This is the precious tidbit you had to offer? This is how you chose to poison my meal?" He retrieved the dagger and wiped its blade mechanically on his thigh. "You dirty little Jew-vermin, you come and tell me tales of Jewish whores with Jewish pimps in barns, do you? I should have turned you over to my men, that's what I should have done. They would have had a time with you that they'd soon have forgotten but that you would have remembered all the days of your life!" He thrust the knife savagely into its sheath and said through his clenched teeth, "Now get the hell out of here and count yourself lucky! Get out of my sight, you Jewish scum, before I change my mind. Get going, I say!"

I turned without a word and without a glance backward. I wanted to run, but checked myself, lest the running incite the squad leader's fury; instead, I walked as quickly as I was able. Behind my back, I heard him barking out orders and then I heard the sounds of his men gathering their equipment together. It was outright flattery to call them men. They were no more than a pack of mongrels who would tear each other to bits for garbage. They were cripples, hiding their deformities under the cloak of Rome. At the first bend in the road, I broke into a full run.

I had reckoned on entering Bethlehem that evening but it did not come to pass. At dusk, at the time when hills and sky mingle and the stars struggle out of their cocoons of oblivion, at the hour when coolness comes and the eyes are soothed by the departure of the sun, brigands set upon me. They were well concealed, and besides that, I had counted myself safe because I was within clear sight of the city. It was a grave error: to be in sight of safety does not mean to be safe.

There were three of them, all husky, all experienced. They pounced on me as from nowhere, as from out of the dusk itself, over-powered me in seconds and carried me bodily into the midst of a copse of acacias off to the side of the road. The trees were in a small hollow, so only their tops could be seen from the way; their leaves were withered and dust-whitened, and a smell of excrement came from among them. I had no chance to resist. I had no chance to cry out, for they stuffed my mouth with dead leaves. Then they bound my hands and feet with rope and shoved me to the ground. Helpless, I watched as they went through my sack and took all of my provisions. They took my bow and supply of arrows, my knife and my sandals. They discovered the pouch around my neck and thought it to be an amulet or talisman. When they ripped it open and found the bracelet, they hugged each other and cried out for joy. Ironically, it was my stepmother's bracelet which most probably saved my life. They were so stunned by the unexpected find that they left me where I was and departed. I had the sound of their laughter in my ears for a long time.

Then there were but the sounds of the night. They were lonely sounds, and for the first time I felt alone. I choked on the dry leaves and vomited and after some length of time cleared my mouth of most of them. There were tears in my eyes; I was glad no one was about to see them, and I hated myself. I struggled with the ropes as best I could. It was not easy, for they were stout and the brigands had tied difficult knots. But ropes and knots were no strangers to me. I put into practice all my experience and struggled with all my strength. Cold-fury lent me a patience beyond any I had ever discovered in myself. At last my hands were free and I could untie my legs. I rubbed the bruises and burns and breathed deeply. I was alive and unfettered. My eyes could see, my hands could grasp, my legs could walk, my teeth could bite, my mind could calculate, my heart could hate.

Above my head, the stars were sprinkled thickly across the black pelt of the sky. They shot blue and green fire at me. I heard jackals calling and jackals answering. A comet opened like a gash in the darkness and then the wound closed. I shivered and hugged myself and walked up and down to keep warm. I reckoned it best to stay where I was. So I gathered the leaves of the copse and made myself a bed of them, in which I huddled. I wanted to sleep but my mind pained me more than my body. Everything had been taken from me: everything but the tiny gold medallion of Rome, which was sewn into my undershirt and which they had not found, and the coin of the Zealots, which they had found but had not wanted. I slept only in brief, fitful intervals: my dreams were turbulent and jumbled, like cut veins out of which spurted shame mingled with rage. I could not remember them when I started awake, for they sank instantly back into the slime of sleep from which they had shapelessly emerged.

I wakened finally, unable to sleep again, as the stars were fading. I rose by the light of dawn and surveyed my surroundings. There was a stagnant pool at the edge of the trees, and I went there to wash the grime from myself. A green and gray bullfrog stared uncomprehendingly at me from the other side, but slid with a plop into the scummy water before I could maim or kill it. I watched the ripples from its plunge diminish and disappear before I straightened up and departed. The sun was in the sky and the cocks were crowing as I neared the city.

Thus it was that I entered Bethlehem, barked at by stray curs—to all appearances a street urchin or ragpicker. The voice of an early-risen vendor of melons carried through the air, mingling with the bray of a donkey and the hoarse, gurgling noises of prodded camels. The smells of food cooking drifted out through narrow window slits; I could hear infants crying and mothers assuring them that there was no need of it. A long line of shaven-skulled convicts came by, shuffling unsteadily, rattling their chains and herded along by yawning Roman guards. The gutters were filled with the prostrate forms of beggars and indigents, some of ·whom sat up dazedly, rubbing the food of dreams from their faces with filthy fingers. Ahead of me a prostitute, reeking of scents and ointments, limped painfully to her lodgings. From a side street scarcely larger than an alley a flock of sheep emerged, bleating, rolling limpid eyes, stirring up yesterday's dust.

From the hinterlands creaked carts loaded down with farm goods; atop their loads the farmers still dozed, looking with their lumpy-fleshed faces and earth-brown hands as if the soil had given birth to them along with their produce. The city grew more crowded, more squalid. The mud and straw hovels were low and often seemed to fall into each other or pile one on top of the next. Everyone was awake by now. Often, through tiny grates I saw families cramped into rooms like caves: coarse, swollen, shapeless mothers, with their grimy, squalling children tumbling over each other like so many swine; stooping out of doorways came the family heads, carrying the tools of their trades. The twisting streets and lanes were littered with animal excrement and human refuse; an overpowering stench filled the air. Wagons of all sizes and shapes, strings of donkeys and mules laden with goods of all kinds, and lurching camels moved in and out of the passageways between houses. A butcher passed, carrying the carcass of a freshly slaughtered sheep, the flies already spotting the bloody flesh.

I walked into a small, open square and stopped. Crossing it were three Roman soldiers, elite troops, on magnificent horses. Their spotless silver helmets were adorned with gleaming golden eagles; they wore bright yellow tunics, silver bucklers and crimson boots; their scabbards and spurs were of the same gold tone as the eagles mounted above their foreheads. I was dumbstruck; I had never seen such warriors, such men, such human figures above humanity. I could not understand how they would deign to ride through these streets, through this city, among this rabble. I could not comprehend how the human offal around them did not melt in their sight. I shrank back against a wall. I was ashamed: I did not want their eaglelike eyes to catch sight of me. Tattered, covered with dust and city slop, I felt myself unworthy to enter their vision. Even with my medallion, it was impossible to come before these incredible beings. They would never believe me, no matter what story I told them; and there was no reason they should. They passed in majestic cadence and disappeared from view. When I looked about me, it was hard for me to believe I had really seen them.

Noon. The sun beat down brazenly on Bethlehem. The city was in a stupor. Its citizens squeezed into strips of shade along the stone and mud walls, sprawled in the gutters and under trees. Doors closed and shutters were latched. The streets became oddly silent; even the beggars left off their wailing, as if midday separated the grief of morning from the grief of afternoon.

An old man seated on a low wooden stool stared at me. He beckoned to me eagerly with arms that had no hands: two glossy purple stumps jabbed through the air. I wondered what they had taken his hands for trying to take. His eyes, running with fluid, blinked, and he leered as he spoke. "Yes," he said, "you're a fine-looking boy, a fine-looking young man! What eyes, so black and with the shape of almonds! What thighs and splendid legs!" He wheezed, "Come closer, let me feast my eyes upon you: ah, yes, you are quite a morsel, my lad! Are you tired? Are you hungry or thirsty? Do you live in Bethlehem? Do you have kin here? Would you like something to eat? A place to sleep? Would you like to make some money? Silver pieces, my boy, even gold ones for a tasty lad like you. It won't be hard, I promise you. Not hard at all. You'll pick up the knack in no time, a quick boy like yourself!" The stumps danced in the air; the mouth gaped; the eyes ran without stop. I turned my back and went in the opposite direction.

A potter's wheel stood still. The potter dozed by his wares, but opened a baleful eye as I came near. The city was flattened by glare and heat, the vast majority of its inhabitants without escape. Only the rich, supine upon the cool tiles of their mosaic floors beneath their high, arching rooftops, behind their thick walls and massive shutters, napped securely and were not affrighted by their dreams. Without knowing where I was or where I was heading, I turned into a narrow street that gave off an odor of wood and dung. I went over to a grizzled fellow sitting on the ground.

"What street is this?" I asked.

His fingers touched the adze on his lap. "The Street of the Carpenters," he said.

"Do you know the man Yosef, a carpenter of Bethlehem?"

The man nodded and pointed down the street. "The last place on the right. You can't miss it, there aren't any houses beyond."

I stopped at length before a broken-down structure, half of plank, half of straw-filled mud; the doors had been ripped off, and I peered into the dim interior, which was littered with wood shavings. A goat stood to one side; at the rear, two young girls were playing with scraps of cloth. I went in. "Is this the house of Yosef the carpenter?"

The girls stopped playing and looked up at me fearfully; neither of them answered my question.

"I asked if Yosef the carpenter lives here? Do you know him? His wife's name is Mara. They have—a child . . ."

The older girl stood up. As she spoke, the younger held to her ragged skirt. "The man of that name used to live here. But that was some time ago. We have come to stay here now—my mother, my sister and I. The man Yosef went away. To the city of Nazareth, my mother said. He took Mara and the child with him. We live here now."

"Who is that?" a woman's voice called hoarsely from behind a partition. "Chana, who is it? Whom are you speaking to? Answer me."

I left and made my way back to the center of the city. I halted in front of a small bakery. The baker, a corpulent man whose red face and clothes were white with flour, was handing up fresh loaves to an assistant who placed each carefully in a large wicker basket. I walked up to the two of them. The assistant, a sallow-skinned adolescent, stared vacuously at me, but the baker scowled. "Get away from here," he growled, "get away from my shop, you little thief! You'd better take to your heels if you know what's good for you!"

I fumbled for the coin I had and held it out. The baker saw and struck at my hand wildly. "A Zealot coin!" he screamed. "You offer me a Zealot coin, do you? May the plague take you! Get away from here this minute or I'll call the authorities! They'll butcher you, you little scum, and sell you to the meat stalls!"

I bent to retrieve the coin which had rolled to the middle of the street. At that instant, a crashing blow landed on my temple and sent me reeling backward; I fell to the ground, clutching my face. When I pulled my bloody fingers away I saw above me the face of my father, black as death, and behind him his chief steward, Avner, with a length of new rope in his hands.

My father did not entrust the task of whipping me to anyone in the household: he reserved the pleasure for himself. He had decided to make my punishment a public spectacle and had ordered all of the servants to assemble in the yard, by the arbor where he had held the feast in honor of the Roman official. My stepmother was there, in a prominent place and obviously by command, for even the satisfaction of witnessing my shame had not been sufficiently strong to distract her from her grief. She was pale and drawn, and her face showed the strain the last months had had upon her; it was as if she herself were about to be lashed. I was led to the yard on a rope which bound my hands at the wrists like a criminal brought to the offices of justice. Most of the servants were silent and empty-eyed, but I could see that some who hated me, like the cook, smirked, though they did what they could to conceal it. I made certain to read each face carefully, for future reference.

Avner set out a wooden bench in the center of the yard and I was compelled to lie over it, resting my forearms on the ground. I had thought that the lashes would be given on my back, as I had seen in the flogging that had taken place in the village square. But my father ordered Avner to expose my buttocks. If at that moment it would have been possible for me to have killed him or by any other means prevent the order from being carried out, I should have done so even at the expense of my own life. There was nothing I could do, least of all cry out. Avner's hands yanked roughly at my clothing; my posterior and, through the cheeks, my testicles were exposed to the gaze of my father's wife, the nurse, the cook and all of the other members of the household. Avner stepped back, and turning my head slightly to the left, I saw out of the corner of an eye my father approaching in his usual brisk, businesslike manner. In his left hand, he carried his riding whip.

It was the finely worked rawhide quirt he cherished so dearly, given as a gift to him by some influential Roman. He knew its properties well—its weight, balance, flexibility; sometimes it seemed to be an extension of his hand. He handled it always with care, with certainty and with a sense of security that he carried it. Rarely did he let it out of his sight. He came at me without hesitation: tall, big-boned, erect, striding with a resolution almost painful to behold. When he halted, I felt his presence almost tangibly, and a shudder ran through my limbs. He did not strike immediately: not to think, I knew that, but to let me think. To let me wait for and tremble before the first blow. I heard the quirt as it rose with faint sound and then the savage swish as it came down. The actual blow was a relief. It exploded at the base of my skull, and the physical pain was so great that it blotted out my shame. As the blows continued, I was completely possessed by a physical pain so sharp it was almost pleasure. It was quite extraordinary. I forgot everything: where I was, even what was happening to me.

Water splashed in my face. I knew nothing. The knot of my hatred had come untied. I smiled. I opened my eyes. I saw Avner's leathery-skinned face peering down at me. His lips were drawn back over his teeth in a particularly repulsive way; his all but lashless eyes were very blue. Then I felt the hate rise in me again and his face blurred. Water splashed into my face once again; I choked and turned my head to spit it out. Avner still stared at me with his clay-mold face.

"Are you awake now?"

I did not answer him.

"I asked if you're awake. Speak to me."

I said nothing.

"Talk to me, say something, so I know that you're conscious."

I kept silent.

Everyone had disappeared. My father, my stepmother, the nurse, the cook, the stableboy and all the rest were nowhere to be seen. The yard was empty. Starlings clustered on the arbor. The sky was very blue and remote. Avner raised a hand that was black against it.

"I'm warning you," he said, "if you don't say a word or two to let me know—"

"I'm awake," I whispered.

I tasted blood in my mouth and wiped my lips, raising my tied hands to them.

"When you passed out," said Avner, "you fell from the bench. It's nothing."

I felt pain, but it was diffuse; it did not explode, it seemed simply to jump at random over parts of my body—my shoulders, legs, feet, back, neck. My buttocks were numb. I felt no sensation at all in them.

"Can you get up?"

I did not want him to touch me so I tried very hard. It was of no use. Each time I made the attempt, I fell back. My head swam. Avner bent over and picked me up: I was completely limp. He carried me to the animal shed. At the extreme right, beyond the stalls, a new chain had been fitted to the wall. He set me on the straw and then put the manacle at the chain's end around my right ankle. He snapped the catch into place, turned the key and slipped it into his cloak. He left without speaking a word and without turning back to look at me. I lay silently on the straw, breathing slowly, trying to guess where the pain would strike next. I shifted the leg with the manacle and my chain rattled. I was almost amused.

Through the many chinks in the roof, sunlight fell softly in mote-filled beams into the dim interior of the shed. Nearest to me, in the first stall, my father's bay mare stirred. She was uneasy and kept

73

tossing her head in my direction. Beyond her, in their own stalls, were the mules and the donkeys. In the last stall was a new horse, one which I had never seen before, most probably brought home when my father returned from his journey. Their hooves struck intermittently at the earthen floor; they snorted and whinnied and let sudden, explosive wind. Their grunting and rumbling seemed the senseless speech of prisoners without hope. I lay listening to their noises and trying to lull the pain. Sometimes the pain was again so keen that it was almost pleasure, just as exquisite pleasure can be painful. Pain and pleasure: they were an optical illusion which kept reversing itself in my mind. I scarcely knew what I felt at times, and it did not matter to me.

I had a vision of my father slumped in a chair, paralyzed, fallen over, his skin scabbed gray and green like the bullfrog at the pool. His face was yellow, browning, like rancid cheese; his eyes were rolled up into their sockets, searching for God knows what tyrant's paradise. He looked dead, ready for the grave, ready for rotting. Only a single blue vein throbbed in his temple, letting you know that he still lived. I was fascinated by the vein: it was blue as Avner's eyes and it twitched like the vein in my member when I had an erection. I watched the vein and wondered when it would stop its impatient stuttering and he would be dead and we could shove him into the earth over which he had walked so arrogantly. My stepmother examined him; her face registered open disgust. She threw his cloak back, exposing his putrefying body. She cast her own robe off and stood naked before him, moving her hips and her belly. He did not respond; she bent forward in anger and tore from his crotch a long, thin object which I thought at first to be his sex organ but which turned out to be his beloved riding whip. "Break it!" I cried out, and she laughed, raised it high above her head in two hands, brought it down over an upraised naked knee and broke it in two. My father's eyes showed great, staring pupils; blood spurted from his ears and mouth; he tumbled from his chair to the ground and gave up his ghost like bad gas. My stepmother smiled, cast down the broken sections of the quirt, and came over to me. I was bent, doubled over the bench. She stroked my buttocks and my testicles with her long, tapered fingers, and called me her son. I wept and pleaded with her to release me, but she said that it was not time, that I must wait until the fruit was ripe. But she comforted me and told me that she would never leave me and knelt by my head so that her nipples grazed my face. And Avner, my corpse-father's chief steward, stood by, looking on all that had transpired impassively with his lidless blue eyes, knowing that he himself would never die but that he would go on serving evil throughout all the generations, forever.

I stayed in the shed more than a month, seeing neither the sun by day nor the stars by night. Avner or another servant brought me food and water, but Avner always made certain he saw me with his own eyes once a day. He never said anything, just looked to see that I was actually there and checked the manacle to make sure it was secure. Maybe he thought I was a devil and could escape by infernal means, or maybe he thought I could bewitch or buy off one of his subordinates. Whatever the case, most likely on my father's orders, he showed up every day. For my part, I never questioned him, never said a single word to him. My father did not once pay me a visit, and I was glad of it. It got colder; Avner brought me an old cloak which I recognized as that of a kitchen worker who had died some months ago. At night I wrapped myself in it to sleep. I seldom woke from my slumber now; I was used to the sounds the animals made and could even distinguish one from the other in the dark. The new horse, which had turned out to be a black stallion, was most restless of all. When the stableboy fed them, the beasts chewed furiously, knocking against their stalls and grinding the food between their great, equine teeth as if they had never known a meal before and never would again.

I grew strangely comfortable in my prison, shut away from all the eyes which had seen my shame. Sometimes in the dark I could feel my soul, almost take it in my hands. In my solitary existence, my soul, which had been seared, had the time and the isolation—the inviolate insulation, I would call it—to harden. I was able to feel it harden, day by day, degree by degree; I was ever the more certain that it would be a soul I could use well in combat. It was a soul that had the keen cutting edge of the dagger, the reach of the sword, the distance and velocity of the arrow, the tenacity of the grappling hook, the crushing power of the mace. I was glad of the poison with which my prison life filled me; I felt there would be an inexhaustible supply for me to draw on in times of need.

Late in the afternoon one day Avner entered the shed. I was sitting with my back against the wall, watching a spider set its trap. To spin a web and snare prey in it: what deep satisfaction the spectacle gave me! So would enemies fall into my power! I had not paid attention to Avner, treating the visit as the customary one. But suddenly I saw that he stood over me, his legs planted apart. I was curious, but I took pains not to reveal myself.

"Listen, you," he said, "you'd better speak up now. Your father commands it. Should I report to him that you refuse, I would not care to be in your place."

I waited for him to say more.

"Has your stepmother been in this shed?"

"What are you talking about?"

"I mean exactly what I asked. Has your stepmother come into this shed?"

"Nobody comes into this shed except you or one of the other servants. Or the stableboy. You know that as well as I."

"Never mind what I know. I'm asking what you know. At night have you ever wakened from your sleep to find her here?"

"What would she do here?"

"Has she ever been in the shed with anyone else?"

I shrugged. "What would my stepmother want with the company of animals?"

"Are you certain of what you're saying?"

"Of course."

"Your father would be, let us say, extremely grateful to you for any knowledge of your stepmother which you may have—past or present."

"What would he offer?"

"That would depend on what you have to tell him."

I smiled. "I have nothing to tell him. Not a thing."

"So be it," said Avner. He turned as if to go, but then faced around again. "Your father," he said, "is thinking of releasing you soon. He asked my opinion on the matter."

"And what did you tell him?"

Avner smiled wryly. "No. But your father is merciful."

"Of course my father is merciful. No one could deny that."

"You have gotten off lightly; I hope you realize it."

"Of course I realize it. How should I doubt it?"

Avner's eyes glittered. "Your sarcasm is truly ill-advised. Had you been my son I should have given you a lesson that would have followed you like a faithful hound all the days of your life to the very grave;

and then it would have sat at the graveside, baying at the moon. But your father's heart is soft clay: it can be kneaded and shaped by those who have the fingers for it."

"But why should my father show compassion toward me?"

"I don't know."

"Does my father know?"

"I don't know if he does. I cannot read your father's heart. It is unintelligible to me."

"But you can read his mind, can't you?"

"I can. His mind is clear; it works logically; it moves toward logical ends. You belong to a dark part of your father, to a part which has no logic."

"Of what use am I to my father? What does he need me for? Why am I important to him?"

Avner shrugged. "I don't know," he said. "I cannot tell. Ask a man why he keeps a viper in his house. Who can say? Some men are fascinated by snakes, drawn to them, cannot leave them alone. It's beyond explanation."

The way my father's chief steward put it amused me. I smiled. "There has never been any love lost between the two of us," I said.

"No," said Avner, turning to go. "But we have left each other alone. What I have done, I have done because it was so commanded."

"And the asp dwelleth side by side with the python," I said.

"I have done as I was commanded," said Avner, already on his way to the door. "So has it been; so will it be."

"Until the command is lost," I said through my teeth.

But my father's servant was gone.

The stableboy who cared for the horses, mules and donkeys and sometimes brought me my food was an orphan who had been with us since he was a small child. Slow of speech, he had red hair, freckles, and a mouthful of rotting teeth. When he was excited or agitated, he stammered so badly it was impossible to understand him. He was fifteen but not much taller than I and prone to fits of extreme depression. I had never had anything to do with him, but during my imprisonment I cultivated him. I would talk to him, spinning wild yarns and inventing fantastic tales, and he would listen

77

open-mouthed, his quivering chin arun with spittle. He became fond of me and hid forbidden food under his cloak for me; once he brought me wine and the two of us drank ourselves into a stupor. He passed out near the arbor and was thrashed the next morning for drunkenness. I told him about the place where I had buried copper coins a year ago, and he went and dug them up. When I told him he could keep them for his own, he wept and hugged me; his tears were hot on my neck and cheeks, and his frail body shook. In return he gave me a treasure of his I had long admired: a slingshot he had made and hunted with occasionally. He also kept me supplied with rocks and sharp stones. I kept my weapon and my ammunition hidden beneath the straw.

When I was alone, usually at dawn or in the late afternoon, I took the slingshot out and used it to snipe at the rats which used the crossbeams as bridges or at the starlings and the sparrows attracted to the food bins. Some days I kept busy at this new pursuit of mine for hours and became far more accomplished with the slingshot than I had been with the bow. Steadying my arm day by day, sharpening my sight hour after hour, in varying light, I reaped bountiful harvests of death. With each kill, a new power seemed to flow into me, and I seemed to feel a keener sense of life. It was odd that out of making death I could have a sense of life, but so it was. The satisfaction was very strong, very heady, almost aphrodisiac. And it was odd in another way: I was the killer and yet somehow in some obscure way I felt as if it were I who was being killed: it was as if I was at once perpetrator and victim; I knew how it was to slaughter and to be slaughtered.

And the killing had no purpose, none at all. I did not want to rid the world of rats, nor did I desire to get rid of starlings and sparrows. In fact, I wanted more rats and more birds. I wanted simply to kill. And to know that the death I dealt out arbitrarily, at my will and in my time, was pointless, meaningless, wanton.

Hunter! Killer! Executioner! Judge of Life! Lord of Death! Black Wind! Final Dawn! Terminal Evening! How thin, how fragile the membrane of life! I could not help remembering Elimelech on his crucifix, nailed to his wood: his breast bared to the sky of day and of night, to its dew, mist, rain, heat; his one sightful eye watching, watching for death to come along the road, trudge slowly up the hill (out of breath at the last), and climb the cross to embrace him and kiss him full upon his withered lips. Irony of ironies! His own lips were wasted, but those of death were taut as buds, full as nipples.

Yes, oh, yes! Death was a kiss. I knew that now as I had never known it all the days of my life. Death was not a savage strike, a brutal blow: death was only a gentle kiss! How clearly I saw to the heart of the matter: the arrow kissed the hare and the doe, the spear kissed the outlaw Ze'evi's throat, my rocks and sharp stones kissed the skulls of rats and breasts of birds. A secret, powerful executioner had done away with Elimelech, my friend Elimelech. He had drawn a bead on the old man, fixed him firmly in the pupils of his eyes, locked him like a spider in his web. "You are going to die," he had whispered. And Elimelech had heard the inaudible words. Heard them and responded: "Amen," he had breathed softly. "I am going to die."

As the days went by, the stableboy, who was called Zvi, became more and more deeply attached to me. He constantly stole food and even sweets for me; he brought me a much-patched blanket from God knows where. He asked me questions about my father and my stepmother, which I did not answer; but when he begged me to tell him tales, I was always ready. Zvi soon realized what purpose I put the slingshot to, but he never breathed a word of it to anyone.

I remembered one morning where I had secreted an amulet I had been given by my mother many years ago—or perhaps had stolen from her, I could not recall, it no longer mattered if ever it had—and I described the hiding place so that Zvi would be able to find it. He could hardly wait to get started, but I cautioned him that he must not be absent from his duties without a justifiable reason. Finally he had the chance to go. He returned, bitterly disappointed, for he had failed to find the object, having taken a wrong turn. I repeated the directions to him, stopping often so that he would fully absorb them. This time, Zvi brought the amulet to me with great pride. It was a worthless trinket, tarnished now almost beyond all recognition, but when I informed him that it was his to keep he was incredulous. His eyes brimmed with tears. He promised me that he would always care for me and always remain loyal to me. He told me that I was dearest to him in all the world. He asked me if I truly cared for him.

"Be assured," I told him. "I care for nobody more than I care for you."

Zvi continued to serve my needs in every way that he could. I wondered if Avner felt toward my father the way Zvi felt toward me, and I wondered exactly what it was that Zvi felt. I tried to question him about it sometimes, but it was of little use. I thought that whatever he felt was foreign to me. Then it was that my thoughts began to be of interest to me: instead of cutting them off as they flowed on, as had been my wont, I let them carry me where they would. I became distracted, subsumed by my explorations, and many times Zvi would shake me by the shoulder and ask if I were well.

One day I asked Zvi if he could manage to bring me writing materials. He said that he would try, that he would bring me anything I wanted if it were but possible. It took him two days, but he made good his promise. I told him that when I was released I would reward him well for his service. But he just shook his head and laughed.

The teacher I had been compelled to visit had instructed me in the characters of the alphabet and had taught me how to form a number of words. I wrote them out. Simple words. I wrote them over and over again. It was strange for me to assemble a group of radicals and make the sudden discovery that the name of an object, or color, or feeling had come into existence; at first I experienced a shock every time I did it, as if I were performing some sorcery. I had, at various times, watched Holy Scribes in the village as they copied out the Law on parchment. I sensed the power in what they were doing, though I had no clear idea what it was, and sometimes moved as close to them as I could without incurring their wrath, hoping that some of the strength would enter me.

I sensed a raw power in words. A fierce, primordial power in the letters from which words were formed. Sentences were beyond my reach, but I could well guess the horizons on which they would open. It occurred to me that a man who read was bound to that which he read, that his thoughts and feelings were caught like fish in the nets that words and sentences spread. Reading could caress a man and words could whip him; words could impell a man to deeds, and reading could restrain him from action. Words lulled men to sleep, and words wakened him to battle. Words could be a mirror unto a man in which he might see himself as he was; and words could be a map of his past which he might study to great profit. A man could write words and die, and the words that he had written might remain after him, yet alive, calling out to other men as if it were the dead man himself crying from beyond the veil of death. Words were stones or gems, slag or rich ore. The Jews could scribble of God, the Romans note down the laws of dominion.

My efforts were limited, primitive. I would write a word and stare at it: I had written it and yet it stood outside of me, living a life of its own. Once written, the word had a kind of new authority: it now carried a weight the reader had to dislodge. If I wrote something as truth, the reader had the burden of disproving it. I had long known what weapons could do; I now became acquainted with the potency of words.

I was fascinated, spellbound, hungry: I wanted more. The next time Avner appeared, I asked that he convey a request to my father: that my teacher be sent to the shed to instruct me. My father's chief steward shrugged impassively. That very evening, the answer came. Permission was granted. I knew that my father interpreted the request as a gesture of submission.

The next day a short, heavy-set man with a full beard and long earlocks came into the shed. He motioned impatiently to Zvi, who had been forking hay into the bins, and the stableboy brought over a wooden stool and backed off, wiping his face of drool as he went. The man, who had a large mole on his left cheek and was missing a finger, seated himself and planted his legs apart. I disliked him immediately; and I also knew that it would be a serious mistake to allow my dislike to be known.

"My teacher?"

The man waved me to silence. "Your teacher," he said in a rasping voice, "was arrested and charged with giving aid to the Zealots. The authorities have removed him. I am the new rabbi. I will be your teacher from now on."

"What will you teach me?"

The rabbi had a nose that had been broken, perhaps more than once, thick, sensual lips that curled around words with a cruel possessiveness, and small eyes—the eyes of a man who sees an opponent in everyone. His fingers gripped his knees as if he had to force himself to remain seated. "What is it that you wish to be taught?"

"Words," I said. "Many words that will make sentences, and sentences that will make tracts."

"And the Holy Books? Do you not wish to study them?"

"I will study the Holy Books if there be need."

"Every child must study the Holy Books. How else can he become a man?"

"As you decree, my rabbi, so let it be. So let us begin."

The rabbi laughed—a loud, long coarse laugh that caused my father's mare to shift nervously in her stall. "Your father says you are no child. Is that true?"

"I have been told that I am no child, that I lack innocence. But I do not believe that innocence exists; I find it an invention of minds that wish to view the world falsely, of men who desire to dupe themselves and others. We are all of us wolves in this world. There are no lambs amongst us: there are only those who choose to see themselves as lambs because they do not want to see themselves as wolves."

The rabbi stroked his beard. "Yes," he said, "I can see what your father means. You are old before your time. One might even mourn for you . . . if one were inclined to mourn." The little eyes burned with fatty light.

The rabbi laughed again; behind him, the mare slammed her hooves into the stall, and Zvi went over to calm her. The rabbi scratched his head. "Do you believe in God, my boy?"

"Does not every Hebrew believe in God?"

"Come, come, my lad," said the rabbi, "the God of Israel does not countenance evasions; the God of Israel calls to account. You ought to know that by now."

I was silent; then I said, "The God of Israel has not seen fit to show Himself to me."

"And the devil?"

"Who is the devil?"

"Who is the devil? How do you ask a question like that? The devil is he who took your childhood from you and slaughtered it as a kid. Try to persuade me that the devil does not appear to you in your dreams and I shall call you a liar."

"What does he look like?"

"What does he look like, indeed? Like the face that peers back at you when you kneel over water! Yes, you know the devil well, you harlot; he has set the mark of his cloven hoof on your forehead, and it burns like sulfur in the night; I smell it even by day—"

"I have sighted the devil, Rabbi: he looks like you."

The rabbi roared. "Like me, indeed! Why, I am nearer to angel than I am to man! I hold converse with the messengers of He who speaks from behind a hedge of Eternal Cloud. The blood of priests bubbles like sacramental wine in my veins. You cannot bait me, little monster: I have met your kind before. Met them and blown them into the air like chaff."

"Though I am as chaff in your eyes, will you teach me?"

The rabbi wiped his lips on the back of a hand. "So you tell me that the God of Israel has not seen fit to reveal Himself to you, do you? To whom then does He choose to show His face? Can you answer that question? Do you know of a single man or woman or child who has seen the Unseeable? Don't you think that I can penetrate your ploy? I know that you are using your question to avoid mine. Do you believe in Him? Answer me directly."

"If the God of Israel is invisible, so is His power. I search for His power, but fail to find it anywhere. But with the Romans, it is a different matter—"

"The Romans?"

"The Romans worship what they can see, what they can touch, what they can hold in their hands. They hold their emperor to be holy because they feel his power—feel it directly, every day of their lives. That is why they engrave his image on their coins and emblazon it upon their arms. Their kingdom is the kingdom of the body on earth. Whatever spirit there is in the world takes care of itself, follows the flesh: they don't worry about it."

"How do you come to know so much about the Romans?"

"I have studied them well: I have sucked the she-wolf's teat from birth. As has my father. As have you yourself, my rabbi."

"As have I? What drivel are you talking?"

"My former teacher has been taken away from the village because he held out his hand to the rebels. This you told me with your own tongue. Then explain to me what you are doing in his stead? Who sent you to take his place? Surely the great seal of Rome has been set upon you."

"The fact that a man does not oppose the Romans does not mean that he is with them. What belongs to the government of Rome must be given to the government of Rome. That's a self-evident proposition if ever there was one." The rabbi rose, stretched his limbs and yawned. "But I must be getting on. Our little chat together has come to an end, and God is still as great a mystery as He ever was. We have solved nothing."

"But when will we begin our studies? Tomorrow? I don't want to put them off. Can we start tomorrow?"

The rabbi's eyes shut almost to pinpoints in the folds of flesh surrounding them. He laughed scornfully. "You didn't really believe that I would teach you, did you? You didn't take my visit seriously, I hope. I'm looking at your face now, and I'm amazed. Amazed, my boy. Your father bade me pay a visit to you to show you what you had lost by your savage and obstinate behavior. That's the long and the short of it. You are not a child, true enough, but you are a fool."

I had miscalculated. I had grossly underestimated my father. For his game of chess was more subtle and more complex than I had guessed. The rabbi was simply a pawn, an instrument of torture suited to my present state. The whip no longer interested my father because I had endured it; imprisonment no longer pleased him because I had grown used to it. He had waited patiently to discover how best he could get at me. Had I asked for a larger amount of food, my portion would have been decreased. Even the hint of release was bait in the trap; had I pleaded for leniency when Avner mentioned freedom, my father would have ordered the term extended. My father made his every move in response to what I wanted. I clenched my fingers so tightly that the nails cut into my palms. "Teach me," I cried out. "Teach me, my rabbi! You must teach me! My father is not king in this village, nor are you his vassal! Instruct me, I say!"

Straining the chain that tethered me, I reached out and clutched his forearm. The skin was like hide—cold, rough, almost reptilian. The rabbi drew back, his face dark with anger. "Take your filthy hands off me!" he said. I did not let go, and with his free hand he struck me in the face. The slap shocked me, but not into retreat. Instead, I sank to the straw and buried my teeth in the flesh of his calf. He bellowed and dealt me a furious blow with all of his might. It knocked me to the wall.

"Pagan!" he screamed. "Pimp! Son of a swine! Your father erred in that he fed you for a single day of your miserable life. Look what you've done! My leg is bleeding. You've wounded me, mad dog. You'll pay for this: I promise you that you'll pay dearly for this. On my life, I'll make you pay." His face had turned purple; he held his injured leg and hopped this way and that, almost comic in his antics. He had started to leave, but I saw plainly there was something holding him in the shed; I saw there was a part of him which could not go, a part aside from that in him which wanted to thrash the life out of me and the wrath out of himself. His lips twitched convulsively, his eyes were the color of phlegm, his beard was spattered with saliva, he was livid with rage; yet there was deep within him something which tied him to me as fast as I was tied to the wall.

All of the animals were disturbed now; they were shifting and knocking about. Zvi, who was standing under the hayrack and holding his pitchfork tightly, his face working with fear and confusion, seemed one of them. The rabbi, whose movements were almost without volition, seemed also to belong to the company of the stable. I felt no pain from the blows, the dizziness left me, my mind cleared. My back was against the wall. My hands slid over the straw. I found the slingshot and groped for a rock; the first one I located I fitted into the pocket. I never took my eyes from the rabbi.

"Rabbi," I said. "You mentioned the God of Israel . . . You told me no one ever sees Him . . ."

"You dare to speak to me? You have the effrontery to mock me? You want me to teach you, do you? Well, I'll give you a lesson in manners far different from the ones you dreamed for yourself—"

"Rabbi, I will introduce you to your God."

The rabbi was so choked with rage he could not speak. Menacingly he took a step toward me; he held two fists before him as the procurer in Bethlehem had held out his stumps. He took another step forward. I sensed he was bluffing. More than that, I sensed that it was he who feared me, he who was afraid of what he read in my face and saw in my eyes. I did not believe he really wanted to take a step toward me: it was his wish not to take it that pushed him to take the second and would push him to take another. Since that day in the shed I have often seen men take revenge on themselves and on others for doing what they do not want to do—by further pursuing the course of the unwanted action.

"You're going to get your just reward, barbarian bastard—"

He never said another word. Nor did he take the step he intended. The hours and hours of picking off rats and starlings had served me well. I raised the slingshot in a swift, smooth motion, sighted as I drew the sling, and let fly. It was the shot of a consummate hunter. All of my strength went into drawing back the sling, all of my skill into the aim. The rock was a sharp one, and it struck the rabbi in his right temple with tremendous force. He fell like a stone. The sound he uttered was no more than that of a rat or a sparrow. He lay face down in straw and dung, his head to the rear of the stallion's stall. Though the animals were noisy and excited, the shed seemed utterly silent. It was as if the inert body of the rabbi imposed a silence beyond the reach of what men usually call sound. I pushed aside the straw at the wall and buried the slingshot under it; then I divided my supply of rocks and stones. When I looked up again, all was as it had been: the rabbi was sprawled out, motionless as a board; the horses were rearing and the donkeys and mules braying; Zvi clutched his pitchfork, blubbering.

"What in the name of God is the matter with you?" I hissed.

Zvi tried to look at me, but did not seem able to focus his eyes.

"Come here," I commanded.

He did not stir.

"Come over to me," I said gently. "Come over to me at once."

Walking as if drugged, he rounded the stalls, gave the body of the rabbi wide berth, and came over to me.

"Sit down," I said, "and listen carefully. We don't have much time."

He squatted, his eyes large and empty. I took him by his shoulders. "Pay attention to me. I will tell you what you are to say about the rabbi, and no matter who asks you, you will repeat the same story." I shook him. "Do you understand me, Zvi?"

Tears ran down his cheeks; his lips, which had turned quite blue, trembled. I held his wrists and drew him closer, staring directly into his eyes. "The rabbi was kicked by the stallion," I said. "The rabbi bent over by the stall of the stallion to fix his sandal, and the horse kicked him in the head. Is that clear?"

Zvi looked at me blankly.

"Say it! Tell me the story you will tell anyone who asks! Say it to me, Zvi, or you and I will never again be friends!"

"The rabbi was kicked by the stallion," said Zvi.

The affair passed off well. I did my part and Zvi did his. He did it perfectly, though as the days passed he grew more and more reserved and uncommunicative; his face grew pale, his body more frail. He worried me. He no longer listened to my stories as in the past, no longer smuggled me food. I kept a close watch on him. From the shed I could often hear the servants talking. The rabbi had been buried with great pomp; the mourners had chanted more psalms, and more loudly, than anyone could remember. A representative of the government had attended the funeral and even bowed his head at the grave.

I was glad enough the rabbi had gone his way, but my dreams frightened me. He kept rising from the earth, and I kept felling him with my slingshot. In some dreams he rose as himself, with small eyes and broken nose and full beard; in others he had a long tail and squealed; in others he was feathered from neck to feet. Sometimes he spoke about the kingdom of God and the angels and cherubim and the celestial radiance beyond the ken of mortals, and other times he talked of the devil's inferno, where men had the forms of animals and were hunted and slaughtered or repeated the hour and manner of their deaths endlessly, crying out for mercy to a great deaf ear that bled from its drum like a hymen but never opened. As soon as I saw him, I reached for my slingshot, loaded it, and shot him dead. But he always rose again, and I woke from each dream in a cold sweat.

I was not sorry for the rabbi. I felt no horror for what I had done. I could not understand why his corpse clung to me like a leech in my dreams. A dead man could not be raised—unless someone drew him out of the earth by talking of the way in which he had been slain. I did not like the manner in which Zvi averted his eyes and face; I did not trust his silence and moroseness; I did not care for the signs of inner suffering that his body plainly showed. I knew that what Avner felt for my father was not what Zvi felt for me. When my father spoke, Avner silenced every inner voice, but Zvi did not. As time went on, he seemed scarcely to hear my voice. I began to feel that I would have to arrange something for Zvi, but how it would be done and when I did not know. One thing was certain: I could not let him drift completely out of my reach. Anything might happen in that event.

I had crossed the line. I had murdered a man, not killed an animal. Yet the release I had expected was not there. It was true that with my own hands I had erased the rabbi, and this gave me a feeling of destructive power I had never had, but it was also true that dispensing with him in the way I did was like ridding myself of a pest. I had not planned the deed and thus had no chance to savor either the anticipation or the unwinding of events. And the rabbi was dead, under the earth. There was nothing more that I could do to him. This, too, was a lesson that I learned and remembered: once a man is dead he is beyond one's power.

I understood why the rabbi troubled my dreams: it was because Zvi had been witness to his death. I did everything in my power to reach the stableboy, to heal the breach between us if I could. I spoke softly to him, entreated him to my side, promised him undreamed-of rewards when I was free. I think he wanted to respond, wished our relationship to be as before, but could not feel toward me as he had. I explained to him over and over that the rabbi had been an evil man, that he had threatened my life, that I had felled him in self-defense, that I had not meant to kill him—only to stun him and stop his advance. Zvi listened to me patiently, not stirring from his place until I finished. But his eyes remained lifeless. It was as if somebody had poured sand over the fire that used to light them.

One night the rabbi again rose from his grave in my dream. He looked himself—had neither tail nor feathers. As always, I reached for my slingshot. But the rabbi put up a hand. He looked quite composed, almost peaceful; his clothing was clean and his beard freshly combed. He said that I must give him a chance to speak, that this was the last time he would appear to me in a dream, that we should never meet again. I had the slingshot in my hand, already loaded, in case of need. I warned him not to come too close, and he agreed. "I can understand your caution," he said. "In your place, I should behave as you do."

He seated himself comfortably before me, stroked his nose with two fingers and patted his beard. "When last we were together," he said, clearing his throat, "we spoke of the God of Israel, the One Who is never seen, the eternally intangible, the mystery of mysteries, the One man searches for always but can never find. I thought you would want to know—"

"Know what?"

"What He is like."

"I want to know. I must know!"

The rabbi smiled. There was almost kindness in his face. His lips seemed no longer to loathe the words they formed. "It is this way," he said. "God is cat-God and man is mouse-man. All his life a man searches for God, never realizing that there is cat-God and there is mouse-man; all of his days a man scampers here and there, to and fro, never knowing that he is always between God's paws like a mouse. God is in no hurry, He has all the time He wants. And when He's through with time, He has eternity. He plays with the man, He licks His chops. Sometimes He puts His paw on the man's tail. The man is bewildered and frightened and cries out in anguish. Something holds him fast, but he does not know what. A predatory breath blows down on him, but he doesn't know where it comes from. He calls out to a merciful God, and God salivates. He trembles and his heart aches so that he feels his chest will burst open, and God licks His whiskers. The man is dazed, confounded, barren. And God lifts his paw. The man breathes again, finds comfort. He gives thanks to a loving, kind God, and God yawns. The man scurries on about his life, running this way and that. And then one fine day God decides that the man has had time enough. Down comes His paw on the tail. The man is terrified, but he remembers how well he came through the last time. He is hopeful; he even struggles, trustful that the Living God will come to his aid. And God, snarling, thrusts forth his jaws and gobbles the man in a single mouthful!" The rabbi spread his hands apart. "That's all there is to it," he said. "Nothing more."

"Nothing more?"

"Nothing."

"Are you certain?"

"I am the living witness."

I sat in silence, keeping a watchful eye on the rabbi. He was very quiet, very respectful; he even folded his hands and placed them neatly in his lap. From time to time he closed his eyes and his features were relaxed; he looked well, better than he had in life. After a while he said, "I'm going to get up now. Don't be alarmed." He stood and said, "Now shoot me."

"I don't understand. You haven't . . . I mean, you aren't . . ."

"You must slay me again. It's the only way I can go."

"You can't just leave?"

"No, you must kill me again."

I had no desire to kill a man already dead, but if he wanted it so, it was his affair. I sighted carefully, taking plenty of time, just as if I were taking target practice. The stone was round and smooth and very cold; I thought it might have come from the bed of a mountain stream. It was a perfect stone, a joy to fit into the pocket. I let fly. The missile flew out straight on its course and suddenly, at the last moment, swerved wide of its mark. I was astonished. I rarely missed a shot, and if I did it was nearly always because I had to get it off in a hurry. I shot again, and once more the stone went wide of the mark at the last instant. The same thing happened the third time. The rabbi stood untouched, smiling.

"You were supposed to go away—forever," I said.

"I will," said the rabbi. "But you must kill me or I can't go."

"You didn't tell me that part of it."

"Does a cat tell a mouse?" laughed the rabbi.

I fired again and missed.

Just at dawn I wakened to an odd sound: it was dry, sharp and rhythmic; sometimes there was a metallic ring mixed in with it. I lay flat on my back in the straw and struggled to interpret the sound. Something blocked my knowledge. I sat up slowly and listened. Then I knew: it was a stonemason at work. When Zvi came into the shed, I called him to me. He was glum and reticent, as usual, but I was determined to get what I wanted from him. I decided I would not let him go until I did. I asked him my question a number of times before he answered.

"It is the hunchback," he said finally.

"What is he doing?"

"He's cutting stones for the house," said Zvi, biting his lip.

"What are they building at the house?"

Zvi either could not or would not tell me. When he left, I thought about it. I assumed that my father was enlarging the house and that it had to do with the prospering of his affairs. The thought of the hunchback chipping away at his pile of stones like a lone maggot nibbling at a corpse made me uneasy. There was something about the man that made me anxious; and the more I considered it, the more I was certain there was some secret the swarthy stonemason was concealing. I knew that Zvi had been apprenticed to him several years ago, but that it had not worked out. The stableboy had fallen very ill—had almost died, in fact—and my father had brought him back into our household and given him his present job. Before the rabbi's death it would have been difficult to get anything out of Zvi about his service with the stonemason; now it was impossible. I recalled the last time I had met the hunchback on the outskirts of the village and the look he had given me: it was the look of a butcher inspecting a calf. I rolled over in the straw, wincing at the sound of the chisel driven into rough stone. I would have to get used to it, though; there was no choice. It would be in my ears every day except the Sabbath from sunrise to dusk. My waking hours would from this day on be filled with the same belligerent rhythm that had cut the characters of "Evenezer" into the lintel of our home.

Since the rabbi's death, I had left off using the slingshot for fear of discovery. Minds like Avner's and my father's might all too readily link my weapon with the rabbi's end in the stable. I occupied myself with thinking and writing the words I knew. I tried, without much success, to assemble the letters in new combinations that meant something. This day the mason's hammering disturbed me so that I could not concentrate, and I was glad as the afternoon drew to a close. At twilight Avner walked in. He came toward me with the usual determined stride and with the usual rigid face that turned back prying eyes and hearts before they ever got started. One thing alone was odd: he did not carry my plate of slop and clay jar of water. I looked up at him. He did not return the look but simply bent and with the key that was already in his hand, the same key that had made me prisoner weeks ago, opened the lock and detached the manacle. I was free of the chain and the wall. My first reaction was to fear trickery, so I did not move. My father's chief steward had already started to leave the shed; when he saw I was not with him, he turned and said to me, as if it were understood, "Your father wants to see you." Somewhat unsteadily I followed him out into the evening, where in the great black bow of the sky stars were hovering like golden butterflies.

My father had grown stouter; there were lines about his eyes and mouth I had never seen. His tone was ironic, but beneath it he seemed pleased with himself. His clothing was new and fashioned of the best cloth; there were heavy gold rings on his fingers. He smiled once or twice during our interview, but his riding whip was near at hand. I listened attentively to what he had to say. He warned me that I had been given my last chance: if my behavior were to displease him I would be sent away, as had been my brother. He lifted an eyebrow and was even more explicit: I should be apprenticed to the stonemason. I said that I understood and that my time alone in the shed had taught me much. He nodded and said the future would tell, then he dismissed me with a wave of the hand.

It was strange to be in my room, a room which I had thought never to see again. I tossed from side to side on the bed. I had grown used to the straw and the noise the animals made that kept up the whole night through: the chamber seemed as empty and silent as a tomb. Toward morning I finally dozed off. Though he had told me I should have to slay him again to make him go away, I had no visitation from the rabbi.

During the days that followed, I discovered many things. The stones on which the mason worked, sending their dust spurting into the air with his chisel, were indeed for an addition to the house. My father was building a large dining room and a number of guest chambers; there was also talk of a bath for which mosaic tiles would be brought from the Galilee and from Jerusalem. His business with the Romans had brought him immense wealth and this would be the finest house in the entire area. Important visitors would be feted here: I could see them already in the glittering light of my father's eyes.

My stepmother was pregnant again; her belly was just beginning to swell noticeably, and she was in radiant good health. She was as busy and bustling and prying as before, as loud, officious and nasty-tempered, and if anything, she was more than ever inclined to use her fists. I saw her, for a trifle, thrash a new scullery maid almost to unconsciousness. The girl, who was flaxen-haired and beautiful and had large, gray, terrified eyes, collapsed at my stepmother's feet; and the big woman had stood over her inert body, continuing to hurl abuse as if there were some quota she must fill no matter what.

My father hired a scholar to teach me, and I soon had my first lesson. The teacher was a thin, pale, wretched fellow, pimply and half-blind with his constant study. He lived in a hovel in the lower part of the village, had crusts to eat, and could barely afford to buy the lamp oil by which to read at night. He was grateful to have my father's wages and so eager to please me in every way. I found him to be a quiet, peace-loving, even docile man—almost an insult to my powers of domination. When he bent squinting over his books, his balding head thrust forward, I often wanted to laugh out loud. He was soft clay in my hands.

As to the stonemason, sitting at his pile of rocks as some Egyptian at his pyramid, he was darker and more shriveled than I remembered him to be. His deformity seemed to have increased in size, as if it were some monstrous growth that was drawing the rest of his flesh into it. Every time I crossed the yard and came near him, he devoured me with his eyes, never taking them from me and sometimes even stopping his work at my approach. I detested him, but I no longer feared him. I felt that I would get at his secret long before he was able to get at me. In the meantime I stayed away from him, giving him almost as wide a berth as did Zvi.

Avner was as always: silent, efficient, devoted to his master as is the plague to death. He seemed to be everywhere in the house and out of doors, to appear suddenly and to vanish without warning, to see and to know everything that was going on. If it had been possible for my father to have another self, it would have been Avner. And I had the feeling that, upon orders from my father, he kept me under his direct personal watch. Toward dusk on the third or fourth day of my release, I walked through the village down to the cemetery. If Avner was following me he was sure to think I was visiting my mother's grave, as does a pious son from time to time. Actually I had a wish to see exactly where the rabbi was buried. I went over to my mother's grave, seated myself on the earth, and looked around until I found the spot. Three crows hopped over the mound of freshly heaped earth, cawing as if they hoped to waken the corpse beneath. I stayed for some time, sitting quietly with my hands folded in my lap. The crows melted into the darkness, as did the graves and the windrows of cypress and blue pine. A single star pierced the rind of the sky like a spear. I sat and waited and listened for a ghost which I well knew had no existence. Once, as I smirked, I even called out the word *ruach*, meaning "spirit" in Hebrew. Nothing. No answer. Of course there would be nothing that called or shrieked unless it came from within me. I laughed silently, got up and brushed myself off, and started for home. I did not look back. Now that I was free and could reckon with Zvi, I did not think the rabbi would ever visit my dreams again.

Seed must dissolve. Fruit must rot. Flesh must putrefy. This is the law of nature. And I saw Zvi as a creature marked by nature for destruction. Though he knew it not, each of the hours of his life had a number, each of his heartbeats had been rationed, the steps he would take were counted out to the very last. He had no idea of what lay in store for him, no idea how his life would end. He could see me a dozen times a day and never dream that within the bone of my skull lay the last of his days on earth. I saw him and I smiled, and he seeing the smile never once knew I was smiling over his coffin, over his open grave.

The matter was pressing, but I had to wait. I had to restrain myself, wait for my chance. I waited until my father and Avner left the house on a journey. They left with a certain measure of trust, that I knew. During the weeks following my release, my behavior had been beyond reproach. There had been nothing exceptional about it, nothing that would have aroused my father's suspicions. To openly profess repentance would have been foolhardy; instead, I gradually exchanged a morose demeanor for one of quiet resignation mixed at times with confusion. It was the perfect ploy, and it accomplished its end. I was less rigidly watched; Avner checked on me only sporadically. The teacher, whom I was sure had to report on me, could give only good reports. My step-mother could find no fault, exaggerate though she might. The spies who were sent after me must return to their dispatcher with empty hands. I knew that Zvi was eaten from within, but his outward behavior was listless, apathetic. I did not have to be desperate, did not have to worry. I could wait for the right moment and then make my move.

The day after the departure of my father and Avner, I took a donkey from the shed and rode through the village to the fields. I wanted to be completely alone and to think. I wanted to think everything through, to miss nothing, to take every eventuality into account. When I had satisfied myself, I rode back. As I had planned, Zvi was in the shed forking the hay. When he caught sight of me, his body stiffened and he averted his face. I tied up the donkey in its stall and spoke to Zvi in the most gentle voice I could summon. I repeated all the old lies about the rabbi and how evil he had been and went over the reason for killing him. Then in a burst of candor I had rehearsed many times over in my mind and even aloud when I was alone in the field, I told Zvi that I understood perfectly the feelings he had for me, that I knew why he had been repelled. I said that I was not and could not be angry with him, and that I only wanted to repay him for the kindness he had shown me while I was incarcerated in the shed. Zvi was silent as I spoke. He had finished his chores, leaned the pitchfork against the wall, and was standing with arms folded across his chest. I sensed that he was unwilling to leave because I blocked the doorway and he did not want to pass that close to me. When I felt that his uneasiness had almost reached a bursting point, I said suddenly, "Zvi, would you like to leave?"

"What?"

"I'm asking you if you would like to leave this place."

"But what . . . what do you mean?"

"I'm speaking plainly, Zvi. Would you like to be free of my father, of this entire household, of me—of the memory of the rabbi? Well, would you?"

"How could such a thing be possible?"

"I have a large sum of money hidden away, Zvi. It was left to me secretly by my mother before she died. No one but you knows I have it." I paused, wet my lips, and went on: "I want you to have it. You can take it, go away from here, and begin a new life. The past will be dead. Only the future will live for you: it will be as if you were just born."

"Why? Why should you do such a thing? I don't understand why."

"Don't you understand, Zvi? It's not only that I want to repay you for what you did—actually, I can never hope to repay such a debt. It's that I know that what happened bothers you, hurts you very much. You will not be able to keep it locked within you forever; someday it's bound to come out in one way or another. The boil will break open, Zvi, and then the both of us will suffer grievously. I will be punished for the deed itself and you for keeping silent for so long. Or else, Zvi, they will think that we planned the deed together, that the both of us lured the rabbi to his death. I know my father, Zvi, and you know him. We both know how suspicious he is and how wrathful he can be. That's why I want you to go. That's why you must go. For your safety, Zvi, and for my own. When you are far away from here, Zvi, when you are living a new life away from these bitter memories, the deed that you witnessed here will fade and die: the rabbi will die, Zvi. And your heart will be free of its terrible burden."

"You really mean what you say? You would really give me the money your mother left for you?"

"I mean what I say, Zvi. The money is yours. The freedom is yours. All you have to do is take them."

"I want to go away. I want to leave and never to set foot in this place again as long as I live."

"You will never see this shed or this village again, Zvi."

Then I explained that matters would best be settled immediately, while my father and Avner were away, that by the time they returned he would be far away and pursuit would be impossible. I told him that he must depart this very evening, and he agreed; I explained that we could not be seen together, that we must separate and meet again at a spot I would designate. I said that he must take no possession with him that anyone could see, that he must do nothing to attract the attention of any person, that no one in the world must know of his intentions or of the money I was giving him. I said that if he breathed a word of what had passed between us, we were the two of us lost. He nodded and promised that he would remain silent and keep his part of the bargain to the letter. He came forward to me, and with tears in his eyes, embraced me. I felt his frail body shudder and patted his back. Then I related to him exactly where and when we should meet, and left the shed.

The sun was sinking. I slipped my slingshot into my cloak, left the village in a direction opposite the one I would eventually take and doubled back to the forbidden path up the mountain, stopping four or five times on the way to make certain I was not being followed. I climbed rapidly and reached a point I had marked out for myself days ago. Three or four yards before you got to the chasm of the corpses there was a boulder; I concealed myself behind it.

I crouched and waited for Zvi to come by. After a time, I spotted him on the path. He was climbing rapidly, and I could discern beads of sweat on his forehead. He passed within scant feet of me, but did not even remotely guess that I was there. There was a strange expression on his face. I could not place it at first, and then I knew that I had seen that look on the faces of pilgrims: it was the expression of a man looking for God, thirsting for God and hoping to see Him soon. Panting, he went up the path and stopped at the very edge of the chasm, as I had instructed him. Zvi had always taken my directions literally and prided himself on carrying them out with exactitude; whenever he failed, he had been very hard on himself. This time, I could see, he wanted to do precisely as I had commanded.

The light of day was failing, but I was able to make out his features nevertheless. I had the strange feeling that his face had its own, secret source of light, a source that came from deep within him. The way he stood and looked about him reminded me of animals I had hunted and trapped, for there was an air of resignation about him; and yet as I stared at him I thought that he had the bearing of a man who, having previously found every path blocked to him, suddenly discovers that all ways are open to him. I was fascinated by him, almost with the fascination I would have had for a supernatural creature. There was no tension in his face, only expectancy. His eyes were wide-open, as if afraid of nothing they might behold, no matter what: it was as if they had already gazed within upon something so strong that no power in the world could daunt it. Zvi's eyes shone, shone with a light so soft and so gentle that had I allowed myself for one instant to forget who he was and who I was, I might have found a sense of myself in their depths.

The sun was very low and the sky a deep tone of red that was already losing its edge: it looked as if the last fire on earth were about to be extinguished and never rekindled. The chill of night had settled into the limpid air; I shivered and crouched nearer the ground. Zvi's lonely figure was red, red as the blood from an opened vein, red as brush of the field fire that, fed by the fury of the wind, seems to burn with a will of its own to be destroyed. A great silence rose from all the flanks of the mountain, as if it had nothing more to say, as if it had given up speech forever in the face of coming darkness. My heart pounded. As I looked at Zvi, I felt myself to be the victim of myself. I had the thrill of awaiting my own extinction. I thought of myself as setting with the sun.

Zvi broke the spell. He lifted his head to the vast expanse of the sky above the mountain peak and chanted in a low, broken voice: "The heavens speak of the glory of God; and the firmament declareth His handiwork . . ."

When he had finished singing the psalm, he glanced toward the pit and then turned his head to the path where he expected me to appear at any moment. I could no longer see his face clearly: I could just make out the shape of his head and his body. Silently I drew out my slingshot and loaded it with the rock I had selected: I had only one, because it would be all I needed. I turned to the left and through the cleft between my boulder and the next took careful aim at the head. I pulled back the sling. But I did not let go. Killing the rabbi had been almost a reflex. He had come at me in fear, and I had been afraid of where that fear would carry him. To stop him dead in his tracks had been instinct. Zvi was another matter. The threat he posed to me was not direct. Up until this instant I had planned every move coldly and logically. I had not reckoned on this final instant, this ultimate interlude. If I did not release the sling I would remain frozen so forever. I broke out in a cold sweat—I could not let go. And then, apparently concerned because I had not yet shown up, Zvi's shadow head called out my name and reminded me who I was.

I released the sling. I was not dreaming. The missile did not turn aside at the last second. It struck home, and Zvi disappeared with not a sound to disturb the silence of the mountain. Next week I would look for his mangled body among the bones of men and beasts heaped at the bottom of the pit. Fruit rots. Seed dissolves. Flesh putrefies. That is the law of nature. Zvi was gone and I would go underground. Zvi would never return, and I would emerge when it was time.

PART

II

Just past my eleventh birthday, my stepmother gave birth to a baby girl. She was a long time in labor, and when the child was at last born it was decided that she be named Hedva, or joy, because there was a great joy in the household that mother and infant were alive and well. But the child was perverse and managed to turn joy into sorrow. Three weeks later, the baby girl was found dead in its cradle by the nurse, green as the bottle flies that buzzed in the room. My stepmother ran shrieking through the corridors. She brandished a large kitchen knife and kept screaming that the angel of death was hiding somewhere in the house and that she must find him and destroy him before he carried off anyone else. It took six servants to trap her, Avner to knock the knife from her hand, and four strong men to hold her down. She kicked and bit and foamed at the mouth and in her agony called out the name of Shabtai the whipper, begging him to come unto her and make her belly rise again. The error was an unfortunate one for the gentle lovers. Shabtai the whipper was seized that very day by my father's men. Nor was he whipped. From a safe vantage point, I saw him led up the forbidden mountain path, and I knew he would become a playmate for Zvi and would enjoy the nameless rest in the chasm. There were no questions ever asked, no accusations ever leveled. My father had always been a disease, but now he was a plague. It wasn't that he was beyond the law: he was a law unto himself.

My father invited me to see my stepmother as I had seen her naked that night through the open door; he invited the rest of the household as well. She was stripped, her skull and genitals were shaven clean, and she was driven forth from the village in a shower of rocks, none of them large enough to put her out of her misery. My father's face was gray and his features were set; he carried his riding whip, though he did not once use it. None of the servants dared approach him after my stepmother had left; even Avner kept his distance in the same way a dog will sometimes do when he senses that his master's pain is apt to spill into his own life if he does not take care. The members of the household stood in their places, waiting for my father to give them the signal to leave. He gave them no signal, neither by word nor by gesture; he simply stared at them, rapping his quirt into an open palm, and then finally, after glancing coldly at the path down which my stepmother had disappeared, went to his bedchamber and shut himself in. Avner waved the servants back to their tasks.

The additions to the house were splendid: a great dining hall with a huge stone fireplace at one end, a half-dozen guest rooms, and the vaunted bath of mosaic tiles which was the talk of the village from the day it was completed. It had stalls, a sunken pool and mirrors in silver filigreed frames; the pattern worked into the tiles showed vines and trees and the fruits thereof in a dozen colors. My father acquired two eunuchs to tend it, and whenever there was a feast, these strange, dour men were armed and stationed at the entrance; the shouts of revelers inside would echo through the house, and once in a while a naked man or woman would come to the door, there to be gently restrained by one or both of the pair.

When the last stone was hewn and set into place and the Hebrew date chiseled in, with the equivalent in Roman numerals alongside it—the first in our village—the hunchback packed his tools and went back to his cave. Not many weeks after, I discovered the stonemason's secret, the one I had known all along was there. The hunchback was a pagan. He only pretended to be a Jew. Inside his cave he kept an idol which he worshiped—a monstrous figure of fecal black stone with a spider's face and two erect male members, one protruding from the crotch and the other from the anus. I saw the idol with my own eyes. The mason was away in Bethlehem, working on a synagogue, and I took the opportunity to visit the cave. It took repeated trips over many days for me to find the hidden spring that opened the door, but I did. The idol stood leering in a niche. Before it on a shelf of rock were grease-covered lamp wicks, the bones of chickens and fish, and the frail skeletons of small reptiles. When the hunchback returned from Bethlehem during the following month, he brought with him a mute boy of eight whom I knew he must use as a part of his service to the idol-god, as he had once used Zvi the stableboy.

When I was twelve, my father openly took the blond scullery maid as a concubine. I knew he had consorted with the girl for a long time, though she never said a word about it to me or to anyone else. My father kept two other concubines, older women, and they were incensed when he took the maid. My father only laughed. "When do they expect me to live?" he said. "When I'm dead?" He installed the girl, whose name was Dalia, in a room not far from my own. I often saw her in the corridors or in the yard, alone. Most of the time she looked bemused or even lost. She was a quiet girl who had no companions and sought none. It seemed to me as though she had learned early in life to expect nothing but pain and to keep the pain to herself, as if it were a kind of treasure she hoarded. Dalia was four years older than I.

On my thirteenth birthday, which actually fell on the Sabbath, I was initiated into the community of Israel as a man by means of formal ceremony. My father, who had become the largest landowner and most influential Jew in the entire surrounding area, saw in the occasion a chance to advance his various purposes. He invited the rich and the powerful from near and far. The preparations were begun a month before the day and only finished at the very last moment. My father spared no expense and no effort. Long ago he had taken me aside and advised me of his expectations: I knew that I must not disappoint him.

As a student, I made rapid progress. My starveling scholar was amazed at the way I grasped grammatical concepts and at the speed with which I picked up vocabulary. As for me, I couldn't learn fast enough. I was a dry sponge, begging for water. Each day I could not wait for my lesson to begin, each day it did not last long enough to suit me. I plagued my teacher with question after question and did not stop until I was satisfied or he mystified. I followed him through mazes and came out the other side almost before he did. There seemed no limit to what I could learn, no boundary to what I wanted to know. My poor teacher, hard-pressed as he often was to feed my voracious appetite, found himself caught in the net of my zeal. There were times when he would lift his head from the text, half blind with fatigue and not knowing what hour had passed or even where he was. My passion ignited his own, but he had not my driving force or stamina. Sometimes, dead with exhaustion, he fell asleep while I chanted a difficult conjugation or expounded a dense text. The bald spot at the crown of his skull shone in the unsteady light of the oil lamp.

He did not last long. Before six months were up, a party of Roman soldiers searching the village for Zealots entered his hovel and ransacked it. He made the mistake of protesting, miserable bag of skin and bones that he was; they promptly burned his texts and precious manuscripts and arrested him for obstructing Roman justice. They dragged him away, but by some superhuman effort he broke loose and threw himself into the fire. In the morning, among the smoldering ashes, they found his charred body, a fragment of parchment clutched tightly in one hand. As a suicide he was buried outside the cemetery boundaries.

Then my father sent Avner to Bethlehem; three days later he returned with a teacher called Nahum, or comfort, and my father quartered him with the servants. He was an older man, with polished ways, a soft voice and a perennial squint. He lacked my former teacher's passionate devotion to letters, but he had stored up considerable knowledge and was willing to share it with me. He walked with a stoop, had a paunch which he patted to reassure himself when he was anxious, and sighed in a melancholy way whenever he saw a buxom wench pass by. I would smile at his mooning, but he would always deny it, claiming that what I imagined was in my own mind. Throughout the household he was known as "the sheep."

With Nahum I studied the blessings over the Law and the portion of the Law I would chant before all who assembled in the synagogue. The occasion was an auspicious one, discussed for weeks before it took place. Our house was bursting with guests, some of whom came from places as distant as Acre and Tiberias. On the day I performed, my thirteenth birthday, hundreds of people had packed themselves into the village synagogue. My accomplishments during the past two years had earned for me a certain measure of distinction. Thus many came out of curiosity, to see if the prodigy whom they had heard about would live up to his reputation. I was very sure of myself and enjoyed the size of the audience and its composition—rich merchants and landowners, elders and notables, rabbis and scholars, Roman officials and even a military commander of high rank who wore his sword into the synagogue.

I knew that I possessed a beautiful voice, a seductive voice difficult to resist. I had always used it to my advantage, had always practiced to perfect it, speaking aloud when I was by myself and listening objectively to the way I sounded, as if I were another person. I strived to achieve certain desired effects and did not rest until I accomplished my goals. I had been scrubbed to ritual purity, had my hair combed and curled, and was dressed in a splendid new tunic embroidered in gold thread. My teacher Nahum fussed over me like a mother hen to the point that I finally had to push him away. "I know you will do well and be a credit to your father," he said. "And to me," he added, wiping the tears from his eyes. I nodded and turned from him to go. "Of course I'll do well," I said. "It would be a shame to waste such a glorious opportunity." Nahum, who scarcely heard what I said, agreed.

The jammed synagogue smelled of incense and sweat. When my name was called out, I squared my shoulders and with blazing eyes ascended the steps to the dais where the Holy Ark of the Law stood, mantled with red velvet on which the Lions of Judah were stitched in silver. There was a stir. I felt a shiver of pleasure run along my spine and walked proudly to the lectern. Throwing my head back, I recited the blessings over the Law. I rendered each word, each note without flaw, loudly and clearly; but I held back the fire, husbanding it for what was to come. My chanting was received with polite attention. It was competent, excellent even, but was this the legend they had come to hear? I saw disappointment on the faces of some of my listeners and I smiled to myself. It was exactly what I wanted, precisely what I had planned for. I wanted to lull the audience with a performance slightly better than adequate and then overturn their socially correct reception with a totally unexpected burst of virtuosity. The old chief rabbi touched my shoulder and nodded, brushing the spittle from his great purple lips with the back of a hand. It was time for me to read from the Law. My eyes swept over the crowd. I saw discreet inattention, dull eyes, and here and there a smirk or even a smile.

I opened my mouth wide and sang: "Return, O Israel, unto the Lord, thy God . . ."

The audience was electrified. A hush so thunderously deep fell over the assembly that for an instant I was dizzy. I sang on. My notes were true and clear and thrilling; they rang out through the hall like the strokes of a bell.

". . . For thou hast stumbled in thy sin . . ."

I held the audience completely in my grip. The rabbis were astounded. The scholars were captivated. The Roman officials who attended as a matter of form looked up in surprise and pleasure. Even my father's faced showed satisfaction.

". . . Take with thee . . ."

Many wept unashamedly. An old man in the rear fainted and there were none able to raise him because of the crowd. The time came and I let the final note fly. It struck the assembly and an audible gasp went up, a shudder as if from an animal that has been hit.

The chief rabbi stroked my head, the Scroll of the Law was covered by a velvet cloth with gold fringes at its corners, and I was given a signal to continue. It was incumbent upon me, as a man of Israel, to expound upon the Law and this I did. I had prepared myself for this task thoroughly as well. I took whatever I could from Nahum and transferred it to my own designs. When I finished, I stepped back, bent and kissed the covered Scroll of the Law, and waited patiently for the mantle to be removed. This was done, and I chanted a final series of blessing and then watched, conscious that all eyes were on my person, as the Law was returned to its Ark. The rabbis on the dais pressed about me, kissing my cheeks with moist lips and brushing against my skin with their scented beards.

The feast of celebration, which began in the midafternoon, lasted through the night. There was music and song and laughter and gorging and wine that did not stop flowing. Merriment and licentiousness were in the air: each male guest promised the satyr, each female the whore. My father brooded a good part of the time, as was his wont. But at one point he rose, made his way through the revelers, and came over to me. He bent over and whispered in my ear, so that no one would hear him but me, "Well done. I have nothing of which to complain." I said nothing, but reddened so that he would know I was pleased. He left, and I continued to eat and discourse with my neighbors. For my part, I was wary of drink and did not more than taste the wines that were proffered; and I was cautious in my conversation, allowing no word that could be misconstrued to pass my lips. When food was served me, I ate modestly of it, often refusing that which I was offered; and I made certain to avert my eyes from Dalia, the youngest of my father's concubines, whose glance, it seemed to me, found my direction inordinately. Toward midnight I approached my father and waited until there was a pause in the conversation in which he engaged; then I apologized, told him that I was weary, and asked to be excused so that I could go to my room and sleep. He drew me aside. His eyes glittered as he spoke and I knew that he had taken too much wine with his Roman friends. "As you are now a man," he said to me, "you may enjoy the pleasure of a woman." He nodded toward the bath entrance leading from the dining hall. "There are women of pleasure in the bath," he said. "I have given orders that you be admitted if you so desire." I thanked my father but demurred. As I left, I saw that Dalia was staring after me and once again I turned my eyes away.

During my fourteenth year, I was awakened one summer night by terrible screams. My first thought was that someone in the house was being murdered. The voice in its agony had somehow lost its sex, for I could not tell whether the victim was man or woman. I slipped into my robe and went out. Dalia was in the corridor—a wrap thrown loosely over her young body, which under my father's attentions had grown almost to full womanhood; her eyes were wide with fear and apprehension. I had no time for her, ordered her to go back to her chamber, and rushed into the yard. Surrounded by milling servants, my father and Avner bent over a wounded Roman soldier. Two torches lit the scene. I pushed my way through the crowd and looked down at the man and his wound. He had received a sword thrust in the abdomen, a great ragged hole from which thick purplish blood gushed. The soldier's face, chest, thighs, legs and arms were smeared with it, as if he were trying to anoint himself with the fluid of his life; as he gasped out his story, blood began to ooze from a corner of his mouth. He informed my father that a battle was in progress not far from our village, on the northern slope of the mountain. His patrol had been checking the area for rebels and had been ambushed. Thanks to the quick thinking of their commander, only two men had been killed in the initial assault; the rest were holding out against a superior force. He had been dispatched to my father to ask for help. I was less interested in the man's story, which I had grasped at almost the first moment of my arrival, than in his face and body. He shivered, his skin was turning blue: he was entering a cold cave. He was breathing his last. A final hiss slid through his teeth, and then there was no more. His body stiffened, almost as a male member. The torchlight appeared as two points in his glassy eyes, which could not project life now but only reflect it. The blood in his gashed belly was hardening.

My father rose. Though he had been close to the soldier, he was unbloodied. His face was frozen; the flame of the torch did not melt it. Avner stood at his side, watching him as I did. We both knew that he had a crucial decision to make. To recognize the might of Rome and to deal openly with its representatives was one thing, but to come actively to its aid was quite another. He had taken the hand of Rome in friendship and commerce; now he was asked to lift a hand for Rome. His eyes had their old hard stare. As much could be read in them as in the mirror-eyes of the dead soldier. His mouth, though—the same mouth that had never been more than a razor slash above his jaw—showed a slackness which I had noticed some time ago and then thought I had only imagined. He drew in his lower lip and I detected a tension— so slight that it took an eye trained as was mine to see it. Either my father had changed, or he had never been in such a situation before— or both. He squared his shoulders, a characteristic gesture, raised his riding whip and touched it lightly to Avner's shoulder. Then he put his head forward until it almost touched his chief steward's and spoke to him gravely, pausing every so often to make certain that he was not overheard. My father spoke with an economy of words, choosing them carefully so that his choice in action would be wider. He invariably kept his intentions hidden as long as he possibly could so that the element of surprise would be added to his advantage. Secrecy, he felt, gave him leverage that would have otherwise been lost. And he never declared himself unless it was absolutely necessary: what was left unsaid could always be denied.

The quirt dropped. Avner nodded a final time and left the yard hurriedly. I wanted desperately to follow after him, but I refrained, much as I had refrained from drinking and from visiting a prostitute at the ceremony of my manhood. I trembled. The wind had shifted and from the north brought the sound of battle to me. The dead soldier was carried into the house, my father following the corpse and giving directions, as if it were a holy man the servants were carrying. Everyone left and I stood alone, listening to the distant shouts and screams. Then, realizing that I must not betray my agitation, I went back to my room and got into bed. I tossed and turned, unable to sleep. The battle stirred my mind to a fever. Over and over, I saw the Roman soldier receive his death thrust in the gut. He lay on the ground, his breath failed, his eyes grew glassy. Nobody could help him, not even the emperor. Then I imagined participants in the battle. Some men inflicted death blows, others received them: it seemed not to matter to me which.

There was a knock at my door. I sat upright, then left the bed and latched my shutters, which I had opened on entering the room in the hope that I would be able to hear the fighting. Then I went to the door. It was Dalia. Her feet were bare, and she wore the same wrap I had seen her in before.

"Why have you come here?"

"What has happened?"

"Nothing."

"Please tell me what's going on."

"Nothing at all."

"Please tell me. I must know."

I related what I had seen and she paled.

"Were there many rebels?" she asked.

I shrugged. "I don't know," I said. "Why?"

"There's no reason. I heard the screaming and the commotion. I wanted to know what was going on. That's all."

She drew her wrap more tightly around her. I could sense the tension, but I did not want to press her. To probe would be to inhibit. Whatever was beneath the surface, I felt, would reveal itself in its own time. A man can endure just so much pressure inside himself, and then he must rupture. "It's all over now," I told her. "Go back to bed."

She stared at me intensely as if there were something she wanted from me, something she wanted me to give her. I pretended not to see and turned away and when I glanced back toward the door, she had disappeared. Sleep was useless. I sat at my small writing table, lit the lamp and took up my quill. The lamp burned badly, though, and I trimmed the wick and then relit it. I had been writing on a regular basis for the past few months, mostly at night and most often when I had trouble sleeping. Sometimes I put down events that had occurred during the day, sometimes thoughts about people in the household or in the village; sometimes I recorded discussions I had with Nahum, my teacher. At other times I put down my own thoughts about the Law, or simply my own thoughts. It relieved me to do so; it pleased me to feel my innermost sentiments flow out of me, even as the flow of semen; it gave me a deep satisfaction to see the shape my feelings and ideas had when they were outside of me. Once in a while, when the mood was upon me, I would write down fantasies or dreams. The other writings, when I read them again, stared back at me as if from a mirror; in a sense I could see my own face in the glass. The latter writings, however, seemed not to reflect but to lead more deeply into the mirror; I saw reflected not me but somebody else, somebody rarely encountered and only dimly recognized.

Most of what I wrote I wanted to preserve, yet I feared lest it fall into the hands of an enemy. I therefore took whatever precautions I could: I never recorded an actual name, choosing a code name instead for every person of whom I wrote. Little by little I developed a code for words as well, so that a given word might represent the opposite of what it expressed—for instance, "good" in my code might stand for "evil." I never set down a place as such, or a date, but transposed them according to the system I had worked out, a system whose key was in my mind and nowhere else. Finally, I kept my writings in a hollow vault I had painstakingly constructed beneath the floor tiles. I had access to my storage box through a certain loose tile over which I always fastened a horsehair in order to know whether or not it had been moved from its place.

I had my thoughts and I had the quill in my hand, but it was not always an easy matter for me to induce thought to hand. Thoughts were mercurial, thoughts were beneath thoughts; thoughts touched the surface of a pond with their mouths, like fish, and when you went after them they dove into the depths; and thoughts crumbled between the fingers like butterfly wings or melted like ice with the warmth of touch. Thoughts could be broken like cobwebs, they could fall apart as soft earth. Like the devil, thoughts could assume all forms, could take on false forms, could pass from one form to the next with the lightness of the prestidigitator's hand. Thoughts wore masks, and when you stripped them off you found nothing; and there were thoughts you touched and thought you had—and when you looked at your fingers found were gone like lizards, leaving you with their truncated tails. The lamp was filled, and its wick burned steadily now that I had trimmed it. I was alone, the shutters were closed. I wanted to write of the dead soldier, of how he had died, of what I had observed and felt about him and about myself. My mind moved, my quill did not. I was uneasy. In the river of my mind, currents moved, swift and powerful, but I was caught in them, I could not control them. I wanted to write of my father, his look and his decision, of Avner his chief steward hastening into the night to do his bidding, no matter what the consequences to himself. The quill did not stir. My wrist remained locked. An unknown force held me captive, and the more I struggled the tighter grew the bonds about me. I felt as if I were suffocating, as if my lungs were filling with poison. I searched for my strangler but found him not. I wanted to write of him but he mocked me: he was formless, shapeless and without substance, and there was no way in which I could encompass him.

I squirmed in my chair and set down a single pronoun: "she," which in my code sometimes meant "I." Then my father's voice rang out in the hall. He called my name, and I did not want it to be called twice without answering. I sprang to the door and shouted back to him even before I opened it. He ordered me to come immediately to the yard, where I was needed. I put on a robe but no sandals. The yard was filled with smoke from the torches, with cries and moaning. Some of our servants were bringing in bodies, others were helping wounded Roman soldiers. The story unfolded in a short time. My father had directed Avner to take a dozen hand-picked men and go to the aid of the patrol. They had rushed to the northern slope and turned the tide of battle in a matter of moments: when the reinforcements arrived, the Zealots fled, leaving their dead behind. Three Roman corpses were laid out to the right and two Zealot bodies to the left. The Roman wounded, three in number, were taken to the house. Then the patrol itself marched in— nine grime- and sweat-covered men and their young, stern-faced commander. Dust boiled up into the red rays of the torches. The officer posted two men as guards and allowed the others to rest. He glanced coldly at his own dead and then walked over to the rebels, over whom my father and a blood-spattered Avner stood. I stood quietly behind my father's chief steward, waiting.

It turned out that one of the Zealots was not dead. He was a tall, thin, bony man with a dark beard and thick eyebrows. He had received a chest wound. He breathed irregularly, and when he did, the blood welled from his cut and there was a hoarse sound in his throat. Cold water was dashed into his face several times; he opened his eyes and blinked. His face was puzzled: he did not know where he was.

"You thought to wake with your God and His hosts?" said the Roman officer. "And so naturally you are disappointed, eh?"

The Zealot closed his eyes.

"That won't help you," said the officer. He knelt down and seized the wounded man's beard in a fist. "Four of my soldiers are dead," he said, "and three wounded. That's a third of my patrol done in by your ambush. I'd better get some information from you or you'll regret it."

The Zealot opened his eyes again, and despite the hand pulling at his beard, smiled. "My words are for God," he said. "Not for swine."

The officer was very young—not more than twenty-two or -three. He reddened and with his free hand pulled his dagger from its sheath. "Four of my men killed," he said. "I'll cut your heart out—"

My father bent and gently grasped the wrist of the hand with the knife. "Let me speak with him, Lieutenant. I know his kind."

The lieutenant looked up.

"You won't find anything out from a corpse," said my father. "Allow me to talk to him. There's always time to cut out his heart or whatever else you wish to do." He smiled, and the lieutenant rose and stepped aside, laying his naked knife across the curly blond hair of his chest. My father pointed his riding whip at the prostrate rebel. "Jew," he said, "do you have a name?"

"*Zavuach*, or sacrificed," said the Zealot.

"I want your real name, Jew."

"And what is yours—traitor?"

My father's lips drew back over his teeth; he bent forward and touched the Zealot's forehead with his quirt. "Do you want us to break it open to find out what's inside it?"

"If you break it open," said the Zealot, "what's inside will escape you. You said as much to the lieutenant before." The wounded man coughed. "And if you're really bent on killing me, why don't you let the gentile do it? They're much better at it, you know. Jews always botch the job somehow. They don't quite have their hearts in it. Except when they commit suicide: at that they are experts."

My father sighed. "Listen, my good fellow. We can reason together. Surely we can do that. After all, we're reasonable people."

"So is the devil," said the rebel.

"Clever," said my father. "Very clever. But it won't get me anywhere and it won't get you anywhere. Now pay attention to what I tell you. There is ample reward waiting for you if you choose to cooperate with us. First of all, there is your life—"

"My life is worth nothing to me if I must live it as a whore."

"Then there is position . . . status . . . rank. And money. You can practically name your own price."

"My price is beyond the reach and beyond the understanding of such as you."

My father slowly shook his head, almost with sorrow, almost as if he grieved for what must be if the rebel did not respond. "You are mistaken, my friend. Very mistaken. And I hope that your error will not prove a fatal one. You see, nothing and no one is beyond our reach. We rise to the heights when we must and sink to the depths when it is necessary. Nobody escapes our reach—ever. You had better understand that fact, for it is a basic fact of life. And you had better understand that I have been very patient with you, more than patient, and I am not known as a patient man. Now talk, and talk honestly. What is your real name? Where do you come from? Who organized your group? How many are in it? What is the name of your leader? What hiding place did the rest of you flee to? Where are you getting new recruits from? How did you come to know about the precise movements of the patrol?" My father tapped lightly with the whip. "These are the things we want to know. Will you tell us now?"

"Where our recruits come from, I won't tell," said the rebel. "But yours come from hell."

"You are keeping an officer of the Roman army waiting, do you realize that? His time is valuable. And you are causing me such embarrassment. I asked him to step aside and let me deal with you, as I am one of your kind."

The wounded man tried to laugh, but choked in his attempt. He lifted a hand; it fell weakly to his side.

"You are a very bitter Jew," said my father. "And I am getting tired of you."

The rebel did not respond. Tiny blood-filled flecks of foam were clustered on his lips; as he breathed they swelled, and some of them burst. The man's eyes, set deep in their sockets, rolled about like those of a horse. The mouth opened but no words came out. Avner, in a blood-stained tunic, moved forward to my father and whispered in his ear. My father listened gravely, soberly, as a judge might listen to evidence. Avner stepped back and my father moved the point of the whip down almost to the Zealot's wound.

"Listen, Jew of mine, there is no reason for your obstinacy," he said. "It's all futile—in vain, worthless. You've been recognized for who you are. One of my men knows you. You were born in Hebron and you live in Bethlehem. You are a cobbler by trade. You are a distant cousin to Shabtai the whipper, who lived in this village but has departed to a land of eternal serenity. You may as well tell us what else we want to know and save your life." My father's voice grew soft, almost gentle. "And if you don't care for your own life, my bitter Jew, you may just give some thought to the lives of your wife and your three children. Two girls and a boy—isn't that correct?"

The Zealot's eyes clouded; his brow was striped with deep furrows. "My wife? My children? What are you saying? I have no wife, no children. I have no friends. I have only God."

My father's quirt skirted the wound, keeping clear of blood. "We know where they are, Jew. Exactly where they are. In Bethlehem. On the Street of the Ram's Horn. How is that for being beyond our reach, Jew-cobbler? We know where they are and we'll get them—unless your tongue loosens . . ."

A thin stream of blood ran down the rebel's chin, slanted across his neck and spilled to the earth. "I have no family," he gasped. "I have no home. I have nothing until Zion is redeemed." The breath rasped in his throat. "I cannot answer your questions. I know nothing."

"Well, then," said my father, biting his lip, "we shall have to refresh your memory."

"I have no memory," hissed the rebel, "until the memory of Zion be restored."

My father signaled to Avner, and two of the servants who had been with the party that routed the Zealots hurried over to the wounded man, lifted the limp body between them, and dragged it in the direction of the shed. Rubbing his chin, the young Roman officer looked after them. My father smiled at him. "Don't worry, Lieutenant," he said. "He'll talk."

"How do you know he'll talk?"

My father bent his riding whip as if it were a bow. "You see, Lieutenant, I've had experience. I know his kind. I know them very well. They start out talking to God and end up crying to men."

They began working on the rebel in the animal shed, those whom my father called his "experts with Jews." His screams came to the house in gusts, as if carried by a wind that the suffering itself generated. Once in a while, I could make out a word such as *Shadai* or *Elohim*, each of them a sacred name for God, a name of special imploring, special meaning. Toward morning the Zealot broke. My father had been entirely correct. The prisoner was badly wounded, but the wound was not so grave that he could not endure the torture, so serious that he would escape with his secrets into death. Nor was he wrong when he told the rebel that in the end he would turn away from God and cry out to men for mercy. It all happened the way my father reckoned it. The rebel stayed on the raft of life and begged to be pushed from it into the waters of oblivion. His howls rang out again and again, without ceasing: it was truly incredible how loud were his screams and how silent was his God.

The man told the "experts" whatever he knew: his real name, which was Baruch, or blessed; his trade, which was cobbler; where he came from, which was Bethlehem; how many men belonged to his group; where their home base was; where they took shelter in time of need. But he could only give the code name of his leader, which was Barak, or lightning, and the code names of his companions. He could describe the leader very well and also a few of his cohorts; then his mind grew fuzzy and his voice weak. He said that he was ashamed and asked to be killed, and his interrogators laughed but he did not know what their laughter meant. Again he said that he wanted neither money nor power nor position, as he had been promised by my father, but simply to be put to death. His tormentors nodded as if they understood. The information he had given them was not excessively valuable, but it was enough on which to base raids and investigations. And my father would make certain to fill in whatever details were missing: they would make the picture look more complete, and it could never be proven that he had provided false leads, as the story came from the mouth of the Zealot captive. As the sky lightened in the east, the four inquisitors left the shed and went to their quarters. No sound from the prisoner followed them.

As soon as the rebel had been taken to the shed, my father brought the entire patrol into the dining hall, where a table had been laid for them and torches lit. The officer, very young, had at first declined my father's hospitality. But my father was very persuasive and the officer weary to the bone and somewhat confused—in all likelihood it was the first combat he had ever engaged in. Food and wine were brought in by the servants, and he gave the order that his men might partake of the feast. "After all," he said, "I am in the house of a comrade in arms." My father smiled and bade him sit and eat. The lieutenant begged to be excused, saying that he must himself abstain until he saw to the welfare of his wounded. This he did, leaving the hall at once. I followed on his heels, trying to keep up with him and direct him to where the injured had been taken. When I first came into the yard, I had helped move the serious case; the other two were only slightly hurt.

When the lieutenant returned, he was in a more relaxed frame of mind. My father assured him that he would not be found wanting in his command, since he had captured a rebel and extracted important information from him, all of which was now being set down by a scribe and which he would receive before he left the house. He asked the officer how many Zealots did he reckon were involved in the ambush and when the lieutenant answered, "Twenty or so," my father laughed good-naturedly. "My son," he said, putting a hand on the officer's shoulder, "there were nearly double that number who fell upon you. We have the exact figure in the report. When you return to your post, you will be greeted as a hero of Rome." The lieutenant sighed, and my father led him gently to the table. "Eat and drink, for you have earned it. Your enemy was defeated even before my men arrived. The Zealot himself told us that the band was beginning a retreat." The officer nodded, allowed himself to be seated at the head of the table, and fell upon his food ravenously, along with his men. "You have beaten the enemy," toasted my father, "and you have beaten death. It is fitting that you celebrate!"

The soldiers became animated and boisterous, dropping food to the floor and spilling wine, which was immediately replaced. My father clapped his hands, and two prostitutes were ushered into the hall. One was a swarthy girl with large breasts and hips, and the other tall, thin and fair. The men jeered at their appearance, and the pair took umbrage and asked to leave. My father was inflexible and said they must stay and serve the Roman conquerors. The women retorted that they would not—that they had been wakened from their sleep at an ungodly hour and thrust into a veritable lion's den. They were paid to consort with men, they said angrily, not with apes. For their part, the soldiers were highly amused by the performance and roared with laughter. Several of them stood on the benches and imitated the manner and speech of the girls while the rest howled. Then a great giant of a fellow with enormous hands like paws left his place and went after the prostitutes; they screamed and ran, inflaming the lust of the whole troop. The Romans rose as one, upsetting benches and knocking plates and utensils from the table, and pursued the girls. They trapped the pair in a far corner of the room, tore the clothes from their bodies and fell upon them frenziedly, as if they had never possessed a female before. Those who stood and watched urged the men who copulated with the whores to finish quickly so that they could have their turns. My father was not in the least amused by what had happened: in the morning he would have the prostitutes flogged and driven from the village.

The lieutenant drank too much. Wine dribbled down his chin, and his mouth fell open in a manner that made him look stupid, like a gaping fish. He rose unsteadily, held to the table for several minutes and then backed away. He seemed not to know where he was. He staggered this way and that, muttering incomprehensibly, and at one point drew his dagger, which Avner, who had been keeping a watchful eye on him all the time, took away so deftly that he scarcely knew it was gone. He showed no interest whatsoever in the prostitutes. My father must have known as much, since a young lad of my own age was soon introduced to the officer. I had never seen the boy before. He had blond, wavy hair that he wore almost to his shoulders, limpid gray eyes and a thin, supple figure. Without shame he went up to the lieutenant and began to fondle him. The officer embraced the boy in return, and the two sank to the floor where they pleased each other.

My father sat in his place, his whip beside him on the table, watching it all. He had tasted no wine; his face was set and somber; and his gaze, as it swept the hall from one end to the other, seemed pensive, much as it had been when he had talked to the wounded rebel in the yard. I looked on the spectacle for some time and then wearied of it. I left the hall. Outside, dawn was just breaking and the cocks were crowing. I was in time to see the four interrogators leave the shed. I waited until they were gone and quickly crossed the yard. I heard the sounds of the animals and then a noise that did not belong. Silently, I slipped into the shed—an instant before Dalia managed to hide herself behind a mound of hay.

"Come out of there," I said.

There was no response.

"Come out, Dalia," I repeated. "I saw you hide."

She emerged, bits of hay sticking in her disheveled hair. She came toward me slowly, her large eyes filled with pain and fear.

"Are you alone?" she whispered.

"I'm alone. What are you doing here, Dalia?"

"Please don't tell. Please don't say anything."

"What are you doing here?"

"Promise me you won't tell anyone. Promise—"

"Why are you in the shed?"

Dalia bit her lip. She reached out a hand as if to grasp my arm, but I was aware of the motion and moved back. She looked at me, her chin trembling. "I came to see a dead man die," she said.

"Go to your room."

"Please . . . let me stay with you."

"I said, go to your room."

"Let me stay with you." She fumbled at her wrap. "Let me be with you—"

"Get out of here!"

I stood at the door and made certain that she crossed the yard and went into the house. Then I closed the door and latched it. The stallion snorted and lashed out against his stall. I walked carefully forward, peering ahead as I went, and halted. My father's men had done a thorough job on the Zealot. His body lay crumpled in torn, bloody straw in exactly the spot where I had been chained to the wall. He did not appear to be alive. My father had promised the rebel his life if he talked, but I surmised that the torture had taken it. I took another step. I was wrong. The Zealot's head, which I had thought buried in straw, had been removed from a gory stump of neck. I looked around me and saw it in a far corner of the shed, its large eyes staring at me from under their thick brows as if at long last they understood.

In the middle of my sixteenth year, I lost Nahum as my teacher. One spring evening a shepherd who went back to the fold to get a forgotten goatskin discovered him straddling one of the ewes in carnal intercourse. My father, who certainly did not consider the offense a grave one, could not let it go unpunished. The next evening, Nahum was flogged, though the whipping was more ceremony than actuality. The crowd of servants and workers who stood in the yard to watch snickered, and even the man who replaced Shabtai —a sturdy, open-faced fellow by the name of Gavriel—had a hard time keeping a straight face as he laid on the minimal number of blows prescribed by law. Nahum endured the ignominy of the public whipping— he had even managed to display a kind of pathetic dignity, as if he were a martyr being sacrificed on the altar of some holy cause—but he could not cope with the aftermath. The members of our household, from cooks to stableboy, and all the people in the village would not let him live his misconduct down. They laughed at him to his face when they saw him, bleated like sheep, and made obscene gestures that could not be misinterpreted; even the children began calling him openly by his new nickname: "the ram." Nahum lapsed into melancholy, lost a great deal of weight but could not keep his food down, went nights on end without sleep and rambled in his discourse. Frequently, when we met for lessons, he would burst into tears and beseech my help. "Tell them to stop," he would implore. "I beg of you, make them stop. You can do it. Your father has the power to stop them. I know he does, if only he wishes. Please tell him to make them stop."

"I can do nothing," I told him. "My father can do nothing. We must continue with the lesson, Nahum."

"But they call me a ram. I am no ram. I am a human being."

"Nahum, the lesson."

He would nod and wipe his eyes. And he would try. But his grasp was shaky, his approaches to problems faulty, his knowledge inaccessible to him when he wanted it. He would stammer, bury his head in his arm in utter confusion, and once again dissolve into tears. I decided to inform my father that I could no longer go on with my lessons in such a fashion. But Nahum himself solved the problem. He took his own life. His mutilated body was found in the sheepfold. He had cut off his testicles with a pruning knife and, as might have been expected of him, had done a poor job of it, having to lie the night through in order to bleed to death. When I saw him together with a group of giggling maid-servants, he looked dwarfish, huddled like a wayward child in the blood-soaked straw. I wondered if on the long road to death he had changed his mind and decided it would be better to live even if the whole village called him a ram and bleated after him. After the knife strokes, there was little he would have been able to do to reverse his decision: he had taken the fatal step and was compelled to lie with his animal paramours the night through, oozing into oblivion minute by eternal minute.

My father told me it was just as well, that he planned to send me elsewhere to continue with my studies. It was summer. We sat in the arbor, the two of us, in the shady cover of the vine leaves. My father was deceptively relaxed, which meant that in an instant he could be ready for almost any eventuality; that was the way he ran his life, always expecting the event least likely to be expected. He had grown considerably stouter; the two furrows running downward from his nos-trils had deepened; there were pouches beneath his eyes; from time to time he would blink and sigh, as if some inner calculation woke to cause him pain.

He had grown in riches and in influence during the past year. His active support of Rome and outright physical opposition to the Zealots had brought him immediate and widespread benefits. Our lands had increased—new fields were added almost by the week; our flocks grew enormously; our cattle waxed fat and multiplied; our grain burst its storerooms. An unceasing stream of visitors, Jewish and Roman, came to see my father, and he engaged a private secretary—a bald, shriveled fellow named Amnon. We built many more new guest chambers, en-larged the bath and built steam rooms, constructed new quarters for the servants who joined our retinue, and doubled the size of the kitchen. The hunchback did not come to work for us—I heard one rumor to the effect that he had killed the boy and sacrificed him to the idol he worshiped, incurring the wrath of the rabbinate and meeting his death by stoning, and another that he had taken the child to Safed to live in a cave at the top of a mountain—but four masons came from Jerusalem and were still not enough, so my father had to bring another from Bethlehem. At the very same time, workmen began the construction of a luxurious villa for him in the outskirts of Nazareth. From time to time, I was sent there to observe the progress and report to my father; I enjoyed the trips and was careful of my behavior while away so as not to lose my father's trust.

The sun shone down brightly on us. My father tapped a knee lightly with the riding whip. With the same ease he displayed when brushing a man from his life, he waved a fly away from his face and stared resolutely at me. He had finished with the business of my education, informing me that I must spend the next few months reviewing my work so that in the fall, when the villa was completed, I could attend an academy in Nazareth. In addition, he told me, I would have a private tutor who would instruct me in Latin. I was elated: I had long hoped for such instruction and had mastered the Latin alphabet in anticipation of the day when I could go forward. I heard the news with joy, but concealed my excitement and nodded calmly. My father saw through my dissembling and chided me. "Scholarship," he said, his face growing grave, "the priesthood, the study of the Law, the written word—these are realms I am not equipped to enter, my son. But they are realms which are necessary and appropriate for my designs—and you, my boy, shall enter them and conquer them as my agent. So have I planned it, and so shall it be." I said nothing and he became silent as well. The fly came close to my face, and I slapped at it. My father's eyes watched every movement I made. He was still tapping the whip. Then, stroking his chin with his free hand, he said quietly, "What do you think of Dalia?"

I responded at once. "I think absolutely nothing of her," I said, "since I have nothing to do with her and no cause to know her."

"I see," said my father. He lifted the quirt and put it to my chest. "Well," he said in the same quiet tone, "would you like to have her?"

"What are you saying?"

"I asked you if you would care to have her as your concubine."

"She is yours," I said.

"I desire her no longer. She bores me. I am bringing three new concubines to live with me—Avner has gone to Jerusalem to get them.

121

I am paying top price for them, and they will be beauties. Dalia you may have as a gift. If I may be permitted to say so, I think she has an eye for you. Well, would you like her?"

My father was a chess player with a deadly strategy and he played for high stakes: you could not afford to miss a single move when you played against him. I did not hesitate for an instant. "No," I replied, "I don't want her. I have no desire for her."

My father dropped the whip. He nodded slowly, yawned and rose to his feet. His bulk loomed large and black against the roof of bright green grape leaves and shards of brilliant blue sky that showed through the interstices. I did not stir from my place. Swinging his whip in a loose arc and looking down at me, my father said, "Had you answered yes, I should have had you thrashed and sent her away. It is not seemly that a son should openly covet his father's mistress, whether his father desire her or not. As you have kept a good head on your shoulders and answered me well, I shall reward you. Dalia is yours. I order you to take her."

Dalia came to me the next evening, as my father had commanded. She seemed troubled or preoccupied and moved about the room restlessly, as if she could not find a place for herself. I glanced at her and told her to undress. She stopped in her tracks and stood gazing at me dazedly, as if she had not understood my meaning. I was seated at my writing table, sharpening a new quill; without turning to look at her again, I repeated myself: "Undress, I said."

She was silent for a moment; then she said, "Aren't you going to embrace me?"

"Take off your clothes."

Out of the corner of my eye I saw that her eyes had filled with tears. She lowered her head, went over to the bed, and slowly began to do as I had bidden her. I watched her garments fall away from her. When she was competely naked, she set her garments on the bed and sat beside them.

"Lie down on your back," I said.

I did not touch her. I did not even get up. The door was latched, the shutters closed and locked, the oil lamp lit. Dalia's body was bathed in a soft yellow sheen. Since the night when, as a child, I had spied on my naked stepmother, I had had occasion to see many women unclothed—maidservants, peasant women, dancers and performers, prostitutes—but it seemed to me that I had never looked on a woman's form until this moment. There was a softness about Dalia, a grace, a subtle harmony of shape and movement that separated her from everyone I had ever seen. They were females whereas she was a woman. My eyes regarded her, lingering again and again over her neck, breasts, round belly and rounder hips, sturdy thighs and strong, supple legs. I was spellbound by a beauty peculiar to her, a beauty that was beyond sex. It was as if her body had an expression of its own, an expression singularly Dalia's. It was as if her body really belonged to her, as if her soul lodged comfortably in it. I trembled and struggled to control myself. I had finished sharpening the quill, and putting the knife down, balanced my writing instrument carefully between my fingers. Dalia's face was rigid as a mask, I ignored it and encompassed her body yet another time with my eyes. Then, making a fierce effort, I dipped my quill into ink and wrote rapidly:

> *My heart is the pulse of time,*
> *It hath no other;*
> *The wind is a friend of mine,*
> *The sea my silent brother . . .*

I took exceeding care in the formation of the letters, finishing each with a flourish. Every stroke I made was precisely and expertly executed; every character I put down had a particular significance that obliged me to perfect it. As for the words they made and the sentences the words composed, I did not know what they meant or why I had written them. I sat with my quill poised. A terrible pain had welled up in me, a pain whose presence I had not known in years—one whose very existence I had all but wiped from memory. I knew that this pain was the pain of my childhood, an agony I had reckoned to be buried forever in the earth of days gone by. I set the quill down and wrung my hands. Why had this happened? I was being fired in the kiln of my present life: why had cracks from my past begun to appear? The lines I had penned seemed absurd. They looked up at me, laughing and piercing me through at once. I wanted to destroy them, but my hands could take no action—they could not even separate from each other.

Dalia looked at me. "What have you written?" she asked quietly. "What have you put down?"

"Words that have no meaning—or that have a meaning which escapes me."

"It doesn't matter, so long as you have written them. Perhaps they will mean something to you one day."

"Do you know how to read?" I asked.

"No," said Dalia. "Read to me what you have written."

To speak the words out loud was strange: they echoed in my ears, as if I spoke them into a chasm. When I finished there was silence. Then Dalia asked, "Why did you write these things?"

"I don't know," I said.

"And their meaning is obscure to you?"

"It is obscure."

"I understand what you have said."

"Then tell me."

"I cannot."

I shivered. I could not explain the state I was in. Part of me felt I had created this strange situation and another part of me felt that matters were beyond my control, that the situation had in a sense created me. I had the feeling that I had fallen into chaos, that I had disintegrated, that I was no longer a being I could point to and call myself. The pain was excruciating and inexplicable. Again I wanted to destroy the writing. But I was afraid of the writing. It had a strength I had not counted on and could not deal with. And another part of me wanted the writing to live. I reached up and picked my knife up from the table. My father had given it to me after the ceremony of manhood. It was a very fine knife: its blade came from Damascus and its handle was inlaid with ivory. It nestled in my palm—sleek, passive, obedient. Holding it, I stared directly at Dalia. I had never possessed a woman, in spite of all invitation and all opportunity. Whenever lust or desire touched me, I restrained myself because with the wish to embrace and draw close came an urge to crush and obliterate. At one and the same time I wanted to plant and wished to uproot. Woman seemed most precious and most abominable.

Now, as I stared, the body of Dalia seemed the body of my mother as I had witnessed it in the dim hum of lost days; and then the body of Dalia seemed the body of my stepmother as she examined herself in the mirror. The blood pounded in my temples and throbbed in my loins. I felt as if a clay mold that had covered me was cracking. I gripped the knife in one hand and touched its point to the palm of the other: a thin spider of blood sprang over the skin. When a woman inflamed me I felt the hopelessness of divided desire: the wish to cleave to her and the urge to tear her apart. I felt no pain in my wounded hand, but the hand with the knife trembled.

"Come here," said Dalia.

I did not move.

"Come here to me—don't be afraid."

Did she sense fear in me? Did I sense it? What had happened to my plans, my armor, my resolution? Did she know I had the knife? Did she have an idea of what was in my mind? Did she know that my self had vanished like a phantom, that I had gone stone-blind and lost sight of who I was? Why did she lie there? What did she want? What was her body saying? Like the lines I had written, her body had a meaning, but it escaped me. Would I ever discover it? Would I ever cast my own shadow again?

"Darling . . . come to me."

I rose from the writing table, half drugged as in a dream where there is awareness of the dream but no wakening. At the bed, I dropped the knife. Dalia's body was below me, wrapped in a mist of light. I swayed. Her arms reached far up and encircled my neck; murmuring gently, she drew me down and onto her. I felt her warmth through my clothes. My limbs shook. No one had ever touched me, save in anger, since my mother died. I closed my eyes. Dalia's lips touched my face, and some terrible, hard knot deep within me melted; there was so much pain that there was no pain at all. I let my hands run over her smooth, hot flesh at will. She pulled at my clothing until I was free of it. Then, moaning as one, we were together.

During the night—I cannot say at what hour—I wakened from sleep, confused by the touch of her body but certain at once who she was and aware of what had transpired between us. I stared, transfixed, at my sleeping partner. The oil lamp had long before burned itself out, but I could still make out the gold down on her neck and arms: her legs and thighs seemed to glow. I roused her and we were together again. It was dawn before we slept. The strong sun of a July day thrust almost angrily through the slats of the shutters when I awoke. I reached out for Dalia, but there was no one. Where her body had lain next to mine there was no sign or mark. I whispered her name, conscious of the futility. Where had she gone? Why had she said nothing to me? Why had she let me sleep on? A bitter sense of foreboding came over me. I dressed quickly and opened my door. Two armed servants were posted there. One of them explained politely that my father wished me to remain in my room until he had a chance to speak with me. There was no choice. I closed the door without a word, sat down on the bed, and held my head between my hands. A kitchen maid brought food, but I let it stand untouched. I noticed the knife at my feet and retrieved it. There was a scar where I had inflicted the wound the night before; gently I pried it open until blood crept forth. My father's voice outside the door roused me. I slipped the knife into my cloak and wiped my hand. I realized that night had already fallen.

My father entered the room briskly, as if he were approaching a horse to mount it. "Why so glum?" he asked. "Is something wrong with you?"

I sat with my head down.

"Answer me."

I said nothing.

"So you want her that much, do you?" He slid his whip under my chin and lifted my head. His eyes glittered. "Listen to me," he said, "that girl had connections with the Zealots. I had suspected as much for some time—the last days confirmed my suspicions. As a matter of fact, her uncle was Baruch, the rebel we executed in the shed last year. Her cousin is Zipporah, an infamous traitor to Rome and to Israel alike. We forced entry to your room during the early hours of the morning and while you slept seized her and bound her. At this very moment she is on her way to the Roman high command. I'm certain they'll know what to do with her."

"Why did you give her to me?"

My father chuckled and sat on the bed beside me. "You fool," he said. "You young fool." Without warning he took my chin in his hand. "Listen, and listen well to what I tell you. I gave her to you to teach you a lesson. A lesson, do you understand? You now know what power a woman may exert over you. Never again stay with a woman for whom you care: it is a luxury you can ill afford. This experience will cause you to lose nothing but a few hours of sleep. The other way—well, you would lose everything. Is that clear?"

"Yes, sir."

"Fine. Then the guards I've posted to keep you from doing anything foolish won't be needed any more. I'll order them to leave."

My father rose and left the room. Outside, a wolf howled. I sat alone with the untouched food.

A month before my seventeenth birthday we moved to Nazareth, to the newly completed villa, the construction of which had been slowed for some months by an epidemic of smallpox. My father would from now on spend most of his time here in Nazareth but would manage a few days out of each month in our old house in the village to oversee his affairs. The new place was more than twice the size of the other. It was situated on the outskirts of the city, on the highest of a group of small, rolling hills whose slopes were planted with vineyards and fruit groves. A long, winding drive led up from the road; it was freshly planted on either side with cypress trees and passed at its final approach to the house through an archway of polished stone into whose crest the familiar "Evenezer" had been chiseled in both Hebrew and Latin characters. An entire wing of the house was devoted to guest rooms, and a separate section to the intimate family, which included the chief steward Avner, the private secretary Amnon, and my father's six concubines. The house was built of stone, and there was a certain part which was sealed off from all but the master and his two trusted myrmidons. This suite was located just beyond my father's bedchamber. It had a number of hidden entrances and exits; under the last of its rooms a cellar, really no larger than a vault, had been hollowed deep into the southern flank of the hill. Behind the house, set in a copse of evergreens, were the servants' quarters, almost as large themselves as the house we had moved from, and the stables.

Our arrival in Nazareth was welcomed in regal fashion. My father accepted the overtures with a gracious and benign attitude, as if he were grateful for it yet knew that it was his due. He gave what seemed to me an interminable series of feasts and entertainments which brought together the most powerful people in the area, requiring of me that I attend them all. The parties bored me, I had no appetite for them, and yet I had to go and behave as my father intended; whatever personal contacts I might have made and turned to my own use were severely limited by my father's designs. I knew my place and my duty and did not once swerve from them. I foiled the machinations of men and avoided entanglements with women. I charmed, cajoled, seduced and flattered that I might better gather intelligence for my father. Sometimes I provoked a quarrel, sometimes I healed one. Sometimes I prevented a man from drinking so that what he told me might not be muddied, sometimes I urged a man to drink so that his tongue would loosen. As for myself, I never lost control nor sight of my purpose.

I had the use of most of my father's horses and spent a considerable part of my time riding through the city and its outskirts. Of my uncle Yosef, his wife Mara, and my brother whom they were raising as their child, I found no trace. They would certainly have known that we had arrived, yet they failed to make contact with us in any fashion. The little family aroused my interest. I wanted to see what my younger brother had become. I asked Avner and got a shrug in reply. I questioned Amnon, who informed me that Yosef and his family had gone to Egypt more than a year ago.

Amnon was a strange little man, birdlike in appearance but venomous as a snake. He had a quick tongue, a ready wit and a flair for language that I admired. He seemed erratic but the trait was false, merely a trap he set in which to snare the unwary. He moved with great speed and energy, and his eyes shifted perpetually from side to side as if he were constantly in search of an escape route. Amnon held a position of trust with my father second only to the place of Avner. Indeed, it was Avner who had brought the acidulous little man into my father's service.

About a week or so after we arrived in Nazareth, I began my official studies at the academy. Whatever foundations I had put down in learning soon seemed to me unstable as I encountered, one on the heels of the other, masters in the Law, theology, philosophy, philology and literature. Up until now I had been swimming in a pond. But everything had changed: I stood on the shore of an ocean and marveled at its vastness and sweep. I did not hesitate to plunge into the water.

Two weeks later, my private tutor arrived. He was received personally by my father and installed in a room in the family section of the house. He instructed me in the language and literature of Rome every day of the week except the Sabbath. His name was Catullus, and he was a thin, wiry, balding man in his mid-forties. He had a hollow-cheeked, pockmarked face, very fine blond hair that lay like a damp rag over his forehead but was sparse over the back of his skull, and a complexion so pale that he always looked as if the blood had been freshly drained from his vessels. He spoke in a low, terse monotone, clipping the words off almost before they left his lips. He was fluent in Hebrew, with a perfect knowledge of its grammar and complete mastery of its idiom, but he spoke it grudgingly, with undisguised contempt, as if he were compelled to hold converse with dogs who were incapable of a higher tongue such as his own. Most of the time his face was as impassive as his voice; I never saw expressions other than hate or anger on it, and even these feelings were difficult to bring to the surface. There were moments when I saw him as a fish, hovering just on the floor of a dark sea, expending as little energy as possible and feeling absolutely nothing, not even the desire to feel.

Catullus' hands were small, with beautifully tapered, elongated fingers whose nails were always manicured. Whenever he touched a text, he stroked it hesitantly as if he were caressing the skin of a woman. There were tiny blue veins on the back of his hands that moved, like little worms wriggling restively beneath the surface of the soil. I would watch them and lift my head and find him staring at me fixedly with small, watery-blue eyes. For an instant I discerned in them a haughty, quizzical gleam which seemed to say, "Do you wonder where these hands have been, what they have done, whom they have held? Don't waste your time wondering—you will never, can never know." And then, almost before it had appeared, the look was gone, the face lapsed again into an expressionless mask.

Catullus was sarcastic with me, but he kept the sarcasm in check through sheer effort of will. If I erred or stumbled, he would sit motionless as a statue. He would remain silent for what seemed an endless time, closing and opening his eyes with lizardlike indifference, and then at length signal me that we were beginning again by tapping a finger on the text. I completely ignored his reticence, his sullen indifference, his hauteur, his moroseness. I knew him for the excellent teacher he was, and that for me was sufficient: he was a bridge over the chasm I wanted to span.

Catullus was not well-liked by the rest of the household. The women avoided him and the men ridiculed him. He seemed oblivious to it all and content to spend his free time by himself. At sunset, or at dawn, I would often catch sight of his lonely figure in the garden by the fountain or at the fringe of an outlying vineyard. In the roseate light of morning or in the lengthening purple shadows of evening, he sometimes appeared to me a Roman god descended from the heavens to probe the affairs of men. My feeling had nothing to do with superstition: it was simply a sense of awe for a man who bore, as some reigning deity, the scepter of Roman learning in his hand—and of course I did not disclose it to him or anyone else. The teachings of the rabbis in the academy, my masters, seemed—though I could fully appreciate the scholarship and skill involved—both insular and impotent: seed that would generate nothing but the feelings of loss and dismemberment. Those teachers were Jews, dreamers in a captive Zion, the sages and scholars of a conquered people, a defeated nation. The future of what they taught lay but in chains and dust.

I had not given up my writing. I kept everything I wrote so that I would have a complete record of what I thought and felt. I no longer hid my writings in my room, since I was certain that it, as well as all others in the house and the servants' quarters, were searched periodically by Avner's picked men. I concealed my writings, wrapped well against harm, in a goatskin that I tucked deep into the hollow of a tree to the side of the drive which led to the house. In that way I avoided all suspicion that visiting a cache might arouse, since I always came to and left the house in the usual manner. My writing now most often took the form of a diary in which I set down the events of the day as if they were puzzles that I had already solved or would solve, when I had more clues, in the future. The journal became so strong a habit with me that I could not fall asleep at night unless I had recorded what had occurred during the day. Sometimes I was sorely tempted to show passages I had written to Catullus, a master of Latin and Hebrew styles alike, but I always changed my mind and was always glad I did. I did not even want anyone to know that I wrote.

I was past eighteen and had been studying with Catullus for more than a year when at the start of a lesson one day he behaved in a strange manner. I had noticed nothing unusual. As was his fashion, he sat with his arms folded across his chest, staring into space, and I did not give him a second glance. I began the lesson, hesitated, stumbled and then went on, at length realizing that I had erred and that he had not corrected me. I looked over at him, surprised that his curt, monotonous voice had not halted me, and somewhat irritated, though I hid the irritation. He had turned his head and was himself looking at me. But what a face he showed! His pale, watery-blue eyes were bloodshot, his mouth was twisted into an open sneer, his chin was trembling; there was even a dull scarlet color in his cheeks! It came to me at once that he had been drinking heavily.

"I didn't do that verb right, did I?" I said.

He snorted, and when he spoke his voice was slurred. " 'Didn't do the verb right?' " he mimicked. "What the hell do you Jews do right— can you give me the answer to that?"

"I'm interested in my lesson, not in your personal opinions of the Jews," I said, knowing fully well that my carefully chosen words would induce him to go on with what he was saying. "I don't want to discuss philosophy with you—"

"Discuss philosophy?" he cried out. "How can a Jew discuss philosophy with a Roman? How can a Jew discuss anything in the world with a citizen of Rome, can you tell me that? Can a Jew have the faintest notion of what error is when he has no conception whatsoever of the truth? It's like a blind man telling a man who can see what the sun and moon are like, or like a virgin telling a mother how it feels to give birth—could anything be more ridiculous, more preposterous? You want to talk to me, do you? You want to talk to me about the lesson, do you? You want to teach me how to teach, do you? Do the conquered presume to instruct the conquerors, then? Instruct them in what, I ask? In the art of defeat? In the science of submission?"

Catullus brought up a burst of low, bitter laughter as if it were phlegm. "Here you sit with me day after day after day for more than a year now, circumcised jackass that you are, sucking at the imperial she-wolf's teat, drawing for all these weeks and months the milk of Roman culture from her udder. Does that make you Roman? Does that confer upon you the majesty of Roman citizenship? And what, I ask you to consider in that filthy Hebrew skull of yours, will the she-wolf do to you when she is ready? Have you ever thought about it, my fancy Jew-student? Do you think she will lower her regal head and put forth her tongue and lick your face, do you? No, my friend, no. She will not lick your ugly face, not a bit of it. It is far more likely that she will devour you alive with her sharp white teeth, however full of her milk you may be!" He laughed again and struck his bony knees with the palms of his beautiful, blue-veined hands.

"Do you find what I have said to you funny, Jew? Is that why you sit across from me and smirk? Is what I have told you amusing to your perverse Jewish taste? I suppose it is, by heaven, I suppose it really is! There is of course no way in the world to calculate a Jewish reaction to anything but to expect that it will be inappropriate, absurd, out of proportion and completely unreasonable. What else can you expect from people who serve an invisible God in a visible world? What else would you expect from a nation whose deity is undefined, amorphous, inchoate, unpredictable?"

Catullus banged on the table with his fists, like a child having a tantrum. "You Jews—you Jews are a monkey people! You spring from branch to branch—from passion to logic, from superstition to the mystic, from hysteria to obstinacy, from reason to lunacy—with never a pause between leaps and never a thought as to where you have come from or where you are going or why. Oh, I know, I know, you don't have to go into the story again—I know it by heart, I know the refrain: 'We have vanquished you, but you are unvanquished. We have beaten you, but you are unbeaten. We have humbled your flesh, but your spirit is untouched.' Yes, I know it all—all the rabbinic clichés, all the priestly truisms, all the rubbish, the nonsense, the make-believe, the fantasies and hallucinations—I know them awake and asleep. But all this Jewtalk, this Jew-gabble is gossamer, do you know? If you want to really know why you monkey-Jews survive, I'll tell you why. You survive because it is Rome's wish that you survive and for no other reason, do you hear? If tomorrow Rome were to decide that you should no longer exist, then you would be utterly destroyed. Is that clear to you? Can your Jewish mind grasp it? Do you understand that if Rome willed it so there would be nothing left of you—not a trace of your priests, your scribes, your Pharisees and your Sadducees, your temple in Jerusalem, your wailing and your whining, your breast-beating and lugubrious passion, your prophetic raving and rabbinic chatter—and your swinish tongue?" And here Catullus scratched his chest and the back of his neck and armpits and loins, puffing his cheeks as if he were a chimpanzee and uttering mock Hebrew sounds which sounded like monkey banter. "All—everything—the lot of it would be gone, vanished, erased. Have you understood me?"

"Quite well," I said. "My Latin is greatly improved since you have come to instruct me."

Catullus was silent. He stared at me as if I did not exist and drew a small flask from his cloak, lifting it to his lips and drinking thirstily from it. It was soon emptied, and he threw it to the floor. "Do you really think that you mock me?" he said, shaking his head slowly from side to side. "Is that what you think? Well, you are wrong. For it is yourself that you mock. All of you arrogant Jews mock yourselves. You jest in the lions' den because you enjoy the gracious hospitality of the lions. But I say to you, beware. Beware, I tell you, for your day will come upon you. As sure as I sit across the table from you, I warn you that your day of judgment will arrive. And then the lions will no longer know you, they will know only their own hunger. And in that hour shall they satisfy their own appetites!"

Catullus cleared his throat and spat. He continued his discourse in Hebrew, his tongue and lips pummeling and bruising it, his voice using the language as he might use a whore in order that he might vent his hatred on her. "Tell me what they teach you in the academy," he said hoarsely. "What is it that the learned rabbis teach you? How to bite the hand that feeds you? How to mock the *goy*? But what idiocy is this? The *goy* you mock holds you in his fist. Or can you really believe the lies the rabbis teach? Can you truly in your heart believe that it is your God who keeps you in His bosom? You dare to laugh at the *goy* to his face and pretend that the face of your God shines upon you? But the *goy* has you safely in his trap, and there is no escape! Does the mouse sneer at the tomcat? Does the lamb mock the mountain lion? Does the rabbit laugh at the wolf? What then do the rabbis teach you? That your God will bend out of the blue sky and blow the *goyim* away like chaff? That the Jews are dreaming and their God will wake them gently from their nightmare and all will be well? That the God of Israel will cure the sick and raise up the dead? Ah, yes, I know, so you do believe and so you persist in your belief, stubbornly and intractably. Ah, you Jews are a stiff-necked, stubborn people, I know—I know. But you are stubborn by leave of the Roman emperor! You skip here and there and beat your chests valiantly like monkeys and pull the sweet fruit of your dreams from the branches. But I say to you—I warn you that Rome has surrounded the trees and one day will burn them to the ground with you in them and will hack away the roots so they will grow no more!"

Catullus waved a hand and opened his mouth to speak, but no speech came forth. His body trembled. His face had gone dead-white, and he gagged. He tried to stand but could not. I rose from my chair to help him. He put up a hand. "Don't touch me with your Jew hands," he whispered. "I don't need your help." He struggled and finally did manage to stand. He swayed and held his balance and took a few wobbly steps from the table. But then he reeled and fell to the floor. I went over to him as he pushed himself into a sitting position. He gasped. His face was covered with a cold sweat.

"Let me help you up, Catullus."

"Get away from me, Jew-parasite! Don't you dare put your filthy hands on me! I'll kill you—I tell you I'll kill you, and the empire will be rid of another vermin-Jew!"

I ignored his words, bent over him and pulled him up from the floor. Saliva ran from his mouth and his eyes rolled in their sockets. I got my arm under him and supported him to his room. He was lighter than I had expected and not at all a burden. He lurched and staggered, several times attempting to break away, but I kept a firm hold. I led him to the bed, on which he fell, panting and exhausted. He muttered in mingled Latin and Hebrew which sounded odd to my ears, as if the languages were coupling in his disordered mind. The room stank of wine and urine. There was a large flask of wine on the table. Catullus pointed to it with a shaking finger. "Don't you touch my wine, you son of a viper," he said. "Don't you lay a finger on it—you'll poison it with your Jewish soul!"

"Do you want some, Catullus?"

"I can get it for myself."

He tried to stand but fell back on the bed.

"I'll bring you some, Catullus."

"I don't want you to bring it."

Again I ignored him and brought the flask over to the bed and held it up so that he could drink. He swilled it in great gulps, spilling it over his chin and neck and splashing the front of his tunic. I held the flask until he pushed it away and turned his head, gasping for breath. I returned the flask to the table and seated myself quietly in a corner. Catullus held one hand to his forehead and stammered, "I'm sick—I'm very sick."

I said nothing. Catullus fell to his side vomiting a thick reddish slush onto the bed. His body shook with great spasms and he continued to retch long after nothing came up. When he finally spoke again, his voice was a reedy whisper. "I'm dying," he croaked.

"A Roman god does not die." I smiled.

A month after this episode, Catullus was no longer in our employ. Two of the maidservants came to my father's chief steward Avner and complained that they had been made pregnant by the teacher of Latin. They said that Catullus had trapped them in isolated spots and compelled them to submit to his desire. Catullus angrily denied the charges and called the girls "Jewish harlots." My father chose to overlook the matter, but Catullus began to drink heavily and did not stop no matter what the warning. He missed lessons. Several times he was found in a stupor on the grounds; once it was obvious from his condition that he had lain in a vineyard the night long. On another occasion he toppled into the pool drunk and nearly drowned; only the presence of quick-thinking Avner saved him. One day at dusk he forced a scullery maid at knife-point into the baths and disrobed her but collapsed atop her before he could penetrate her body. I did not want to lose Catullus because I knew that a teacher of his caliber could not easily be replaced. I used whatever influence I had with my father to keep him on, and even followed him about when I could to see that he came to no harm. I argued that it was merely a passing episode. I told my father that because I had studied with the man for more than a year, I knew his character fully and was certain he would recover from whatever madness afflicted him. Many a day I tried myself to talk to Catullus, but he vilified me and the Jews and gave no heed to what I said. Then one night he burst into the dining hall and interrupted a party my father was giving in honor of a local dignitary. He was very drunk, his hair was disheveled, his tunic stained with wine and with excrement; he wore no shoes and his feet stank of the dung of the road. In foul, blunt gutter Hebrew he heaped abuse upon me, his Jew-student; upon my father, his Jew-employer; upon Avner, his Jew-jailer; upon the rabbis of the academy in Nazareth, whom he called the "bearded scum of the earth"; upon the scribes and the priests, whom he termed "God's termites"; upon the people of Israel; upon their Messiah, whom he said was the "one who appears never to appear"; and upon the Jewish God, whom he referred to as the "absentee landlord." He reserved a special epilogue for the tetrarch of

Galilee and his "myrmidons, sycophants and decadents." My father had issued an order immediately on Catullus's entrance that he not be removed, that he be permitted to speak as he wished. This was a very clever move, a shrewd gambit allowing the teacher of Latin rope enough with which to hang himself. So Catullus did. His speech thickened and became slurred, his gestures grew ludicrous, his breath came in short gasps, his ideas became fuzzy, and he rambled until his audience displayed restiveness and then derision. There was a final spasm of oratory in which the words "Rome" and "Jerusalem" buzzed like horseflies and which no one in the hall could decipher, and then he collapsed. Catullus was lifted unconscious from the puddle of his own vomit and carried, with his belongings, through the arch and down the drive to the main road leading to the city. He never came again to impart knowledge of the Latin language to me, but he often haunted my dreams, descending like a supernatural creature from the skies of dawn or dusk and alighting on the earth: a wondrous figure endowed with the everlasting wisdom of Rome.

My father said he was not sorry that Catullus was gone. He called the Latin teacher "a troublemaker Roman," a man who was enemy to Israel and the empire alike, and said that his departure was of no "real consequence," since I had studied enough Latin for his purposes. My father told me that when I finished my course of studies at the academy I should be sent directly to the court of the tetrarch of Galilee. There my official capacity would be interpreter: actually I would represent my father's affairs and interests, much as an ambassador does in a foreign court. This was the first open disclosure of my future, though I had surmised what it might be for some time, and I welcomed it with an equally open display of pleasure, a measure I felt entirely appropriate to the occasion.

In a rare show of feeling such as I could scarcely recall, my father grasped my right arm at the elbow, squeezing my flesh and bone with his long, powerful fingers. "I spoke to you a while ago of the fields which are barred to me, my son. But soon, very soon, they will be open to my presence, for you shall enter them as my personal emissary. And, my son, you shall make harvest of the grain therein—and a rich harvest it shall be, a harvest bounteous beyond all manner of reckoning, for what the ultimate yield may be no man can say." My father pressed my elbow until tears started in my eyes. "No," he said, "there is no way to measure in wealth the naked power to which you will have ready access and which you may draw unto you as does the pond the forked lightning of the sky!"

We were sitting at the time in my father's private chamber, a large, splendidly appointed room with deerskin rugs and carved furniture of oak, mahogany and teak. Across from us, before a great hearth, at a huge table heaped high with parchments, seals, quills, sacks of coins of gold and of silver, sat Amnon, frowning heavily as he wrote. My father released my arm as suddenly as he had taken it, picked up his whip from his lap, and rested its point against a cheek. "From the time you were a small child," he said, "I sensed the power of the word in you. The power of the word: calculated thought, reason, stratagem, plan. And I sensed as well the power of the deed in you. The power of the deed: execution, impulse, passion, blind fury. And I knew and I understood that if these two powers would fuse in you, then I should have an advocate, a stalwart, a second right arm, and an heir. Balance, my son, balance is what you needed—and balance is what you are now acquiring. Boundless will be your rewards if you can but achieve that balance and sustain it. If—" He broke off abruptly, without explanation, and rose to his feet. "Amnon," he cried out, "Amnon, have you prepared the accounts I wanted?" A wave of the quirt bade me quit the chamber.

During this period of my life, in my nineteenth year, I made the acquaintance of the daughter of a neighbor, a rich Jewish landowner and merchant who had made his fortune selling stolen cattle and horses to the Roman military. His daughter was a slight, pale girl with auburn hair, light-green eyes and a shy smile that stole unawares to her lips with the softness and sweet stealth of a spring rain. One day I had sighted her as I was walking, had approached her in a polite and friendly manner, and had introduced myself. She smiled and spoke to me, and I accompanied her to her home, a sprawling villa almost as large as ours but built in execrable taste. We sat on a bench beneath a willow and watched her father's peacocks strut.

Her name was Tzila, or shadow; she was a year younger than I. Her mother had died while she was still a small child, and a governess had raised her. She spoke with the merest trace of a strange accent; when I mentioned it to her, Tzila told me that she had spent a good many years with an aunt's family in Alexandria, where she had been fortunate enough to receive an education. Tzila knew Egyptian fluently, could both read and write Hebrew, had acquaintance with arithmetic and geometry, and was fairly well-versed in Latin. In addition, she had pursued the arts of ceramics, weaving, mime and the dance. I liked her face and slim figure and her intelligence and learning, and told her of my life what I deemed it proper for her to know. She listened to me with perfect attention and poise, radiant with the smile that lit her features every now and again. Then she rose and said she must return to the house lest her governess wonder what had happened to her and take alarm. I asked her when I might see her. She reddened and shrugged and answered that she did not know, but she was certain we would meet soon. She left with the sad, gentle smile on her lips and puzzlement in her light-green eyes.

I mentioned Tzila that same evening to my father. We were at supper. He stared at me, lifted an eyebrow, and pushed his plate, which was still half full, away from him, nearly upsetting a wine goblet. "Have you forgotten the lesson of Dalia?" he asked. He sat looking at me and drumming his knuckles softly on the table's surface. "Well, did you forget?"

"No, I haven't forgotten. On the contrary, the lesson is quite clear in my mind. But Tzila is hardly Dalia."

My father said nothing, and I did not know what to think. Later while we were playing chess, he said without lifting his head from the board to look at me, "No, the only daughter of Avinoam is scarcely to be compared to a Zealot slut. The proposition is an interesting, I should even say a fascinating one. Such a marriage, if it were ever consummated, would in fact have many advantages: Avinoam has great wealth, much influence in political and military circles, and no other heirs to his fortune. But the time must be ripe." He sighed heavily, lifted his queen from the board with two fingers and set it down again gently, as if he might do harm to the piece. "But, see, you have left your king completely unprotected. How clumsy of you, my son. And how unlike you!"

My father smiled and the game was over.

I saw Tzila again several times, and with each visit my first favorable impression grew stronger. Her delicate beauty, her softness and charm, her cultured intelligence held and heightened my interest in her. Only once did she disturb my equilibrium, and after that single experience I was never bothered again. We were sitting on the bench beneath the willow; the peacocks were moving sedately across the sward, the brilliant colors of their plumage rippling in the sunlight; the air was filled with butterflies, which looked as if they had torn loose from the birds' feathers, and the scent of Tzila's young body was in my nostrils. I saw the full swells of her breasts and felt the curve of her thigh against my own. A lethargy began to steal over me, a weakness that was at once physical and spiritual. I sensed within me the possibility of my own dissolution, my own decomposition, as if all that I had worked and struggled for in my life were of no account and could be pushed aside with ease and abandoned forever. The feeling gave rise to an intolerable anxiety, to a fear that was beyond any fear I had known. To die was one thing: to be destroyed alive was quite another. And then it seemed to me as if I were observing myself from a point outside myself, and that what I saw offered neither comfort nor hope. I felt as if I were a stranger unto myself, someone alien, remote and uncertain, someone altogether unconnected to the person I had been until now. I felt that only by some supreme effort of the will could I return to the boundaries of the self with which I was familiar. The languor persisted and deepened—I could not rid myself of its grip. A longing came into my heart, a yearning so powerful and so painful that I felt an urge to destroy the person who had called it forth. At that moment Tzila leaned forward and touched my shoulder with the tips of her fingers. "What is that look in your eyes?" she asked. "It frightens me. What are you thinking?"

I knew that I had exposed a naked blade to the girl, and that angered me even more. I was so tense I thought I would burst apart: first, with the pain itself which seemed unbearable and immitigable, and then with the shame and the folly of my exposure. There must be no further revelation. Of that I was certain. All that I truly thought and felt had to be hidden from the eyes and heart of the girl, lest by another's recognition it gain an external life of its own and become a plague and a threat to my existence. I struggled with all of my strength, exerting every last measure of will power I commanded. Inwardly I gasped, choked, spun on the brink of oblivion. Then the crisis passed as suddenly as it had come upon me. The strange, deformed, yearning self shrank, withered and disappeared. My familiar outlines asserted themselves and claimed their due. Order was restored: every altar and abattoir took its proper place. Tzila would never again evoke my chaos-self: I was secure.

"Tell me—tell me," said the girl. "Please tell me what was in your mind just now."

"I was just thinking how beautiful the peacocks are," I said.

Tzila's father was a squat, barrel-chested man with a broad, muscular back, long arms and great, hairy-backed grasping hands; all of our servants called him "the bull." Avinoam's yellow, egg-bald skull was creased down its center as if an axe had struck it but failed to penetrate; his squarish, ugly jaw had been shattered a number of times in brawls, and the nape of his wide neck was packed with a sausagelike roll of fat. He walked with a quick, furious and curiously indecisive stride, as if at any given instant he might change direction in midstep; spoke in low, guttural tones that trailed off unpredictably into grunts; and stared with small hot eyes at people as if he wished to incinerate them on the spot. He was a blunt, gross, ruthless man who talked and looked like a peasant and lived like a king.

He knew my father, and it was obvious from the first that he regarded me as my father's delegate and so viewed my visits to his daughter with favor. After I began to pay court to Tzila, he called on my father several times and was in turn invited to attend a number of our fetes. Avinoam was a lusty eater and inveterate drinker. He banged the table, spat into his plate, spilled wine and picked his nose whenever he felt so disposed. In company he was loud to the point of obstreper-ousness, rude to the point of obscenity and cunning almost to the point of theft. But with others or alone, he was always a formidable enemy, withdrawing when he wished into impenetrable silence. In the presence of his daughter, he was reserved and appeared resigned to some sorrow fate had thrust upon him. It was safe for Avinoam to pretend with his daughter that he was docile, for she asked little or nothing of him.

Tzila seemed not to have the slightest aversion to her father, nor to harbor any resentment toward him. She had no idea of how her father had amassed his wealth or of what he did to preserve and increase it. She cared for Avinoam, but as one would care for a wayward child who is beyond redemption. His mercilessness she saw as simple brusqueness, his cruelty was to her ignorance, his cunning was cleverness. Tzila not only altered reality to suit her needs but needed very much to alter it. If she bore wounds, they were so deep and so covered over with scar tissue that she no longer felt their pain—or perhaps no longer even realized they existed. Her light eyes and the smile that came so often to her lips reflected sadness, but it was gentle and quiescent, without relation to her present and future. I saw her as a sheltered young woman who had no desire whatsoever to rid herself of her shelter; I saw in her a wife who would serve her own most desperate needs in her unquestioning service to her husband.

I cared for Tzila, though not at all in the way I had cared for Dalia. Tzila was never again strong enough to evoke in me my alien self, to induce disarray, or to throw into question the rigid lines of my identity. Tzila was safe: there would be no eruption from within her, nor revolt, nor even the initial skirmishes that lead to conflict. I spoke to my father with increasing admiration for Tzila's attributes and left him to consider the numerous benefits deriving from an alliance between our fortune and Avinoam's. My father's eyes narrowed when I talked, and I thought I detected in their depths sparks from the fiery vision of the Galilee within his reach. I was pleased. If I could ultimately help to bring my father the power he dreamed of, who was to say what power would one day be in my grasp?

On my twentieth birthday, I successfully terminated my formal studies at the academy. Though he lay on his deathbed, the chief rabbi, whose favorite I had been since I began studying in Nazareth, sent for me. He lay in a small, low-ceilinged room lit by oil lamps. It was so silent that I could hear the wicks sputter from time to time. His closest aide, a tall, stooped man by the name of Amatzya, took my elbow and steered me to the dying man's side. His eyes deep in the recesses of their sockets, his wasted face more a part of the world beyond the grave than this one, the chief rabbi beckoned for me to bend over him. He gestured with his bony hand, saying, "My dear son, do you see him?"

"Do I see whom, my rabbi?"

"The angel of death, my son. He's there—in the corner. The only reality in this world. I see him so clearly. Do you? But surely you must.

He's reading the Holy Law and laughing. And why does he laugh, my son? Because this is what the Holy Law comes to in the end. Do we not read as much in Ecclesiastes? Then why should men be surprised by his laughter?" The old man's voice shook, but his body was calm, even tranquil. Amatzya wiped his lips with a wet cloth. "Stay close to me, my son, and do not fear. There is nothing to fear, nothing at all. For the angel of death comes to every living thing upon the earth. He is with us each day of our lives. He follows on our heels like a faithful dog.

"You have graduated from this academy as a luminary, my son. You have drunk of the bright waters of wisdom and have yourself become a fountainhead. But I charge you to remember that this same angel of darkness was in attendance at your graduation. When you spoke, this black angel listened; when you sat on your bench of honor, he did rest himself; when you walked, he went after you on your path; when you drank the wine that is the blood of life, he waited patiently for you to finish . . ."

The old man groaned, and Amatzya and another, themselves old men, came forward, but he made sign that they approach no nearer. "Can you still hear me?" he whispered, and when I nodded he continued, "Do you remember," he said, "that when you came into the room I told you the angel of death was in that corner?" I nodded again, and he said, "Now he has put down the Holy Law, my son, for he is finished with it and so am I. He is no longer in the corner. But if you gaze into my eyes, you will see him there . . ."

It was as he said. In the wells of his sockets, the old man's eyes were like final drops of water. I watched a pale film draw down over the once brilliant pupils: the last points of understanding left them and they became no more than stones, objects at one with the vast blind array of the universe. They would never look at the Holy Law again, at the oil lamps, at me, at the angel of death. Amatzya and the other devotees wept and rent their garments, and I left the room. I had the feeling that I was being followed, but there was no one.

My wedding was set for a Sabbath night when the almonds would be in full bloom. Tzila wished it thus, and so it was agreed. For weeks carpenters, gardeners and other workmen busied themselves on Avinoam's grounds.

A curious event introjected itself into the preparations for the wedding. A detail of Roman soldiers accompanied by a delegation of three priests brought the hunchbacked stonemason to our house early one morning. He had been accused of molesting a child in the vicinity of Safed. The authorities found the floor of his cave littered with bones. He denied that he had done any wrong, but the priests were calling him an idolater and murderer and demanding his death. The mason had used my father's name as a character reference, and the Romans brought him to my father in deference to his position: they wanted his opinion as to what they should do. I was present when they led him in chains into the yard. He caught sight of my father, uttered a little cry, and fell at his feet in the dust.

"Save me," he cried out. "Save me, master!"

The stonemason had much changed since last I had seen him. His skin had grown darker, his deformity had twisted his body completely to one side, his face was marked with scars, and he had gone blind with a cataract in his left eye. He snaked forward on his knees and tried to clasp my father's legs and kiss his sandals, but my father stepped back. "Why should I bother saving you?" he asked.

"I have done nothing, your honor," the hunchback whined. "I have not transgressed the law. Everything I am accused of is false—my enemies have borne false witness against me. The idols in my cave are works of sculpture: surely you know that I carve in stone. And the bones that were found are the bones of slaughtered animals. I molested no child, but simply found the boy lost and brought him on his path. You see, everything can be explained."

"Come, come," said my father. "That's quite a speech for a tongue-tied man, a man of stone. But it is foolish to pretend with me. I know very well who you are. I've made it a point for many years. I don't give a damn if you're guilty or not. I simply want to know why I should help you. That's all."

The stonemason's one good eye fastened to my father's face. "I have always been your loyal servant and trustworthy artisan—my lord, I have ever kept your welfare close to my heart. Did I not toil for you for many long, hard years? Did I not shape your stones? Was it not I who spied for you? Who was it then that whispered into your ear of Shabtai?"

"Shabtai?" said my father.

"Shabtai the whipper, from the village that gave you birth. It cannot be that he has passed from your memory."

"Of course I remember," snapped my father. "But I'd like to know what you recall. Do you remember what became of him?"

"I do. And it was a fitting end for him!"

"Would you choose it as an end for yourself?"

The hunchback's jaw quivered. "No, good master. That is why I told the authorities of you."

My father rubbed his chin in silence. "I should not choose such an end as Shabtai met with for you either."

"I thank you, my lord. I thank you from the bottom of my heart!"

"It is much too good for the likes of you," said my father.

The stonemason was appalled. His face fell, and tears started from his red-rimmed seeing eye. "What are you saying, master? Surely you are jesting? My lord, consider that you are killing me!"

"I have considered."

The hunchback's callused, blunt-fingered hands scratched in the dust of the yard. "For the sake of your son who will be married before the month is out," he blubbered. "For the sake of the comely bride. For the sake of their issue. I beg of you, oh master—"

"You are wasting your breath."

"For the sake of the God of Israel against whom I have sinned. For His sake, my master, spare this sinner. For I know now the evil of my deeds. I plead with you, your honor."

"Do with him what you will," said my father to the Roman officer.

The mason burst into great, racking sobs. But when the commander bent over and touched his shoulder he stopped abruptly and stared up at my father. He did not remove his gaze. "It is not I who am a man of stone," he said. "It is you."

"Come on," said the officer.

As he was led off, the hunchback looked over a shoulder. "It is not I who am deformed!" he called out. "It is you."

One of the priests spat in his face and he fell silent.

Next morning I rode out on the bay mare. She was spirited, tossing her head and almost dancing as she trotted on the road. Dawn was just breaking. To the east the sun flamed in the sky as in a vast hearth, ready to reach out its arms and kindle the earth. The eastern hills were deep blue, and their ribs stood out boldly in gray and white streaks.

The road was unusually crowded for so early a time of day. Peasants on donkeys, farmers on horseback, and inhabitants from the neighboring villages packed into carts were all making for Nazareth and the *skilah*, or stoning, of the hunchbacked mason. Further search by the authorities had brought to light a secret vault, cleverly and pains-takingly constructed by the hunchback, which was packed with the corpses of children. Some of the bodies were badly mutilated; others had small stone idols thrust into their mouths or into other orifices. Even the Roman troops that had come upon the cache, men schooled in brutality and inured to it, were shocked. On the road to Nazareth, I heard that people were calling the mason the devil.

I did not share this view, did not see the little hunchback, with his lopsided body and blind eye, as an incarnation of evil itself. To me, he was simply a man like any other man who had certain impulses to which he had given himself over. In my opinion, he was guilty only of errors—two of them, to be exact. The first lay in his choice of impulses, for in choosing the way he did he had strayed so far from society's appetites that there was no way for him to mask or camouflage his desires, no way in which he could *use* society to hide his desires—as did so many others. His second error was in getting caught. When a man plans to break the rules of society, he must know them so well that they can never be used against him, or come as a surprise to him. A man must know how the authorities think and think ahead of them so that when they come for him, he is already fled. No, to me the hunchback was no devil. He was only a fool.

By the time I arrived, Nazareth's public square was already crowded with spectators, some of whom had been there a considerable while. Over all, in the air, solitary and imperial, the Roman eagle glittered, seeming not to catch the rays of the sun and reflect them but to be their very origin. A full battalion of crack cavalrymen were on duty in the square. At the northern end, a large pile of stones had been heaped; beside it ranged a group of priests in long black robes. They were the ones who would execute the sentence of *skilah*. It seemed ironic to me that the hunchback who had lived by stone would on this day die by stone.

A trumpet blast rang out, and the crowd grew still. A centurion wearing a black-plumed helmet read out the sentence. Another blast sounded, and the prisoner was led into the center of the square. I had expected the groveling worm who had importuned my father in our yard. But I was wrong. Never had the hunchback stood so straight, nor looked so proud. Flanked by the soldiers, he marched with a quick, bold, steady step. His head was held high, his good eye flashed, there was even the hint of a smile on his lips. The High Priest approached him to hear his confession, but the stonemason waved him off. "Get on with it," he called out gruffly. "I am more than ready to leave this dog's earth!"

The roar of the crowd drowned all else out. The first rock struck him squarely in the forehead. He staggered back, his arms flung out. The second caught him in the mouth. The priests were throwing with a vengeance now. The hunchback lurched like a drunkard, his hands pressed to his mashed face. Then a great lout of a priest hit the back of the stonemason's skull. It opened like a mouth, and great gouts of blood, bone and brain whirled through the air. The hunchback fell to the dust. Like locusts in their robes, the priests converged. Then they withdrew, and the corpse of the hunchback lay mangled and still in the sunlight. The centurion, together with the High Priest, kicked the body and pronounced it dead. The trumpet blared, the battalion rode off, and the crowd dispersed.

"Behold, thou art consecrated unto me . . ."

The rabbi spoke the words of the marriage ceremony, and Tzila looked up at me. More than anything else, her delicate face expressed trust. She seemed too frightened to show love, or perhaps the water of love had gone underground. Tzila appeared more than ever to be, as I had observed her to be on numerous occasions before the wedding, a creature of resignation, a woman who would bend with what came, no matter what. Women were called butterflies, moths, nightingales; Tzila was a chameleon. She seemed to shrink, almost in horror, from any course which would in any way define her as a person. Even her betrothal and marriage to me were accepted passively, as if what she feared most was to assert that within her which gave her uniqueness: thus the very methods by which she hid herself became the person known as Tzila. I knew that she was apprehensive about the marriage, which had been arranged for her by her father, but I knew that she was even more afraid of opposing him. Above all, she wanted to be left alone, wanted to be left to her simple pleasures, her brooding and her daydreams. At times she seemed to be gossamer, blowing here and there on the air with virtually no will of her own. Her smile, with its gentle, enigmatic sadness, lent to her features a look of mourning which I decided after a time was for herself. If she cared for me, I knew it was because she felt I would never disturb the near-perfect equilibrium she had so laboriously struggled for and so painstakingly achieved.

"According to the law of Moses . . ."

Tzila touched my hand lightly. Even in her touch I felt her hesitation, her diffidence, her readiness to comply and to acquiesce. I was relieved, even happy. Out of the ashes of Tzila's self-immolation I would rise anew.

Our wedding was the largest and most extravagant within memory of the inhabitants of Nazareth and the surrounding villages. The almonds were in full blossom and looked like stars caught among the dark branches of the trees. The torches burned brilliantly, the roasting sheep and oxen and calves turned on the spits, the great casks spurted wine, the servants hurried to and fro without cease. The mighty throng that pressed its felicitations on us was jubilant, raucous, lustful and obsequious. We responded correctly, without warmth or real interest. The higher officials, Jewish and Roman, kept aloof and waited for us to approach them. As we greeted the titled, the rich and the powerful, I watched each face and marked its strengths and weaknesses well. I recorded in my mind, never to forget it, each glance of scorn and greed, hate and jealousy, lust and envy so that one day I might use the information for my purposes. Nothing escaped me: hesitation, doubt, fear, desire, anger, perversity, obtuseness, anxiety. I made note of them all and of the measure they held sway in whom they lodged. I made my appraisals and knew that I was appraised in turn: everywhere about me were calculating eyes, making their own notations.

Only one discordant episode marred the feast. Avinoam, his jaw slack and his eyes glassy with drink, attempted to pull the clothes from a tall, beautiful woman, the wife of a neighboring landowner. Her husband became aware of what was going on and threatened to thrash his host, shouting loudly that Avinoam had violated the basic tenets of hospitality. There might have been real trouble had not my father intervened and put things to right. His stern, unflinching eyes, his strong hands, his regal bearing and firm, unswerving manner settled matters

147

before they got out of hand. Avinoam, muttering distractedly, was diverted and led away without his knowing it, the husband was pacified, and all was well. The woman, a striking beauty with chestnut hair and a magnificent bosom, followed my father with admiring eyes, but he did not so much as glance at her in return.

It was nearly dawn when the wedding feast ended. The fires in the ovens were dying, the torches burning out, the servants exhausted. Almond blossoms littered the sward where here and there a stupefied guest lay breathing hoarsely. Many of the guests were staying at Avinoam's house and had gone to their chambers. Others were too swollen with food and drink to bestir themselves and sat at their places with glazed eyes and spittle running over their chins. Still others were leaving, and their shouts and the clatter of their horses filled the air. The marriage canopy still stood and fluttered in a gentle breeze.

Holding Tzila tightly by an elbow, I steered her among the remaining dignitaries to bid them good night. Finally I took her over to Avinoam, who sat slumped at the head of the great table, alternately belching and snoring; when I spoke to him, he opened his beady, fat-clasped eyes and became sentimental, weeping and calling me his long-desired son, then lapsing into a stupor from which it seemed he would never waken but from which he miraculously roused himself the next instant, beginning his tearful ramblings from their start. And then to my father, who took Tzila's hand gravely and pressed it, assuring her that he as my father and I as his son would hold her dear to us, would cherish and protect her from every harm. Tzila flushed and bowed her head and promised to be a faithful daughter to him and a loving wife to me. It seemed to me almost a formal declaration between the two and could have been rehearsed.

We were finished with our obligations. Both of us mounted on the bay mare, we rode slowly through the misty night. The stars were obscured, the air redolent with the scent of the almonds; scarcely an hour of darkness remained. We reached my house, where a weary groom took the mare. My father had especially appointed a room for us in which we would live until we departed for the court of Herod. The light of the fresh dawn was just breaking when I latched the door behind us and threw off my cloak. Tzila stood across the room, by the bed; she looked pale, slight, vulnerable. She stood without moving, as if she did not know where to go or what to do. For an instant in the uncertain and unearthly light, she looked as though she were drowning. Her fingers plucked idly at the bedcover, her eyes were cast down. The sad smile played fragilely on her lips: she was looking inward, as if whatever life had in store for her could come only from inside her. I could see that she had forgotten me, forgotten the world. Slowly I crossed the room to approach her. For her, there was no choice: she must always be available when I wanted her. I touched her shoulder lightly. She started and looked up at me. Trust and then a terror I had never seen before mingled in her great, glistening eyes. She trembled.

"Undress yourself," I said.

She complied.

I dreamed that the hunchback sat at the foot of God's throne. He was as he had been before the *skilah*, his body whole and untouched. Even his deformity seemed right and natural, given the battered corpse I had seen. He appeared to have been waiting a long while in silence, as if he had to summon the courage to speak from deep within him. At length, he looked up and said gently, "O Lord, am I not Yours?"

And God did not hesitate but spoke at once to the hunchback, saying, "My hands have shaped you as they have shaped all other flesh: for there is none alive that the Lord God did not fashion with His own hands . . ."

"Then it was You who shaped my deformity, was it not?"

God smiled. "What is it that you mean when you say the word 'deformity'?"

"I mean the lump of bitter flesh I carry on my back as does the dromedary his hump, that foul mound of meat which causes men to jest to my very face and snicker behind my back—and women to turn their eyes away from my form lest the sight of me bring my malady upon their unborn children."

"But what folly do you speak? Your flesh is as all other flesh. Of what importance is the particular shape it has? As I have created the flowers and the trees, the birds and the insects and the beasts with many shapes, so have I done with men. Can you not understand that fact?"

"But men mocked me for the shape I had."

"Then they are twisted, not you."

The hunchback was silent. He seemed to be thinking, so deeply and so intensely that his eyes filled with tears. Then, turning his face away from God, perhaps so that He should not see his distress, he said, "And my other deformity—what have you to say of it?"

God was puzzled. "Which other deformity do you mean?"

The hunchback said nothing, but hid his face in his hands.

"Speak to me," said God softly. "Tell me what you mean."

"I cannot," sobbed the hunchback.

"My son," said God. "You can trust me."

"Am I Your son, then, O Lord?"

"You are my son."

And the hunchback opened his mouth to speak, but the words did not come forth and he bent his head and wept sorely. And an archangel drew near unto the throne of the Lord and whispered in His ear. And God's face grew grave and He waved the angel from His presence and spoke unto the hunchback, saying, "I know now of what you speak." But His voice was cold and His eyes stony.

And the hunchback recovered himself and said to God, "Tell me, Lord, did Your hands shape that?"

And God was silent.

"I asked you a question," repeated the hunchback. "Was it You who shaped that deformity?"

And still God did not answer him. And the hunchback rose from his stool at the foot of the throne of Glory, and he trembled and pointed a finger at God and cried out so that all in heaven heard him and were witness: "You must tell me! Did You fashion that monstrousness as well? And if You did, why? Tell me the reason why!"

God said not a word in reply to him and summoned instead two great archangels, each of them with bulging forehead and fire-rimmed eyes and six pairs of wings that were black as night. And in their hands they carried flaming swords, and they led the hunchback away from God's throne to another place that was cinder and pitch underfoot and stank of burning sulfur. And they walked on hot ash until they came at last to a throne of black flint where the devil sat.

And the devil, who was a bent little old man with shifty eyes and a tic in one cheek, spoke unto the hunchback, saying, "Why have you seen fit to blaspheme the Lord?"

"I intended no blasphemy," said the hunchback. "I simply asked God a question which He did not answer."

"It is hardly your place to decide for God which questions He will answer and which He will not, my son."

"Am I your son, then, O Satan?"

"You are my son."

The hunchback sat deep in thought, and the devil grew tired of waiting and prodded him, saying, "Now, tell me the question you asked."

"I asked Him if He was the one who made my deformity—not the one on my back but the other, invisible one. The one for which they sentenced me to death."

"I see," said the devil, frowning. "And what was that?"

"I cannot speak of it," said the hunchback.

And one of the devil's myrmidons drew near unto him and whispered into his ear, and the devil threw back his pinched little head and laughed squeakily. "So that's what is eating you," he chuckled. "And eating God as well!" He slapped his knees with merriment.

"Did you shape it?" the hunchback said.

"Excuse me?"

"Are you the one who shaped my monstrousness?"

The devil's face grew sober, then darkened with anger. "Did I shape it?" he mocked, scowling as he spoke. "So that's the game God is playing, is it? He wants to fix the blame on me, eh? Well, it's not going to work, I'll tell you that."

The hunchback shrugged.

The devil snorted. "He won't get away with it," he said. "I won't allow it." A malicious smile came to his lips. He whispered to an aide, who nodded and left. Then he motioned the hunchback to sit on a rock at the foot of his throne.

But the hunchback would not, saying, "Of stone I got my bread. Of stone I carved my idols. And of stone I met my death."

"Stand then," said the devil. "I don't care. We'll soon settle matters. But in the meantime, tell me some more about yourself. For instance, do you feel that you belong to God?"

"I don't really know."

"Do you feel you belong to me?"

"I don't know that either."

"When you—when you did what you did—what was it that you felt?"

"Evil," said the hunchback. "I felt evil."

"How then do you define evil?"

"Hate. Hate without regard for the culpability of the hated. Hate that has nothing real to do with the hated. And terror—"

"Terror of what?"

"Terror of feeling greater terror. Fear—fear of pain. Pain inside of myself, pain beyond anything I had ever known or experienced before, pain which I felt would destroy me, crush me to death! Did you ever have a dream which seemed to clutch you by the throat, to stop the very beating of your heart? Well, that was the feeling that impelled me to kill."

"I never dream," said the devil.

"Impelled me to murder, I should say," the hunchback said, ignoring the other's remark.

"Then you distinguish between murder and killing?"

"Of course I do. There's a difference between the two, you know."

"I know," smiled the devil. "I know very well. It is difficult to live and not kill . . . something. But murder is, well . . . optional."

"To avoid the pain of my inner self," said the hunchback, "I struck outward. I murdered others to wipe out the pain inside myself."

The tic in the devil's cheek jumped. "Well," he said, "whatever the case may be, I will not have the blame put on me. We shall come up with something, I'm sure. In the meantime, be patient."

The hunchback nodded. He looked drawn and pale, a little weary. Once in a while, he reached up with a hand and touched the deformity on his back, but for the most part he stood silently, not moving. The devil went about his business, which consisted mostly of his interrogation of prisoners. There seemed to be an unending line of them, and they trembled, quaked, vomited and even defecated. Some fell at his feet and wept, others fainted and had to be revived. The devil himself was reserved, at times a trifle morose, but never raged or lost his temper. At length, the aide he had sent away returned and spoke in his master's ear and the devil nodded and beckoned the hunchback to approach him. "Listen," he said, a little abruptly, "we have reached a decision about you. You are to have another chance."

"Another chance?"

"Quite so. You will have another chance to decide to whom you belong—to God or to myself. You will be sent back to earth, to mortal life, and there you will start anew. You will have a form other than the one you have now. And no man on the earth will be your father, but instead you will be the Son of Heaven. However, your soul will be the same as it is now; and likewise your pain will be the same. You will live again, and you will decide to whom you belong." The devil rubbed his chin. "Well, how does that strike you?"

The hunchback had turned white. "I don't want to go," he said.

"You have no choice."

"I won't go," whispered the hunchback. He shrank away from the devil's throne.

"They all say that!" laughed the devil.

My life at the court of Herod, tetrarch of the Galilee, began on an even, tranquil note. I kept my bearing modest, was circumspect in my relations with all whom I met, and did my work conscientiously and well. Above all, I made absolutely certain to enter no clique or circle or group, and I was scrupulously careful to form no alliances. I wanted to be a friend to all, an enemy to none. I soon became known for my listening ear and my closed mouth. People came to know that they could confide in me, could tell me their problems and their secrets, and that their confidences would remain inside my skull and go no further.

I set for myself the task of getting to know as much as I could about each person I encountered. I learned about the preoccupations of each, open and covert, and I stored the information in my mind and in my journal. Sometimes, as I had done when I was a student, I would assiduously go over what I had written down, comparing early impressions with later ones. Or I would compare one personality with another, noting similarities and differences. I passed many hours in this fashion, studying people as I had once studied the Law, philosophy and literature. I wanted to know exactly with whom I dealt so that to the extent it was possible I could control the relationship to my advantage. And I discovered that in reading through the journals again and again I got important insights into my own nature so I could strengthen it.

157

Of course, most of what I had written up to this point in my life I kept in the cache at Nazareth, exactly where it had always been stored, in the hollow of the tree by the drive leading to our house. I brought with me that which I had written since the marriage. Immediately upon our arrival at court, I set about prying loose one of the stones in a wall of the suite of rooms to which we had been assigned by the major-domo. I split it, wrapped the larger section in a cloak and got rid of it, and used the hollow space I had created in the wall as a vault. There I could safely store my documents. Not even Tzila knew of the hiding place, and I was relieved. For I knew that if Avner had searched our home regularly, the surveillance at court would be a thousandfold more rigorous.

Tzila did not take well to her new life at court. Very little was required of her, but she managed even that with great difficulty. She was shy, reticent and uncomfortable. She became suspicious of all who approached her, attributing the basest of motives to each without real basis for her fears. I spoke to her several times, once or twice at length, but my words did not seem to help at all. She grew cunning and tried to hide her misgivings from me, sulking alone or weeping at night when she thought I slept. Of course it was impossible for her to maintain the façade for any extended period of time. When I sat up one night in bed and confronted her openly, she broke down and confessed that she was bitterly unhappy and did not know what to do. I told her there was nothing to do, that she must adapt herself as best she could, and that in time she would get used to life at court. Tzila knew that she had no recourse, that my word was final and unchanging, that it would serve no purpose for her to persist in her woe. She accepted what I told her passively, apologized for her outburst and for having wakened me, called herself a "silly goose," and pressed her slight but shapely body against mine in an expression of tenderness that I knew was a direct result of our physical intimacy.

Tzila found considerable pleasure in carnal union. She had taken to it instantly, with a patent enthusiasm that was unusual for her and with an unguessed-at freedom. As the nights went on, she became more and more adept at pleasing me and herself and looked forward eagerly to our embraces. She had been altogether a virgin when I married her; she was wholly a woman now. Sexual union seemed to soothe and comfort her, to bear her away to distant shores where ghosts long familiar and dear to her paraded without cease. As for myself, I enjoyed

Tzila. She gave me warmth, not fire. And that was good. I did not wish to be burned.

Tzila did make an effort to change. She spoke to a number of the women at court and attended several social functions. But she did not seem able to get hold of herself, did not seem able to alter. Though she controlled her unhappiness and no longer wept or sulked, she kept to our rooms a good part of the time, read much, and slept many hours into the day. Occasionally she went out for walks by herself, but she went with trepidation, for her surroundings were unfamiliar and strange. Sometimes I thought she was like an animal pulled from its natural habitat and so confounded. I was concerned about my wife, but I did not let her know of my concern. I pretended that I felt she had adjusted so that I could more easily keep watch over her.

My immediate superior at court was a man named Nachman. He was a lanky, sallow-skinned Jew with hair that was gray but had not thinned, a pointed, well-cut beard that was still shot with black, large eyes that brimmed often with lust, and an engaging smile. He hoarded his smiles for private life, however, and at work carried himself gravely and put a somber look on his handsome face. He spoke in slow, deep, grave tones that sounded like the tolling of bells, and often cupped his chin in his hand as if he were caught up in thought so burdensome he must support the head that entertained it. He would never answer a question directly if he could possibly avoid it, preferring, as he put it, "to cogitate on the matter" in the hope that the questioner would either forget what he had asked or go away. It was all an act. Nachman cared little for his work and nothing for anyone else. Whatever he had left of his mind was elsewhere. His greatest asset, as he had come to realize, was his sonorous voice. After it came his handsome face and lithe body.

Nachman was chief interpreter at the court of Herod. He had been in this position for many years and was regarded as a fixture. While others in higher ranks had been purged and replaced, he had remained —partially because his job conferred no real power on him and partially because he was not an intriguer. And then there was the story that he had pleased Herodias much as her lover but that he'd had the good sense not to gossip about their relations and not to protest when she tired of him and sent him packing. He was good medicine for Herodias: he reminded her of her pleasures of the past without ever disturbing the present. Nachman's actual usefulness, if indeed it ever existed, was long gone. I saw him as a kind of extinct being, a kind of fossil. He preserved a polished exterior, but inside he was like a blown egg. And he was lazy, so lazy that he grudged each step he took and each word he spoke; sometimes I thought he grudged each breath he drew. What he could possibly defer doing, he deferred. What he could avoid doing altogether was even better.

Nachman had a young mistress called Zahava, whom he referred to as "my voluptuous one." He had been married for a long time to a woman who died under mysterious circumstances after he met Zahava and began an affair with her. Many at court said that his present mistress had poisoned the older woman or had pressed Nachman to do so. The chief interpreter adored Zahava and devoted most of his waking hours and all of his energy to pleasing and serving her. He seemed to me a man who had buried his life in sloth and squandered his manhood on a cheap slut, but I subsequently saw many men who had yielded to the same maladies. I reckoned Nachman to be untrustworthy and his paramour to be dangerous. Zahava was a buxom girl with a live body and a dead soul. She had narrow green eyes always filled with virulence and scorn she did not care to or could not hide. She took great delight in taunting and controlling Nachman through the obvious use of her breasts and hips. At times, she would try to exert her "charms" on me. I found her antics grotesque and distasteful, her feminine "schemes" ludicrous in their simplicity, her conversation stupid. Nachman would regale me with stories about her beauty, sensuality and cleverness, and I would listen, hiding my contempt behind a mask of polite attentiveness. He also described his love-making with Zahava in great detail, sparing neither himself nor his partner; I found this practice grossly obscene.

It became apparent in my first few weeks at court that Nachman would gladly divest himself of his responsibilities, and I made the most of this desire. As far as it was possible within my limited means, I gave what he asked for, procured what he wanted, supplied what he lacked. He grew more and more to lean on me: to seek my opinions, to draw on my knowledge, to delegate authority to me, to confide his fears and troubles to me. I served him well and requested nothing in return. All the while I kept a very close watch on his mistress Zahava and soon knew exactly with whom and when she betrayed her lover. I kept what I knew about her a strict secret so that unsuspectingly she would supply me with more incriminating evidence and so that one fine day she would walk completely unawares into a trap I had set for her.

Nachman was extremely jealous of the girl, but that did not prevent him from noticing and desiring other women. Several times he invited me to his apartments, asking that I bring Tzila along with me. I refused his invitations as gently and diplomatically as I could, explaining that both Tzila and I were too new at court—that too many other cares weighed upon me and that Tzila was ailing. I said that some day in the future we would be glad to visit him. Privately, I knew what he was after. Tzila had touched his fancy, and he wanted to entice her his way. I knew that he would go to considerable lengths to have her—even to, say, putting a potion in my wine or something of the sort. But he knew nothing of Tzila, less of me. In essence, I found Nachman a dull, hedonistic fool whose pleasures as well as vices lay in entirely predictable quarters. He was a man far too lazy to be greedy, a man too lazy even to recognize his laziness and make adequate provision for it. Nachman suited my purposes well: he was a fruit so rotten he could be picked any time at all, if he did not fall first of his own accord.

My duties at the court of Herod were varied. Sometimes I served as interpreter at social functions, standing unobtrusively at the right hand of the host, there when I was needed. At other times a court official, once in a while even a minister, would require my presence. At still other times I rode out to Jericho or Hebron or Schechem with a purchasing agent or even with a military detachment. I performed well, never complained, and above all never thrust myself forward. As the days and weeks passed, I established a reputation for excellence, tact and reliability. At first I had often been referred to as the "son of Evenezer," but now people began calling me by my own name. Courtiers nodded when I passed, court ladies turned their heads to flirt, and servants stood respectfully at attention. I kept my eyes and ears open, and whenever it was possible to advance my father's causes in a respectable fashion, I did so with zeal.

My father wrote to me at least once a week and frequently far more often. He sent the letters by special couriers who always arrived as if the devil himself were after them—and I was inclined to believe he was. One day at dusk I received a short note informing me that Avinoam had met with an unfortunate accident and fallen gravely ill. Tzila's father had been kicked by a horse and lay in a coma, my father wrote, and it would be a miracle if he lived. My father advised that I spare my wife the news, as there was nothing she could do and it served no purpose for her to suffer needlessly. I quite agreed and hoped for Avinoam's speedy death. I also doubted the story about the horse. What matter? One story was as good as the next. My spirits were lifted. Only a finite number of breaths and heartbeats kept my father from being the most powerful civilian in all Galilee.

One morning shortly after daybreak there was a knock at the door of our apartment. I drew a robe on and hurried to answer, certain that it was news of Avinoam's death. But it was a page by the name of Elazar, a small, dark-haired boy of twelve whom I paid to spy and do errands for me, bearing a summons for me to appear at the ministry of war. I was ushered past soldiers of Herod's elite palace guard through marble and stone-walled rooms into the private chamber of the minister himself. The room was silent when I arrived. The minister, a portly man whose visage was circled by a nimbus of thick black hair, was sitting behind a great marble-topped table absorbed in the study of a document. At his right, a white-haired scribe sat waiting patiently. At length the minister, who was called Zerubabel, looked up. His face was broad and swarthy, with a thick nose and wide, flaring nostrils from which little tusks of hair protruded—I heard it told later that Zerubabel was proud of these protrusions and never allowed them to be cut by his barber. His eyes were large, ringed in black, topped by bushy brows and had a peculiar blank expression in them: looking into them one felt as if one were staring at a wall. The minister's lips were also large and were curled in a perpetual sneer; often his strong white teeth bit into the lower one with great force, as if to tear it from its place. Zerubabel cleared his throat, and the scribe poised his quill, ready to write.

"So," said the minister in a surprisingly high voice that made one think immediately of a eunuch, "so you are the son of Evenezer."

"I am, Your Excellency."

"Come closer, then. My eyes are not what they used to be."

"Yes, Your Excellency."

"That's better. So . . . you are every bit as handsome as they say you are, are you? And then some!" Zerubabel nodded his head in a curious, jerking motion that seemed almost involuntary, as if some outside force had caught hold of him and was exercising its power as a kind of joke. His brows knitted and his lips tried to smile, but all they would produce was a leer, as if in the struggle between inner selves this was the only possible resolution. But the minister caught himself, the interest died on his face, and his eyes took on their blank look once more. "Nachman swears by you," he said, letting the document he held drop to the table, "which is an excellent reason for never laying eyes on you as long as I live. But there are other reports on you that I've been receiving: they run from good to superb. Some of them, I must say, almost make a supernatural being out of you. Therefore I believe I can conclude safely that you're a fairly decent interpreter and moderately trustworthy. Would you go along with my assessment?"

"Yes, Your Excellency, I would."

"Fine. I thought as much." Zerubabel leaned to one side of his chair. "Now pay attention to me. I have a job, an important job for a good interpreter—and for a good man. This assignment is important, and it's also dangerous. It means going into the field with a large Roman detachment. They're going to sweep the Hebron area, where the Zealots have been quite active in the last few months. I need someone to accompany the unit—someone who can really talk to the people who live in the area, someone to ask the right questions, to sort out the real answers from the false. I need someone to interpret the language, yes, but far more than that I need someone who is perceptive enough to interpret people and events, to interpret signs correctly, someone who will help the mission accomplish its purpose. I thought that you might qualify for the job, son of Evenezer. But let me hear how you feel about it."

"I'd like to go, Your Excellency."

"You would?"

"Your Excellency, yes!"

"You are fully aware of the risks?"

"I am aware, Your Excellency."

Zerubabel leaned forward and sighed deeply. He set his elbows on the table and clasped his thick-bearded chin between his palms. He was silent for some time and so very still that he looked like a round idol. Something flashed in his eyes but disappeared before I could make out what it was. He cleared his throat, and when he began to speak his voice was so high it cracked before he could bring it under control. "I mean," he said, struggling to keep his voice within bounds, "I mean, are you fully prepared to accept all of the risks this job entails? You must understand that there are certain, shall we say, inconveniences that you will incur even before you commence your assignment . . ." His voice trailed off and once again he sighed.

"As I stated before, I am fully prepared to accept all risks, no matter what they are and when they occur, Excellency."

"I see," said the minister of war. He sat thinking for several moments, and his eyes slowly filled with an ugly light as if they were filling with stagnant water. He turned his head slightly in the direction of the scribe and dismissed him with a cursory motion of his thick, blunt-fingered hand. The old man rose instantly, and despite his age hurried with incredible speed through a small door set in the wall behind the table. The door closed with a sharp sound that echoed through the huge chamber with its tapestries and wall maps, its charts, globes, burnished weapons and military paraphernalia arrayed in symmetrical displays. Then silence returned, to match the bitter, withdrawn silence of the war minister.

It was impossible to be a day at court without hearing a new story about Zerubabel. Of all Herod's ministers and inner coterie, this man was most feared, respected and despised. From a number of sources I had heard the story that he had killed his own brother in combat, hurling a javelin into his back in the thick of battle, to attain to his present position: his brother, so went the tale, was his arch rival, and Zerubabel had treated him so and as such sent him from this world. Another widespread rumor was that Zerubabel had captured the fancy of Herodias but had spurned her advances, a course of action for which many men had paid with their lives: but Zerubabel, through cunning and villainy which matched hers and often outstripped it, had parried each and every thrust and survived the first furious gusts of her rage until finally they tapered off when she found another prey. Still another story, which was confirmed by many people at court and by many of the military, recounted how Zerubabel had shut the families of a dozen Zealot suspects into a barn and with his own hand had set it on fire in front of their eyes so they could watch their wives and children burn to death; this he had done during an abortive Zealot revolt in Samaria to some men who were only suspects and knew nothing and to others who cried out before the torch kindled the blaze that they would openly confess all that they knew.

What his origins were nobody really seemed to know for sure. Some said he was not a Jew at all, but an Egyptian who had come to Judea with his parents as an infant; when his parents died in a plague, so went the account, he had been adopted by a Jewish family which in later life he betrayed to the Roman authorities. Others related that he was the son of a rich merchant in Acre and had been banished from the family for seducing a sister and getting her with child. One courtier insisted that he had no father in the human sense but was the spawn of a vain, lustful dowager and some nocturnal creature of Satan, claiming that he knew servants who had actually been present at Zerubabel's birth and had seen that horns had to be cut from his forehead and a tail severed from his spine with the blade of an axe. Nachman said that he was a poor Jew from Jerusalem who had learned his lessons well from the Romans and won his present rank by lying, cheating, stealing and slaughtering everybody and anybody in his way—as did the majority of rich and powerful men in the world.

Whomever his parents were and whatever his background, Zerubabel exerted an enormous influence over Herod. He was a key figure always in the deliberations of the tetrarch's inner sanctum, was granted private audiences when all others were not, and was privy to every decision the tetrarch made, whether great or small; there were even those in court who said that Herod never went to sleep without first consulting his minister of war. Herod had conferred upon Zerubabel much direct military authority, almost unlimited tribunal powers and considerable latitude in matters of appropriation and tax levying. During the years of his office Zerubabel had thus amassed great wealth. He was often referred to as "the octopus"—a man with tentacles everywhere and a reserve of beclouding fluid behind which he quickly retreated when attacked. He was also called "Herod's wet nurse," and I had occasion to see several caricatures in which Zerubabel was depicted as giving suck to the tetrarch from a distended, snakelike tit.

Sitting before me now, the man looked more than anything else like a monstrous frog, with his round shoulders, swollen face and big, unblinking eyes over which now and again the heavy lids with their metal-like sheen fell as of their own accord. Zerubabel folded his hands and sighed as if this movement had cost him great effort. He held stubbornly to his silence for some time longer and then, clearing his throat as usual, said, "I am pleased to know that you have come to such a wise and advantageous decision, my boy. Very pleased. I'm certain that you will be satisfied and that I will be satisfied. And that's what counts in life, isn't it, my boy?"

"I suppose it is, Your Excellency."

"You suppose, do you? Well, that's fine, that's splendid!" Zerubabel sighed. "But tell me, my handsome fellow, did you know that my apartments are but a moment from here? They're capital, really they are—especially the bath! It's done all in pink marble, the finest Rome has to offer! And I had the best architect in all Judea do it—what's his name now? Well, it doesn't matter, he's long gone from this world, and may he derive greater enjoyment from the next!" Zerubabel chuckled and rose by spreading his hands out on the table in front of him and pushing himself up slowly. His next words were spoken haltingly and in an unsteady voice. "The scribe is gone, he shan't return. I've dismissed all the servants, and they won't disturb us. You see, I've thought of everything so the two of us can be alone, just you and me. Actually, my boy, I've had my eye on you for some time. 'Who is that lovely young man?' I asked the first time I ever saw you in court. And they told me. And I knew that one day, when the opportunity presented itself, we should be friends, just you and I together." He sighed and left the table. "Would you care to have a bath with me first?"

"Yes, Excellency."

He grunted and I followed his wagging buttocks out of the chamber.

The mission ran smoothly, with characteristic Roman precision. Four battalions of cavalry at full strength rode out from their base and reached the designated area of search in record time. The target was a small village southwest of Hebron where a rebel band was thought to be in hiding. Three of the battalions completely surrounded the village, which sat atop a hill, and held their positions through the night. At dawn the fourth moved up the hill, and by the time it was light, they were in full command of the situation. A house-to-house search was begun, and with the help I was able to give to the commanding officer, several dozen suspects were rounded up. The soldiers brought them to the bottom of the hill where the cross-examinations were held in a little wadi under a towering wild date tree. I played a major role in this part of the operation, keeping pace with and frequently outdoing the examining officer. I was exacting, relentless and brilliant in my stratagems: I thoroughly enjoyed my work— enjoyed confounding the miserable, terrified Jews we had caught like so many fish in our net, enjoyed frightening them out of their wits and cracking them like nuts. Whenever a man broke down, I experienced particular pleasure, almost sensual in tone, for the power of my voice or the look in my eye were sufficient to make him crawl on the earth and beg for his life. Sometimes a man would offer me his wife, his sisters, his mother, his children if only I would let him go free.

We had failed to capture the Zealot band as we had hoped; most of its members, we surmised, had moved on to the Sea of Salt some days earlier. But we had taken about two dozen suspects, men whom we felt had actively aided the band or men who could give us information on the rebels' activities. By the time the sun reached its zenith, we had released all but nine prisoners. Then the intense interrogation and torture began. Four more men were freed—bloody but alive and whole. Two perished under the torture methods—one whose lungs burst and another whose heart stopped. That left three, all of them strong possibilities. I exerted all my efforts, as I wanted the men to be cogent and lucid enough to give us valuable details: fingerless or toeless men generally did not talk as well as those left intact. My exertions were crowned with success. One confessed all he knew immediately, and the other some fifteen or twenty minutes later. That left the third, out of whom we had been able to get not a thing all morning. The soldiers were sweating and disgruntled, and their officer very close to losing his patience.

The two who had confessed had been given water and food and removed; they would be taken back to the base for further questioning. That left the lone holdout, a bent, shriveled little man with warts on his narrow, grimy face and a mouth devoid of teeth. I had my good reasons for believing that this man had been harboring Zealots on his farm for years and that he had personally harbored several members of the band which had fled the village. The old man had somehow managed to endure all of the punishment we had dealt out, fainting every once in a while but always recovering. It was by now nearly midafternoon and the Romans were very weary. They had held the old man's head under water continually for nearly an hour, broken the fingers of his right hand at the knuckles, and severed a toe—but they had gotten nowhere. Now the consensus was to kill him quickly and "get it over with."

I felt compelled to interfere. "Don't do away with him yet," I said to the officer in charge. "Let me question him by myself." I approached the prisoner. The old man was on the ground, half unconscious and lying in his own blood and excrement. I stood over him as many years before my father had stood over the Zealot in our yard in the village. Then I knelt beside him. "Listen," I said. "Pay attention. I'm Jewish. You can trust me." I jerked a shoulder in the direction of the Romans. "I won't let them touch you."

The old man's large blue eyes regarded me with a puzzled insolence.

His mouth moved silently several times before words came out. "A drink," he whispered with his cracked lips. I had water brought immediately. When he had finished drinking, he asked, "Are you really a Jew?"

"Do you want to see that I am circumcised?"

The old man stared at me—first in disbelief, then in belief, then in horror that he believed. "You could be my son," he said at length.

"I am not your son."

"Are you a son of God? A son of Satan? To whom do you belong?"

"Old man, you don't seem to realize that your life is in my hands!"

"My life is in God's hands."

"Arrogant nonsense!" I waved my arms. "Your life is in the power of these men about you. Why do you have to confuse the issue with your talk of God?"

"That is the issue," said the old man slowly. "The spirit of God on earth—"

"Come now, we can talk honestly, as fellow countrymen. You and I and the Roman authorities know that you have been consorting with the rebels for a long time. And now we have caught up with you. We found a rebel in your barn, didn't we?"

"You found a man in my barn, that's all. I didn't know who he was when I brought him there. He was hungry and homeless. I gave him food and drink and temporary shelter—according to our commandments. I didn't ask about his politics, I don't give a damn for them."

"That isn't what the man said."

"I don't care what he said."

"He's confessed, old man. He's told us all."

"You tortured him and made him say whatever you wanted him to say."

"You can help us very much, old man."

"I've told you what I know," said the prisoner.

"If you tell me the whole truth, old man, I can fix things."

The old man smiled weakly. "Fix what things?"

"I can get them to let you go. And I can get them to spare the lives of the other two. They're young men. They have families. You don't want them to die, do you?"

"If they must die to live, then they must die. That's better than a living death—like yours."

"What will you profit by your obstinacy? A ditch for your grave? The Zealots talk prettily, old man. But talk is wind, and Rome is a fist."

"If talk of the Law is wind," said the old man, "it is holy wind."

I rose and looked down at the prisoner. He seemed absurdly small, in his shredded clothing almost like a heap of rags. "Your years have brought you no sense. You will die for your obtuseness."

"It won't be the Romans who kill me," said the old man. "It will be the sight of a Jew turned renegade."

I shrugged and walked over to the officer in charge. He was furious when he heard that I had gotten nothing out of the prisoner. "Jews are damn leeches," he said, struggling to his feet and waving to the torture detail. "They suck your blood and they waste your time! Finish him off quickly—I want to get out of this hellhole!" As the sun touched the crests of the hills, I saw a lone cavalryman ride south. Behind his mount, tied by a long taut rope, the old man's corpse dragged: it would be left in the open field for the vultures. A fitting end for a jackass, I thought.

We rode through the night toward our base, taking our two manacled prisoners with us. They were heavily guarded, as if they were treasure. The air was chill, the dark sky thickly sprinkled with stars. None of the Roman officers addressed me, and I had much time to reflect. In spite of what the interrogating officer had said to me, I knew that I had done a superb job, that the two prisoners would yield important secrets, and that word of my success would reach the highest circles of Herod's court. I also felt certain that the Roman hierarchy would hear favorable mention of my name and skill. Ahead of me and behind me, the cavalrymen sang hoarsely in the night, exalting Rome and reviling Jerusalem, praising the gods and mocking the unseen God of Israel. Beneath my swaying body, the powerful legs of my horse struck at the earth in an unbroken rhythm. Above my head, the sinking stars glittered as if they were knives being sharpened on the revolving wheel of the heavens. Inside my heart, a small voice spoke clearly and confidently: "Your time will come. Hold fast—for your hour is sure to arrive."

A week after I returned from the mission, Avinoam died. The end came suddenly, just after two physicians from Jerusalem had visited him and pronounced his condition improved and directly after a group of priests from Nazareth had blessed him and predicted complete recovery. Though it was long past midnight, Elazar brought word to me as soon as he had it himself from the spent courier: like others in my employ, the page, who was shrewd beyond his years and reminded me somewhat of myself as a child, knew that those who served me well were rewarded well. Tzila was distraught when she heard the news. She fainted twice, and when she recovered wanted to set out immediately for Nazareth, but I forbade it. I lay with her through the night, listening patiently to her lamentations, and early the next morning sent for the court physician to examine her. She was four months pregnant and I wanted to be sure that she was fit for the journey. The physician assured me that she was, but warned me that excessive grief might be injurious. I therefore spoke earnestly to my wife and related to her what I had been told by the doctor; I made it clear to her that I would permit her to accompany me to Nazareth only if she exercised control over herself and did not give way to undue mourning. I sat with her until I was certain she understood my meaning and had given me her promise that she would restrain herself.

We set out from the court at noon in a carriage drawn by six swift horses and followed by two soldiers of Herod's mounted palace guard, purple pennants fluttering at the tips of their lances. We stayed that night in an inn on the outskirts of Schechem. Despite her promise to me, Tzila was feverish and restless, and I was compelled to warn her that if she did not regain her composure I would send her back. She agreed and appeared to doze off for a few hours, during which time I put down my day's observations in a small diary I carried with me; later they would be transferred to my journals and stored in my vault.

At daybreak we set out again with fresh horses. The countryside was radiant, freshly washed by a spring rain that had fallen during the night. Farmers and peasants appeared in the fields; now and again we passed merchants bearing their wares to market. Everywhere along the roads, travelers and workers fell back when they saw us, and the royal colors of Herod were saluted. We encountered many Roman patrols, but they waved us on without halting us for search. Only once during the entire journey were we detained: at a crossroads where a long train of convicts in transit from one military camp to another was resting. Lying in grass at the side of the road, shaven-skulled and gaunt, they looked like animals. The officer in command, a burly young man with a somber voice and merry eyes, apologized for the delay. He had orders, however, to halt and search all passers-by in order to prevent a Zealot raid aimed at freeing his prisoners. I nodded at his explanation and smiled when he flushed in returning my salute. We rolled forward and picked up speed again. Tzila was asleep against my shoulder, as I had given her a potion the physician prescribed.

Late in the afternoon, we reached the Jezreel Valley. I had never seen its fields and vineyards so lovely—it looked as if the world had been fashioned anew especially in honor of our journey. And I could not help feeling myself a king traveling through his demesne. At the roadside, sparrows were settling into the branches of the cypresses and eucalyptus trees. In the distance, a flock of sheep moved lethargically in from pasture, a shepherd at their head and a shepherd following after, each piping on a flute whose shrill sounds now and again reached me on the wind. Then I spotted a squad of Herod's foot soldiers marching in single file toward us and ordered the driver to slow the carriage to a halt; when the line came abreast of us, the leader barked out a command and his men presented arms, their spears flashing blood red in the light of the dying sun. I returned the salute, the driver whipped the horses into a gallop, and we sped on. Against my shoulder, Tzila stirred from her stupor and asked thickly, "Are we there yet? Have we reached Father?"

"I'll let you know when we arrive," I replied. "Sleep now . . ."

As the last rays of the sun were fading from the sky, we reached the outskirts of Nazareth and drove past the hill atop which my father's house stood guard. A group of weary peasants, their scythes resting on their shoulders, stared dumbly at us as we approached, and the dust of the road swirled back and settled on them as we rolled swiftly by. The first stars were out as we came to a stop in front of Avinoam's villa, the horses pawing the earth and snorting with exhaustion. I half carried Tzila from the carriage, refusing the help of her governess and the other servants who pressed forward, weeping as they came.

Avinoam lay in shrouds on a bier in his great dining hall, which was lit by lamps of mourning. I thought it entirely appropriate, since he was now fit only to be served as a meal to the maggots. The room was packed with priests and rabbis paid to mourn, with neighbors and acquaintances come to make certain for themselves that the rumors were true and that he was really a corpse, with business associates concerned with the settlement of outstanding debts, with competitors there to lament in public and gloat in secret, and with villagers and peasants drawn by curiosity. These latter wanted to know how a rich dead man looked, how a powerful dead man looked, how a man who had ruled over them with a cruel and unrelenting hand, who had crushed them as a vineyard owner crushes grapes, who had threshed them as a farmer threshes his grain, who had spilled their blood and called forth their tears while he was alive and breathed the air of the earth—these latter wanted to see how Avinoam looked when the breath of life had ebbed from him and the leer had frozen forever on his face and his eyes had gone everlastingly blind and he lay a cadaver upon his bier, naked and vulnerable before the gaze of their living pupils. They found that he was very dead, dead as any other man or woman who dies, rotting as any other flesh and blood born of woman; that he stank and was silent and would be shoved into the ground as would they some day. And they realized that he had hidden this mortality from them and from himself like a shameful secret behind his iron mask, his wealth, and his whip. And their hearts were glad he was dead. And their hearts consigned him to the nethermost regions of *geheinom*, hell. And they muttered the words of the psalms gratefully.

My father had been expecting me, and when he caught sight of me, he nodded his head; I left Tzila in the care of her governess and the others of her household who cared for her and edged slowly over to him. He drew me into another room, and for a time the two of us just stared at each other, for it was the first time that we had been together since I departed for the court of Herod. My father had aged some, there were ash-gray lines in his hair, and he had put on some weight. But there were no signs of weakness in him, no indications that his faculties were lessening. His keen, stern eyes raked me like talons, taking stock of everything he saw and boring deep into mine as if to pry loose any covert information. There was a trace of mockery on his lips, but it died at birth, almost before it could be identified; and if it was there, it was because my father desired that it should appear and vanish upon its very appearance. My father did not speak, and the silence grew strained until I realized that he wished me to speak first. "So it's all over with Avinoam," I said.

"It's over for Avinoam," said my father. "And beginning for us."

"You phrase it well."

"It has worked out well, my son—because I have made it work out well. The property, the money, the holdings, the debts owed to Avinoam —they are your wife's now. And so they are in your hands, my son, and through your hands pass into mine and merge with what I have: and then what I have becomes the Galilee—its fields and vineyards, its mountains and streams, its men and beasts. Evenezer will be Galilee!"

I said nothing.

My father touched my shoulder and then let his hand drop, as if he had touched fire. "You've done well, my son, very well. I've heard your name spoken exactly as it should be spoken—with respect and a touch of fear." He smiled. "You are a paragon, a watchword, a symbol of probity. You are excellence and energy, shrewdness and sagacity. The balance I spoke to you of, my son, the balance. Your knowledge and your, shall we say, practical skills fit hand into glove—and though none may yet realize it, the glove is mailed. But enough of this talk for now. We must give the dead what they deserve. I shall expect you tonight so that we can attend to the living and their needs."

I followed my father back into the dining hall, which had become even more crowded with those who chose to appear as mourners. Tzila had been brought forward to the bier and had swooned on her father's body. I ordered her removed to her old bedroom and there instructed her governess to administer the physician's potion in a cup of wine and to wait by her side until I should come for her; this the faithful woman promised to do. I returned to the chamber of death to mingle there with the guests whom I considered of value to me. I kept away from my father, avoiding him as if he were a stranger; I knew that my father approved of this course of action. The royal sash of Herod's court, whose purple silk I wore across my chest, served me proudly and well. I found that I was sought after and pursued. Several Pharisees approached me; a number of Roman officers engaged me in conversation, including the deputy vice-commander of a legion which had seen service in Syria; and finally I was drawn into a discussion with a special envoy of Pilate himself—a bald, wizened little old man who squinted, shook and cackled almost without cease. But I remained on my guard, for I knew that when a clever man willingly plays the fool he does it for no other reason than to entrap the unwary. I stayed with him until he departed, impressing him with the range of my knowledge and the sharpness of my linguistic skills. I remained in the dining hall until all the guests had left. The professional mourners were droning like bees, and I passed among them to take my last close look at Avinoam's corpse—a great, swollen lump of putrefying flesh that would melt into eternity. Then I quit the room, had Tzila borne unconscious to the carriage, climbed in after her, and ordered the driver to take us to my father's house.

When Tzila was safely put to bed, I went to my father's private chambers, where he awaited me. He immediately dismissed Amnon, who had been going over accounts, much to the scribe's open displeasure and my masked amusement, and himself made certain that all of the doors to the room were secured. Then he poured wine for the both of us and sat on a divan opposite me. He sipped from his cup, sighed and set it down on a table whose surface was inlaid with ivory. "Yes," he said, fixing his intense gaze on me, "through you the Galilee will pass into my hands. But it must stay securely within them once it is there. There is, my son, one lone impediment that must yet be removed. Do I make myself clear?"

"Of course."

"You understand to what—or should I say to whom—I refer when I speak of impediment?"

"It is quite clear to me. I had reckoned on such a move myself."

"Well, my son, it appears that we did not play chess together in vain."

"Certainly not."

My father put up a hand. "But you must wait. There is a propitious hour. It would not be seemly for father and daughter to follow each other to the other world, howsoever closely they were tied to each other in this life. Do you agree?"

"I agree. It would not be seemly."

"When I feel that the time is ripe, I will send a courier to you bearing a message. There will be one line and one line only: the last line of the prayer of mourning. Amnon will copy it exactly as it is written and there will be no other sign or mark on the parchment; nor will I affix my signature to it. You will read it and know that the hour has arrived, and you will destroy the message." My father stroked his cheeks. "Then you will do what is required of you—in the manner you choose as fitting. I trust you will use a method that will call forth no suspicion."

I nodded and rose to go.

"Sit down," said my father.

I seated myself again.

"Some more wine?"

"No. I've had enough."

"Fine. I'll pour some for myself, then." He filled his cup and raised it to his lips, but then changed his mind and put it down. "There is one other matter I'd like to talk to you about. I've known about it for some time now, perhaps a month, but I decided to wait until I saw you to impart it. I wanted to relate it personally." My father crossed his legs. "It's about my brother, Yosef," he said. "He has returned to Nazareth to live, and I have seen him. He makes his home once again on the Street of Carpenters. I believe you sought him there when we first came to Nazareth, did you not?"

"How did you know that?"

My father shrugged. "Those who do not know are surprised."

"And his wife?"

"Alive and well."

"And my brother?"

"Also alive and well."

"What does he do?"

"He is apprenticed to a master carpenter in the quarter, a man by the name of Naftali. He lives there—in a shed at the rear of the house."

"Is he learned?"

"I believe he is able to read and to write the Hebrew language. No more."

"How does he stand in politics?"

"He has no stand that I know of. He's like his stepfather." My father drank off his wine and smiled. "Is there anything else you'd like to know about him?"

"What does he look like?"

"He's slight and rather short for his age. His face is badly scarred by the pox, and he's hollow-chested—in fact, he has none of your mother's good looks or mine. You wouldn't notice him twice on the street. I've always said it does no good to raise a child in Egypt. It's a land of the dead—for the dead." My father yawned. "Well, does that satisfy you?"

"Entirely."

"Be frank—does your brother worry you in any way?"

"Why should he?"

"I asked you if he does, not if he should."

"My brother gives me no cause for concern. I do not, after all, allow myself to be troubled by carpenters' apprentices." I stared directly at my father. "Does he worry you? After all is said and done, he is your son."

My father's face darkened. "I have only one son," he said. "He sits alone with me. One son. Is that clear?"

"Transparently clear." I rose once more. "Well, the journey was difficult. I'm weary. And I must attend to my wife—to the woman whose spirit I partake of, whose body I embrace, whose worldly wealth I share."

"Attend to her," said my father.

Six months later, my superior Nachman was involved in an altercation, seriously wounded almost to death, and subsequently removed from his position as chief interpreter of the Court of Herod. It was Nachman who spent many years preparing for his own downfall, and it was I who arranged for the final events that led directly to it. The matter was actually quite simple. I knew, of course, precisely with whom Zahava was in bed when she was supposed to be out riding and exactly where they lay locked in carnal union. All I had to do was to send the page Elazar with a spurious message from Zahava to Nachman, and the rest followed of itself. My superior arrived at the love nest, burst in upon the pair, drew his dagger and rushed straight for, not his paramour's lover, but the naked Zahava herself. The other man, one of Herod's top generals and a brawler of renown, rose gallantly to the girl's defense, rapping Nachman's skull from behind with the heavy handle of his broadsword and coming within a hair's-breadth of dispatching him to his eternal rest. My superior lay in a coma on the brink of death for three days and three nights, wakened from it without warning on the fourth, waving his arms and babbling of his mother long ago swallowed by the grave, and fell in a pool of bloody vomit to the floor when he tried to get out of bed to embrace her. Nachman lingered on, alternating between comatose and raving states, and then gradually got well. But he never recovered from the blow the general dealt him. I visited him several times. He smiled broadly in greeting, did not know who I was, and called me by the name of his dead wife, Shoshanna. He sat up in bed, rigid, his empty eyes staring at visions of the blind.

In Herod's own hand came the order ousting him from his position;

and in Herod's own hand came the order instating me as chief interpreter of the court. This turn of events caused no little sensation among the courtiers. There was a stir in every circle and on every echelon because Nachman had fallen from his height, would end his days in the gutter and would finally be found an all-but-unrecognizable corpse in some forsaken alley; and because a newcomer such as I should inherit such a coveted place, passing over the heads of scores of contenders who considered themselves infinitely more deserving of the honor. There were those who instantly sought to curry favor with me, who offered gifts and favors to me and who pressed invitations on me— most especially Zahava, whose sinecure had come to a sudden and jolting end. And there were those who turned away from me and from the decision in disgust, envy and anger, not bothering to conceal their bitterness and hostility—those who would at a later time return to the fray, hellbent on my destruction.

As for me, I was greatly pleased and satisfied, though I did not feel my selection was undue; on the contrary, I felt that the honor was warranted, for I had long been a prop and a mainstay to Nachman, covering for his gross deficiencies and compensating for his scandalous errors. In short, I had kept him afloat until I thought it was time for him to sink; I had made certain that he kept his office until I had built enough of a reputation to be named his successor. I was aware that my father's standing, greatly increased since the death of Avinoam, had contributed in no mean way to my elevation, but I knew with equal conviction that this factor would not of itself have been sufficient to raise me above the other candidates. What I had gained, I had gained on my own merits. Proudly, nobly, conscious of my worth and of my determination, I donned purple robe and silver sword, and was installed as chief interpreter at an elegant court ceremony by Herod's special designate, the tetrarch himself being indisposed at the last moment and unable to officiate. A declaration in the monarch's own hand, bearing the royal seal of his exalted family, was my compensation. As soon as I could decently detach myself from the banquet that followed the installation, I hurried to my apartments to store the official parchment away with the rest of my documents.

Tzila was late in giving birth, and the physicians did not know why—even the famous "Doctor of the Dead" who had journeyed to the court from Egypt to examine her and pronounce his judgment. A week after the ceremony, which she was not able to attend because she had been confined to her bed, Tzila cried out that her time had come at last. The labor pains seized her during the early hours of the morning and I quickly wakened Elazar, whom I kept close at hand in case of emergency, and sent him for the doctors and the midwives. By the time they arrived the baby had emerged from my wife's womb—stillborn. I saw the baby only once and for a brief time: a tiny, shriveled, monstrous-faced female who looked as if she had been born a thousand years ago and was glad to die. At that instant a strange and powerful urge came over me. Though it was already dead, I wanted to kill the infant. The desire was sudden and overwhelming: I wanted to snatch the baby from the arms of a midwife who held it like some filthy rag and dash it to the stone floor. It would have given me great pleasure to have seen the skull split and the foul brain matter and fetid blood run out. Trembling in all of my limbs, repelled to the core of my being, I turned my face away. One of the physicians squeezed my shoulder. "I know how you feel at this moment," he said, "and I sympathize with you. But don't worry. The sorrow will pass. You will mourn for your lost child for a time, and the wound will be healed. Speak to your wife for a few moments and then get some rest. And let her rest—she needs it badly."

I went to the other bedroom, where I had been sleeping since Tzila's confinement. I lay in bed but did not close my eyes for a moment. I knew that the time to deal with my wife had come. The physicians had informed me that Tzila was gravely ill and that her chances for recovery were poor. This would be common knowledge at court and would simplify my task considerably. I wanted to act, but could do nothing until I got word from my father. I did not even dare to communicate with him, but as it turned out, there was no need. Two days after the stillbirth and an hour after the "Doctor of the Dead" told me in private that there might yet be hope for my wife, Elazar hurried to me with a message just delivered by a courier who had ridden at "breakneck speed" from Nazareth. I broke the blank wax seal and read the single line: "He who maketh peace on high will give peace to us and to all Israel. Amen." The message bore no signature. I dismissed my page and fell instantly asleep. I wakened at noon, attended to my duties at court, and returned late that night by a private entrance to the room where Tzila lay.

She slept in a darkened chamber, one arm under the cover, the other thrown across her moist forehead. Her skin was very pale, and the hollows in her cheeks and about her eyes were so pronounced that it seemed her entire face must collapse. Her breathing was shallow and labored, and each breath seemed loath to part from her lungs. The lamp had burned low, but whatever light it gave annoyed me and I went over and snuffed it out. Faint moonlight showed at the shutters. I stood by the bed and calmly watched my wife as she slept. I felt sure that she dreamed and that her dreams carried her back as on a river current to the distant shores of her childhood, to the times when she walked alone in garden and meadow, secure in her inviolable solitude. The pulse in her neck was slight, almost nonexistent. What a narrow line there was between her life and death! I felt as if I could almost blow her over to the sleep from which she would never rise. Gently I touched her cheek and ran my fingertips over the down. She did not stir. Slowly, carefully, I slid my hand down to her neck. The flesh had only faint warmth, the skin was pathetically wasted. I brought my other hand up to her neck, encircled it in my fingers, and closed them very tightly and very surely, scarcely straining myself. There was no struggle, no appreciable reaction. As she had always done in her days on earth, Tzila seemed to submit passively to the grip that would end for once and all her passivity. For an instant I thought I even detected her shy, sad smile, but I could not be certain. Then I felt a spasm. It was slight, a mere casual shudder and no more. But something had gone out of her body forever. I removed my hands. They did not tremble. I bent over Tzila. There was no bruise or mark on the skin, nor should there have been, for I had been extremely gentle. I straightened up. All was still. The fire in Tzila's flesh was extinguished: it would cool, harden, and then begin to dissolve into the stuff from whence it came. Her face was peaceful, tired, a little pinched. She would be found that way, dead of natural causes in her sickbed. I left the room. Tzila must not be disturbed. She must be alone, wrapped in the final, unutterable loneliness. I was certain that even her Maker would respect her wish to be by herself and would wait for a time before He sent his dark angel to extend to her the peace He had promised to her and to all Israel.

After Tzila's death, I submerged myself in my work. Following religious custom, I made no attempt to remarry. I frustrated Zahava's desperate and persistent attempts

to consort with me by obtaining a writ which enjoined her from trying to contact me under pain of imprisonment or worse. I went secretly
to whores who dedicated themselves to the court and found that I got
much enjoyment in beating and pretending to strangle them when I
lay with them. There was one girl whom I took particular pleasure with
—a thin, blond girl brought by the Tenth Legion to Judea—who
committed suicide when I began negotiations to take her exclusively for
myself. I was sorry to lose her, as I found no other who satisfied my
desires as had she.

Then I wearied of the whorehouse and its tiresome stable of
females. I had befriended a man named Achitofel, a deputy to the
minister of finance, who was an expert in matters of carnal fulfillment,
and I asked him to procure for me a number of concubines whom I could
keep in my apartments, which were now much larger and more lavishly
appointed, as befitted my rank. This he willingly did and I paid him for
his efforts, desiring that I be not beholden to him or to any man. I
found concubines satisfactory and convenient, though I preferred not
to keep any particular girl for more than three months at the maximum,
for I wanted no attachments to develop and no involvements to result.
Moreover, I did not wish any other human being to become overly
familiar with my intimate habits. I experimented with the girls I had
in my service, refraining from the beatings and the mock strangulations;
essentially I wished for pleasure, not trouble. I titillated the girls and
urged upon them the innovative spirit so that they might bring
amusement to me and take amusement for themselves. Constantly
replaced, they were pretty objects, delightful playthings whom I used
and thrust away. I was very strict about limiting my sex to one, or at
most two girls at a time; I frowned heavily on, and would not permit
myself ever to indulge in, the orgies that were in vogue among court
circles. And I was scrupulously careful in my consumption of wine and
in my use of other drugs, for I knew well how easily they might steal a
man's life from under his feet. In short, I steered by the true star of my
ambition and avoided all pitfalls.

In my service as chief interpreter I exceeded by far my previous
record. I was a superb planner, excellent administrator and assiduous
worker. I was decorous, completely efficient, rigorous in the performance
of my duties, indefatigable and totally beyond corruption. Men in
higher positions feared when they came into my presence, and many

courtiers approached me for my advice and opinions. Gradually, by slow degrees, I purged my staff of its dead wood and of those who had been loyal to Nachman or to someone else or to no one at all. In place of those whom I had rid myself of, I introduced hand-picked subordinates allied to my spirit and my cause, men who did not love me too much to fear me nor fear me too much to love me. I played no favorites, nor did I appoint a single incompetent or unreliable person. I desired that those who were out to attack and defeat me find no chinks in my armor, no imbalances in my stance. As to my father's interests, I remembered them always and pursued them with constancy, but I worked at them with discretion and a sense of proportion and never allowed them to take precedence over the management of court affairs.

I had not yet finished a year at my new job when one evening I received a summons from Zerubabel, the minister of war, requesting that I meet with him in his private chambers. As my bodyservant dressed me and readied me for the visit, I wondered at the purpose of the invitation. The war minister and I had little or nothing in common and less to do with each other. What he wanted from me, he had gotten long ago and was no longer interested in getting. In fact, I had the distinct feeling that if a man of his nature could be said to be embarrassed, I was a source of embarrassment to him—as perhaps all the half-a-hundred young, male, one-time lovers he had possessed since me were as well. I was certain that, had it been fashionable, Zerubabel would have kept a harem of male concubines.

When I arrived at his place he was sitting at a small, ornately worked ivory writing table, arrayed in a white toga with gold trimming at the neck and on the sleeves. He looked more than ever the idol: puffy, grim, bilious—an idol ravaged by wind, weather and the wear of many indifferent hands. He showed no visible emotion when I was shown into the room and gave me a limp, dead hand in silence, indicating with a nod of his head where I was to sit.

Before we got started, a young boy of ten or eleven came into the room; Zerubabel's face showed a strange greed which I had never seen until then, and the war minister called the boy to him and ran his fingers through the child's brilliantly black hair. "He is called Gur," said the minister of war. "Isn't he beautiful? See the lashes and the chin—what a fine dimple the chin has!" He touched it. "He's a poor orphan and I've adopted him," explained Zerubabel. "Say hello to the chief interpreter. Don't be shy—he won't bite you!" The boy said nothing, but stared at me with huge black eyes as if I were an ogre. "Charming, utterly charming," murmured the war minister, and he drew the boy to him, whispered to him in his ear and sent him off with a pat on the rump. Zerubabel chuckled and followed the child's lithe young body until it was out of sight. "Excuse the interruption," he said, turning to me, "but it was a lovely one, wouldn't you say?" I nodded, and Zerubabel's features grew serious and the color drained from his cheeks, leaving them sallow as before.

He drummed with the tips of his fingers on the table. "Let me speak directly to the point," he said gruffly, knitting his thick brows. Herod's minister of war, who had never fought a war and most probably never fought a battle in his life, began with a long-winded, rambling, diffuse paean to my abilities, skills, loyalty, dedication, ardor and more; he delivered the speech in a shrill voice that turned lugubriously falsetto whenever he became excited, which was often. It was odd to have such mercurial tones jump out of the war minister's great figure of stone. I listened to the almost totally disorganized preface with only half an ear and watched the drumming fingers. When they stopped, I knew the proposition would begin in earnest. I was right. Zerubabel's voice dropped, and his words became level and calculated. He was once more the cunning, ruthless infighter whose victories had been scored at the tetrarch's court. His proposal was that I become the head of a new department which he wished to establish as a part of the ministry of war. I would be directly responsible for the functioning of the department to him, and to him alone. I would continue as chief interpreter, and none but the war minister would know of my new appointment.

"What are you driving at?" I asked.

"I am talking," Zerubabel replied, "of a special, secret police service with sweeping investigatory powers, a service which would silently and covertly plant its agents everywhere: in every branch of government, in all of the units of the army, in the hierarchy of the court, in the priesthood, among the Pharisees and Sadducees, among the scribes. In short, no aspect or facet of the nation's life would be overlooked or bypassed. The purpose would be to inform the minister of war of any disloyalty or treason before they could do harm." Zerubabel leaned forward. "To discover the poison at its source and be rid of it before it had a chance to take effect," he said, enunciating his words with great care and staring to see how I received them before he went on.

"The members of the service would be organized in cells, and the cells would work independently of each other. Operatives in one particular cell would have no knowledge of the identities of those in another cell, and no idea of the work the other cell was doing. Certain cells would be designated to investigate the other cells—and though they did not know what they were doing, this would be the sole purpose of their existence. We would select our operatives secretly and with the greatest care, demanding absolute loyalty and obedience on the pain of immediate death. Our recruits would undergo rigorous indoctrination and be trained to endure torture and privation. They would be courageous and self-reliant, yet respond blindly to orders, carrying them out with dispatch and without the slightest hesitation. They would know discipline, zeal and complete devotion. They would infiltrate every group, know everything—"

"And the Zealots?" I said. "Would they infiltrate the Zealots as well?"

The war minister stared at me coldly. "The Zealots? Yes, of course they would infiltrate the Zealots. What did you think?" He paused, as if to consider certain aspects of the matter by himself, and then, satisfied that he had worked the details out, went on. "Our headquarters will be small, compact, totally efficient, instantly transportable. Our files will be coded. Each member of our elite inner circle will carry poison upon his person at all times and use it before he divulge any information. We will have a chamber for special interrogation and torture, but our main remedy will be death. We will be cognizant of all and tell nothing. That is the only way to truly manipulate events—don't you agree?"

I nodded.

"I see. And what does the chief interpreter think of the plan?"

"It is an excellent one. Excellent in conception, excellent in formulation. And it will be excellent in operation. The nation will profit well from such a spy system."

"But . . . ?"

"But what?"

"But what is the chief interpreter's objection?"

"Who says that I harbor one?"

"Come, come, Chief Interpreter. We are colleagues too long. We were colleagues before we ever met, were we not?"

I leaned forward. "And the tetrarch?"

"What of the tetrarch?"

"Where does the tetrarch fit in?"

"He does not fit in."

"Why is that?"

"Because, Chief Interpreter, he does not need to fit in—and we do not need him to fit in. Can I make it any clearer?"

"It is entirely clear."

"The tetrarch exists solely in his own universe," said Zerubabel. "And woe be to the universe that touches his, for it will crumble and fall asunder. It is best that the tetrarch not be disturbed—lest he disturb those who work for his own benefit. These are loyal words, Chief Interpreter, make no mistake: the solemn words of the most loyal man in all the kingdom."

"I receive them in the spirit that they are given."

The minister of war folded his hands. "But this discussion has become abstract—and, God knows, I am a man not fond of abstractions. I am a man, Chief Interpreter, who is interested in the concrete. Birth is concrete, death is concrete, life is concrete. Power is concrete. I'm interested in power. I am interested in a network of spies that will lie over the land like an iron spider web, a web that I can draw tight at will." Zerubabel held up a fist which he clenched so that the blood ran from the knuckles. "I want this country in my hand, do you hear? I want to squeeze this country whenever the fancy or the need comes over me, and when I do, I want to hear it cry out in anguish, do you understand? Let me ask you a direct question, Chief Interpreter, because I am a direct man: have you ever caught a man by his testicles, eh, and squeezed them together and crushed them to a bloody pulp, have you? And have you heard the screams that came out of him when you did, have you? Well, those are the screams I want to hear from this country, Chief Interpreter, because they are music to my ears!" The minister of war let his hand fall. "I don't like metaphysical discussions and I don't like monologues. I called you in here to ask you if you would take charge of my network, and I want your answer."

"There is only one answer I can give."

"What are you saying, Chief Interpreter?"

"Surely the minister of war knows that in telling me about the clandestine department, he has already made me party to it and thus a part of it. Surely the minister of war realizes that I cannot know of such an operation and be outside of it."

The war minister shook his head. "You can indeed be outside of the network, Chief Interpreter, but you cannot be outside of it and remain alive." Zerubabel touched his nose thoughtfully. "It would most certainly be a pity to eliminate you—it would truly be a shame. You are such an asset to the court. And such a brilliant ornament. Yes, the ladies like you, Chief Interpreter, the ladies enjoy you—you are a constant delight to them. Even the noble Herodias has cast a desiring eye upon you. And Salome—they say that the sap runs down her thighs when she but sees your shadow on the floor! Well, like mother, like daughter— isn't that the way the saying goes?" The minister of war pointed a finger. "But you—you stay aloof, you don't bother with them, with any of them. You don't give them a tumble, as the saying has it, and I admire you for it: I admire your independence and your strength of will, you don't find them around every day. You turn your pretty nose up at the court ladies and concentrate on your wenches—ah, yes, you're quite a homebody with your wenches, aren't you! Well, it's best that way—I must say it's for the best. You occupy yourself with your own playthings and leave the intrigues to others. That makes sense, Chief Interpreter, that makes supreme sense!"

Zerubabel wiped his lips and frowned. "I'm waiting for your answer," he said in a slow, deliberate voice. "I am waiting for you to give me an answer, and I am a man who does not like to be kept waiting."

I rose to my feet and as deliberately as the war minister had spoken saluted formally. "Your Excellency wishes a web, does he? Well, then I shall be his spider!"

"Capital!" exclaimed Zerubabel, a red flush creeping into his cheeks as it had when he fondled the boy Gur. "Splendid! I congratulate you, Chief Interpreter—I congratulate you on a wise decision! You will never regret it. I promise you that you will live never to regret it—on my life, I make you this promise!"

"Nor will you regret it, Excellency." I smiled. "Long live the tetrarch, Your Excellency! Long live the emperor!"

"Long live the emperor, Chief Interpreter!"

I was standing at the door when the minister of war's voice stopped me. I turned. Zerubabel was seated at his writing table, his face devoid of both color and expression. "Listen," he said hoarsely. "Would you like to try the boy?"

I did not waste a second in beginning the organization of the war minister's spy service. I made each successive move cautiously and calculatedly, and I built one move squarely upon another: I desired an unshakable foundation and I got it. First of all, I assembled my inner circle, those from whom I would build outward. I wanted hard, cruel, shrewd material, capable of fanaticism if there was need, and I got it. I reviewed the members of the court and excluded them one by one, using the journals I had compiled to help me in my assessments. Only two people associated with the court passed the tests which I had painstakingly devised. One was the page, Elazar, whom I felt would go through fire for me and if he came through alive would go back again the same route; and the other was the pimp Achitofel, who was the kind of man I could use and who as the deputy minister of finance would be useful in money matters.

I wrote to my father and requested several men, explaining the sort of men I needed without letting fall a hint of my plans. My father complied, and by the end of two months I had the nucleus of the system ready to operate. One trustworthy fellow, veteran of many a battle and brawl, a one-armed Galilean named Melech, I dispatched to the prisons. Under the war department's writ, he was authorized to remove prisoners for "labor duty," but of course he was recruiting for me. I would receive frequent word from him by courier from all parts of the country, informing me that he had been fortunate enough to locate "prize material." By the end of four months, I could report to the minister of war that I had a rudimentary operation going, an operation founded on rock.

My own, overt department ran almost of itself, I had set it up so well, so I was able to devote most of my time and energy to my new pursuit. I threw everything I had into the creation of the system—all of my mental acumen, all of my intuitional prowess, all of my passion and my zeal. I wanted a corps the likes of which were unknown, a body that could not be reached by Judean standards, by Roman standards, by any standards. I personally set up the headquarters section, and followed it up by establishing the recruiting section, supervising the selection of the initial recruits who would later on establish cells of their own. I was scrupulous almost to the point of obsession, hard as tempered metal, uncompromising in my demands and untiring in my efforts. I spent entire days and nights on end, sleeping only in one- or two-hour intervals and waking as refreshed as though I had taken my usual rest. For me, the department was the fulfillment of an unconscious dream. In its creation, my most fertile imagination was kindled, my inner heart of hearts stirred, my most intense being touched.

I did not content myself with the idea which had been presented to me: I used it only as a point of departure. For I envisioned in the plan possibilities far beyond those the minister of war had discussed. He had conceived of a monster: I would bring forth a colossus. He had dreamed of a creature of the dark: I would bring forth an army of the night. My hand-picked men would in turn enlist hand-picked men of their own. The minister of war would take pride in the fact that the reins were moving outward to a thousand horses, but in his pride he would ignore the fact that it would be I who held them and controlled the horses. The minister of war would believe that he drove as he wished, but would be unaware that he drove no one but me until such time as I was ready to drive. No man in the world would know what I knew about the organization and its cells: no man would be able to fathom or control my phantom power. Thus I had brought to the central headquarters section a strength far beyond the strength that was intended for it.

And I hit upon a plan that both followed my own bent and pleased the minister of war, who in his arrogance failed to see where it could lead. I conceived of creating a central terror squad that would be composed of the most ruthless, most obedient men that could be found. For the realization of our purposes, the minister of war opened the coffers of his department and provided almost unlimited funds. Zerubabel, to whom I was constantly expected to report and to whom I gave glowing but carefully censored reports, looked with extreme favor on this pet project, considered it of supreme importance, and was more than willing to provide any money that was needed to carry matters forward. I saw to it that the war minister always had accurate details about our progress, so that his spies would be able to substantiate what I told him, but made certain that he would not divine the true shape of developments. I kept him informed about certain trees, drawing his attention to many facts about their nature and growth. But I never let him see the forest.

I never squandered a penny of the money Zerubabel allocated, for though I often advanced my father's interests when an opportunity presented itself, I had no special concern with financial gain. I made certain that funds were well spent, that they produced results, and that the results were readily demonstrable. This was a prime factor in allaying any fears that the minister of war might harbor. Ability, ardor, rectitude, credibility: these were the spikes with which I would hang the war minister on the cross of my intent.

Melech the Galilean had proven himself a superb recruiter over and over again, and I detected in him an inflexible disciplinary sense which I felt would be useful in training a certain type of man. I therefore entrusted him, after a series of lengthy interviews, with the creation of the network's striking force, its elite guard, which I called by the code name of *Patish*, or hammer. I needed a training ground for *Patish*, a place that would be hidden not only from the eyes of men but most of all from the notice of the minister of war himself. To escape detection, I hit upon a brilliant device. I approached Zerubabel and asked him for the use of his own villa, explaining that I needed it for the headquarters section. The war minister was delighted and, swollen with pride, readily agreed. He also agreed, for obvious reasons, to visit the villa only at infrequent intervals and to notify us when he and his retinue were coming so that I could take adequate precautions. What better way to conceal prey from a lion than by taking it to his cave?

Zerubabel's huge, rambling country home was located in rugged hill country and set in the midst of a dense forest of pines and spruce. The men of *Patish* would be able to train in the enormous dining hall of the villa, in its many large rooms and on the sprawling, secluded grounds which I ordered put under immediate heavy security. At the very start, I went up to inspect the training facilities. Archers were posted in hidden positions which overlooked and dominated all approaches. They had standing orders to kill on sight any intruders, and I learned to my great satisfaction when I arrived that they had already slain a number of curious interlopers. Word of what had happened spread to the neighboring villages, and the villa became taboo for them. The villagers knew only that they must avoid the "eyrie" of the minister of war on the pain of death. They had long ago learned that there were very many matters about which it was best to keep silent, so they viewed this as yet another harsh fact of life that they must blindly accept. Even from the first moments of my tour of inspection, I was greatly pleased with all aspects of the program: with the idea itself as I had conceived it, with the man I had chosen to head it, with the fortresslike villa, with the harsh, isolated physical surroundings and with the men who had been selected for the group. With Melech and several of his subordinates I rode out over every inch of the grounds. And I spent a number of days meeting with the recruits. I desired and obtained firsthand, intimate knowledge of the character and composition of the force. And I saw to it that I created a personal link with me.

Before I returned to court, I spent almost a full day with the man I had picked as leader. Melech the Galilean had survived the pox and the plague; the loss of his right arm, which a peasant gone berserk had lopped off with a scythe when he was still a child; the death of his father in a tavern brawl; the rape of his mother and sister by a troop of Roman cavalrymen; and years of virtual servitude with a vicious landowner who had "collected crippled servants" as an entertaining pastime. He had worked his servants without mercy and sometimes used the women but most often took his pleasure in watching the deformed people cohabit, punishing them severely if they refused his wishes. Melech had ended his service abruptly by poisoning his master's food and escaping in the subsequent uproar. He had been in every part of the country, hunted boars and mountain lions in the north and survived on desert plants, snakes and lizards in the wilderness of the south. He had saved a unit of the Tenth Legion from an ambush by the Zealots and been commended by the authorities; and he had beaten a Roman soldier almost to death in a quarrel and spent a year in prison. He always said that he had been close to death so many times that death was "almost his best friend"; he had survived because of his fierce will to live, his extraordinary courage, which came just short of being reckless-ness, and his uncanny sense of the right word, gesture and action he needed at precisely the right time. What I liked best about the man was the fact that, being well-schooled in terror since early childhood, he knew the effect that terror had on an opponent and knew how and when it could be instilled. I felt that my choice of Melech the Galilean for leader of the terror squad was fully as wise and as fortuitous as my father's choice of Avner, and it seemed to me that the two men were similar in a fundamental way. More and more I grew to see that, as was the case with Avner, the essence of this hardened, cold and unquestioning man lay in subservience. Melech the Galilean was mine for the asking. His body and mind begged to be commanded, his anchorless fury to be directed, his chaotic will to be harnessed, his explosive life to be summoned to a clear form of expression. It had become his nature to see himself only insofar as he served a superior incarnation of himself; whenever he grew anxious about himself, his unfailing inclination was to find relief by subjecting himself to a loftier command. He had no responsibility for his actions, since what he decided was always what he was commanded to decide. He was perfectly capable of accounting for his own life, but he lived only by pretending it was not so.

Melech the Galilean fascinated me as a strange snake or reptile that one has never seen before would fascinate. The night before I left the villa for court, I tried to draw him out. We were sitting in a great stone room whose walls were bedecked with weapons; the bolted door was guarded by two armed sentries; a fire roared in the fireplace; and Elazar, whom I kept more constantly with me, poured hot wine for us. "Melech," I said, "tell me. Are you fond of women?"

"I am fond neither of men nor women."

"Do you like animals?"

"I never consider them."

"What about—insects?"

"I am one."

"Do you like yourself, Melech?"

"I neither like nor dislike myself. I am myself. I do not have another choice."

"Were you ever married, Melech?"

"I was."

"When?"

Melech shrugged.

"Where?"

"In Syria."

"What happened?"

"I left Syria."

"Do you have children, Melech?"

"I don't know. If I do, I hope I never see them."

"Why?"

"My seed repels me."

"What about the Romans, Melech?"

"They are strong."

"And . . . ?"

"They are here to stay."

"To stay forever, Melech?"

"Nobody stays forever."

"Would you fight the Romans, Melech?"

"If I thought I could win."

"Do you think you can win against the Romans?"

"Not by fighting them. Only by letting them think they are too strong to fight. Then they will fight themselves."

"And the Zealots, Melech? What do you think about the Zealots?"

"They are insects. Like me. But they are smaller insects."

"Melech, what about God?"

"Sir?"

"What about God?"

"Whose God?"

"The Roman gods. The Greek gods."

"They are children's toys."

"And the idols—the creations of the idolaters, the *goyim*—the 'works of the hands of man'?"

"He who worships idols—it is as if he worshiped his own excrement."

"And the God of Israel?"

Melech turned his head away.

"The God of Abraham, Isaac and Jacob, Melech?"

"Sir?"

"I asked you about the God Who is 'king over all the land and sanctifieth Israel.' What about Him?"

Melech shrugged. "Where is He?"

Quaestoris was the one Roman who had to know something about *Patish*. Like the minister of war, he was informed of particulars but had no idea of the overall meaning or dimensions of the group. I had known Quaestoris since my arrival at court, striking up an acquaintance with him that had the overtones of friendship because of my mastery of Latin and interest in Roman culture. I sensed that this tall, aloof envoy, with his iron-gray hair, eagle eyes, squarely molded chin and lithe body, had an interest in me that went far beyond official court functions and duties. Sent by the governor of Judea, Pontius Pilate, as personal representative and trusted servant, Quaestoris held enormous power in his hands: he was the link between the court of Herod and the authority of Rome. He was constantly seen at court, seldom heard, but eternally sought after. A knot of flatterers, favor-seekers and sycophants continuously surrounded him, pressing their attentions upon a nature that was essentially unassailable and inviolable. The envoy would hold audience patiently, his face lit by a solemn but amiable smile, his eyes expressionless but not vacant, his fine hands lifted often in mock dismay. He never encouraged his suitors, but neither did he deny them the right to press their cases.

He had been in the diplomatic service for more than three decades —in Syria, Egypt, Macedonia and other lands, coming finally to Judea under Pilate, who had known him in his youth, kept track of his career, and requested his presence in the Kingdom of the Jews. His forebears were patricians for generations, wealthy landowners, military men and politicians, and he traced the family lineage back almost to the founding of Rome. I had desired from my very first day as interpreter to cultivate this remarkable man, but had reckoned the obstacles at that time as formidable, if not impossible. However, I knew that it was important to bide my time, to wait for the right opportunity. I knew that time was on my side and did nothing to mar my future chance. The combination of my own ability and Nachman's indolence threw me into unusually frequent contact with Quaestoris, who already knew me by reputation. Still, I kept to my place, held fast to the reins of modesty. I limited my conversation to business, sought favors for no one, did not thrust myself forward. Naturally, gradually, as the ore turned over in the course of duty, I let the precious metal in me gleam. The veteran diplomat had a keen eye and sensitive ear—I did not go unnoticed and did not play upon this fact. Now and again Quaestoris drew me aside and questioned me. Several conversations more than confirmed his initial appraisal. Many times during our interchanges I saw his eyes sparkle and a warm smile come to his lips; once or twice he threw back his noble head and laughed out loud—laughed, as he told me, as he had not laughed since he was "a young man in the capital of the empire." I received his compliments in good grace, but I knew better than to press myself. Though the world would never wait for a man, a man had to wait for the world.

If the Roman envoy admired my knowledge, skills and suavity, he valued my humility. I sensed that my silence was often more appreciated than my speech, my retirement from the scene more than my presence on it. When one is constantly surrounded by geese, one cherishes a pheasant. Shortly before Nachman's descent and my appointment to the post of chief interpreter, Quaestoris invited me to visit him at home in his villa, and I accepted with a restrained warmth that pleased the diplomat. It took me over an hour, riding at a swift pace, to reach his home, which was built of white marble and located in a forest of delicate willows planted near man-made ponds. Four elite cavalrymen in gleaming helmets and breastplates met me at the gate and accompanied me as a guard of honor up the stately drive that wound in sinuous curves to the villa, over whose red-tiled roof the golden eagle of Rome glittered in the morning sun. Quaestoris waved his servant away and himself came to the door to greet me as I dismounted and gave the reins to a groom clad in scarlet and silver.

"Welcome!" the envoy called out in his deep, resonant voice. "Welcome to my humble abode, whelp of Judah!" His white teeth shone in a broad smile. "Come, do not tarry—I am hungry for your company!"

"And I for yours—lion of Rome!"

Quaestoris opened wide his arms and embraced me.

We sat on opposing divans placed beside a pink marble pool in which three fountains played, their jets shot through with tiny, evanescent rainbows. We had finished a hearty, protracted repast, washed down with wines of rare vintage, and the servants were clearing away the leavings. Quaestoris's eyes were moist and a deeper tone of green than I had ever seen them before. He sat silently, looking at me with unabashed fondness—and yet I felt that he was absorbed in some inner reflection which had nothing whatsoever to do with me. He was the kind of man who was used to living on many levels and in multiple worlds at the same time. I returned his look, regarding his fine figure with keen, almost biting pleasure; and I held my silence in turn, not wishing to interfere with his mood. I relaxed and let my attention wander. A lethargy stole over me; I half closed my eyes and let the world filter in through the brilliant colors that danced on my lids. I seemed to be gazing upon a universe that was perfect and indestructible.

"It really doesn't exist," said the envoy softly.

"Excuse me, I did not catch your meaning."

"I said that it does not exist—the perfect world which you think you behold. At least, it doesn't exist out there in front of you, out in nature." Quaestoris nodded. "For the outer world is nothing other than chaos—blind chaos in every sphere. Only the ordered minds of men like ourselves impose a harmony on it."

"But you flatter me."

The diplomat put up a hand, as I had seen him do so many times at court: it conveyed eloquently a dismay that it simultaneously denied. "I flatter neither you nor any man. I do not try to make mint coin out of slag—one can scarcely pay his bills with the result. I am not a man who gilds, for life is far too short for sham. No, young man, I have known you long enough to be certain that you are the possessor of a well-tempered soul, an harmonic mind, a true heart. Sitting here and watching you, I could not help but recall my own youth. It seemed to me that I was very much like you, though perhaps not as diligent or as ambitious."

"Then you detect ambition in me?"

"I certainly do. I sense in you an underground river of ambition, an explosive force that has yet to be released in public, an iron discipline that is as close and as familiar to you as your very shadow. I feel that essentially you keep your powers stored away safely until such time as you need to draw upon them." The envoy smiled his warm, frank smile. "I have learned in this life to measure carefully, exactingly. Otherwise a man will find that nothing fits, not even the skin he wears." The envoy's eyes narrowed. "I have been watching you for a goodly time now. I have followed your life like a hunting dog with the scent of quarry in its nostrils. Sometimes after I have seen you in action, I am mystified. 'But he cannot be Jewish,' I say to myself. 'He must be Roman.' And I smile at my foolishness, because of course you are Jewish. But again the same thing happens, and I wonder if you are not a Roman . . ."

"What do you mean?"

"I mean that you do not strike me as being a Hebrew. I mean that you are somehow the antithesis of being a Hebrew. And the proposition fascinates me—the thought of a man growing up in one culture and ending up alien to it, ending up a foreigner."

"How do I seem to be a Roman?"

"Essentially, you are hard with the hardness of Rome, harsh with our harshness. You know that under the veneer we keep the brute ready to act. You are not afraid to take another's life into your hands as one takes the dust of the earth and grinds it to powder between one's fingers and scatters it to the wind without guilt, compunction or worry. You are ready to smash another's face to bits rather than see a single scratch on your own. You care as little for religion as do we: for you, as for us, it is a sop that one throws to the weak, the infirm, the unsteady, the starving and the lost. You never lose yourself in hyperbole, nor do you find yourself in flights of poetic invention—all that is mere rubbish to you. When you look into the mirror, you see you and not some creation of your fancy. And when you look at the world, you see the world for what it is and not for what you would like it to be or for what you dream it is. You gauge your chances in life by the fear that you can inspire in men and not by the love you can evoke from them. For you know that fear is reality and love phantom. You know it is the baser passions that men live by, not the higher. You have a Roman's appreciation of force —you know that society crumbles without it. You are well aware of a basic Roman axiom: what words may take a year to do and in the end still not accomplish, the fist will settle in a day. And above all, you know that while your appearance is mild, your heart is a battlement of granite."

Quaestoris leaned back on his divan. "Well, now," he said, "I have answered your question. Have I answered it well?"

"As you answer all questions well, so have you answered this one. Roman or Jew, I am myself. That is how I see it. But you, Quaestoris. What are you doing here? Why did a man like you come to Judea?"

"Pontius Pilate and I were acquainted in our youth. After he had been in Judea for a while, Pilate reckoned he could use me. And I wanted to see for myself the contrast between my Romans and your Jews, to experience at first hand how the black sets against the white." The envoy paused. His face took on a strange, somber cast. "I have always," he said in a low voice, "been interested in the play of opposites —the thrust of the tangible against the substanceless, good against evil, life against death. Did you know that I sculpted?"

"No," I said.

Quaestoris looked at his long, powerful, well-shaped fingers. "Yes, I sculpt. I have been at it for nearly thirty years now. To me, there is no greater play of opposing forces in the world than that which I find in sculpture: the play between everything—stone—and nothing—air."

The envoy held his fingers up in front of him and stared at them. "You know," he said, "I have no desire whatsoever to squeeze any spirit out of stone, for I do not believe that there is any in it. I am content to let stone be as it is. I don't burden myself with transformations nor plague myself with transfigurations. I allow matter to be matter and do not pretend that it is something else. All I do when I sculpt is to give matter another shape." Quaestoris dropped his hands to his lap. "Would you like to see some of my work?" he asked.

"Very much."

First Quaestoris showed me the small figure of a shepherd boy playing his pipes set in a garden to the rear of his villa, a garden so tiny it was almost an alcove. The statue was cut from a marble so white and so pure that, when seen against its dark background, it dazzled the eyes of the beholder. The face had not much expression—indeed, had almost a blank look—but the body, which was unclothed, was well-realized. Of all, I found the hands, which were obviously bringing music forth from the instrument, to be most beautiful. They reminded me of the artist's own hands.

"I call him David, the shepherd king," said Quaestoris. The envoy held my arm firmly. He took me next to view the figure of a horse which he had done in a pale-green marble. The animal stood on a raised platform in the center of a circular room. It was a stallion—muscular and lithe, with the genitals featured prominently: they had been rendered in greater detail than had any other part of the body. We stood silently before it for some time, and then went on through the house. The envoy showed me several more busts, none of them very appealing. However, there was one of Pilate before which I halted in recognition. "That was done over three years ago," said the envoy, "when the procurator was in better health and in a much better frame of mind. It took me a long time to finish, since he was not very often willing to come and sit for me. Much of the work I had to do from sketches. All in all, I think it a decent likeness. Don't you think so?"

"I'm afraid I can't say. You see, I've never actually seen Pilate."

"How droll," said Quaestoris. "How perfectly droll! So you've never really set eyes on Pontius Pilate! It's silly of me, I know, but I keep forgetting you're a Jew and young and newly arrived at court!" Quaestoris sighed and touched the forehead of the figure gently with a finger. "But enough of Pontius Pilate. You will in due time have ample opportunity to judge him for yourself. Come along and I will show you my masterpiece!"

The last work of sculpture was where I was sure it would be: in the envoy's bedchamber. Set in a fluted niche in the wall opposite the bed, so that the envoy had a full view of it from the front when he was at rest, was a slightly larger than life statue. It was cut of very fine white marble shot through with pale yellow veins that faded into capillaries and then emerged again unexpectedly; and it was polished to an incredible luster. The figure was a nude male, an athlete—perhaps a discus thrower or a runner. It was so prepossessing that one involuntarily stepped back so as to recover from the first shock of seeing it.

The hair over the well-rounded skull was curly—a little like the tendrils of the grapevine. Though precisely carved, the face once again was all but devoid of expression. The broad, muscular chest was smooth and hairless, and the nipples pronounced. Altogether, the torso was exquisite—lithe and sinuous, the thighs flat and rounded, the legs strong and well-shaped. But very obviously the most meticulously carved and fully realized part of the body was its genitals. Every pubic hair curled crisply in stone, and each vein stood forth, wormlike, on the skin of the scrota which stretched tightly over the swollen testicles. Nestling comfortably on them was the large, thick, half-tumescent penis, its head hidden from view by a delicately worked foreskin. As I stood gazing at the statue, Quaestoris moved very close to me.

"I only finished this statue about four months ago," he said, "after working on it for more than a year. During the last stage of what grew to be an increasingly difficult process, something paralyzed me." The envoy's voice trembled. "Then," he said, halting before he went on, "something happened and I was able to work again and to finish . . ."

"What happened?"

"I saw you at court." The envoy grimaced and then his entire face contracted; for a moment I thought he would cry out in pain. Swiftly he leaned over to me and softly kissed the lobe of my ear.

After Quaestoris and I had slept together in his bed, we were massaged by the eunuchs in his bath and then we swam naked in the adjoining pool. Then we sported once again,

197

visited the bath to freshen up and finally were perfumed and dressed by bodyservants. Arm in arm we strolled into the grotto-garden at the rear of the villa, where an oval table with silver candlesticks, dishware and utensils had been set out for us. On noiseless feet, the servants brought out the repast. The scent of jasmine and of roses wafted to us through the air, the stars glittered down at us, and often one fell, staining the darkness with a long streak of fire that seemed to dry instantly, like a tear on some false lover's face. We feasted on squab, pheasant and a dozen other delicacies brought from the far corners of the land, and we drank of the best wines the empire could offer.

Quaestoris spoke in a tumultuous rush. His words seemed not to come quickly enough out of his mouth for him; his sentences were rambling and disjointed and frequently left unfinished, and his movements brusque and erratic. The polish, hauteur and control that I had so much admired in him had almost completely disappeared, and like the procurator of Judea he had spoken of only a few hours ago in so cynical a tone, the envoy seemed a little boy himself. A number of times during the meal, he got up from his place, came over to me and embraced me warmly, declaring eternal love for me and swearing that he would be with no other man or woman, that he would care for me alone and exclusively. He told me that he would demonstrate the strength of his feelings for me and the depth and constancy of his love by dismissing all of his concubines and by ridding himself of the servants and slaves with whom he consorted. He had desire for me alone: for my body, my mind, my soul. I was the Hebrew spirit in the Roman body and then the Roman spirit in the Hebrew body, I was beauty incarnate, I was a lifelong dream come to fruition, I was divine —a gift of the gods to a careworn servant of the empire and weary subject of the emperor. Quaestoris ate and drank and raved, at times flinging out his arms excitedly, knocking food and drink from the table. The servants hastened to retrieve what had fallen, and Quaestoris chided them for their clumsiness and pinched their buttocks. His face was suffused with color, spittle ran from his mouth, his tunic was bespattered.

The moon was over our heads—a pale-gold disk three-quarters full which stood in majestic solitude, surrounded by fleecy, tendril-like clouds that stayed apart from it as if in awe. From it came a diffuse, tenuous light that flooded down and washed tenderly over the miniature garden with its trees and hedges at the borders, over the statue of the shepherd king with his pipes, and over the drunken sculptor who had fashioned it with his hands. I knew very well that Quaestoris would return to his senses, that he would reclaim his identity as the suave, scholarly, imperturbable diplomat I had known all along. I knew that this was a departure for him, a digression, an escape: I knew that he had been bitten by the moon as by a mad dog, that he had been bitten by my delicious young body; by the lust that had been building up in him, like water in a cistern that can only take so much pressure, for days and weeks and months; by the rare wines and the overwhelming scent of the roses and jasmines. I knew that he would emerge from the spell, that he had not the slightest intention of getting rid of his con-cubines and his slaves or of making love exclusively with me—and it did not bother me in the least.

I knew that though the love he showered upon me was exaggerated far beyond reality, he would continue to desire me and pursue me, and I was sure that I could exploit his desire. When all was said and done, Quaestoris the Roman envoy was no Zerubabel, no puppet war minister, no Jew-flunky to King Herod. Quaestoris was a man of noble parentage, the scion of a great and aristocratic family, a man of considerable influ-ence and power, an artist with impeccable taste, a citizen of culture. He was not a creature who needed a tight rectum for a night, a hole to thrill him because it was new, a blind orifice into which he could pour the filth of his body and his mind for the fleeting moment. Quaestoris needed companionship as well, a full relationship—I knew that I was correct in this feeling. I was perfectly willing and able to give him what he wanted and to take what I wished in return. The sculptor had will-ingly and of his own volition exposed himself to my sharp-edged chisel, and I meant to cut away at him as it suited my interests. I understood, of course, that I would work carefully and intelligently so as not to mar or injure the form I was shaping.

Quaestoris kept up his antics, falling occasionally from his divan to the grass and being helped up again; the servants came and went like shadows in the moonlight; sometimes as I gazed at it, the statue of the satyr-shepherd seemed to breathe and move its limbs; two lutists and a reed-flutist serenaded us; two towering Nubians, wearing gold earrings and loincloths that barely contained their swollen genitals, served us melons, honey, figs and dates. A naked dancing girl with a single ruby in her navel performed for us by snatching objects up with her vagina. Quaestoris uttered idiocies in his trance. I smiled to myself. The envoy was quite a man indeed. But he was far from a god.

After the founding of the spy system and *Patish*, it was essential that a Roman know about them, and I selected Quaestoris as the one man to tell. Of course, I told him exactly what I wanted him to know, and he asked no questions. What I did politically in Herod's court was of no consequence to him—his interests lay elsewhere. As I wished, he passed on whatever information I fed him to Pontius Pilate, and Pilate in turn told his military commanders. Once the military knew, they were satisfied and permitted the organization to function freely, even ordering their field commanders to cooperate when requested. The generals did not consider any military machine Herod might build up as a threat, immediate or potential. As far as they were concerned, Herod's troops were bedbugs and they were out after scorpions—the rebels. I could not help but be immensely pleased at the success of my schemes, for the Romans had sanctioned the secret service and the secret service would now sanction the Romans.

Toward dusk one evening, the page Elazar brought me an urgent message from Melech the Galilean. My secret service had apparently scored a major success. One of the members of a cell, a clever man who was called Shimon Hanegbi and whom I recalled meeting at the villa on my very first visit, had infiltrated a large Zealot band after months of intensive work. He won the trust of the group, worked with it for some weeks and awaited his chance. When it came, he managed to get word to *Patish* at our headquarters, and Melech ordered a raid against the rebel band which he personally led. The raiding party struck at night and caught the rebels completely by surprise. The guard was overpowered without a sound, and the others, who were asleep in a large cave, were overrun before they knew what was happening and captured almost to the last person. Two were able to resist but perished in a brief, bloody struggle; a third, who was a young woman, succeeded in committing suicide with her dagger. Choking on the words, she cried out the familiar "Hear O Israel, the Lord our God, the Lord is One!" and died as the *Patish* warriors in the fury of their frustration stove in her skull with their boots. The rest of the band, seventeen in number, were taken alive and brought in oxcarts to the villa. Each had been bound hand and foot with stout rope and blindfolded.

Upon receiving the message, I gave instructions that my carriage be readied and hurriedly had myself dressed for the journey, pausing only to write a brief note in Latin to Quaestoris explaining that I had been called away on pressing business and would be absent from the court for a day or two. I assured him that I loved him and would miss his caresses dearly. When I returned, so I wrote, he would find my ardor tenfold increased, as I would long for him during my absence. I begged that he remain faithful to me as I would remain faithful to him. I sealed the note with the sign of Herod the King and handed it over to Elazar to deliver. "Do not fail to deliver the missive," I told my page, "but wait until I have been gone two or three hours—and above all, do not tell him where I have gone or what matters engage my attention." Elazar kissed my hand and departed. I smiled as I went quickly down the stairs and out to where the carriage stood waiting. Quaestoris was extremely jealous of my movements at court and of my contacts, male and female. I took great care never to fan the flames of that jealousy to an immoderate degree if I could possibly help it; on the other hand, I was just as careful never to let the fire go out.

The horses were straining at their bits, and I sprang into the carriage and gave the command to start. The driver cracked his whip, and we were off, rushing through the darkness at tremendous speed. The sky was heavily overcast—not a single star showed its light. At times rain fell in a light shower but stopped, leaving the air parched and charged with mounting tension. We rode at a fierce pace, accompanied by six Herodian cavalrymen, three to the fore and three following behind. All along the way, riders of the night fell back at our approach and the roads were cleared for our swift passage. We arrived at Zerubabel's villa at dawn, in a driving rain that had slowed us somewhat. Dripping, the sentries halted us and examined our credentials. They were scrupulous, suspicious men who interrogated us—expert archers and ready killers. They did not go by personal recognition: as far as they were concerned, I might just as well have been the devil masquerading as myself until I proved otherwise. Under escort, we drove to the villa itself, where Melech came bareheaded and with sandals out into the downpour to throw his arm around me and clasp me to him.

Once in the villa, I told him how pleased I was with everything—

the raid, the capture, the sentries, *Patish*, the entire service. "It was all that I planned and more," I said, letting a servant take my cloak. "And you are to be congratulated for your part in making it so!" Melech grunted. "When you see for yourself what fish the net has brought in," he said, "you will be even more pleased." He gripped my shoulder with his one hand. "But first you must eat and rest."

"To hell with the meat!" I said, grinning. "Let us go directly and see the fish!"

Melech nodded and turned, indicating that I should follow after him. He led me through several corridors, turning this way and that, until at length we came to a massive door, bolted across with wide strips of armor plating. Two *Patish* guards, in black hoods and wearing the emblem of the dreaded hammer on their arms, stood at attention as Melech himself fitted the key into the lock, turned it, and shoved the great door open with his powerful shoulder. A torchbearer led the way, and we descended a flight of steep stone stairs in single file. Melech was in front of me, and he turned to caution me at every step. I laughed. "I haven't stumbled until now—and I don't intend to stumble in the future," I said. At the bottom, there was another door and before it another pair of sentries on duty. They carried naked broadswords and also wore black hoods, out of whose slits their eyes glittered with restive light. "I keep them hooded," said Melech, "so they won't be recognized. And so they recognize themselves only as warriors." We passed through the door and into a vast underground vault whose porous rock walls dripped with moisture in which the torchlight trembled. Chained to the far wall were the seventeen prisoners whom Melech's raiders had brought in. Slowly I walked over to them and Melech fell in step behind. Its tip resting over my right shoulder, I carried a new riding whip with a large, beautifully carved silver handle—a gift that Quaestoris had given me but a week ago.

The rebels were a ragged, bedraggled lot. They looked like corpses and stank like animals. They were chained to the wall by collars clamped around their necks, and those that slept did so with their heads against their breasts because the chains were not long enough for them to lie down. Several dozed fitfully, snorting and muttering, neither asleep nor awake but floundering in some tortuous middle sea between the two and unable to reach either shore. I walked with a measured, deliberate step along the row of captured Zealots, prodding each face with my whip so that it lifted and I could see the pair of eyes in it stare at me with fear and hatred.

At the end of the line I found two females, both of them wide-awake. They interested me, and I called for a torchbearer to bring his light forward so that I could see them clearly. The woman next to last was the older of the two, perhaps the mother or the older sister of her companion because I was certain I detected a family likeness. I turned my attention first to her. She was tall and thin, her hair stringy and matted with blood, her face wasted as if by a long illness. Her eyes met mine directly, and I saw in them no fear, only intense hate. The younger woman, who was the last prisoner in the row, was half naked. Her clothing had been ripped so badly that only shreds of it were left. Her neck and shoulders had great bruises on them, and there were deep welts, still oozing blood, over her back and her chest. I saw that the hooded men had subjected her to extremely harsh treatment, but I could understand why. There was something about the set of her features and the appearance of her body—every part of it—that expressed defiance. I could see how it must have aroused the fury of her captors, how it must have goaded them into punishing her. And I knew that the more they punished her, the greater her defiance must have become. I was sure there was a sexual aspect to the punishment. I desired to inspect her more closely. "Move the torch down," I ordered. I bent further into the flow of reddish light and extended my whip, touching one of her nipples and then the other with its heavy tip.

"Get away from her!" hissed the older woman.

"So," I said, "you still have a tongue in your head, do you?"

"A tongue, a heart—and a conscience."

"Very pretty," I said. "And what is your name?"

"*Asura*," said the woman; the word meant "captured" or "forbidden."

"I see. And what is the name of this lovely female?"

"I don't know."

"But she's so lovely, is she not? Only see her breasts and her thighs. Everyone must know her name. Come, now, think hard. What is it?"

"I don't know her."

I caught a piece of the younger woman's tunic with the whip and tore it, so that her left breast was completely exposed.

"You'll pay for that!" said her companion.

"We all pay for everything. The point is what, and when."

The younger woman, who had until now averted her face from me, turned it squarely to my own. My first impression was that of a visage which showed enormous strength, a strength exceeded only by obstinacy. In that initial instant when our glances met, I understood that we should never break through the barrier that this girl had put up, do what we will: I understood that this was a face from which death itself would draw back in defeat. I knew that I had met a person in whom the suffering of a lifetime had one day transformed itself into limitless and indomitable courage. We would be wasting our time with this girl. There was absolutely nothing to do with her except finish her off and be glad she was dead. Then I recognized her.

I was startled by the recognition, even shocked. But of course I did not show my reactions. The young woman was Dalia, the same maidservant whom my father had sent under guard from my youthful bed to Roman headquarters in Bethlehem. Whether she had escaped en route, fled her imprisonment later on, or been released for whatever reasons, I could not guess. But of one thing I was certain: that her experience at the hands of the Romans had helped considerably to mold her into the bitterly defiant, fiercely intractable creature whose unflinching gaze would have withered me to dust had it the power to do so. Our eyes seemed unable to break the hold they had on each other, and we continued to stare at each other in silence. I was positive she did not know who I was, but I knew her face and I knew every inch of her body. At that moment I recalled the past clearly in its every detail, but the past had no power over me. I remembered the emotions I had once had for Dalia, but they were hollow, only memories, no more than last year's dead leaves. I saw the past as having happened to two different people. The Dalia for whom I had felt something was dead. The self which had felt something for Dalia was dead. I had before me only a hostile, recalcitrant mind that would go unbroken unto death, and the beautiful, fleshly form of a female. Where the soul led, that body would go without complaint.

I touched the whip to my chin. There was a routine prescribed for the occasion and I was perfectly willing to go through with it. At times, routines were useful. They gave a man time to think ahead.

"What is your name?"

"*M'chulelet*," Dalia replied immediately, meaning "defiled."

"No. Not an imagined name. I want your real name."

"I have none other in your hands."

"Of course you do," I said softly. "Now tell it to me. Be sensible."

"My name died when Rome occupied this soil," said Dalia.

"It is ridiculous for you to keep up this pretense," I said. "We're going to get to the bottom of your mystery sooner or later. There's absolutely no use in your postponing it."

"It is equally as ridiculous for you to persist in your attempts," said Dalia. "Your comrades tortured me and got nothing. Do you think you will talk to me and get something?"

"My comrades, as you put it, did not even begin to torture you. As a matter of fact, neither have I begun—"

Dalia's eyes narrowed. "Who are you to speak Hebrew so well? I've never heard a Roman speak it so fluently, so free of accent."

"How do you know I'm not a Jew?"

The older woman spat. "No Jew would do what you are doing. He would kill himself first."

I smiled. "For prisoners," I said, "both of you are very free with your words."

The older woman, who now seemed familiar to me, closed her eyes—perhaps to pray in silence. "Leave us alone," said Dalia quietly. "You are wasting your time. No matter what you do, you'll get nothing. In the end, you'll kill us and still have nothing."

"No," I answered. "On the contrary, I already have something. I already have a lot. Listen to me, my dear, and I will tell you your real name—the name your Jewish mother and father gave you when you were an infant and they thought you would live to a ripe old age—"

"Your ruses won't help you," said Dalia. "We are always one step ahead of you."

"Take off her clothes!" I commanded, slashing down with my whip and cutting Dalia across a cheek.

Two hooded men sprang forward and ripped whatever clothes Dalia had left from her limbs. The older woman stiffened, but Dalia remained impassive, as if her body meant nothing, as if in the struggle for her soul's freedom she had committed her body to the dust, as if when the soul has no other food left it must devour even its body to live.

"Unchain her!" I commanded.

Melech himself had to unlock the iron collar at her neck, as no other had the key.

"Stand up, bitch!" I said to Dalia. "I want to see a Jew-whore naked!"

Dalia attempted to rise, but could not. "Your men have injured me, I cannot," she said.

"Lie down then," I said. "On your back!"

She did as I commanded.

"The torch. Move it down!"

I squatted and peered at Dalia's prostrate body, searching it from head to toe for signs of the past. There was nothing. Even her beauty was remote and had no meaning for me. I felt that I could destroy it easily, without a qualm, as one destroys an object that, for one reason or another, must be dispensed with. I rose and said slowly, "I just wanted to make certain. You are called by the Hebrew name of Dalia. You come from a small village outside of Bethlehem—"

"And you are the spawn of the devil!" said the older woman.

Turning to her, I went on: "Your name is Zipporah, and this is your daughter. Your husband was a notorious traitor, an enemy of Israel and of Rome. He died a mongrel's death on a hilltop, crucified for all to see beside three other criminals. And the same kind of death awaits the lot of you."

Dalia sat slowly, raising herself from the floor with great effort. She said nothing, but her large eyes were moist. I saw no fear in them, only a sorrow that was beyond any I had witnessed before. I did not like her look—it was unfocused, eerie, a look that had no right to be on this earth. I rapped my whip against my thigh and turned to Melech the Galilean, who stood waiting quietly. I sighed. "There is nothing more to do with either of the women. They are a bad lot. Dispose of them. Make an example of them. Maybe one of the others will break."

Melech shrugged, his stump rising oddly. "What does it matter? We have not cleared the garden but we have pulled out some ugly weeds. One day they'll all be gone."

"Get about your work!"

Melech barked out his brusque commands. The vault echoed with them, as if its very walls heard and answered in obedience. The hooded warriors of *Patish* hurried back and forth, casting colossal shadows that kept pace with them. One of the torchbearers hurried to the wall opposite the one to which the rebels were chained and thrust his burning brand forward in the darkness: in an instant, a giant red mouth opened up, roaring as if with insatiable lust. I knew it to be the great oven where Zerubabel's bakers had toiled for days on end to feed the war minister's guests. I had seen them several times, half naked and covered with fiery sweat, stacking the loaves and chanting guttural songs that lost themselves in the crooning of the oven fires.

Melech freed Zipporah. Dalia was raised to her feet. Silently, without a struggle, the two women were led across the room. The prisoners were all awake now; I could see them stir. One of them—I could not tell which—cried out the opening words of the prayer of mourning: "*Yitgadal v'yitkadash* . . . Magnified and sanctified . . ." The rest took it up, comforting themselves with the chant. But Dalia, naked and ruddy with flame-light, put up a hand. "Zealots," she called out. "Zealots, no! They tell me that at my birth I made no cry; and it was as a sign of wonder to those who were present. They said I would be a blessed child, a child who loved life. It is so. I do love life and I am blessed. Let me then leave this world as I came into it—without a sound. Let silence speak for me, absorbing pain and anguish and despair. Let silence be a comfort—as the sea and the sky are comfort. Zealots! Be not afraid of death! And even more—be not afraid of the life that leads to death, that lives in death." She turned to Melech. "I have one request. Let me go first, that I may not see my mother die."

Melech the Galilean looked over at me.

"Let the mother die first!" I said.

Zipporah's body went into the fire feet-forward and a terrible wail broke from the throats and chests of the other Zealots. But for Dalia, as they had promised, the rebels were silent. Dalia's body, which seemed unnaturally long as it was seized by the hands of the men in hoods, had gone limp—perhaps she was unconscious, I didn't know. They shoved her head-first, and in the tremendous heat the hair on her head and at her genitals burst into flame even before she was actually in the oven. I watched her molded flesh: the fire licked it, tongued it, slid cozily over it and finally wrapped it in a moaning cocoon of flame. The flesh turned dark, shriveled, grew black. Nobody moved or spoke: all were fascinated by the sight. It was I who broke the spell. "Close the doors!" I commanded.

Metal grated. The great red maw which had devoured the two women disappeared. I thought it appropriate: women who devoured men were in the end devoured by men. The devouring maw swallowed itself. Melech the Galilean, accompanied by a torchbearer, came toward me. A cracked voice arose from the rebels. " 'How art the mighty fallen!' " it cried. And another voice added: " 'Pleasant and beloved were they in life—and even in death they were not parted. . .' "

Upstairs we had a splendid repast. Food was without end. Wine and mead were served as if from an inexhaustible source. The men of *Patish* were exuberant. They ate and drank, stuffed themselves and vomited, laughed and caroused, sang together and beat the huge wooden tables. At one point, an emaciated little fellow with a mouth that was pulled to one side in what seemed a perpetual leer stood up among the rest. It was obvious that he did not belong to the striking force, and I recognized him as Shimon Hanegbi, the man who had infiltrated the Zealot band and informed. He held his drinking cup aloft and cried out, "A toast to our leader!"

The others roared assent and lifted their cups.

"A toast to the man who has nourished our most secret dreams, fed our deepest urges, and given voice to the screams that were so long silent within us—"

Amidst the shouts and bellows, the men drank, their eyes fixed—as one—on me. But Shimon Hanegbi was not satisfied. Still he stood and still he held his cup. "This toast means nothing!" he screamed. "It is the toast of sucklings and old women! It signifies neither our character nor our intent! We must give of ourselves to the toast as we give of ourselves to the leader and to the organization!" And with that he slashed at the wrist of the hand that held his cup, cast down the mean little knife to the table, snatched the cup with his left hand and set it to the vein in his right wrist from which blood gushed. "A toast to the leader!" he croaked, and glassy-eyed, reeling, he put the cup to his lips and drank of his own blood. One of the physicians fished him out from the forest of feet surrounding him and dragged him out of the hall to bind the wound. Melech and I laughed at the uproar.

"A devoted servant," sputtered the Galilean.

"A potential leader!" I observed.

The celebration went on. The great feast tables were danced upon by large, leathery feet that scattered dishes and utensils in all directions. The men jostled and shoved and cuffed each other, and then they stripped and the wrestling began. The torches smoked; the rafters trembled; the hairy bodies streamed with sweat that was the color of blood in the firelight. I gnawed at a venison bone. "This is delicious," I said to Melech. "Where did you get it?"

"We shot an uncommonly large buck yesterday," he replied. "And roasted it entire in the oven last night."

Quaestoris had consumed much wine. He lay naked on his back beside me, one hand indolently fondling his flaccid phallus. He raised himself on an elbow and looked down thoughtfully at my naked body, lifting a hand to caress me and then changing his mind and dropping it. "Sometimes I think you do not love me at all," he said.

"You doubt too much."

"Sometimes I feel there is no such emotion as love—that it is only a phantom born of aching flesh. . ."

"You are far too pessimistic. And what's more, you turn your pessimism against yourself—most unlike a true Roman."

Quaestoris sighed. "I should like to carve you one day," he said, lying down on his back once again. "I should like to carve you in blood-red marble. The red of the fetus. The red of slaughter. But the marble would have the transparency of glass so that I could see into it, see into you and know what goes on. And then I should erect a temple on a lonely hill, and I should set the statue in the temple and come every day to worship it at dawn. And on the last day of the year I should arrive at the temple not at dawn but at dusk, when the evening star stands forth in the sky like the first spot of leprosy in a body. And I should put my chisel to the throat of the statue and with a single blow of my hammer knock its head off."

"The wine has muddled your mind, Quaestoris."

"Are you saying I'm drunk?"

"I never said that. I said you're not thinking straight. You've had too much to drink."

The envoy sat up again. He had aged considerably in the last few months. His skin color was bad—a pasty white; his belly protruded; the muscles in his arms and legs sagged. He stared at me, his eyes narrowed and filled with a mean light, his face puffed with childish arrogance and spite that he would be sorry for later on, his lips pouting. "I hate this country," he said thickly. "I hate this land and this people, I'm fed up with them, I'm sick of them. What are the Jews but ticks on the hide of the empire? We are going to pick them off and crush them"—Quaestoris snapped his fingers—"like that!" He pointed a shaking finger at me. "And you? You're one of them! You don't love me, you never have! You use me, I mean nothing to you, I am an object in your Jew-hands and nothing more! You are insolent, you are faithless, you are hypocritical and dishonest! You have misled me." The envoy buried his splotched face in his hands and began to sob. "I'm sick of circumcised dogs, I'm sick of life . . ."

I stifled a yawn and sat up, putting an arm about his quivering shoulders. "There, there . . . don't take it so hard. Sometimes life does seem bleak. But the feeling will pass. Lie down now and sleep it off. That's the way . . ."

Quaestoris lay on his back once more, but he did not sleep. Staring up at the domed ceiling in whose vault satyrs sported with nymphs, he said, "Pilate and Herod hate each other, but that is only because they so much resemble one another. They care for nobody in the world and for nothing on this earth but themselves. I can well understand this, except for the fact that they do not properly know who they are. Both are hedonists, opportunists, creatures of the moment. Both blow as the wind blows, turn as the tide turns. I run back and forth between the two, and sometimes I think I run to one man alone. They are cowards both, shadows both, and both fear discovery more than anything else in the world. The same poisonous milk fed them and the same punitive hand raised them." Quaestoris struggled to sit up again, and though I tried to dissuade him, finally managed to do so.

"There is a difference, though. Yes, there is a difference. I know," said the envoy. "I see them both and I know. You see, King Herod fears retribution, and Pontius Pilate does not know the meaning of the word. Herod imagines hell, and Pilate has no imagination. Herod sometimes feels remorse for an action, while Pilate cannot feel at all. In other words, Herod is a Jew and Pontius Pilate a Roman. Just as you and I are . . ." Quaestoris smiled sadly. "The only trouble is that I no longer seem to know which of us is which. Don't you find that amusing?"

I did not answer.

"Why don't you laugh? The hyenas laugh, Jew. Haven't you learned yet from them?"

I said nothing.

The envoy reached over and with a trembling hand grasped my

forearm. His touch was cold, his eyes wide-open, his jaw slack. In a tiny voice that reminded me the sparrow's chirp, he said, "I know I am evil. I know I am worthless. I know I am ungrateful. Whip me—"

I stared at him.

"Beat me. I beg you."

I climbed out of bed and went over to the statue of the naked athlete, in whose upraised hand I had placed the silver-handled whip.

I was twenty-nine. I was getting ready to strike at Zerubabel at last. I had friends and supporters at court and a spy system that was dreaded from Hermon in the north to the Red Sea in the south. I had the stamp of political approval from Pilate's inner council and was seeking an active understanding with a top Roman military man. Through the good offices of Quaestoris, I had arranged a meeting with a most respected member of the High Command, the illustrious general Livinius. I was elated that the meeting was set for a week's time and was preparing for a bath and festive supper at Quaestoris's villa, to which intimate and influential friends had been invited, when a servant approached me.

"I told you I wasn't to be disturbed!"

"I can't help it, Excellency—"

"Can't the lot of you leave me alone?"

"I must inform you, sir. I can't—"

"Out with it then, you fool! Must I listen to your stammering?"

"Elazar has a message for you. He says it's urgent—"

"Why are you delaying, numskull? Show him in!"

Elazar was flushed. His brow was covered with sweat. He handed me a note whose seal I broke at once. I looked up at the page. "My father is dying. Ready the carriage. And send ahead for a change of horses. Carry the tidings to Quaestoris, and tell him I will get word to him from Nazareth. Be quick!"

I was exhausted and dozed often during the journey. I rode with ten cavalrymen as an escort now and with a trumpeter: it was the latter's horn which jolted me out of my sleep. I sat erect, bracing my back against the rear of the carriage. "Faster, drive faster!" I cried out. I stared out into the harsh gray morning light at the countryside which rolled swiftly by—citrus and fruit groves, windrows, vineyards, terrace walls bending around slopes, open fields and meadows, flocks of sheep and herds of cattle, villages clinging to the crests of hills as if in vertigo, peasants, farmers and merchants setting off on their day's work. The landscape and the people I saw seemed pale and unreal. I arrived in Nazareth at dusk and at my house shortly thereafter; I sprang from the carriage almost before it had stopped rolling.

My father's chief steward, Avner, stood in the doorway—leaner, grayer, tighter-lipped than when I had seen him last, but sounder, harder, more silent than ever. Behind him, framed by torchlight, was the figure of the scribe Amnon, bent almost double now, his high, reedy voice piping shrilly as in alarm. I brushed past both of them and went to my father. He had ordered them to move him from his bedchamber to his private office, where I found him on a divan under animal skins, his eyes sunk in deep hollows, his cheeks furrowed, his skin eaten by fever. I approached him, and though he did not turn his head, I knew he had been aware of my entry from the moment I crossed the threshold. Though he could scarcely move, though his arms and hands were wasted, his eyes still had their keen appraising glance and had lost none of their sharpness. He wet his lips and said, "I would like to borrow from you of the life you have left to live, but I cannot, so then let it be as it is—welcome home!"

"I'm sorry to find you so ill, Father."

"I'm sorrier, you can be sure of that. But you haven't made the trip from the court of Herod to Nazareth for an exchange of pleasantries. We have a lot of ground to cover before I die, you and I, and there is no time to waste."

"But you will not die, Father."

"I will surely die. I do not speak to you as the victim of an illusion but simply as one who imparts a sober truth—and that only if one chooses to accept that truth soberly. I will certainly die within the next few weeks or days or hours. They will say that I am gone before my time, but that is sheer folly. One always goes in one's time, no matter when it comes. I will die and the reins will pass into your hands. And if you manage it properly, the reign will be yours as well."

"What are you saying, Father?"

"We will go into that shortly. But let me say a few words to you now, while I have them ready. I want to tell you that I am not displeased with the gains you have made, the strides you have taken. For a time, when you were a very young child, there was weakness in you, softness, hesitancy, indecision. I must tell you that I was troubled sorely by these flaws. I feared greatly that the other, harder part of your nature would wither and die even before it had properly taken root; I was afraid that the firmness in you would crumble. And then"—my father lifted an emaciated hand that did not seem to belong to him— "then you ran away from home. You stole the weapons and left home while Avner and I were on a trip. And I was encouraged. And then I chained you in the animal shed, and one day in your fury you slew the rabbi with your sling. And then I was certain—certain that you would be what I wanted you to—"

"You knew that I murdered the rabbi?"

"Did you really think for a moment that the rabbi or Zvi would escape my notice? Did you really so underestimate me? How then can he who sires the panther be ignorant of the panther's ways?"

"And you considered the rabbi the turning point?"

"Yes, for you that was the turning point. I knew clearly then in which direction your nature would go. From that point on, what was needed was balance. Balance and restraint. In a way of speaking, I might say that your lava had to be contained under a shell of rock. The veneer of scholarship, of learning, of culture, of pedigree, of status had to conceal the—you will not mind my saying it, I'm sure—monster underneath."

"And now?"

"And now it is up to you, my monster."

"And you?"

"What do you mean?"

"And you—now that you face death, now that you know you will die: do you reckon your investment worth it?"

"Worth it? Do you mean by that, would I do it all again in the same manner? Well," said my father, "that seems to me rather an idle question. If I were to be again myself as I was, I would do everything just as I have already done it. But if I were to live again as another, then I would do things differently." My father closed his eyes for a moment and then opened them. "But I am growing weary. Bid Avner and Amnon draw near to me now. We have a way to go before I reach the pit."

Avner came forward then, close-mouthed, his face impassive, looking in a way more dead in life than my father would look when he died. And at his heels came Amnon, limping with gout, muttering his perpetual complaints with relish, as if he kept on living solely for the purpose of complaining. The scribe groaned, sat himself at a desk which had been drawn up to the divan and wrote as my father spoke. Avner and I stood and listened in silence. My father talked without interruption for nearly two hours. His voice weakened at times but never faltered or stopped; it dropped now and again, but it was never indistinct. His discussed his affairs with clarity and coherence and I knew that his mind had lost none of its grasp. Whatever the beast that stalked his flesh, it had not been able to lay a claw on his mental powers. At length he finished and fell silent and rested.

Then he spoke again, saying, "Avner will retain the house keys so he can carry out your instructions as you wish. But I want you to take the key to the underground vault from my neck and keep it safely on your person. I charge you: let it not fall into the hands of others." As my father had directed me, I unfastened the chain with the key to the vault under the house from his withered neck and locked it about my own; when he was satisfied that I had done so, my father said, "Now bid Avner and Amnon to take their farewell of me and retire, so the two of us may be alone."

The chief steward's farewell was brief and inaudible: though he stood near my father, he did not reach out to touch whatever warmth there was left in his body. But the scribe wept and fell on his knees by my father's side and would not take leave of him until Avner placed his hands upon him and drew him back by main force. As the two of them were departing, the scribe turned his head at the door and cried out, "Evenezer, do not leave us!" and my father answered him, saying, "If it is my time, I will indeed leave you, for in his own time so does every man take leave of this earth." Then the door shut and my father signaled for me to set the latch in place so no one would open it and disturb us in our meeting. And I did as I was bidden and then stood again at my father's side.

"What is in the vault," said my father, "is essential to the empire of the Galilee. You must use it to build a greater empire—Judea and beyond."

"I shall, Father."

"Amnon will provide you with a record of all that I have spoken this night. It is indispensable to you; it will help you plan the future. Have you understood me clearly?"

"I have, Father."

"Do you have any questions?"

I hesitated.

My father lifted a hand and let it fall. "This is no time to be coy. Death is not shy. Ask what you will, but ask it now, for you cannot question a corpse."

"Who else knows about the rabbi and about Zvi?"

"Avner," said my father. "Avner, who supervised everything at my behest. And my scribe Amnon, who has put it all down in my journals. Yes, I've kept journals as well as you have. Are you surprised? Amnon recorded what I had to say, word for word, line for line. And my journals are in the underground vault with all the rest."

I was silent.

"Why do you ask me who knows?"

I did not answer.

"Will you kill them?" my father said.

"I will."

"Good," said my father. "I am satisfied with my handiwork. I am pleased you know that men with dangerous knowledge turn into dangerous weapons. While I am alive, these two men are loyal, as they have always been. But once I am gone, well—one cannot really expect loyalty to a corpse, can one?"

My father closed his eyes and fell silent. I knew then that he was in great pain, that pain ran through him as flame through a parched field of hay. I could see him struggling and see that little by little his will was weakened. When he was able to look at me again, I saw for the very first time in all my life that his eyes had lost their cutting edge. Like the scum that forms on the surface of a stagnant pond, a strange film was forming over his pupils. I sensed that my father had stopped struggling against what was happening to him: that was very much like him, for he never expended effort in a hopeless cause. Several times he tried to speak, but could not get the words out of his mouth. At length he was able to whisper, "You will obey my commands to the letter in all that I instruct you regarding my death—"

"I shall, Father."

"Then hear what I say. Let there be no service for me of any kind: let neither priest nor layman speak. And let there be no grave for me. For I desire that my body be not committed to the bowels of earth, but

215

rather be cremated and the ashes scattered to the winds. This is my wish and my command."

"Father, what you ask is against religious law."

"When I am dead, what have I to do with priests? For me, as you well know, religion was never more than another power structure." My father compelled his pain-wracked face to smile. "But my corpse is surely beyond the power of men, religious or not."

"And what of the world hereafter?"

"It is no different from the world before a man's birth. It does not exist. A man's life comes to him when he is born. Nothing exists but the life we know on earth." My father coughed. His breathing was labored and sporadic. A foreign sound had entered it, a sound like pebbles make when they are scattered over a tile floor. "And now, say to me what you must say, for my time is short."

"*Requiescat in pace!* is what I will say for the man whose loins begat me."

"You have learned to speak the language of the gentiles well, my son." My father sighed. "And now leave me. For I would die alone, with no man present to see me yield."

"Will you die now, Father?"

"I will die now."

My father's hands lay motionless on his cover. His face seemed to retreat; it had become so sharp that I could see the skeleton peering through, as if it were longing to come forth and show itself. His eyes were open, but their look was clouded and turned inward. "I am a specter," whispered a voice I did not recognize as my father's. "I am a specter, my son . . ."

I turned away from the divan and left the room without looking back. As he wished to go from this world, so I would let him go. At dawn Avner entered the room, found him dead and came to notify me. Immediately, I ordered the carpenters to make a simple pine coffin and I sent to Nazareth for the burial society. The chief steward, who was acquainted with my father's wishes for silence and cremation, stared at me.

"I do not wish the priests against me," I said. "And further, I am not pleased with the tacit opposition of the chief steward. I charge the chief steward to remember who is now master in this house!"

It rained that night. The sky was lit by great spider webs of lightning, the air filled with long, rolling waves of thunder. I paced up and down through the corridors of the house, unable to sleep or even to stretch myself out. I descended alone into the underground vault to make certain that all was safely shut away. And then I made my way to the private chamber where my father's corpse was being washed, found his riding whip, took it to the great dining hall, broke it and cast the halves into the fire. And then, far past the hour of midnight, when except for the guards all the household slept, I went outside and stood in the downpour, my head bared to the storm as if I would gather it to me. Sometimes, as it raged with such force that it seemed it must destroy the world, I did not feel separate or apart from it. And often when the lightning flashed, I saw strange shapes in the sky above me— shapes I could not decipher, shapes which might have been from my past. Once, a huge, bone-white bolt of lightning opened out of the blackness like a sword, reached down and struck a giant fir tree that stood on the hill next over. It was a tree that had dominated the landscape about Nazareth for as long as I could recall, but the bolt split it in twain as if it were a twig and sent its upper half crashing to the ground. I was very much pleased. I did not know why, but I was satisfied and relieved. The tension that had drawn my body and my mind taut to the breaking point was gone. I felt that I could go into the house and sleep. I threw my clothes off, wrapped myself in a robe, and reclined in one of the huge armchairs in the dining hall, where as a youth I had attended so many of my father's fetes. I closed my eyes and dozed dreamlessly.

At dawn Elazar woke me. He had a message from Quaestoris, which the envoy had insisted he bring to me personally. I was glad to see the page. I did not look at Quaestoris's note, but immediately sat and wrote a coded message which I sealed and gave to Elazar to take to Melech the Galilean. I bade him take his rest and set out on his journey to the commander of *Patish* as soon as his strength had returned to him. Elazar kissed my hand and left. I took Quaestoris's note over to a window and in the rain-washed light of the morning read it slowly and carefully, alert always for the language beneath the language. As I had expected, the note was little more than a jumbled outcry, the plaint of an infant. It told me that Quaestoris loved me madly, terribly, that he could not abide my absence, that he would die of grief if I did not return in haste. It begged me in the name of "our holy love" to come back without further delay, to "fly home on wings of speed" to the "bosom that longed for" me with a longing that "few mortal men would be capable of imagining." The note ran on and on—it must have taken the envoy hours to compose. The language was polished to almost a poetic finish, and the envoy had put it all down in his own demented scrawl. Typically, there was no mention at all of my father. I reread it, decided that Quaestoris had been uncommonly active with a number of lovers and was feeling especially guilty, tore it up and threw the pieces into the fireplace where the glowing embers turned them at once into ash.

My father was buried late that afternoon on a grassy knoll to the rear of the house. The ceremony was simple, brief, and private. Only members of the household and the professional mourners I had hired attended it. Wrapped in its linen shroud, my father's dead body looked small, almost dwarfish. I was surprised that so much venom had fit into such a diminutive vessel. Some of the servants wept, but most stood and stared silently. Avner stood quietly, his hands clasped together in front of him. Amnon was nowhere to be seen. The wind bent the tops of the cypresses, the earth quickly filled the hole into which the body had been put, and the last words of mourning were spoken by those who were paid to speak them. The crowd dispersed and a startled flock of birds, which had grown comfortable in nearby branches, took fright and flew suddenly into the lowering sky. I ordered the officer in charge of my escort to assemble his detail and then took my leave of the chief steward, giving him my last instructions until I should be in touch with him by courier. Then, returning the salute of my men, I sprang into the carriage, raised my whip in the air and started out for court as the trumpeter's blast rang through the still air. As my conveyance sped forward, I went over in my mind the coded orders I had sent to Melech the Galilean by Elazar the page. The first called for the immediate arrest and summary execution of the chief steward Avner and the scribe Amnon. The second called for the immediate seizure and detention, in a secret security cell, of my "long-lost" brother, the "son" of Yosef, carpenter of Nazareth, and his barren wife, Mara.

The Roman general Livinius was a bull of a man, a swollen-backed mountain of flesh with huge, meaty hands which most often unconsciously cradled his protuberant belly, a great, round, raw, sunburnt skull that was always shaven down to the scalp, and a broad smile that readily pulled an eruption of coarse laughter from his ample chest. This was a man of the forced march, the massed phalanx, the corpse-littered battlefield, the common grave, the hypnotic dirge; this was a born fighter, a seasoned combat soldier, officer and commander, merciless in his thinking, direct in his approach and utterly frank in his speech. It was true that his eyes were frequently lit with amusement and that his laughter came often and loudly. But I was not in the least deceived: I knew that beneath it all was a malevolence that had no bounds. When he fixed an objective, he would spare no effort nor would he rest until he had attained it. In battle he was calculating, tenacious, unrelenting until he had the "enemy's guts safely in hand."

There were many stories about him. One had it that in the midst of a bloody fray whose outcome was in doubt, an aide came to him at his command post, asking whether or not to commit the last available battalion to combat. "Why do you ask me?" said Livinius. "Because if we send it in, it will be caught between two units of the opposing army— only by a miracle will it pull through!" the aide replied. Livinius held his belly, laughed long and loudly, and then snarled, "Put it between the millstones, then, and let the corn be ground!" The battalion was ordered into battle and slaughtered almost to the last man. But the other Roman troops, weakened and decimated as they were, took heart and redoubled their efforts. The hill that Livinius was after fell to him at dusk. "There is little corn left," joked the general. "But we have the cornfield." From this particular incident, his nickname "Millstone" was derived.

Livinius and I were sitting in a small hunting room in his mountaintop villa. We faced each other across a chessboard of polished bone, engrossed for more than an hour in a difficult end game. I had come to see the general in secret and spoken to him but a few moments when he invited me to play. The game began almost in routine fashion, developed with unexpected rapidity and then plunged into a bitter, protracted conclusion. Livinius sighed often and heavily, at times swearing under his breath or even aloud. But I was quiet. There was no victory in sight for either of us. But I was waiting. I was confident my move would come suddenly, without warning. And it happened that way. The general set down his piece and leaned back in his chair, his bulging, pitted brow furrowed, his jaw thrust out.

In a flash I saw before me a picture that was strange yet familiar.

Livinius's last move had put a whole new construction on the board: it was as if a star had shifted and completely changed the shape of a constellation. In that sense, what I saw was different. But it was also familiar, because I saw in my mind a board on which, as a youth, I had played against my father. It came to me in an instant that I could use precisely the same move by which my father had defeated me to gain a victory over the general. I raised my queen, moved it gently through the air, and set it down. "Checkmate," I said quietly.

Livinius was thunderstruck. His eyes raked the board as if they were claws. He saw what happened, saw what he had neither seen nor suspected before, but still could not believe it. "It's impossible!" he grunted.

"No," I said. "It's actuality."

Livinius's hands clutched the arms of his chair with such force that the knuckles were white. Slowly, unwillingly, his craggy face looked up from the board. Before he had a chance to mask his feelings, I saw into the very heart of the man: saw through the bitter metallic gleam in his eyes that was meant to frighten away all inquiry, deep down into the pit where the murderer stirred restively, waiting to crawl out and do his deeds. The general stared straight at me. For an instant he sneered—the imperial sneer of Rome, the sneer of the conqueror with his foot planted on the chest of his defeated foe. And then his lips twisted, of their own accord it seemed, into the good-natured smile I had come to expect, though I never put even the slightest faith in it. "You play at chess very well—for a Jew," he said.

"You lose at chess very well—for a Roman," I countered.

I knew that I had taken a risk, but the risk was calculated and I did not think I would lose. My instinct proved correct. The Roman general Livinius, stung by my victory in the game, was amused by the triumph of my wit. His laugh was full and hearty and genuine. He slapped his knees. "We shall make capital conspirators, you and I," he said gleefully. "I am much impressed—by your methods and by your metaphors." And with that, the general reached out and with a hairy forearm the thickness of a tree branch swept the chess pieces from the board to the floor, where they scattered in all directions. "Come with me into my war room, and we shall lay our plans!"

The war room, which adjoined the hunting room, had in it everything from skulls to bludgeons, from maps to maces. We sat facing each other, as we had during the game of chess, at a large oak table whose surface was so polished that it almost reflected our faces. The general Livinius toyed with a silver-handled dagger as I spoke, running his fingers back and forth along the gleaming blade as if their touch was sufficient to whet it. Within the limits I had prescribed for myself, I discoursed freely and at considerable length. I was explicit, but not overly detailed or repetitious; I allowed myself broad conceptual grasp, but was never vague.

When I had finished, Livinius nodded as if pleased. "You have spoken well and to the point," he said. "You have covered everything without covering everything up. I have a clear idea of where you are going and why you want to get there." The general threw his dagger to the table. "You will need help to accomplish your coup—I will give it to you: you have the word of Livinius, and that is better than the gold of the empire." He cradled his stomach in his hands. "Of course, you must understand that my troops will not interfere in the battle itself— you are on your own in the arena, and what your men do or fail to do will decide the issue. But my soldiers will make absolutely certain that no rescue forces or reinforcements arrive and that nothing unforeseen hinders or thwarts your attack. And when the ambush is finished, when you have accomplished the coup that you describe so well to me, I shall throw the full weight of my influence on your side. You can be certain that there will be much opposition to your plan, and scheming from many quarters, but together, my chess-playing Hebrew, we shall sweep it aside—as I did the pieces of the game! What do you say to that, eh? Have we struck a bargain?" The general seized the dagger from the table and sheathed it in a lightning motion that was unconscious and perfect. "When you assume command of all Herod's forces and unite them with mine, there will be little in all Judea to stop us!"

"There will be nothing in Judea to stop us."

Livinius roared and rose from his seat, nearly lifting the table with him. His belly shivered, his small eyes gleamed like coals, his craggy face twitched with excitement, like that of a hunting dog fired with the scent of the prey within range. I looked at him with a sense of pleasure. His stance now, and I was sure wherever he was, had the cast of war. This was truly a man who revered the blood bath, who rested in conflict, who fed on famine, who lived on death. Livinius came round the table and took my shoulder in a crushing grip that had great power and no warmth whatsoever: it was the clutch of a reptile. "To victory!" he cried out. And stepping back, he gave the Roman salute. Without a word, I returned it.

Four of his crack cavalry units, men who had been with him in campaign after campaign and had been carefully briefed by Livinius himself, blocked the roads that led to the wadi. To the south, the road to the court fortress was cut off; to the north, the road twisting down from Jerusalem was sealed; to the east and west the specially selected Roman troops cut off the trails that led to Herodian military encampments. The minister of war Zerubabel always traveled with at least two platoons as his escort. "It is far better to prepare for the worst while you are alive," he said, "than to have mourners when you are dead say that you failed to prepare for it!" He was full of homilies and parables these days—which did not prevent his troops from being the toughest, most battle-hardened, most trained and most heavily armed. "Words are fine," he would say with a grin. "But they won't split skulls." Sometimes before he set off on a trip, he would personally review the men of his escort, marching along the ranks like a plump pig, pinching biceps or patting rumps along the lines. "I like to feel what I'm getting," he would say with a wink.

When the war minister traveled, no matter what his purpose or his destination, he traveled well. There were always many carriages and other equipages, wagons and pack mules, the latter trailing the main convoy by a half or whole day's journey. Zerubabel was fond of taking with him a goodly number of female concubines and male slaves, dozens of Roman and Jewish friends and sycophants. He liked being surrounded by a host of admirers and flatterers, and he enjoyed merriment and jest, for which he was sure to include several jesters in his entourage. "There is more than enough time for solemnity in the grave," he would say. "There is place in this life for frolic and entertainment— a man who has not these cannot truly be said to live." Although he was a staunch patron of the spirit, the minister of war was sure to take along a lavish supply of food and wine—in part because he was afraid of being poisoned and in part because he feared there would not be enough food for him to eat when he reached his destination.

Every so often, almost with the regularity of a menstrual cycle, he would announce that he was taking a brief vacation from, as he phrased it, "the many, grave cares of court." He was frequently heard to say that of all King Herod's ministers and high officials, he worked the longest hours "at the most difficult and most trying tasks." He would then groan, throw up his hands, and say solemnly, "Another man would have cracked long ago under the strain of my office. Only a workhorse like me can stand up to the pressures." This time Zerubabel was heading for the sea on what he termed an "official trip of weighty significance." His purported aim was to "inspect the coastline from north to south" and report back to his monarch on the advisability and possible location of fortifications, which the Romans would then be asked to construct. Everyone at court knew that the story was patent nonsense concocted by the minister of war almost on the spur of the moment. Zerubabel himself was aware that he was not believed. But he did not care. Nobody cared. Everyone enjoyed the little game. The war minister was glad he was going and the court was glad to see him go, just as the minister would be happy to return and the court happy to receive him.

There was even an intimate gathering to wish him well on his journey. Of course I was among the invitees, and I made certain to attend. The party was held in the minister of war's spacious, elegant salon where the revelers allowed themselves to sink wholly into the lascivious, abandoned mood which their host knew so well how to create. At one point in the evening, Zerubabel—as I had known he would—drew me aside and asked me to come with him into a small, private chamber where we could talk as "allies and conspirators." I smiled to myself. Since the time of my father's death, the minister of war had been going steadily downhill. More and more of his time was spent in pleasure and dissipation; the cares and concerns of office were being neglected. I had sensed that a soft spot in the war minister had gone rotten, that he was yielding to his weaknesses; that he was plunging into a quicksand of spiritual anarchy from which he would never emerge. I had reasoned that my hour was at hand and I had to take advantage of it before another saw fit to do so. It was this chain of logic and events which had led me to the home of Livinius.

Zerubabel closed the door and turned to me. "Be seated," he said. I sat, and though I protested that I did not wish any, the war minister poured wine for me. Lifting his own goblet in toast he said, "Chief

Interpreter, you are doing well, extremely well. I am a man who is not given to lavish praise, as you know, but for your accomplishments I have only superlatives. Our spy system is bringing in excellent results. Herod is pleased. The Romans are pleased. I am pleased. The trinity of power in Judea salutes you!" He set the goblet to his lips and drank it off in several long draughts.

"The latest reports of progress which have come to my attention are superb—there is no other word that will adequately describe them. The monarch himself has been asking me who is responsible for such stunning achievements." The minister of war laughed nervously. "Of course, given our requirements of strict secrecy, I could only evade his question. But my mind—my mind, Chief Interpreter, pronounced your name with respect and even—if I may say so—with a degree of reverence." Zerubabel poured himself another goblet of wine. "That is why on the very eve of my departure for the sea I have seen fit to call you to me and to inform you of what is in my heart."

"Excellency, I do not quite understand what you are driving at—"

The war minister waved a hand, spilling his wine. "You will, you will understand directly. Just let me unburden myself and all will be revealed to you." Zerubabel paused and cleared his throat. "Chief Interpreter, I wanted to tell you before I left. I have been considering the matter for some time, and I have at length come to a decision. I wish to appoint you deputy war minister in the court of King Herod, second in the department of war only to myself. I am overtaxed with responsibility and overburdened with care. I need a capable man whom I can lean on for advice and for aid, and I need a loyal man in whom I can safely place my trust. I know of only one man who qualifies—and that man is eminently suitable. I announce this to you with great personal respect for your abilities and with deep personal fondness for your nature. 'Deputy minister of war.' How does that strike your ears, Chief Interpreter?"

"I don't want it," I said.

The minister of war dropped his goblet and rose from his seat. "What's this?" he cried out. "What are you saying? What rubbish! What foolishness! You don't want to be deputy minister of war? Why, there are men in the court of Herod—"

"Few of them," I said.

"—there are men in the court of Herod who would gladly give their right arms for such an appointment!"

"Then take their right arms."

"You cannot be serious—"

"I have neither time nor inclination for jest."

"But why—why would you refuse such an offer?"

"Sit down," I said. "Sit down, Excellency, and I will tell you."

Zerubabel lowered himself into his chair. His round, flesh-gripped eyes stared at me as if I were an apparition.

"I want to stay exactly where I am, Excellency. It is essential that I remain in my present situation. I have perfect camouflage: I am totally invisible. Nothing—nothing in the world, Excellency, must disturb that. As I am now, in my present post, I can run the spy system safely and efficiently. There is no tie between the two of us; our work has no relation, one department to the other; you and I are not even friends in the proper sense of the word, but merely members of the same court. For your sake and for mine, and for the sake of our mutual interests, I want to keep it that way. There must be no overt connection between the war department and myself—between you and me. Is that clear? Do you see what I mean?"

Zerubabel shook his head. "You are ashamed of me," he said mournfully.

I saw that the minister of war was drunk. "No, no, Excellency—how could I be ashamed of a man like you?"

"You do not love me as once you did . . ."

"To love a man is to have his best interests at heart, Excellency. As I have yours."

"Will you miss me when I am away?"

"Most grievously, Excellency."

"I shall miss you," said the war minister in his lugubrious voice. "I shall miss you very much."

"But I shall be with you, Excellency. I shall be with you in spirit every step of the way."

"Nicely put, Chief Interpreter. Very nicely phrased. I want you to know that I thoroughly enjoy your language, that I wholeheartedly enjoy your polish. It is a pleasure to deal with you. You are an educated man, a scholar, a welcome relief from the boorishness I am compelled to endure day in and day out. Such stupidity! One can scarcely believe that such charlatans and ignoramuses run the affairs of state! That is why I so admire you. Why, in talking to you, the unsuspecting person would never in his life suspect that you are a killer."

"Thank you for the compliment, Excellency."

The minister of war waved a hand. "Don't mention it—it is only a small part of the tenderness I feel for you. But tell me, Chief Interpreter —have you ever been to the sea?"

"Not since I was a small child, Excellency."

"What a pity!" Zerubabel clapped his hands together. "I have a capital idea—would you like to come along?"

"Thank you, Your Excellency. Your concern moves me. But I cannot come with you. I have work to do. Work that affects both of us, work that will determine both of our fortunes."

The war minister frowned. "It's a damn shame you can't come. You're too serious, that's your main trouble. You don't know how to live. You have too much of the Jew in you and not enough of the Roman." The minister of war winked. "Take it from me, Chief Interpreter, the goyim know how to enjoy themselves; they don't mind dying because they really live while they are alive. You'd do well to take a lesson from the Romans. Change your habits—too much work can corrupt a man, destroy his health and his peace of mind. That's why I'm going. *Mare nostrum* is a magnificent healer. A wonder-worker. Ah, yes, the ocean is wonderful—restful—you cannot conceive of the serenity it brings. The waves, the sand, the majestic coastline: why, all of this is—a gift of God. What do the sages say again?"

I shrugged.

"Well, no matter. Never mind what the sages say. How much did their prattling mean when their heads lay on the block, eh? It's sufficient that we enjoy the ocean, that's quite enough—and to hell with the sages! *Carpe diem*, as the Romans have it. And we do. Why, sometimes when the moon is bright and we are certain about security, we go down to the sea, the whole lot of us, and we plunge into the waves as naked as on the day that our mothers showed us the light of this world! Yes, even some of the soldiers join with us in our frolic—those whom I select as worthy participants. I know you would revel in it." Zerubabel stroked his chin.

"But enough. Enough of the trip. I am digressing and the hour is late. The appointment—I take it that your mind is made up, that there is no changing it at the present moment. But why don't you think it over? Perhaps by the time I return to court you will have altered your decision."

"By the time you return? When will that be?"

"Two weeks. Three weeks. I can't say for sure. But perhaps when I return, things will be different."

"In two or three weeks' time," I said, "things will be different."

The war minister nodded ceremoniously and rose unsteadily to his feet. His eyes were bloodshot, his hands shook, his splendid tunic was splotched with the wine he had spilled. "Come with me," he said hoarsely. "Come with me, my friend, back to the party. They have missed us sorely as we have missed them. Come join the revelers once again. And I will introduce you to a very beautiful couple: a lovely man and a lovely ewe. They have agreed to let us watch them as they perform the most intimate rituals of love. What do you think of that? Are they not generous to share their conjugality with us? And to think—I bought them for a song!"

"Some other time, Excellency. I thank the minister for his generosity and for his solicitude. But I must go. The Romans, whom you mention with as much love as envy, can afford to relax and make sport —they are in power. While such Jews as you and I—"

Zerubabel belched. "Until we meet again," he said.

I said nothing.

Herod's minister of war left the private chamber by one exit, and I departed by another. I galloped home. Elazar stirred in the anteroom as I entered and rose from the bench on which he lay to hand me a message from Livinius: it told me that all was in readiness, the troops already gone. I dismissed my page and destroyed the note. A courier arrived with a communiqué from Melech the Galilean informing me that the men of *Patish* were deployed in position. I destroyed it as well and threw myself fully dressed on my bed. The room was stuffy, and I rose to fling open the shutters. Still I was uncomfortable, so I walked onto my terrace that I might fill my lungs with air.

The night was velvet dark, and the great immaculate hive of the sky filled with a swarm of stars. The moon was up, much as it had been the night so long ago when my father had feted the Roman official in the arbor and I had dreamed of glory. From my perch, I had a clear, unbroken view of the landscape all the way down to the basin of the Sea of Salt, whose northernmost tip glimmered spectrally. I put a hand on the railing of the balcony. On the ramparts below, I could hear the rattling of weapons and the faint clash of armor: the guard was being changed. In the stable, a horse whinnied. From an invisible point in the darkness came the moan of a wolf, as if the night itself were crying out.

Glory. The stars glittered with it. It shone on the dead waters of the Sea of Salt. The moon infused the night with it. And like the night, it was both light and dark. Its victories were radiant, but they left deep hollows of shadow: the brighter the light, the denser the darkness. I gripped the railing with both hands. I wanted no leper spots of darkness left; I wanted the world to drown in my effulgence. I did not want glory. I wanted to be glory.

The hour had come. I had chosen it well. Zerubabel was sliding ever more swiftly and irrevocably downhill, and there were others who knew it; Zerubabel was wounded and there were others who could smell the blood. His wish to appoint me deputy war minister was a move of desperation, a gambit born of panic. He felt that with me close at hand as his deputy minister, the department would clearly reflect my accomplishments and that he personally would shine in reflection. The deputy would reap, and the harvest go to his minister. Herod would no longer have to ask him from which quarter the excellent reports came. The critics would keep silent, the opponents retreat. And the war minister would find it easier, if I were directly under his thumb, to keep watch on me. He would surround me with spies and know my every movement almost before I did. And if he ever decided it was time to remove me, that would also be accomplished with greater ease—once in his department, I should be swallowed at will, without a sound. But I had forestalled his plans. I had made every move carefully and well, guarding against every conceivable reaction and countermove. And now my forces were arranged for a master stroke. The cavalry of Livinius sealed off the arena. The men of *Patish* waited to swoop down from the heights. Within the next twenty-four hours, two pasts, two destinies beginning with the moment of birth of each of the protagonists would meet. Under a slightly altered sky, they would lock in battle and for a brief time would merge. Only one would come forth to continue its journey under the stars. I smiled into the vast cavern of space that floated down from the fortress of the tetrarch to the cold fire of the Sea of Salt which lay at the very bottom of the world; I smiled into the loneliness and endlessness of the night. I was not worried in the least. For I was certain that Zerubabel's time had ended and that my hour had arrived.

PART

IV

Melech the Galilean, commander of the striking force *Patish*, gave me a full account of what happened. Under no circumstances did I wish to make personal contact with him during the period of turmoil and internecine struggle that came in the wake of the battle, and I had therefore instructed him to transmit to me, as soon as it proved feasible, a detailed report. It read as follows:

My lord and master, as you know, we had reckoned on the war minister's hurry to reach the coast and on the full moon to keep his caravan in motion. So it was on the first night. At an hour past midnight, we glimpsed the first party of the war minister's scouts. We next saw the first units of the minister's main escort. They were two enlarged platoons, with fully fifty men in each. It was clear that our plan of battle would have to be executed swiftly and without flaw. As soon as I saw the first equipage of Zerubabel's convoy move into the wadi, I gave the signal for attack. The assault, as you know, was two-pronged. The first unit which I sent out, which bore the code name of *Macah*, or blow, struck at the advance platoons. The second, bearing the code name of *Helem*, or shock, attacked the forces of the war minister in the rear of the convoy.

My lord and master, I can joyfully report to you that the assault was a complete success: it caught the enemy completely by surprise and led him—in his frantic haste to hit back—into the very defeat he sought to avoid. To the front and to the rear were the war minister's ramparts pulled slowly, steadily, subtly from him. I waited for precisely the right moment, and when it came signaled the attack on the convoy itself, leading it personally. Except for a few great louts whom Zerubabel kept near for wrestling matches, and a number of pretty fellows the war minister kept by him for love-making, the convoy's flanks were exposed. My hooded riders swept down squarely into the center of the target, riding forward under a covering fire of arrows from the reserves on the heights. In accordance with the plan, my men did not enter any of the wagons, but surrounded them quickly and within minutes put them to the torch.

Taking a dozen of my best men, I rode over to the minister of war's personal wagon. At the rear was a small balcony, over whose rail the Herodian flag was draped. Suddenly a figure clad only in a loincloth stepped out onto it. I recognized the portly figure of Zerubabel. He stood gaping at the flames billowing from the wagons of his convoy, at the charred corpses littering the wadi floor, at the hooded men of *Patish* as they pursued their tasks. I turned to my right-hand man, Ichavod—a fellow I can safely entrust my bones to in any scrape— and he raised his great bow, bent it back and let fly an arrow that struck Zerubabel with such force as to pin him against the wagon wall. Then I gave the signal for the firing of the vehicle. This last was the most spectacular of all the fires. Within a short time, the domed roof shivered as if with fever and then erupted in a tremendous burst of flame, collapsing with a roar on the remains of those penned within.

There was little more for us to do other than watch. And this we did—we patrolled the area ceaselessly for signs of anyone who might escape. And when the dawn finally came, my hooded soldiers made a last, thorough search among the smoldering debris. They poked with their spears and javelins among the corpses. They touched neither body nor object. Thus, my lord and master, did I carry out your express command that no spoils or loot be borne away from the carnage, lest in some manner the attack be connected with your person. When I was convinced that neither man nor beast had survived the holocaust, I gave the signal to quit the field of battle. As we rode for the home base, I turned in the saddle and looked back for the last time. A great, spreading pall of smoke hung like a curtain in the morning sky: I saw in it a sign of Zerubabel's epitaph and my master's prologue.

Back once more at the home base, I can report to my lord and master the following: that in this conflict, we lost seven men. All of the corpses of the slain warriors were recovered and burned in the oven in the vault beneath our headquarters. Eleven of our troops sustained wounds in the struggle. All are expected to live and return to serve in *Patish*, except for one man whose legs were amputated at the knees: he will be killed, as we have no further use for him. Also, six horses were slain in battle.

And with these words, my lord and master, I end my report to you.

The Roman general Livinius was correct in his political speculation: a fierce struggle for the vacant position of war minister began after the carnage in the wadi. Zerubabel's adherents and friends, such as were left, proposed a distant cousin of their deposed hero, Azavi, a Judean aristocrat who had spent a good deal of his life in Egypt, a thin, high-strung, dissipated man in his early sixties with a lean, horselike face, bony hands that shook continually and scruples that were no firmer: Azavi was an orator, a master of rhetoric, and could rouse an audience to bloodshed with the sound of his voice alone. His fame at stirring the rabble had spread far and wide, and his proponents considered him eminently suited to government. "What else does a ruler need," they said, "besides an attractive voice?"

The minister of finance, who fancied himself a military man whose genius had been overlooked, who hunted whatever animals as were within the range of his weapons, who practiced at archery constantly and took up the art of swordplay as if the prophet Moses had commended it as holy, proposed that he be given the post along with his present post. "War and money share the same bed," he would say with a smile. "When one cannot sleep, then the other is restless as well." And again: "The hand that fills the coffers must be the hand that empties the purses. But there is no purse that shall be emptied, except that the sword shall command it so!"

The priests were not to be left out of the jockeying; they too had

233

a candidate of their own: an obese, ungainly man by the name of Ikutiel whose father had been slain in the Temple of Jerusalem defending the High Priest against a deadly attack by a madman. Ikutiel was slow-moving, slow-spoken, and slow-thinking, and had so prodigious an appetite that one imagined he might constantly be at war in order to capture the provender necessary to his sustenance. His credo, simply stated, was "Religion is obviously for everyone, none must be left out. Therefore, those who are not religious should be exterminated." The priests pushed their favorite aggressively, for they realized that he would be a tool in their hands, that if they procured for him the produce of earth, Ikutiel would secure for them the rights of heaven.

Among the Romans, the political adversaries of Livinius had their candidate: a sycophant Jew who, as it was said, trembled at the sight of a Roman and fainted if one addressed him. The story was told at court that the mother of this man, who had taken for himself a Roman name and was called Tarquinius, gave him as an infant to a Roman woman that she might nurse him at her breasts. "For," said the mother, "the milk of Jewish women is poisoned!" One notorious wag improved upon the tale by saying that Tarquinius had been suckled by a Roman man.

King Herod, who could be counted on to vacillate in any situation, was in a complete quandary. Zerubabel was a man who had been acceptable to virtually all factions except the priests, and Herod had been much pleased by the fact—it was undoubtedly the major reason for keeping the minister of war in office. Now that Zerubabel was gone and the furor had started, the monarch was irritated almost beyond his endurance. He had indulged himself in a number of tantrums so violent that his personal servants had fled his chambers in terror.

Besides the pressures of the warring groups, there was of course the matter of Zerubabel's manner of death. Herod was a man who detested violence, unless it was the violence of personal relationship, the structured violence of the army in combat, the ordered violence of government in its routines or the tamed violence of contest and game. But the specters of assassination, riot, rebellion and ambush haunted him always. For days after the slaughter in the wadi, he hid himself away in the depths of his fortress and would see no one. It was said that even Herodias was barred from his presence; and Quaestoris himself told me that he had sought to obtain an audience with the tetrarch several times and had been turned away, being told that Herod was "gravely indisposed." King Herod issued orders immediately—orders that were to be carried out "to the letter, on the pain of death." The fortress guard was doubled. No stranger was allowed within a mile of the fortress. All servants were subjected to a search of body and sleeping quarters. Leaves for military personnel and servants were canceled without exception. All communications from and to the fortress were to be examined by a censor personally selected by the tetrarch. All supplies reaching the fortress were to be checked by a special detail. The tasters of Herod's food and drink were increased from two to four. And no group of more than three persons might gather together on the fortress grounds. There was also a rumor stemming from well-placed sources to the effect that the monarch had sent urgent word to Pontius Pilate, requesting that units of the Roman army be dispatched at once to protect his person, since it was quite obvious that his own forces were incapable of adequately defending their rulers and leaders.

In theory, the rebels stood accused. In fact, a new wave of searches and roundups began: Herod's forces swept the country from north to south with a dragnet that brought in everything conceivable—except Zealots. At one point in the wake of what came to be called "the swift war against the slow war minister," Quaestoris was summoned to Jerusalem for a secret conference with the procurator of Judea. Both the envoy and I had reckoned on this possibility and had planned to use it to advance my interest in obtaining the vacant post.

Quaestoris later reported to me in detail on his audience with a disturbed and sullen Pilate. The envoy told me that he had suggested me and in support of his suggestion had listed my numerous abilities and accomplishments with great care and at great length, sparing not even the most minute point that might contribute its weight to the overall balance. Pilate had been morose, then listened with a cool reserve which changed to mild interest as the envoy went on praising my attributes. When Quaestoris at last finished his catalog, Pontius Pilate remained sitting, head in hand, in thoughtful silence. The envoy, sensing what he thought to be hesitancy on the governor's part, hastened to add several additional points, which he had kept in reserve for just such a situation. But the procurator raised his head abruptly, waved a hand to silence his emissary, and said in irritation; "Never mind all that trash—is he good-looking?"

"Your Highness?"

"Come, come, it isn't necessary for you to stall—I've been around you too long, my good man, much too long. I know all the ruses of your diplomacy by heart. Is the fellow good-looking or is he not?"

"I fail to see the point—"

"To hell with what you fail to see! Answer my question, will you? Or have you been too long among the Jews to obey my orders as they are given you?"

"The man has an appearance which is not . . . altogether unpleasing to the eye, Your Highness. But it is the inner substance of the man which mandates that he be chosen."

"Is that so?"

"Yes, Your Highness."

"Which means, I suppose, that he is ravishing. Tell me, my tongue-tied diplomat, have I seen him at my court?"

"No, Your Highness. Unfortunately, he has never had the pleasure of bathing in your radiance."

"Which displeases you greatly, I am sure."

"I wish to say—"

"Do you sleep with him?"

"Your Highness?"

"So first your speech and now your hearing fails you, Quaestoris. Perhaps you are ill. Perhaps Jew-sickness has laid you low. Perhaps you are no longer the man to stand in my stead in the court of Herod the Jew-king? I am told by authorities who ought to know that one needs very sharp ears in that court—have you heard as much, my ambassador?"

"Even a deaf man knows what jackals sound like, Your Highness."

"That was well said, Quaestoris!"

"Yes, I sleep with him."

"And that is well done, I am sure. So, you sleep with a candidate for the position, do you? Well, from this moment on, Quaestoris, you shall fill Judea's new minister of war with the seed of Rome! Pilate has commanded and Herod will obey!"

Thus—according to the word of Quaestoris—was Zerubabel's ministry secured for me: I should have the spy system, *Patish* and the war department all three under my command; and I should have the firm alliance of the general Livinius to buttress and support my aims. Some days later, a messenger who rode behind the glittering eagle of Rome bore a message made fast with the imperial seal of the empire to King Herod, whose haste in issuing an edict naming me war minister was exceeded only by his reluctance to deliver it in person to the subjects of his court. For in the interim, the struggle to obtain the ministry had grown even more furious, with the scribes, Pharisees and Sadducees adding their own favorites to the list of candidates. In addition, still another foe of Livinius, the general who commanded the famed Tenth Legion, had advanced the cause of his choice—a man by the name of Shimshon Hanatzri, a half-breed Jew who was known for his traffic in drugs and slaves and was much respected and feared.

Herod's edict caused a storm of protest, as the tetrarch knew it would. A hundred voices called for Herod, a thousand hands stretched forth to him. The king wanted no part of it. He stayed in seclusion, under heavy guard, and a scribe took down the complaints patiently and then burned them in secret as he had been commanded. The outcry rose to a peak, but it was not heard by the ears for which it was intended. Herod's friends called him "the fox." His detractors called him "the mole." King Herod cared nothing for what he said was babble. Shut away from "the horde," he listened instead to the incantations of sorcerers, the sagacities of soothsayers, the harmonies of minstrels, the adoration of lackeys, the lullabies of whores. The grumbling lessened and grew faint: everyone knew that the will of Rome had been done. And, as the protestations subsided, the protestors turned their attention to me, their irate voices growing sweeter by the hour. However, like the tetrarch whom I was to serve, I became deaf to all entreaties.

The investiture came a week later in a full court ceremony, with hundreds of courtiers, officials and guests in attendance. The Romans were there in force—Livinius and a number of other generals and high-ranking officers, two senators on a visit from Rome, a proconsul on a mission from Damascus, Pilate's military adjutant, representatives of the priesthood and of the major parties. The palace was magnificently decked out, and a large number of Roman troops, in dress array, had marched in to stand in review along with Herod's soldiers. The trumpets blared, lances and spears glittered, shields and swords clashed in unison. I walked slowly along the walls of living men on the parade ground, taking the salute with the full knowledge that it was due me. If a soldier passed out and lay in my path as I walked, I stepped over his body as if he were a corpse; and I ordered the unit commander to have the man flogged. The presence of so many Roman units eased Herod's fears, and the monarch appeared, first on the parade ground, where the entire field presented arms in one crashing stroke, and later inside the palace, where he was to personally officiate.

A purple carpet led from the ivory-layered doors of the great throne room to the opposite end, where on a marble dais the King of the Jews sat on his throne, staring morosely out at the assembly as if he wished it to disappear before his very eyes. Beside him, stiff of body and heavily made up, was his Queen. As I moved down the carpet between the twin rows of spectators, I observed the pair, slowing down as I neared them so that I could have more time for observation. The tetrarch bit his nails, touched the tip of his nose and his chin with a finger, fidgeted with his scepter as if it were a poisonous snake. He was a tall man with a rounded back and high shoulders that made him look uncomfortable, as if he had never been completely at ease with his body, as if even after all the years he had spent with it he still found it alien to him. He had a long, thin, hollow-cheeked face with skin the color of aged meal. His eyes had oversized lids the color of lead, but the eyes themselves appeared colorless and seemed to focus only with considerable difficulty; his nose was thin and severe; and his lips were no more than two lines over a receding jaw, so fleshless that they seemed to have been painted on his face as an afterthought. His hands were puffy—they looked like the bellies of toads—but the fingers were short, blunt and cruel: they looked the sort that could do any mischief they chose. Altogether, King Herod gave the impression of being a man who was uncertain of the next breath he must needs draw. He struck me as a man for whom hidden bells of terror tolled interminably within his mind: he seemed terrified, haunted, volatile, erratic—a soul in search of an existence which, like a butterfly, kept dancing outside his reach. I thought it would not serve a man well to fall into his hands, for this was a man whose first impulse was to kill, and a man who had no earthly reasons to check his impulses. As I marched down the long aisle, I looked directly into his face, but he averted his glance. I reached the dais, and with all eyes watching me, ascended the twelve steps which signified the twelve tribes of Israel; at the top, I went down on my knees and bowed my head reverently. There was a pause. I waited. In the silence I heard the monarch snicker. And then the scepter touched my shoulder lightly and a reedy, wheezing voice said, "Arise, thou whom I have appointed Judea's minister of war; arise, O son of Abraham, and make thy way in peace . . ."

I stood to faint applause. The king's cheeks, as I could see, were faintly scarred by pockmarks. On his hairline lips was a smirk whose meaning I, and perhaps the tetrarch himself, could only guess at. On her throne beside her husband, Queen Herodias leaned forward the better to scrutinize me. She was almost as tall as her mate and heavier of limb. She wore a gold tunic with two slits out of which her pointed nipples and the tips of her breasts protruded. Her fleshy arms were circled by dozens of bracelets fashioned of silver and gold, and the nails of her fingers were very long—perhaps two inches or more—and lacquered with gold. Earrings the length of a dagger swung from her lobes, her mouth was painted scarlet, the lids of her eyes were iridescent. She stared at me coldly, setting her tongue—which looked like a third nipple—between her dark lips and slowly, with a kind of sullen insolence, studying me. I backed down the stairs, my eyes locked to the glittering stare of the Queen of the Jews. Then it was over. The trumpets wailed. The guards in their splendid attire wheeled about. Herod and his wife were gone—vanished as though they were apparitions who could remain only an allotted time and must then disappear. I was surrounded by a small number of well-wishers and by a larger number of those who wished to appear well-wishers. The general Livinius pushed and shoved his way through the crowd to get to me. He pressed my hand with his iron grip, put his big, bald head close to mine, and whispered only a single word: "Checkmate!"

Late that night Quaestoris and I lay in bed, sated with food, wine and sex. He stroked my cheek gently and said, "Well, darling, we have won at last—as I promised you."

"No," I said. "No, we haven't won at all. But now at least we have a chance to win."

Quaestoris was silent for a time. Then he said, "You mean to go far, don't you? Very far."

"As far as I can."

"But—"

"But what?"

The envoy hesitated.

"Out with it, Quaestoris! Say what you mean!"

"But you are Jewish."

"So I am Jewish. So what?"

Quaestoris shook his head. "It is not a Jewish world," he said.

I smiled. "Then one of two things will happen," I said. "Either I will change myself for the world . . . or the world will change itself for me."

"You are very arrogant, my little Hebrew war minister."

I ignored Quaestoris. "Or perhaps," I went on, "or perhaps the world is ready for something else—something neither Jewish nor Roman, something new sprung of both. What do you say to that?"

"I don't see it," said Quaestoris, sliding his hand down my body to my loins. "I don't see it at all."

I shrugged. "You don't have to," I said. "As long as I do."

Ten days later, a day after my thirty-third birthday, the war ministry guards who stood duty at the doors to my private chambers opened them to admit Elazar, who gave me a message bearing the seal with the hammer of *Patish* on it. I sat at the great olive-wood table before which men bowed, scraped, groveled, trembled and swallowed anger that later gnawed at their vitals and kept them awake the night long. I broke the seal and read the communiqué:

My lord and master, in accordance with your orders, I have as of this day apprehended the son of Yosef, the carpenter, resident of Nazareth and his wife, Mara, who is himself a carpenter residing and working in the city. He is safely in the custody of *Patish*, unharmed as you have yourself ordered, and shall remain so until you shall direct otherwise.

Also in compliance with your command, the chief steward of your late lamented father, called Avner, and your late father's scribe, called Amnon, were as of the day before yesterday apprehended and as of this date executed by the men of *Patish* under my personal command. May I add, as an eyewitness to all that took place, that the two men were taken in the dead of night, in complete secrecy and entirely without resistance. They were brought directly to headquarters where they suffered death by garroting and where their bodies were incinerated in the cellar oven and their ashes sold with those of other slain men for fertilizer.

My lord and master, so was thy will done. And so ends my report.

I instructed Melech the Galilean to have the prisoner, the "son of Yosef, the carpenter, resident of Nazareth," bound, blindfolded and transferred to the underground vault which my father in his last years had also dug in our old home on the village mountain slope south of Bethlehem. As soon as I had the opportunity, I wished to journey there and speak with my brother for the first time since he had been taken away more than two decades before. I had formulated no clear or definite plan for his future, feeling that the decision on how I was to deal with him would come out of our meeting.

I did not have a chance to go to Bethlehem for more than a month. There was much urgent work that had to be done, and I was not able to leave Herod's fortress—even to pay a visit to *Patish* headquarters in the villa, to which I had taken title by law. Of primary concern was the war department, which Zerubabel had sorely neglected for many months and which as a result had deteriorated. The whole ministry had to be overhauled from top to bottom, its dead wood removed and new personnel installed. Though *Patish* was to remain essentially as it was— an independently functioning organ—I wanted to better integrate its activities with those of the ministry and to coordinate operations so there was no overlapping. I called this phase of my work "Operation Two-Headed Cobra."

I worked long hours and I worked hard, and even after a short time, I was able to see the results of my effort. I tightened the reins, unified the command, purified the hitherto muddied policy of the department. Everyone in the department feared me by reputation, obeyed me by instinct, knew me by sight. There was not a single official, whether top echelon or petty, who had not received my praise or felt my sting. I was everywhere at once—or I made certain to give the impression of being so—and I was as inflexible in my demands on myself as I was on others. I never flinched from duty and expected as much from subordinates. In short, I was a leader and saw to it that those who followed never lost sight of that fact.

By the end of the fourth week, the ministry seemed like a corpse which had sprung to life again. My success filled me with new energy and with greater zest. I threw myself frenziedly into my tasks—so much so that Quaestoris began to complain bitterly, arguing that I had "fallen in love with a mistress far more demanding" than he could ever think of being. Once or twice, he actually came to my private office at the ministry seeking, as he put it, to "extricate" me from "my folly," but I had him turned away without seeing him by the guards. He was greatly incensed and threatened me with many and assorted punishments, ranging from suicide at one end of the scale to a full denunciation before the procurator of Judea at the other. Of course none of his threats were carried out. The next time we met, he wept like a child and begged my forgiveness—which I gave only after thorough enjoyment of his misery. I made love to him with a fury that left him half-unconscious, patted him on the rump and called him a "bumpkin." When he fell asleep, I departed, leaving him a note that was calculated to cause him fresh agony. During the last few months I had come to realize that the envoy was more a source of amusement than of pleasure. I confessed this realization to no one.

Several times during this period I met in secret with the general Livinius in order to draw up plans and to fix a timetable for their implementation. The general was well pleased with the progress I had made, but was also cautious in his assessment. "We've just gotten started," he told me with a smile. "The opening, I should say, is rather a routine one. No formidable opposition up until now. However, you will see that the game will soon become complicated—and that the finale will be nothing short of a maze." He laughed heartily. "Well, my Hebrew war lord—does it sound at all familiar to your ear?"

"Quite familiar, general."

"And we must needs keep in mind," said Livinius, rising to go, "that we are taking Judea away from the Jews—not the Romans!"

I said nothing, but answered his salute with one of my own.

At the very first opportunity I ordered my conveyance readied and drove with all haste to Bethlehem. Through the night, as we rode, I went over in my mind passages from my journals, which I had reread the night before. The man who was overseer at the Bethlehem estate was the man I would eventually replace Avner with at Nazareth. Called Onan, he had worked for me when I was chief interpreter at court. He was a very short, slight, taciturn fellow with slanted eyes and a diffident smile whom I had nicknamed "the asp" the first time I ever saw him; though we rarely exchanged more than a dozen words when we met, we had a great respect for each other's deadliness.

The dungeon room in which my brother was detained had in one of its walls an aperture which could not be detected from within. I put my face to the wall and fitted my eye to the hole. I could see my brother clearly. He was sitting on a low wooden stool in the far corner. At his feet were a rude bundle of clothing which had come undone, worn sandals and a staff rubbed smooth with use. The young man whom I watched seemed to have nothing in common with the boy of whom my father had spoken the last time that the subject arose. He was a good head taller than I, of slight, almost fragile build, with soft round shoulders between which he appeared to hunch as if for protection; his waist was narrow, his knees angular, his legs long and lean. His face was very well made, with high cheekbones accenting it, a finely modeled nose that was not quite aquiline and a round, cleanly clefted chin: it was a face that had both delicacy and strength and a cast of beauty that was almost feminine. His hair was sand-colored, and his eyes a deep brown that seemed at times black, but turned again when he moved his face and the light struck them differently; as I watched him, his gaze shifted, and I saw that his eyes had in them a strange, diffuse look whose meaning I could not decipher. I found that the more I watched his eyes, the more they puzzled me. On his lap lay my brother's striking hands. They had pronounced, beautiful veins on their backs, suggesting both the masculine and feminine; and the fingers, which were extremely long and tapered, moved with deftness and surety. As he sat, my brother joined his hands together: they looked like good, intimate partners that had worked long and hard together, would live peacefully with each other always and would never part. I found that I was quite fascinated by them. Oddly enough, when I realized the attraction, the thought that ran through my mind was "Cut them off!" but I had no idea why I thought such a thing. My brother's feet were bare, and at times he rubbed the instep of one with the heel of the other. Thus I stood, face pressed to the aperture, for a long while—longer by far than I had intended—watching my brother sit quietly, lost in distracted thought. What was in his mind, I had no way of guessing. At length I drew back, turned to Onan, and said, "All right, open up now."

Alone, I stepped into the dungeon and signaled that the door be shut. It closed behind me with a loud, grating sound that did not disturb my brother. I walked slowly forward, clearing my throat, but my brother remained as he was on the stool—silent, immobile, staring into the air. He did not seem to know or care to know that someone had come in. A smile appeared on his lips for an instant and then vanished as suddenly as it had arrived; the light in his eyes intensified and then disappeared. Scant feet from his outstretched legs, I stopped. If the prisoner saw me, he gave no sign. His head was bent slightly forward, and I noted that despite his youth the hair at the crown of his skull was already thinning. The scalp was raw and scaly in spots, and there were the marks of nails in it. Up close, I saw that the cheeks were faintly pitted and marred by evidence of old wounds. At their corners, the lips were crusted. And the hands, too, though fine, were callused, their knuckles bruised, fingers torn, nails black and broken. I had given strict and explicit orders that my brother not be harmed in the slightest, and I was certain that Melech had seen to it that they were carried out. It was clear that life had ill-used my brother, that he had taken many a blow, received many an insult, that he had been abused and maltreated, that he had struggled and suffered for his portion of bread. I examined him again, and try as I would, could find no resemblance between him and me. No one in the world would have called us brothers —neither in body nor in spirit.

I smiled, and with my silver-handled riding whip reached out and tapped his right shoulder lightly, much as the King of the Jews had touched mine with his scepter in the throne room. My brother looked up at me. He smiled. "Who are you?" I asked.

"Who are you?" he returned.

"You don't quite understand. I ask questions—I don't answer them. Now tell me who you are and be quick about it."

"I am nobody."

"And I am the man who has imprisoned you. If you wish to leave your cell alive, you had better answer me truthfully."

My brother shrugged his shoulders. "I am the son of Yosef, the carpenter, and Mara, his wife."

"What sort of people are they?"

"They are good, they are evil. They understand, they fail to understand. They hope, they despair. They try to live without denying life to others."

"What is their political persuasion?"

My brother looked puzzled. "They have no political—persuasion, as you say. They have nothing to do with politics. They believe that one government is as corrupt as another. They believe that the rulers are for the rulers and none else: that the subjects are as fodder in their hands, as dust under their feet. They trust neither the man with the sword nor the man with the scepter. They believe that the man who says he speaks for the welfare of the people lies, that in truth he speaks only for his own welfare."

"They say these things? To whom do they say them?"

"They would not know how to say them. And who would listen to them if they were to speak? They are old and ailing. Yosef's back is bent almost double. And Mara's legs are going; she can scarcely walk to market."

"Then how do you know they believe them?"

"I feel it," he said.

"In other words, it is your own interpretation. These thoughts are in your mind, are they not?"

"Perhaps. They come to me. I don't know from where."

"I see. Were you born in this country?"

"I was born in Bethlehem."

"Your parents were wealthy then?"

"They were poor. Very poor. And they are still poor. There are those who wish them to be poor—"

"And who would they be?"

"It's obvious," said my brother. "Those who are wealthy."

"I see. Do you have sisters—or brothers?"

"I am the only child."

"You have lived all of your life in this land?"

"No, I lived with my parents in Egypt for some years."

"Why did your family sojourn there?"

"I don't know. I have asked Yosef many times, but he is silent. And Mara cannot or will not explain it."

"Were they ever in trouble with the authorities—in Judea or in Egypt?"

"They left the authorities alone and the authorities left them alone. It's best that way, you know—best to leave the authorities to their own devices."

"This is your—own theory?"

"This is my belief."

"I see. You do a great deal of thinking, do you not?"

My brother shrugged.

"And you draw many conclusions?"

"It seems that the conclusions reach me—almost of their own accord."

"Are you literate?"

My brother's eyes widened with interest. "I can read some . . . and write too."

"When you returned to Judea from Egypt—what then?"

"We settled again in Nazareth, the city we had departed from.

That sometimes happens in life—return to a point of departure. But it is never the same."

"And what did you do?"

"I was apprenticed to a master carpenter in the city. As my father did before me, so I learned to work with wood." My brother looked away dreamily. "I wanted to work in clay, to turn the potter's wheel, to fire the kiln . . . but Yosef insisted on wood. So I set myself to work with wood."

"And with men?"

"Work with men? How do you mean?"

"With the spirit of men?"

My brother spread his hands. "Am I God that I should work with the spirit of men?"

"Do you go to the synagogue? Do you keep the fasts and the holy days? Do you observe the Sabbath? Do you pray? Do you believe in the Deity?"

"If you ask me about rituals, I consider them merely that. If you ask me about my belief in God, it is easy to say yes—too easy. To believe in God a man must commit his life to that belief."

"I am not accustomed to your kind of answers," I said. "I pose my questions clearly; I expect clear answers. Now, tell me. What is your religion?"

"It is not yours."

"That's not good enough! What is your religion?"

"Human."

"Meaning—?"

"That a man's religion must be for himself. That a man must save himself if he is to survive."

"Save himself from whom?"

"From his worst enemy."

"Who is?"

"Himself."

"And the government—is it an enemy as well?"

My brother's hands locked and fell apart, joined and came apart. "The government will fall. And the government that takes its place will fall as well. And the government which succeeds that one, it shall also collapse in its time. And always . . . man will be left to face himself . . . to do battle with the ultimate enemy: himself."

"Have you spoken to people? In Nazareth? In the villages where you do your work, your carpentry? Have you spoken and have they listened?"

"Who would listen to me?"

"I am listening. Very closely and very well."

"But you—you are a gentleman and a lord. You are an authority. Perhaps you are the king, I don't know. The people in Nazareth and in the villages have often laughed at me."

"You believe—that I am the king?"

"Perhaps you are."

"What makes you think so?"

"You look like a king."

"And how does a king look?"

"Like there is nobody on earth before him."

"And why would the king listen so carefully to you when the others mock you?"

"Because the king wants to understand every person over whom he rules."

"Why would he want that?"

"So he can know better how to deceive his subjects."

"And have you told people this idea—the one you have just told me?"

My brother shook his head. "No. They would not understand."

"And what if—you were king?"

A shudder went through the prisoner's body. He started violently, closed his eyes and then covered them with a hand. "God is King," he whispered.

"What's that?"

"God is King," he whispered. "But I cannot see Him. He will not reveal Himself. He will not speak to me. He will not listen to me. Perhaps He laughs . . ."

"You—hold converse with God?"

"If I can know His will? Yes. But His will is that it be my will."

"Does He ever appear to you in your dreams?"

"If dreams are sent by Him? Yes. But I must unravel them." My brother stroked his chin. "It always ends up with me," he said. "It begins with God and ends with me."

"What do you think of the priests?"

My brother laughed loudly. "Priests? Priests are monkeys! They swing from their tails, they thump their chests, they scratch their rumps, they screw up their ugly mugs and chatter from morning until night. They stuff their fat bellies, satisfy their lust, pick lice from their scalp and dance about God's Law. But they have nothing to do with it, nothing at all! They have not the faintest idea what it means!"

I tapped with my quirt on my open palm. "And the Zealots? Do you know about them?"

"Everybody knows about them. In Nazareth, in Tiberias, in Safed, in Acre, in the villages—wherever you go, there is talk. But the talk is in secret, the talk is private, when people are sure no authorities or spies are around."

"What kind of spies?"

"But you are an authority. Surely you must know that the country is overrun with spies?" My brother smiled. "They are worse than locusts. Only the priests are worse—yes, the priests are a plague. The others ignore God openly, without subterfuge. But the priests pretend to love God—and instead pervert His Law."

"Do you know any Zealots?"

"No, but I hear about them. I hear that people are joining them. Old men who say they want to die in freedom. Young men who say they want to live in freedom. I have heard the talk everywhere, and beneath the talk the whispering, and under the whispering the silence which is louder than all."

"And the Romans?"

"The Romans," said my brother quietly, "honor the fist. But the fist is flesh and will decay. They honor the sword. But the sword is brittle and can be broken. They put their trust in armor. But armor rusts and chinks appear in it. They worship gods of wood and stone. But wood and stone have no feeling and cannot understand the heart of man. They put their faith in empire. But empire unravels at its edges, as do the threads of a great rug. The Romans take stock only in what they can see and touch. But the senses alone deceive."

"Tell me who you are!"

"A man," said my brother.

"Whose son are you?"

"I am the son of man."

"And woman?"

"What about woman?"

"Have you been with a woman—have you known a woman carnally?"

248

"I have not."

"Why not?"

My brother shrugged. "I don't know. Perhaps it is not time yet. I have wanted a woman, but I have not found one. Neither would I consort with prostitutes."

"Have you stayed with a man?"

"Never."

"Have you spilled your seed alone?"

"I have."

"Did it satisfy you?"

"No." My brother shook his head thoughtfully. "The seed of man," he said, "is spirit. And spirit must be planted." My brother looked up at me, his eyes clouded. "Please tell me now—now that I have answered all of your questions—why have you arrested me?"

I smiled. "That's simple. Because you are human."

"What will you do with me?"

"Keep you," I mused. "Yes, keep you. You are an interesting bird, and I shall want to keep you caged for a while. So that I can study you. Do you have any objection?"

"My parents will worry. And I shall worry about them. Yosef cannot work as he did. And Mara is ill. Besides her legs, her eyes are going. She will be blind one day soon."

"I will see to it that your parents are provided for. Is there anything else?"

"I don't know."

"You don't mind being shut away?"

"Shut away from whom? I have no one except for Yosef and Mara. No other relatives. And no one calls me friend. I have no woman, as I told you. I am no shepherd—my flock will not miss me. I cannot be shut away from myself—I am with myself always. And God—God is everywhere."

"God is in your cell?"

My brother smiled. "God is everywhere," he said, closing his eyes and rocking to and fro on his stool. "God is nowhere."

The war ministry had a number of special detention cells under the minister's direct authority, and I ordered my brother transferred to one of them so that I could have access to him whenever I chose. Three days later, Elazar brought me a message from *Patish* that my order had been carried out. The message came to me at seven in the evening, while I was taking supper in my office at the ministry. I had two more appointments scheduled after supper and had planned to leave for Quaestoris's villa, but the news of my brother's arrival made me change my mind. I was drawn irresistibly to see my prisoner. My final visitor of the night was Aquilius, a veteran Roman brigade commander in the Tenth Legion; he was visiting the fortress at the express invitation of Queen Herodias, and I had asked him to drop in and see me. Of late, I had taken to the study of military tactics, was reading extensively on the subject, and linking the theory to discussions with field officers whenever I could get hold of competent ones. My aim was, of course, to fashion out of Herod's forces—which were used primarily in actions against the rebels and to demonstrate that Judea had a measure of autonomy—a disciplined and efficient fighting machine. I listened to Aquilius talk in his blunt, disorganized, self-laudatory fashion, gleaning what I could from his blustering monologue and then finally making my excuses as politely as I could.

I scribbled a hasty note to Quaestoris and handed it to Elazar to carry, scarcely bothering to seal it. Then I locked my notes and maps away in the vault and left my office. Herod's fortress in its lower levels was like a beehive in rock, and the block of cells in which my brother was imprisoned had its location deep in the heart of the maze. All of its prisoners were kept alive by the State for one reason or another, although there were a number against whom the charges had long ago been lost or forgotten; and there were even a few whom time had proven innocent but whom nobody had bothered to set free.

The special detention block in which my brother was kept consisted of a small, gallerylike cavern in which there were four individual cells. I, together with the warder and several guards, passed the first, in which there was a naked woman no more than twenty who paced to and fro without stopping and without seeing us. Her body—which had quite obviously been beautiful once—was scarred from neck to ankles with the mark of whip and cane. This was a former bodyservant of Herodias who had been accused of trying to poison the queen and cast into the dungeon.

The next two cells in line were empty. Two prison servants were busy scrubbing the floor and walls of the second cell. The warder confided that Kalbi, the head jailer, had that very morning disemboweled the inmate—a convicted rapist and murderer—with a broken stick in a fit of rage: now, the cell had to be cleaned.

In the last cell of the block, beyond whose far wall the excavation did not extend, was my brother. There was no window in the cell, but a fissure in the sheer face of the mountain had been widened with a chisel to admit light. My brother was sitting directly beneath the fissure, his head bathed in the moonlight that fell through it so that I could see every feature of his face.

The door swung open and the warder drew back.

My brother looked up. A smile lit his face when he saw me—I thought that he was glad I had come. "Come in, come in, my brother," he said. "Come in and be seated—"

"Your brother? What are you saying? Who put such madness in your mouth?"

The prisoner was puzzled. "All men are brothers," he said in a quiet voice. "Have you not understood that much in life?"

"I see—I see what you are driving at."

"All men are brothers," the prisoner mused thoughtfully. "God, our father in heaven, created us all one family. As it is written in the prophets: 'Have we not all one father?' "

I seated myself on the chair near the door, resting my whip across my knees. "Do you know what cell you have the honor of occupying?"

"A prison cell." My brother smiled.

"In this very cell a famous prisoner was kept for many months. He was called Yochanan the Baptist and he had visions of God. Do you know of him?"

My brother shook his head. "There are many of whom I know nothing," he said.

"He used to perform a strange ritual in which he immersed his adherents in running water," I said. "Have you any idea why he did it?"

Again my brother shook his head.

"He wanted to drown them in God!" I laughed. "Yes, he was in this very cell for many months—the last one in the block. And then one fine day the queen decided that she would part his head from the rest of his body. Which she did. Unfortunately, Yochanan's soul could not abide the separation and departed from this world. The queen kept his head for a time, amusing herself in her own inimitable fashion, and then she wearied of the sport and disposed of it. A truly unhappy and grotesque episode without a shred of political significance. What did the State gain by removing a charlatan's head? Nothing. What political purpose did it serve? None whatsoever. It was all whim. Caprice." I snapped my fingers. "Doesn't that frighten you?"

"I have no fear of ghosts. Only living men can harm me—and I will not fear their harm before it comes."

"Are you not frightened that I will do the same to you?" I persisted.

"You are my brother." The prisoner smiled. "I have no fear."

Then my brother rose up from his stool as if to come over to me and embrace me. He took one step forward, yet did not take another. His face turned deathly pale and a violent trembling seized his limbs.

"Are you ill?" I asked. "What's the matter with you?"

My prisoner did not answer me, so forceful was the seizure. His body shook with agitation as if it must come apart. Then his knees gave way and he slipped to the floor, moaning as he fell. I got up and walked over to him. Then I heard his first words. "Violence . . . corruption . . ." The breathing was labored and harsh, like the sound of the wind rushing through a canebrake. "Violence . . . corruption . . . whoredom—everywhere . . . everywhere . . ."

My brother whimpered and was silent. But then his lips moved, and he spoke again. And his voice was gentle and lilting and seemed not the voice of my brother as I had heard it before. And he spoke from the depths of his silence, saying, "The poor sigh and the rich make sport of them, saying, 'Why do these ingrates vex us with their sorrows—have we not troubles enough of our own?' The people groan with their burdens and cry out for amelioration, and the government pretends that it does not hear their cries. And the poor are downtrodden and craven 'and depraved . . . and in their depravity steal even from each other, crying, 'Mine—all is mine. As nothing was mine before, so all shall belong to me now.' And when refuse, stinking garbage falls into the street from the rich man's passing wagon, then poor men run out with lust in their eyes and murder in their hearts and clash and roll in the dust and give up their lives in the bitterness of the dust."

My brother's voice dropped almost to a whisper: "Yes, the rich man and the government are the two great millstones between which the bones of the people are crushed to powder; and, lo, the poor cry out in their agony: but when did pain ever stop a millstone from its grinding? And the poor say, 'Enough, enough . . . we are naked and have nothing left to give except our very skin and bones, except the eyes of our wives and the limbs of our babes!' And the landowners hold out their hands and say, 'Give more!' And the government holds up its sword and says, 'Give more!' And the poor say, 'We cannot.'" And the tears crawled down my brother's cheeks slowly, as if loath to leave them; and he sighed heavily and whispered, "Oh, my pity . . . my pity is boundless even as the sea . . . My pity is vast even as the sky . . . Oh, that with the strength of the pity in my heart I might heal the sick and the wounded, make whole those that are crippled, make straight the lame, give back sight to the blind, make pure again the leper . . . Oh that I might bring life again to those who are dead."

My brother moaned softly, the muscles of his mouth and jaw relaxed, his body went slack, his eyelids fluttered and his eyes opened. Their pupils were large and very dark and yet radiant, and a look of sereneness was on his features, as if the storm that had been was gone and fled.

I turned my back on the prisoner and went to the chair and sat in it.

"Is that where your political ideas come from?" I asked.

"What do you mean?" my brother asked.

"Do you get your political ideas from your trances?"

"What political ideas?"

"The rich—the poor—the government—the priests—oppression: the lot of it."

"I have nothing to do with politics."

"What you say does, my prisoner. Or do you claim, as do some of our—rabble-rousers, that you are not responsible for what you say, that you are possessed by an angel—or by a devil?"

"I claim nothing."

"These cures, these miracles you speak of—do you claim that you have performed them, that you perform them now?"

"I claim nothing."

"Can you make the lame straight?"

"My own steps are crooked."

"Can you restore sight to the blind?"

"I dwell in darkness myself."

"Can you make the leper clean?"

"I am leprous myself."

"Can you give tongue to the dumb?"

"My own tongue stumbles."

"And the dead—can you quicken them?"

"I can scarcely stir my own body."

"Then, my prisoner, what is it you claim?"

"I claim nothing, my brother."

I left strict orders that my prisoner not be harmed, that his needs be looked after and that if anything untoward happened I be notified at once. And I went a step further— I left a special order that the female inmate in the first cell not be touched by any prison official on the pain of severe punishment. The head jailer Kalbi lifted an eyebrow when I mentioned her. "The female prisoner in the first cell of the special detention block? But, my lord, she is the queen's own captive. Nobody says anything about her except the sovereign."

Kalbi was a short, squat, bull-headed man in his thirties who went about, winter and summer, bare to the waist, revealing his bulging arms, broad chest and muscular back, which were totally hairless and covered with strange-smelling grease. His skull, too, was completely bald; his front teeth, lower and upper, were gold—the other officials said he stole it from corpses; and he wore thick gold earrings that flashed in the prison torchlight whenever he moved. He had a habit of ducking his head as if he were a weasel and peering up at one with ugly, yellowish eyes whose irises looked like scum. I disliked the man intensely and would have gotten rid of him except that he was under the protection of the king and his removal did not seem to me worth the trouble it would occasion.

"No prisoner," I said, shaking my whip in irritation, "belongs solely to the queen or to anyone else. As head jailer, you ought to know that very well. And if you don't, I'll refresh your faulty memory. Every inmate in this prison is the property of the State. As war minister, I have my own State reasons for wanting no—accident to befall her. I charge you, Kalbi, to see to it that no fate such as overtook the unfortunate prisoner in the second cell overtakes her. Otherwise, Kalbi, you will find yourself forced to deal with me—king or no king. Do I make myself clear?"

Kalbi turned pale. "I understand, my lord," he said.

When I arrived home, my chief butler, who was visibly on edge, told me that I had a guest. I realized that it must be Quaestoris, was greatly annoyed but refrained from chastising the servant, who had obviously been browbeaten by the envoy. I dismissed the servant and went directly into my bedchamber, where Quaestoris was sprawled on a divan. I saw that he was in a state. His clothes were rumpled and stained, his hair disheveled, his cheeks unshaven, his eyes red-rimmed and bloodshot. The skin of his face was gray and puffy, and he had cut himself on his right temple. He looked altogether distraught. "It's late," I said angrily, throwing off my cloak, "it's late and I'm tired and I sent you a note explaining matters, damn it. Now, what the hell are you doing here?"

"Yes," said the envoy. "It is late. Very late."

"Never mind the damn histrionics—just tell me what you mean by coming here at this hour. Can you tell me that much without putting on a Greek tragedy?"

"You speak to me—you dare to speak to *me* that way?"

"How the hell do you want me to speak to you? Look, it's not as if I didn't send word. I wrote you a note—"

Quaestoris winced and put a hand to his brow. "Why," he said hoarsely, "why? Tell me why you didn't come as you promised?"

I sat on the bed and removed my sandals. "Listen, you make me weary—weary with your damn whining. I've told you once, twice—a thousand times that I was busy. I'm not going to go into it again, and that's final."

"No, of course you're not going to go into it again. Not now, not when you're high and mighty, not when you're a lord, not when you're a Jew-minister sniffing the king's private parts!" Quaestoris sat up, trembling. "But who put you there—who, you dog? Who lifted you from the sewer and set you on high—who, you ingrate? Who pulled you from a flunky's livery and suited you in armor—who, you swine?"

I shook my head. "You helped me, of course. That doesn't mean you own me."

"Helped you?" choked Quaestoris. "*Helped* you? I *made* you, Jew —and I can as easily unmake you!"

I rose from the bed and removed my tunic. "Now just a moment, Quaestoris. Aren't you going a bit too far? Calm yourself—"

"Too far? No, I've not gone far enough. And don't try to calm me, because it's beyond that—beyond that, do you hear? I've taken enough

255

from you—too much from you—and I'm fed up, finished. I'm not going to let things slide any longer—I'm not going to overlook them. You may very well be Judea's war minister to the puppet court of a puppet monarch, but to me you're no more than a little Hebrew whore—no better than a thousand others!"

"You're drunk," I said. "You're stinking drunk. Get hold of yourself, Roman. I'm in no mood for your tantrums."

"Tantrums, are they? Tantrums, eh?" The envoy tried to rise, his face flushing with an ugly scarlet color, but fell back exhausted on the divan. He breathed with difficulty, and when he had regained his wind somewhat, wiped his lips. "I promise you," he gasped, "I promise you you'll pay, and pay dearly—"

I smiled. "I know your promises, Quaestoris. After all, you're a diplomat—you speak for the State."

"They were good enough to install you as minister of war, Jew-devil! They were good enough for that, weren't they?"

"You're a child, a spoiled child. And you're having a tantrum."

"So I'm a child in the throes of a tantrum, am I? Well, perhaps you and your whore-lover can laugh this tantrum off!"

With shaking fingers, the envoy drew forth a crumpled document which he held out to me. I let it hang in his fingers while I removed my underclothes and then, naked, went over and took it from him. He smirked and then laughed. I glanced at what Quaestoris had written. It was quite apparent from the first words that the envoy had penned a scathing denunciation of my person. Written in Latin and in transliterate Hebrew, the text was a garbled and scarcely legible attack which accused me of every crime imaginable, from high treason against the emperor to necrophilia. I reread it. I did not think that anyone in his right mind would pay serious attention to the diplomat's drunken scrawling; nevertheless, I was quite disturbed that Quaestoris had conceived the denunciation and actually written it down. To me, it set a dangerous precedent. For Quaestoris to malign me in speech, however virulent the attack, was one thing; to set forth his allegations in a written text, which would begin to live an independent life of its own, feeding on time and on the scrutiny of hostile eyes, was entirely another matter. A very grave one, I believed.

"Well?" Quaestoris smirked. "Well, are you satisfied? Are you convinced now?"

"Why did you do it?"

"Well, do you still think I'm a child? Do you still think I'm bluffing? Is it still a great joke to you? Am I still a laughingstock to you and your lover?"

"Move over."

"What?"

"Move over and let me sit by you on the divan."

"I don't want your honied words—I don't want you! Stay away from me, you're killing me—"

I touched the envoy's head. "Now, now," I said softly, "there's no need to be so disturbed—no need at all. You know in your heart that I have no lover other than you, no one other than you."

"I know nothing," said Quaestoris in a choked voice. Then he buried his face in his hands and sobbed.

"There, there," I said, stroking his hair, so that in the midst of his weeping he shivered with pleasure. "There's no reason to cry. You Romans don't really believe in your tears anyway."

"Nor you Jews in your laughter," said Quaestoris through his weeping.

"Why?" I whispered close to his ear. "Why did you do such a thing? What did you mean to do with it when you had finished?"

"To give it to Pilate. To end your career and your life—and to end mine!" Quaestoris's body shook with a fresh spasm of grief.

"Come to bed," I urged.

The envoy shook his head vigorously. But he allowed me to pull him up from the divan and lead him there. His weeping grew less as he lay on his back, and his body went limp. As I spoke to him, I began to remove his clothes. "It was very foolish of you to write such accusations, Quaestoris—don't you realize that?"

"You drove me to it—you drove me to it with your harshness!"

"I drive you nowhere, Quaestoris. You drive yourself. You create your own hell, your own avenging gods. You plague your own mind with fantasies and jealousies that have no basis in reality. And the poison within you makes you mad—and so you spill it forth. But don't you realize, Quaestoris, that when you allow the madness of your mind to best you and compel you to write such scurrilous stuff that you not only malign me, but yourself as well? Everyone at court knows exactly how close we have been and how close we are—and so you are bound to be guilty by association. You hang the both of us with one noose. And for what? For the excesses of a diseased imagination? For the faltering of a sick will? I am disappointed in you, noble Quaestoris; I am disappointed and ashamed."

"You gave me your solemn word that you would be with me tonight," sniffled Quaestoris. "Do you know how I waited for you? Do you have any idea of how I longed for you?"

"May the gods of Rome forgive you for this lapse, Quaestoris."

"Do you know what I went through—do you?"

"I know . . . I know. Unfortunately, as you above all people should realize, in lives like ours, matters of State must take precedence over matters of heart. Though I wish it could be otherwise."

The envoy was completely undressed now. I ran my fingers lightly over his chest and smiled affectionately. Though I kept it a secret, I had no use for Quaestoris's body. Its skin had gone gray and coarse, its flesh ran to fat, its muscles were wasting away, even its genital parts were bloated and unsightly—like some foul thing the tide brings ashore after a storm. As if he divined my thoughts, the envoy said plaintively, "You love me no longer."

"Of course I love you, noble Quaestoris! Why do you speak such foolishness? Perhaps it is you who no longer loves me."

"But I do—I do love you," protested the envoy. "More than ever. More than I dreamed I could ever love. It isn't right that I should care for you as much as I do. My love is a leech on me, it sucks me dry, it destroys me. And I know that you do not return it. I know that you have another. I know that you were with your lover tonight, though you deny it a thousand times over."

My fingers slid to the envoy's flabby middle. "You completely fabricate or misinterpret events, Quaestoris, and on the basis of your erroneous interpretations draw conclusions that are utterly false. I have no lover to replace you—no lover could. As for a tryst this very night—I was at the prison. You can substantiate my words with the head jailer, Kalbi. Ask him, if you will—if you dare."

The envoy laughed bitterly. "Verify your words, indeed! Your words are what you wish them to be at the moment, and nothing more! Whatever you say and whatever you do, what has taken place in your life a year ago, a month ago, a day ago or ten minutes ago changes according to what your wish or pleasure is this instant. Your soldiers, your servants, your agents, your spies, your thugs, your murderers are in all places. They are everywhere—there is no respite from them and no escape from them; they cover the earth like a pestilence. And they do your bidding without question, without hesitation—though your bidding bring them death. You control events and the memory of events. You are like a god: you shape the world in the image you choose it to be."

"Ah, Quaestoris! Noble Quaestoris, how well you speak, how like music your speech is! Surely it is one of the many reasons I love you so well!"

"And your speech . . . your words . . . they are lies," said the envoy dolefully, "all lies. But that is because you are a lie yourself—or a succession of lies. You are lie after lie after lie, and at the end of all the lies is the great lie that there is an end to the lies."

"You sculpt in words, my dear Quaestoris—why have you never written?" I slid my hand along the envoy's thigh, and he closed his eyes and moaned softly as though he were in pain and enjoying that pain. "I had to be in prison tonight, my jealous diplomat. I had to interrogate an inmate."

"The minister of war had to personally interrogate?"

"The minister of war does what he decides it is necessary for him to do." I lifted my hand, paused a moment, and then brought it down and lightly touched the envoy's member for an instant and then drew my hand away. "Tell me, that whore of a maidservant in the first cell of the special detention block—do you know whom I'm speaking of?"

Quaestoris shook his head. His lips were parted, his body trembling.

"The bodyservant who tried to poison the queen. Surely you remember her?"

The envoy smiled thinly. "Yes, yes . . . I remember her very well. I remember being sorry that she failed in the attempt. Well, what about the bitch? I thought she would have been dead and buried long ago."

"No, she's quite alive. The queen—amuses herself by playing games with her. What I'm asking is whether the queen is particular about her —possessions?"

"What are you driving at?"

"Could I get hold of her?"

The envoy stared at me. "So she is the lover for whose sake you have abandoned me? A slut of a convict girl! A murderess!"

"Fool! Roman blockhead! If I were consorting with the girl, would

I speak to you openly of her? Where is your balance, your Roman reality?" I clutched him by the shoulders. "I need her—I need her for my purposes! Can I get her? What do you think?"

Quaestoris shrugged. "I don't know. It's possible. Anything's possible. It's even possible for a Roman noble, an adviser to proconsuls and governors, to fall in love with a peasant Jew—for the scion of one of the empire's oldest and most revered families to chase, like a bitch in heat, after a Judean mongrel!" The envoy bit his lower lip. "But why ask me about Herodias? Am I married to your whore Judea? Am I a member of your bastard royal family? Am I some circumcised fop of a courtier? Herod had a plaything in Yochanan. Herodias has a plaything in the girl, whom—if the truth were ever known—she herself probably tried to poison, rather than the other way around! You want to know if it's possible to get the girl, to trade for her, to make a deal for her? Why come to me, whom you hold in such poor esteem, whom you reject? Go to the queen!"

I smiled and placed my hand directly and firmly on the envoy's member, squeezing it with my fingers. "Quaestoris, you will say a word to Herodias about the girl, if I ask you? Quaestoris. My own . . ."

"What?"

"My gifted sculptor, my architect of words, my Roman god—my own love. You will talk to the queen about the girl—I know you will, I know you cannot refuse me."

I caressed his stirring organ gently. Quaestoris began to weep again. "You know I cannot refuse you—you know it and you take advantage of it. You use me as you use everyone and everything. But even with this knowledge clearly in my mind, I cannot help myself, I cannot free myself from bondage. I love you. I obey you, my darling, my Hebrew faun—" The envoy's racking sobs choked off his voice.

"What's the matter? Why are you crying so?"

"I'm sorry," gasped the envoy. "I'm terribly sorry for what I've done. For the accusations I wrote. For the things I've said. I meant none of them. I beg—your forgiveness."

"You mustn't weep—"

"Please forgive me . . . I implore you."

"All is well. Quaestoris, stop. The wound is healed. You will mention the prisoner to the queen, and all will be forgotten. All will be as if it never happened."

"I am evil . . ."

I looked down at the envoy. Though somewhat swollen in my hand, the envoy's penis was still limp, was nowhere near being erect. I withdrew my hand and said softly, "I know . . . I know how evil you are."

"I am very evil."

"You are. It is true. You are evil, vile, abhorrent."

The envoy's penis began to stiffen. "I am a child," he said with spite in his voice. "A spoiled child. You were right in what you said."

"I know I was right. You are disgusting, abominable."

"I deserve to be punished—punished severely."

"Yes, you do."

Quaestoris's penis stood. Gently I rolled his naked body over. His flabby, gray, shapeless buttocks were laced with the marks of countless beatings; some of the welts were fresh and raw, others were old and faded. I got to my feet. "You are a very evil child," I said in a harsh voice, "and I am going to punish you. I am going to whip you until you bleed—until you scream for mercy."

"Be merciful," pleaded Quaestoris. "Beat me!"

I sent word to Melech the Galilean for Ichavod his stalwart that the warrior of *Patish* might come to me at Herod's fortress and serve me as my personal guard and defender. Within forty-eight hours, the great, battle-scarred giant arrived at the palace, having worn his mount to exhaustion with the ride. He had not a tooth in his mouth, and when he smiled and his small eyes were swallowed in scar tissue, his face was corpselike. I kept Ichavod with me constantly, finding in his person precisely the qualities I desired for the task I had assigned him. He was incredibly strong of limb—able to lift a tree trunk or a boulder by himself—and I had once seen him crack a calf's skull with his own bare fist in a single blow; he had the mental cunning of the shrewdest of predatory beasts and never failed to outwit them in the forest or the desert; he had almost legendary endurance and had been known to walk a hundred miles without a rest; and above all, he had a passion to maim and kill that seemed almost an instinct. And there was another reason I wanted Ichavod so much: when he was thirteen, an enraged centurion had cut out the lad's tongue with a dagger for slandering the emperor. With my warrior at my heels—supremely silent as if he were some martial god gloating in the soundless thunder of battles gone by and battles yet to come—I set about reconstructing Herod's army with feverish determination and zeal, subverting all else to this central purpose.

One of the major stumbling blocks which obstructed my efforts was the army's commanding general, a gaunt, bandy-legged, dried-out little man of sixty-five, with the sting of the wasp in his words—and nowhere else. Pompous to the point of absurdity, senile and vindictive without a thought for the consequences, the Judean general Achiazav was a distant relative of the king's, on his mother's side, and kept a strangle hold on his sinecure by virtue of that blood relationship. The popular saying had it that "What virtue could not, blood hath wrought!" But the commander-in-chief himself, who heard no insults and brooked no criticism, was fond of saying (always as if he had thought of it for the very first time), "The king is Judea . . . and I am the army." With Achiazav at the helm, there was little or no opportunity of radically transforming the army into the fighting machine I wanted it to be. I knew he had to go. And I knew who had to do it. And I knew how it must be done. And I knew I could delay no longer.

Ichavod, of course, had free run of the stables. One day, as we were preparing to ride out to a camp south of the fortress to look over a regiment that had recently returned from duty in the Negev, I diverted both the supreme commander and his chief groom, a man who had cared for the general's horses when he himself was a lad and whom Achiazav trusted as he trusted his own right hand. I held their interest with a fanciful story I told about a device with great cutlass blades that could be fitted over the spine of a battle-horse. The inventor, I said, was a Jew who had come from Syria a short time ago and wanted to sell his invention to the army of Judea. "How do you know that it will really work in battle?" asked Achiazav. "And how can you be sure he has not sold it elsewhere? And how do you know it is not a trick to incite the Romans? Or even a trap cleverly devised and set by the Romans?" While I gave shrewd answers to a fool, Ichavod walked calmly into the stable and with the blade of the hunting knife he never was without carefully slit the girth of Achiazav's already saddled steed.

There is little more to say. When my warrior Ichavod fixed his eye of death on a target, the prey was as good as gone. While riding down a rocky descent an hour later, I spurred my horse forward. Achiazav on his roan stallion could not be left behind; he touched its beautiful neck with his hand and in a matter of seconds outdistanced me. Seconds later, the girth split, the commander-in-chief shot forward, a final frozen scream on his lips; and death won the last race Achiazav ever rode.

"Where's Kalbi?"

The warder shook his head dumbly.

"I asked you where Kalbi is."

Still the warder did not speak. His lips trembled, his mouth opened —but no words came out.

"Have you lost your tongue? Or do you want to lose it? Tell me where Kalbi has gone?"

"My lord, I don't know."

"Ichavod—"

The giant warrior stepped from my shadow forward and pinned the warder against the wall with the side of a wrist as if the old man were an insect. I saw the blade of Ichavod's hunting knife gleam like a maleficent star in the gloom and come to rest against the bared throat of the victim; my warrior awaited only the signal to cut.

"Old man, I know that you love your God well. The question is, Do you want to meet Him now or do you want to wait?"

"My lord, have mercy—"

"I have mercy, old man. But you alone will decide whether I use it or not!"

"My lord, let him remove the knife. I will speak."

I nodded. Ichavod sheathed his knife and stood aside. The warder shook so that he could hardly stand. I nodded again to Ichavod, and he brought a prison stool. Breathing heavily, the old man sat—one hand in his lap, the other clutching his throat.

"Now tell me where your superior has gone."

"To the south, my lord."

"Where in the south?"

"I don't know. Hebron . . . or perhaps Beersheba . . ."

"Why has he gone there?"

"My lord—"

"Did he command you to be silent?"

"My lord—"

"And you fear him more than you fear me—a louse more than a lion? Old man, ask yourself well if there is any sense to such reckoning."

"My lord, he is to set up a prison in one of those cities."

"But we have a prison here. And another in Jerusalem. And in Safed and Tiberias and Acre. Why in the south? And under whose orders does he act?"

The warder shrank into his cloak. His lips had turned purple, and he kept blinking, as if he were staring directly into the light of the sun. "I cannot answer these questions, my lord," he whispered.

"No, I suppose you cannot. You are the tail and not the head of this scheme." I touched the old man's head lightly with my riding whip. "But tell me, warder, what happened to the girl in the first cell? She was unconscious when I passed. Who did it?"

"My lord—"

"This is a question to which you know the answer, old man. The beekeeper knows the hive. Old man, I will not tolerate your silence. Who did it? The queen—or Kalbi?"

"Kalbi, my lord."

"Why?"

"In anger, my lord."

"Why?"

"He desired her, and she resisted when he tried to enter her."

"Did he kill her?"

"I think not, my lord."

"With what did he beat her?"

"With his fists, my lord. He cried: 'Daughter of a whore—mother of whores.' And he struck her again and again about the head and face with his fists until she fell to the floor where you saw her now. That was last night. She has not risen since. But I do not believe she is dead, my lord. I heard her groan this morning."

"Unlock the last cell—and then attend to her. See that her wounds are treated and that she is made comfortable. I make you responsible for her recovery, warder. Do you understand?"

"Yes, my lord."

I left Ichavod outside the door and entered my brother's cell alone. My brother was at the far end of the cell, under the aperture through which the light of day filtered in, on his hands and knees. His head was bent over something he had in his hands.

264

"What have you got there?" I said.

He looked up at me without surprise, as if he had known all along that I was there. "A moth," he said. "It came in through the fissure. But it hurt itself and fell to the floor. I thought that perhaps I could save it, but I was wrong. It died."

"Then bring it back to life."

"I cannot. It is quite dead."

"Are you not the man who can raise the human dead?"

"No."

"But that is what you told me the last time I was here."

"I told you no such thing."

I smiled. "Perhaps you don't remember," I said. "But that is what you told me."

"The moth is dead," said the prisoner. "I cannot resurrect it. But I can send its soul to heaven."

"Moths have souls?"

"Oh, yes," said the prisoner. "Moths have souls. All creatures have souls. The grass has a soul. All life has a soul. All the living world *is* a soul."

"I see. You have a philosophy of religion as well as a political philosophy. Have the priests heard your views on—the soul?"

"A priest laughed at me once, and I never talked to another."

"When was that?"

"Many years ago, when I was a lad."

"How would you like to speak to one now—a High Priest?"

"I think not," said the prisoner. "For my soul has its own priest who dwells within it. We get along quite well." My brother looked again at his clasped hands. "A tiny corpse," he said. "But still it lived, it was animated by spirit. Now that spirit is fled—back to heaven from whence it came. This is a mystery. A holy mystery. Will you kneel?"

"Kneel?"

"Yes, we will celebrate its journey back to the source."

"Do you know who I am?"

"The king. The emperor. It doesn't matter. There is life in you, there is spirit, there is holiness. Will you kneel?"

"I do not kneel before nothing."

"I am kneeling before everything."

"Men kneel to me!"

265

"And you must kneel to spirit."

I laughed. "Go on with your nonsense. I'll sit in this chair and observe you."

My brother nodded. "As you wish." And then he began to chant. He had a fine tenor voice which he managed with delicacy and ease; it obeyed him well, lifting at times with unexpected power or breaking in a kind of convulsive sob like that of some glittering mountain stream which knows it feeds on vast underground lakes whose dimensions will never be revealed. He sang snatches of the liturgy, bits of psalms and the prophets interspersed with a text that was wholly his own, a text that he seemed to compose as he went along. He stopped as suddenly as he had begun, opening his hands and letting the dead moth fall to the floor. "There is no flesh without spirit," he said. "For without spirit, flesh decays and is as the dung in the field. Therefore the flesh is spirit."

"The flesh is the flesh, the spirit is spirit—the two can never be reconciled."

"Except that the spirit inhabit the flesh, the flesh is nothing," said my brother. "It is scarcely worth bothering about."

"Without the flesh," I said, "the spirit has no home. It cannot exist. It does not exist."

My brother said nothing. He bent far forward and kissed the dry little corpse of the moth on the floor. Then he got up and went to his stool and seated himself. He stared at me for some time and his face wore a puzzled look. At length its features became calm, and he said, "You asked me before if I knew who you were and I said that I did not. But I have been thinking about it. And now I know."

"Who am I?"

"The devil," said my brother.

"The devil? How do you know?"

"It was not easy knowledge to come by. But I sat and I watched you, as before you had watched me, and it came to me. A voice spoke to me and said: 'This man has neither cloven hoof, nor horn, nor tail. He has in fact the appearance of a mortal human being. But be not deceived. He is the devil.' And when the voice had spoken so, I looked at you and perceived that what the voice told me was indeed so. You are the devil."

"You doubt neither yourself nor—the voice?"

"No. The devil is always for the flesh. The devil always denies the spirit. Just as you have. I am certain that you are the devil."

"Aren't you frightened?"

"No. The devil is with me often. I expect him to come because I am his enemy. He is drawn to me because I oppose him, because he must keep watch over me and because he wants to win me over to his side. He assumes many guises and forms, some of them quite subtle. Sometimes he even clothes himself in my thoughts: then it seems to me that I am fighting myself, though actually it is the devil against whom I struggle. But I am not afraid. I know I will prevail. I am spirit, and I will conquer him. The devil is always concerned with power over other men; I am concerned with power over myself. I will win."

"That remains to be seen."

The prisoner smiled, but his eyes glittered: they had in them the same look that had bewildered me so many times before. Without uttering a word, he bared his right arm to the elbow, held it up before his face for some moments and suddenly sank his teeth into the flesh above the wrist. Then he took it from his mouth and displayed it so that I could see: the deep bluish-purple toothmarks he had made were slowly filling with blood, which he licked almost as animal licks a wound. "I eat of my flesh," he said in a voice that sounded drugged. "And I drink of my blood. For I am spirit—eternal spirit."

I laughed. "You are a man," I said.

"But I was not born of man," said the prisoner.

"What do you mean?"

"My father never entered my mother to give his seed unto her womb. My mother conceived of spirit alone. I was born in the hay of a shed in Bethlehem. And a star that did not move but was as if frozen in the sky announced my birth. Wise men came to pay me homage for they realized I was a child of spirit." My brother put his wounded hand to his head, moaned and slipped from the stool. I called to Ichavod, who picked up the prisoner from the floor as one would pick up a husk and laid him on the cot. Then I summoned the warder, who brought water and fruit. A quarter of an hour went by before the prisoner revived. He drank, but would not eat of the food. He tried to sit but was too weak. "I had an evil dream," he said at length. "I am unclean."

"What was the dream?"

"I had carnal union with a woman."

"What is so evil in that?"

"The devil often assumes the guises of a woman. In the dream, I knew the woman was the devil. Still, I could not resist her. I succumbed to her charms. I penetrated her. Then I could not get loose. For she had closed her female jaws on me and I was trapped."

"Would you like a woman?"

"What do you mean?"

"Would you like to have a woman?"

"How—how could that be?"

"I could arrange it. As a matter of fact, I have a particular woman in mind. It would interest me to see the both of you together. I hope that my plan will work out—it depends on the queen."

"A woman," mused the prisoner. "It would be strange. I have thought of it many times. But women are frightened of me." A troubled look came into his eyes. "I caused a woman to miscarry once. In a village outside of Nazareth, I think it was. The men were angry. They wanted to set their dogs on me, to stone me to death. But my father pleaded with them and saved my life." He stared at me with peculiar intensity. "Do you know who I am?"

"Of course. You are the son of Yosef and Mara."

"I don't know," shrugged the prisoner. "But I know who I am not!"

"Who are you not?"

"God." The prisoner laughed. "But in my dream, I was God. And the naked woman was the devil. And I knew the woman and she conceived. And she brought forth a child who was the savior of all mankind—a child who loved men and comforted them in their times of sorrow."

"Do you dream often?"

"Always. By day and by night. My dreams are a burden, a torment, a torture. I cannot escape them. They crucify me. When I die, then I shall awake."

"Tell me, do you have any real idea of whom I am?"

"I know who you are not."

"Who am I not?"

"The devil." The prisoner laughed. "You are an angel. I dreamed that God sent you to me because I am very lonely. No one visits me but the holy ghost."

"What is the holy ghost?"

"He, too, is a messenger sent by God. But he has not the form of an angel, nor does he speak. I can neither see him nor hear him but I know he is present. I can feel his breath on me—it flows from his nostrils like the winds of earth."

"I'll tell you who I am, my prisoner. I am Judea's minister of war—"

"And I am Judea's prince of peace."

I rose to leave. "We shall meet again, my prisoner."

"So we shall, my brother."

I could hear his hysterical laughter even after I had gone from the block of special detention cells.

As he had promised when he was in the throes of desire, the envoy Quaestoris approached Herodias and spoke to her of the convict girl, who was called by the name of *M'gadlah N'shayah*, or "beautifier of women," as she had indeed been a hairdresser for the queen and her intimate retinue. Herod's wife, as Quaestoris had recounted to me, had been in a receptive, even a gay mood—highly unusual for her of late—and had talked to the diplomat at considerable length; he had hoped—given past experience with the queen—for an affirmative answer during the interview, but just as he was about to broach the matter of an immediate decision, the queen insisted on a personal meeting with me. The envoy had not been able to dissuade Herodias; she was set on seeing me and had fixed a meeting in her private chambers in a week's time. "The queen commands that he attend!" was the way she put it as Quaestoris left. The diplomat made a sour face. "Once you are in her den," he said, "she is sure to lust after you. I know her well: it cannot fail to happen. But beware—if you give an inch, you are lost, for she will suck you dry as a bone is sucked of its marrow!" I laughed. "Don't worry," I said. "I can handle myself. Herodias may find that she is the one who is sucked dry." Then I pretended to chafe at the delay and even berated the queen to the envoy's face, though the truth was that I was inwardly elated, for I had long wished for an intimate audience with a monarch who was as thickly surrounded by devotees and claimants as a cactus fruit with spines. I pressed Quaestoris to my bosom and called him "My good Roman friend!"

I plunged into my military efforts with even fiercer zeal. Since the "unfortunate accident" that had befallen Achiazav on his descent to the desert, I had made great progress with the revitalization of Herod's forces. I had arranged to meet with Livinius and a number of other generals, explaining—as they already knew—that the state of the army was deplorable, was beneath all acceptable standards, and that as Judea's minister of war it was my first task to overhaul it so the nation's troops could stand side by side with Rome's legions in the event of war or civil uprising. The Romans welcomed my endeavors warmly. They called me "the Jewish eagle" and the "lion cub with teeth," and they clapped my back and toasted me with "Jews' wine." The Romans respected intelligence and the ability to put it to practical use, and they knew I had both—and energy as well. They gave me advice, and one of them, Tarquinius, even asked me on maneuvers with his troops. My overall tactical plan was to build a unified, disciplined fighting machine unit by unit, as the general Livinius had counseled. "If the bricks are not solid," he would say, "the edifice will not stand." Or "If you build with rotten blocks, you build debris." I therefore reviewed my regiments one by one. Wherever I found a commanding officer who was lethargic, vacillating, overbearing or derelict, I got rid of him immediately; wherever I found a capable, eager, courageous junior officer, I upgraded him at once. I overturned the tables of seniority. I dispensed with nepotism and social status. I recognized no standard other than that of merit. For me, the past was dead—only the future counted. My appointments were based strictly on ability to command and zest for combat. Nothing else counted. There was nothing in the world I wanted less than an army which was a reflection of Herod's court.

The malcontents multiplied like lice. The protests of the ousted and the demoted swelled like a chorus of hell. I didn't give a damn. I picked a booby officer to whom they were to address their complaints, one and all, and had him burn them when they left. The title of commander-in-chief I took for myself, as chief executive officer. For the day-to-day operations of the army I picked a deputy from among the best of the line officers. He was a man of forty named Akrab—a born soldier who had joined the army when he was fifteen and fought his way up through the ranks. He was the son of a peasant who had been hung—on the basis of false testimony, so Akrab contended—for burning down a neighbor's barn. As a sergeant in the infantry, Akrab had settled the score by hanging the falsifier as a rebel. That was when he was still young. As the years went by, he had killed many times over in order to stay alive and had come near to being killed enough times to know the value of killing first. With a lithe, hardened body, iron-gray hair, scarred face, keen blue eyes and an incisive mind, Akrab was a symbol to me of the new army I was building. Riding out to inspect a regiment with me one day, my deputy had leaned over in his saddle and said, "I have an appetite for death—the death of others." It was true. He hated "Jew and Roman alike," and had "not the slightest use for the entire despicable race of humans, with its monstrous vanity and abominable behavior. The less of them the better," he would say. "And I am here to see that there are less!" I was proud. I felt I had made a superb choice.

As each new appointment of officers was made, I sent a coded message to Melech the Galilean, who in addition to commanding *Patish* had been more and more entrusted with overseeing the operations of the spy network. Melech had the report decoded and lost no time in assigning an agent to the new commander. So scrupulous and careful was I in my efforts that there was not a single high-ranking officer in the army of Judea who was not constantly watched. But the full dimensions of my plan I revealed to no one. In my mind alone I saw it in completion. Not a day passed without my thinking of the plan; not a day passed without my advancing toward my goal. As in a game of chess, I had mapped my moves out; as in a game of chess I made them methodically and exactly. I had gained the war ministry and so the army of Herod. Herod's army would become my army. I would use that force to take on Herod and defeat him before he knew that he was being attacked. No force of his would come to his aid, no matter how loyal, for the general Livinius was my firm ally and would aid me as he had in the massacre of Zerubabel. Herod would be deposed. No other Jewish force would be strong enough to rally against me. I would be king not alone by Roman sanction, as was Herod, but by my own right and cunning. Quaestoris would sway Pilate and I would obtain full political approval. My name would fly to Rome a sparrow and return an eagle. I would sit on the throne of the Jews and they would know— every last one of them, be it man, woman or child—that I was there: they would know because they would feel my weight on their backs and my whip on their skin. This would be no puppet monarch, no fop- king, no fool with a crown. This would be iron, fire, burden—the shod hoof of a horse in the face. The groaning of the people in the past would be as silence before what was to come; the outcries would seem as whispers. The vial of my hatred had filled slowly, drop by drop, over the passing years, and when at last I emptied it there would be no end of pain and suffering. No matter what sorrows the people had seen in the past, they had seen only joy in comparison with what the future held for them. Only when it was unleashed would the world know how much hatred I had in me and how long I had waited to express it.

By his complicity, the general Livinius would gain his own end—not military power, which he already had in sufficient measure, and not political stature, which he realized was beyond his grasp, but the vast treasure which his army career had denied him. On its military heroes Rome conferred honor, but it denied them wealth: I offered Livinius generously of the loot seized from the tetrarch's vanished kingdom. This was our solemn agreement: I would have the throne of Judea, the general would have Judea's wealth—the treasures which Herod had heaped up and which were beyond all reckoning save that of the monarch's diseased imagination.

Of course, my own ambition went far beyond the plan to which we had agreed. Once I had the throne, I would have the power that went with it. In one hand I would hold the scepter of political decision, in the other the sword of military strength. I would hold on my tongue, like dew in the chalice, like venom in the adder's sac, the word that meant peace or war, life or death, building or razing. By my command, thousands would eat or starve, drink or perish of thirst, harvest their crops or reap the wind. Justice would stumble at my feet, mercy beseech me in vain, compassion whisper into a deaf ear. Men and nations alike would tremble before me. My options would be numberless, my choices unlimited. If I did not like the look of a man's face, he would die—and his family would be erased. If I did not like the sound of a man's voice, he would go to prison—and his wife and children would rot. There would be law in the land—iron, inflexible law: law that went no higher than myself. I would have full, untrammeled freedom to maneuver, manipulate and weld together a conglomerate force that would make its reverberations sound even to the very gates of the Eternal City. Foreign alliances would be within my grasp; secret treaties, pacts, agreements and understandings would be mine to make at will. All of the acts that I had played out throughout the days of childhood and youth on petty stages I should now be able to show on the grand stage of history and nations. He who had denied my mission would find his very existence refuted, he who had opposed my will would find the very memory of his opposition vanished and flown. I was confident, I was secure. I knew that I had planned well. My army, though steadily improving, would never be counted a threat by the Romans—Herod in his profligacy had seen to that. And the Romans themselves, being Romans, could not imagine a force that would oppose them in battle.

At night, when the stars began their descent into the chute that led to dissolution, at the bitter end of the night when the mists of dawn began to churn in their cauldron and I lay abed for the hour or two of sleep I allowed myself, I saw myself in those last moments of clairvoyant wakefulness a titan, a colossus, a giant on the earth casting a shadow that fell like an axe across the empire. I saw myself besting Rome at its own game just as I had bested its general Livinius at the chessboard. Each move I made now brought me closer to Herod, and each move toward Herod brought me closer to Rome. The "little Hebrew whore," whom Quaestoris in his lover's anger had reviled, would make his countrymen eat the dust they deigned to call their own property! Many times over during those nights had I phrased my plan in words, though I had never taken a quill to write them down: "The lion will pluck the raven clean and then—wonder of wonders!—will swallow the eagle!"

A coded message came to me from Melech the Galilean. Our agents had been successful in locating Kalbi. He was in Hebron, where he was indeed setting up a prison. The report went on to inform me that the head jailer of the fortress prison was in the secret employ of Aquilius, the Roman brigade commander, who had for years wanted a legion for himself and who was apparently plotting a move of his own: what it was exactly, the men of my system could not tell. I was extremely pleased that my network had uncovered the scheme so quickly; I would now be able to follow its developments and quash it when it best suited my purposes. Whatever the particular gambit of Aquilius, I knew it would be somehow aimed at Livinius, his rival and enemy, and thus at me. Quaestoris brought me reports that confirmed what we had already found out. His own sources informed him that Aquilius was seeking the top military post in Judea and wanted Livinius out of his way in order to advance. He was about to begin a vigorous series of sweeps in the south, to take hundreds of "rebels" prisoner and to incarcerate them in the detention camp that Kalbi had established for him. I sent immediate word back to Melech that the watch on Kalbi was to be increased, and that if we could manage it, the movements of Aquilius must also be monitored.

We had a number of Romans working for us in special spy cells. They were an odd lot, mean and dangerous all—misfits, malcontents, seekers of vengeance for real or imagined wrongs by the Roman hier-archy against them or members of their families, out-and-out mer-cenaries, hardened criminals who had been able by murder and pillage to escape Roman justice. We screened our Roman agents even more rigorously than we did our Jewish spies, and even when they were accepted for service we kept them strictly isolated. We did not want them to infect our men with their diseases.

I saw the queen at the appointed hour on the appointed day, though she had not yet risen. She "did not want to detain me, knowing the burdens that were on my shoulders," so she received me in her royal bedchamber, a privilege—so I was informed—"accorded to few and at rare intervals." The room was high-ceilinged, with great cedar rafters ribbing it from end to end, enormous windows draped in gold, a sunken bath with tile approaches, and magnificent Persian carpets on which immaculately groomed cats and a chained ocelot lay, switching their tails. She lay under a cover of crimson silk with only her eyes and head showing and greeted me from beneath the blanket in a muffled voice, explaining in a simpering drawl that she was "weary with the cares and exigencies of life" and tired of her "dull and meaningless existence." The bed was a giant, four-posted affair, ornately carved and inlaid in ivory and jade, "her majesty's favorites." I stared at the reclin-ing monarch and saw that she was half asleep, but scarcely indisposed. As we chatted, she seemed more and more to waken, as if her conver-sation with me drew her steadily from the depths of a deep and treach-erous pond into which she had unwittingly stepped and sunk. "I'm so very, very glad that you could come and see me!" she would murmur in her smothered, lilting voice every time there was a lapse in the talk, as if she felt that silence was somehow a breach of good faith. "Oh, yes, I am so pleased that you are here at last!" And she would laugh. Her large, protuberant eyes, once free of the censorship of their lids, seemed to roam over my face and body like jungle beasts; there was in them the look of the demented, the look of those who are haunted by their own nightmares, of those who in fact produce their own night-mares so they will be haunted by them. She moved up on her pillow so that her entire face was visible now. She grimaced. Her nostrils dilated, her cheeks twitched and her mouth pouted, and every now and again she bit her lower lip so that in the end it bled, and her thick, pointed tongue emerged like a rat snout from her mouth to lick it dry and clean.

"Blood is good," she laughed. "It feeds one's dreams as it nourishes one's womb."

There were mirrors in all parts of the room, mirrors large and small and of various shapes—behind the divan on which I sat, on the mosaic walls, hand mirrors on the dressers and tables, and over the bed itself a huge oval mirror whose frame was decorated with cherubim and flushed, smiling seraphim. All the time we spoke together, Herodias would glance out of the corner of an eye or openly at one or another of the images of herself, as if seeking reassurance from a dozen different surfaces. Her preoccupation with her reflection amused me. I could sense in this queen a spiteful little girl, a vicious little girl who delighted in evil the way a child does, without the slightest regard for consequences or ramifications, not as a part of a plot or a scheme, not for gain or aggrandizement—but simply for the sheer instant of perverse pleasure to be squeezed out of the evil deed. I thought that as long as this queen might live, as old as she might get, the malevolent little girl in her would never atrophy.

"It's so very lovely that you surprised me and came all this way to spend your valuable time with me!" Herodias yawned. She giggled, she twisted this way and that, she belched, she covered her mouth, she sat bolt upright so that her nightgown slipped from her shoulders and her pendulous, hard-nippled breasts were completely exposed; she laughed disconsolately, touched her nipples with her fingers, covered herself again with the silk and then began to manipulate herself in sight of my eyes, writhing and showing the whites of her own eyes until she spent in a shuddering, half-hysterical paroxysm that terminated with what sounded like a wail of regret. She threw the cover to the floor and lifted her nightgown and gazed at her reflection overhead. She called for a maid to cover her and asked my pardon.

Herodias sighed, stared at me wide-eyed, pouted, and then said, "But whatever in the world do you mean to do with the girl in jail? She's a killer—you know that, don't you? She's rotten to the core."

"I want to study her," I said. "I believe she's mad. I want to study her madness."

"Study madness?" The queen burst into laughter. "Why in the world do you have to shove your snout into the dung of a prison?"

"I have another prisoner there. A male. He's mad as well." I smiled. "I'm going to mate them. I'm going to breed madmen."

The queen ignored me. Her voice was shrill, strident. "Now, tell me the truth," she said in a brittle, aggrieved tone. "I don't like to be lied to. I will not be lied to by any man on this earth! What do you really want with the girl? What does she mean to you? What will you get out of her? Will she perform secret rites for you? Have you a potion that will drive her crazy with lust? Do you want to watch her rut with the stud you have picked out for her? Will you sell her to a whoremaster who makes a specialty of murderesses? Is there a priest you want to please who wants her? Answer me! Remember I am the queen and speak the truth!"

"Your Majesty, Your Majesty, I—"

"You do desire her! I can see it in your face! You are bloated with desire! I can smell it—I tell you I can smell it!"

I was silent.

"So . . . it is true. What I have said is true. What I suspected is correct."

I said nothing.

"Isn't it correct?"

"Yes."

The queen sighed and was still for a time. At length she cocked her head and said: "Well, I can't say that I blame you. No, no . . . I don't really blame you."

I nodded solemnly. "The desire came over me suddenly," I said. "I hardly knew what had happened to me. I had passed her a dozen times and felt nothing. And then it was different. I saw her and I wanted her. I felt I had to have her—or burst!"

"What do you feel like?" the queen asked. "Do you have much trouble sleeping?"

"I am extremely restless."

"So am I," sighed Herodias, "so am I. I cannot sleep—I cannot sleep for weeks at a stretch. My nights are a bane, a torment, an affliction. And when at last I do sleep I am plagued with terrible dreams, with dreams I cannot unravel for the life of me. I wake in terror, and in spite of my exhaustion, I will not sleep again for fear the nightmare will return to claim me." She stared at me. "Do you reckon there is a king-dom of dreams to which a mortal can be taken, there to remain forever? What an ugly, horrifying thought—to be trapped in a dream for all time!" The queen shuddered.

"Last night," she went on, "only last night, I dreamed of the evil one himself. It was ghastly. I was in a great scarlet room. I was naked as the day my mother bore me and I lay on a rug of white fur. And the evil one came to me in the form of a huge fish, with copper scales and eyes the color of bad phlegm and a laughing mouth from which white foam gushed as he slithered forward, hissing as he moved. And I saw him and was affrighted and I asked him what a fish was doing on the dry land, and he laughed and spoke unto me, saying, 'Why are you not in the water?' And I was puzzled and said to him, 'Why do you mean?' And he laughed and replied, 'Surely, you must know that one of us is bound to come to the other; since you have not come to me in the water, I have come to you on dry land.' Then before I had a chance to grasp what his intention was, he leaped forward in a mighty copper flash and slipped between my parted legs and into me. I felt him thrash about and the sensation was neither pain nor pleasure but rather a mingling of the two of them that left me confounded. And I called unto him, 'What are you after that you have penetrated my woman's place and entered into me? What is it that you seek in your fury and your folly? Do you think that you will find the source of me in there?' But there was no answer from him, and I cried out again, 'If you do not answer what I have asked you, I shall cross my legs and prevent you from going out and you shall be locked within me forever and see no more the light of day or the face of man!' But still he did not reply to me, so I shut my legs together that he might not escape. And then I felt him strain and surge, and in a great convulsion he burst up and into the very space of my womb. And then I heard him sob in the voice of a child, and I called to him but he did not speak, so I called to him once more and then his voice came to me as the voice of the evil one, saying from within the darkness of my own womb: 'Mother, I am home at last. Here was I born and here will I die.' And I cried, 'Tell me more!' But he said to me, 'There is no more to tell. All that must be said has been said; and all that must be done has been done.' And he ceased to speak and to move and was silent and restful in the chalice of my womb. And I, too, ceased my agitation and sighed a long, restful sigh. And I whispered to myself, 'At last I am peaceful . . . at last I am at rest. My womb is hell and I am with child.' But even as my mouth was uttering these words did the evil one fly out of it in the form of an enormous black crow, bruising my lips as he took flight and scattering feathers black as coal and dung the color of blighted corn as he soared into the sky. And his voice came screaming back at me, cawing, 'Barren! Empty!

Seedless! Sterile! Fruitless! Daughter of a whore! Mother of whores! Mother of whoredom!' And he dwindled into a speck and I saw him no more, but the memory of his words was like a wound in my breast; I fell upon my knees and wept black tears, and I knew that the evil one had swallowed my womb as a kernel of wheat and would return it no more . . .

"So I wakened and called to a servant to come to my bed—man or woman, I didn't give a damn!—and lie with me, but it did me no good, was of no comfort to me. And I tossed in my bed until the dawn and slept no more until weariness claimed me just before you arrived." Herodias hid her face in her hands. "This dream disturbs me," she said through her fingers. "This dream tortures my mind and my heart. Can you—can you tell me what it means? I have no faith at all in my inter- preters—they are a pack of liars and fools! Can you explain it? Can you?"

I was silent. The queen's eyes narrowed. "If you can unravel the dream for me," she said, "you shall have the girl. Tonight—this very night you will be able to do with her as you please!"

I stared directly into the dead malevolence of the queen's eyes. "I can tell you exactly what the dream means," I said slowly.

Herodias sat bolt upright in her bed. Her entire body stiffened as if it were being stretched on the rack.

I leaned forward. I cleared my throat and spoke in a calm, modu- lated voice: "The evil one of whom you dreamed is in reality someone in the court of the king whom you loved dearly and called a friend. He entered into you—that is to say, you took him into your confidence and put your trust in him. Into your womb—that is, you admitted him to your innermost sanctum. You were with child—that means your love, your passion was reborn in this relationship. You were peaceful, secure. But what did this evil one—this false lover—do? Did he justify your faith? Did he return your trust? Did he sanctify the home you had pre- pared for him?" My voice dropped to a whisper: "No, no, my queen, he did not. Few there are in this world who can return a love as strong as yours. As I am fond of saying, 'Many will taste of the wine, but few can make it.' Thus, my queen, did this evil man, this false lover, this betrayer of your goodness reject and make a rank mockery of your womb—your warmth, your tenderness, your love nest—and desert it! Scarcely had you spoken of the fruit of your love—your child—when the evil one, the deceiver, took wing—that is to say, abandoned you.

And as further insult to your person, this man attempted to hide his own base and shameful emptiness by heaping abuse on his victim; that is why he cried out to you, 'Barren! Empty! Seedless!' And so forth. He accused you of the very fault of which he himself is guilty." I leaned back. "And thus, my queen, the meaning of this dream is made manifest and clear to you."

Open-mouthed, the queen stared at me. She seemed dumbfounded. "The evil one in the dream was a false lover then."

"Of course."

"But why was he a fish?"

"Is not a fish slippery? Can you grasp a fish in your hands?"

Herodias shook her head. "What you told me," she mused, "what you explained to me makes sense. Yes, it does. There was such a man. I gave him my love, heart. I gave him my body, my—" The tears welled up in her eyes and she choked.

"Well," I said, "have I kept my word?"

The queen looked up. "Bravo!" she said harshly. "So you have."

"Do you know now why the dream troubled you?"

"I know," said the queen. "Men are whores."

"All is clear?"

"Yes," said the queen hoarsely.

"And the girl—she is to be mine, as her majesty promised?"

"The slut is yours," said the queen. And she called for a scribe, who appeared in the bedchamber and took down the message to Kalbi, the head jailer, which Herodias dictated to him; and when he was finished the queen set her seal on what he had written and handed it abruptly to me. "The slut is yours," she repeated. "Choke on her!"

Elazar took the order immediately to the fortress prison and delivered it over to the warder, who saw to it that the girl in the first cell of the special detention block was transferred to the last cell, wherein my brother was kept. Kalbi, the head jailer, was still gone, and latest word informed me that my agents had unfortunately lost track of him for the moment, though rumor had it that he had fled the country for Egypt—an agent traveling in a caravan on the coastal route from Alexandria believed he had seen him among the journeyers. I gave full and explicit instructions for the care and welfare of my brother and his female cellmate and charged the warder with the responsibility for their safety on pain of death. In addition, I ordered Melech the Galilean to assign two men of *Patish* to guard the cell day and night. I was anxious that no harm befall either of my prisoners. And I wanted very much to visit them, but the pressures of my office and a reluctance to disturb the couple in the first phase of their conjugal life combined to keep me away from the prison.

I was engaged in a strenuous round of negotiations with the leaders of the various parties and sects as a part of a concerted effort to raise funds for what I had come to call "my army of the future." In the dung-spattered world of politics, my past was clean. I had an irreproachable record, years of government service that were unassailable; I was attached to no political party, and my performance as Judea's minister of war was superb if I was to be judged objectively, spotless if I was to be judged with the bias that meant to find fault and wrongdoing.

I was everywhere and I oversaw everything. My own personal probity in all of these dealings was exemplary. The lack of corruption in the war department, no matter what the echelon of service, and in all ranks of the army itself was nothing short of enviable. The severity and thoroughness of my initial purges of the ministry of war and the military had paid off handsomely; and I had followed through by ruthlessly and methodically punishing every and any wrongdoer, no matter what his station or rank. My scrupulousness and zeal, my intelligence and efficiency—above all, my constantly increasing power—persuaded all but the most blindly prejudiced elements to throw political and monetary support to me.

I was now approaching the zenith of my powers. What I had desired so in my childhood, fought for in my adolescence, struggled for in my young manhood and now labored with such intense effort for in my time as a man was within my scope and even sight. I was undisputedly the most wealthy and largest landowner in the Galilee, with properties that ranged from the Hermon to the Sea of Galilee in the east to Acre and the Great Sea in the west and even south unto Nazareth—vast fields and lush meadows and young forests and unworked swamplands and orchards and fruit groves where exotic saplings were tended; and the lands were worked by thousands upon thousands of peasants and sharecroppers who tilled the soil with plow and harrow, bound the vines in the arbors, brought in the sheaves of barley and wheat and oats and rye, planted the melons and heaped up the grain from vast acreage in huge storehouses that strained in their seams with the ripened harvest of the rich earth. And I had herds of cattle and flocks of sheep and goats that were almost beyond reckoning, and with them entire families to tend and watch the beasts and wander with them where they went in the pastures; and my animals multiplied and their numbers increased year by year, and they grew fat and sleek and were the praise of the country. No one had herds like mine, nor cattle tenders nor shepherds like mine, nor water holes and fresh streams like mine, nor pasture lands and sweet grass as had I.

I was owner of the great, sprawling villa in the outskirts of Nazareth, the second home of my father Evenezer to which I had added rooms and guest chambers and tiled baths and a concert shell in which musicians might play and actors perform, and the grounds of which I had improved with rare plants and shrubs and trees and fine grasses and pools of marble brought from afar in which fish of all colors and shapes swam and strange corals glowed; and my gardeners were from Jerusalem and Tiberias, Rome and Florence, Damascus and Alexandria, and they made of this property an Eden in which visitors gaped and wondered and forgot that they lived upon the dismal earth of man. No one had earth like mine, nor plants like mine, nor gardeners like mine. And I was the owner of the house in the village south of Bethlehem where I was born, and where my brother was born, and where my mother had died, and this home, too, I had enlarged and beautified; little by little over the years the village had come into my possession, until now it could be said that I owned it as my own, from the highest point on the mountain, where the chasm of the dead plunged into its flank, to the lowest in the valley, where the cemetery was in which my mother lay buried and not far from her grave was that of the rabbi.

I owned many other houses throughout Galilee and even further, and many vineyards and lakes and wild, untended fields and slopes and sprawling desert land and even several caravans of camels and the drivers thereof. And my servants were of all kinds, including those who labored for me and received wages in payment for their labor, and those who were my slaves, whom I bought and sold as it pleased me; these latter numbered in the thousands and were like unto a mighty host, and no one had bodyservants nor houseservants nor scullery maids nor butlers nor concubines like mine. And over all of this that was solely and wholly and without dispute mine and mine alone, I set Onan as overseer, for Onan had proven himself a more than worthy successor to Avner and even exceeded the latter in his performance.

And I was Judea's mighty minister of war, the most powerful and influential member of King Herod's cabinet, the most listened-to man in his inner circle, privy to all decisions of state and consequence, pillar of the nation and friend of Rome. Among my intimates I counted the king and queen; Quaestoris, who was envoy of the procurator of Judea, Pontius Pilate, to the court of Herod; the Roman general Livinius, who had won his laurels in historic battles, and others too numerous to mention, among them priests and scribes, Pharisees and Sadducees, merchants and landowners, judges and military men, sculptors and scholars, painters and poets.

And I was supreme commander-in-chief of the new army of Judea, whose strength and reputation grew day by day, week by week, year by year—an army that through the ceaseless toil of my mind and un- flagging efforts of my body had been transformed from the effete and all but useless toy of a doting and foppish monarch into a ruthlessly effective machine of destruction.

And I was sole and secret commander of the dreaded spy system that had its tendrils and its tentacles everywhere, and its striking force of hooded warriors, *Patish*. Through these networks and the hundreds of devoted agents who labored in them without surcease, my glance was the glance of the falcon, my touch the touch of the boa, my sting the sting of the yellow scorpion.

Thus did I end the thirty-seventh year of my life and begin the thirty-eighth . . .

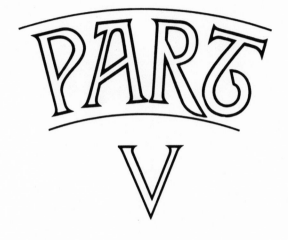

PART

V

It was at that time Quaestoris began a statue of me. He began it in a little courtyard of his home, a charming little place with high walls of glazed brick over which ivy trailed in rich profusion and with a small rectangular pool in one corner, in the emerald-green water of which great, fan-finned goldfish swam with majestic poise. Mimosa and pepper trees surrounded the yard and threw the shadow of their delicate leaves onto the paving, which was of pink, amber and salmon-colored Jerusalem stone. The envoy had a huge block of carmine marble set in the yard, breaking down a complete wall to get it in and then having it rebuilt when the block was set in place. He would rise early every morning, sometimes far before the sun was up, and begin his work when the light of the dawn was strong enough for him to see. Often, when he was not at court, he worked through entire mornings and even past the hour of noon, wearing a straw hat to keep off the sun or seeking shade under an awning which the servants put up for him. His face had a look of absorption on it, and he communicated an intenseness that I had missed in him for a long time; at times when I spoke to him, he seemed abstracted, distant, lost in the contemplation of some inner vision. Many times I tried to discuss his work with him, but he was loath to talk about it and murmured apologies.

285

Whereas formerly he had been anxious about my visits and made unrelenting demands on my time, he now accepted my frequent and at intervals prolonged absences calmly, almost with disinterest. He stopped his bitter attacks and rebukes, smiling sadly and even somewhat disinterestedly when he saw me. He did not look well, with the purple-gray shadows around his once luminous eyes and with hollow cheeks whose sallowness even his mornings in the fresh air and sunshine of the courtyard did not seem to help, but he had lost somewhat the marks of dissoluteness which had begun to decay his features badly; serious illness or even death was present in his appearance, but the deterioration was halted or postponed by a mysterious force that pushed him to sculpt day after day. His hands grew callused once again, his muscles firmer, his eyesight a little keener, his speech less halting, his words less cynical. Once in a while, he even joked. Once in a great while he even made love to me with warmth or had a good word for my ardor. He still drank, but less than before. He ate well, but stopped gorging himself to the point of nausea. Now that he was sculpting, he slept better. And he sharply restricted his social life, seeing only me and a few intimate acquaintances of long standing. A host of sycophants and unworthy callers upon whom he had frittered away precious time and strength were no longer allowed to press their attentions on his person.

"I'm glad to see that you have finally got hold of yourself," I told him one evening when we were having supper together.

"I'm glad that you are pleased," said Quaestoris bemusedly.

"I was quite worried about you for a time."

"Ah, yes," said the envoy, sipping wine. "I did not seem to be doing very well."

"You were slipping—you were plunging downhill at an alarming rate. To me it seemed that you had quite lost your grasp on the real world. I expect that from Jews, and I'm not really surprised when it happens. But from a Roman? Especially a Roman of your stature and mettle—no, it's just not logical."

Quaestoris shrugged and set his half-full wine glass down carefully on the table, quite as if he were playing chess and making a crucial move. "Logic," he said. "What has logic got to do with it? Do you think that human life is logical?"

"Life," I replied, "is life. Neither logical nor illogical, neither meaningful nor meaningless. But the men who live it have to be logical. Isn't that what Rome has taught us?"

"I don't know what Rome has taught you," said the envoy. "But she has taught me that I cannot understand Jerusalem." He stared into my eyes, a melancholy smile on his full lips. "It has taught me that I will never be able to understand you, or perhaps any other human being. Perhaps I should be grateful for that knowledge—I really don't know and lately don't care to know." He picked up his glass again and drank slowly. "I'm working again. The chisel is in one hand, the mallet in the other. The marble is taking shape. I'm grateful. It's enough for me now."

"You sound as if you are alone, Quaestoris."

"I am alone."

"But you are not. You have me."

"Except for the statue-being-born, I am quite alone."

"Except for the statue, you say?"

Quaestoris nodded. His food lay unfinished on the plates before him, but he did not eat; instead he quietly folded his hands on the table. In the last insubstantial light of the day, he looked suddenly like a very old man—like a man who has successfully battled the ravages of age for years and then all at once capitulated. "The statue," he said. "Yes, the statue is my company . . . and my consolation. And also, I am sorry to say, my executioner."

Up until this moment the envoy had stubbornly refused to discuss his new project with me or to show me what he had done on it; I had not had the most remote indication or expectation that the evening would bring a change of heart. "You're very dramatic about your work," I said, "but I'm sure you realize that I don't have the slightest idea of what it is you're doing. You can't possibly mean that you are doing a figure of an executioner in the literal sense—that's quite obviously alien to your taste and your nature. Are you trying to tell me that the struggle to complete your work is killing you? Is that what you're trying to say?"

"Hardly," said Quaestoris, "hardly. As a matter of fact, this work does not tax my strength at all. On the contrary, I find it relaxing. As odd as it may sound to your ears, the work seems to be completing itself; I am merely the instrument through which it will be realized. *I* finish *it*?" The envoy unclasped his hands and picked at a morsel of food, casting it aside again without putting it to his lips. "My feeling is that the statue is completing me."

"But what exactly is it?"

Quaestoris closed his eyes for several moments, leaned forward and remained as he was without answering; at length he opened them, looking somewhat refreshed. "Would—would you like to see it?" he asked in a stifled voice. "Would you like to see what I have done—what has been done?"

"Yes, of course! That would give me great pleasure! I've been waiting for you to show me your project for some time."

"Well, yes," said Quaestoris. "I certainly hope it will afford you pleasure." He smiled uncertainly. "Tomorrow, then. In the morning, when the light is strong and the air exceptionally clear. Shall we say ten-thirty, perhaps? Eleven—would that be better for you? I needn't be at court until three in the afternoon."

"Tomorrow? But that's impossible! That's out of the question! I'm meeting with Akrab tomorrow morning. We shall go over some plans, and then he wants me to go out with him and review the Seventeenth Brigade. It's a special assault unit that we've been developing for more than half a year. Akrab says he has good reason to believe it may revolutionize cavalry warfare. We're going to watch them demonstrate an attack that involves fording a river and storming a fortress on a height. They're going to launch it just at the break of day—Akrab and his senior officers are very enthusiastic about it. The commander of the brigade is a remarkable lad—not a day over twenty-five! Comes from the Bethlehem area, where I was born. His father was a priest who turned pagan and was killed in a religious brawl. The son is a born leader—they say he'll be a general before he's thirty. Especially if there's a war . . . " I laughed. "What do you think about the possibility of a war, my noble Roman friend?"

"I think more about peace than about war."

"Do you think there will be a rebel uprising in the next . . . say, year or two?"

"I think about my mallet and my chisels," said Quaestoris. "And my marble."

"And after the demonstration," I said, "we shall review the unit and talk a while with the entire brigade staff. Akrab tells me there is some general staff material among them, and I want to see for myself. 'Trust a man to see things,' I always say, 'but use your own eyes to pick them up.' And then in the afternoon, I have to be at the war ministry to receive a deputation of merchants from Samaria, among them a man who did much business with my father and knew him quite well; I saw him only as a child and it will be—novel for us to meet now." I chuckled. "They want to discuss the sum I've asked them to raise for the army; they sent word to me several weeks back, and I sent word back to them that they were to come ahead. They were delighted that I had asked them to visit me—they think it means we'll talk things over and I'll agree to a reduction of the sum." I laughed. "Actually, I think the amount I asked for is ridiculously low. I'm going to request a far greater contribution. They'll come into my office all smiles and good cheer and go out livid with anger—and fear: I'll have Ichavod do a few of his stunts for them. And then, in the evening, the High Priest has requested that I meet with an emissary—"

"Then tomorrow's out."

"Well, yes, dear friend . . . tomorrow is an extremely busy day."

"And the day after?"

"Filled—filled, my dear comrade. They're all filled for a month—for two months! But you know that. And you know why—surely you know the reasons why! We don't have to go over it all again, do we?"

"No," said Quaestoris quietly. "No, we don't have to go over anything any more. I know: the cares of office, the pressures of state, the responsibilities of leadership, the spur of history, the fateful hour—have I left anything out?"

I ignored the sarcasm. "What about now?" I said.

"Now?"

"What about seeing your work now?"

"Impossible!" snapped the envoy. "There's no light! You know that very well!"

"I'll view it by torchlight."

"It can't be done! It can't be seen!"

"Of course it can be seen. There's no question that it can be seen."

Quaestoris smiled grimly. "The minister of war decides an issue . . . and there is nothing more to say on the subject. Do I state matters correctly?"

"You do."

The envoy put his face in his hands and at length removed them. He sighed heavily and then rose from his place with an abrupt awkward motion, upsetting his wine glass and spilling its contents. Languidly he dropped his napkin into the deep scarlet stain that spread slowly over the white tablecloth. In a low, firm tone that was instantly obeyed, he gave his orders to the servants. Then he turned his attention to me once more. "All right," he said. "It shall be as you wish. Just as you wish, my lover and tormentor. We'll see the work. Just as you say . . . "

I did not reply but rose in my turn, threw my napkin to the floor, and followed him through the house. We gained access to the small courtyard where he did his sculpting through the bedroom. Night had fallen and the court lay in darkness and silence. A faint breeze stirred the branches of the trees that overhung the walls; high above their shadowy crowns, the stars were lazily gathering in the sky and soon the silver sickle of a moon would show. Quaestoris walked ahead of me over the flagstones to the pool, where in the hush I could hear the sounds the invisible fish made when they broke the surface of the water. I stood by the envoy and looked toward the shapeless hulk that was the unfinished statue. "In a moment," said Quaestoris softly. "In a moment." I detected in his voice a strange tension which I had never heard before. We stood together, side by side, without touching and without speaking. We stood together and waited.

A short time later there were voices and footsteps. The envoy's bent and gnarled old major-domo, who had been with his master for as long as both could remember, even since Quaestoris had gone into the diplomatic service, and whose whimsical charm and unsurpassable suaveness were talked of everywhere the envoy had been posted throughout the empire, came limping in through a gate. He was followed by six strapping servants in loincloths, each of whom bore an unlit torch. The major-domo waited until all had passed into the yard, then closed the gate and locked it. Quaestoris spoke to him, and he in turn directed the others to their positions in a circle around the marble's bulk. The envoy cleared his throat and fidgeted uneasily. "Prepare yourself to look upon my nemesis," he said.

"I thought it to be your salvation."

"My salvation?" Quaestoris laughed bitterly. "It was once my inspiration," he said. "It will be my nemesis."

"Well," I said, "let it be what it may—I am prepared."

Quaestoris gave the signal and the major-domo limped from one torch to the next, kindling each as he went. The flames blazed up brightly, illuminating the entire yard even to the walls, the side of the house, the pool and the dark shape that dominated all else by the sheer fact of its presence. But the envoy's sculpture was not yet revealed to me: it was draped and the major-domo had to uncover it, fumbling at the ropes until at last they were free and he could haul the shroud aside. When he did, I saw what Quaestoris had been working on every day of his life for the past several months.

The figure, whatever it was, stood headless. It was taller than any man, perhaps nine or even ten feet, and had outstretched arms, as if it were begging or beckoning—I could not make out which. There were two female breasts on the torso—large and well-rounded, but one of them had a nipple on it and the other did not. Below the navel, the genitals were those of a male; they were disproportionately large, and even from where I stood I could see that the penis was circumcised. The legs, thick-thighed and muscular, were finished to the kneecaps but directly below ran into rough stone. In the red cast of the torchlight, this half-formed hermaphrodite with no head took on a color darker than the carmine of the marble of which it had been carved: it looked like fluid blood, its finished surfaces running liquescent and raw, like a fetus plucked freshly from the womb. I said nothing, but I was both puzzled and displeased with what I saw. I walked slowly to one side, skirting the pool, so that I could see the statue from behind. Quaestoris stood where he was. From the rear, the sculpture seemed to have been carved in reverse: the figure's chest was flat and male, while the sex was female. But the legs, which were female in shape, were completely realized, even to the formation of feet with slender toes and toenails. Altogether, the statue did not attract me: it seemed grim and bleak, vaguely cadaverlike, as if the sculptor were a ghoul who had pried this hideous figure from the grave and not carved it above the earth.

"So," I said, turning to Quaestoris, "so you have complete power. So that's why you do it—so that's why you sculpt."

"Complete power? What do you mean?"

"Complete power to form something exactly as you wish, exactly as you desire. You start from nothing and you can go anywhere that you want—anywhere. Whatever you wish to bring forth from chaos, whatever you want to extract from the darkness, whatever it is that you choose to allow into the world—there it is! You will it and it exists— monster or angel, cripple or athlete, beast or man, myth or mother, child or corpse, devil or seraph! You are the god who holds the *fiat* in his hot hands!"

"All those shapes," mused the envoy, "or any combination of those shapes . . ."

"Or any combination of them, precisely! You alone are sole judge and sole arbiter. You alone decide limb and feature, species and sex: all . . . all is in your mind and in your fingers. And all the world outside of you must accept whatever it is that you have chosen to bring out, like it or dislike it. Even if they detest it, it is still there—it has still taken its place in the world, and all creation has been compelled to move back and make room for it. Nobody can change it before it appears, nobody can alter it the instant it is revealed. What you show is what you have chosen to show—every molecule of it. What power, Quaestoris, what enormous power! I can well understand why you pursue your work so avidly."

"Yes, yes," said the envoy. There was irony in his voice. "Yes, my friend, and I too understand very well why you pursue your own particular—work. You are searching—for the very same power, no? You want absolute dominion, do you not?" Quaestoris coughed. "But I do not think you will find what you are looking for."

"Oh? And why not?"

"Because there is nothing in the world that you do that bears your own stamp, that is why. Because nothing of your work is you, that is why. The power that you have is power over other men, not over yourself. You can command a hundred men, or a thousand, or ten thousand, or an entire nation, or an empire—but you are you and they always remain themselves."

"On the contrary, my friend Quaestoris, the men whom I command become an extension of my will."

"And what is your will other than to command them?"

I laughed. "As the representative of an empire which has deified the power of arms, you must realize that you are hardly qualified to lecture me on personal morality."

Quaestoris shrugged his shoulders. "I would derive no personal satisfaction from delivering a 'lecture,' as you phrase it; neither do I now—or for that matter, have I ever labored under the illusion that moralizing is of any use whatsoever. I am simply conveying to you an observation based on my own experience. You can take it in any fashion you see fit."

"I think," I said, "that you are getting old, my friend."

"Yes, yes," said Quaestoris. "Old and senile. My talons no longer rip into flesh as they did in the past, nor can my beak tear apart prey as once it did. But, to tell you the truth, during the past few months I have stopped missing my predatory days altogether."

"I've heard that said before—it's the epitaph of every aging beast."

"No," said the envoy, "you're wrong. Even if you are the infallible minister of war, you're wrong." He snorted and then said in a low voice, "My friend, I am very sorry now that I did not heed the call of stone, that I did not pursue it wherever it led!"

" 'Stone is stone—and spirit is spirit!' A man by the name of Quaestoris once told me that. I don't know what ever became of him."

The envoy ignored what I had said. "My life," he said, "has come together very recently in a strange way . . . a very strange way. I don't know if I can explain to you what I mean, what I'm driving at. But I think that I have touched something inside me whose existence I did not even dream of; I think a man has a center that he can reach if he works at it assiduously enough. My friend, having discovered this force, this core, this—as it were—being inside me, I have been able to discover spirit where I never knew there was any, or where I thought there was none. The world of matter has fallen back in awe—I don't know how else to express it . . . Oh, I know that you're going to laugh."

"No, Quaestoris, I am going to cry. I always weep at the funeral when a sane, rational man chooses to bury his sanity. Perhaps you were right, Quaestoris, perhaps your first impulse when you arrived in this country was correct—perhaps you should have left it when you wanted to leave, or perhaps you should never have acceded to Pilate's invitation and come here. This country has gotten to you, has shattered your nerves and clouded your mind. You'll be seeing visions before long, like the madman I keep in the fortress prison! You've deteriorated, my friend, you've slipped badly. You are but the shadow of the man I met a few short years ago!"

"I rather think the man you met was shadow."

I laughed. "Quaestoris, it's not too late. The descent is not irreversible—you can still change your course. You'd better see where you are heading—if you don't take care, you'll find yourself converting. The priests will smell you out and come running to snatch your soul from under your nose!"

"They shouldn't want it," said the envoy in a melancholy tone. "Whatever soul I have left is not, I can assure you, worth snatching. It is shriveled, rancid, rotten, worm-eaten! Even the curs in the street would turn away from a soul like mine."

"What you call your soul is up to you, Quaestoris. If you choose to become an old woman who cringes at imagined ghosts in corners, it's entirely your affair. There is no greater ruin in life than that which a man brings upon himself. And there is none to save him from it but himself. 'The call of stone?' That's the nonsense a child talks when he's frightened of the dark! Stone has no voice. Matter has no voice. Most men who walk the earth have no voices—they are silent tombs whom a strong man must fill with his echo! The mallet and the chisel are no more than instruments a strong man uses to gain an end, to gain control —just as the weapons of war are no more than instruments a strong man uses to establish his absolute authority! Only the strong man has a voice—and that voice is power: raw, naked, brutal power! It is incredible that I must repeat this particular lesson to you, a Roman and a venerable servant of the emperor, of all people!"

There was a prolonged silence in which I heard the major-domo approach Quaestoris, coming from behind a torchbearer over to his master and remaining several moments to talk with him. The servant withdrew, and the envoy stood alone. "Have you finished looking at the statue?" he asked abruptly.

"No, I have not."

"My friend, I am weary."

"Leave me alone, then, and I shall join you in the house when I am through."

Quaestoris shook his head. "I should prefer to stay here in the yard with you until you know—"

"Know what?"

"—know more about the statue."

I shrugged. "I don't give a damn . . . Suit yourself." I walked past a torchbearer and went closer to the stone figure. It was evident that the sculptor had been working on the side now facing me, since not only were the legs completed but a long, slender neck had been carved out and there was even the beginning of a chin in the marble above. I found the chin extremely disturbing, but I did not know why. I was irritated. "This work is—most unlike you," I snapped.

"You mean that it doesn't resemble me?" said Quaestoris.

"Nothing of the sort, damn it! I meant that it was not in your usual style."

"And what is my style?"

"Lucid. Direct. Unemotional. In touch with reality."

"Take a look at the other side again," said the envoy.

"Why?"

"Because I asked you to."

"As you wish." I went around to the other side of the figure with a feeling of sudden impatience, with a wish to get the statue out of my

294

sight and out of my mind. Again I saw the chest with the one nippled breast and the second that had none; again I saw the scrupulously realized male genitals. But now in the formless stone that should have been or was to be the head my eye caught something heretofore unseen. There were chisel marks I had not noticed. I went still closer and peered up. In the flickering red pall of the torchlight, a pair of stone eyes gazed back at me in icy disdain. I could not help but recognize them. Quaestoris laughed shrilly. They were my own.

Despite all of the pressures and the frenetic pace of my work, I now began to visit my brother and the woman, whom in my mind I had begun to call his "wife," with unbroken regularity once and sometimes twice a week. I always took Ichavod and three or four other trusted warriors with me and left them stationed outside the door of the cell. The first visit had surprised me. My brother and the woman seemed all but unaware of each other's existence. My brother occupied his part of the cell and did not leave it; the woman sat on the cot that had been installed for her comfort and stayed there, quite as if she lived in another room or house or world. My brother had greeted me cordially, calling me his "prodigal." We spoke easily, but he did not once refer to the woman or to the fact that she had been brought into the cell to live with him. He told me that he had been very busy since my last visit and had little or no time to think of me, though he "loved me" as his "own flesh."

"What has occupied you?"

"God has visited me," he said. "Several times."

"God visited you—here in this very cell?"

"Yes, my brother."

"And He spoke to you?"

"He spoke to me, my brother, just as you speak to me now."

"Did you see—God?"

The prisoner hesitated. "Four times," he said after a time, "He came to me in my cell. Three times He could not be seen. He said that my eyes were not opened wide enough to perceive Him. So I simply heard Him speaking to me. But then, on the fourth visit, I became aware of His divine presence. I was terribly frightened and coldness ran through my limbs; I felt I must faint, but a strange inner courage buoyed my spirits. From my cot, I watched as He gathered in that corner"—the prisoner pointed with a trembling finger—"He gathered there slowly, as the gray clouds gather over the great sea before a storm breaks. And I plucked up courage—I know not from where—and said: 'O Lord, my eyes have been sharpened, for I detect Your awful presence.' And the Lord sighed, 'Yes,' even as the wind sighs in the cypresses at the coming of the dawn. And I said, 'Lord, my eyes are sharp, for even as I say these words, You gather.' And the Lord answered me, saying, 'Now then, sharpen your heart and serve me as I direct you.' And He bade me obey to the letter all that which He commanded me to do."

I grasped my silver-handled riding whip and said to the prisoner, "But what are you telling me? You know very well that the God of Israel has neither shape nor form, nor does any man know the place in which He dwells. Even the prophet Moses, who brought the Holy Law down from the mount, did not look upon His face. How then did it come to pass that you saw Him?"

The prisoner gazed at me calmly. "Nevertheless," he said, "I saw His presence. As the spider spins his web, so did He spin Himself out of the unseen world where He dwells in His glory."

"I see. And what is it that He commanded you to do?"

My brother smiled. "I cannot disclose it—at least, not now."

"I understand." I gazed at the girl. She was sitting on her cot, motionless as she had been since I entered the cell, her eyes fixed to my person. There were apprehension and strain in her face, but she looked far better than when last I had seen her. Most of the wounds from the vicious beating Kalbi had given her were healed, but there were pronounced scars on her face and neck from that thrashing and from the "games" the queen had played with her which would never fade. I slapped the riding whip against my thigh, and she started as if I had struck her. "Relax," I said. "I'm not going to harm you." I smiled, but the girl seemed even more frightened, like some animal that has been violated beyond the point that will allow it ever to trust again. "Were you here when God appeared to him, as he says?" The woman did not answer. "Did you see God's presence in the corner?" Still the girl said nothing. She sat without moving and stared at me wide-eyed, clenching her fingers tightly. My brother seemed to wake as from a dream. For the first time he looked over to where the girl sat and smiled gently.

"She means no offense," he said. "She is afraid of you. She does not have trust in you. She does not know what a good man you are."

"Did she see God?"

The prisoner shook his head. "No, she was asleep. God in His great mercy touched her with His hand and caused a deep slumber to fall upon her that she not be affrighted with His terrifying presence."

"I see."

"I'm glad," said the prisoner. "I knew you were a man of understanding heart."

During successive visits, my brother revealed—a little more each time, it seemed—some of the tasks that God had given him. One evening he told me that because the world was so evil, "because like a garden it was overrun with weeds and vile blights," because the world was like "a leper gone mad with terror of death and tearing its own pustulating flesh to shreds in the desire to die and end its suffering," because the world was "a beast who devoured its own young in blind, uncontrollable rage," because the world was "a scorpion swollen with venom, that—finding no other victim—stings itself to death with its own tail," God had bidden the prisoner to come to the world and cleanse it of its scarlet sins and purge it of "its rank iniquity." The prisoner clasped his hands. "Consciousness of sin is the first step," he told me, "but only the first step. Once consciousness of the world as a miasma is established, action must follow. God has ordered me to act. I am His soldier, His sword, His scouring agent!"

The prisoner stared at me with blazing eyes. "Will you kneel and pray?" he said. "Will you kneel and pray to the God of Hosts for the strength to act boldly and wisely in His name?" I refused, and he knelt on the floor of the cell where he was and prayed out loud to his "Father in heaven," who had "instructed and inspired him" in dream and fancy, by day and by night, and who had in "His mercy and His loving kindness" made "His divine presence manifest in a cloud of transcendent glory" that even the "darkest night of hell could never dispel." The prisoner smiled in his prayer. "Even the tiniest spark of God," he chanted, "could illumine an entire universe of darkness." The girl, who had gradually come to accept me as a visitor who meant no harm, sat on her cot and watched him, a look of strangled pain in her large eyes and in the twisted, stubborn set of her lips.

The next time I paid a visit to the prison, I was surprised to find my brother and the woman together. He was sitting on her cot beside her prostrate form. At first glance I thought that perhaps there had been conjugal union between the two of them, but then I saw from the look

297

of consternation on my brother's face that something was amiss. "What's wrong?" I said.

My brother grimaced. "The devil," he said through his teeth. "The devil has seized her. We must fight for her soul! Do you understand? We must fight for her soul!"

I went over to the cot and saw immediately that the woman was very ill. Her face was haggard and flushed, her eyes glassy with fever that convulsed her limbs every few moments. "How long has she been this way?" I asked.

"She cried out in her sleep last night," said my brother. "I thought she had a nightmare and spoke to comfort her. But she continued to groan and I rose from my bed and went to her, and when I looked into her eyes I knew that the evil one had come for her and was trying to take her from me. I went down on my knees and prayed to the Lord that He might descend and save the woman from the clutches of the evil one. But the Lord spoke unto me and said, 'I will not descend to save this woman, for you are my vicar on the earth. Have faith in Me and in My holy name and lay your hands upon this girl and the devil will leave her tormented body and she will rise from her bed and be well. The Lord has spoken to you, and now harken unto His words and do as He commands.' And I was greatly puzzled and I said to the Lord, 'What manner of thing is this that you command me to do?' But the Lord did not see fit to answer me, and I thought that He had turned His face away from me because I had questioned Him and His ways. But I rose from my knees and bent over the girl and laid my hands upon her head, as I had been directed, and called upon the evil one to quit her burning body. But the girl cried out in agony and remained as she was, and as I bent over her I feared for her life: I feared even in the night that her soul would leave her and the devil would snare it and bear it away with him to infernal regions."

"Then your hands have not cured her?"

"No, they have not."

"And why is that?"

"Alas, my brother, that my faith in the Lord was not strong enough to heal her!"

"Will she die?"

"No!"

"How do you know?"

"She cannot die!"

"Why?"

"Because I do not want her to die!"

"And why is that?"

"Because—because I love her!"

"Ah, so that's it. I understand—I understand very well."

"I knew you would."

The girl's condition worsened. Great pustules appeared on her flesh, and when they burst, black fluid ran out over her skin. She lay in a coma and the breath rattled hoarsely in her chest, coming in fits and starts, as if uncertain that it would continue. I left orders for the physicians to be allowed into the cell to do what they could. They prescribed what medicines they could and gave her up for lost. My brother never left her side during the illness. He sat with her day and night, administering the herbs the doctors had left and giving her certain potions which he said "God had instructed" him to mix. The fever rose in spite of his efforts.

One night when I came in, I saw that he had removed all of her clothes and was bathing her skeletonlike body with water. He held her gently and sang to her in an odd, high-pitched voice that kept cracking, though she lay unconscious and could not hear a note he sang. When I asked him what he was doing, he told me that he was "holding on to her soul, lest it be tempted to fly away." He said that the "devil's own smell came out of her orifices" and that he knew "the baleful one was within her." He rocked her to and fro and told me that he "would not let go," that he would "sustain her in life," that he would die himself rather than surrender "to Satan and the powers of infamy." When I asked if I might help him in any way, he told me that I must not draw near, for I was not "strong enough" to combat the influence of "the arch fiend who rules in hell." But he said if I wanted to pray, that "would certainly aid" in his struggle.

I repeated what I had seen and heard to the chief physician, and he marveled that the woman was still living. "According to my diagnosis," he said, "she should have been dead long ago. This is really nothing short of a miracle." My brother persisted in his vigil, in his care. When she was in a coma or slept, he prayed without surcease. "Let my imploring voice never leave the ears of God," he said. When she was awake, he spoke and sang to her and caressed her to comfort her in her pain. "Do not fear," he whispered to her. "I am with you. I will not let you die. I will not allow the evil one to spirit you away from this earth, away from my arms and my mind. My heart will defend you against darkness." When she had the strength and was able to swallow, he fed her, sometimes chewing her food for her before she took it. Several weeks passed, and gradually the fever subsided and the pain left her. "God has heard me," he said. "God knows what is in my heart and has answered my prayers. The infernal one, who delights in death and agony, has not prevailed. I have prevailed. I have advanced God's cause on this earth." My brother hovered over the recuperating girl as if she were an infant; he could not do enough for her. "I will nourish her with my love," he said. "I will heal her with love."

One day at noon when I entered the cell, the woman was sitting up again. She was very pale, and her face and limbs were wasted. But her eyes shone. She was well. My brother was ecstatic. "She is returned!" he cried. "She is returned from the vale of the dead! She is risen from the dead! Praise God for the wonders He works, for His infinite mercy, for His everlasting glory, for His power, before which the universe is as a mote of dust!" My brother's eyes blazed. "As the Lord has done with this woman, so shall I do with the earth. Where there was death and decay, I say to you, there shall henceforth by my hand be the resurrection and the life!" The prisoner rose from the cot where he had been sitting with the woman. "Will you kneel with me and give thanks to the Lord?" he said to me.

I laughed. "You ought know by now that I do not pray."

"It does not matter, my brother," said the prisoner. "I know that your soul is good."

The next time I came, the prisoner was praying at the far wall. The woman, who was fully recovered now, was kneeling on the floor beside him. From the aperture, a soft light fell upon both. "What is this?" I asked.

"She wishes to see God," said my brother.

The girl did not turn her head to see me or move from her position. She had bent her head far over so that it grazed the stone of the wall, and now as I observed her, she covered her face with her hands. Her body rocked to and fro and her shoulders shook; I could see that she was overcome with emotion. "Will God show Himself to her?" I asked.

My brother nodded. "He will—if she has sufficient faith."

On a subsequent visit, I asked the prisoner if he had engaged in connubial relations with the woman. He looked puzzled. "Have you entered her, as a man enters a woman?" I asked.

He shook his head slowly.

"Why not?"

"God has commanded union of the spirit, but no more," he said.

"But surely your spirit must whisper to you of carnal desire?"

"No, if that happens, it is only because the devil infiltrates my spirit and speaks to me thus."

"Tell me, my brother," I said. "For I should like very much to know. How is it that the devil came to be?"

"Only the devil knows that," the prisoner smiled.

"And God? Surely God knows something about it?"

"God knows. Yes, God knows all. But He reveals only what He chooses."

The next week I walked into the cell at an hour past midnight. I was astounded to see that the prisoner was lying with the girl on her cot; both of them were completely naked and plainly engaged in the coital act. The woman gasped audibly. She was openly ashamed and thrust my brother from her gently but with firmness and quickly covered her nakedness. My brother sighed and sat up slowly, a dreamy expression on his face. His eyes were moist and shining; he saw me but did not seem to recognize me or to know why I had come. "What is it that you are doing, my prisoner? Can you explain it to me?" I said.

"—God's prisoner—" my brother muttered to himself. And the words that followed were indistinct.

"What have you just done with the woman?" I asked. "Have you engaged in an act of sex? Did the devil enter your spirit and take possession of it? Or has God changed His mind about physical union? Does He allow today what He forbade yesterday?" I laughed. "I had no idea that God was so fickle-minded."

The prisoner looked dazed, as if someone had struck him a blow across the head. He rose from the cot and stood meekly before me in his nakedness. I saw clearly for the first time how ravaged was his thin, frail body. His round shoulders, scrawny neck and pathetic, almost childlike arms were crisscrossed with scars—the marks of the cane and the whip which I knew so well. His hollow chest and protruding rib cage were spotted with the vestiges of bruises and welts; and there were the unmistakable traces of burns on his thighs and legs. His manhood, which was still wet from contact with the woman, had not escaped punishment. I was able to detect without the slightest difficulty where the pincers had bitten into his member and to observe that his left testicle had been crushed in torture. It was markedly evident that my brother had run afoul of his fellow men, the men of earth he so earnestly hoped "to save" many times over in his three decades of life.

During my visits, he had often described to me the manner in which he had been abused and beaten in his travels through the countryside and in the villages. Sometimes dogs had been set upon him and his flesh had been torn and mutilated. In upper Galilee, children had pursued him through the streets of a small village and just beyond its perimeter had thrown stones at him with such savagery that he had lain unconscious in a ditch for two days and had been picked up and nursed back to health by a farmer, who had then tried to enslave him. Another time, in Acre, on the coast, a gang of rowdies had bound him to a stake and threatened to burn him as a disciple of the devil; fortunately for him, the authorities had happened upon the scene and rescued him from death or maiming. Once he had been picked up in a sweep by Herod's troops and interrogated for three days and three nights in a military prison; the soldiers, so he told me, had selected him "to find release for their manly fluid" and had wanted to keep him for that purpose, but had been prevented from doing so by an irate officer bent on disciplining his men. And once the Romans had locked him up for "suspected rebel activities" and for "blatant sedition." They threatened him with dismemberment and crucifixion if he "did not talk," but after cross-examining him only beat him "into a coma" and threw him out of camp "like a sack of bones." Always, he told me, always and wherever he went he was the "butt of a joke, the point of a jest, the target of anger and spite, the perennial scapegoat—the scorned, mocked and despised." And when I asked him why he thought God allowed this to happen to him, he replied simply, "He knows I can take it." And he smiled.

And when he turned for a moment, I saw that his back and buttocks bore the marks of the lash. He had told me that often during his wanderings he had been picked up by local authorities; sometimes it was for an embarrassing theft which needed a culprit, other times it was for arson, vandalism, lechery and a host of other petty crimes—or simply for "vagrancy" or because the police "needed an outlet for their hatred." Once, so he told me, he was arrested for rape. He had not even been in the town when the rape had been perpetrated, but it did not seem to matter. The police seized him, the girl identified him as her attacker and lifted her cloak to show the court how she had been mauled, the judges overruled everything that he said in his defense, several townspeople testified that they had heard him plotting the assault in a local tavern. The sentence was brought in quickly: he was to be stoned to death on the morrow. He was led away to jail in chains, the spectators in the courtroom spitting in his face as he passed. Luckily, the jail was attacked by a mob and burned down during the night, and he was able to make good his escape during the confusion.

Once, so he told me, he had been incarcerated for "profaning the religion of Israel." This was because he said in a public place that "God did not need rituals and had no use for burnt offerings and sacrifices." He did not remember what else he said, but he was later accused of "defaming the priesthood" and of "heaping abuse, insult and slander upon hallowed institutions and holy practices." He was punished by being publicly flogged. The whipper was a gigantic fellow, a professional wrestler and an athlete from childhood days, who struck so viciously with his knotted and barbed whip that my brother "left the world" on the first blow.

"I journeyed straight to the heavenly throne of God," he told me, "where I threw myself on my face before His blinding presence and wept. I described in detail to God the baseness and cruelty of men, their narrowness, their arrogance, their vanity, their lust for power, their boundless delight in inflicting pain upon others. 'Why,' I asked Him, 'cannot they translate the anguish they cause others into the anguish they themselves would feel in similar circumstances? Why do they hide from their mortality? Why do they put their faith in ownership of things, which passes from them as the dew dries from the grass in the heat of the day? Why do they devour others in greed, not seeing that greed devours them? Why do they beat and bludgeon and crush and destroy, when each blow they deal and every wound they inflict drains them of the worth of life?' And I wept tears that were very bitter and asked Him further, crying, "Why do the rich prey upon the poor and the strong upon the weak and the cunning upon the naïve? And when will it end? Lord, tell me when there will be an end to it?' And God answered me and said, 'My son, you will make an end to it.' And I said, 'Am I your son then, Lord?' And God replied, 'Yes, for I am the Father.' And I said, 'But how can I bring an end to the evil in the world, how can I stop the wicked from oppressing the innocent, how can I stop death from feeding on life?' And God said, 'Fear not, but believe in me and I will send you forth as a scourge and a flail and the men and nations of the earth will yield to your word.' And I said, 'When, Lord, when should I go?' And God said, 'Go now.' And instantly I was back in the marketplace where I was being whipped, hanging on the post, and the onlookers laughed to see that I was awake, and the whipper struck again and then there was darkness, only darkness.

"And when I wakened again, it was evening and my face was in the dust, in the dung and straw, and two men—town drunks—were staring down into my face; they spat into it and then took me by my legs and arms and carried me to the wadi where the garbage was cast and laid me there with the rats and the maggots." My brother's fingers played softly over his chest. "And once, in Judea," he said, "for a punishment the villagers tied me to a post in a field and said, 'This is our scarecrow; surely he will frighten away the crows and the starlings!' And they were much pleased with what they had done. And the children of the village threw scraps of refuse and cried out, 'He is crucified! Our prisoner is crucified!' " And then my brother was silent, he spoke no more, and the look in his eyes was distant and diffuse.

His forearms and neck had always been dirty, but I saw now that my brother's flesh was clean and white; I was certain that the woman had washed and cleansed him as he had done for her when she lay ill. I bent my riding whip. "Answer me," I said. "Tell me how you cohabit with this woman when it is forbidden?"

My brother shook his head. "It was not I who lay with the woman," he said. "It was God who lay with her and entered her. He found her desirable and He wanted her." The prisoner smiled. "It was very beautiful. I watched as the two of them made love and there was no shame. They moved as the waves on the shore, as the wind in the fields of ripening grain, as the stars dancing in their constellations, as the sun mounting the bride of the morning sky from the east. God was a burst of glory and the woman received His embrace with the smoking arms of night . . . " The woman, clad in her prison garb, looked up at my brother with love in her eyes; she reached out and softly touched his arm and he started as if he had been stung and turned his head and stared down at her. "What is it?" he said in a voice that was low but very clear. Her eyes shone, her lips moved, but she spoke no words that were audible. Nevertheless, he nodded and took his prison raiment from the floor and put it on. His lacerated flesh was gone from sight.

During the following visit, he told the girl that I was the ruler of Judea and that one day I "would be the ruler of all the nations of the world." And he laughed happily, completely, as a child laughs. "And I shall know him and he will listen to me and bring forth good in his kingdom." Then his face grew serious, and he told the girl, "He is the king. He rules over all the land: free man and servant, female and slave, beast and fowl. God has seen fit to place the scepter of earthly power into his hand and entrusted him with our welfare. God has blessed him with kindness of heart and with wisdom of mind." The prisoner pointed to me. "God is lightning," he said. "The king is a tall tree on the mountain."

And I visited my brother many times and heard many stories that he told me: of how he rose to heaven and descended to the bowels of the earth, of how he flew in the air and walked on the waves, of how he made the blind see, the deaf hear, the mute speak, the lame walk, the leper clean-skinned. And once he told me that he had raised up a man who lay dead in his bed so that the corpse breathed again and lived as any other man. And I recorded much of what he said and entered it in my journals, which were kept stored in my most secret vault.

The pieces were on the board and I was ready to make my move. The army, which I had labored so long and so hard to resurrect, was in superb shape. The Seventeenth Brigade was only one of a dozen assault units trained to move quickly, strike hard, and crush all opposition. Backing this attack spearhead were well-disciplined regiments of infantry and cavalry with energetic, highly motivated line officers to lead them. The general staff was superlative: I knew every officer on it, and many of the younger men were budding generals. Akrab spent long evenings with me, poring over maps and battle plans. "Our army is a mastiff," he told me. "A razor-fanged, iron-muscled mastiff. You have only to give the orders, and it will fly at an enemy's throat!" I thanked him for his enthusiasm, but bade him go over our forces with a "fine-toothed comb," if necessary. "When we cast the dice," I told him, "we want the surest hand possible. If we are certain before we make a move, we can be certain of every move we make. Check everything again and again, and when you know it is right, check it once more." Akrab laughed and showed his strong white teeth. "You can be proud of what you have wrought with the army," he said as he left my office, "just as the army is proud to have you as commander-in-chief. If we must die, it will be for someone who truly understands the need to die." I returned his passionately delivered salute, and when he was gone sat down to go over the last *Patish* report I had received on my deputy. It showed that he was fine, that there was no reason to suspect him.

Melech the Galilean informed me that *Patish* was at full strength and "drawn as a catapult." He wrote in code that "when its power was released," the opponent would feel "force and fury beyond imagination." He went on to say that he experienced difficulty "only in restraining the men" and that when they were at last given the signal for combat they would "accredit themselves as legendary warriors." I was much pleased with the report, and I trusted the commander of my spy system implicitly; still, I made a special trip by dead of night to the villa that had once belonged to Zerubabel to inspect my elite striking force for myself. Melech had aged, but aging had made him harder, shrewder, more ruthless, more eager.

"The soil that will in the end receive my corpse . . . " he told me as we rode about the grounds to see the men as they trained and would train until the final moments before the battle, "I want to soak it well with blood"—he exploded with laughter—"so that I can sleep soundly!" Set in his flinty, weather-seamed face, his small eyes blazed with what he often described as "lust for combat." He would swing his one arm in a wide arc as if wielding a sword and say, "Some men like women, others like drink, still others yearn after gold—as for me, I like spilling an enemy's guts onto the earth!" After we had reviewed the men under his command and gone over plans, contingency plans, codes and the like, we sat together from midnight until the break of day as we had sat together when *Patish* was founded. We ate of the flesh of a boar slain "with the single spear thrust of one of the men"—a miraculous achievement, for it usually took the combined efforts of many men to bring that animal down, and—as Melech said, wiping his lips of grease —"a portent of what is to come, a sign that the beast of Judea will come to a similar end!" We drank the best of wines—wines still left from Zerubabel's cellars—and we toasted each other in the spirit, as Melech put it, of "fiery comradeship." As the dawn opened the eastern sky like a wound, Melech the Galilean rose and lifted his glass high: "If death be waiting on the fateful day of conflict, our victory will be in submission; and if life, our victory is in defiance!" And he laughed, drained his cup and flung it at the wall.

In the upper reaches of the Galilee, in a hunting lodge once owned by the war minister I had displaced—a structure of natural unhewn stone set high on a mountain crag that overlooked the inland sea—I met in secret with the general Livinius. He was accompanied by senior officers of his staff while I came with my deputy commander, general of the army, Akrab and a number of staff officers. We had all of us traveled incognito and with almost no escorts and arrived at the lodge during the night. We rested from the journey for two hours and at the start of the new day began our meeting. Hidden in mountain crevices and in canyons, concealed in forests and swamps, the hooded warriors of *Patish* surrounded us, unbeknownst to anyone but myself. They were the best of the elite, hand-picked by Melech the Galilean himself for this assignment. "You shall have protection, a guarantee against treachery," Melech wrote back when I sent him my orders. "For I will provide you with a group of the finest cutthroats, butchers and murderers— bound in blood to your service!" These were men who were ready on command to slay any intruder or rally against any perfidy. With the knowledge that they could be summoned to my cause at any instant, I was fully secure.

We sat together at the long oak table in the large dining hall of the lodge, Romans and Jews, to plan the downfall of Herod the king. Livinius jokingly suggested that the code name of the monarch be "ostrich," and although the name was offered in jest we adopted it. The time selected for the coup was Herod's birthday, six weeks away. The king was sixty, a number he said to his courtiers was "swollen with significance." After a series of lengthy meetings with his spiritual counselors, diviners, astrologers and sorcerers, Herod announced that because the number sixty was "ripe," was "big-bellied with promise," and "heralded new constellations of glory for the monarch and his kingdom," the day would be a national holiday, a fete. "For Jew and for Roman alike—for all brothers in Judea—the day would," proclaimed Herod, "be a time of joy and celebration, of merriment and carousing. For the valley of death is deep," said Herod, "and the hour of man on the earth short and swiftly flying: therefore when it is a time of gladness, let him be glad!" We saw the monarch's birthday as an excellent time for him to die. Livinius said he would even be happy to say the Hebrew prayer of mourning for the king, and we all laughed except for Akrab, who said that the only prayer deserved by Herod would be recited for him by the jackals, at which we laughed the harder. But my deputy Akrab did not laugh: Herod had executed his two brothers for a crime they did not commit, and he hated the king with all of his heart, referring to him always as "the rat of Judea." The day, then, was fixed: it was a logical choice, for the king and his subjects would be preoccupied with the gaiety decreed by royal edict for all.

The plan was essentially a simple one. The army, directed by me, loyal to my command, would seize control of every major city by force of arms: Beersheba, Hebron, Jaffa, Bethlehem—where my brother and I were born—Jericho, Schechem, Acre, Safed, Tiberias. Everywhere the army would depose the civilian authorities appointed by the "ostrich" and institute a military command responsible directly to me as the highest officer in the land. Opposition would be instantly trodden underfoot; anyone who dared raise hand or protest would be struck down without hesitation. I gave to all officers the right to conduct summary trials in the field, and the power, by authority of the sole, indisputable and uncontestable decision of each, to execute. The general Livinus concurred wholeheartedly with my thinking. As the cities fell into my hands one by one—"like ripened fruit," as I put it to the others—troops would be diverted from each to take part in the main assault on the capital city of Jerusalem. We expected no trouble of any serious proportions in any but the "City of God," where King Herod maintained a special force of several thousand troops that were not under my jurisdiction and answered only to his direct orders and where the priests and the other parties all quartered armed contingents of their own. "Jerusalem," I reasoned aloud, "had to be softened like an apple with the introduction of worms." By this, I referred to the men of *Patish*, whom I described simply as "my agents." Once they had infiltrated into the city, I said, "they would burrow like termites into the defense structure and undermine the entire foundation." When the main attack came from my forces outside the city, the warriors of my secret striking force would rise up from within and deal a blow in the rear that must stun the defenders and "reduce them to utter dismay." With the fall of the Holy City, my star would ascend. To my own troops would be added the surrendering forces who would pledge their loyalty to me, the regiments of mercenaries in the hire of the various political factions, who always went to the winner when their own employers became losers, as well as thousands of the city's inhabitants whom we would call up as conscripts on the pain of death. Every party in the capital would flock to me and throw its support my way, fearing the reprisals that would follow if they did not. "Jerusalem," I told my listeners, "is a delectable course—the most succulent of all the cities of Judea. But unfortunately she will not be the main course. She will but whet our appetite for a morsel even more delicious—Herod's mountain fortress. With Jerusalem, as it were, under our belts, the way will be clear to the lion's den!"

At this point an involved tactical discussion took place, in which Livinius and his aides reviewed the attack plans Akrab and my general staff had prepared along lines I had suggested. The talk grew heated. Some of the Roman generals favored an all-out frontal attack, with ramps, catapults and other engines of war, and tens of thousands of soldiers taking part. Most of our staff advocated guerrilla tactics, with night raids and surprise forays. Livinius rose and in his bass, rasping voice pointed out the defects in each approach. He strode to the wall and advanced his own theories. His strokes were swift, his hand certain, his eyes cold and deadly. The talons of his mind grasped the battle as they grasped the chessboard. As a spider spins out of itself, so did his extraordinarily keen mind slowly but brilliantly web its plan: the lines on the wall had a shape whose meaning was clear only after he had finished drawing them. He sat, and there was silence. One of the Romans coughed politely.

Then it was that I rose and offered my own critique. As once, long ago in the past, I had astounded and overwhelmed the assembly in a synagogue with my mastery of the Law, so now did I bedazzle the foremost military men of Rome and of Judea with the laws of armed combat. Long before I had suggested the outlines of the plan to Akrab and the others of the general staff, I had reckoned with Livinius's cutting, well-tempered mind. I had come to grips with the crafty general at the chessboard and knew the subtleties of his reasoning thoroughly. My plan had been purposely devised with inherent weaknesses I knew he would discern, though of course none were obvious. Behind the plan that was presented was another plan, meant to supersede the one I knew Livinius must advocate. My ideas were so direct and so lucid that I needed not a single line to make them apparent: the mind of itself understood immediately what I was driving at. All were amazed, and several hands reached out to congratulate me. Livinius himself, flushing a deep scarlet, jumped up. "What a pity they took the foreskin from this one's pizzle!" he cried. "He should have taught great Caesar himself a thing or two!" And he moved over to me as the others fell back, and clasped me to him. "This is my brother!" he shouted, so that the hall echoed with his drawl. "This is my brother in battle! We are infernal seed, we are—spawn of the devil, poison to the race!" And he roared and called for wine and food "—and good hot whores, if they are to be found!"

While the meal was being brought in by slaves who would—unbeknown to them—be slaughtered when the parley was over because they had been on the scene of a meeting too important for them to be left alive, we went over the task of the Romans. Essentially it was much the same as it had been in the massacre of the war minister and his party in the wadi. In the Galilee, in the Jezreel Valley, in Samaria, Judah, the Shefelah and the Negev, the Romans under Livinius would move to head off any possible interference. Roads, junctures and bridges would be guarded; forests, mountain passes and wadis would be watched so my forces could move forward and take their objectives. If Herod were to call for help, Livinius would see to it that the calls never got through, and if they somehow did, that help never got through to him. Whatever the Roman general had to do to insure the coup, he would do. He wanted the wealth that the coup would bring him; he wanted revenge on adversaries and rivals who would be discredited by Herod's fall; he wanted to ally himself with me in the extermination of the rebels which I would be able to achieve once I had the reins of state securely in my hands. For him, the coup was a gamble, but it was a gamble he both wanted and had to take. Enormous wealth and certain advancement were his as reward if the coup succeeded; banishment as a rich man if the plot failed.

Livinius was, so he had told me many times over, a "cagey old beast of battle," now grown "weary of the fray, tired of spilling entrails and tacking stuffed heads to the wall." He had squinted at me a dozen times and said, almost in a whisper, "I've had enough pleasure out of lopping off arms and legs like so many stalks, enough of breaking sieges and taking cities, more than a bellyful of blood and flies and corpses! I want to be a power, to wear diamonds on my breast, rubies in my ears, a bit of sapphire in my nose. Yes, I want a jeweled sword and a retinue and a harem—I want to be a military commander who yawns when they bring him the plans and waves a hand and, sipping wine, says, 'Yes, yes . . . it's fine . . . it's all fine. Go on and do as you think best—I have every confidence in your judgment.'" And he would wink every time.

If Pilate and his military command were able to view his moves, his "passive" or "tacit" part in the coup, as deriving from what it was fashionable to call "personal exigencies" that could be "contained within the arena of Roman foreign policy" and explained to the powers in Rome "in the language of the Hebrews"—that is to say, if the procurator of Judea was able to look the other way when Herod fell—well and good! Livinius would have made a successful gamble and would be on his way to new power and influence. If, however, the coup aborted, Livinius was prepared to flee the country for his part in the failure: to remain in such circumstances would spell downfall and perhaps death, for it was "always easier for an enemy to step on a head which is on the ground than on one which is in the air!"

For the very first time since I had assumed direction of the war ministry and command of the army, I permitted funds from the levies I was collecting from the populace to be diverted for purposes other than those directly connected to the expansion of my war machine. A small shipment of gold, silver, and other precious metals and jewels was packed carefully in clay jugs, fastened to a mule's back, and transported by night to a cave in a remote part of Samaria which had been picked by the general and me as a cache for the payments due him. Livinius was there personally when the shipment arrived—so Elazar, who had traveled with it from the time it left Herod's fortress, told me—and took immediate possession of many of the smaller items, rings and the like, so that if it became necessary for him to leave the country he would be well provided for until more came. If worst came to worst, we had designated Alexandria as the secret rallying point for further action against Judea and the "ostrich."

Livinius had, of course, assured me of his complete support not only in the field but on the political scene as well. There was much feeling against the "rat of Judea" among the Roman authorities in the country and also in Rome itself and the general meant to exploit this sentiment in our favor.

Quaestoris, too, though grudging and reluctant, was drawn into our service. "I want no part of this butchery!" he had told me bluntly. "But you already wear a butcher's smock!" I answered with equal bluntness. "You already have a part—you are part of me!" After a series of bitter and sometimes violent quarrels, he had finally agreed to communicate with a number of senators with whom he was on intimate terms and press them to rail against Herod. We called this "preparing the soil out of which the coup would spring." As the days went by, the envoy seemed more distant, more reserved, less and less interested in the company of others. He wanted me, but less often, and there were times when I failed to arouse him at all. "You have grown cold," I said to him. "Yes, the fire's sunk," he answered. "You are almost a recluse these days," I said. "I have my statue," he answered. "You cannot make love to a marble figure," I joked. "No, one certainly can't," he replied with a bitter smile. He lived an austere, lonely life and began to appear at court less frequently. There was the usual gossip. One person said he had a fatal disease ("I agree with that," said Quaestoris), and another that he had a new lover whom he was hiding from all eyes—"an animal, of Judean descent," the story ran. One courtier recounted that the envoy had "retired from the world to serve a strange, new god" who had manifested himself in the marble in which Quaestoris sculpted. The diplomat found this particular story "fascinating" and said that if he had been able to find the inventor he would have rewarded him well. "The fool who told the tale is obviously passing it on, and no more than that," sighed Quaestoris.

However vigorously the envoy "pursued his destiny in stone" and struggled to "find himself in the crowd of his selves," he did not and "could not" choose to rupture his ties with me. When he resisted my demands, I threatened to terminate our relationship, and in the end he yielded to me. I explained to him over and over again that once my objectives were secured, we would see each other more often and that things would once more be as they had been in the "halcyon days" of our love. Quaestoris exploded in harsh laughter. "The past? The past is gone," he said, "gone irretrievably . . . and I find myself beginning to wonder whether or not it ever existed. As for our future together, I can only say that it looks—bleak. Your sort of triumph, my dear friend, will not release you for me; on the contrary, it will only lay further claim to you." He put forward a hand as if he meant to touch me, but then for some reason reconsidered and pulled it back. "The only victory that would be a real one for you would be a victory over yourself—and that is not easily forthcoming; in fact, it is not forthcoming at all." I shrugged. What did it matter if the envoy spoke such words? I was interested in what he did. I recalled his face when, after a particularly lengthy and violent quarrel, he had suddenly reversed his stand and agreed to help me attain my ends. "I have wanted to break with you for so long a time," he told me, "but I—I simply cannot. Cannot, do you hear? You are some self-inflicted disease which I find myself unable to destroy without destroying myself." There were tears in Quaestoris's eyes. I reached out and touched his cheek—half a caress and half a slap—and saw the warring passions struggle over the features of his face. There was joy and loathing: joy that I had deigned to touch him and loathing for himself because my touch meant so very much to him. I saw clearly that the last words he had spoken to me were true: he could not get along without me and he hated himself for his inability to break away.

In the hunting lodge, the slaves staggered into the dining hall under huge, smoking platters of mutton, venison and beef and the meal began. Despite Livinius's demonstrative and boisterous embrace, the repast was scarcely a festive one. Romans and Jews sat soberly, even sullenly at plate: a mood of ugly rancor prevailed. Steam curled upwards from the food as it was served, blood dripped from the meat to the table and the floor, fat sizzled, utensils clashed, and feet scuffed impatiently. Strong teeth ripped into the crackling skin stretched over roasted animal flesh, knife blades glittered, wine trickled into beards and jaws that could form on the words which would send men to their deaths as easily as most men ask directions to the market chewed steadily. But the eyes of the diners were distant and brooding: they already beheld the bloody specters of war before them. There was a drone of talk in the air that petered out to grim silence. The generals and staff officers drank, but no man drank excessively and the wine did nothing to relieve the tension. The meal was dispatched quickly, and when we finished we rose from the table and adjourned to another, smaller room where we formulated in detail the battle operations, stage by stage, fixed our timetable of events, and assigned areas of responsibility.

It was nearly midnight when we left the room so subordinates could work up the maps and plans for us to take with us when we left. Out on the wide verandah, the night was sultry and thunder smoldered in the distance. We had a clear view from the lodge all the way down to the Sea of Galilee below, on whose moody black surface starlight glittered like shattered armor. The Roman and Jewish guards who had ridden with us as covert escorts to the meeting had stripped and were wrestling to pass the time. Their soft grunts slipped sluggishly into the air, and the fine sweat on their muscles in play stirred with the same restless fury as the light of the stars on the waves far beneath them.

To me, at that singular moment, the night became a vast crucible in which the future was being compounded. Out of this fertile darkness surrounding us would come the kind and degree of power I had sought all of my life: the power to plunge the world into cataclysm at will! Beyond the operation against the throne of the puppet king, the doll monarch, Herod, was concealed my own master move against Rome itself. I had thought it all through carefully and reviewed it over and over again in my mind. When Judea was safely in my grasp, I would move immediately to end party and factional quarrels: I would wipe out altogether the internecine wrangling that drained the country. Once that strength-sapping plague was gone, I would go after the rebels tooth and fang, sparing no effort to root them out wherever they were and sweeping them from the board in a single stroke. The all-out campaign against the Zealots would serve me well as a *modus operandi* for doubling or even tripling the size of the army and raising the level of its operational effectiveness. Within a year or two at most, I would head a nation free of civil strife and would command a powerful fighting force that had gained its strength and its experience freeing that nation. Under the very nose of the Roman conquerors, I should have built up the might to upset them.

If Livinius survived the coup politically, and I had not the slightest doubt that he would, I would approach him with a censored version of my plan. I would enlist his aid under the guise of removing one of his rivals, not as a move against Roman occupation per se. But once he had committed his troops to battle, the results would be exactly the same for me. "When Romans fought Romans," as I put the matter in my mind, "only Romans died!" I saw no reason in the world why Livinius's first taste of political and economic power should not whet his appetite for more, no reason why he should not join with me in a further exploit. For Livinius appeared to me to be no lover of Roman soil above all other soil, no slave of some mythical "empire" in which he had some mythical stake, no cultist of the blood, no necrophile, no worshiper of sacred ashes, no dupe of emperor or ancestor, no lackey at the altar. Rome to Livinius was precisely what Rome, or for that matter Jerusalem, was to me: the hilt of a sword that was mine to grasp, the handle of a whip that was for me to wield. Rome was the eternal boot in the face, toe in the kidneys, heel on the skull. If Livinius continued to feel thusly, I would use him to go further. If not, I should find someone else who did—an adversary of his, perhaps Aquilius or another like him.

Or else, if my war machine had built up sufficient strength, I should go it alone: plunge my troops into head-on battle with the Romans, and carried forward by the element of surprise, drive them from the land.

"You who spoke so eloquently and so lengthily . . . are so silent," said Livinius, coming up to me at the balustrade. "What are you thinking of?" He snickered. "Chess moves?"

"Perhaps," I said.

"What do you see out there in the darkness?"

"The future."

"And what is the future?"

"Whatever we make it."

"And what will you make of your future, my Hebrew gamecock?"

"An impregnable fortress, my Roman crocodile."

Livinius yawned. "Yes," he drawled, "you will stand this mongrel land in good stead when you are king. I'm certain of it!"

"It is myself I wish to serve—and no other. But why do say what you have said?"

"Because, my friend, you have clarity and confidence. And a very firm hand, if I may say so. A hand which knows how to use the whip and the sword even before the mind instructs it to use them."

"The rod is my measure, Livinius. I use it to gauge all men."

"So I've seen." The general leaned forward on the rail beside me and peered down into the great dark bowl at whose bottom lay the sea, astir with the tremulous reflections of the stars. "When I was a young boy," he said after a long silence, "I used to dream all the time of being high up—of being on what I used to think of as on top of the whole world—with the gods . . . "

"And now you will be there."

"I don't know. I'll be on top of the world of men, but I don't know about the gods. The world is a puzzle without a solution, don't you think?"

"The world is a chessboard—no more and no less."

"Spoken like a Roman!"

"Felt like a Roman!"

The general straightened up. "Well," he said, "well, it doesn't do to brood, there's no profit in it. The dawn will soon thrust itself into the darkness of night and show us what it will."

"Show us what we will," I said.

A noise behind us on the verandah made us turn our heads to

look. It was a sharp sigh that had gone up from a circle of onlookers that had formed about two men. The wrestling bouts that had gone on while we were meeting had produced their champions, who were now squaring off for the final match. The Roman contender was a tall, square-shouldered, strapping fellow, white-skinned and blue-eyed, with long hair the color of new-mown hay. He was pitted against Ichavod, who moved around him in a slow, ungainly fashion, his lips drawn back over bared gums. "Well," said Livinius, rubbing his hands together, "so it's Rome against Judea once again, is it?"

"Always."

"But your man is unfortunate," said the general, clucking his tongue. "He's matched against Marcellus, the military champion. He's never lost a bout, he's crippled a dozen men in the last year alone, he's vicious, and there's not another man in the legions who can touch him." Livinius grinned broadly. "And he hates Jews."

"I see."

"And your man? He's your bodyguard, isn't he?"

"Yes."

"Well, how is he?"

"Adequate."

The general rubbed the back of his thick neck. "Would you care to wager on the outcome? You may bet me that your man will not be crippled, and I will bet you that he will."

I shook my head.

"And why not?"

"I don't like games of chance," I said. "I prefer relying on my own skill. Besides, there is no wager. I am absolutely certain my man will win."

One of the Roman staff officers standing near had overheard me. "How can you be sure?" he asked.

"Because you know your man by reputation, from hearsay. Perhaps you've seen him in action a number of times. But I know my man because I put my life in his hands every day. That's why I'm certain."

"A certain wager," said Livinius, "is assured wealth. But have it as you wish." To his officer, he said, "There's no way to understand these Jews, no matter how long a time you're in their country."

The Roman wrestler feinted, but Ichavod did not react; he seemed slow, even sluggish. The Roman smiled, his face hardening as if the smile had an effect opposite of relaxing it, and his adherents, who had seen him wrestle before and were familiar with his careful, feinting style and sudden lightninglike bursts of magnificently timed fury, smiled as well and waited for him to strike. In contrast to the fluid grace of the Roman champion, the big Jew with his angular shoulders and protruding rump was awkward—even a trifle ridiculous. Marcellus baited him: "Jew, Jew, why are you dancing? Do you think this is the temple at holiday time? Do you think the priests will come out and anoint you?" He screwed up his handsome face and mimicked Ichavod's homely one. "You're so pretty, Jew, you're wasting your time here. Why aren't you out with the girls? Don't you know they're pining for you? Don't you know the virgins of Jerusalem are panting for your embrace?" He made obscene gestures. "Jew, Jew, are you sure you were circumcised properly? Why don't you take it out and make sure? Or is it gone? Did you lose it? Did the cat get your pecker—is that what happened?" Ichavod opened his mouth, but of course he could say nothing. Marcellus knew he was mute. "Did the cat get your tongue as well? Then what can you possibly do with the women? How can you please them?" He turned his eyes to the sky. "Why don't you call upon your God to help you? He's a very obliging God, I've heard tell. Though no one can see or hear Him, He's everywhere at once! That's quite a trick, Jew, isn't it? You Jews are full of tricks, aren't you? That's the reason I love Jews. Did you know that I love Jews? Only ask my friends— they'll tell you. I love them like the plague!"

The Roman's sickly smile turned to a sneer, and then without warning he danced with tremendous light-footed speed about Ichavod before the latter had sufficient time to turn with him. Only half facing his adversary, Ichavod was off-balance when the other feinted once again, and then, as the Jew seemed to flounder in an attempt to regain his footing, the Roman shot a long arm forward and caught his shoulder. A shout went up from the Roman spectators. A split second of imbalance and one hold was all their man required to crush an opponent; they had seen him do it a hundred times before. But as quickly as it had come, their approbation died in their throats. Ichavod's "slow" turn was his own private, unorthodox feint, the calculated and deadly movement of an animal so skilled in stalking prey that the prey has no idea it is being stalked. What had seemed inert came to sudden movement; what had seemed dead came abruptly to life. Ichavod thrust his own arm out, clutched the hand at his shoulder in an iron grip, and before the Roman veteran knew what had happened, jerked it with his enormous strength; then, stooping and using his powerful shoulder as a fulcrum, Ichavod spun Marcellus around like a top. His knee rose in a flash to the Roman's back, striking it squarely at the center, and then the Jew yanked, grimacing as he did. There was a sullen crack, as of a tree trunk splitting in a storm, and Marcellus fell in a limp heap to the floor of the verandah, his spine snapped in two. A sigh went up from the Romans, and one of the escort guards began to weep and had to be led off by comrades. Ichavod stepped back into the group of Jewish guards and officers, shaking fine, needlelike drops of sweat from his glistening brow and the muscles of his naked body.

Livinius spat. "That's not a man," he growled. "That's not a man at all!"

"He looks like a man," I said.

"What does that mean?" The general scowled. "So do you!"

Later, we watched the slaves who had served us our meal herded out of the hunting lodge and down into the yard. The servants were altogether calm; they had been told that they were being transported to another location, and they believed what had been said to them. When they were all assembled in the center of the yard, torches were brought out, supposedly so that they could be counted and chained; an instant later, a dozen guards on horseback charged into them at full gallop, swinging swords. Screams filled the air and the dust boiled up. We had a perfect view from the verandah and saw how the terrified slaves, dashing here and there for their lives, were cut down in their tracks. One by one they fell. A Roman officer leaning over the rail was showered with blood from a severed arm which sailed through the air with the force of the blow that had parted it from its torso and sent it spinning up like a juggler's baton.

One slave, a tall black man, managed to elude the horses' hooves and the blades and plunged into the nearby woods. Shouts followed him. The torchbearers rushed forward across the yard. Several riders sprang from their mounts and pursued him. We could hear the cracking of twigs underfoot and the thrashing of branches. Then there was a hideous cry, and silence. Moments later, one of the guards emerged from the trees carrying his sword in one hand and a leg, dripping gore, in the other. A second guard came out with an arm stuck up over one shoulder like a pike. He was followed by two men, swearing and bearing between them a mutilated body. Then the last guard came out of the forest with the black slave's head jammed onto the point of his spear. The torchbearers brought their lights closer so that all could see clearly. Livinius yawned and stretched, and we turned to receive the maps and battle plans, which were ready now, from our aides. As we left the lodge, the general made a point of saluting me formally, but I did not knowledge it. He looked displeased. "So," he growled, "so the Jew ignores my salute, does he?" I was about to climb into my equipage, but I stopped and stared at him. "Don't worry," I said. "It will be returned on the field of conflict."

When I returned from the conclave to the war ministry, Quaestoris was there waiting for me.

"I'm not receiving callers, not at all—and you know that. Why are you here?"

The envoy's face was impassive, masklike. Only his eyes, under their plucked brows, betrayed his pain and agitation. His voice when he spoke was low and even, and though he had come on an obviously urgent mission, it did not once break or falter; oddly enough, it had a dead quality about it. "I must see you," he said. "It's as simple as that."

"Have you completely taken leave of your senses? Don't you know what's going on? Don't you realize what the coming weeks are to bring? How can you thrust yourself on me at a time like this? How can you jeopardize what I am doing? I should never have expected this kind of behavior from you—especially since you've been so understanding of late."

"You must come home with me—you must, if only for an hour!"

"Impossible! Out of the question!"

"But you must—I won't keep you for more than an hour. You— have my solemn word."

"And the trip there and back?"

"You can work both ways. I shan't disturb you. I promise you that as well."

I saw that underneath the surface calm, the envoy was extremely distraught. "Quaestoris," I said, softening my voice. "Quaestoris, you are very dear to me. You know that. I don't have to prove it—"

319

"Never mind all of that. I don't need you to profess your love and concern. Just do as I ask. Come to my home. It will take an hour, perhaps less. Certainly no more than that."

I was silent.

"You needn't fear," said the diplomat. His cheek twitched. "I'm not luring you into a trap—I'm not somebody else's bait, and I would not harm you of my own volition. You can come with as large an escort as you see fit—you can even send an advance guard if you wish! I don't give a damn and I won't be offended." He laughed bitterly. "And I'll even taste the food and wine before you—or better still, you don't have to eat or drink! Is that satisfactory?"

"Dear Quaestoris—"

"Please. We're wasting time."

"When do you want to leave?"

"Now."

"This minute?"

"This instant!"

"But there are pressing matters I must attend to. I can't just walk away from them."

"Attend to what is urgent."

"Fine. Then I'll meet you at home."

"I'll wait."

"Wait? Where?"

"Here. Where I am. In the anteroom."

"But—this is absurd!"

"Quite. Still, I'll wait."

I shrugged. "As you wish. The anteroom is at your disposal. If there is anything you want—"

"Nothing."

I left Quaestoris pacing in the anteroom and went into my private office, locking the door behind me. I glanced quickly once again over the maps, plans and the code and then stored them in my vault. I summoned Elazar, who entered through a secret door, and through him sent word to Akrab and to Melech the Galilean that all leaves were herewith canceled, without exception. I also ordered that the guard be doubled at all army posts, military camps and at *Patish* headquarters. I commanded that all suspected rebels, informers and spies be executed immediately and without trial. Then I checked to see if there were any urgent communiqués which had arrived during my absence, found there were none, dismissed my faithful page, and went back to the anteroom, where I found Quaestoris seated on a chair in a corner, his face buried in his hands.

"Quaestoris, my dear friend. Are you grieved?"

He looked up, his eyes clouded.

"Are you ready to go?"

"Yes, of course," he said. "We'll start. I have my carriage waiting."

"I prefer to use mine. But you may join me if you wish . . . "

The envoy nodded. "Fine," he said. "I'll travel with you. But I won't interrupt you."

He kept his word and did not utter a sound during the entire trip. At the outset I said a few polite sentences to him, but he did not answer. I soon became absorbed in my own thoughts and forgot he was there beside me. Again and again my mind went over the plans we had formulated at the hunting lodge, seeking any weaknesses that might have eluded us and searching for possible improvements. Then I reviewed the code for perhaps the hundredth time to make absolutely certain it was foolproof. I was startled when the envoy touched my shoulder and said, "We're here."

"So we are." I smiled.

The envoy's face was grim. His skin was gray, and out of it, as grubs in the clay of a graveyard, his eyes peered at me: they were open but their dull gaze seemed to register nothing; though they saw and I knew they saw, they appeared to be the eyes of a blind man. I stepped out of the carriage before him and then waited to follow him into the house. "Remember," I said to him, "that I have no more than an hour to spare. You've made a bizarre request and I've granted it on the strength of our dear friendship. But I will leave when I must leave. The coordinator of the general staff is coming on a matter of first priority. And the Seventeenth Assault Brigade needs some refining—slight, but most necessary. And then there are the communiqués—I must be on hand when the communiqués come in. There's really no end to them, you know."

Quaestoris made no reply. He walked resolutely, if a trifle shakily, into the house and down the corridors that led to the courtyard where he sculpted. At one point, the old major-domo came limping out and approached the envoy, but his master waved him off brusquely and the servant fell back, looking as if he would weep. When we reached the entrance to the yard, I said, "Do you mean to say that you've brought me out here at a time like this to show me the statue? Can that be the truth?" The diplomat ignored my questions, went to a small table near the pool, and took up a hammer and a large chisel. Ichavod was of course with me as always, and out of the corner of an eye I saw him stare coldly at our host: I knew that my bodyguard was reckoning precisely how many steps it would take and what sort of blow would be necessary to break Quaestoris's skull should he mean to do me harm. I had no fear of the envoy, but Ichavod had no faith in him—or for that matter in anyone. The yard lay under an immense sea of sunlight; among the roots of the water lilies floating on the surface of the pond, the fish flashed to and fro like arrows of gold. The shadows of the trees danced on the flagstones; in among the leaves of their outer branches sparrows flitted.

The major-domo appeared in the doorway, and Quaestoris signaled him to remove the shroud. The old man limped dutifully to the sculpture and, sighing, yanked the cloth away. I was astounded. In daylight, the marble was the most unusual color I had ever seen: it was a raw crimson, like the flesh exposed by a gaping wound. Its outer surfaces were wet, as if drenched by the fluid of birth. "Don't be afraid to come closer," said the envoy. "It will not hurt you. It's only stone, you know; it can't move or speak."

"I'm fine where I am," I said.

The creature that Quaestoris had wrought was spectacular. The sculptor had surpassed his every previous effort in workmanship. Breasts, male and female genitals, arms, legs, hands, feet: all had been rendered with consummate skill. There was not a single flaw to be be detected, except for the intentional ones: the nippleless breast on one side of the Janus-bodied figure, and a scarred female part on the other. Muscles, veins, finger- and toenails—all seemed to hover on the very brink of life itself, as if all that were needed was some living person who would clasp the marble to his flesh and pass the warmth of animate existence to it. Quaestoris laughed nervously. "And what do you think of the likenesses?" he said. He was referring to the faces, one to each side of the statue. The front with the breast that lacked a nipple had my face; the other, with the marked vagina, had his. I went to each face in turn and examined it. Both were excellent, even beyond that. Quaestoris looked in stone precisely as he was: haggard, wasted, vacant-eyed, weary of the breaths he had to draw in order to keep on living. My own visage was assured, haughty, self-contained, exacting, inflexible:

322

my eyes had the cold look of the avalanche before it falls. I was much pleased with the manner in which the sculptor had chosen to do my face; I enjoyed looking at it—it had a kind of hypnotic effect on me which I found relaxing. "Well?" pressed the envoy.

"I am very pleased with the way you've done my face. It's—well, it's a magnificent portrait. My congratulations, dear Quaestoris! It's quite obvious that the muse truly dwells in your soul!"

"What about the totality? What do you think about the whole statue?"

I laughed and spat into the fishpond. "What do I think? What should I think? It's a monstrosity!"

"That is your—honest opinion?"

"My dear Quaestoris, I'm sure you know what I mean. The workmanship is superb—I might even say quintessential. You've outdone yourself. The subtleties, the delicacies, the fineness of detail—each segment in and of itself is nothing short of a masterpiece. Only see your outstretched arms and mine that are folded across my chest! I've seldom set eyes on such extraordinary skill. I really don't know how you managed it—it's almost unearthly, do you know that?"

"Yes."

"But as a whole the piece is an abomination! It's a damn shame that all of your individual heavens have produced an overall hell!" I shook my head. "I'm sorry to put it to you so bluntly, but there is no other way."

"You needn't be sorry," said the sculptor. "There is no other way. And you need not regret what you have said. I am in total agreement with you. The piece is vile." His forehead was covered with sweat, and he wiped it on the back of a hand. "It is—an abortion. It never should have been conceived in the first place, much less born." He glanced at me, then around the courtyard, and then to the statue. "But we can rectify that soon enough, can't we?"

In the doorway the major-domo stirred. He lifted a tired hand and said softly but distinctly, "Master . . . master, I beseech you—"

A look from the envoy silenced him. Carrying the hammer and the chisel, Quaestoris went up to the gleaming red marble monster. "It has no tongue, but it speaks," he said, addressing no one but himself or perhaps some invisible presence in the air. "It has no brain, but it plots. It has no heart, but it lives . . ." There were tears staining his cheeks. "It is indeed a monster, but it came to be in the world. Why did it come into being? Why did it grow day by day, week by week, month by month? What does it mean that it is here? It is enigma, cousin to the Sphinx. It is folly, sibling of the idol. It was mine to bring forth and it is mine to destroy, mine to create and mine to abolish. There was no one to exult over it when it was here, and there will be no one to mourn it when it is gone. The pain of birth is mine alone and the pain of death belongs solely to me. The sun is mine and the shadow is mine: all is in my hands."

He fell silent, and in a swift and perfect movement lifted the chisel to the neck of the statue on which the double-faced head was poised. Strangely enough, I had not noticed the neck before this moment: it was slender, supple, perhaps a trifle overlong—deliberately, to support the burden of two faces—and the marble was undoubtedly the most exquisite I had ever seen, with a texture like glass and an inner glow. The sculptor put the point of the chisel to the throat, and then struck it with a stroke of the hammer whose power I should not have thought the envoy capable of summoning. I saw the hammer flash in the sun, and the next instant the head struck the flagstones of the yard with a crash that pushed the fish to the depths of the pond and sent the birds screaming through the air. Quaestoris dropped his tools and wept openly. The major-domo disappeared. Ichavod leaned against a far wall. The blood-red figure stood grotesquely with a jagged neck that looked like a truncated phallus. And the head lay dumbly in the yard, stone on stone, in its own torn splinters, with my face staring directly up into the blazing sun.

I began working eighteen to twenty hours a day, seeing to the final preparations for what I had come to call in my mind the "Day of Wrath." Coded messages came and went without cease between my office at the war ministry, Melech the Galilean at *Patish* headquarters, Akrab at his field command post between Jerusalem and Jericho, and Livinius, who had joined his legion in central Samaria—a pivotal position from which he would be able to maneuver with great effectiveness when the operation started. I was no longer able to visit my brother and the woman in the prison because, as I said jokingly to myself, I too "was a prisoner of the momentous undertaking I had mapped out." I had not once seen

Quaestoris since the day he had struck the head from the Janus statue—
the "glorious abomination," as I termed it; I had written him several
brief notes, telling him that though circumstances forced us to be apart,
he remained always in my heart and that the day would come when
we "would be reunited in the harmony and ecstasy of love." The
envoy did not see fit to write back, but I had no time to concern myself
with his shifting moods. My sole occupation, my sole passion was the
coming attack on Herod—my bid for supreme power in Judea. My
schedule was ironclad; I had sequestered myself in my office, sleeping
there for scant, fitful periods of an hour or two a day; and I received
no visitors except those few who came on matters of extreme consequence relating to the coup. I even neglected my journals, which I
had kept faithfully and well throughout the years, no matter what
external pressures there had been.

Late one night as I worked, Elazar slipped into the office through
the hidden panel he often used with a message which he said was of
great urgency. I looked up from a sheaf of documents that pertained
to ordnance and transport for the battle; there were a number of
arrangements I was not completely satisfied with and wanted to revise.
Looking weary, Elazar handed me the communiqué. It was a message
from an operative in Herod's fortress prison, informing me that a
mysterious raid had freed a group of inmates, including my brother
and the woman with whom he shared his cell. I set the message before
me on the table and reread it slowly and carefully, though I was already
certain of its content. But I could scarcely believe my eyes. It seemed
absolutely impossible that Herod's fortress prison had been penetrated
and convicts taken from it: there was no more inviolable citadel in all
Judea! Slowly I turned the matter over in my mind. My first thought
was that the message was some kind of hoax or ruse meant to lure me
into a trap. It was true that the operative's signature was bona fide,
that the code was ours, that the code mark of the day and month was
accurate, and that the seal of the spy system was valid. But all of this
did not rule out treachery. Perhaps one of our men had talked under
torture and revealed his secrets? Perhaps someone had turned on us for
gold or a woman? Perhaps an agent had been forced to write the message? We were and always had been extremely careful in screening,
training and constantly checking our men; our methods were the best,
our surveillance unwavering—but there was always a margin of error,
chance, mishap. I ordered a detail of security guards to investigate the

situation at the jail and report back to me as soon as possible. Within the hour I had a report that confirmed the earlier message and erased any suspicion of a snare. I left at once to see for myself what had happened.

The attack had been carried out only several hours before. Nobody seemed to know how it had happened. The greater part of the prison, which was extensive, had no idea that the raid was taking place. In all, twenty-seven cells had been opened and their prisoners released. Nobody could say how the intruders entered or how they got the inmates away. The main gate and the gates at all of the other cellblocks, except for the block that had suffered the raid, were intact. Several warders and a number of guards had been overpowered and killed; their keys had been taken from them and used to unlock the cells. I saw the bodies. In the special detention block, the doors stood open. My brother's cell stood empty. The cots were overturned, the stool where my brother sat was broken, the chair in which I sat and tapped my riding whip was smashed. The two *Patish* agents had been hacked to pieces—their blood was smeared over the floor, spattered on the walls and even on the ceiling, and their corpses lay in the corridor. They had obviously fought to the last breath. Down at the very end of the corridor, the old warder lay. He was still alive, and I went over to him. "Old man . . . "

He was lying on his back, the blood oozing slowly through a rent in his grimy cloak.

"Old man, can you hear me?"

He did not answer.

"Can you understand what I'm saying to you?"

His eyelids fluttered and his tongue ran over his cracked lips. I motioned to one of the guards, who knelt, lifted the warder's head, and set a cup of water to his mouth.

I raised my voice: "Old man, it is imperative that I ask you some questions. Try to collect yourself."

The warder's eyes opened. The light of life was sinking in them, and they were filled with terror. "I know nothing—I can answer no questions—I know nothing at all."

I smiled. "Don't be afraid, my friend. You will live."

"I will die," said the warder.

"That is not so. I promise you. The physicians have been summoned. They will be here shortly and will heal your wounds."

"No. It is the angel of death who has been summoned to heal my wounds."

"Old man, you must get hold of yourself. I want to know what happened here. I want to know the whole story."

"There is nothing—for me to tell. The prison tells its own story."

I crouched and touched the warder's forehead with my whip. "Listen to me, old man. You may feel that the angel of death is here for you and may have reconciled yourself to the fact. But you have sons and a daughter. And grandchildren. Your sons live in Jerusalem, your daughter in Hebron. Your grandchildren—well, you wouldn't want the angel of death to pay them a visit, would you?"

The old man's chin trembled. He began to weep hoarsely.

"Well, would you?"

"What . . . what do you want to know?"

"Tell me what happened. Exactly what happened."

"They—they broke in—suddenly, they were—they were here—"

"Stop blubbering! Who was here?"

"The attackers."

"Who were they?"

"I—don't know."

"Who do you think they were?"

"I don't know. My God, I don't know. Zealots, perhaps . . . "

"But how did they enter? How could they enter? It is impossible to get into this prison! This is an impregnable fortress!"

There was terror in the warder's eyes. His lips moved but there was no sound. "I—I can't—"

"Your grandchildren, old man. Have you forgotten your grandchildren? The angel of death is quick with little ones. He stuffs them into his cloak"—I snapped my fingers—"like that!"

"There is an entrance."

"An entrance?"

"Yes."

"An entrance? What entrance? Where? Why didn't I know?"

"A secret entrance. A passage."

"Where is this passage? Tell me where!"

"Herod built it. In case of emergency . . . "

"But where is it located?"

"Only a few people know about it. Kalbi—knows . . . "

"Do you know?"

The warder choked. Blood trickled from his mouth. His eyes looked bewildered.

"Answer me! I must know! You must speak!"

"The king built it many years ago—Kalbi knows—I never—"

Without thinking, I had drawn my whip back and raised it. The warder's glazed, confused eyes, the tears coursing down his filthy cheeks, his trembling chin and halting, half-coherent words infuriated me and abruptly I brought the quirt down across the upturned face. The old man's mouth fell open and blood spurted from his nostrils; his nose began to swell and become discolored. But oddly enough, the warder seemed relieved; he even stopped crying.

"Where is it? Who else besides Herod and Kalbi knows where to find it?"

The old man smiled, the blood that leaked from his nose spreading over his teeth.

"Old fool, tell me where the passage is!"

The old warder sighed. "Ask the angel of death," he whispered, closing his eyes.

I saw the final shudder and knew that it was over. Whatever more the warder knew, he had taken with him. He was pleased to have escaped. I was certain he felt that I would no longer have any interest in his family. But he was wrong. My threat was not an idle one. I rose, and tapping my whip against my thigh, gave orders that his sons and daughter and their families be arrested and brought with all haste to the prison, where I would deal with them at a suitable time. Death might have released him, but it did not release his family. If there was a world to come, as the devout were so prone to believe when things got too difficult in this one, and the fool of a warder could hear the converse of earth from it, their cries would jolt him from the eternal rest he had been promised.

I then ordered an immediate search of the entire prison for the passage. "Let this whorehouse be turned inside out until it is found!" I thundered at the captain of security. "And if it is not, I'll turn you and your men inside out! Do I make myself clear?" I felt that it was inconceivable that such a secret should exist and I should know nothing about it. And further, if the fortress were penetrable for the raiders, my discovery of the passage would make it vulnerable to my forces when the time came for the attack on the "ostrich" in his nest. It was essential that the entrance be located as soon as possible. On the way back to my office, I mulled the entire matter over in my mind. Who were the attackers? The warder had suggested they were Zealots. But he could have been mistaken, or lying. How would Zealots have come into possession of a secret like the whereabouts of the passage? Perhaps the raiders had masqueraded as Zealots? But why the hoax? Whom had they sought to deceive?

Back in the ministry of war, I had a strange but extremely compelling hunch. The more I thought about it, the more certain I became. I felt that Kalbi himself was behind the break-in and liberation of the prisoners. It was a logical consideration. He knew where the entrance was, was familiar with the workings of the jail, and had probably done it to suit Aquilius's or his own purposes. Either the attackers pretended to be rebels, or else for some reason Kalbi had turned the secret over or sold it to their forces. I sent a top-priority communiqué to Melech the Galilean which ordered him to put every available man on Kalbi's trail, even if it meant searching him out in Egypt or Syria, where the most recent rumor placed him. "Bring in the dog dead or alive," I wrote. "But bring him in, for I suffer from his fleas!"

When the order was on its way, I considered further. Which prisoner had the invaders come to get? For what reason did they want him? Was it possible they had come for my brother? But why? What use would they have for a madman? Could it have to do with my interest in him? How did they interpret my interest? Perhaps they thought my brother and the woman possessed some vital information. I rose from my table and paced my office from wall to wall, sometimes pausing at the window to glance out at the guards in their helmets and armor, pacing to and fro as I was. It could not have been that someone had discovered the connection between my brother and me—no, that could not be. It was impossible. But even if it were so—and I could not see how in the world it could be—what difference would it make? Did they hope to get at me through him? In what way? Did they think I would shed a single tear if he were cut to ribbons? Did they think my tie to him was anything but curiosity? I stopped at the window and parted the drapes. The silver spearheads flashed in the sunlight. To the east, the mountains shimmered with heat. A new day had come into being without my realizing it. In his corner, Ichavod stirred, glanced at me, scratched his neck and went back to sleep.

An aide brought me the list of missing prisoners I had requested.

I went over it with great care. There were several inmates who might have been of interest to various groups. One was a wizened old Zealot named Uziel who had been arrested many years ago and within the first few weeks of his incarceration had been beaten into a stupor from which he would never emerge. Since he was still a symbol of courage and integrity to the rebel forces, he was kept alive as a possible exchange for men of Herod's forces who had fallen into enemy hands. Another possibility was Zavua, a Jew who had been born in Syria and had been imprisoned as a dealer in smuggled goods, poisons, potions and stolen weapons. Still a third convict was a man who had been a rebel in his early youth, had risen in the ranks, and had deserted to our side, causing much havoc among his comrades. He had been warmly accepted by Herod's forces, risen in favor, and then—to the consternation of his new allies—reversed himself again and sold out to the rebels.

I put the list down, and starting with the first conjecture, reviewed the possibilities. It occurred to me, of course, that the raid had a meaning entirely different than any I had considered. Life . . . war—call it what one would—was a strange game. One stared at a certain configuration on the board and calculated the risks, chances, opportunities, dangers. One felt that everything was taken into account and that the solution to the problem was there, within reach. And then suddenly it became evident that one was not playing at the right board. The board with which one had preoccupied oneself was a dummy, a decoy, a ruse. The game was being played on a different board, which had been only dimly apprehended. I picked up my whip and toyed with it. I concentrated on the other boards I had not heretofore examined. But a strange feeling introjected itself, a feeling I had not planned for or expected. I rested my chin on the tip of the quirt, feeling it give slightly, like a phallus when it is grasped firmly. The loss of my brother annoyed me, irritated me—even depressed me. I could not explain the effect it had on me. Though the incursion into the prison had baffled and infuriated me, it was—in the total scheme of things as they stood—all but inconsequential. Herod's hidden escape route, though I did not yet know the location, would be found in time—I would rip the fortress prison apart brick by brick to do it if I had to. The millstones of the coup had begun to turn and my enemies would one by one be crushed in the unrelenting embrace of the process. The scepter of Judea was within reach. And I knew that the scepter of Judea was also the rod that would drive the Romans forth from the land. "An empire is no more than a chain," I reasoned. "And when a link is thrust into the forge, turns white with heat and melts, then—the chain is no more!" Who could say what other links would follow my lead? Who could tell what other links would come to me for leadership? My mind was charged with energy, my heart was vibrant, my body as resilient as the silver-handled whip. I felt that I could and would live a thousand years—that life would support me as a log is supported in a river because I understood it, understood what was needed to live, what was required to survive. And I felt that death would keep his distance from me, because he had no real business with me.

But my brother, my brother. The loss haunted me. The loss angered me. I felt that my brother belonged to me, that he was my property—not that he was a servant or a slave but that he had no right to a life other than the life, the existence I gave him. I resolved to push all thoughts of him out of mind. But Elazar entered and gave me a scrap of parchment that had been given him by the captain of the security detail combing the prison. It was covered with a strange scrawl. The writing was barely legible and almost every word was misspelled. It was the first time I had ever seen anything written by my prisoner. It read: "Understand me: my brother, I am seeking freedom." He had no ink. I knew the message was written in blood. I put it down on my great table, littered with the documents of office. Ichavod was still in the corner, squatting on the floor as if in the forest or the desert. As I moved away from the table, one of his eyes again opened to make sure all was well; when he saw that it was, he returned to the light, elastic sleep of the animal world wherein the slightest sounds signal the difference between life and death, security and danger. I went to a small cabinet and from it took a decanter of extremely rare wine, given to me by a weapons supplier who had procured from me a lucrative contract, and poured perhaps a third of a glass. I savored it slowly, trying as one should always try to make the most of pleasure when it comes—just as one should make the most of power. The parchment. The words in blood. The awkward, childish scrawl. The wretched spelling. What exactly was it that I felt about my brother? Why did his absence disturb me? Why could I not banish all thought of him as one would dismiss the thought of a flea? How did he come to have influence in my life when he was nothing, when he had been totally in my power, when he would again be totally in my power one day soon? Why did he leave the message? What did he mean by "freedom"? What did a madman know of freedom or captivity, when it was all one to him? Why had my brother really fled? What in his disordered mind had pushed him to it? Where had he gone? Or had he been spirited away? I swallowed my wine in a single gulp, set the glass down and seated myself on the divan where I slept when I worked through the night. I decided to rest, since the level of my concentration had sunk. I felt a bit feverish—but I knew I would not be ill, I would refuse, no matter what.

Thoughts of Quaestoris entered my mind. Once again I saw the chisel at the statue's throat, I saw the hammer strike. Again I saw the breast without a nipple—perfectly, wonderfully formed, but without a nipple: no infant could ever suck at such a breast. I saw the female part, which looked as if a talon had ripped into it. And I saw the Janus-head lying on the stone of the yard in the frozen blood of its own marble chips. The fish darted away once more, the sparrows were startled into unexpected flight. The limping major-domo wept. There was the head, hurled by its creator from its height! The sculptor's face was smashed; mine was whole, intact, turned to the living sun! That was the way it should be! It made me want to laugh. A sign of ascendancy, a sign of supremacy! I wondered idly what had made the envoy do what he had done. Was his mind, like my brother's, disordered? Would he allow himself to be lured away into the shadows? I had a very strong hunch that once the statue was gone, Quaestoris would go as well. Perhaps it might be wise to speed him on his way. What he could do for me, he had in essence already done. His influence was on the wane—in some circles he was even a laughingstock. They called him "hermit," "recluse," accused him of being "demented" and a "deviate." There were those who said he was first "marked for circumcision" and then "for death." A man who had been close to the envoy for many years said, "A Roman does not willingly seek extinction—but Quaestoris is no longer a Roman." Even in Rome, there were many who predicted his imminent downfall. I had even heard a rumor which said that the procurator wanted him replaced and was in the process of negotiating for a successor. And then, in the final analysis, once the coup had taken effect I would be a power in my own right, a force to be reckoned with on my own. Perhaps it was high time to put the chisel to Quaestoris's throat. In a certain sense, it would be doing him a favor. He would be spared the trouble of suicide. I smiled. The thought of the envoy dead was not unpleasant.

I had not slept in forty-eight hours and more. I stretched myself out on the divan. The fever burned fitfully, even comfortably, and I closed my eyes.

When I opened them once again, my father sat across from me at a chess table. He smiled, then vanished, and my brother took his place. He was thinner than when I had last seen him. He had grown visibly older, and his hair was sparse upon his skull; he smiled in recognition— a faint, hesitant smile, not without a trace of bitterness—and then his face became solemn. "It's your move, brother," he said quietly.

"How did you get here?"

"I am here. There is no more to say."

"But Father was here."

"I am his son."

"He has but one son."

"I am the son."

"Where have you been?"

"Within myself."

"Where?"

"Within every man."

"What have you done?"

"You know what I have done."

"What?"

"I have walked on the waves and calmed them when there was storm. I have given bread and meat to the poor and bade them eat to their fill. And the thirsty, who have crawled across the deserts to reach me, I have given them drink. And the blind I have returned to sight; and to the mute I have given tongue; and to the deaf I have taught hearing. And those who came to me lame I have enabled to walk straight. And the lepers I have made pure as snow. And even those which were dead and had begun to stink of the rot of the grave, even those whose hearts had stopped and became as stones, even those who had started on the road of eternal silence: even to them I gave life again, life with breath and heartbeat and sperm and milk of the breast and the sap that swells anew in the veins each day the sun rises. And I did it all with the firm touch of my hands and the gentle kiss of my mouth. This is what I have done. Do you understand?"

"No."

"It is not clear?"

"No."

"I did not expect it to be." My brother smiled sadly. "I did not think you would understand."

"Why—why did you leave the prison?"

"It's simple. I wanted freedom."

"What have you to do with freedom?"

"What every man has to do with freedom. It is the search of a man's life."

"But every man is bound to himself."

"No. Every man is free to find himself."

"You mean that every man is free to—find his own chaos. Isn't that it?"

"Yes, freedom leads to chaos. But chaos leads to creation."

"Chaos is anarchy, dissolution, madness. Chaos gives rise to the fear that destroys a man."

"Chaos engenders the humility that releases a man from the necessity of believing in his own infallibility. When he is humble, a man does not have to act on what he does not know as if he knows it."

"He who pursues chaos . . . pursues death."

My brother smiled, again only for a moment. "There is no reason for a man to run after death. Death waits—he is patient, more patient even than life." My brother waved a hand, gently, without irritation—but firmly. "But we have talked enough for now. The game is unfinished. We must play. You must make your move."

"I had no idea that you played."

"Of course I do."

"Had I known, I should have played with you in prison. We should have set your freedom as the stake."

"You could not, nor will you ever be able to grant me or withhold from me my own freedom. That power is mine, and mine alone."

"But I am the king."

"It does not matter. But enough. Let us play our game—the first and the last."

"All right."

But when I looked down at the board, I saw that it was empty. I called to Ichavod for the pieces, but he did not come. I was much disturbed. "How can we play without pieces?"

"We will play."

"But how?"

"With my spirit and your body."

But as I gazed at the board, puzzled as to what my brother meant, the woman appeared. She was no longer dressed in prison garb, but rather in decent raiment; she was clean, her hair was washed and combed, and she seemed in excellent health. As she approached my brother, her face grew soft and a light as of the morning dew in the sun shone in her eyes. Though she had never spoken in my brother's cell, she touched his shoulder now and said, "It is time to go. The poor await you . . . and the downtrodden . . . and those who are oppressed . . . and the cheated and duped and misled . . . and the outcasts and the rejected . . . and the bitter and the despondent . . . and those who mourn though mourning is of no avail . . . and the agitated and the unrestful and the unresting . . . and those sick at heart and those sick of mind . . . and those whose bodies betray them at every step or breath . . . and the crushed and spat-upon . . . and the lost and the enslaved . . . and the confounded and the mutilated and the maimed . . . and the starving and the parched: all of them await you."

"And what do they wish of you?" I said to my brother.

"To eat his body and drink his blood!" said the woman.

My brother waved a hand. "Hardly—they hardly want that. They want only that I help them."

"And when you go to them—and when you help them," I asked, "what awaits you?"

"Myself."

"Come," said the woman, touching his cheek. "It is time."

My brother rose. "Yes, it is time. It is more than time."

"And the game?" I said. "What about the game?"

"You will finish it."

"But when?"

"When the hour arrives, you will finish it."

And both my brother and the woman were gone, vanished as if they had never been with me. And I was alone, alone as if I were the only living creature in the world. And it was as if I were once again a child and on the dusty street in my village on the way down to the cemetery where the dead kept faithful vigil over eternity. And I was calm and unfearing, and when I entered in among the graves I sat on the earth and slowly, carefully drew forth from my cloak a rag that was worn but clean. And so I unfolded it and turned what it held onto my palm and gazed down at the tiny medallion on which was engraved the image of the emperor. And the sun struck its surface and leaped up from it as if it were flame. And into that fire I thrust my heart, endured the pain, and drew it forth again tempered as metal . . .

I wakened on the divan, feeling refreshed; Ichavod now stood at the window, arms folded across his chest. I then got up and went back to work.

Quaestoris's suicide came as no surprise to me—if anything, I was surprised he had waited as long as he did. Elazar brought me the news one day just at dawn. I had worked the night through, but the work had taken no toll; on the contrary, it had filled me with an even greater energy. Elazar gave me a complete report, omitting not a single detail, as I had charged him. Quaestoris had been found at dusk on the previous day in the small, enclosed courtyard where he had done his sculpting and where for the better part of a year he had formed his loathsome Janus-statue—his mockery of man and sex, of life and ambition, of will and power: his all-too-obvious denunciation of our relationship. The body of the envoy, as I would have supposed and perhaps even as the suicide had planned it to be, was discovered by the old, lame major-domo, who had gone in search of his missing master. Already yellow, spongy and bloated from its immersion in water, the corpse was floating face down in among the lilies of the pond, with the fish nibbling unceremoniously at the ears and nose. The faithful servant of so many years and so many assignments in so many lands had completely lost his poise and run shrieking through the house, calling on the gods of Rome and Greece, on the pagan idols, on any deity that had come to his muddled mind, for help. So the Roman and then the Jewish authorities had been notified.

"And there was no special call for me?" I asked my page.

"No."

"There was no note or any other sort of message to be delivered to me?"

"No."

"And the major-domo gave you no private word for me?"

"None, master."

"I see. Continue, then."

"They are undecided about what to do with the body," Elazar related. "I have heard that some want to bury it here in Judea, that others wish to preserve it and send it back to Rome where his family lives, and that still others want it cremated and the ashes placed in an urn for his relatives. He seems to have left no instructions regarding the matter."

I burst into laughter. "Why don't they stuff him and set him on display in Pilate's palace?"

Elazar, who knew my moods well, was silent. His clear-featured, copper-skinned face, which grew more beautiful as each day went by, registered no emotion.

"Is the procurator distraught?" I asked.

"Most terribly, master. I have heard that he is considering a national day of mourning to be observed by Romans and Jews alike. He says that while it is a sad day for Rome, it is a devastating night for Judea. He says that Rome has lost a son, but Jerusalem has lost a lover."

I smiled. "Well said—well said, indeed. I'm certain that Pilate never uttered a word of it."

Elazar's large, moist brown eyes regarded me coldly, just as they regarded everything: man, beast, or object alike. "Will you attend the funeral, master?"

I nodded. "I must. I haven't a choice. There would be suspicion and repercussions if I did not appear. Yes, my loyal page, I'll attend the funeral of Quaestoris and I'll weep—weep as no one has seen a minister of war weep! I will fairly drown the corpse once again in tears. I will do whatever it is necessary for me to do and say whatever it is necessary for me to say. I shall pay my deepest respects to the corpse of the renowned diplomat, or to his mortal remains, whatever form they may take; and I shall do it gratefully, for the departed has spared me—and for that matter, himself—a great deal of unnecessary trouble by doing away with himself. He deserves my homage well." I took Elazar's wrist and gently drew him to me, so that I could stroke his cheeks and his fine hair. "And how did the court of the noble Herod react to this tragedy?"

"Some say that Quaestoris was mad, that his stone had cast a pall over his mind; others say that he is dead of love, that he succumbed to the fatality that lurks in a certain sort of love; still others, though they do not say it openly, hint that you are the one who drove him to it . . . " Elazar hesitated.

"What is it?"

The page bit his lip.

"Speak, damn you!"

"And there are a number who have dark thoughts—evil thoughts."

"What are they?"

"That somehow you—managed to kill him—and to fling his body into the pool."

I ran my hand over Elazar's tight, supple buttocks—lightly, as if simply to make certain they were there. "Well, that's fine . . . that's only to be expected. If there were not a measure of that kind of talk I should begin to wonder. Well, well . . . so they hint at murder—that's excellent." I chuckled. "Perhaps those who spread such rumors abroad fear me—perhaps they fear I shall arrange such an end for them as well, eh?"

"But in truth, master, most say that Quaestoris is dead of love."

"No one dies of love."

"They say he is dead of love unrequited."

"No one dies of unrequited love either." I smiled. "The suicide dies because the only life possible for him is in death."

"Did you love him, master?"

"Love him? He was but the shell of a man. How can one love a shell?"

"Do you love me, master?"

"Love you? Of course I love you, Elazar. Why do you ask?"

"You seldom want me any more, master."

"It has nothing to do with you or with my desire, Elazar. It is the task before me, the hour of decision. The time for us will come, my faithful page. But it is not now. It cannot be now."

Elazar's eyes stared at me coldly. "When I am dead, will it be with me as it is with Quaestoris? Will my death mean nothing to you? Will you mourn me at all?"

"You have a long life ahead of you, my boy. A very long life. And when the power is mine, I shall raise you up—raise you higher than ever you have dreamed."

"Will you grieve for me when I am dead, master?"

"My love for you will never change, Elazar."

"Do you mean what you say, master?"

"I mean it." And I patted his taut rump and through his garment squeezed his firm little phallus and dismissed him. After he had left the room, I thought how curious it was that through the years he did not seem to change. His boyish face, almost feminine in its delicate beauty, never altered. His large, melancholy eyes with their long, fine lashes, his nose that was slightly turned up, his full sensual lips that could frame a sneer more subtly than I had ever seen, his splendid little chin with its dimple that was so reminiscent of the female cleft—all had remained exactly as they had been the first day I set eyes on him. Even his beautifully molded and perfectly proportioned body had increased only slightly in its size; it was as if nature wanted to preserve him as a flawless child that time would never ravage or even touch. If there were any alteration whatsoever, it was in his look—which had become colder, harder.

The final two-week period before the zero hour was upon me. It seemed I needed neither food nor rest: I was like a flame that fed upon itself, needing no fuel to keep it burning. During this time, a time when I was confined almost exclusively to the war ministry, I attended the funeral of Quaestoris, exactly as I had said I would to Elazar. The decision as to arrangements for the body had come at last: Quaestoris was embalmed, and after the funeral services in Judea was to be shipped back to Rome, where he would be interred in the family crypt. I thought that Quaestoris looked very well indeed as a corpse—it suited him splendidly. As I gazed down on his scrubbed and lacquered form I felt that he might have been a statue carved by another sculptor. It was ironic, but he seemed to have turned into the very stone with which he had been preoccupied and then obsessed all his life long. I viewed his body without any feeling of grief or pain, without regret, without a sense of loss. I felt absolutely nothing, for even the relief I had experienced on learning of his suicide had completely faded away—now that he was securely dead there was no longer any reason for its existence. Of course I wept—as I was expected to weep, knowing indeed that a considerable number of people had come to the funeral expressly to see me weep. My shoulders shook, my hands trembled, and I sobbed with such gusto that my hot tears dropped to the cold cheeks of the deceased, whose face and body the cosmeticians of death had worked on with amazing success, lending to Quaestoris a bloom that I doubted he ever had while he was alive. And as I grieved —seemingly unable to tear myself away from the bier—I saw the eyes of score upon score of courtiers on me and saw the lips moving, fashioning stories that had as much to do with the truth as did the cadaver before me with the living.

The funeral had attracted hundreds, as does a flame the moths; even Pontius Pilate, the procurator of all Judea, had honored the dead with his presence. He stood close to the bier on which his mute friend and colleague lay, awaiting only the eulogies and transportation back to the mother city and the paternal vault—tall, sharp-shouldered, angular-faced, sour-fleshed, ungainly in his stance and in his movements because he had no interest in and no need for grace. His eyes were screwed up into tiny knotholes, his brow was furrowed, his lips were puckered as if they had come unexpectedly on something unpalatable. He was surrounded by a large number of guards and aides, who though they seemed anxious to shield their master from all could not prevent the spectacle of death from penetrating their solid phalanx. When I finished what I considered a sufficient and seemly period of public mourning, I withdrew from the bier. The proconsul was uneasy; he fidgeted and his face grew even more dour, as if the bile in his mouth was beginning to spill through the rest of his system. Herod was present as well, surrounded as well by his protectors and his myrmidons, and looking dejected and fearful. But the queen was noticeably absent, because, as the stories went around, she was "utterly devastated" by the "shocking and untimely demise" of her beloved Quaestoris.

I remained at the funeral as long as the procurator and the tetrarch were there and departed immediately after they went. I had very much hoped to have one of the envoy's works of sculpture, for he was genuinely talented, but his last will and testament—which was strictly adhered to under the guard of troops dispatched to the domicile of the departed by Pilate himself—directed that all, with no exception, should be destroyed. Elazar reported to me that workers with sledge hammers devoted several days to carrying out the order and left nothing of the sculptures I knew but rubble. Quaestoris's papers and other personal effects were packed so they could be transported together with the body to Rome. I reckoned that the diplomat in his bitterness and

340

in the furor of his mental condition had left me nothing. But I was wrong. Two days after the funeral a small, sealed strongbox arrived at the war ministry in the hands of a Roman lieutenant, who saluted smartly and then presented it. The cover of the box was inscribed with the words: *Dies irae.* There was no key and I ordered Ichavod to break it open for me. Inside it, were two objects—both of marble. One was a female nipple, obviously the one that was missing from the breast of the Janus-statue, from the side that represented me. The other also came from my side: it was the male member, but it was run from mouth to root by a deep crack. I removed both objects with distaste. Underneath them, I found a message in Latin, in Quaestoris's own hand— which had greatly deteriorated. It read:

> *How twisted is the lonely path . . .*
> *That leads but to a day of wrath.*
>
> Q.

The old major-domo came limping to my office to see me the next day, and thinking that Quaestoris had sent jewels or gold that he wanted no one else to know about by the hand of his most trusted servant, I had the guards seize and search him, as I wanted to grant him no audience. But nothing whatsoever was found on his person, not a ring, not a single copper, and it was obvious that the old fellow had come only to find some solace in talking to me. I had him turned out. The next morning Elazar brought me word that the major-domo had been found dead in his bed. From that moment on, I gave Quaestoris not another thought and concentrated solely on my work.

I received a communiqué from my deputy Akrab that all was in readiness for my final inspection. That was the way I worked and had always worked: I liked to see and know for myself. Under the guise of routinely inspecting the army, I spent the next few days reviewing the assault units which would spearhead the attack on Herod. Akrab accompanied me everywhere, and we rode together as companions. His body was leaner than ever—like a whip, I thought; his blue eyes were the color of water in which a man drowns because of the cold; his movements were extraordinarily quick, but had the calm of total certainty about them; he spoke in a voice that tolerated no question or rebuttal. His weather-worn, seamed face had taken on a look of anticipation. Always laconic, when we reviewed the troops he was silent—almost indifferent, I thought. I asked him about it once and he replied, "What need is there for me to speak? The soldiers will talk for themselves!" When at length we had completed our rounds—ending with an inspection of the seventeenth assault group, which under its brilliant young commander Achaz had become the flower of the entire army—he pressed my hand warmly and bade me farewell in a voice that for the first time betrayed emotion. It was dusk, a dry wind blew over the face of the desert, raising dust in pale clouds that caught the last rays of the setting sun; and beneath us our mounts stirred impatiently. "Until I send word of victory, my monarch," he said.

"Monarch? Aren't you anticipating?"

"No," he answered. "You are the king. It is only a matter of making it official."

"I know you are sincere, Akrab. And I know that you are capable. And I am sure you will succeed. Rest assured that I will reward you well."

"My work is my reward," said Akrab.

And I knew that he meant it.

I met one last time with the general Livinius in a forest halfway between Jerusalem and Bethlehem. The day was sultry and overcast; there had been a wind in the morning but it had fallen off toward noon, and the forest, with its pines, firs and birches, was strangely still. Livinius was looking fit, he had lost some weight, his complexion was ruddy from his life in the field, his eyes were bright and even mirthful, his features were relaxed. I commented on his appearance. "Why not?" he boomed, slapping a thigh. "The battle is drawn—it remains only to be fought! And for me it will be the last as a field commander." He laughed heartily. "Yes, from here on I mean to skim off the cream and leave the rest for the others—whatever's left will have to be good enough for them!" He threw back his large, powerful head. "May their bones rot! The gods know their hearts have rotted away long ago!"

We seated ourselves on a fallen log and compared notes, discussed last-minute plans, reviewed adjustments and changes, and confirmed for the last time the signal for the coup to begin: I was to withdraw from Herod's party, dispatch Elazar to the war ministry, where the couriers would be waiting to move out to the field commanders with orders to strike, and then leave immediately for *Patish* headquarters, from which I would direct the progress of the battle and maintain contact with Livinius. The general leaned forward and squeezed my shoulder. "The end of this affair," he said, "will see you king—and your enemies carrion!"

"To the wealth, power and honor you so well deserve!" I returned.

Livinius nodded. He rubbed his brow. "What do you say to a game of chess, my Hebrew tactician?"

"A game of chess?"

"You've not forgotten the game, have you?" The general laughed.

"Hardly! But when?"

"Now."

"Now?"

"This minute."

"And where do you propose we play?"

"Here, of course!"

"Here in the forest?"

"Precisely! There's no better place for solitude or concentration than the forest. My aide will bring the board and the pieces—I never travel without them, you know. As a matter of fact, I never go into battle without them!"

"But my schedule—"

"It will wait for you."

"This is your wish?"

The general's eyes gleamed. "This is my wish."

"Then we shall play."

"We shall play indeed!"

Livinius clapped his hands, and an aide brought forth the board and laid it on the log between us and set out the pieces—the white to my side and the black to the general's. Then Livinius held out his fists. I tapped the right and thus chose the black queen, so the aide turned the board about. The general guffawed. "You've chosen the color of Judea!" he said.

"How do you mean?"

"I mean the color of the king's heart."

"Which king?"

"Since there can be only one king at a time, I am obviously referring to Herod."

"To the ostrich," I smiled.

"To the ostrich—may he smother under the sand!"

"I dreamed of chess the other night," I said.

But my opponent did not hear. His face was grave, intense. Already his mind was on the contest between us, and on that alone. Above our heads, birds moved fitfully in the branches of the trees. A smell of dry rot came from the log on which we sat. The thick, unstirring air came alive with the sounds of insects. Somewhere nearby a frog croaked wearily and then fell silent. Ichavod had removed his hunting knife from its sheath and was patiently scrutinizing the blade. The general sighed, cupped his chin in his hands and contemplated his opening gambit. After a time, he moved and I followed suit. We were both absorbed in the game, drawn into its arena to the exclusion of all else. The light in the forest filtering down through the trees grew fainter, the outlines of the trees and the giant ferns blurred, the sounds of the insects diminished. At length, the blue-violet shadows of evening swallowed all: we could no longer make out the board. The game was well advanced, but had not been decided. The general had the advantage of one piece—a knight—but mine was the stronger position. "Well," said Livinius, yawning, "we shall have to resume play at another time. Will you remember the board?"

"Have no fear—I will."

"Excellent—so will I!"

He extended his hand and I took it.

Mounting his horse, he said a single word: "Victory!"

"Victory!" I replied.

That night, at the war ministry, I received an urgent message. It came from Melech the Galilean and informed me that the head jailer of Herod's fortress prison, Kalbi, had at last been found—dead. Our agents had discovered his whereabouts several weeks ago in Jericho and had followed him from that city to Hebron, where he had gone under heavy escort. Unfortunately, his trackers had lost sight of him there, and only some days later in scouring the area had come upon his mutilated body in a wadi outside the town walls. They had driven a pack of jackals off to get at his corpse. I put the message down: it was clear that whoever had needed Kalbi needed him no longer. I sent word that the body be brought to me immediately, and so it was. I had it placed in a small stone chamber in the cellar of the ministry and went down to view it the first spare minute that came my way: I always derived singular pleasure from

344

the sight of a dead enemy. I was satisfied—it was Kalbi all right, and he stank to high heaven. Though my aides held their noses, I went closer without lifting a finger to my face. One of Kalbi's ears had been completely chewed off, his chin was ripped open to the bone, most of the nose was gone—but it was definitely Kalbi and no other. Even mutilation and decay had not erased the arrogance of his appearance. I should have preferred it if Kalbi had been taken alive, so we could have pried his secrets loose and then slowly and expertly led him to the province of death, giving him ample time to experience every stage of the transfer, but if this was the way it had to be, it was sufficient for the moment. "Better bury the rabid dog than chase him!" I always said. What Kalbi had known would become manifest, whom he had worked for would be discovered, the passage into the fortress would be found—all in good time. I could enjoy his corpse, which—fittingly enough—the jackals had begun feasting on. I stood and gazed down on it with deep satisfaction, while behind me my aides shrank back. Then I turned, and leaving the room, said to the keeper of the cellar: "Burn it!"

It was Tuesday morning. Herod's great party was set for Wednesday night, a night which the king's astrologers and necromancers had told him was "singular" and "charged with significance." An agent went to the chief of couriers, who woke Elazar, and Elazar came to me in my office with the message: the men of *Patish*, working in twenty-four-hour shifts and literally turning the prison inside out, had discovered the passage in and out of the fortress. Ironically enough, one end was located scant feet from where I had often sat in my brother's cell—in the floor of the chamber directly beneath the aperture through which the light came in. As always, I wanted to see it with my own eyes but did not have the time. Fortunately the report was detailed and accurate. I read it through several times over. The floor panel was opened by cleverly concealed hinges. From that point, a tunnel, with ridges for footholds, had been cut into what was actually a large underground cavern in the mountain itself. Once in the cavern, the going was easy and swift enough; there was room to walk, and one simply followed a spring which fed from an unknown source. The spring led gently downwards to a point a hundred feet or so below the floor of the cell and there disappeared into a sheer wall of rock. Here Herod's men had cut a small doorway into the face of the mountain. When it was shunted aside, one passed through it out onto a shelf halfway up the mountain's flank. From there one could descend a narrow trail, partly natural and partly hewn by the hand of man, which clung to the cliff down to a tiny ledge scarcely large enough to hold a single person. The ledge was thirty or forty feet from the ground, and had carefully hidden projections for a rope ladder to be hung. Thus a man could wend his way to the base of the mountain, or by activating the ladder from below, could make his way upward. The route was a perilous one and could be used only by those who knew its every feature well—but it was certainly a way in and out of the fortress: it was this very route that had been used by the raiders to liberate the prisoners.

I rose from my table. I was jubilant. Elazar, who had been standing quietly by all the time I was going over the report, stared at me. I felt enormous power course through me. For this was a major breakthrough —and it had come at the most crucial of hours! With this knowledge, I could introduce my own forces into the fortress and block any attempt that Herod made to escape! I began to pace the room. I knew that it was essential for me to stop Herod and Herodias from fleeing. The king and his queen had to be exterminated—there was no other way. If they stayed alive after the coup, there was always the danger that like hydra, they would spring up again and thrive. The only way to be rid of them was to rid the earth of them! And with the escape route unveiled, my task would be that much easier. I went to my table, sat again, and devised plans for the use of the route which would be transmitted to Melech the Galilean without delay. And then, briefly but with emotion, I wrote out a citation for the men who had uncovered the passageway; when the time came, they would have their reward. I gave both to Elazar and sent him on his way.

That night I left the war ministry and went to my apartments. All that could be humanly done had been done. The coup awaited only my signal. I had now to collect myself, attend Herod's birthday celebration, and launch the attack. From that instant on, I would be wholly absorbed in its direction. It was strange for me to be home again— everything seemed almost unfamiliar. I summoned my servants, whom I had not seen for so long, and had them bathe me in leisurely fashion, dry and perfume me, shave and comb me. "I must shine like the morning star at the party!" I joked to Ichavod, who watched impassively. I looked at my bodyguard's large, crude face: it was scarred and seamed, the nose had been broken and had mended many times over, the lips were thick, the jaw was massive and set stubbornly—it too had been smashed and had healed more than once. The eyes, under brows that were broken by scar tissue, were not cruel; they were only blank, with the blankness that one sees in the eyes of an animal. I wondered what he thought, and then decided that like an animal he chewed his thought and swallowed it. At about ten I posted Ichavod outside the door of my bedchamber and summoned Elazar. He looked weary and was rubbing his eyes; I thought he was surprised that I had sent for him at my home.

"Undress," I said.

He looked at me.

"Why do you stand and gawk?" I said. "Undress."

As always, he gave his tender young body to me to do with as I wished; whatever my desire, he submitted to it without protest and often, it seemed to me, without interest. I lingered over every pleasure this night, even the most minute, for I had completely abstained for many weeks and would again once the coup had begun. Perhaps Elazar sensed this, for he was especially responsive. His nakedness was white and smooth and supple with the sap of youth, and he offered me all of it, without reservation. Afterward we lay side by side, spent and comatose, each of us lost in private dreams. At length, I stirred and summoned the servants, who brought us a rare Greek wine that had been chilled, roasted pheasant, fruits and sherbets prepared by a cook I had managed to lure away from Herod's palace kitchen. We ate on divans and then returned to my bed.

My page lay on the silk sheet, open to love again. I caressed him slowly, languorously, dwelling on each of his body's secrets as if I had discovered them for the first time. My ardor awakened the hidden fires of his own lust, and I found in him a passion I had often suspected but never thought to taste. I enjoyed myself thoroughly, though I observed in myself the wish to punish and to inflict pain. Other lovers had sought punishment from me, and depending upon my mood at the time, I had acquiesced. Elazar did not wish to be punished; he wanted only gentleness and was always submissive—yet there were moments when the desire to hurt, maim or even throttle him were overwhelming. The fact that he gave himself over to me with such complete abandon aroused in me fury and hatred. Thus far in our relationship, I had not yielded to my wrath, but the longer we continued to be lovers, the more difficult I found it to restrain myself.

It was past midnight. We lay in each other's arms. Elazar was asleep, breathing deeply and regularly, but no sleep came to me. Slowly, carefully, I disengaged myself from his embrace so as not to waken him. Naked, I went to a dresser and took from it a gold-handled knife with a long blade of the finest metal and workmanship. I touched it very gently to the palm of my hand, not applying the slightest pressure, and drew blood. I glanced over at the bed. The youth was still asleep—his arms flung out, his legs apart, as if he were on a crucifix. With a single stroke of the knife I should have been able to slit his jugular or pierce his beating heart through or sever his limp member or slash away his testicles. A part of me wanted to do one or even all of these things, but another voice said no. For a time, I teetered as on a precarious perch, feeling that I could as easily go one way as the other. Then, with a groan that came unexpectedly from some place deep within me, I tossed the knife onto the dresser. I went over to the bed, grasped the page by a shoulder and shook him roughly. His large eyes opened and he gazed up at me impassively. I squeezed the shoulder, and though he tried to contain it, I saw the pain on his face.

"Get out!"

"Master, I—"

"Get out! Quickly!"

"Master, yes . . . of course . . . "

He rose from the bed and I flung his cloak at him; he began to put it on.

"I said get out of here!"

And I shoved him through the door, naked as he was. Ichavod looked inquiringly at me, but I slammed the door in his face. I could not tolerate the sight of another living creature. There was a small bowl on a table in one corner of the room, and in the water was a rare fish that had been presented to me by a landowner from Tiberias; I got up and smashed the bowl and stepped on the fish with my bare foot. Then I drew on a robe and went out onto the terrace. The sky was very dark, darker than I had ever seen it, and covered with a rash of harshly brilliant stars. Tiny tongues of light, like those of poisonous serpents, shot out from them: green, blue, yellow and red—cold as ice, hot as flame. The same star breathed both, the same star exuded both. I looked up at the heavens until I felt calmer, until I no longer felt the pressing need to use the knife on human flesh. In the profound darkness before me, I heard the guards pacing the ramparts, calling out to each other regularly as if to confirm each his own existence. I stood and listened

348

and the sounds comforted me: the military barking, the heavy footfalls, the jangling of weaponry. Once a torch flared and I saw the captain of the guard, arrayed magnificently, swirling his cape and spitting out a rapid series of orders. The torch was snuffed out and the night became blacker than before. It was past three when I left the sky, giddy with its constellations, and the vast inkwell of the earth that had only sounds to offer me, and went inside again. I extinguished my lamp and stretched out on my bed. The smell of Elazar, the smell of perfume, the smell of sperm—all of them were on the sheet. I ripped it off and flung it to the floor. Then I walked in darkness to my dresser, crushing shards of the fish bowl underfoot, picked up my knife and returned with it to my bed. I set it on the mattress by my head, the long, thin, chill blade pointed downward to my feet. I reached out my hand and grasped the handle. Thus we slept, my bride and I.

PART

VI

I wakened early and again, drawn to the outdoors, went to the terrace. The sun was just up, flooding the great basin that lay between the fortress of Herod and the Sea of Salt with colors and nuances that seemed to come alive only at the break of day. In the distances, on the slopes and spines of the hills and on their ridges, flocks of white sheep and herds of black goats roamed, already in search of pasture. Here and there were the clustered houses of villages, paling steadily in the light, and sometimes an oasis that did not seem real. The morning air was clear and limpid and birds glided through it with a strange lethargy, as if they were moving through water. I was calm once again, serene; my blood had settled, the evil dreams which had tormented me were blown away like cobweb. I stood for a long while at my rampart and envisioned everything I had planned, the entire coup—and all of it was one great panoply, one spectacle, from start to finish, coeval in time, begun and accomplished, conceived and executed, as if what was occurring and what would occur were set forth on a scroll meant for my eyes alone.

I was giddy with the vision, and then felt a desire to see the scroll of my life set before me in the same way. As hurriedly as I had gone onto the terrace, I left it and went into my house vault and opened it and brought forth my journals that I had kept for so many years. And I

353

seated myself on a divan and began to read in them, beginning with the earliest, tentative entries of my youth and going on to my courtship and marriage and through my position at court and my life there. My entries were sharper, keener, took on weight and depth and complexity; frequently I became so absorbed in the character studies I had drawn that I felt myself shifting uncannily into their souls. But then I came back to myself and went on, and the story of my life from my village days until the present unfolded for me. Oddly enough, what I read about myself had little or no living meaning for me: it was all but completely removed from me, vastly remote, the story of an age or ages long gone by and never to be revived again, tales of a world fled forever and of interest only to the most pedantic of historians. It was as if the past were a shell and I some creature of the sea that had emerged from it and left it behind—an object now altogether foreign—to dry and rot in the sun among the stones of the beach. I grew weary and bored, and though I was accustomed to read for hours on end without tiring, my eyes began to blur and smart and my attention wandered.

At length I put the journals aside, went back to the vault, rummaged through various effects, and finally withdrew the single object that through all the years had not lost its meaning for me; I had stumbled upon it now in my idle searching, and yet I could not call the discovery an accident. As I held it in the palm of my hand, I recalled that I had dreamed about it not long ago as I lay asleep in my war ministry office. I smiled with a measure of bitterness, remembering the day on which and the circumstances in which it had been given to me. It glittered yet, as brightly as on that day so long ago: the tiny medallion of gold engraved with the profile of the emperor, placed in my hand by a Roman officer who was most probably dead or retired. It was a curious thing how little of my life—aside from, say, this minuscular symbol— had survived, how little of it was left for me, how little what had gone by mattered: it was almost as if the person who had lived that life was dead and another person had taken his place. Even now—except for the bottomless, inexhaustible hatred I felt, except for my insatiable long- ing for power—there was a disturbing deadness about my life. I shook my head and felt a shudder pass through my body and once more the taste of evil dreams in my mouth and the urge to kill, to kill without rhyme or reason or even pleasure—just to kill; and I rose hurriedly and gathered my journals together and stuffed them back in the vault where they belonged and closed and locked it and went into another room.

There I summoned a servant and ordered him to bring a gold-smith to my apartments as quickly as possible; I wanted the little medallion affixed to a chain so that I could wear it about my neck, so that I could feel its slight but awful weight against my naked skin. "And you'd better make it fast—if you have any regard for your hide!" I called after the terrified servant as he departed. It was just past noon and the smith arrived within the hour, bent—or so I assumed—on spar-ing his bones. Half frightened out of his wits, he began work in my salon, looking up every moment to see if the torture he feared was about to overtake him. I sat opposite him on a chair, watched him work, and calmed him with quaint observations about "precious metals and more precious hands." He settled down to his task and soon had the job finished. I held the chain up and let the medallion dangle delicately against the light streaming in through the window. It was a beautiful sight. I told the smith so, paid him with my own hand a sum far in excess of what was due him and had the servants send him—laughing and chattering like a loon—on his way. "What a bore was the smith," I told the servant who helped me clasp the chain at the nape of my neck, "but what a delight was his work!" I stood before the mirror and saw the medallion's gold on the whiteness of my breast. I was calm, my heart was at peace, my mind flowed as a river that knows its course.

I yawned and clapped my hands, and when the servants came flying again had myself washed and dried and powdered and perfumed; and I commanded manicure and pedicure and combing and curling, and when I was relaxed and satisfied with the grooming of my body, I had my valets dress me. Actually, my attire was simple: a deep purple robe with silver trim on the sleeves and hem. Over my heart I wore the emblem of the commander-in-chief, wrought in purest gold. At my right side I wore a regulation army broadsword, the handle and sheath of which were, however, jewel-encrusted. My wide belt was of simple silver and was fastened with an emerald buckle. My sandals, too, were of silver-worked leather with buckles of emerald. I wore nothing in my thick, wavy hair. The servants stood back when all was finished and said that I was "splendid," "magnificent," and "radiant as the dawn"—but of course they were servants and the comments they made were expected. I gazed at myself in the mirror: I was a trifle drawn, my eyes were somewhat sunken, my jaw had a bit too rigid a cast—but I was imposing, I was formidable, I was leonine!

I summoned Elazar, and when he arrived, promptly as always, I dismissed all of the other servants and sent them from the room.

"Master," he blurted out before I had a chance to address him, "master, forgive me—" He went down on his knees.

"What is the meaning of this?"

"Master—I implore you—I beg of you—pardon . . . "

"But why do you ask my pardon?"

"Last night—last night . . . "

"Last night what?"

His lips trembled. "Last night I displeased you, did I not?"

"You displeased me," I said.

"But what did I do? Or what did I fail to do?"

I shrugged.

"Tell me, master—that I may not repeat the offense."

"Never mind."

"But how, master, how did I cause you displeasure?"

"It is unimportant," I said angrily.

Elazar stared up at me. The coldness had left his eyes, and a terrible fear, which I had never seen before, replaced it. I was fascinated by the revelation. "You are afraid . . . Elazar, I can see the fear. Of what are you afraid, my page?"

Elazar bowed his head, and his shoulders shook. "Of losing you, master," he said in a whisper.

I laughed. "Of losing me? How droll! You will never lose me, you little fool! Never! Now, listen to me and listen to me well—" I took his chin in my hand and lifted his head even higher, as one might do to a dog of whom one is fond. "It is unimportant, completely unimportant and inconsequential that you did not please me last night; perhaps it wasn't even your fault. But what is important is that you serve me well this night—and you know it, don't you?"

"Yes, I know it, my master!"

"And you will serve me faithfully—as always?"

"Oh, yes, master, yes! I will serve you!"

And I was certain that he would—even to the death. In his own way, he was as attached to me as Melech the Galilean, Ichavod, Onan or Akrab. There was some fatal attraction I had for a particular kind of man who in losing himself to me somehow found a web of actions that gave him a sense of perverse purpose, of denial. And that denial, that immolation was everything in life to him. I smiled, and leaving my page on his knees as if he were at prayer, I went over to a dresser and from a hidden compartment took out a ring. "Extend your right hand," I said, returning to Elazar. He did as he was directed and I slipped the ring on to his index finger. It was a signet ring—a gold setting that held a flat ruby with my emblem cut into it: the Hebrew letter *ayyin*, which was the first letter of the name Evenezer, cleft diagonally by a sword on whose blade was inscribed my own name in Hebrew and Latin script; below it was the code sign of the coup, which was an adder poised to strike. "Wear this ring, my page, as a sign of my love," I said. "And with it you have safe conduct wherever it is necessary among all of my forces and among the forces of the general Livinius." It was the same ring I had given to Melech the Galilean, to Ichavod, to Onan and to Akrab—a ring I called in code "the noose."

Elazar gazed raptly at his finger. "I accept it, master. I accept it in love, as it was given."

"Yes . . . yes, of course: 'in love as it was given.' Of course." And I dropped the page's outstretched hand, which had grown cold.

Elazar was silent; then he said, "But if I die, master, if I die in the difficult days ahead, I beg that you mourn me, that you remember me, that you do not allow the light of my name to be extinguished in your heart!"

"Foolish boy! Again you speak of death!"

"Master . . . master . . . " He held out his hands to me but I did not take them, did not touch them. "Master, I have no one—no one in this world but you. Remember me."

"You will not die. I promise you." I stared directly into the troubled depths of his eyes. "But what will happen if I should die? If I should not survive the days ahead, what then?"

"You cannot die!" the page cried.

"But if I do? Will you mourn me? Will you weep for me? Will you remember me? Will you serve another master?"

Elazar shook his head. "You cannot die, master. You will not die. I am certain of it."

"Come, come, what nonsense are you saying? What foolishness is this?"

"You will never die, master."

"I will never die? Never?"

357

"No."

"How did you—arrive at such a preposterous notion?"

Elazar was silent.

"Well, how did you reach such a conclusion?"

"I dreamed it, master."

"When? When did you dream it?"

"Many times. Many times over, master."

And he wept. I stroked his head gently, but the touch of his hair revolted me and I withdrew my hand. "All right, Elazar," I said. "I will not die." My voice hardened: "Now go to your post and wait. And let nothing thwart you on this night of nights! Go—and I will see you at the appointed time!"

Elazar rose in silence and left the room without looking back. I watched him, knowing that he did not exist except in the performance of his mission, except in me.

A thousand tapers flared and burned and shot sparks and sent wisps of fine-spun smoke up into the colossal dome of King Herod's grand ballroom; a thousand royal pennants swayed and fluttered and waved; a thousand lances glittered in the hands of the palace guards, who lined the walls, erect with pride and pomp, resplendent in purple and gold. In cages hung from the arches, peacocks spread their fans, and monkeys clad in the spangled garb of clowns cavorted without cease. A great band of minstrels played, and dancers slithered to and fro among the jewel-bedecked instruments. From the very instant a guest entered the enormous foyer through which one had to pass on his way to the ballroom itself, a horde of servants and slaves besieged him with lavish attentions. They fluttered before the gold- and silver-framed mirrors and in and out among the soaring pillars of varicolored marble, converging upon the guest in ever-renewed bursts of energy, welcoming him "in the name of the most revered and exalted monarch, Herod," who had "by the grace of God" attained to the "glorious and blissful age" of three score years, an age "blessed again and again in legend and lore." In their frenzied desire to please, Herod's vast retinue of ancillaries succeeded most often in irritating; in their frantic wish to flatter, they most frequently offended. The harried guest was compelled to flee their overpoweringly repetitious offers of food and favors, pleasure and excitement—all extended through the "gracious and bountiful offices of his royal majesty," whose "lofty and magnanimous heart brimmed over with joy of the occasion"! The little speeches and salutations had been taught to the servants and rehearsed by them for many weeks, but still there were many who forgot their lines altogether or garbled their phrases beyond recognition—and there were those who spoke in accents so strange that it was impossible to understand them. In the huge hall itself, long tables had been set out end to end and ran the entire length of the room from entranceway to the raised dais, with its intricate grillwork and festoons of fresh flowers from every part of the country, where the king and queen and dignitaries were to be seated. Between the rows of tables, wide aisles had been left for the servers; and in the very center of the hall was a large circular arena for entertainments. Slowly the guests filed in, each of them announced by the clash of cymbals and the calling of his name by the royal criers, whose piercing voices circled the room like bats. My own place was of course on the dais, and I was led to the scarlet-carpeted stairs that ascended to it by a pair of Ethiopian slaves, male and female, naked but for gold-clothed loincovers. I had been seated between the Judean minister of the interior, one Yirachmiel by name, a fat, red-faced bore who was renowned at banquets for his gluttony which often caused him to soil himself and collapse—to the dismay of his neighbors—and a tall, hump-backed high priest by the name of Shmaryahu, who belonged to the inner circle which revolved about Annas and Caiaphas. It took nearly an hour for all of the guests to be seated, during which time I exchanged inane pleasantries with the men who flanked me and those who came over to greet me. Most complained that I "worked too hard" and "was not seen nearly enough at court" and that my presence at various social functions "was sorely missed." I tendered my apologies in most humble fashion, regretted that the "situation could not be helped," but hoped that "better times were ahead." My admirers assured me that they were.

At length the festivities began. Herod's master of ceremonies stood up with a torch in his hand that blazed with a dozen different colors— red and crimson and blue and green and yellow and orange and other hues—and from the four corners of the hall came young children in white attire, two boys and two girls, with garlands of flowers in their hair, bearing the goodly fruit of the land which, kneeling, they laid before Herod's place. All eyes in the packed hall were on the monarch as he rose and blew kisses at the children, who retired, bowing as they went. All eyes were also on the empty block of seats at the dais table—those meant for the procurator and his courtiers; people looked, but no one dared utter a word. As the king seated himself again, there was scattered applause. Then the master of ceremonies gestured with a gold baton, and a great burst of music came forth from the artists of the king's own court—a perfect thunderstorm of sound that rumbled down from the balcony to the left of the dais, where they were ensconced. There was a pause, again the baton pointed, and these same musicians, using trumpets and drums without restraint, accompanied a chorus of singers stationed on a balcony to the right; the choral offering was "a solemn hymn of praise and thanksgiving, composed especially for this exalted occasion" and expressing the "boundless love of the people and the court for the adored monarch, Herod." The song also extended the "nation's most profound and heartfelt wishes for the king's continued health and happiness" and its gratitude for the "numberless benefits and blessings of his exceptional rule, unparalleled in the memory of man."

There followed next, in the center circle, a pageant performed by naked actors and actresses depicting the conception of Herod, his birth, the years of his childhood in Samaria, his noble youth, and finally his marriage to Herodias, his ascendancy to the throne of Judea, and the birth of his daughter, Salome. The great hall had been darkened for this performance, with only a circle of massed torches held by slaves suspended from on high to illuminate the bizarre spectacle, during which the players engaged in heterosexual coitus as well as intercourse of the male and female varieties; they also performed other erotic acts, "with admirable gusto and with exceeding good taste," according to the opinion of many spectators.

Herod, at whose side torchbearers stood all through the pageant because he was notoriously terrified of the dark, was clearly visible: his eyes shone hotly, his face was flushed with excitement, and his flesh had an unnatural tone, as if it were made of wax that might melt at any instant. On his left sat his wife, the queen, her bare breasts caught in gold netting, her hair studded through with gems—diamonds, pearls, rubies, sapphires and emeralds that looked as if they had been scattered there at random by a hand that did not care what it did. Her eyes rolled, her cheeks twitched, her lips moved without stop whether she conversed with anyone or not, her hands flew this way and that like birds run amok: she looked quite mad. Next to her sat Salome, with the same look of demented abandon on her features. The two women were in fact like twins who shared the same disease and kept infecting and reinfecting each other with it. I smiled inwardly. This loathsome trio would be wiped out before many days had gone by. This foul trifoliate plant would be cut at the base of its stem and the roots pulled out— that it might never spring up again! And it was my firm resolve, as well, to comb the land and seek out every member of that abhorrent family, be he close or distant, and exterminate him in order that the name and memory of Herod be expunged for all time! *Patish* would serve me well in this enterprise, and I decided that one of my first projects when I ascended the throne would be this.

The pageant finished in one great shuddering paroxysm of carnal release, and then the flares and the torches all about were relit. A small, bent, wizened old man in black rose and lifted his silver goblet. It was Caiaphas, the high priest, with wrinkled forehead, knife-blade nose, and skin the color of soot to match his black robes. The hundreds upon hundreds of guests rose in turn with uplifted cups to offer their toast. The old man muttered his words, spitting them out curtly as if he were loath to part not only with them but with the breath he needed to launch them, and the audience gave its response with a roar that had the force of an avalanche. "Blessed be Herod, king of the Jews!" And the guests thundered back: "Blessed be Herod, king of the Jews!" Many were already drunk, though the drinking had not officially begun. "On this joyous day and on every day of his life; may it stretch its wings until one hundred and twenty!" And the audience echoed the response as if its own length of days depended on it. "Amen!" said Caiaphas, spitting, wiping his purple lips and seating himself as the guests did the same.

Then the cymbals clashed three times over and the food began to arrive, for the most part being wheeled down the aisles in carts. There was food and drink of every description, in vast quantities, and the guests began to gorge themselves, reaching over each other and jostling one another to heap plates which were already loaded. I did little more than taste my meal, and I drank not a single drop of wine. "What's the matter with you," asked the minister of the interior. "Are you ailing?" But he continued to shovel the food into his mouth without waiting for an answer.

Halfway through the initial course, a series of strident trumpet blasts announced the arrival of Pontius Pilate and his entourage. Toppling goblets, upsetting plates and knocking servants to the floor, the entire assemblage rose as one, stood at attention, and sang the Roman anthem as if their throats must burst. Even Herod was on his feet, tottering uncertainly and gesticulating, and beside him the bitch-queen, Herodias, her bejeweled hair blazing, and their slut of a daughter, Salome, whose nipples had been capped in ruby sheaths. They all stood, the whole horde of them, and sang, sang with all the blood of their hearts and marrow of their bones—sang harshly, raucously, with a cacophonous abandon that was nothing short of diabolical. Preceded by special ushers and elite Roman troops, the procurator of Judea and his retinue made their way slowly up an aisle that had been cleared and carpeted for them; children dressed up as cherubim strewed flowers in their path, and to both sides of their feet the torn and crushed petals scattered.

The trumpets rang out again. The procurator and his entourage ascended the dais and took the seats reserved for them, for the late arrival they were bound by protocol to make. Trembling, red-faced, glassy-eyed, Herod turned to the procurator and embraced him; and Pilate returned the embrace stiffly, backing off just as soon as decorum permitted it. "Roman brother!" "Hebrew brother!" These were the salutations their thieving mouths uttered, though I was in no way near enough to them to hear what they said. But I knew—knew as surely as I knew that Herod and his kin would be gone! Behind the two, on the wall, were the two gigantic bronze figures of the lion and the eagle: the former's mouth was open wide and the latter's wings were spread. The assembly of guests applauded and cheered. Queen Herodias curtsied in her lopsided manner to Pilate, her netted dugs swinging as she did so, and after her, Salome, upon whose features was stamped a grin of imperious inanity. Pilate seated himself to Herod's right and next to him sat the functionaries he had brought. Still, I noticed a vacant place, though it was set with gold utensils as were all others on the dais and its goblet filled with wine and food served into its plate. When I asked about it, I was told by my neighbor, the High Priest, that it had been left so in "in tribute to and memory of" the departed Quaestoris, whose "immaculate spirit" the Romans felt was "present among his comrades." I yawned into the speaker's face, and he turned away from me, obviously insulted. The meal seemed interminable—course after course was wheeled in, carried in, borne in by slaves whose flesh was sheeted over with sweat. Guests were continuously being led and carried out of the hall. Some slumped onto the tables, others slipped to the floor. Between the endless courses, which became more and more lavish and exotic, there were acrobats, jugglers, magicians, sword- and fire-dancers, animal and bird acts. At times the great throng of guests burst into song, suddenly and inexplicably, without rhyme or reason, struggling in their drunken and bloated frenzy to reach heaven or hell with their words, which of course went no further than the confines of Herod's hall.

At the hour of twelve, a fanfare of trumpets sounded, their clarion tones cutting through the din and at length silencing it. The drums rolled. The day that marked the auspicious birth of Judea's Herod had actually begun. The trumpet blasts—three to symbolize three score of years—died away and the monarch got to his feet, looking more than ever like an old crone. There was no announcement, no introduction. A profound hush fell over the audience. In halting words, half of which were swallowed and half of which were garbled, the king spoke lengthily of the majesty of his reign, in which the "lion and the eagle clasped each other in love and regard." He recounted the countless blessings of his regime: progress, plenty, peace, security; he talked of the "welfare of the people," of the "calm and equilibrium which rested upon the land," of the "contentment and prosperity that prevailed, even from the Great Sea unto Galilee, and from Hermon in the north to the Negev Desert of the south." In short, he boasted of everything that his kingdom lacked and would never have. Then he turned to his "own poor and austere life," which was characterized by the "purity of his unswerving dedication" to the "people, the land, and the nation." He praised his "adored spouse," his "regal wife, beloved mother of the realm," and his "ethereal and saintly daughter," the beauty of whose body "was matched only by her soaring spirituality." And then, turning his face to the right and to the procurator, whom he addressed as "most august and illustrious personage" and "brilliant symbol of the empire and its everlasting glory" and "ever more noble Roman," he paid unsparing homage to a Pilate who looked half asleep in his seat. He called Pilate the "progenitor of the halcyon" and hailed him as a "mighty artificer of advancement whose name and works would never be forgotten as long as the race of man held sway on earth." Pilate's head sank to his breast, but the monarch went on. Finally, he was through—with Pilate, though not with his address. He faced front once more, and spreading his hands so he resembled a rooster about to be slaughtered which flaps its wings for one last time before the end, spoke directly to the audience. He delivered a long, rambling monologue on the mystical significance of his age, mixing together every bit of patent nonsense that had entered his head and stuck. Some of the guests wept, without knowing why or simply because they wanted to or felt it was expected of them; others sat in a daze, blinking and belching; still others succumbed to stupor. When the king at long last finished, few knew what he had said and fewer cared. Scattered applause broke out, forceful only among the Roman contingent, who responded with what they felt to be proper decorum.

Herod, who was still on his feet, raised a hand, and the audience grew silent. The procurator of Judea rose. Dull-eyed, his prune-textured face gray with weariness, he began his response in sepulchral tones that fell upon his listeners like lead weights. He spoke in Latin—a bald interpreter translated what he said—with neither the polish nor the fluency of his late-lamented friend for whom the token place had been laid out. Ill-at-ease before the crowd of revelers, gruff, speaking with graceless and even tasteless monotony of one who was used to unchallenged command, he was very much, it seemed to me, the rhinoceros paying tribute to the tick. His speech was brief, formal and dull, lauding Herod as a ruler who "had the wisdom and the foresight" to "read the text of Judea's future . . . in the handwriting of Rome." Nothing much more had to be said, and it was not. He passed on to few weakly deferential remarks about the "matchless charm of the queen" and the "unsurpassable delicacy" of the princess, who flushed with patent pleasure over his references to them. The talk ended almost before it had begun, almost before anyone realized it was over, and Pontius Pilate sat, with evident relief, while the "ostrich" continued to stand and lead a thunderous ovation that seemed only to build on its own momentum as the minutes passed.

At last Herod too took his seat and the applause died away; almost at once, as if by some prearranged signal, the revelry—which was orgiastic in tone, now that the last "duties" had been performed—commenced. Pandemonium broke out. Guests crawled onto the tables and thrust their faces into platters of food like swine; they snatched up carafes of wine and drank steadily until they passed out; they swarmed into the aisles and seized male and female servants for whatever appetite or purpose suited them; they exposed their genitals or disrobed altogether; they ripped the clothes from each other; they abandoned or completely lost their continence. The musicians struck up a wild, lewd melody meant to inflame; the monkeys screamed on high and the peacocks dashed against their cages. The sea of guests became a hundred twisting currents. Actors, mimes, dancers, acrobats, jugglers, jesters, male and female prostitutes mingled freely with the audience. A magician produced a flock of doves from his cloak and then killed them in flight with tiny darts; a snake charmer turned his reptiles loose among the screaming revelers; a fakir flung up hot coals and caught them in his hands and mouth; fortunetellers babbled the future in a dozen tongues; a whore spread her legs and slipped a dagger blade between her thighs into her human sheath. The noise was deafening, the movement bewildering—the total effect staggering and unreal. Lining the side walls were Herod's palace guards, and massed shoulder to shoulder before the dais were Pilate's elite troopers—they stood ready against any unruliness that might pose a threat to their masters.

The time had come. I rose from my seat and, unnoticed, made my way to the rear of the hall and passed through an exit into a small anteroom where personal servants, security agents and assorted liaison officers milled about quietly, as if the sounds they made might somehow interfere with what was transpiring in the great hall. His face composed, his eyes set with their usual cold fury, Elazar awaited me in a corner; I could see immediately that he had given himself over wholly to the passion of his assignment. Into his hands I pressed the small metal disks with the code word for attack on them that I had taken from my robe; he slipped them into his pouch, turned without a word or other sign, and left for his rendezvous with the couriers. The door closed on him. Within a matter of hours, my forces would launch the attack. A new lion would swallow the old.

The night was very dark; heavy clouds hid the stars. Noiselessly Ichavod brought the horses from the special section of the war ministry stables. We mounted and rode swiftly out of Herod's fortress to a citrus grove several miles to the north. There my hand-picked escort from among the members of the seventeenth assault group waited, well-concealed by the trees with their ripening fruit. The unit was under the command of a young captain who came highly recommended by the brigade commander, and who had distinguished himself again and again on maneuvers and in actions against the rebels. He saluted smartly and led me to a makeshift table, where I sat and by the light of an oil lamp whose flame did not once waver in the windless dark made a number of last-minute computations. The first of my troops to launch the attack would do so in the north, in the Galilee, where my influence and my power held sway. They would make for the cities of Safed and Tiberias. Once the north was in my hands, the troops would move to the south—to Nazareth and into the Jezreel Valley and along the coastal area of the Sharon. Beersheba, Hebron, Gaza and Bethlehem would fall from the south, while Jericho would be taken from the north. With Livinius blocking interference, the noose would now be drawn around Jerusalem.

I finished my work. Round the lamp's knifelike flame, the fat night moths whirled and dipped; I watched a goodly number of them plunge headlong into the fire, as if the others had picked them for sacrifice. I smiled at the sight—so necessary, I thought, in human affairs—and rose, nodding curtly to Captain Achzari, who instantly gave the order to move out. We left the grove, thick with the scent of the fruit, and rode into the sultry darkness. Our route was a circuitous one, avoiding main roads, crossings, towns and villages. We stayed clear of ridges and other high points, from which we were visible from a greater distance, and from wadis and ravines in which we were easy prey to ambush. I had calculated long and thoroughly and did not anticipate an attack. But I wanted to be ready for any eventuality—experience had taught me again and again that expecting surprise was the only method of disarming surprise. My objective was, of course, to reach *Patish* headquarters as soon as possible. There my communications and operations center for the entire coup had been set up: into it would come reports from every part of the country—communiqués which I would study and evaluate. Out of it would go the orders for the furtherance and progress of the coup. We rode in complete silence for more than an hour. Then suddenly the contingent, which was of platoon strength, halted. I was riding with Ichavod in its center and did not know what had caused the delay. With Ichavod close behind, I rode up front to the captain, who was talking earnestly to a scout.

"What seems to be the trouble, Captain? Why have we stopped?"

Achzari's voice was tense. "My scout, sir. He's just come back—"

I turned directly to the soldier. "Why are you here? Tell me and be quick about it!"

"There's a patrol ahead, sir. Just over the next rise."

"A patrol?"

"Yes, sir. Over the rise."

"What sort of patrol? Whose patrol?"

"Roman, sir," said the scout.

"Are you certain?"

"Absolutely certain."

"Then why are you back here?"

"Why, sir?"

"Yes, why, damn it! They must be men from the southernmost brigade of Livinius's legion! Why didn't you give the code word? Why did you come back?"

Rattled by my tone, the scout fell silent.

Reining his restless mount in, Achzari spoke, "With your permission, sir, my scout tells me that he did not use the code word—"

"But why not? Those were his instructions! I'll have him court-martialed on the spot!"

"He could not make contact with the patrol at all, sir."

"Not make contact? And why not?"

"Because the patrol aroused his suspicion, sir. When he discovered them, he discovered they were deployed in a hostile manner. In ambush positions, sir. The Romans were supposed to show their presence, not hide it." The captain nodded toward the scout. "This man is a veteran, sir. I assure you that he is one of the best scouts in the army. I'd stake my life on him."

"I'm not interested in your life—I'm concerned with the patrol. Get on with what you're saying, Captain!"

"He was suspicious, and in order to confirm his feelings he managed to penetrate the Roman lines."

"Penetrate their lines?"

"Yes, sir. Precisely." He turned to the scout. "Tell him your story, soldier."

"Well, sir, as the captain said, I was able to get inside the perimeter of the ambush. I had spotted two of its lookouts and reckoned I could get between them without being seen. So I left my horse a couple of hundred yards back and went forward on foot. I had to crawl the last fifty on my belly. And then I knew the lookouts were behind me on the rise and that I was safely inside."

"So you made certain it was an ambush?"

"Yes, sir. Certain. As certain as I'm speaking to you now."

"It is true," I said to Achzari. "Livinius's forces were not to be deployed in ambush—only in visible patrols. Their job was to head off trouble, not start it." I shook my head. "This is not according to plan. I don't understand it—I really don't understand it! Perhaps some miserable platoon commander took it into his head to start a war of his own? I just don't know!" I rapped my riding whip on my thigh. "Well, go on, soldier! What happened then?"

"I had a look, sir, that's what happened. I had a good look. It was a big patrol—a big one, maybe two platoons, maybe even more! And there they were in ambush, waiting to have a crack at whoever came along. I saw exactly what was what. Why, I got so close I could have slit a half-dozen throats without anyone being the wiser!"

"How could a general like Livinius allow this?" I said.

"Sir," said Achzari. "Sir . . ."

"What is it? Don't just gape at me, Captain! Say what you mean to say!"

"They were soldiers of the Tenth Legion, sir," said the captain quietly.

"The Tenth!? Impossible!"

"With your permission, sir," Achzari repeated. "They were soldiers of the Tenth."

"But the Tenth is—Aquilius! And Aquilius is in the south—I know he's in the south! He's been there for months, for half a year." I stared at the scout. "How can you be sure of what you're telling me?" I slashed at my boot with the whip. "If this is a mistake, soldier, then you've made a mistake with your life!"

"If I'm wrong, sir," said the scout, "I don't want my life."

"What this man says," said the captain, "he knows. There is no guesswork about this man and no nonsense—and there never has been." He extended a hand. "Here, take this—see for yourself, sir."

I took a small feather from the captain and examined it: it was yellow and had been torn away from something at its stem. "What does this mean?" I asked.

"There was a helmet on the ground—on a rock, that is. I tore it from the plume. It's yellow, sir, as you see—"

"The color of the Tenth," said Achzari.

I held the feather in my palm. "Yes, it is the Tenth," I said slowly. "It is Aquilius." I looked up. "And you can't say exactly how large a force there was? Or whether there were others?"

"No, sir, I cannot say. I simply marked the one perimeter and identified them, sir. And then I crawled out, thankful to be alive."

"Were you observed? Did anyone see you?"

"No, sir, they did not. Or I shouldn't be talking to you and the captain now, sir. The Tenth is a bloody bunch, sir."

"Captain," I said, "can we get around them?"

Achzari considered the matter. "I know the hills to the north very well—better than they do, I'm sure. We might be able to squeeze through. It's a risk, sir."

"Dismiss the scout, Captain."

Achzari sent the soldier away.

"We must get through, Captain. Something is seriously amiss. Aquilius belongs in the south and nowhere else. I had assurance that he would remain there. The presence of his legion here is ominous. Something has gone terribly wrong. I've got to get through and find out."

"I understand the urgency, sir. My men are the best. And they'll give it everything they've got. My suggestion, sir, is that we send out a party with the scout and if the way through the hills can be negotiated, they send us word. Then we can move ahead."

"And to the south?"

"There's the wadi, sir, as you know."

"Could we make it?"

"Assuming that the Tenth has no patrols in the area, we could. But it would add a day and a half, maybe two."

"I need the time, Captain. We'll try the hills."

"As you wish, sir."

"How long before we'll know?"

"Two hours, maybe three, sir."

"Not sooner?"

"I don't see how, sir."

The captain rode off to give his orders. I remained where I was with Ichavod. The overcast had grown thicker, the night darker—it seemed that the moon and stars could never have existed. The air was close and stifling; I wiped the perspiration from my forehead. I dismounted and for a time walked the earth, crushing the yellow plume-feather between my fingers. Suddenly a cry rang out. I sprang on my horse and with Ichavod rode to where the captain was.

"What is it?" I said.

Achzari did not answer my question but pointed in the direction of the hills. The scout and another soldier were riding at full gallop up the slope. A hundred yards behind them lay four comrades and four dead horses, hit by Roman archers. Behind them were the Roman troopers of the Tenth Legion, whom we could not yet make out. The scout and his lone companion did not make it. Invisible arrows pulled them to the earth and to a darkness deeper than the night of earth. But now shouts rang out from our lookouts east and west.

"He was observed," I said. "They let him through on purpose. They're coming at us, Captain!"

"Sir—"

"I *must* get through, Captain."

"Sir, I—"

"Must, do you hear?"

"It's a larger force than we reckoned—far larger—"

"The fate of Judea hangs on my getting through."

"Ride to the south, sir. There are wadis—canyons—you can hide in them by day, if necessary, as the rebels do. We'll hold them off here as best we can!" He dug his spurs into his mount's flanks and began barking orders to his men. From all sides came the sounds of battle—the whistling of arrows, screams of the soldiers, neighing of the horses. "A safe journey!" cried the captain, dashing past us. "Long live Judea!"

"Long live Judea!" I snarled as Ichavod and I galloped southward.

We got clear of our own lines. A cold fury gripped me. I could not mark the dimensions of what I knew, but one thing was apparent: I had counted on the Romans, and the Romans had failed—or worse. And now I counted on the darkness, and it too failed. The clouds parted and light from a pale, ghastly moon shone down. Moments later, six Roman soldiers made their appearance. We caught sight of them first, and Ichavod waved me aside; as he drove his horse forward, I took cover behind a hillock. Ichavod was upon the Romans almost before they were aware of the fact. The cavalryman in the lead thrust a spear at him which he caught by its shaft and butted back into his opponent's face: I saw the Roman's head go limp as he fell, and knew the neck was broken. Using the spear as a club, he swung it at the second Roman and hit his throat with such force that the jugular opened in a spray. The third man, who had his sword upraised and thought to strike Ichavod, received the spear with all of the power in the giant's shoulders and back: it shattered the soldier's breastplate and breastbone at once; vomiting blood, he toppled from his mount. All of this had taken place within a number of seconds—with such incredible speed and precision that his enemies scarcely realized half their troop was gone. It was as if a secret voice spoke to Ichavod from deep within his being, a voice that his mind and every part of his great body heard at the same time. Ichavod whirled on his horse. The Romans who were left, thunderstruck by what had occurred, reined in their mounts. That was a mistake, as it always was a mistake to hesitate in the presence of my bodyguard. Thinking to attack their lone adversary, they never thought that he would attack instead. Goading his mount to top speed, he charged directly at the trio, raising his great sword and passing between two of the cavalrymen as they started forward to meet him. Both Romans miscalculated his reach, for as he rode, he leaned first to the left and then to the right, slashing the faces of the troopers with strokes so swift they seemed one. Two bodies spun twisting from their mounts as the last cavalryman came screaming at him. Ichavod had just time to arch his torso as the outthrust sword pierced his cloak; he turned backward in his saddle and with his counterblow severed the trooper's leg at the thigh. The leg went one way and the Roman the other, and Ichavod trampled him with his horse; he then signaled me to come out of hiding and into the carnage, which I did. We left the six corpses basking in the grisly light of the moon. "Long live Judea!" I said bitterly as we rode off. Ichavod said nothing; he was satisfied with silence.

We took shelter in the cleft between two giant boulders in one of a series of canyons that led into each other like a maze; it would have been impossible to find us there with a thousand men. Ichavod removed his cloak. His body was caked with grime and blood—the last Roman cavalryman had, after all, wounded him—but the cut, which was across his rib cage, was no more than superficial, and he attended to it with herbs gathered from nearby crevices. When he had finished, he put on his cloak once again and sat cross-legged on the earth to sleep the sleep that he could shed in an instant like water from the skin. I seated myself on the ground under the sparse branches of a stunted terebinth.

A thousand questions went through my mind, but they did not matter. What help would it be if I knew the answers to all of them? What good would it do me if I was able to explain the reason for everything that had happened? In one, single, devastating stroke I had been cut off from my power, separated from the vast machinery by means of which my will expressed itself, my spirit held dominion. The reins that I had picked up one by one, painstakingly and exactingly, over the years and bound into one mighty and inviolable knot of authority— had been struck from my hand. In one, blinding, unfathomable instant I had been jolted from the driver's seat of a juggernaut I had expended a lifetime of care, energy, effort and calculation in building. I was like a man all of whose senses, developed through his own agonies of mind and body to incredible levels of acuity, had been torn in one lightning blast from him: I had been rendered deaf, dumb and blind—left only with the capacity to slowly, steadily and inexorably realize the extent of my wounds and the magnitude of the damage to my person. The horror of my situation enveloped me as a coffin would a man who still lived. Parted from the apparatus of power it had cost me so much and taken me so long to fashion, I was only a man—a man limited solely to the immediate strength of his mind and body and exercising command over a dumb colossus of a fellow, more beast than human and loyal only out of secret urges and instincts that no one, including Ichavod himself, understood. Severed from army and state, I had control over no one but myself and a half-savage brute—and was myself subject to the wanton vagaries and capricious cruelties of the elements and the men who struggled in them as eels or tadpoles struggled in littoral mud. I was weary; I was beyond weariness; I was beyond the redress that weary men sought after and could manage to find; I was beyond comfort, solace, relief, revenge. I was no more than mortal dust, prey to every madcap wind that blew from every and any blind alley in the world: I was a man awake in a nightmare.

The first streaks of daybreak were beginning to appear in the sullen mud flats of the sky. In the distance a jackal called, another responded, and the walls of the canyons built a fugue of their screams. Sparrows flitted through the webbed gray of the air. The sky lightened and grew more intense; ribs of color began to show. Ichavod sat cross-legged, motionless, head sunk on breast; flies were crawling across his forehead. His eyelids were closed, but behind them there was wakefulness. He was coiled, complete—a part of the desert like a lizard or a cactus. A morning breeze had sprung up; it sobbed along the rock faces and stirred the branches of the terebinth. I felt myself dozing . . .

Lamentations filled the great ballroom, rising to the dome like a flock of ravens. The long tables were set out as they had been for Herod's birthday fete, but they were draped in black and the guests who sat at them in stiff rows, as if they were soldiers, were dressed in mourning. On the dais, the chairs were set out as they had been, and all the dignitaries sat in rigid order, but they were faceless. I thought it was because I was at the rear of the hall and could not see them well, but though I walked forward down one of the center aisles they remained featureless. There were none of Herod's men stationed along the walls, nor were any of Pilate's soldiers positioned in front of the dais; in their stead were dancers, magicians, acrobats, mimes, fortunetellers, actors, musicians, courtesans and street whores—none of them moved in their places, for they were frozen like statues. I approached the dais and saw that there were two places empty; I understood that one was Quaestoris's and realized that the other was mine. When I reached the dais stairs, the weeping rose to a great pitch and then died away, like the sighing of the wind in pines. I wished to ascend, but found I could not lift a foot to reach the first step: my leg was paralyzed.

"I must get to my place," I said.

And a voice spoke to me and said, "Stay where you are."

"But my place is empty," I said. "I must reach it."

"You will fill your place," said the voice.

"But when—when will I fill it?"

"When it is time."

"And when will it be time?"

"You will know when it is time."

"It is time now!" I was furious, but I calmed myself and said, "Why am I being punished?"

"How are you being punished?" asked the voice.

"By being kept from my rightful place."

"No. Your place is there for you. It cannot be kept from you, since you are the one who chooses it."

"But I know I am being punished!"

"If you are punished, the punishment is in the fact that you do not, or do not choose to, know the time for your place—not in the fact that you are barred from it."

The voice was coming from the center of the dais, where Pilate and Herod—the "fox" and the "ostrich"—had sat, and I looked toward it. "Who is speaking to me?" I said.

"You don't recognize my voice?"

"It—it sounds like mine. Like my own voice."

"It's hardly your voice."

"Then whose is it?"

"You don't know my face?"

"All the faces are blurred."

"Look again—more carefully."

I craned my neck and strained to see more clearly, but at that moment there were three loud, mornful blasts of the trumpet. All of the guests turned their heads as one toward the entrance; I did the same. The polished brass doors, with their bas-reliefs of upright lions, of candelabra, and of the six-pointed star, swung open, and a huge oak and burnished copper coffin appeared, borne by eight naked slaves, four male to one side and four female to the other. Slowly, to the beat of drums, and to the stifled mourning of the guests, the coffin was carried forward. Along the walls, the entertainers began to perform: the acrobats to tumble, the jugglers to juggle, the magicians to prestidigitate, the mimes to ape the follies and furies of men, the musicians to simulate play, the courtesans to mince and the whores to spread their legs and roll their hips—but all to the rhythm of the muffled funeral drums. Only the strutting peacocks and the gibbering monkeys in their cages on high ignored what was going on below.

"Who—who?" I cried out. "Who has died?"

"You don't know?"

"No one has told you?"

"No."

"No one? Not Herod? Not Pilate? Not Livinius? Not Aquilius?"

"No one has informed me, I tell you!"

"Well, then," said the voice, "it shall be I."

"Tell me!"

"The minister of war, of course!"

I was amazed. "Do you mean Zerubabel? Of course he died—or

was killed, unfortunate man. But that was long ago—that was years ago."

"Not Zerubabel—may he rest in peace—" said the voice, "the other. His successor. The one whom all Judea knew. The one who was talked of even in Rome—yes, even within the walls of the Eternal City!"

"But that's impossible!"

"No."

"That cannot be, I tell you!"

"And why not?"

"Because I am the minister of war!"

"Are you?" said the voice.

"Of course I am!"

"Are you indeed?"

"I am the minister of war. There is no other!"

"Prove it then."

"Prove it?"

"Yes, prove it."

"But how?"

"Make war!" said the voice.

"That's ridiculous."

"Then ascend the dais—join the authorities. Go ahead, let me see you do it."

I struggled with all of my might, but again my foot was frozen. It was impossible for me to mount the stairs. My wrath was great, but I could do nothing. My hands were empty—I had not even my riding whip. I stood silent and motionless.

"Are you angry?" said the voice.

I did not reply.

"With whom are you angry?"

Still I did not answer.

"Think about it," said the voice. "Consider it well."

At that moment, the coffin reached the front of the hall and the slaves set it carefully down before the dais; they did not leave, but stepped back from it—the four males to one side of it, the four females to the other—and waited. The great room grew very still, except for the thin, lone voice of a woman lost somewhere in the crowd. It was evident that she was trying to restrain herself, but could not: into the vast vault of the ceiling her repressed sobbing flew like a bird which attempted to but was unable to escape. The sound unnerved me, and I twisted my

375

head to see who the grieving woman was; in the sea of black-cowled, blank faces it was impossible.

"Are you wondering about the woman who mourns?" said the voice.

My own voice stuck in my throat.

"Do you want to know who she is?"

"Yes."

"Is her voice familiar?"

"Yes—and no . . . "

"What do you mean?"

"I've heard it before—but I don't know when. Perhaps a long time ago . . . "

"A very long time?"

"Yes—yes, a very long time ago. When I was—"

"But what woman would mourn over you? And why, since you say you are not dead?"

"I am not dead."

"Look in the coffin, then."

"No!"

"Look in it, I say."

"I will not!"

But a strange invisible force propelled me: I could no more resist it than I could the whirlwind. In an instant, I found myself at the foot of the coffin. The slaves, whose bodies—male and female—were perfect, were like the most superb Greek statues, but whose faces were the faces of mummies, of corpses, lifted the lid and bore it away. An unseen hand shoved at my back and neck; I peered inside. The coffin was empty.

"You see!" I cried out in triumph. "You see, I am not dead!"

"But you are—and this is your place!"

"No! My place is on the dais—with the mighty and the powerful!"

"The places there are filled."

"Not so!"

"They are taken. None is vacant."

I looked up and saw that what the voice said was true. In my place sat a man with a blurred face. In Quaestoris's place sat—Quaestoris himself. He smiled to see me and nodded, as if we had parted the evening before and had agreed to meet on this day. I was astounded, shaken, bewildered, troubled.

"What do you feel?" asked the voice.

"Nothing."

"But what do you feel?"

"Nothing at all."

"Are you afraid?"

"No."

"Then why do you tremble?"

"I do not."

"Then why are you pale?"

"I am not."

"Then why do you lie?"

"I tell the truth."

"Get in the coffin."

"No!"

"Climb into the coffin."

"I will not!"

The force began to push. I struggled with all of my strength. My knees knocked against the wood. I screamed. The force desisted.

"Why did you scream?" said the voice.

"I did not scream."

"Then listen." The echo of a scream drifted down to me from the dome of the hall. "Well," said the voice, "do you hear it? Do you hear that your scream of terror lives? Do you?"

"It is the scream of an idiot—not mine."

"You deny it is yours?"

"It is not mine."

"You deny your terror?"

"I am not terrified."

"Then crawl into the coffin."

"A living man does not belong in a coffin."

"It is your coffin—it has your mark. Only see."

Once again my neck was shoved down. At the bottom of the coffin, under writhing maggots, I saw indeed the mark of the coup—the same mark carved into the rings I had given Elazar, Melech the Galilean, Onan and Akrab.

"Have you seen?"

"I have seen nothing."

"Nothing?"

"Nothing at all."

"Neither your life nor your death?"

377

"Nothing."

"So then I must show you!"

And in an instant I was inside the coffin, among the maggots, and the slaves were fitting on the lid. I wanted to scream, to howl, to shatter all of creation with my cry, but there was no sound or word or even thought that could frame what I felt. The lid closed and I felt my heart stop, my lungs cease, my senses depart—yet I was alive. And there was still the voice. It was very small and it was within me: it lived within me like a tiny worm. I felt it gnawing, gnawing—gnawing through skin, tissue, bone, marrow. It bore into my brain, pierced my bowels, cut into my genitals. It never stopped, not for a second.

"Do you hear?" it said.

"I want to get out."

"Is that what you want?"

"Yes—to get out. I want to get out."

"Is that what you really want?"

"Yes. To get out. I must get out."

"There is a way."

"Then I will take it!"

"Are you certain?"

"Yes!"

"No matter what?"

"No matter what!"

"Admit your terror!" said the voice.

I was silent.

"Confess your fear!"

I said nothing.

"Say you are human!"

I bit my tongue until it bled.

Then the voice, for the first time, faltered. "Say it—say you are human . . ."

I uttered not a word.

"Say—confess—admit—" said the voice weakly.

And in the darkness and the stillness of the coffin, I sneered. And then the voice broke and the voice wept, and then the lid of the coffin flew off and light and air and sound broke over me as torrents of fresh water, and I was on the dais and sat on the throne there and I was the king and in an instant I summoned my troops and destroyed the guests, every last one of them even to the foolish woman who had wept for me and whose face I had not been able to see and whose voice I could not identify and whose name I had buried, and I had the slaves strangled with the belts of the soldiers and the entertainers quartered with axes and the trumpeters disemboweled and those on the dais with me pinioned to their seats with spears, and then I commanded that the necks of the peacocks be twisted and even that the monkeys be brained. And then I ordered that the soldiers who had obeyed these orders respond to the final command, which was to fall each upon his own sword and die where he was. And when it was done, all of it according to my wishes, I threw back my head and laughed. And I heard the voice that had spoken to me even in the silence and blackness of the coffin no more: it had died.

A hand grasped my shoulder, a hand that despite its great strength shook me gently, almost timidly, and I opened my eyes. I stared up into Ichavod's face with its large, square, scarred chin, its twisted nose, its alert but vacant eyes: it was a face, I thought, that did not belong to mankind, that shared none of man's troubles or even his joys, that seemed to have no part in man's destiny. It was a face that reflected no inner life, a face over which flies or ants or spiders could crawl as they crawled over stones or logs. Indeed, Ichavod was as silent and as inscrutable as nature: he could say nothing, not "Master, wake up, you have been sleeping," nor "Master, are you well?" nor "Master, I am ill—"; he could say nothing at all. He was dumb—dumb as sand or straw or clay or stone, dumb as the very earth itself. He was—I thought as I stirred and saw the crooked branches of the terebinth above me, and far above them the sky, tarnished now by afternoon like metal—the perfect companion for a man who could no longer use speech to command: we were comrades well suited to each other, I thought, each of us having been struck silent by the unspeaking monstrous fury of fate, which has no need to define itself or to explain its actions.

I roused myself, raising my body on an elbow. I had fallen asleep by the trunk of the misshapen terebinth, which suffered my body as it would have suffered some animal that had paused to rub its itching flanks there and clean its hide of parasites. Twenty or so yards away, our horses stood, drooping their fine heads dejectedly and sniffing at hard, barren earth they knew could yield them nothing. Between them and the tree, in a little circle of stones, there burned a small fire that one could see had been expertly made and carefully tended. Already much of the dry wood Ichavod had gathered for it had turned to fine white ash. Over it was a crude spit fashioned of branches that he had pruned with his hunting knife. While I slept, overtaken by exhaustion, Ichavod had gone foraging in the area—not so far that he was out of earshot should anyone approach or threaten me, but far enough for him to kill a good-sized snake, three or four lizards and even a hare which he had brained with a perfectly aimed stone. He had even found enough water for the horses, though I failed to see a drop of it anywhere about. He told me all of this with his large, coarse, yet singularly expressive hands—the same hands that had dispatched countless men and beasts to the other world.

I rose and joined him, and the two of us sat together by the fire, listening to the twigs crackle and spit as they burned, watching the thin, sinuous lines of smoke as they rose serenely into the air and smelling the roasting flesh of our prey as it sizzled in the flames. Ichavod lifted the slender spit from its forks and pulled the meat neatly from it without once burning his deft fingers. And so we ate, the two of us, seated in the narrow alley between the boulders in which we had taken refuge, the sky a roof over our heads. And so I ate, though I had been sure I would never be able to eat again. And so I chewed and savored and swallowed and even enjoyed the food, though I thought I would never enjoy a meal again. I would digest it and it would enter my body as new strength, as the strength to go on. Why not? I had been cut off from my power—that was true—but I did not know, could not say for how long.

And I realized that the road to power ran in two directions: if I had walked away from it now, that did not mean I could not reverse my direction and reach it once more. I had been wounded—that was true—wounded deeply and grievously by enemies I did not yet know and in a manner I could not yet fathom, but I was not finished, I was not dead. Some grim force had tried to close the lid of a coffin over me, but—as in my dream by the terebinth—it had flown off: I was alive, I was well, I was determined! I had lost the reins, they had slipped from my hands, they dragged helter-skelter over the ground—but I could pick them up again and that was exactly what I proposed to do. I chewed and swallowed and the juice of tender, roasted flesh ran down my chin and even to my neck. I bit ravenously into the morsels Ichavod handed me, and my robe was stained with the savory fat. And then Ichavod gave me a goatskin and I lifted it and from its spout drank water—tepid water that tasted strangely of animal and herb, but water nevertheless; and my hunger was satisfied and my thirst quenched. And as did my bodyguard, I belched and let wind. I asked Ichavod where he had found the water, and he laughed without sound and in his pupils were tiny reflections of the dying fire. Using his hands, he explained that he had collected it from a pool he had discovered—a pool left over from the last rainfall. He had brought it back for the horses—and for us. And so I had drunk from the same skin vessel as did my chattel and from the same stagnant pool as did the beast I rode—I who had toasted with kings and proconsuls, I who had sipped the rarest of wines with generals and statesmen! The thought caused me great bitterness, yet a part of me was amused and I smiled; Ichavod stared at me, though there was no sign in his eyes to tell me what he thought or did not think.

I had slept long, for the sun was already low in the sky. Overhead the clouds were bloody, drifting on a sea of gold and purple. Out in the canyon, the rocks were rust and amber and deep crimson, and something seemed to stir in them as if they were animate. I wiped my mouth and was about to hand the goatskin back when suddenly Ichavod was up on his feet, risen in a movement so swift and so fluid that it was hard to believe he had moved at all. He cocked his head and listened intently. I listened as well but heard nothing. He signaled me to be silent and remain where I was, and then, drawing his knife, made his way noiselessly to the mouth of the rock passageway. He stood for a while without moving a muscle, craning his thick neck and shading his eyes. Then I saw his body relax, and he motioned to me. I rose and joined him. A hundred yards down the canyon to the south rode a lone priest, his clothes worn and patched, his possessions tied on the back of his slow-footed donkey.

I explained to Ichavod what I wanted done; he nodded once and was gone. He sped in silence over the floor of the canyon, running as the black wind of night might run over it or as an animal might streak forward to overtake his quarry. In a short time he reached the priest, sprang up at him and with one blow from behind knocked the fellow from his mule. The priest lay unconscious among the stones and pebbles and Ichavod stooped and calmly stripped him of his clothes and sandals while from a distance the terrified donkey stood and gazed at the scene, rolling his eyes. Ichavod brought back his booty, and I removed my own garments and put on the priest's. Ichavod gathered more wood and built up the fire, and I handed him my robe to burn. The sun was dying now, giving the last of its sacred blood to the men of earth who scarcely knew how to appreciate it. The insignia of commander-in-chief, the silver-handled riding whip and my Roman medallion I had Ichavod bury and mark the spot where they were put under the ground. The sun set. Darkness was upon us. The fire still burned, and I watched as it consumed the last of my robe of command; the cloth curled and twisted, as if in agony, and at last disintegrated into flakes. So I had watched the bodies of men burn in the basement oven in Zerubabel's villa, where the headquarters of *Patish* were. So the bodies of the men who had brought me to this act would burn: it was a promise I made to myself—a promise I would keep no matter what.

Dressed in the purloined robes of the priest, with Ichavod beside me as a servant, I headed southward, and then just at the entrance to a great valley, swung to the west; eventually I would begin to move to the north. We rode rapidly, enveloped by the vast silence of the wilderness. The night was cool and very clear, the stars large and swollen like ripe fruit that one with a little effort might reach out and pick. The moon rode with us, gilding the crests of the hills and plunging the hollows between them into impenetrable darkness. We urged our mounts on as much as we could: it was imperative that I reach *Patish* headquarters and find out from Melech the Galilean exactly what had happened so that I could make the necessary countermoves.

We must have been on our way for a couple of hours or so when, by slow but steady degrees, I sensed that Ichavod was growing tense. Out of the corner of my eye, I saw his body lean forward in the saddle and his head strain to catch some sound that was beyond my hearing. I had instructed him that unless we were directly attacked, unless our lives were clearly in danger or unless I gave him actual orders to the contrary, he was to make no move against anyone we encountered; and I had commanded him to bury his bow and sword alongside my insignia and whip. Moments later, my ears picked up what he had already heard: hoofbeats. I glanced at Ichavod and then to the north. Over the nearest rise, their helmets and weapons gleaming like quicksilver in the moonlight, rode a detachment of Roman cavalry. They spotted us immediately, and we made no attempt to hide or flee: we rode straight ahead. I heard the lieutenant in command shout his order. The detachment halted just under the crest of the hill, and the officer, together with a soldier on each flank, rode slowly forward. They wore the green plumes of the Eleventh Legion, a force that Pilate often used in special police actions. The officer called out for us to halt in our places and we did. The lieutenant and his escort themselves halted.

"Stay in your places!" he ordered.

"We will not move, sir," I said.

"Dismount at once!"

"As you wish, sir."

Ichavod and I dismounted and stood by our horses.

"What is your name?" the officer said to me.

"Pinchas," I said.

"And your occupation?"

"Priest."

"And you," said the officer to Ichavod. "What is your name?"

"With—with your permission, sir—he is a mute."

"What is his name, then?"

"Amatzya is his name, sir."

"You—Amatzya or whatever your twisted devil's name—step forward: that's it—over here—be quick about it!"

Ichavod stepped forward, and one of the soldiers leaned down from his saddle, and prying my bodyguard's mouth open, peered into it, spat, and straightened up. Frozen-faced, Ichavod backed off.

"It's as the other says, sir," the soldier reported. "The big one's a mute. His tongue's gone, sir. Cut clean off at the root."

The officer nodded curtly. "It's lucky for you you're telling the truth—had you been lying, you should have fared poorly." He cleared his throat. "But why are you out?"

"Excuse me—"

"What are you doing out? Answer me quickly!"

"I do not—grasp your meaning, sir."

"Don't you know there's a curfew in effect?"

"A curfew?"

"Anyone caught outside his home after the hour of sunset is subject to imprisonment—or death," said the officer. "By the order of Pilate himself."

"But my servant and I had no knowledge of this, sir. We did not know."

"And how do you explain that? Everyone knows about the curfew!"

"With—with the lieutenant's permission, sir: we were in the desert, my servant and I. We had been there for more than a month, praying and fasting and serving the Lord. We had no word of this curfew or any other, none whatsoever." I hesitated, then spoke slowly and carefully, as if choosing each word: "But why, may I ask, is this curfew in effect?"

"There is rebellion in the land, Jew-dog!"

"Rebellion?"

"Rebellion, you devil's-seed!"

"Is it the Zealots, sir? Are they behind it again?"

"No, not the blasted Zealots this time . . . this time it's one of the confidants of your puppet king, he-with-the-face-of-a-swine!" The officer laughed bitterly. "But it was indeed a Jewish rebellion: it died at birth. We are merely mopping up the slime."

I was silent.

"Did you hear me, pig of a priest? Your puppet king's puppet aborted!" He shook his head. "Are you as deaf as your friend is mute, then?"

"No, sir."

"Did you understand what I said to you?"

"Yes, sir."

"Then repeat it so I know you're alive—or maybe you won't be alive to repeat it!"

"There was a rebellion."

"Excellent."

"It is—over."

"Capital!"

"There is a—curfew."

"And that means?"

"No one may be out after sundown."

"Splendid, splendid! How quickly you Jews learn!"

I bowed my head.

"And now, my learned priest. Tell me where you are going, you and your handsome servant?"

"We are going home. We live in Acre, on the coast, sir."

The Roman officer was silent. He sat astride his horse, tapping lightly with his riding whip on the saddle. He was thinking. How well I knew what was in his mind: the scales, the delicate scales—tipping first to belief and then to disbelief and then back to belief, swaying up and down like the wings of a bird. And how well I knew the enjoyment he was tasting: the pleasure in the power he exercised. Before him were all the alternatives: to release us as free men, to arrest us and take us off to prison, to torture us until the torture became a bore, to slaughter us and leave our corpses for the beasts and the birds. He had only to select the course of action which pleased him most. None but the hard stones of the earth and the harder stars in the sky above, nothing but the emptiness and silence of the wilderness could pass judgment on his choice. He was accountable to no one in the world but to himself; his subordinates were less than spectators, less than observers, less even than animals—they were but marionettes who moved just as he directed them to move, who spoke the words he chose for them to speak. Alone in this night and in these circumstances, he was undisputed ruler, absolute monarch. I could see the shifting light of rumination in his eyes, see his nostrils dilate with pleasure, hear the thrill of authority when he cleared his throat as if to speak and then did not. And I knew that he was delaying his decision as long as he could; I knew that he derived immense pleasure from this fact as well. For each moment of uncertainty and indecision made of him a god with all of chaos in his hands to fashion of it what he wished: in a sense, it was not really the decision that mattered to him, but the power to make it. Drawing the air in greedily through his long, curved nose, he said crisply, "Your name again?"

"Pinchas."

"And the name of your manservant?"

"Amatzya."

"And your—occupation?"

"Priest."

"And your home?"

"Acre."

"And you say you have been in the desert for a month, praying and fasting and—how did you put it?"

"Serving the Lord, sir."

"Ah, yes." The lieutenant smiled. "And to serve Him you must have sought Him—is that correct?"

"Yes, sir."

The officer grimaced. "You Jews are always sniffing after God! Well, did you find Him?"

"Yes—and no, sir."

"That's a proper Jewish answer," snarled the officer. "Well, you may not know whether or not you found Him, but I'm quite certain that He did not find you!" He guffawed. "We did!"

I bowed my head. "May we go, sir?" I said. "We're expected at home and if we are delayed any longer, they will worry—"

"Never mind that they—the plague take them!—may worry: it's you and your beast of a servant who have cause to worry!" The officer's voice had taken on a tone I knew very well—a tone I had bred in a thousand officers of my own. He leaned down from his saddle. "Strip!" he said.

"What's that?"

"Strip your garments!"

"But, sir, we are unarmed. I am a man of God . . . and my servant—"

"Do you wish us to do it for you?"

I removed my garments and Ichavod did as well. We stood, the two of us, naked under the flashing ice of the stars above, stripped to our bare flesh before the horseborne god in whose hands our fate lay. The lieutenant's lips curled in disdain. "A fat, white grub of a priest and a mute ox!" he said. "Some catch!" He spat to the ground, turned his steed about, and rode slowly back to his detachment, his helmeted twins behind him.

We managed to avoid further patrols. By dawn, we had ridden half the distance to our objective; another night's ride would get us there. It was far too dangerous for us to be traveling by day, so at sunrise we took shelter in a large forest of pines. Ichavod found a spring and the horses drank thirstily. Then he went off by himself after food and fodder and I stayed behind to rest. The forest was filled with a soft light, as green as the depths of the sea. From the branches of the trees a dozen different kinds of birds sang, and in among the sap-stained trunks, butterflies of brilliant hues flitted. Over the carpet of brown and yellowed pine needles and cones, tiny insects of every sort crawled, bent upon their objectives. I stooped to watch them for a time. It was curious: one could take up a twig and bar an ant's way whenever one felt the urge. But stubbornly, unyieldingly—almost purposefully, one might say—the ant pursued its course, as if drawn by an invisible string so tough that no one could snap it. I wondered, as I watched, where the purpose was. Within the ant itself, or somewhere outside it, beyond it? How obdurate and tenacious these tiny creatures were! Indeed, they seemed all but indestructible—for what real power did men actually have over them? It was said that man "had dominion over the beasts." Yet he could no more contain these insects than he could snare the ocean waves or trap the wind! He hemmed them in and they escaped his obstacles as if they were nought; he crushed them, burned them, tore them to bits, and they came again and again, more numerous than before— plentiful and durable as the very stars in the heavens above. I watched them carefully—the ants and the spiders and the beetles—and it seemed to me that all of the world, the heart of the entire world . . . was power. Even the dust of the earth and its mites had power of their own and were in their own way invincible.

Yes, I thought, the world was one vast hierarchy of power, a giant pyramid of authority that ran from the apex, where there were kings and lords and princes and ministers and generals, down to the base where there were servants and slaves and chattels. The higher a place one had on the pyramid, the less weight one had on one's back; the lower down he was, the greater the pressure upon him. With a stick, I began suddenly to crush the insects at my feet. Here and there— wantonly and indiscriminately, at random—I blotted out the little creatures, as once long ago I had stepped on a toad when I was a child. I understood very well why children committed such acts: it gave them a sense of power. Essentially, the power they felt was not over other creatures—no, that was not the heart of the matter—but over life itself! Thus it was, I knew, that grown men established dominion over other men—not because the fact that they held sway over them meant anything in and of itself (after all, if one despised utterly those over whom

387

one had power, what did it matter that one could command them?),
but because it gave them a power over life, power to control life. A man
of great power and authority could not be crushed in life as I was now
crushing the insects on the earth.

I heard Ichavod returning through the forest, cast the stick aside
and rose. He came with a heavy tread, with a doe slung over one
shoulder, its head rolling loosely, its legs dangling. How he had managed to kill it with only his hunting knife, I did not know. He threw
the carcass to the earth and with his blood-stained hands explained
that he had lain the morning long in the branches of a large silver pine,
one whose top I had seen as we entered the forest. He had waited there
patiently, downwind of the animal, until it passed below and then had
dropped upon it from above, plunging his blade into its neck at the
base of the skull. He squatted and with fine, precise movements
eviscerated, skinned and quartered the doe. He dug a pit in the earth,
lined it with rocks and stones, and kindled a low fire over which he
roasted the venison on a long, pointed stick. We ate slowly of the meat,
and there were berries that he had gathered as well. Ichavod tore at his
food with short, fierce, predatory motions of his head, as if it were his
last meal on earth but that fact did not disturb him at all. Then he
covered the raw meat that was left with pine boughs and squatted a
distance away, closing his eyes. The horses ate of shrubbery he had
given them. Flies buzzed lazily in the air. Long shafts of sunlight
reached down to the forest floor. Through a lacework of pine, I could
see the sky—immense, covered as if with pearl, cloudless, dazzling. In
its vault, a spiral of minute specks whirled—vultures. The fire had died
out. A wind had sprung up, spinning its ash about and stirring the
branches of the trees; it carried on it the smell of putrescence. Somewhere not too far away, there was a corpse which invited the scavengers
of earth and of air to invade it and celebrate. I dozed . . .

I was sitting upon my throne: the throne that had been decreed
mine since the day of my birth. A servant, who bore a close resemblance to my page, Elazar, ushered an endless stream of petitioners
into my audience chamber. It was judgment day, and I enjoyed it. One
after the other, they entered—subjects all—and I dealt with them as I
saw fit. A scribe read out their petitions and I made my decisions as I
saw fit. I awarded land to some and took it from others; I increased the
taxes of one merchant and decreased those of another; I released a
number of inmates from prison and sent another group into servitude:

I was harsh and lenient, rewarded and punished, granted life to this man and decreed death for that one. The afternoon wore on and the scribe's voice wore out with his reading; thinking that I had exhausted the list, I sent him away. But the usher opened the door once again and stood hesitating.

"What is it?" I asked.

"There is still another—the last," he said. "Will His Majesty see him?"

"Who is he? Why does he come so late?"

"I don't know, Your Majesty."

"What is his name?"

"He will not say."

"Has he ever been here before?"

"I have not seen him, sire."

I tapped my knee with my scepter. "It doesn't matter. Send him in."

A figure in rags appeared and approached my throne.

"What outrage is this? Who permitted you past the palace gates? What are you doing here? We do not allow beggars in our midst!"

"I am no beggar."

"You do not belong here! Leave at once lest my wrath be aroused!"

"So . . . you don't know me?"

"Know you? How should I know scum like you?"

"But you do know me, surely you do. You have seen me many times."

"It is impossible—but I am kindly disposed today. Approach, that I may view your face more closely. But know that if you are lying to me, you will face the consequences."

"There are always consequences when we lie—to ourselves or to others."

"You are nearer but still . . . I cannot make out your face."

"Perhaps the fault lies in your eyes?"

"You take liberties!"

"What else can one take?"

The ragged figure, with its sore-incrusted hands and bare, filthy feet, came even closer. The clothing—if indeed it could be called that —was torn so that it barely held together and was stained with the wear of nights spent in fields and ditches. The man's body shook in all of its limbs, as if in palsy, and a terrible stench arose from him.

"You are an affront!" I cried out. "You are a rank offense to the majesty of my person and an insult to the throne. I say to you that for your villainy and your grossness I shall purge the earth of your miserable carcass! But that you may not go down nameless into the pit, tell me who you are!"

"Isn't it obvious?"

The man, standing now at the foot of the throne, lifted his head to me and I saw the face clearly: it was my brother. He had changed much for the worse. His look was haggard, his eyes sunken and blood-shot, his sickly yellow skin covered with sores that bled and ran with pus. When he opened his cracked lips I saw that all but two or three of his teeth were gone.

"Well, do you know me?"

"Of course!" I laughed heartily. "You are my prisoner! You thought to escape me, but I knew they would bring you in again one day!"

"I am the prisoner of no man," said my brother gravely.

"No, my poor madman, no. If you say you are not, then you are not. But who or what are you?"

"I am the king," said my brother quietly.

"Rubbish!"

"I am the king."

"Nonsense!"

"I—am—the king," my brother repeated.

"Do not irk me," I said. "You are trying my patience sorely. Hold your fool's tongue!"

"I am king."

"Treason!" I shouted.

"Truth," said my brother.

"Guards!" I called out. "Remove this insane man! Take him off to prison where he belongs! Get him out of my sight!"

But no guards appeared, though I continued to shout.

"It won't help," said my brother. "It won't help a bit. There are only the two of us. We must settle matters as best we can between us."

"This is—absurd!"

"Not at all. Just listen to reason. There can only be one king, surely you agree to that. And since there is only one king—I am he."

My brother smiled his calm, sad smile; I was about to protest when, suddenly as in a dream, our positions were reversed: he sat on the throne of gold, with the great gold lions of Judah crouching muzzle to muzzle above his head and the lions' claws of gold for him to rest his arms upon, while I stood at his feet. But though our places were changed, I still wore my crown of jewels and carried my scepter while he was still clad in his stinking rags and carried only the bent stick he had come into my chamber with. I stared up at his pathetic figure, twisted and emaciated and dwarfed by the throne, and howled with glee.

"You see . . . you see!" I cried out exultantly. "It doesn't matter if you sit upon the throne or not: I wear the royal robes and carry the baton of power while you—you are crowned with thorns and dressed as a scarecrow of the fields!"

"Your raiment is as unmown straw that rots in the sun and your rod but a broken reed. I am the ruler," said my brother, "in Judea and on earth." He flung his stick aside and tore his clothes from him so that he was gaunt and naked for me to see, and he looked as he had looked when he was naked in his prison cell with his whore of a woman. "I need no outward signs of power, no external trappings which signify authority. My strength is the strength of my spirit." His eyes blazed. "Don't you realize that the spirit is supreme—on earth and in heaven?"

"What's that? What madness are you saying?"

"I say the truth: that spirit rules all."

"Spirit?" I sneered. "Spirit is nothing."

My brother ignored me, semed not to be speaking to me at all. "Spirit," he said, "is boundless, shapeless . . . unfettered by matter, by that which has material substance and form. Matter reproduces; spirit creates. Spirit in chaos is . . . the very breath of life itself: out of its holy flux come all earthly changes and all heavenly glory. Matter decays, but spirit is everlasting, indestructible: since only spirit can create, only spirit can destroy—all but itself, since by its very nature there is no matter in it to be destroyed. Matter rots, putrefies . . . because matter is bound to form, because matter *is* form. But spirit, being without form, can never lose form. Matter changes . . . but only spirit can transfigure." My brother's face shone with a profound, pure radiance. "Though a man be confined to the deepest and darkest of dungeons," he said, "though he be whipped and flayed and lashed, though he be tied to the stake and burned or nailed to the cross and crucified . . . yet may his spirit dwell in the most supreme of heavens."

"Lunatic! Rabid cur! You were always mad—that is why I took you prisoner and kept you in a cell. Yes, I kept you as man keeps a bizarre pet by which he is fascinated—a monkey or a leopard or an exotic snake or an oversized tarantula or a fish with a human face! I held on to you because my instincts told me that some day—some day in the distant future . . . somehow, in some way—I should make use of you! Yes, use! The way a man uses a tool to his advantage—a spade, an axe, a hammer, a knife, a pen."

My brother was gazing at me. "But why am I mad?"

"Why? Because I say so, that's why! Why is anyone mad—except that another says so?"

"Do you mean that my spirit is sick? Because if that's what you are saying, you are wrong. My spirit is well . . . My spirit is eternal life, eternal resurrection." My brother's voice dropped to a whisper: "Spirit lives forever . . . even after the race of men is gone from the earth. Even after the hierarchies of angels have vanished from the skies of men's imaginations." And now his voice was musical—it was almost as if he were singing: "First the spirit . . . and then the water. And then the spirit 'upon the face of the water.' "

There was a noise behind me and I turned my head. The usher had reappeared. And with him were two burly guards, with drawn swords. I smiled triumphantly, though my brother seemed to notice nothing. I motioned the guards forward, signaling to them not to make any warning sound. When they had moved stealthily up the aisle to the foot of the throne, I roared, "Seize him! Seize the maniac!"

The guards sprang up to do my bidding, but the instant they touched him with their hands his flesh began to melt away: it melted and sloughed until we saw before our astonished eyes the skeleton of a man propped up on the throne that had been destined to be mine since the hour of my birth. And the guards were amazed and affrighted and fell back as if to flee the horror, but I held them fast in their places with my command. "Arrest the skeleton!" I cried out. But again, when their hands were upon the bones, they crumbled to dust which blew away into the air; and there was nothing before our eyes but an empty throne. And when I made as if to ascend to it and assume my rightful place, I found that I could not, for as in my dream of the previous day, my feet were paralyzed and I was locked fast in my position. And when I strained with all of my might to break free of whatever force it was that held me back, lo, the throne vanished—and then the guards and the usher and the chamber itself and then there was nothing: nothing but the continued consciousness that I was myself and none other.

I wakened with a start, my face and my body covered with a rash of fine sweat. Rubbing my eyes with my knuckles, I sat up. A small green worm had crawled onto my forearm and was wriggling along it. I flattened it with a finger and flicked the pasty corpse to the ground. Ichavod was cleaning his knife, wiping the blade carefully with leaves. He finished, sheathed it, and went over to the horses. In the saddlebags he packed whatever meat we might need and then fixed the bags in place. A soft, wine-gold light filled the forest, as if it were a giant goblet. The needles and cones on its floor shone with an unearthly glow that began to fade the moment it was struck. I left Ichavod and walked alone among the trees, thinking of *Patish*, of Melech the Galilean, of the couriers on their way, of Livinius—and then inexplicably of death. I saw my corpse laid out, yellow-marbled and carved as if by the hand of a master sculptor: I saw it clearly in my mind and I did not suffer—I felt nothing except faint amusement and faint boredom. Death was boring—nothing more. Then I thought of Aquilius and of what could have gone wrong. There was no use speculating, no use conjecturing —I had to have information on which to base my future moves. I turned and walked back slowly, with measured steps. By the time I got to Ichavod and the horses, it was already dark. The evening star turned like a maggot in the sky. We mounted, Ichavod and I, and rode off toward headquarters and the reins of power retrieved.

Long before we had reached the midpoint of the slope that led to the villa, we should have been challenged many times over by the cadre of guards who were my pride and my singular delight: the incredible hurlers of javelins and spears and the archers who could perform wonderful feats with their bows. There had been nothing. Nothing but the soft thud of our horses' hooves and the erratic sounds of night animals rustling through the brush. A feeling of uneasiness came over me, and I could sense Ichavod straining; he, as well as I, knew that something was amiss. Suddenly he raised his hand and we halted. Then I heard it too—the sound my bodyguard's ears had caught: a low, involuntary moaning that was repeated again and again. We dismounted in silence. Ichavod signed for me to stay where I was with the horses, and he went forward, bent low, passing noiselessly through the undergrowth as if through water. The moaning continued—low-pitched, insistent, monotonous. It was not a call for help or a plea for mercy: it was far beyond that—simply a statement of pain and despair that forced itself, of it own volition, out of shattered flesh and bone. I stood and waited. Ichavod's head appeared suddenly between two trees; he waved for me to join him. He led the way, I followed. We had not far to go. Under a fir tree was sprawled the body of Shimon Hanegbi, one of Melech's most trusted henchmen. One could tell immediately by looking at his face that he was near death. But he seemed to recognize me and even to be glad to see me.

I knelt beside him. "Shimon Hanegbi," I said, "what happened?"

"It's you," he breathed.

"Yes, it's I."

"My lord . . . it's really you . . . I do not dream."

"You do not dream." He reached up with a hand, though it cost him great effort, and grasped my shoulder, but I drew back; I could not suffer the cold, trembling fingers. "Shimon, what happened here? Tell me as quickly and as completely as you can—it is imperative that I know as much as possible!"

The wounded man tried to speak but could not. Ichavod raised his head and gave him water from the goatskin, but he could not hold it and it spurted out and onto his blood-soaked tunic. He struggled to regain his breath and his voice.

"Master," he said at length, "master . . . I am fortunate. I have found you . . . found you as Melech charged me . . . "

"Describe what happened, Shimon."

"They came upon us, master . . . They came upon us as a storm, as a flash flood, as a forest fire . . ."

"Who came, Shimon, who?"

"Aquilius . . . soldiers of the Tenth . . . They attacked . . . full brigade. We tried, master, we tried . . . but we could not stop them . . . could not . . . "

"How did it end, Shimon? Tell me how it finished!"

The dying man choked. Blood flowed thickly from his mouth and nostrils. His entire body shuddered. He had always had a slight, misshapen frame, and now, in the throes of death, he looked like one of the insects I had crushed in the forest.

"My lord and master, it is too late. I . . . am finished. All that I have to say now . . . is not for human ears: it is only the sound of the wind sucked across the battlefield . . . the sound of sod slipping into the graves of warriors . . . the wail of wasted old mothers who know they will never give birth again. I cannot . . . tell you . . . what you want to know. What I can tell you . . . you will not know until . . . the hour of shadow lies over you." He coughed and large clots of blood tumbled from his mouth. "But Melech . . . Melech . . ."

"Melech what?"

"Melech ordered me . . . find you . . . give you report—last report . . ."

"Where is it, Shimon? Where?"

He pointed to his tunic and Ichavod lifted it. The document we sought was fastened to his waist with cord. Above it was a wound in his chest so large that one could have easily put both of one's fists into it; it welled with blood that came lazily, as if it knew its way out and was in no particular hurry to escape. I took the report. Shimon's tiny, crooked frame shook, and then, with a sob that did not seem to belong to him, he died. I found a rock, seated myself on it, and held the document close to my face. This is what it said:

My lord and master, I salute you!

King of Judea, ruler of the Jews, I embrace you!

My lord and master, I know I write to you for the last time, for it is clear and apparent to me that I will not quit this place alive but will certainly perish here, where I have lived and where I have served you and your interests for so long. I will never desert you or our cause but will, as long as there is life left within me, stay at my post in your name and in the name of your command.

My lord and master, this message I will dispatch to you with my able lieutenant, Shimon Hanegbi, in whom I place my complete trust, knowing that he will discharge his duty and his commission though he pass through the fires of hell. I have charged him, master, to seek you out and to deliver this report to you by his own hand.

My king, I grieve to tell you that we are betrayed!

This morning at dawn the forces of Aquilius which we supposed to be in the south, comprising a brigade in full strength of the Tenth Legion, launched an all-out attack on our headquarters. Never once did we consider surrender or capitulation in any form or manner, though the offer was extended to us several times by means of messengers who came through our defenses bearing the white flag of truce. For answer, my lord, let it be known to you that we trampled the mes-

395

sages in plain sight of the legionnaires and their officers, burned the
flags and sent the Roman messengers, with hands bound at the wrists
behind their backs, turned to the rear on their mounts, down the slope
in disgrace. Into the mouth of the last messenger who was sent we
stuffed the message and did strip him naked; and then, my lord, we
circumcised his member with a dagger and sent him back to his masters on foot, dripping blood all the way! This was our response to the
Roman forces which surrounded us on all sides.

My lord, within the hour after this response, the enemy began his
full assault. They spared nothing in the battle to take us; we knew it
was a conflict to the death. And there was no man here who was not
willing to die, no man who was not willing to yield his life rather than
to yield his honor. The Romans began with catapults, my lord. They
had positioned them on the mountain with the bald peak, which has,
as you know, a slight advantage in height over us. The boulders and
rocks came crashing in, and some of our men were wounded and
killed. But our warriors sang and hurled defiance at the legionnaires,
and a special force led by Naphtali, a stalwart and hero of many a battle, attacked the men of the catapults, destroying many of the engines
of war and exterminating their crews. Of course, none of Naphtali's
party returned to our midst.

My master, then did the Romans fill the sky with arrows, as if it
were a plague of locusts that was upon us; and there was nowhere we
could see that was not thick with arrows, and if a man stood to look,
he was lost in the swarm of them. And after the barrage, the cavalry
of the enemy came, and it was heavily armored and the soldiers were
clad in chain mail and carried shields and great swords and axes with
which to hew the saplings and cut the brush so that behind them the
infantry could move ahead, company after company of them, with
huge square shields and lances and pikes. My lord, they came like the
waves of the sea; there was no holding them back and no stopping
them. We did what we could, each man to the limits of his body and
his strength, but the monstrous tide rolled on, crushing all in its path.
In among the trees and bushes, on the slopes and hillsides, upon the
crags and heights I could mark from my command post in the tower
the guidons and pennants and flags of the Tenth Legion, all in the
yellow of canary with the eagle of Rome emblazoned on the cloth in
black. And I thought: It is the black of death's angel.

My master and lord, when I say that we resisted with all the power and courage and endurance we could marshal: I wish you to know that my words are true. I cannot possibly record for you the single acts of valor which I, with my own two eyes, witnessed from this tower—acts which even had I the time to set them down would defy description. Nor can I record the tales of heroism which my couriers from every section of our fortress and our home recounted to me. But I can tell you that our fighters displayed the courage of lions and the ferocity of panthers. And they were tenacious. Every inch of ground that the Romans took, I can assure you, they paid for dearly. And there are many of their number who will never walk their native soil again, nor breathe their native air, nor hear the songs of their wives and mothers in their ears again. My lord, on these slopes and in these ravines, there will be a goodly crop from the Roman blood which has soaked the earth.

My master, by noon they were at the gates of the house itself. The combat was hand to hand, but how can one prevail against a noose of armor that draws tighter with every passing moment? Over the walls they came, and even through, with their battering rams and with other machines whose likes I have never beheld before this time. Our men were hacked to pieces. I mean this statement literally, my lord, for I saw it happen again and again. Their archers knelt, row on shining row, and fired directly into the villa with flaming arrows. And our fort, our castle, our redoubt, our beloved home began to burn. I saw a number of our finest warriors emerge from the house, burning as human torches; enveloped in flame as in priestly robes, they spread their arms to heaven and turned black. Reports came that the house itself, our sanctum, was invaded in the wings that had not been touched by fire. Our men were speared to the walls, butchered in the corridors, slaughtered like swine and cattle in the great dining hall in which so often we had celebrated our victories and triumphs in your name and honor. Some retreated, battling every step of the way, to the basement where the oven was alight, as we had been disposing of prisoners the night before. When it was plain that all was lost, our men—your faithful servants, my lord—elected to kill themselves rather than be taken by the Romans. Some fell upon their swords; others used the daggers that had been as loyal comrades to them through the years; still others cast themselves into the inferno of cremation. One cried out: "Let the Roman who dares follow me . . . do so!"

My master, there was no longer time. The couriers stopped com-

397

ing. That meant they were dead—to the last man. Wherever I looked from the tower, there were only soldiers of the Tenth Legion and the bodies of our slain: the corpses of martyrs who had acquitted themselves gloriously against forces outnumbering them fifty to one, or more. The carcasses of horses and of mules lay about, but the bodies of the dead Romans had already been carried off, as if it were not seemly to let them lie on Judea's earth.

My lord, Shimon Hanegbi stands before me as I put down these final words. He is a hard man, my master, a bitter man. I have seen him dash an infant's head against a stone and not flinch. But there are tears in his eyes—tears in his eyes that do not cry. I have spoken nothing to him, but he knows we have been betrayed. I have said not a word to him, but he knows all is lost. I will simply give him this last report and send him forth by the secret route that he may find you and deliver this to you by his own hand.

As for me, my lord and master, the hand—the one hand I have—that writes these words will take up my knife when Shimon has left. Do you remember the knife, my lord? You yourself gave it to me as a token of your love and a sign of your trust. On its handle is the letter *ayyin* for Evenezer, your father, and the sword that cuts it diagonally in twain—the sword whose blade bears your name in the Hebrew and in the Latin. This is the knife which I will bury in my heart, seeking with its point the dream we have lost.

My beloved lord and master, I salute you . . . I embrace you . . . I serve you to the last. I ask only—if it is possible—that you seek vengeance for my name and for *Patish*!

And it was signed: "Melech."

Ichavod and I withdrew, leaving the corpse of Shimon Hanegbi to rot slowly into the mountainside on which he had lived and on which, felled by a stray missile, he had perished. There were still Romans, soldiers from the brigade that had attacked and wiped out *Patish*, in the area; we often heard their voices and the neighing of their horses and braying of their mules and donkeys. But never once did we hear the sound of Hebrew being spoken or the screams of a Jew being tortured, and I knew that every warrior of *Patish*, to the very last, had died there, and that no man had fled or tried to escape. The Romans were jubilant: often we heard them singing and once in a while we saw their campfires flickering through the trees. We were relatively secure, even though the forces of Aquilius were so close at hand, for we knew every crack, chink and cranny in the terrain, and it would have been virtually impossible to entrap us there. Once I waited with the horses while Ichavod went on ahead and picked off a pair of sentries who might have caused us trouble or considerable delay. He came back wiping his hands on leaves he had picked up, explaining with his hands that he had, in his wrath, severed the heads of both men from their bodies. This act, he told me by sign, would never bring back his dead comrades but it made him feel better. I understood what he had done and what he meant by the deed, but it did not make me feel better. Romans—like Jews—were insects to me, and I felt no satisfaction in crushing them blindly, one by one, in single acts of revenge.

We left the area of the broken ant hill of *Patish* headquarters. We traveled steadily northward, moving always by night and taking shelter by day in caves and forests, in canyons and groves, and sometimes in fields of grain. Always we avoided towns and villages and other human beings. But once in a while, when I deemed it to be safe, I would talk to an itinerant priest or a farmer or peasant or servant girl at the well, just before the sun went down. I had Ichavod conceal himself so that the other would feel no fear, and using my soft, sincere, ingratiating tones, would pick up important bits and pieces of information. I learned, for instance, that the rebellion—which had come to be called in popular terminology the *nayfel*, meaning "miscarriage" or "abortion" —had been, as the people said, "nipped in the bud" or "choked to death before it had uttered a cry." I learned that the curfew had been lifted, that citizens might travel freely between cities and by night. I also found out—this from a merchant whose caravan I had approached meekly and who had even given me alms, though I had not asked— that a great Roman general, who had complicity in the plot to over- throw the mighty Herod, had been thrown into prison and would be "sent back to Rome where he belonged" to stand trial because he "had meddled with the affairs of the Jews." The merchant said that the general had attempted "to thwart the will of the empire," and for such a crime "would be severely punished."

So, I thought as I rode away from the caravan, Livinius was in prison. I had thought as much many times, had expected news of this sort, but assumption was a far cry from fact. Ichavod and I rode side by side in the deepening dusk. A light rain fell, and to both sides of us, the fields glistened in final daylight and then turned black. Livinius incarcerated. Livinius in disgrace. The hard-bitten old war-horse, the scar-covered veteran of a hundred campaigns, of a thousand-and-one bloody encounters, was cooped up like a criminal in a cell that stank of the sweat and urine of men he had swatted like flies. I knew well what it meant. And I also knew what would happen. He would be shipped like a beast back to Rome and tried by the Senate for high treason. The Senate would consider his conquests, his laurels, his entire record—and the Senate would find him guilty: they would have no choice. And he would be sentenced and the sentence proclaimed publicly, that his humiliation might be complete, and then it would be carried out before the eyes of all who had the time and inclination to watch—by men and women who were not fit to lick the dust from his boots. He who had scattered thousands in terror, who had caused entire populations to flee in panic and enemy troops to turn back from the field of battle when they but heard mention of his name, would be marched under the guard of pismires, of sucklings, on to a crude platform in a central square of the city and decapitated. And then his gore-dripping head, that craggy lion's head, would be rammed onto the point of a pike and stuck up for crones and children to gawk at and for crows to peck and flies to befoul! This would be the justice of Rome!

The rain continued to fall, harder now; the horses bowed their heads and so did we. Now and again lightning flashed and the countryside stood forth in detail like some landscape of the dead. Livinius—warrior of warriors, soldier of soldiers! What irony, what travesty, what ignominy that one such as he should die this domestic death, this ritual household slaughter of a barnyard animal! We rode for hours that night, Ichavod and I, into the pouring rain, and we were soaked to our skins and the hooves of our mounts sucked as they lifted from the mud of the road. And I pledged myself to take revenge on Judea for Melech the Galilean and on Rome for the general Livinius.

And from a priest whom I encountered some days later I learned more—about myself. He was a tall, gaunt fellow whose long, skinny legs dangled from his mule almost to the ground. He was most eager to impress me with his "vast and penetrating knowledge of politics and the affairs of men and state" and informed me haughtily that it was the "infamous" minister of war of "Judea itself" who had been "solidly behind" and "directly responsible" for the "whole plot" and the "collapsed rebellion." When he learned, much to his surprise and to his "incredulous disbelief," that I knew nothing of the revolt, he forgot the matter at hand and began plying me with irrelevant questions which I made haste to answer with proper humility. "You see," I said, "I have been in the desert these past three months."

"In the desert?"

"Yes."

"With the snakes and the lizards?"

"Well, one might put it that way if one were so inclined."

"And what did you do there, my good man?"

"I fasted and prayed and meditated."

"Ah, yes. I see." The priest looked disturbed. "And did you have visions? Did the evil one appear to you? Did angels descend from the sky and visit you? And did the Lord see fit to whisper in your heart?"

I shook my head. "Nothing of the sort occurred," I said humbly. "I experienced nought but hunger and thirst, loneliness and boredom."

"Then why did you remain for so long a time?"

"Ah, well, I hoped things would—change."

"And they did not?"

"No."

The priest's face looked grave, lugubrious. "Alas, then you wasted your time."

"No," I said in a low, urgent tone, "for I learned that the company of God is best found in the society of men."

"Well put." The priest smiled sadly. "Very well put. I understand your meaning and I congratulate you on your understanding. Think of it," he muttered, almost piously, "only think of it: three months in the desert among the scorpions and the kites . . . in the sands and the burning east winds."

I stirred my feet in the dust and then stared soberly at him. "But this—this minister of war you were telling me about—what happened to him? Was he judged? Did the king kill him? Did the Romans put out his greedy eyes and sell him for a slave? What was done to him who hatched and spawned the abortive revolt?"

The priest scratched his head. "I don't really know," he said, twisting about in his saddle. "I don't think anybody knows."

"How can that be? Surely the villain's end is a matter of record for all decent men to study and make moral profit from?"

The priest shrugged. "It's a mystery, what else can I tell you? Life is strange sometimes"—he lowered his voice—"even enigmatic. Some say that the scoundrel was captured at Herod's own birthday fete on the very night the rebellion began and that he was cast into a deep dungeon in the king's fortress—the same dungeon in which the madman Yochanan the Baptist was kept until the day he was disposed of; they say he is still there at this very hour, awaiting Herod's sentence and punishment. Others say that, with the aid of his friends and accomplices at the court, he made good his escape and fled to Egypt, where now, in the great desert, he is assembling a vast army of mercenaries whom he will lead against Judea when the time is ripe." He sighed. "Others say that Herodias has hidden him in a secret place and shields him from the wrath of her husband because he is her most potent lover and she cannot part with his pleasures for the world. She is a great whore, you know," said the priest, "and it is widely known that she will do anything for the sake of carnal bliss." The priest reddened. "I do not know if this is actually so," he said apologetically, "but I am acquainted with those who are in a position to verify it." The priest stroked his chin. "And then there are folk tales," he said, "which make the minister of war out to be a sorcerer, a magician of supernatural powers. They say he bewitched the entire court and sped away to hell . . . or that he changed himself into a bird or insect and escaped thusly . . . or that he slipped into the body of another—a cabinet member or general or ambassador—and from his hiding place pursues his diabolic ends." He spat. "I don't believe this sort of nonsense, naturally, but these are the rumors which are abroad."

"The rubbish that one hears these days."

The priest nodded vigorously. "To the ears of an enlightened man, such stories are truly incredible."

"Incredible," I repeated, and thanking the priest for his kindness, went on my way.

And so we continued on our way, Ichavod and I, riding together as priest and servant. Ichavod was a master at getting food: there was always fowl or meat to eat and sometimes fish; and for the horses there was hay and often oats or rye. No farmer or peasant ever missed what Ichavod took until we were far away. And if the opportunity arose for him to waylay a lone traveler and take his purse, Ichavod did that as well, and then we bought whatever provisions he could not steal without endangering us. And sometimes when I slept, he would creep out across field or meadow or marsh and kill a Roman or two. "Because it made me feel good," he explained to me in sign language. I felt I could not easily deny him this pleasure, that somehow to forbid it would rob him of nutriment as necessary to his well-being as food. I grew used to the bloody ear or finger or nose or even penis he brought back as token or talisman and watched with interest as he spitted his souvenir on tree or bush for the birds or beasts or insects to make life of. In this manner and after this fashion we came out of Samaria, crossed the Jezreel Valley, and entered the Galilee. An odd, slow song arose in my blood as we headed toward Nazareth. I felt I was home again.

I would go to the great house on the hill. I would visit the grave of Evenezer, my father. I would emerge from my home as lord of all the Galilee and from this rung reach out for my power again. These were the feelings I had—all of them irrational and unreal, all of them emotions which I burned from my system as a man cauterizes the wounds where a poisonous snake has bitten him. I had talked to many more citizens of Judea on the way north; I had listened carefully to what they told me, filling in meanings of which they were ignorant, interpreting motives that were beyond their scope. I knew that I was wanted. I knew that I was hunted. I knew that both Herod and Pilate were after me with all of the force and energy they could command. I knew that a price had been put on my head—an enormous price that would bring the military and citizenry of Judea after me like ants to honey that has spilled over the ground. I knew the reward for my capture was so great that no one, neither Roman nor Jew, could resist it. Ichavod and I bypassed Nazareth and rode on up into the wilds of Galilee.

I ordered my bodyguard to extract three of my front teeth. I had him break my nose so that its shape was altered. We found a cave that was safe from even the most cunning intruder and put up there. Ichavod gathered herbs from the forest and boiled them to make a paste, which when applied to my scalp made the hair fall out in clumps so that I became half bald. I grew a long, unkempt beard and allowed a mustache to grow as well. And the sun and wind and rain darkened and creased my face. There was a rock pool not far away and when I peered into it one cloudless day I saw the rude, season-worn face of a hermit-priest. Only the cold eyes were mine.

So we began a new life. The cave was large and we installed the horses at the rear. At one point, there was a break in its ceiling, and by prying a few boulders loose, we were able to provide ourselves with an emergency exit. Ichavod slipped easily into a life he had known many years ago. He set snares and came back with captured prey of every sort, from rabbits to wild pigeons. Sitting on a log or on the ground with his hunting knife, he would fashion the delicate trigger mechanism or cage for a small trap or the lethal wooden spikes for a large one, for fox or mountain lion or wolf. He would pare a long, flexible branch deftly and spear fish with it in the mountain streams. Using stones, he made a cooking oven for us at the mouth of the cave, and of pine and fir boughs he made pallets. He fashioned his own bow and arrows and shot deer and once a boar that almost killed him in a death charge before a final arrow in its eye dropped it. And for me he built an altar at which I performed my "priestly" rituals. Every so often he left our mountain perch and wandered among the cultivated farms and peasant villages outside the city of Safed. There he stole, or with stolen money bought what other supplies we needed. Ichavod satisfied our physical needs and ran the household while I read and thought.

In the calmness and isolation of my retreat, I had begun anew the philosophical pursuits I had abandoned so many years ago. I sent Ichavod on a number of waylaying missions over a period of weeks and set aside the money he had taken from unwary merchants and farmers. With the sum, I had him purchase a copy of the Law and some Roman religious texts so that I could study again. Then I asked him for writing materials. He prepared and sharpened quills for me, as many as I needed. Using berries he gathered, he made ink, and I kept it in several of the clay vessels he had fired in the little oven. And then he stretched and cured animal skin for me upon which to write. It was good to put down my thoughts once again and to take comfort in them when I read them over as a man takes comfort when he sees the face of a trusted friend or servant. I had formed the habit of writing in the morning, even before I had eaten my breakfast, of reading and studying the length of the afternoon, and of rereading what I myself had written that day by the light of an oil lamp which Ichavod had made. The days slipped by one after the other, seemingly with greater and greater speed, and there was nothing to disturb me.

For his pleasure, Ichavod kept up the custom of killing Roman soldiers. He took them unawares, even in broad daylight, and made certain always to bring back a little keepsake from the carnage; but I strictly forbade him to keep his souvenirs in the vicinity of the cave, so he began for himself a grisly mortuary in a small cave some miles off. Often when he had completed his chores and I was busy at my work and had no need of his services, he went to his "cave of the dead" and stayed in it, sitting on the floor and staring at the severed body parts he had fixed to the rock walls. I never questioned his interests, as he never questioned mine.

One evening he did not come back. Ichavod stayed out after dark infrequently and would most often let me know that he was doing so. However, there had been occasions before when he had been absent for a night or two without notice. He had more and more become a creature of the fields and lived in obedience to a mysterious inner rhythm of his own. I reread what I had written that morning—a new train of ideas on the manner in which words could be employed to achieve power—closed the wooden gate Ichavod had built for the mouth of the cave so that with a stick he could lift the latch from outside, put out the lamp and went to sleep peacefully. I had been troubled by dreams the past few weeks—dreams of Livinius's noble head, the noble head that had inspired fear and awe and love, impaled on a pike and covered with flies; dreams of Melech the Galilean fallen in the tower of the villa with my dagger in his heart; dreams of Shimon Hanegbi rotting slowly into the flank of the mountain where we had left him by night. But this was a dreamless sleep, an untroubled sleep, a sleep from which I arose refreshed and renewed. Ichavod's pallet was empty. I was surprised, but not concerned. I began my writing, expanding on the effect that words had on the minds of men.

"In effect," I wrote, "words are like soldiers: they can go forth with irresistible force and conquer cities, nations, empires. They have a life span far beyond that of mortals and can do battle, can raze and destroy long after their authors have disappeared from the earth . . . " I continued, deeply engrossed—as always—in what I was doing. A fly buzzed heavily by me; outside the cave ravens called. At length I wearied and pushed my writing implements from me. I rose from the rude chair Ichavod had built of pine, walked to the cave's mouth and threw open the door. The sun had already passed its zenith. Behind me, a sheer wall of cliff rose several hundred feet into the sky; in front of me, the slope of the mountain—covered with dense growth—plunged to a gorge beyond which stretched a swamp; far below it was the valley and its cultivated farms, groves and vineyards; and in the extreme distance, hazy with heat, was the city of Safed, home of mystics and scholars. I shaded my eyes with a hand and looked the landscape over from right to left: there was no sign of Ichavod nor of anyone else. I went back into the cave, ate a noon meal which I washed down with a berry wine Ichavod had made, and started my studies. I had been interested of late in the concept of man "being created in the image of God" and was pursuing this idea through the books and tractates of the Law and in Roman philosophy.

It was evening before I looked up again. The cave was all but in darkness, and yawning and rubbing my eyes, I lit the oil lamp and set it back on its shelf of rock. Usually Ichavod served me with a meal of cooked meat, fowl or fish, but tonight I dined on cheese and olives and on wild apples my bodyguard had gathered the week before. I was puzzled at Ichavod's absence, for he had been gone almost two days. I wondered if something had befallen him—if he had been wounded by an animal or had slipped and hurt himself or been struck by a falling tree or boulder. I could not imagine that any human had entrapped him or otherwise brought him low: his were the uncanny instincts and magnificent powers that made certain animals legend—beasts that men sought and pursued for decades but that no hunter ever slew.

A wolf cried out from afar and I stood for a while in front of the cave gazing up at the black flint of the sky on which the stars blazed like sparks being struck by an unseen hand. I mulled over my thoughts of the afternoon. If God had no form, how could man be formed in his image? Did that mean God could be all things and thus man all things? If man was incorporated in God, could God be incorporated in man? Who was the devil? Did he have any form, or was he formless as well? How did he come by his power? Who granted it and why? The stars flashed—restless, like flotsam in the sea; the wolves howled and then the jackals began to cry, as if to compete with the others; I returned to the cave and took out what I had written, but uneasiness came over me and I could not concentrate. A thought that had not previously entered my mind came to me: what if Ichavod had deserted me, had run away?

I shook my head. I did not believe it, it was not possible. Why should he do such a thing? He had nothing in his life, absolutely nothing but his service to me. His life meant nothing to him except insofar as it served my ends. Then why would he leave me? What would he gain by such a move? My head ached—I rubbed my brow. The reward. Perhaps somehow, in some way he had gotten wind of the reward and had gone to the authorities to turn me in. I could not believe that he would do such a thing, for great wealth seemed unimportant to him; he had been surrounded by it for years and it had made no apparent impression on him; he was a man of field and forest, of mountain and desert—a man of knife and sling, of dagger and spear: for what material goods would he trade this life in? But if he had—if he had, for some unfathomable reason, for some reason known only to his innermost processes—done such a deed, committed such an act, then what was I to do? Should I leave the cave? To go where? To do what? Would I be able to fend for myself in the wilderness? In which direction would I go? The questions seemed elementary, yet they were baffling in a way I had not experienced before.

I stretched out on my pallet, intending to rest and make a decision of some sort in the morning, but I tossed fitfully, unable to relax. At last I fell into a troubled sleep through which passed the same parade of ghosts that had disturbed my dreams for the last several weeks, but added to the list now was Ichavod. I saw him—tall, ox-shouldered, his face set like a devil's mask, plodding heavily yet agilely, gracefully away from the body of a man he had just slain. And then I saw the corpse: it was me. The Romans were jubilant; they crowded about him and congratulated him, offered him rank and honor in the army. The Jews were grateful as well, and Herod's emissaries pressed gold and silver and jewels upon him. Herodias sent Salome, who told him unashamedly he could have the "jewel between her legs." When she looked him over from top to bottom, she said that if her mother ever saw him she "would chew every morsel of him up" and "never let him go again." But Ichavod refused it all, waving his great hands in apology and backing off. In his cloak he had secreted my testicles, which he had sliced from my torso in a single stroke.

The mobs of Roman and Jewish admirers fell away, and we were back in the wilds that he loved so and in which he felt at home. He went swiftly through the foliage, his feet seeming not to touch the earth at all; and I followed him—a wraith, a spirit, a dead man. I knew

407

where he was going and I was right: to his grisly cave. Once inside it, he seated himself on the floor of earth and rock. About him, fixed to the walls that dripped with moisture, were the body parts he had cut from Roman cadavers—or perhaps from men who were still alive, I did not really know—and he gazed up at them lovingly, as if each brought back to him a moment of rapture. Then he unfastened his cloak and drew forth the sacs of manhood he had taken from me. He stuffed them into his mouth and began chewing them, licking the blood from his lips and his chin. When I questioned him, he explained patiently with his blood-stained hands that it was "good to eat of the dead," especially the dead whom one had himself "created." I was surprised to hear—though he did not, of course, actually speak, it seemed to me in the dream that I could hear him nevertheless—him use the word "create" in such a context, but upon reflection found its use very apt. I had never entertained the idea that one could "create" dead people, but it certainly seemed to fit the affairs of men well and even to give to them a new dimension. Ichavod went on to explain that eating of the dead, and particularly of "one's own dead," gave one "new strength" and "new joy." I told him that this concept was not an original one, for warriors of savage tribes often ate from the bodies of men they had killed in battle in the belief that they could in such a fashion incorporate the strength of their enemies into themselves. He replied that he had not intended that meaning at all. "No," he said, his eyes lighting up in a way I had never before seen, "what I meant to say is that the flesh of the dead one has created is holy and therefore sanctifies the man who eats of it!" What he said was that such an act communicated "a sacredness." And he called this act, not the "cannibalism" I had expected, but rather "communion." And in its strangeness, the word remained in my mind and did not disappear, though it did not become conscious again in my life for a long time after the dream. I told him that he had betrayed me, but he only laughed and swallowed the remains of my genital sacs. He shook his head. "No," he said, "I have not betrayed myself and thus have betrayed no one." And he went on to say that it was fruitless to argue the point, and I was forced to admit that it was. And so my dreams flowed on through the night: muddy, turbulent, savage, filled with refuse—torn tree roots and the bloated caracasses of goats and camels—like the violent flash floods of winter that take a wadi by surprise in an instant, drowning and sweeping before them all the men and animals who happen to be in their path when they strike.

I awoke with a start at dawn and immediately glanced over at Ichavod's pallet—it was empty. I rose in a surly, confused state and upset a chess set which Ichavod had carved for me at my direction. The crudely fashioned pieces fell to the ground from the board, and I did not bend to retrieve them, though I valued them greatly and spent many hours with them, solving the most difficult and complicated problems. I even trod upon two of them—one that Ichavod had stained red with a paint made of berries and one that he had left in its natural wood state. Still, I did not stoop to pick them up. A curious, gnawing hunger agitated me and I breakfasted at once—contrary to my custom. I devoured half a loaf of bread which Ichavod had made himself with stolen flour which he had transported up the mountain on his back, the remainder of the cheese left over from yesterday, and wild scallions —all of which I washed down with cold, clear water from our large clay jug. I rinsed my mouth and spat to the earth. Then I hastily stuffed some supplies into a shoulder bag, took up Ichavod's bow and a supply of arrows, and selected one of his favorite spears from a stack which he kept in the corner. I had resolved on a plan of action—one that was simple and direct. It was this: I would sweep the area before the cave for some sign of my missing bodyguard. If indeed he had been hurt or crippled in some accident, I should discover it and help him: one way or another I would manage to get him back to the cave and nurse him back to health. If, however, he was missing because he had betrayed me, if he had descended to the valley or even to Safed to inform on me, he and the party sent out to arrest me would find me gone when they arrived, and I would have an excellent chance of detecting them on their way, for I was certain they would never expect me to have quit the cave.

So I began a wide and scrupulous sweep of the mountain slope, descending steadily as I combed the area for evidence. Very often, as I moved through the underbrush, I encountered traps which had caught small animals—and so knew that Ichavod had not visited the area. One, just by a clump of wild fig trees, had caught a good-sized hare, which— snared by a hind leg—endeavored vainly to escape. I saw the familiar gleam of terror in the animal's eyes and stopped for a moment or two to examine the phenomenon more closely. The tender pink nose twitched; the mouth seemed to curl back on itself, revealing the sharp, white teeth; the eyes bulged out and rolled to each side successively as if to discover the escape that had thus far eluded them but must be there; and the noosed rear leg jerked spasmodically in its rawhide thong, raw and bleeding from stubbornly repeated attempts. I stood quietly, in the midst of my own terrible search, gazing down at the entrapped creature. I was as fascinated by the spectacle of fear as I had been when I was a small child. I sometimes thought that fear was actually a living being which entered the minds and the bodies of men and took possession of them. I felt this strongly now, much as I felt that words were attack forces sent forth by their commanders to carry out the orders given them. Which commander was it, then, who sent out fear to do his bidding? The hare trembled with fear and defecated. It was mute—like Ichavod; it made no sound except that of its leg scraping the ground. I stood and considered. I had three choices: one was to ignore the animal and go on my way; the second was to cut the thong and release it; and the third was the one I chose—in a single motion I brained it with the butt of my spear!

And so I went on with the search. Noon came and went—there was no sign of Ichavod. I worked my way slowly down the slope, from right to left and back again; by late afternoon I was a good distance from the cave. Suddenly I halted in my place. Three or four hundred yards in front of me a thin, gray spiral of smoke curled lazily into the air. It was obvious that whoever kindled the fire did not care that it was seen, but that fact did not lessen my caution. I made my way downhill with great care, ready for a sudden attack; silently I crept forward until I was but scant feet from the fire. The smell of roasting flesh filled my nostrils. Gently, I parted the foliage with my hands. A small, gaunt man—wizened as a prune through exposure to the weather—sat on the earth, greedily devouring the meat in his grease-stained hands. He was dressed in rags, and at his bare feet, bones and feathers were scattered. When he spat into the flames, I could hear the fat sizzle. I could have bypassed him, but I decided against it: he was apparently alone and unarmed, except for a knife in a sheath; there was a chance that he had seen or heard about Ichavod; and there was also something familiar about him, something that drew me irresistibly —with a force I could not easily shake—to him. I stepped into the little clearing and coughed. He turned and at once I saw that he was old; he stared at me stonily, one hand on the handle of the knife.

"You won't need that," I said.

He seemed uncertain. "You startled me," he said. "I didn't hear you approach."

I shrugged. "Silence is an ally," I said. "But I will not harm you —I'll stay right where I am if you're more comfortable that way."

The little gray eyes glittered. "The traps," said the man. "The traps are yours, are they?"

I stared at the meat in his hands and realized that he had been poaching and feared that I would cause him trouble. I shook my head. "No," I said. "They're not my traps. I'm just passing through myself and came over when I saw your smoke. It's not often one meets another human being in parts like these." I kept examining his face, working at a recognition I knew was there but could not reach. In turn, the stranger gazed intently at my face. "Why are you here?" I asked.

"Are these parts forbidden, then? Does some great lord own them?"

"To my knowledge, they belong to no one but the king. But no one ever comes here except trappers and hunters—and they come because the king's gamekeepers are not sufficient in number to patrol the lands properly. You don't look like a hunter or trapper."

"Or gamekeeper," said the stranger, with a bitter laugh. He squinted. "I'm a wanderer," he said. "And you? Are you really a priest? You don't look like a priest to me."

"And how does a priest look?"

The stranger's face had turned deathly pale. His pointy little chin, grown over with gray-white stubble, trembled. He seemed to breathe with difficulty.

"Well," I said, "speak up. Is there any particular way a priest should look?"

"A priest," stammered the stranger, "—a priest should not look— should not look like—like—my master."

"Your what?"

"My master," said the stranger in a voice so low I scarcely heard it. "My lord and master." Tears welled in the stranger's eyes. Suddenly, he flung the uneaten food in his hands into the fire, swung himself around so that he faced me, and lurched—evidently with great pain— onto his knees. "Master," he said, "master, don't you know me? Don't you recognize me? Have you forgotten me then?"

"What are you saying? Are you out of your mind?"

"Master—I should know you anywhere, anywhere, master—even in hell! I know you—I know your eyes: there are none like them in all this world—or in the next!"

"I have never seen you before in all my life! You don't know what you're saying! Either you're insane or you're confusing me with some-one else."

"Master . . . I am your servant . . . your trusted servant, Onan—who was faithful to you even when I believed you to be dead."

It was true: the stranger was Onan, the overseer of all my lands and estates. How he had changed! If it were possible for a man to die and yet walk the earth, then such a man would be the specter I saw before me. "Yes," I said, moving a step closer. "Yes . . . on my life, you are Onan, after all!"

"I have seen your eyes in my dreams . . . many times, master." And with those words, he began to weep, holding his withered face in his hands.

"Calm yourself," I said. "Calm yourself, Onan, and tell me your story. Perhaps it will be of help to me."

Gradually my overseer regained control and began his report. He related how Herod's troops had come to the great house at Nazareth on the day after the king's fete. They had swarmed over the grounds "like rats out of the rotten corpse of a horse or cow," surrounded the stables and the servants' quarters, and overrun the adjacent vineyards and farmlands. "And the commanding officer who led them"—so Onan told me—"rode his horse even into the dining hall where you and your father before you celebrated with guests and ordered me—on pain of death—to open for him all of the doors of the mansion. 'Your master is dead and under the earth,' he said, 'and so will you be if you do not comply!' And I saw, master, that it would not avail to resist, for if I did not open the doors he would certainly smash them in with his soldiers and put me to death as well. And I did precisely as he had commanded, and he shouted orders and the troops rushed through the corridors and rooms of the house like madmen, carrying off the furniture and rugs to the last stick and last thread, the ornaments and adornments, and even the moldings of the walls and the wood of the floors and the tiles of the baths and flagstones of the walks! But I did not open your private suite, and the officer said to me, 'Open it!' but still I would not, and he said, 'Open it or I will burn you alive and then open it myself!' and I knew that he would do as he had threatened, so I opened it and, master, I wept as he went in with his troops. And they tore the rooms apart, and even the vault beneath the floors, and took everything they thought valuable, leaving the place stripped bare as one sees the carcass of a camel stripped bare by kites. And what they could not carry off as plunder, my lord, they smashed utterly.

"Then they led me back into the room where you and your father before you had so many times over held converse and played chess and made plans, and there the officer said again that you were dead and that it was of no use whatsoever to withhold information from him, and I replied that indeed I had no information to give whether you were dead or whether you lived. And the officer said, 'Tell us where the treasure is!' And I said, 'What treasure?' And the officer told me that you had buried a vast treasure in the vicinity—'a treasure vaster yet than King Herod's and stolen every coin and jewel of it from the crown and the people of Judea!' And he told me that I must lead him to it or I must die—one or the other. And again I said, 'What treasure? I know not of any treasure that my master has buried.' And the officer drew his sword and put its blade to my throat and said, 'Talk or die!' And I knew that if I said I did not know I would die at once, but that if I pretended to know and to lead them I should postpone the hour of my death. And then I said to the officer that I would lead him to the treasure as he wished, but that we must wait until it was dark before we started. And he said, 'What folly is this? Do you mock me, traitor?' And I said to him that I was in earnest, that the place in which the treasure was buried was marked by a stone which glowed in the darkness, and that was the reason we must wait. And so we waited. And so I heard the cries of the servants as they were rounded up for deportation —the screams of the servant girls, whom the soldiers raped repeatedly; the howls of the manservants, who were tortured for sport; the neighing of the horses as they were taken out of the stables; and the crackling of the flames as the stable buildings were put to the torch. And, my master, they took every horse and every servant away, even to the last scullery maid and groom. And when it was night they took me out, and I saw as I crossed the yard that the stables still burned and that the soldiers were roasting sheep and goats and geese and ducks which they had slaughtered from among your herds and your flocks. I saw it, master, and my heart was grieved and I wept bitter tears . . ." Onan was silent, as if lost in the memories.

"Go on," I said.

"And so I led them on, my master, even into the wilderness so that they knew not where they were, even into land which was as familiar to me as the palm of my own hand. And there accompanied me as guards twelve men and the officer who had directed me to find the treasure, and I drew them further and further from the house and from the burning stable that lit the sky. And there was no moon, and the stars were hidden by cloud, and in the hills high above the mansion I plotted and managed my escape." Onan paused. "It was not an easy matter to arrange," he said, "but I had resolved that I would die free of them, or in the attempt to be free, for only death awaited me in the hands of these men. And so I led them to the gorge—you know the one of which I speak, I'm sure—and when we reached it, master, I threw myself over the precipice without warning, and there was nothing they could do. They had roped me to a pair of soldiers and the two of them, taken completely unawares, went over with me. The drop is fifty or sixty feet, not more. I was fortunate, master: I landed on top of one soldier, who died instantly of a broken skull. The second man was badly shaken up, and I managed to crawl over to where he lay before he came out of his daze—perhaps he was injured as well—and to get his knife out of its sheath and cut his throat like a lamb. Then I took the dagger and cut the ropes that bound me, and I was free. There was no way that the remaining soldiers above could find me or even know what had befallen their comrades." Onan supported himself on his hands and stretched out a leg toward me, wincing as he did so. "My leg was broken in the fall," he said, "and it was very painful for me to get around—but I did, I did and I lived, master, for when death breathes on the back of one's neck . . . then much is possible, much! I lived on berries, roots, wild fruit and even insects until I was well enough to hunt and fish. But I survived—and even fashioned myself crutches to use until I had no use for them."

Onan scratched his matted hair. "At first, master, I thought to seek news of you and help from among the men who had known and respected and supported you through the years, and even among those who had known your father Evenezer before you. But then I thought the better of it, for those men were under suspicion themselves and would have been glad to sacrifice me to prove their loyalty to the regime. All of them—all who had dealings with you—were interrogated, and had it not been for their wealth and influence and for the lavish contributions they hastened to offer the crown, would have been finished off in short order. Indeed, a few of them—despite their wealth and rank

—disappeared from sight and were not heard from again. No, I did not choose to tempt any of those powerful men with the pardon and approbation that would come their way for turning me in; thus I subsisted in the wilds as best I could until my leg healed as best it could." Onan smiled grimly. "I am a wanderer, my master . . . but I have wandered back to you."

I nodded. "And the coup," I said. "What do you know of it?"

"I have been able to learn a great deal in the months that have gone by," said Onan. "I don't think they ever found the corpses of the two soldiers, so it was assumed that I was dead with them—a suicide who had taken others on his lonely journey. And so I was able to move about the area in relative safety. Though their masters were out of bounds to me, I knew a few overseers and servants who were willing to talk to me and even at times to give me shelter or help. They knew many things: mice in the pantry, they say, often know far more than the cat."

"Go ahead," I said impatiently. "Go ahead."

"The rebellion," said Onan, "was stopped at its inception. All my information leads me to believe the Romans must have known something about it in advance: some vital details were missing, of course, but they knew what was coming and prepared for it. There was an acquaintance of mine, a man whom I have known for thirty years or more, who has a cousin in the employ of Pilate himself. I spoke to my friend at great length—"

"The story, Onan! Tell me quickly."

"Knowing what was in the offing, the Romans ordered the Tenth Legion, the legion of Aquilius, up from the south. The general Livinius, who was in command of the Eighth Legion, was on the morning after the king's fete stripped of his rank and sent to the Roman prison in Jerusalem."

"Do you know what happened to him?"

"Within a week, master, he was on his way back to Rome, charged with high treason."

"Did they try him? What was the verdict?"

Onan shook his head. "I don't know, master—"

"Then tell me what you do know!"

"Everywhere, there was Roman power, Roman might. If there was to be a coup, the massive presence of the Romans prevented it. There was not a Judean commander in the whole country who did not know his unit would be cut to ribbons if it moved so much as an inch out of line!"

"Are you telling me that there was no revolt at all?"

"In two places there was action against the Romans."

"Where were they?"

"The first was on a mountain to the north and the east of Jerusalem. There, a secret Jewish force held out for almost a whole day! They were completely destroyed by the attacking Romans."

"And in the other place?"

"That was south of Jerusalem, master, near Hebron. The Seventeenth Brigade of the army of Judea was surrounded there. Asked to surrender, the Seventeenth fought for two full days. It was the same in the end, master—the brigade was wiped out. There, the Jewish general, Akrab, died in battle—he who was your loyal servant and comrade."

"And then? Proceed!"

"And then, my master, the army of Judea was purged—from top to bottom. Hundreds upon hundreds of officers and noncommissioned officers were removed from their posts and straightaway sent under heavy guard to internment camps in the south—those same camps set up by your enemy, Kalbi." Onan wet his lips with his tongue. "As for your own lands, my master, the crown seized them all: in Nazareth and the Galilee, in Bethlehem and Judah, and elsewhere in the country, master, down to the smallest parcel. And to mention your name, my master, was forbidden!" Onan looked up at me and his eyes were wet. "That is all I know, master . . . all I can tell you."

"But how the rebellion was betrayed—you have no idea?"

"None, master, none. Except—"

"Except what?"

"Except nothing . . . It's only rumor, master."

"What's only rumor?"

"It's folly . . . sheer stupidity . . . baseless invention."

"What are you talking about?"

"Master, I—"

"Tell it to me no matter what you think. Onan, speak!"

"They say . . . Master, there are those who say that a highly placed Roman gave the authorities the word that a revolt was brewing—"

"Highly placed Roman?"

"Yes—yes, master—someone who was very close to Pilate . . . "

"Why are you hedging, Onan?"

"Master, I—I don't know how to tell you . . . "

"What Roman? Of whom do you speak?"

My overseer screwed up his eyes and hunched his head down between his shoulders. "They say . . . master, they say—"

"Yes, Onan."

"They say," Onan blurted out, "it was—it was—Quaestoris!"

"But Quaestoris is dead!"

"I know, master," whispered Onan. "I know."

I had no choice, really. With the price that was set on my head, I did not have a choice. The fewer people in the world who knew of my existence, the better the chance I had of staying in it. Onan had served me well in his life; now he could serve me only by dying. That was the decision I made, almost without thinking. I asked him to fetch me some food as I was hungry and had not eaten since early morning, and when he turned to the fire to do so, I bent and picked up a rock. His back was toward me, his head bent over. In three or four swift, silent strides I was across the clearing and in another instant directly behind him; I lifted the rock high and brought it down with all my strength upon his skull. He pitched forward and fell face-first into the flames. His hair caught fire and the brain matter oozing from the cracks in his bone sizzled. I thrust his body from the fire with my foot and then turned it over: his face was burned and spotted with ash. The eyes that had recognized mine in a face that even my mother should not have known would recognize them no more. I went through his threadbare garments quickly. I found only one object that was of importance to me: he had carried it in a small pouch sewn into his cloak at the thigh. It was the signet ring of the coup. I left him lying there on his back, collecting flies by the minute, and hastily retraced my steps; I halted at the edge of the swamp and pitched the ring into the scummy water and slime. Then, giving the clearing where Onan was a wide berth, I continued down the slope, not thinking a thought, not devising a plan—but losing myself in sheer physical exertion.

By evening there was still no sign of Ichavod. I seated myself on a mossy rock by the bank of a swiftly flowing brook and ate of the provi-

417

sions I had brought with me. There was a wild fig tree nearby, and I ate of its fruit as well. The day ended, and as darkness crept over the wilderness, I climbed high into the branches of a large oak for whose shelter I had picked this spot. Far up in a roomy crotch of the tree, with darkness rushing over me like the billows of the sea, I bedded down for the night. There, for the first time since I had heard it that day, I considered the incredible story Onan had told me about the envoy. "They say it was Quaestoris," Onan had said. Five simple words. Five unbelievable words! And yet I had no reason to doubt that the story was true, nor had I any cause to doubt my own reason. I had learned in life many times over to believe in the unbelievable. Often one could not believe solely because one had not all the facts to judge. Quaestoris had not returned from the dead—that I knew, that was certain. The logical deduction that followed was that he had never died in the first place. But I had seen his corpse, had I not? I had attended his funeral and wept over his carcass, had I not? Herod had blubbered and even Pilate had sniffled. It had all happened; it had all taken place . . .

An owl hooted—once, twice, three times—the cry sliding into the darkness and losing itself as in quicksand. From above, a hyena called. He had undoubtedly discovered the feast awaiting him in Onan's body. I considered the matter. I had seen a dead man on the bier, a dead man who resembled the envoy—but how did I know it was actually he? It occurred to me that the master hand of the envoy might well have sculpted "himself" dead so that he could live on in secret. But for what purpose, toward what end? For one thing, the diplomat's "death" would have protected him from any attempt on my part to do away with him. I was quite certain that he sensed such an intent on my part, though he never came out with it directly. Any increased protection he had requested from Pontius Pilate—which he certainly would have received—would have aroused my suspicions and put me on my guard. That he knew. Just as he knew that a trip to Rome or to foreign parts by him would have been suspect. I knew very well how much he loved Judea and how much Judea meant to his art. And there was another important point—or so I reasoned, putting myself for the moment in the envoy's place: his "death" could only have served to hasten the rebellion, since I would be more confident with Quaestoris safely out of the way. That was very true. The moment I learned he was dead, there was a new birth of certainty in me.

The owl hooted again, at a greater distance now. Through the leaves and the branches of the oak, I caught sight of the stars, stuck like maleficent bits of glass into the flank of the night sky. I had the strange sensation of being suspended between heaven and hell, as in the case of a dying man whose final resting place has not been determined. If Quaestoris had indeed "died" so that he could live on, sheltered from harm, and destroy the revolt, he had made quite a move! I could, through the glacier of my hatred, almost admire the consummate cleverness of such a gambit. I knew that Livinius, if he knew, would surely applaud it as a stroke of political genius. I shook my head. But it was hardly the last move of the game. It was my turn to move now. An icy calm stole over me. I rested my head against the trunk of the tree. Almost immediately I fell asleep. And in my dream-tortured, dream-strangled slumber I saw Quaestoris rise again and again from the dead. Bits of grave clay were caught in his matted hair and stuck to his bloodless face. "How is it you are alive," I asked him, "when I plainly saw you lying dead upon your bier? Were you really dead, then?"

"I was dead," he answered.

"Then how do you come to be here, among the living?"

"I was resurrected from my grave," said Quaestoris.

"But how could such a thing be accomplished?"

"God can accomplish all."

"You have embraced the God of Israel, then?"

"He is the God of all the universe."

"But you have embraced Him!"

"In His love and His compassion, in His boundless mercy and His infinite goodness, He has embraced me."

"But why do you appear before me now to breathe and to move and to speak?"

"God has sent me to earth."

"Why? For what purpose?"

"To bring salvation to erring man."

"But why you?"

"Because . . . I am His choice."

"But why did He choose you? You are a pagan—even more than you are a Roman! You are a profligate, an unbeliever, a cynic, a hedonist, a whoremaster!"

"You don't know why?"

"No."

"You can't guess?"

"No—tell me!"

Quaestoris laughed. "I am His son," he said. "That is why."

I wakened in my tree-bed. On every side the leaves murmured, stirred by a breeze from the west. Weary with their night watches, the stars overhead were slipping from their ramparts. The hyenas were still —Onan was eaten. Below me, a night animal screamed in terror; I knew it had been struck by a predator and would scream no more—its elegy was silence, the all-embracing silence of darkness and of dust. My eyes closed and once more I slept. Once again, Quaestoris emerged from his grave. "You don't belong in this world," I cried out. "You are already a part of the other! Why have you come to plague it?"

"He has sent me."

"Who sent you?"

"God, the father!" said Quaestoris. "He whose holy spirit . . . whose holy ghost fills the universe from end to end."

"But why—why have you been sent here?"

"To rid men of sin. To redeem the world."

"But it is God who created the world—and all that is in it!"

"God created only choice. All the rest is dependent on choice. And men have chosen falsely, wrongly. They suffer the guilt of their wrong choice. Now I have come to expiate their guilt . . . to wash their hands clean of scarlet sin. As it is written: 'Though thy sins be as scarlet as blood, yet will I cleanse them white as snow!' "

"But how will you do this thing?"

"How will I do it?" Quaestoris sighed and cast his eyes down. "I will die. I will die for mankind. I will give my body and my blood for mankind. And my death will atone for the evil that men choose."

"You mean to sacrifice yourself for mankind?"

"God will sacrifice me. I will be His lamb."

"You, Quaestoris . . . you who were once the wolf?"

"I who had fangs once . . . will become as the suckling calf."

"And you will truly die?"

"Verily, for he who dies so that truth may live will himself live by the act. I will be crucified . . . and I will die . . . and my flesh and my blood will sanctify the lives of all men."

I shook my head. "No," I muttered. "No."

"Why do you doubt what I say?"

"Because, Quaestoris, you are dead already. A corpse cannot live again. And he who does not live cannot die. Nor can one man atone for the evildoing of another. Each man alone is responsible for the purity of his heart and his hands."

The envoy stared at me. "Your words—your words amaze me," he said. "You who are a moral leper among men! How then does the devil learn to speak with the tongue of an angel?"

"That is the devil's business!" I smiled. "But I will tell you. I have confessed it to no one in the world, but I will tell it to you, for truly you are not of this world. I have a brother—would you believe it? After my mother died, he was sent away from home by my father—he was still an infant. My uncle, a carpenter in Bethlehem, raised him. I spent many years searching for him, and at last I found him and had him arrested and cast into prison. There I found him a wife. It pleased me to observe him and his wife. I've never told this to anyone else: you are the only one who knows it. It is good that you are dead."

Quaestoris said nothing.

"It was my brother who taught me this kind of speech: 'purity of heart and hands' indeed! You see, he's a madman. It was curiosity that pressed me to seek him out, and his madness that prompted me to keep him prisoner. He was quite a specimen—I enjoyed watching and listening to him, for it gave me insight into the soul of man. He used to imagine that he walked on the waves and tamed the wind, that he changed water into wine and multiplied several loaves into a vast number; and he would recount to me how he healed the sick and gave sight to the blind—and even life to the dead." I laughed. "Perhaps it was my brother who raised you up from the grave?"

"No one returned me to life from the dead but God," said Quaestoris, "and no one will send me back to the grave but man."

I laughed loudly. "Quaestoris, Quaestoris, you are my dream—my dream and no more!"

"Though you but dream me, when you waken again you will not be rid of me."

"Quaestoris—"

With the name of the corpse-man upon my parched lips, I wakened. The sounds of the wilderness tumbled about me; I could scarcely distinguish one from the other. The leaves of the oak glittered with light. Far above, the sun's rays ran through the sky like a comb. I sat in the crotch and ate sparingly. Then I descended to the ground and began my search for Ichavod again. I crossed a patch of marshland, following a path that my bodyguard had once shown me, and came to a level plateau, beyond which the mountain fell steeply away to the valley far below.

At the plateau's edge, on a slight rise in the earth, I saw a towering crucifix. Nailed to its arms and straight stem was the figure of Ichavod. Though I could not make out the face, I knew at once that my search had ended, that it was he and that he was dead. I reconnoitered the surrounding area for more than two hours and when I was satisfied that nobody was about, I made my way toward the rigid body, black against the brilliance of the new day. I reached the cross and stood at the bloodless, mutilated feet of the man who had guarded my life and served my interests for so long a time. In most deaths, I knew from my experience, the body of the dead man shrinks—retreats, as it were, from the dimensions of life. But Ichavod's cadaver seemed to have grown larger, was in fact almost monstrous in size, as if the true stature of the man lay in death. He had been terribly mutilated, and I immediately surmised, from my knowledge of wounds, that he had been tortured extensively and at length while he still lived. I gazed upwards and was surprised. Ichavod's large face had on it an expression of horror —a look of bottomless, unfathomable terror that I had not once seen on it all of the days we had been together. I wondered what vision it was that had wrenched such a look from his features—always calm, always impassive. One eye had been gouged out, and it was the remaining eye that bulged insanely, as if for both. It shone glassily in the morning sunlight and I spotted in its depths the expression that comes to a man when for the first time in his existence he experiences pain and fear he believes to be beyond his strength. And his mouth, Ichavod's mouth was wide open, locked open that way, as if on a scream! For an instant I actually believed that his tongueless mouth, which could not so much as utter a single sound, had screamed! Both of his ears had been sliced off and his nose had been slit from end to end longitudinally. His chin had been burned so severely that no flesh at all was left to cover the bone of the jaw. The hands, which were nailed to the crossbar through their palms, were fingerless—only the black-blooded stumps remained; and his feet were missing all of their toes. The corpse was entirely naked, and where the great thighs converged was the most violent wound of all: Ichavod's genitals were missing completely. There was nothing to see there except for a huge, jagged hole gnarled with clots of dry blood. It looked as if he had another mouth now, this one between his legs and tongueless as well. Beneath his feet a parchment had been fixed to the cross, and I moved closer so that I could see it. Its message was written in both Latin and Hebrew. It read as follows:

PROCLAMATION

The Roman army of occupation in Judea proclaims that on this day it has nailed to the crucifix a monster which it apprehended after many months of pursuit—a Jew-monster! This beast preyed upon the soldiers of the empire, maiming and killing them in a premeditated campaign to spread terror and anarchy throughout the land. Let it be known to whomsoever reads this proclamation that this particular bird of prey was a difficult one to snare: but as is always the case, no matter how long it takes, he was caught and arrested after a fierce but futile struggle with the imperial forces.

For his traitorous and vicious acts and activities against the troops of Rome in Judea, against the Procurator of Judea, His Excellency, Pontius Pilate, and against His Exalted Majesty, the Emperor . . . this dog's Reward was death. But death was not given to him gratuitously: he had to earn it, stage by slow stage. And in the end, after two days of hard labor and earnest efforts, the Reward came: both for the criminal, who so devoutly sought it out, and for the army of Judea, whose Reward it was to be rid, once and for all time, of this blight upon the land!

Thus let the death of this Jew-monster, this pestilence among men, this cancer upon the face of the earth . . . serve as warning to each and every citizen who might consider, in folly or delirium or for personal gain, a career of crime and treason similar to his. Let this death proclaim, by order of the military commander of the area of the Galilee, in whom is invested the imperial power of Rome, that such a fate and such a punishment shall befall any man who attempts in any way or manner to thwart, frustrate, damage, inhibit or in any form whatsoever evade or avoid the will of Rome! Anarchy will never be tolerated, nor chaos countenanced, nor treason—from the greatest act of open defiance down to the smallest sin of secret thought—be permitted by the Imperial Government of Rome. Let it be herewith remembered at the crucifix that the people of Judea, as the other peoples of the Roman Empire, live but by the sufferance of Rome and perish but by the wrath of Rome.

As for this Jew nailed here—we have circumcised him again, and this time we have done the job properly! His back is turned to the valley, to the living land of Judea, because in his traitorous acts and in his villainous deeds . . . he has condemned himself to the land of the dead! He thought to escape the net that Rome casts, but he erred—as do all criminals—and was taken—as are all criminals—and punished according to the statutes of Roman Law. For the eye of Rome is all-seeing, the heart of Rome eternal, the voice of Rome all-penetrating, the will of Rome irresistible, the hand of Rome firm in its grasp and unfailing in its justice . . .

Long live His Excellency, the Procurator of Judea!

Long live His Imperial Majesty, the Emperor!

And it was signed with a flourish by the commanding military officer of the Galilee, who had personally made the trip up to the spot to be present at the crucifixion and to dictate the proclamation, and in a neat, cramped hand by the scribe who had written it down on the parchment at his behest. And beside their names were the imperial eagle of Rome and the skull and crossbones.

I decided that under no circumstances would I return to the cave: if the Romans had managed to find and torture Ichavod to death, they would not be long in finding—or perhaps had already found—our hiding place. My main objective now would be to stay hidden until the road back to power was open to me once again. I did not quite know what form this new power would have, but I was certain that one day I would possess it. Slowly, patiently, borne almost as an autumn leaf that is carried carefully by the wind, I drifted. The lore of the wilderness, which I had observed Ichavod put to use for so many months, became my lore. As once while a child, I had taught myself to use the bow and excelled at it, so now I taught myself all of the myriad and invaluable secrets of forest and field, marsh and swamp, mountain and ravine. As the days and the weeks went by, I felt more and more confident of my ability to survive. For hours at a time I would observe the creatures of the wild—bird and beast and fish—at their variegated pursuits, as they struggled to survive; and then I would apply what I had seen and

learned to my own life and my own struggle. I had a great deal of
time to think, and though I did not actually record my thoughts as
when I kept my journals, I worked through, clarified and resolved a
great many of my ideas. One day as I sat in a copse of birches, I
fashioned for myself of bark and twigs a miniature chess set. I now
spent endless hours devising problems and working out solutions for
them.

As time passed, I felt my position to be safer than it had been and
drifted farther and farther down from the hills to the valley and the
fringe of "civilization" proper. The peasants were at first very suspicious
but gradually became accustomed to me and accepted me. Those who
began by fearing me and even by driving me off with stones and with
their dogs came after a while to be amused by my presence. The children looked forward to my arrival and kept up a constant watch for me.
They called me the "man from the mountain" and "mountain goat"
and "uncle of the forest." Their parents, who seemed more and more to
be taken with my ways, called me "the wise hermit," "the priest with no
flock," "tumbleweed," and after they knew me for a time, "the philoso-
pher" or "the weaver of words." They asked me again and again why I
had no fixed abode, why I subsisted as a "beast of the field," why I had
no wife and no children, when I would no longer "roam the earth like a
wraith." I answered them simply, in a manner they could understand.
"I live the way I do," I said, "because God commanded it so. When He
desires it to be otherwise, I shall obey His command." They were much
satisfied with my answer and murmured approval; word of what I had
said spread through all the villages. Then I was welcome wherever I
went. Sometimes they gave me shelter in a barn or haystack or food
and drink, in exchange for which I gave them advice about matters
which troubled them, or wrote petitions to the authorities for them, or
pronounced priestly blessings on their infants, animals or crops.

I began to observe their life as I had studied the life of the animals
in the wild. I saw how poor they were, how docile, how malleable; how
open to command they were, how bound to superstitions of all kinds
they were. They always warned me when Herod's soldiers or when the
Romans were coming. The first time it happened, I told them that it did
not matter if the troops found me, that I "was a man of God" and had
nothing to hide or fear. But they laughed and told me I was a fool—that
soldiers made trouble "even when there was nothing to trouble about"
and that they abused newcomers or strangers "just for the sake of

abusing them." I nodded and took their advice and in that way became closer to them, as if one of them. They often invited me to their hearths, especially if some good fortune came their way—as it was inevitably attributed to my presence and influence. "You have a way with God," they told me. When a barren woman became pregnant, her husband had a sheep slaughtered in my honor; when a cow gave birth to twin calves, the owner named both of them in my honor. One fellow, whose "poisoned" leg grew well after I had stroked it and muttered the first Latin words that came to mind, offered me his daughter as a "wife" or as a "bride for the night." I declined graciously, and word of my "gentle refusal" went far and wide.

More time passed. I thought it safe to move more freely and announced my decision to leave. The peasants were grieved and pleaded with me to stay on. "I must go now, dear friends," I told them, "but I will return. I promise you. God tells me to go now, but I am certain that one day He will tell me to return." This statement satisfied and comforted them. I had come to see what enormous power the word "God" had over these people. On the dusty road that led away from their scattered villages, down deeper into the Galilee, I thought that the peasants were grapes and that there was no end to how much a man might squeeze out of them. If one pressed them properly, they gave and gave and gave; even in their death they gave—as manure.

I approached Safed. Occasionally I was stopped on the way by a patrol—Roman or Herodian. But I aroused no suspicion. They questioned me and I answered. My demeanor was humble, my tone gracious. I rolled my eyes to heaven. Herod's troops gave me the proper deference, the Romans the correct measure of respect. God worked wonders. The narrow streets and alleyways of the city were crowded with miracle workers, itinerant preachers, peddlers, merchants from near and far, farmers with produce, students of the Law who had nothing to eat, artisans and craftsmen who worked when they could, madmen vociferous and silent, mendicants of every size and shape and appearance, beggars who slept in the gutters, burnt by the sun and rotted by the rain. One of them attracted my attention. He sat in the street before a large Academy of the Law and held out his hand for alms. I had some coins which I had myself begged along the way and dropped one of them into his palm. He thanked me in a dead voice and continued to call out his woes in a monotonous singsong.

"Alms . . . for the love of God, alms! Help a poor cripple, an orphan who is alone in the world! Alms . . . "

He was legless and sat with his naked stumps out, from time to time slapping the flies from them. He had large, beautiful eyes which were sunk so deeply into their sockets that it looked as if they would retreat into his skull if they were able. He was young and had once been exquisite but he looked old far beyond his years and his face was withered and splotched—like blighted fruit. I stood watching him for a time and then walked up again and put another coin into his palm. He thanked me expressionlessly without looking up.

"What is your name, my son?" I asked.

He did not answer.

"Will you tell me your name?"

He said nothing.

But I persisted. "I mean you no harm, my son. I am a priest from the hills and wish to know your name. What is it?"

"*Bli-shem*," he answered sullenly.

The term *bli-shem* meant "no name," and I chided him. "Why are you so stubborn? A young man with eyes so beautiful as yours—"

"Why do you ask my name? It is my body you want, is it not?"

I smiled and bent over to whisper in his ear: "Yes."

"Do you have money? What will you give me?"

I took out my purse and shook it so that the coins that remained jingled. His eyes lit for an instant and then went dull again. His lips curled. "What is it that attracts you—my eyes or my stumps?"

"Both."

He nodded and explained where I was to meet him. "At sundown," he said. "Not before. I will not leave this spot—it is mine by the law of the street," he said. "Do you understand?"

"Yes."

"Then off with you—you lecherous garbage of a priest!"

I spent the day wandering through the steep streets of the hill-hugging city. I observed everything, studied all that I saw. The ways of men were as the ways of the beasts and birds and fish: one had to analyze the patterns of human behavior so that one could establish domination over them. Brute force gave one dominion—that was certainly true—but that kind of power could be so easily and so readily subverted, lost. One's own spear could be shattered by the spear of

427

another; one's own army could be bested by the army of an opponent. Power had to have a firmer, more certain, more stable, more enduring base: a base that was rock—immovable rock. I walked through the streets of the city and considered: what had the kind of power I was seeking? The word. Yes, the word: time and again I had seen what it could do to men, how it could affect them, how it could change and shape their lives, how it could persist and endure. I had seen how, like fire, it could consume men and civilizations; how, like water, it could seep under foundations and topple fortresses. But it had to be the right word. The word that could not be easily refuted. The word that touched the right nerves. The word that burned into the mind like a brand, that burrowed into the heart like a cankerworm. My step quickened, my breath came in spurts. I bumped into passers-by and toppled a heap of fruit. The word. The right word. I would find it. It would be the way back to a power far greater, far more enduring than the power I had commanded! Aimlessly my feet wandered where they would, while inside me my mind relentlessly pursued its goal: the Word!

The sun's rays slanted down into the city streets, igniting the stone and mud dwellings with ephemeral gold. Here a mirror glittered, there a bauble flashed. The vendors gathered their wares, the shopkeepers fastened their shutters, the merchants mounted their mules and donkeys, the farmers and peasants headed for home on foot. Dust rose from the final flurry of the day's activity and hung, sluggish and golden, in the air. Students of the Law, half starved and old before their time, headed for their hovels. From behind crumbling walls came the cries of mystics, calling out their adoration and complaints to the invisible God of Israel. Did He hear? Did He know? Did He care? Perhaps it made not the slightest difference to the supplicants. They did as they felt they must: that was all.

Out at the edge of the city, out beyond the cemetery, with its dusty firs and drunken gravestones, was a refuse dump. Rats crawled boldly through it and buzzards wandered casually, without fear, as if promenading. The crippled beggar had dragged himself there on his stumps. He spat when he saw me.

"All right," he said. "Give me the money and let's get it over with!"

"But why are you so curt?" I asked. "Why is your mouth so filled with venom?"

"Let's get it over with, you scum! And mind you, no tricks. I've brought a good friend along. He carries me when I'm tired of slithering. And he deals with anyone who tries to play tricks."

Sure enough, sitting on a rock several yards away and picking at his yellowed teeth with the point of his knife, was a great street oaf with the arms and back of a hewer of wood. I gave the cripple two coins.

"More," he said.

I added another.

"That's not enough!"

I added still another.

"Empty your purse!" he said.

"What is the meaning of this?"

"Empty your purse, priest-whore!" ordered the cripple. "And be quick about it!"

"You cannot do this . . . "

The great hulk rose and grasped his knife menacingly and took a step forward. The sun bloodied him and his naked blade and the refuse and the arrogant rats and stuffed buzzards. I tossed my purse down into the cripple's lap.

"There. Are you satisfied?"

"That's better."

"Will you tell me your name?"

He stared up at me. "My name? You really want to know it?"

"Yes."

"What for?"

"I knew it once."

His eyes narrowed. "Rubbish!"

"And you knew mine."

He laughed. "You're crazy!"

"No," I said. "I'm quite sane—Elazar . . . "

The cripple's face turned deathly pale. Holding my purse, his fingers shook. He stared up at me in amazement and disbelief. "How—how did you know?"

"I know."

"Who are you?"

"Look into my eyes, Elazar . . . "

"Master!" Elazar seized my hand and kissed it.

"So . . . you know me."

"Master . . . it's you, it's really you! You did not die . . . You are among the living! How I wished for this day, but never thought I would see it!"

"I knew you at once, Elazar."

"Then why didn't you tell me?"

"It was not time."

"How I've thought of you, master! How I've ached for you and longed for you! How many times I've thought of doing away with myself!"

"Doing away with yourself? Would you have sought me in the other world, then?" I laughed.

"Do not jest, master!"

And Elazar's hot tears fell upon the back of my hand. I touched his once beautiful hair—it was filthy and brittle now, and I removed my fingers.

"Can we talk alone?"

Elazar nodded and spoke to the street oaf, telling him to return to the city and come back in an hour or so. Without a word the fellow left. I sat beside Elazar, who continued to hold my hand tightly.

"Master, I should have recognized you but—but I scarcely saw you. Or anyone, for that matter. There was a wall of hatred before my eyes. I glanced up at you as I should have glanced at a tree. And your appearance, master. What happened?"

"Never mind my appearance, Elazar. It doesn't matter. I am alive. That is sufficient." I smiled. "But you? Tell me what happened to you."

Elazar's eyes clouded. "The memories are not pleasant, my master. I reached the couriers, as you commanded me, with their orders, and they left. Some of them never reached their units, but were detained and arrested en route. Others got through, but the orders they transmitted were never carried out, for the Roman show of strength was too great; and it became obvious that the support of Livinius was gone. Except for two battles—one for the headquarters of *Patish* and the last, desperate, futile stand of the Seventeenth Assault Brigade of which General Akrab assumed direct command—there was nothing. Nothing at all, master."

"But to you—what happened to you?"

"I was picked up on the evening of the day after the king's fete. In obedience to your command, I was riding to *Patish*. The roads were swarming with patrols—Roman and those of a militia Herod had conscripted in Jerusalem and the surrounding villages. Although I had changed my garments as you directed me, the officer in charge of the patrol—one of Herod's—thought he recognized me. He brought me immediately to his superior in Jerusalem, who confirmed his suspicions. I was instantly taken under guard to the fortress palace which I had quit not more than eighteen hours before. Herod's chief of intelligence, Gedaliah, interviewed me—do you know him?"

"I know him. Go on."

"He threatened me with the most hideous tortures, master, but I told him nothing. I told him that I knew nothing. I told him that you confided nothing to me. He laughed. He said that I was small, but that I held within me much poison. And much knowledge. He said that if I did not answer his questions, he would send me to the special chambers of the secret service and there I would be made to talk. I told him that it didn't matter, that I had nothing to say because I knew nothing." Elazar's voice shook. "They took me downstairs, master. To a room I had never seen before. There were hooded men there, master—special men. Men who know the body well and how to make it hurt. Master, they—they did many things. I fainted many times and always they brought me back. They brought me back and did more things. I thought I would die, master, I wanted very much to die, but I did not. They did not wish me to die, the men, they wished me to live—and to talk. They hurt me, they hurt me more than I thought it was possible to hurt a human being, inflicted pain that I did not think a human being could stand—but they did it carefully, as if I were a precious vessel that must not be shattered. Do you know what I am telling you, master?"

"I know."

"But I told them nothing, nothing of your plans, master, not a single word! That is the truth, master, the holy truth! You must believe me, master, you must know how much I suffered for your sake, master, how much punishment I took—" And Elazar wept bitterly, bowing his head.

"I know. I know how you suffered, Elazar. I know how much pain you endured for my sake. I am grateful. Go on."

"It was later. How much later, I don't know. Hours later, days later. Who can say? Gedaliah was there. And he had brought with him a little man, a strange little man with a crooked nose and a great wart on his forehead and a mincing little walk, like a dancer's. Gedaliah referred to him only as 'the butcher,' and the little man smiled oddly to hear it, as if there were some hidden meaning in the name. Gedaliah told me that the man would take me apart, 'piece by piece,' if I did not tell him what he wanted to know. He said it was my last chance to confess, that I would have no other. He warned me that the road would lead 'straight ahead' to 'dismemberment' if I did not reveal the secrets I knew, that 'as God had put my body together' so his 'friend would take it apart.' He commanded me to speak. I refused." Elazar wept again. The nails of his grimy hand cut into my flesh, and gently I took my hand away from his grasp.

"It is important for me to know the whole story, Elazar. Continue with your account."

"Forgive me, master. It is difficult—"

"Nevertheless, I must know."

He nodded. "Yes, of course." He regained control over himself. "The little man took off one leg," he said. "I saw what he had done. They picked up my head so that I could see. The little man's hands and arms were bloody. And his smock was covered with my blood. They held my severed leg up for me to see. And then they threw it to the floor. The little man smiled and took up his instruments—I suppose he was a butcher, or a surgeon. I don't know. I lost consciousness. But they wakened me with water. 'I am dreaming,' I said. 'No,' said Gedaliah. 'You are not dreaming.' I shook my head. 'But I must be dreaming,' I said. 'This is not possible.' Gedaliah laughed. 'It is real,' he said. 'Quite real.' I passed out once again and when they wakened me they showed me that my other leg was gone and even brought it close to me and made me put out my hand so that I could touch it. And Gedaliah asked me if I had changed my 'addled mind' and would tell him what he wanted to know, and I replied that I would not, that I would never talk, that I could never talk because I had nothing to say, knew nothing that would be of value or interest to him, and he said that it was a shame to see such a pretty body cut up and 'fed to the fishes,' a body that could be 'used for so many pretty things.' And the little man laughed and once more took up his instruments, and still, my master, I did not betray you. And then—and then—" Elazar's voice wavered.

"And then what?"

"—and then the door opened—and—"

"And what, Elazar?"

"—and Herod himself came in—and—"

"And?"

432

"—and Quaestoris."

"I see. Quaestoris. Alive and well."

"Alive and well, master. As you are now."

"What did he say? Why was he there? Why was Herod there?"

Elazar shook his head. "I don't know, master. For I fainted once more . . . " He paused and then went on, "When I awoke, I was no longer in the torture chamber, but in a prison cell, a cell under heavy guard—there was even a warder by my bed. But I scarcely knew what was going on. I was consumed by a raging fever. People came and went. I could not eat, but vomited up all they gave me. Day ran into night and night turned to day: I did not know how. I was not sunk to the bottom, to the muddy bottom of death, but I was somewhere below the surface of life—struggling, as in water, gasping for breath until I thought my lungs would burst. It must have been weeks before I returned to my full consciousness. The pain in my—in what remained of my legs was great. But I could eat. I could think. I could worry about you, master, about what had happened.

"Then one day the door opened and Quaestoris came in. He was accompanied by many aides and soldiers, but he dismissed them all and he ordered the warder to leave the room as well. We were alone—just the two of us. He brought up a chair and sat by me. He looked well, master, but aged: he looked like a very old man—his hair had gone white and his eyes were dim. And there were lines over his entire face and deep lines about his mouth. He spoke slowly and with deliberation, as if I were a child he needed to be patient with. He told how the revolt had been aborted and the two pockets of resistance—'the two chancres,' he called them—had been wiped out. I asked about you, my master, and he told me that you had disappeared and not been found and that there was a great price set upon your head. I was relieved, master, relieved to learn that you were not dead, but I was terribly concerned about your welfare. Quaestoris sensed what was going on inside me and told me that I should no longer concern myself with you or your fate. He said that it was because of his intercession, and because of that alone, that I had been spared. 'They would indeed have fed you to the fishes,' he said to me. 'Literally. Gedaliah has a pond behind his home and keeps the fish in it fat on prisoners!' He told me that he had learned of my predicament from one of Herod's aides and rushed to the torture chamber to save me. The king had come along out of curiosity and because it took his personal presence to get into the room where I was detained. I thanked him for his efforts on my part. And then I asked him why, why he had saved my life? He said it was because he did not feel I should be punished, because he did not feel I was guilty. He said—he said—"

"Yes . . . what did he say?"

"Master, he said—"

"Said what?"

"—that—that I was 'a dupe' of yours, as he had been. And that I should not be made to suffer and die for it. He said that I would be kept in prison until I was well and able to get around. And that then I should be set free. He said that he had petitioned to Pontius Pilate and to Herod on my behalf, and that his petition had been granted. And it was as he said, master. When I was well enough to get around, I was released. And I was even given transportation to Safed, where I grew up. The words that Quaestoris spoke to me in my cell, he kept, even to the last of them."

"I see. And did he speak to you at all of his 'death'?"

"Yes, master. He spoke of that at once since I was terrified at the sight of him. He explained that he had 'died' in order to hide from you and in order to be in a better position to prevent, or failing that, to quell the revolt. Though he did not know the details, he knew the substance of your plans; though he was not sure how and when, he was certain of your intent. 'Your master's heart is a fortress,' he said to me, 'and it is death he keeps imprisoned there!' His 'death' was merely a cover, a shield. Pilate and Herod knew that he had not, indeed, died, but the secret was kept from everyone else."

"But how was it accomplished, Elazar?"

"The prison raid—do you remember the prison raid, about the time of which the head jailer, Kalbi, disappeared?"

"I do. Proceed."

"It was staged for two reasons. The first was to secure the services of a master embalmer, who was among the group of prisoners which 'escaped.' This man, held for grave-robbing and other acts against the dead, was used to aid Quaestoris prepare his 'corpse.' The body was actually that of a murderer who was executed. The face was a creation of Quaestoris and the embalmer, who after he had accomplished his task, was placed on a galley sailing for Venice. A large group of prisoners was released so that the identity of the only man really wanted would be hidden from you."

"And the second reason?"

"To divert your attention from Quaestoris and Rome and to throw it to Kalbi and the Jews. They wanted to divert you. They knew that the secret passage would divert you as well. And they knew that you would find it. They wanted you to find it. They felt it would increase your confidence. And that it would encourage you to make your move. They wanted you to make your move—so that they could make theirs."

"And so the rebellion died at birth."

Elazar was silent. His eyes stared off over the refuse dump, which lay in ever-deepening shadow. Without his being conscious of their movement, his fingers played idly with the strings of my purse.

"And what else have you to report?"

My voice seemed to waken him from a stupor. He looked up, his lips twisted into a melancholy smile. "Nothing, master. Nothing that would be of worth or of interest to you. I came to Safed to find that my parents were dead and my family scattered. Quaestoris had given me some money, and when it was spent, I took to the streets. I have done comparatively well, for there are those who starve. Taxes are high—if Pilate does not levy them, then Herod does—work is scarce, the crops failed this year, and then there are the Zealots and the Roman reprisals, and there is the military conscription, which tears many families apart, and the plague was in these parts but two months ago. But I've managed to survive. I teamed up with that—fellow whom you saw before; we work together and share profits. I still have nice eyes, and there are those whom my crippled body tempts far more than a flawless one would: all in all, it hasn't been too bad. But I missed you, my master, I yearned for you so terribly; I prayed that one day I would find you again. And my prayers were answered."

"Did Quaestoris say anything else about me?"

Elazar's brow wrinkled. "About you? I don't know. I really don't remember."

"Try to think, Elazar. It's important. Every bit of information I gather is important to me. It takes many single threads to weave a tapestry. I've told you that many times."

"Yes . . . yes, you have. Let me recall." Elazar held his head. "Yes," he said at length. "Yes, there is one thing."

"What was it?"

"He said—he said—"

"Said what? Out with it!"

"He said that if ever I were to encounter you, if ever I were to meet you . . . I must remember that—remember that you—"

"That I what?"

"—that you are—how did he phrase it?—that you are . . . 'the weed of destruction,' that you are . . . 'the cup of death.' He said that I must avoid you, that I must have nothing to do with you, that I must—that I must report you immediately to the authorities. He said I must give the nearest authorities a description of your person and your last known location. And he told me I must not fail in this, if I hoped to live. He said that if I complied, I would not only live but that great wealth and important recognition would come to me, that the government would reward and honor me until the end of my days, which would be long and fruitful in the land of Judea. And he said that if I did not harken unto his words, surely I would meet with a terrible end."

"And you believed him?"

"No, master!" Elazar cried out. "Oh, no! Only witness how much joy I have had in the very sight of your person! Only remember how quickly I dismissed my friend!"

"Perhaps your friend went to inform, eh?"

"How could he? He does not know who you are!"

"Perhaps you gave him a secret sign?"

"Master, what are you saying? You wound my heart!"

"He will return, your friend, will he not?"

"He will. But—"

"Perhaps you will warn him then? Perhaps you will set him on me, and he will seize and bind me?"

"Master, how can you speak so? After the way I have suffered for you! After all I have endured for your sake! Your words are poison to my soul! Master, have mercy on me."

He was ready to weep afresh. I bent and touched his hair, loathsome as it was to my hand. I softened my voice: "I'm sorry . . . I'm sorry, Elazar. Please forgive me. I know I have hurt you. But I did not intend to do so. I know you are a faithful servant; I know that you love me as dearly as your own flesh—"

"As my own soul, master!"

"Then forgive me, dear Elazar. I have been through much; I have suffered greatly as well." I forced tears into my eyes. "Let me embrace you, dear friend . . . Let me kiss your mouth, dear loyal Elazar."

His eyes were wet and shining, and he looked up at me with an expression of boundless love and devotion and opened his arms. I bent low and then in a swift and sudden motion grasped his neck in my hands and squeezed it with all of my strength. His eyes bulged as if they must burst from their sockets, his face turned purple, his little legless body thrashed in the dirt, its naked stumps striking my thighs and loins. I set one knee upon his chest and bore down on him until the muscles of my arms and back ached with terrible pain. One second his body was a single sinew of resistance—and the next it went limp. Still I kept squeezing. "Die, you little worm, you little whore-bastard," I whispered. "And may Quaestoris die with you!"

I let go. The twisted little corpse slid from my grasp and rolled in the dust. I kicked it—in the crotch, in the face, in the head. It lay still, bloody mouth buried in the dust. Then I stooped and quickly stripped it of whatever coins there were. My purse had fallen and come open during the struggle, and I recovered its coins as well. Money too, I thought, was power. But money could be lost as easily as this little crab had lost his legs and then his life. I wanted a power beyond money, beyond brute force: the power of the undying Word. I stuffed the coins into my cloak and ran quickly from the refuse dump into the hills. The evening star shone down on me as I ran.

PART

VII

There were two men left alive whom I had to fear, two men who would recognize me no matter how I changed my appearance, who would recognize me if hell itself were to twist my shape into another: one through the power of his sanity—Quaestoris; the other through the power of his madness—my brother. Before I could begin my ascent to power again, I had to put each of them in his place: the grave. In the case of my brother, I felt it would be easy—it would merely be a matter of finding him. Quaestoris would present more of a problem, he would be a serious problem. But I did not reckon his end as beyond my will. Nothing was beyond my will. There was a secret entranceway to Quaestoris's villa, which I had often used when we first became lovers and wished to hide our faces from spying eyes; I reckoned that the diplomat would have it watched carefully lest I use it now. But his reasoning might carry him further: he might think that since I knew it would be guarded, he would not have to keep it guarded, and then—so he would figure—I would actually use it again. Therefore he would keep it watched. It was all a game, a game of mortal chess in which it was imperative to know how one's opponent reasoned. I would find a way to the envoy, it would take me time, but I would find a way and achieve the security that only his death could bring me.

Slowly, without hurrying overly much, watching and observing— always observing as I went—I journeyed southward from Safed to Tiberias and then across to Nazareth, where I went directly to the great estate that had been seized from me, to the house and lands that had belonged to my father, Evenezer, before me. As I plodded along on foot, approaching the driveway that led up the hill and to the mansion, a gaily dressed, cheerful hunting party rode out the main gate on splendid mounts. They rode past me without so much as glancing in my direction, their dust rolling up in huge clouds into the air and then slowly settling—covering my clothes and hair and even entering my nostrils and my mouth. I stood where I was, staff in hand, and stared at them as they cantered on down the road; not one of them turned to look back. I turned and went on. At the gate, as I had expected, I was halted by armed guards.

"What is it you want, beggar-priest?" said their captain. "We have no alms for scum like you! Be off!"

I showed no anger or fear; instead, I smiled and said softly, with gentle humor, "What do I want? Excellencies, it is not alms, for I am no beggar. Simply . . . to sleep in the bed of the master!"

They took no offense, but found what I said extremely amusing and laughed until they held their sides with the pain of it. Meanwhile, I stood relaxed and regaled them with humorous stories and incidents which kept them in good spirits and then praised them for their good sense and remarkable taste. They were soon in the palm of my hand. When I felt the time was ripe, I asked them for a favor.

"What is it, good friend?" said the captain. "If we can help you in any way, we will."

"I wish to pray at the grave of the former master of the house, Evenezer. I will not stay there long, and you may watch me all the time I stay."

All of the guards paled.

"Which master did you say?" asked the captain.

"The man who built this house—Evenezer," I said.

"You knew him?"

"Yes. I was a young priest in this area when he was alive. He was good to his servants, who were as numerous as the sands of the seashore. And he was very good to me, very generous. I loved him well. And I was even present at his funeral: I saw him go into the earth. I beg of you, good friends, allow me this favor. It can harm no one, but it will make my heart glad. I beseech you: let me pray for his soul for a few moments, and then I will depart in peace."

"But—but the gravestone has been smashed."

"There was a tree at the grave."

"It was cut down."

"The stone smashed, the tree felled?"

"By order of the crown."

I shook my head and sighed. "It doesn't matter. As long as I can pray at the site for a little time. It would ease my troubled spirit so very much," I said gently, "if you would only permit it . . . "

"But you must be silent about it. You must tell no one."

I assured the captain that I would breathe not a word of it. The other guards looked at him uncertainly, but he nodded and slowly the great gate swung open. I walked between two guards to the site of my father's grave. They had indeed smashed the stone but left its broken pieces lie where they fell—a warning of sorts, I supposed. The tree, too, had been cut and its trunk left sprawling on the earth. Actually, it was the tree I had come for—I had no interest whatsoever in visiting Evenezer's grave; his moldering bones would do me little good. At its base there was a hollow in which, years ago, I had secreted a pouch with a number of jewels in it against a time when I might need them. I began to pray in a loud voice, rocking back and forth and beating my breast as I did so; the guards who had accompanied me stared off into space, and slowly, as if overcome by grief, I went down on my knees. The guards glanced at me, looked embarrassed and turned away. Quickly I thrust my hand into the hollow of the trunk. Leaves and cob-webbing came out. My fingers plucked at rot. Then I felt the pouch! I pulled it out and shoved it into the folds of my cloak. Then I cried out in a voice of anguish, "Oh, God—give this good soul rest in Your heaven above!" And I buried my head in my hands and wept. One of the guards touched my shoulder. "Worthy priest," he said. "You must leave now. You must get hold of yourself and go. We wish no trouble." I stifled my sobs, got to my feet with the aid of the guard's hand, and went back to the gate with the two of them. I blessed the captain and all of them as I left. When I sold the jewels, I would have enough to live on for a long time to come.

I recalled that Quaestoris must be at his summer villa on the coast of the Sharon. So I set forth for the shore. The sun beat down merci-lessly; the July sky was cloudless and glassy with heat. There had been a severe drought; the crops were parched and withering from brown to black; the peasants were hard-pressed and in dire need. They stared at me, red-eyed and sullen, as I rode by them along the dusty road on the mule I had bought with some of the jewel money. Sometimes a mother held up a starving or even a dead infant for me to see—as if I could do something—and sometimes an old man or woman begged me to help— in what way, I could not imagine. But for the most part, the peasants were stoop-shouldered and silent, and one fancied they ate of the dust one left behind. There was power in each of them, power in all of them together—if one but could release it!

My journey was uneventful, even placid. On a farm in Samaria, I bought a peasant's young son for a night and gave rein to my long-repressed lust. I left the child half conscious at the break of day and rode forth, much relieved. When I was several miles away from Quaestoris's summer place, I rode into a small mountainside village that reminded me very much of the village in which I had been born and raised. I secured lodgings with a grape grower whose vineyards had been blasted by the drought; he was glad to have the handful of money I offered him. As I counted out the coins one by one, testing each as I did so in order to impress him with my honesty and frugality, I explained that I was embarked on a long journey, a journey that would take me eventually "all the way to the desert" where I would encamp to "pray to the God of Israel for the welfare of the suffering land and its sorely oppressed people." The farmer stared at me. "But why the desert?" he asked. "Can you not find God here?" I smiled sadly and shook my head. "The wickedness of men chases the spirit of God from the cities and the villages," I said mournfully. "I must be off by myself in the wilderness in order that I may seek and reach Him." My host himself tested the money, and finding it good, said, "I understand. I know exactly what you're talking about." And he turned his back and went off, leaving his stout, red-faced wife to show me to my quarters. I explained to her that I planned to stay for several days or perhaps a week "to rest and to recuperate from my arduous trip from the north, where I lived," and to prepare for "the exhausting trip to come."

I wasted no time in befriending the five children of the house— children are very useful, if handled properly. They gathered around me that afternoon in the dusty yard, sat in the straw at my feet, and listened intently to the stories I told them. They answered all of the questions I put to them in a casual way I had perfected, vying with each other for my attention and my favor; I patted all of their cheeks and heads with impartial fervor. I mentioned many places to which I had traveled, cities at the other end of the country and even foreign places; I told them I had met great princes and dukes and asked them if they ever had. Their appetites were whetted. They told me, speaking almost with one voice, that "a great Roman lord—perhaps even a king—had come" to the area not long ago and "lived in a palace up in the hills." And they pointed vaguely to the northwest. I asked if he were alone, and they answered that he had come with "many soldiers —perhaps even an army." I asked them if he had ever visited the village. "Never," they told me. "The village was too poor for him to visit, and besides it was Jewish. Romans never visited with Jews." Then how did they know him? They explained that he "liked to hunt in the valley," where they went sometimes to catch a glimpse of him "from afar." To see him, they told me, and to see "his soldiers on their steeds, each with shield and spear and armor as bright as the sun." Did they see him only in the valley or was he visible to them elsewhere? They said they also saw him at the shore, but "from a very great distance," for they were compelled to "keep to the bluffs and go no further" by his soldiers. But by darting in and out among the dunes above the beach, they saw him "bathe in the ocean, naked all of him," with the "young boy" who was his constant companion. Did he hunt or bathe most often? They did not know, they thought it was about the same. I thanked them, gave them sweets, and sent them off.

I had a small room above the barn in which my mule was kept. I went to it, locked my door, and lay on my pallet considering what I had learned. Beneath me, the sounds made by the stirring animals reminded me of my imprisonment at the hands of my father so many years ago. As then I had plotted the death of Zvi, the stableboy, who knew too much, so now I planned the death of Quaestoris, who would never miss my eyes if he were but to see them. The envoy had pretended to die in order to protect his own life and to hedge mine around; now I would oblige him and make his death a reality. It would be either at the seashore or in the valley: I would examine both possibilities carefully and decide which. I rose and lifted my cloak: into its lining were sewn a slender, supple bow—the best that money could buy—and six razor-tipped arrows. I set the cloak under my head as a pillow and fell asleep at once.

At dawn I ate my breakfast with the farmer, explaining to him in my most gentle voice that I wished to be out-of-doors at "the break of the new day" so I could "rise with the sun and give praise to the glory of God." The farmer mumbled into his porridge and I saddled my mule and left. I rode first to the coast, for the distance was the lesser. From the bluffs, which were forty or fifty feet high, I had a clear view of the yellow-white stripe of the beach, running as far as the eye could see in both directions: to the north it curved outward like a scimitar, and to the south it ran straight as a plumb line. As the sun lifted into the sky, the gray water turned steadily green, at first pale, then a deeper and deeper jade, with an unbroken fringe of white where the line of the advancing waves came in and shattered, spilling thick foam like sperm over the clean sand. That was where Quaestoris went bathing in the surf with his "young boy," the two of them naked. I knew at a glance that hitting my target from that distance would be impossible: every arrow that I shot, assuming that the guards were not upon me imme-diately, would fall far short of its mark. There was no point near enough and no point hidden enough for me to make an attempt. It would have to be the valley then.

I set out at once, spurring my mule on, and reached my destination by midmorning. After an initial survey, I found that the prospects were scarcely more favorable. The way from Quaestoris's summer home to the valley where he hunted was open, and anyone who approached from any direction would be stopped long before he could get the diplomat in range. I went carefully over the terrain, taking everything into account. There was only one place, I calculated, where a successful try might be made. A deep gorge separated the envoy's villa from the val-ley; it could only be crossed at a single point, where a narrow defile— with room enough for horsemen to pass in single file—cut into it. Who-ever entered the defile was subject to attack, if he were not well-guarded on his flanks. I stared down into the path from above. I could hardly imagine Quaestoris riding into such an obvious trap without soldiers on either side, commanding the heights. I turned my mount back, back-tracked for about a mile and a half until I reached a spot where I could enter the defile and did so. Slowly I rode down it, crossed the gorge and moved up the other side, observing each detail as I went. Soon I was out in open country again, close to the valley hunting grounds. I faced about again and studied the situation from this vantage point. A trumpet blared and I saw three Roman cavalrymen emerge from the defile. I remained in my place as they rode unhurriedly toward me. I squinted. They wore the silver plumes and embossed breastplates of Pilate's elite guard: it was apparent that Quaestoris had been greatly honored by the empire for his part in uncovering and halting the revolt.

"Hey, priest!" shouted one of the soldiers. "Move out of this area!"

"Eh?"

"I said, get out of the way, Jew-priest! This entire area is barred to civilians for the rest of the day! You must leave—at once!"

"May I ask why, sir?"

"There is no why! Just do as you're told and don't ask questions, if you value your worm-eaten hide!"

I nodded and bowed my head respectfully and prodded my mule. They were perfectly right, I thought. There was no why. Those who made the rules and could see that they were obeyed, those who gave the orders and had assurance they would be carried out to the letter . . . had not to account to anyone. They did not need a reason for anything they did: the very fact that they existed and were in power was reason enough in itself.

Some miles away, having watered my mule at a nearby well, I sat in a ditch by the side of an open field and ate my lunch. The sun blazed in the sky, scouring earth and heaven with its rays: before me, the crop that some miserable farmer had sown in the sweat of his brow drooped dismally, withering away by the hour. There was no wind, not the slightest breeze; there was nothing and no one to be seen. Even the birds and insects seemed to avoid the field as if they sensed the inexorable approach of death. I tossed the scraps to the dry, cracked earth, mounted my mule, and rode off again for the coast. When I reached it, I rode down from the bluffs to a little seaside village, with nets drying in the sun and naked children playing in the skiffs drawn up on the sand. At the edge of the village, I found a fisherman who agreed to do business with me. He was a small, bent fellow with gray hair, red-rimmed eyes and skin like leather. In a voice so harsh it hurt the ears to listen, he haggled over the price for his services. We finally compromised and I paid him half the sum agreed upon. As before, I counted out the coins one by one, and he tested them with his sharp, rodent's eyes and with his strong white teeth. We shook hands again. I stepped over the worn net he was mending and left his tiny hut.

I returned to my lodgings after dark, ate my meal alone and went directly to my room, explaining to the children who followed me that I was extremely weary because I "had prayed all day to God in His heaven." The night was stifling. I stripped off my clothes and stretched out on my pallet, the heavy, regular sounds of the animals rising up through the floor to my ears. As I had once planned a mighty campaign against Herod and against Rome, so I now plotted against a single life. But my concentration on and devotion to my goal were the same. Whatever I did, I did meticulously and well. I did not close my eyes until I had worked out every detail of my plan, down to the smallest. Then, satisfied that I would succeed, I closed my eyes and fell asleep immediately.

Almost instantly, or so it seemed to me, I began to dream. I saw myself walk unchallenged through the gate of Quaestoris's summer home. The old major-domo limped forward to greet me, and I asked where his master was; he smiled, bowed his head, and led me round the side of the splendid house to where the envoy was sitting in his magnificent rose garden, surrounded by flowers of every hue and color. A wind from the west stirred the bushes and brought with it a scent of the sea. At Quaestoris's feet, the "young boy" reclined on the lush grass. He was stark naked and though lying in the sun—obviously for some time —had not become tan: his incredibly smooth flesh was white as milk. His eyes, under arching brows, were large and dark—rather like Elazar's, I thought; his body was supple and unblemished. He glanced up at me and then turned his eyes away; his lips pouted, he seemed to be brooding. The envoy gazed at him fondly, hungrily, and then looked over to me. He was completely relaxed on his divan and he smiled as he motioned me to sit beside him.

"Well," he said. "Well, this is fine. I've been expecting you to pay me a visit; I've been expecting you to come for some time." He laughed with genuine pleasure. "Do sit down and make yourself comfortable."

I shook my head.

"Are you certain? Will you have a glass of wine?"

Again I shook my head.

Quaestoris picked up a glass and sipped its contents. I looked him over carefully. Elazar had told the truth: he had aged considerably—his hair was gray, almost white. But his eyes glowed with a deep, inner satisfaction I had never seen in them before. "You've come here to take me, then," he said, "is that it?"

I nodded.

"I knew it . . . yes, I guessed as much." He yawned. "Well, I'm ready to go. I've nothing to take along with me—just my own skin and bones and that's all."

"You aren't frightened?" I said.

"No. Why should I be?"

"You aren't—unwilling to go, are you?"

"No."

"Why not?"

The envoy shrugged. "Of what use is life?" he said.

"But you are very much alive," I said. "I've been told that you hunt in the valley and bathe at the seashore. And here you sit outside your palatial summer villa and sun yourself, ringed about by these exquisite flowers. And then there is—the boy. You certainly enjoy him and you certainly enjoy life—you sip it as you do your rare wine! How can you leave it all so quietly, so docilely?"

"You have named but diversions," said the envoy. "The pleasures you have listed are slight . . . They are surface pleasures. Actually I hate and loathe life! Life is futile, empty, meaningless. People live it only out of habit . . . or out of the fear of death. People live only to spite others . . . or to spite themselves." The envoy sighed. "No, my friend, I have no further desire to live. I'm weary of life, altogether sick of it. I shan't at all be sorry to go."

"Let us be on our way, then."

Quaestoris rose and then bent to kiss the boy upon his forehead, but the boy did not respond in any way. I led the envoy out of the garden and through the beautiful grounds about the villa, with their parks and ponds, their arbors and groves, their banks of exotic blossoms, their willows, pomegranates and lime-trees. No one said a word to us as we passed; no one made an attempt to stop us: all the guards we encountered stood aside and watched us dumbly as we went. At the main gate, manned by a full squad of troopers who kept massive hounds straining at their leashes, the captain saluted smartly and said to the envoy, "When will you be back again, Your Excellency?"

Quaestoris regarded him for some moments. "Never," he said quietly.

"Farewell then, sir," said the captain.

"Farewell," said the envoy sadly.

The gate swung open and we walked through. We soon left the villa behind us and then the fields and the meadows and occasional peasant huts until we were alone, trudging on earth that was wild and uninhabited by men. Under the darkening sky, we ascended a lonely hill whose top was bald and strewn with jagged rocks. Exactly on the crest, I had gathered stones and built a small altar of the sort that pagans used for sacrifices. I halted when I reached it, and the envoy stopped with me, sweating and a little out of breath.

"Is this the place, then?" he asked.

I nodded.

"Have you sacrificed here before?" he asked.

"No. You will be the first."

"I see."

"Are you frightened now?"

"No."

"You are not afraid to die?"

"No. What is human life on this earth but *vanitas vanitorum?* I have no fear. I am going to meet God . . . why should I be afraid? After all, it is God who created me. I trusted Him with my birth— surely I can trust Him with my death."

"Is it into the hands of the God of Israel that you go?"

"Yes," said the envoy. "I am finished with Rome. The gods of Rome are but puppets manipulated by the fingers of men."

"And are not men puppets manipulated by the fingers of God?"

Quaestoris shook his head. "No," he said. "For the God of Israel stands aside and lets men play their own games. When the pieces are swept from the board, He stoops to pick them up."

"As you wish," I said. "Believe what you will. But, my friend, your time has come. Approach the altar and heed my instructions."

The envoy did precisely as I directed him to do. He knelt before my altar and thrust his aged but still handsome face onto its rough surface. Evening had come to the earth. From the branch of a nearby pine, a nightingale sang poignantly. Quaestoris looked up at me. His face was composed. The evening star's silvery light shone in the pupils of his moist eyes and along the blade of my upraised knife.

"May I pray?"

I nodded. "The victim always prays—what else can he do?"

"Thank you." Quaestoris lifted his countenance to the great, soft,

450

unfurled tent flap of the sky. In a low, clear voice he chanted: "Blessed art Thou, O Lord our God, who hast created man in His image . . ."

He had not need to say "Amen" because I cut his throat.

I had purchased a large skein of fine fisherman's cord in the seaside village, and having concealed it in my cloak, I left my room above the barn before sunrise that morning. The farmer was up, milking a goat. I bade him good morning and asked to borrow an axe. "An axe?" he snorted. "Why does a priest need an axe?" I laughed. "To build an altar in the forest," I answered, "at which I can praise the Lord God for the beauty of and the sustenance afforded by all growing things"—I clasped my hands—"just as yesterday on the shore I praised Him for the vastness of the sea and for its limitless bounty." He shook his head, muttering to himself as he rose from the goat's teats and set his pail aside. He went into the toolroom and came out again. "Are priests never tired of praising?" he said as he handed the axe over. "Do farmers never tire of harvesting?" I asked. I could hear him mumbling a reply as I left.

I saddled my mule and rode swiftly to a small hillock covered by a copse of fir trees that commanded a view of the defile at its entrance, reaching it before the day was wholly light. I did not emerge from among the trees the day long but labored with axe and with knife, recalling carefully the method of construction Ichavod had used to build the device I wanted. The sun was a fiery flail in the sky, beating at me as I worked—even through the cover the firs provided. I was quite certain that Quaestoris would visit the seashore today, or else remain at home, but even if he did choose the valley it did not affect my work, for the hillock—though it afforded a clear view of the defile where it began —was too far from that passage for any weapon to be used from it: as long as I stayed among the trees, I was safe. I worked steadily and carefully, keeping Ichavod's finished product as a model.

By evening the trap was completed. I ate and rested until darkness had fallen. Then, leaving the mule tethered in the copse, I hoisted the device on to my back and began walking toward the defile. For so lethal an object, the trap was surprisingly light. As I pressed forward, the moon rose—a glowing fetus in the black womb of the sky. I reached my

451

goal and discovered to my pleasure that I had more light than I had anticipated and so could work more swiftly than I had calculated. Still it took me more than three hours to finish my task. When I did, I fastened one end of the fisherman's twine to the trap and then led it expertly out of the defile, often walking backwards as I went. I paid out the cord all the way to the copse, there tying its other end to the branch of a tree. I was through: there was no more to be done now. I threw myself to the earth to rest and to wait. I lay on my back on a carpet of fir needles, not at all sleepy, not even tired, as if the work instead of wearying me had refreshed me; I stared up through the lacework of branches at the moon as it rolled silently through the sky, now naked and now covered by silver-ribbed clouds, like a mill wheel. Silently, unswervingly—leaving no mark or track behind it—it went on the way that was decreed for it—like Quaestoris's fate. As in my dream, a night-ingale sang, giving the night a dimension it had not before, and I thought I would be hearing its song long after the envoy heard it no more. The hours of the night sped by with uncanny speed, for there was nothing to hold them back, nothing to which they were anchored; and I was filled with a profound calm. Just before the break of day, I got up and patiently carved the mark of the Zealots on the trunk of the tree to whose bough I had affixed the end of the twine. Then I breathed deeply of the fresh, dew-moist air.

The day dawned cool and overcast. Through the limpid morning hush I could hear roosters crowing in a neighboring village. It was, I thought, a perfect day for the hunt—Quaestoris's and my own. I slipped easily onto my knees, striking an attitude of prayer or meditation, in the event that someone should stumble into the copse and find me. The sun rose, but clouds hid it. Below me, on the road that ran parallel to the defile, two peasants carrying bundles on their shoulders trudged heavily, their legs white with dust. I wondered where they were going, if indeed they had any idea of where they were going: walking so, bent under their loads, they seemed the eternal peasant on his endless way. I knew that with proper handling, they could be turned in any direction one wished for them to go in, and that the man who learned to handle them with skill would have enormous power. Even after they had disappeared from sight, walking southward, they seemed to me to be still on the road: and I could no more banish their image than I could renounce my appetite for authority. I knelt by the tree and waited, though I had not long to wait. Perhaps half an hour later, the first soldiers of Quaestoris's advance guard came into view. They were men of the same elite guard which had ordered me from the area but a short while ago. Two squads of them rode in single file on either side of the passage; a third picked its way along the defile itself. I rose slowly to my feet, stood by the tree, and cautiously unfastened the fisherman's cord that was tied at its other end to the release mechanism of my trap. With extreme care, I pulled it to me, hand over hand, until I felt that it was taut.

The advance guard went by and a full platoon of archers rode into sight, half to one side of the pass and half to the other. Lightly armored lancers rode below them. I rested my hand on the trunk of the tree, reckoning that the envoy would make his appearance soon. He did, riding a spirited chestnut mare and turning to converse with his young "companion," as the company was no longer able to travel side by side or in groups. The boy—he must have been thirteen or fourteen —was, as far as I could make out from my post, exquisite, with pale blond hair; I was certain that Quaestoris enjoyed him thoroughly, in the hundred subtle ways he knew so well and had practiced so long on so many lovers. Even at this distance, I could see that the boy was remarkably beautiful and that the envoy himself looked well: sleek, solid-fleshed, finely groomed and attired in a white-and-gold toga. Though his hair had indeed turned gray—almost white—it was obvious from the way he rode and tossed his head that he had lost the despair which had gripped him when last I had known him, and taken a new lease on life. The advance guard had by now reached the gorge, and the flanking squads ranged themselves back to the archers, who halted. In the distance behind, the first units of the rear guard were forming to move into the defile as into the mouth of a funnel. The envoy was heavily protected in an area known to be "clean" of Zealots, so much I could see, but his protection would avail him nought against my zealous hand. I readied myself for the moment of the strike.

The trap, modeled after Ichavod's well-proven device, had been set with great precision in the branches of a tamarisk that grew out from the right bank of the passage to the gorge; it overhung the defile, and several of its lower limbs had been removed long ago by peasants or farmers in the locality in order to facilitate movement beneath. I was not at all anxious; I was sure of my plan and certain of my ability to carry it out to the letter. The last lancer passed under the tamarisk with its cleverly camouflaged trap. Then the chestnut mare stepped beneath its boughs. With all of my strength, as I had strangled Elazar in the refuse dump, I pulled the stout, near-elastic cord in my hand: in one instant the trap dropped and sprang shut.

An amazing transformation took place: one second there was Quaestoris—the brilliant diplomat, the polished courtier, the venerable scion of a noble family, the heir to fortunes unguessed-at, the veteran servant of emperor and empire, the consummate aesthete, the master artist, the darling of the inner circles of Pilate and Herod alike, the lord of the chessboard, the arch politician, the queller of revolt and rebellion, the lover resurrected in the ardor of his new-found love . . . and the next, a hideous, mutilated monster with arms outflung and flailing, covered with a tide of his blood and spattered with his own gore! The trap had long wooden teeth like needles which had locked his face and neck in their murderous grip. Shouts filled the air—shouts of the soldiers beating their horses and brandishing their weapons in vain. Screams rang out—the screams of the boy whose horse had reared and pivoted, flinging him from his saddle as if he were an insect. Chaos and confusion prevailed. The captain of the escort whipped his horse, turned this way and that, shouted orders that could be heard a mile away, but there were no orders that could overturn or undo what had just happened.

I wanted to remain and watch the little play I had arranged go on, but I well knew my place was elsewhere. I threw down the cord, untethered my mule, leaped on his back and rode rapidly down the rear of the hillock which had been so kind to me and whose hospitable firs I would remember until my dying day. Once at the bottom, I rode away from the copse and then—slowing the mule almost to a walk— moved directly and methodically toward the scene of the catastrophe. My heart was light and singing; I recalled the report of Melech the Galilean to me describing the "massacre in the wadi" that had carried me on its crest to the position of minister of war. As I drew nearer to the mouth of the defile, I saw that the soldiers were bringing Quaestoris out of the pass, his body limp, his head and neck in the loving embrace of the trap. They were carrying the body of the boy as well— either he was unconscious, a prey to shock, or he had been seriously injured in his fall from the horse. My heart was buoyant and my mind chanted praises of Ichavod, whose hand—it seemed—could stretch forth even from beyond the grave. Two soldiers galloped furiously toward me, one of them drawing his broadsword as he came. "Back!" he screamed. "Go back! Turn your nag about and ride away from here!"

I halted the mule. "What has happened here?" I called out.

Breathless and sweating, the troopers rode up to me.

"None of your business!" screamed the first. "Just turn your flea-bitten mule around and get the hell out of here, Jew-priest, before we lose our tempers!"

"Has someone been injured, sir? Perhaps I can be of some assistance."

The first soldier hesitated. He glanced at his companion, who looked me over and said, "Can you heal wounds?"

I nodded. "I have done so many times over in the villages," I said. "But I must examine the wounded man first before I can tell you anything."

"Come along with us," said the second soldier.

And so I rode along behind the two, keeping at a respectful distance and halting when they drew near the knot of cavalrymen gathered about the prostrate forms of the envoy and his tender paramour. The soldiers dismounted, went up to the captain of the escort, and saluted. They spoke eagerly to him, gesturing in my direction. At length, the tall, lean Roman officer with scarred chin, thin lips and pocked cheeks walked up to me, slapping his thigh with his quirt as he came.

"You are a healer of men?" he growled.

"I have healed many a sick man in my day, sir."

"We have a badly wounded man here. Do you think you can help him?"

"With the captain's permission—how did it happen? An animal? A quarrel? If it was a quarrel—I am excellent with sword wounds. Or did he fall from his horse?"

"Follow me, Jew!" said the officer.

I dismounted and did so.

Quaestoris was flat on his back like a whore—sprawled on the earth with arms and legs outflung, almost as if the sod were a crucifix to which he had been pinned. The so-called punishing mechanism of the trap, which the soldiers had cut loose from its frame among the branches of the tamarisk, was clamped tightly over his face and neck. Its teeth, which I had taken great pains to sharpen, had sunk deeply into his flesh. One had entered the left eye; a second had gone into him through

455

his mouth and come out again through its roof and his nose; a third had plunged into the back of his neck at the base of his skull. His throat and chest were sheeted with blood. So were the hands and forearms of the soldiers who bent over him and knelt by his side. Even the boy, lying several yards away, had been spattered. I glanced over at him curiously: he was very beautiful, as delicate as a maiden, and his hair was the color of molten gold.

"He is still alive, your wounded man," I said.

"Yes. He is alive. I did not bring you here to have you tell me that, Jew. I want you to do something. Well, is there anything you can do?"

"What have you done already?"

"We did nothing except bring him up from the defile where the trap sprang upon him as he rode by," said the officer. "We are afraid that if we touch him, he will die. There is a tooth in the back of his neck, just under the skull. We fear that if we move it improperly, it will—"

"I see," I said, bending closer as for a better look.

"Well, can you do something? Can you heal him? Or at least make it possible to move him so that a physician can see him?"

"I can try." I looked directly into the officer's eyes. "It is clear, Captain, that if nothing is done for him, he will die soon."

"I realize that, Jew. That's why I brought you."

"Then there is nothing to lose."

"Nothing."

"I will try, Captain."

"Try."

I stepped over to Quaestoris and knelt. His eyes were staring up, and he did not see me until I was directly over him. Then his one remaining eye gazed up at me through the savage teeth of the trap in which he was caged. The initial instant was one of confusion, of doubt, of incredulous groping—and then in a flash, unmistakable recognition broke in on him. He knew! Yes, he knew! He knew it as clearly as a man knows the hour of his death! His eye wanted to retreat, to crawl back into his socket, to melt and be as blind as its partner. But it could not—it could not! It was locked into my stare, locked into the knowledge of who I was! I imagined for myself how he must feel, what horror there must be in his mind, what fear in his heart! He could not speak, he could not cry out, he could not tell the devoted men of his escort—who would willingly lay down their lives, to the last soldier, for him—who it was that was bending over him! He was in my power, totally in my hands, and there was nothing he could do about it, nothing—not all the might of Rome, not his newly won glory and newly found grace could help him now! How superbly ironic it was: to be at once so close to help and so far away from it, to be lost, utterly lost in the midst of admirers and protectors. The moment was one of supreme triumph for me, and to make the triumph even sweeter, the victim knew it. I hung over him, suspended myself over his helpless form so that he might have a final look at the proportions human hatred could take on before he departed for the world of the dead. Then, bending lower, I stretched my fingers toward the trap. But there was no need for me to touch the long wooden teeth or the victim: I saw clearly that the look of terror in his single, bulging eye had become an eternal one.

"Well," barked the officer. "What the hell are you waiting for? Are you going to treat him or not?"

"It doesn't matter," I said, straightening up.

"Are you insane, Jew? Are all of you people insane? Do you want your mug smashed in? Do you want to be cut up into quarters and sold for meat in one of your filthy Jewish stalls? What is this insolence?"

The officer raised his quirt.

"He's dead," I said, cowering. "He's dead, sir—please don't strike me."

The officer bent forward. "So he is," he murmured. "So he is." And waving his quirt, he began shouting orders to his men, who galloped out at once to comb the area for suspects.

I cleared my throat. "May I—may I pray for his soul, sir?" I asked, turning my eyes piously up to the sky.

The officer spat and turned his head away in disgust. "Save your Jewish vomit for Jewish faces," he snarled. "This face is Roman."

"And the boy, sir? Would you wish me to look at him?"

"Get him out of here!" screamed the captain. "Get him out of here before I slaughter him on the spot!"

The two soldiers who had brought me seized me by the arms and propelled me roughly to my mule; they shoved me up onto its back and then one of them whacked its rump soundly with the flat of his sword: the animal shot forward and broke into a frenetic run. As I rushed by, I heard a trooper shouting, "The Zealots! The Zealots! We've found their mark on the trunk of a tree in that copse. And this cord—it was fastened to a branch . . . "

The voices died away; there was no sound but the rapping of the mule's hooves on the earth. I did not look back. I smiled as I rode, and my heart lifted with untrammeled joy. My plan had worked perfectly, from start to finish, without a single hitch or flaw. I had conceived of it and I had executed it. None had been with me, no one had given me his advice or help. So I wanted it: so it must always be. I must depend on no one in the world but myself: then my power would be boundless and complete. I smiled and then I broke into an open, unrestrained laugh. In one stroke I had settled a score with Rome—Quaestoris . . . and with Jerusalem—the Zealots. So I would continue to settle my scores!

I whipped my mule and in a short time reached the village at the shore of the sea. I went into the fisherman's hut and waited there until darkness fell. Then I roused the old man, who had fallen asleep on his nets, followed him outside, waded into the surf and climbed after him into his skiff. We put out to sea at once and set sail for Acre. The journey was not unpleasant—the sea offered a comfort that land did not. The old man picked his scalp for lice and sang ballads I had never heard. He told endless stories out loud, but they were for himself—not me. It was a shame I must drown him when we reached our port, but nobody must be alive to say where I had gone when the soldiers came asking. The old man smiled his toothless smile and sang to the creaking of the boat while I planned his death.

One last enemy remained: he was my brother. I felt he would be in the Galilee, perhaps in Nazareth, and resolved to find him no matter how long it took. I had enough money to live on comfortably, so I did not have to play the scavenger, and I bought myself a small, modest-looking mare and a staff. Since my brother had often mentioned Nazareth, I went first to that city to seek him out but did not find him. I inquired, and though I did not locate him, discovered that people knew him vaguely. An old hag, whose greed I kindled with a silver coin, told me that she had ministered to the "madman's" wife when the woman was unwell, and that the couple had "gone north."

I set out immediately for Safed and beyond, to secure the aid of my peasant friends to whom I was known as "the man of the mountains." They were overjoyed to "behold my visage" once again, told me that they had missed me sorely, that they had suffered during my absence with "a host of misfortunes" that had come suddenly on them when I departed. I told them that I had been "far off," that I had penetrated "to the very heart of the desert," where while I was asleep on the earth, an "angel had appeared to me in a vision" and brought me the word of God, which was that I "return at once to my friends in the north to bring them aid and succor." They fell upon my neck, embraced me warmly, wept unashamedly and called me their "savior." I spoke to them at length, treated their sick, blessed their flocks and their huts, caressed their children (whom I called "lambs of the Lord") and asked them if perchance they knew of the man I was seeking. I asked them if they had seen or heard of a "madman" who claimed to perform "wonders and miracles like no other man on earth, even to the raising of the dead." A good many of the peasants shook their heads, but it was obvious to me that they were lying for one reason or another—perhaps because they had believed in the words of my brother and felt that by doing so they had betrayed me. Others nodded moodily, explaining that they "knew who the madman was" but that he had gone away and that they "did not know where, as the country was large and could swallow a man as the haystack a needle." Could they ask other people? Could they help me find him? Could they start at once? They nodded and told me they would try and that they hoped they could succeed because they "loved me" as one of their own and wished me the "fulfillment of all my desires."

One of them by the name of Rachamim—a great, swarthy fellow with matted hair and beard who was called "the ox" because of his enormous strength and his limitless patience in the face of adversity—said that he had heard of the "madman" only a few weeks ago: someone —he did not exactly remember who, but he was certain he would— had told him about an incident in which the "madman" had fed a "large crowd of people" from a single basket of food out of which poured an unending supply. Rachamim, who was known and respected as an eminently practical fellow and a man of keen intelligence, finished recounting the tale with a shrug.

"But this sort of nonsense is heard every day," he said. "And it is never true. It is simply what people want to hear, what they wish to be true. Today, it happened to a neighbor, a friend, an acquaintance. Tomorrow they hope it will happen to them—the fools!"

"But people believe such stories nevertheless," I said.

"They believe what they want to believe," said Rachamim. "Which does not make what they believe any truer."

"The 'madman,' " I said. "He has many followers?"

"Somebody leads," said Rachamim, "others follow. That's the way of the world. Surely you know that?"

"Have you ever seen this man perform the miracles that are spoken of in the stories about him?"

Rachamim bent double with laughter. "Of course!" he sputtered, wiping tears of merriment from his eyes. "Of course I have! That's why he's so rich and well-fed and why his adherents are so reputable!" Rachamim looked soberly at me. "As I told you before, I don't know exactly how many are his adherents or disciples—or whatever he calls them—but any man, let me tell you, who promises relief from pain, who promises the end of despair, who promises an easier or better or saner life—without any real cost—will have his admirers."

"He convinces others when he speaks, does he?"

"His voice is pleasant and his manner—soothing. I have heard that he tells tales that lower the heavens and raise the powers of hell! He can bewitch willing souls, that he can! Some even call him Messiah. But they are the same people who last year or only last month called a jackass the Messiah!" Rachamim stroked his beard. "As for myself, I think that Messiah is like the carrot that one dangles before the poor, exhausted donkey."

"You were yourself not convinced by him?"

The ox snickered. "Me, convinced? I should as soon be convinced by a snake charmer or a sorcerer!"

"Can you find out for me where the man is now?"

"I can. Of course I can. But what do you want the fellow for? Does he owe you money?"

I patted his broad shoulder. "God has spoken to me of him," I said.

"Well, if God Himself has spoken to you of him," said Rachamim, "then I must find him by all means, mustn't I?" He shook his huge head.

"Though it's strange that God did not see fit to tell you Himself where the fellow is."

A week later, Rachamim found me in a little woods I visited often. I was sitting on a tree stump, engaged in solving a chess problem I had posed for myself—it was the first time I had put the set I had fashioned during the last few days to use.

"I didn't know that priests played games." The ox smiled.

"This is not the game of chess as you may know it."

"Isn't it?"

"No, my friend," I said. "Most certainly not. This is a struggle I am working out: a struggle between body and soul, flesh and spirit, Satan and God, evil and good, past and future, death and life."

Rachamim smiled and stroked his beard. "I'm certain it is as you say."

"Well—do you have news for me?"

"One could say that I have news."

"Some information?"

Rachamim nodded.

"Then speak! Tell me!"

"It's not that simple."

"What do you mean, not that simple? Why isn't it simple? Tell me what you know!"

Rachamim rolled his eyes. "Heaven," he said, "is without cost. All know that. But on earth . . . well, on earth it's a different story. And since I see . . . with my sharp eyes that you have become a rich priest—well . . . "

I smiled, drew out my purse and took two coins from it; I pressed them into Rachamim's palm and he put them into his cloak without looking at them.

Rachamim sighed. "He's up at the Sea of Galilee. At Capernum."

I set out that very day. On the way, I inquired of the "madman" of the peasants and farmers. Some gave me blank stares, but others were willing to talk, especially if I stimulated conversation with a coin or two. As I traveled, I heard a good number of stories, since it seemed my brother had been in the area for quite a while and had acquired a reputation of sorts. Some of the peasants smiled and tapped their foreheads or their skulls when they spoke of him; some had seen him or heard of him but were indifferent and could give little information;

some talked but were careful about what they said, fearing that I was some kind of a government agent out to entrap them; some seemed to be fearful of my brother himself, whom they referred to as the man "smitten by God" or the "man with the wind of God inside his head"; some praised him as a "gentle soul" or "good spirit"; and there were some who were altogether in awe of him and called him "God's anointed messenger" or "the angel of God on earth."

I reached Capernum at midafternoon. I asked for the "madman" and was told that I might find him at the synagogue, where he had been preaching for the past several days. I went to it immediately and found it to be a handsome structure by the shore of the Galilee. The sun shone brightly, and one could see the cheerful blue waves of the inland sea glittering all about as if someone had showered down fistfuls of silver coins upon them from above. A wide flight of stairs led up to the main entrance of the synagogue, and my brother was standing at their midpoint. Above him stood several priests and officials robed in black; they seemed alternately bored and amused by my brother's remarks. To their left, leaning against the end columns, were two of Herod's internal police officers; they wore looks of patent disgust on their faces, as if they were being subjected to a routine they had been through many times before in the past. There was a group of people at the bottom of the steps listening to my brother speak, perhaps twenty or thirty in number. I spotted the woman whom I "had joined" to my brother in prison among them—she looked better than when I had last seen her, tanned by the sun and roughened by exposure to the weather, poor but fit. Her belly had swelled, and it was apparent to me that she was pregnant. A strange feeling came over me, and for some moments I could not remove my eyes from her round, ripe stomach. Long ago, before I had attained to the age of seven, my mother's belly had looked so. I recalled the time clearly and felt horror, sadness and rage within me before I was able to take my eyes from the sight. The woman was gazing up at my brother—who was obviously the father of her unborn child—lost in his words and oblivious to all else. She hung on every syllable that came forth from my brother's mouth, as if God Himself were speaking to her.

My brother had changed appreciably in appearance. It was more than the fact that his prison pallor was gone and that the gaunt look of the dungeon had left him; there seemed to be a certain calmness or peace about him that had never displayed itself before. The hysteria that had always wrapped about him like an invisible cocoon had gone —or was not at present discernible. He was thin and hungry-looking, but he was clean—dressed in a patched robe—and well-groomed, as if somebody paid attention to his bodily needs. His head was bare, even in the strong sun, and he was clad in worn sandals which had on them the fine white dust of the summer roads. His head was turned a little to one side—as if he were straining to catch words that came only to him—and he was speaking slowly in a soft but remarkably clear voice that carried for a considerable distance. He was, as I gathered, expounding on the Law, on the relationship of man to God, whom he referred to as his "holy Father in heaven," and on the duties and responsibilities "men had to the Holy One, blessed be He." The speech was even in tone and delivery, erratic in nature and content. Some of it could be understood, given a certain religious point of view, but most of it was what I chose to call "visionary gibberish." I had heard some of parables and stories my brother recounted before, when I had visited him in the prison in Herod's fortress; other tales he told and examples he cited were new to me. One thing was clear: the speaker was in love with what he had to say—there was enormous pleasure, even relief, for him as the sentences came rushing out from some inexhaustible source that he alone could tap. His eyes, seemingly larger and brighter than ever before, rolled upwards frequently, his nostrils dilated, his jaw quivered, his arms swung out in wide circles and figures. Lost to all and to everything but the voice that called out "from above," as he described it, he rambled on, digressed, discoursed—fitting parable into parable until one sometimes had the feeling one had toppled headlong into a bottomless well—drew parallels and developed analogies that often disappeared in the complexity and convolutedness of obscure and esoteric references that it seemed he could not do without. His speech seemed without beginning and without end, as if it could start and stop anywhere, at any time—nor did he particularly care where and when. It was as if he watered a garden which brought forth weeds—and now and again a flower. It did not appear that he distinguished, or even desired in the least to distinguish, between the two. All of these things were true, but there was something else as well: he had imagination and he had feeling.

And I also saw that his audience sensed as much and listened raptly to what he had to say. When they could not understand him, they reckoned it as their lack; when they had difficulty following him, they blamed themselves. I saw that the idle hangers-on, the brazenly curious, the mockers and the hecklers had all left long before, and that those who remained were utterly serious. I looked them over: peasants, farmers, fisherman, a merchant or two. I was fascinated by them. They stood open-mouthed and wide-eyed as my brother spoke, suffering under the blazing sun, the sweat standing forth in great beads on their skulls and foreheads and dripping down their faces and necks. Flies and gnats bit them, mosquitoes from the rushes on the shore plagued them without letup, the soldiers above them gave them black looks of scorn and annoyance, the priests stared contemptuously down on them: but it made absolutely no difference to them—they stood in a group as if transfixed, as if locked in a prison cell by a jailer without force of arms. What held them so? What spell were they thrall to? Why did my brother and his often patently deranged words have such an effect on them? What strange power had he put into operation? What was their hunger to believe, their thirst to give credence? I watched their eyes, their lips, their hands, their feet carefully. There was no denying it: nonsense or not, chimera or no, absurdity or fact: they did believe. "The ox" had told me that they believed because "they wanted to believe." But it was more than that: they believed because my brother made them want to believe. I observed their every response, every reaction. They had faith in my brother. They loved him. They worshiped him. They would have fought for him, bled for him, died for him. There was a bond between speaker and listeners. A bond greater than any I had ever seen. These listeners were slaves to my brother as Melech the Galilean, Onan, Akrab and Elazar had been slaves to me. These listeners existed only in my brother as my servants had existed only in me. Except that when my servants died, there was nothing left. And when these servants died— there would be something left. What was it? I knew, of course. It was the word. The word that survived famine and pestilence, fire and sword, battle and massacre. It was that which I had come to realize was the ultimate and indestructible source of power: the undying Word . . .

An hour passed and still my brother talked—as diffuse as his speech was, it grew still more chaotic and disorganized; his face turned pale and his cheeks became hollow. As I watched, the whole structure of his face seemed to sag, almost to break, and he took on the look of a man in a trance: and as he withered, so did his listeners wither as well, at times groaning aloud and weeping. The hysteria which I had felt was gone now surfaced, but though it came from the speaker it did not appear to be within him—it was instead a kind of tension which built up between my brother and his audience, a nerve-straining atmosphere that was the result of one force acting upon the other and that I felt could not swell beyond a certain point without bursting. Perhaps the authorities felt this as well, for I saw the priests turn their heads to the soldiers and nod; the soldiers did not waste an instant but moved at once down the stairs, and taking my brother by his arms, moved him down to the bottom. The crowd murmured disapproval, but my brother raised a hand and all grew quiet. The listeners, rubbing their eyes as if waking from sleep, milled around and then dispersed. My brother, together with the woman and an odd, bedraggled lot of men, trudged slowly southward in the waning light of afternoon. I knew I would easily be able to overtake them, since I was on horseback, and stayed behind to make inquiry.

"Excuse me," I said to one of the soldiers. "I'm a stranger in these parts—hailing from Hebron myself—and I happened to overhear part of what this—preacher-fellow was saying. May I ask how the government allows such speeches to be made?"

The guard who answered was a surly corporal. "Though it's none of your affair, and though you'd do better to meddle with the problems of God and not of men, I shall take the time and trouble to reply—not that you deserve it!" He winked to his partner and then said to me, "If we had to arrest every maniac who opens his mouth in this country, one-half of the population would end up watching the other in jail! That bird's so harmless that even the flies bite him as he speaks—"

"But those who listen to him?"

"They pass the time of day that way, no more—"

"But those who went with him?"

"A pack of beggars and charlatans! Drifters . . . scum . . . riffraff: the kind it's not worth locking up because you have to feed them and keep a roof over their lousy heads!" He laughed. "We let him hang about here with his gang for a few days, but this afternoon we closed the circus and sent them all packing."

"And you will not follow them?"

"Only the field mice and the starlings will follow them—to pick up the crumbs they drop." The corporal stared at me coldly. "Why so many questions? Are you a spy?"

"If I were a spy, would I turn to the police for information?"

"Well spoken, my clever-tongued priest! But save your jokes for your Heavenly Father! Those on earth may not see much point to them, if you get my meaning!"

I bowed my head and backed away. The guards watched me for a few moments and then sauntered away. I waited until they were out of sight and then entered the synagogue, where the priests were busy with their affairs. One of them—a stout, bald man with bushy brows and a bulbous nose—came up to me immediately.

"What is it you wish?" he said in a tone of extreme annoyance. "We have no positions here, there is no shelter for you, and we haven't enough food to take care of our own!"

"Just a few words with you."

"Make it short, then—we have work to do here: the synagogue does not run on prayers, you know!"

"That fellow—"

"What fellow?"

"The one who spoke on the steps."

"What about him?"

"How does the priesthood allow him to speak?"

"What does it matter what he says? He speaks as does the wind into the void."

"But some of his ideas—they contradict the Law. How is this permitted?"

"The Law is the Law. Nothing can add to or detract from it. We cannot concern ourselves with the drivel of every fool: if we did, we would have time for nothing else."

"But there are those who listen to him!"

"There are those who listen to the woodpecker and the cuckoo. What are we supposed to do about it?"

"But there are those who walk with him, who follow him. I saw them myself. What about them?"

"Those who would follow him are better off with him than with us. We have no use for drifters . . . idlers . . . mountebanks."

"But the Law must suffer," I said. "The Law must suffer by his words."

"The Law is a fortress," said the priest, turning away so that I knew he was finished with me. "The Law can withstand any attack. Surely the Law will not trouble itself over a flea, a gnat, a moth."

"But if he is a termite, or a locust?" I said. "What then?"

But the priest had disappeared into the gloom of the synagogue. An old sexton shuffled up to me. "May I show you the way out?" he said.

"I suppose so."

"It's this way."

I overtook my brother and his party just at sunset. They were on the road that skirted the Sea of Galilee, walking south from Capernum in the direction of Tiberias. The air was sultry, stifling, as if we were breathing a stagnant residue—that which had been used over and over before. The sea seemed thick and sullen, its surface lit dully by the dying sun. A great flock of starlings passed overhead, dwindling rapidly into motes of dust and vanishing in the distance. I slowed my mare to a walk and followed the party without addressing it until the sun went down and it left the road to sit at the foot of three barren date trees. I halted my horse and looked the group over. It was comprised of my brother, the woman with the baby in her belly, and eleven men, each of whom had one thing in common with the next: the stamp of self-willed thralldom.

I sat in my saddle silently as the vast bowl of the sky darkened and the first star of evening rose. From the shore of the inland sea, I could hear the ceaseless lapping of the waves. Objects, I thought, what were objects? In their false infinitude, they inevitably turned out the same. They were inexhaustibly pursuable, yet in the end what did they bring a man? A great mound of junk, like the pyramids of stone built in vain by witless Egyptian Pharaohs, for when the Pharaoh died what did his stones matter to the men who came after? Would they be moved by those futile stone dung piles? Would they be swayed, influenced, commanded? What would the stone say to them except that it was stone? What could the size of the pile say to them except its mindless size? And who, seeing nature, would not laugh at this miserable fecal offering of mummies long ago turned to dust not unlike the stone that sat above their sarcophagi? No, endlessly multiplied objects could not bring real power to a man: he could not even keep track of them, let alone put them to use. The real power lay not in matter—but in spirit. If one could capture the spirits of other men—that was booty worth having! I gazed over the faces that ranged in a semicircle around my brother, who sat cross-legged and relaxed, his back against the trunk of the tallest date tree. A fire had been kindled and the faces seemed to have been shaped out of the darkness by its ruddy hands. How the eyes shone greedily with awe, as if they could not get enough of their leader, as if they would devour him if they could! But how did one devour the spirit which held one enslaved? One submitted to it . . . allowed oneself to be impregnated by it! A woman and eleven men. Each one of them had been infected by the spirit of my brother: each one of them carried him within as a disease! Each of them would go out in turn and infect others with the disease! I marveled at the prospect. Imagine an army of such people—a vast army of them spreading the disease! I had said "termite" or "locust" to the priest in the synagogue, and I meant it: such termites could undermine the most impregnable of forts, such locusts could wipe away the growth of centuries! The woman had been cooking something in a battered earthenware vessel and now she ceased stirring, removed the vessel from the flames, and with her spoon began to apportion it among the half-circle of men; each had a wooden or a clay plate which he thrust forward. She had wanted to serve the "master"—my brother—first, but he had shaken his head and only after all, including the woman, had been given their ration did he hold out his own dish. There was little of the mush, or porridge left, but he smiled to receive it and his face, now weary and lined, was wreathed in the steam that rose from his plate. How clever! How brilliant! What a gambit! The gentle smile of the man who had waited until last to be served his portion and who had received least for his patience cast its spell on each member of the group: one and all they were caught and held fast in his invisible net! I nudged my mare's flank and turned it from the road to Tiberias; slowly I rode toward the campfire.

"Weary travelers," I called out in my warmest, most ingratiating voice. "Good evening! May I join your beneficent company?"

My brother shared his food with me—as I knew he would do. I sat next to him and ate; the woman was on his other side. In the dim, uneven light of the small fire, I did not expect to be recognized immediately by the "master." But I was

468

wrong. After the introductions to his followers, which were—in my brother's style—tortuously long and involved, treating with individual life histories, God, angels, creation and apocalypse, and the meal, which was brief because there was little to eat, and grace, which my brother intoned after his own manner, the "master" drew me aside into the night.

"It is good to meet you again, my brother."

"What are you saying? I'm not your brother."

"You are my first brother."

"I don't know what you're talking about."

"Don't pretend. There is no use in pretending. I know you." The "master's" voice dropped to a whisper: "But you needn't worry—I shan't reveal your identity to anyone. It will remain with me and with me alone. It will be our secret and ours alone, so long as you wish it to be so."

"How did you recognize me? It has been a long time. It is dark. And my appearance has altered. How do you know me?"

"It is your voice, my brother. I would know it anywhere."

"But you have not heard it for so long a time."

My brother laughed quietly. "You're wrong. I heard it always in my dreams. And even when I am awake and there is silence around me, I hear it speaking to me. Do you understand?"

"I do."

"I knew—that one day we would meet again. I knew that it—had to be so."

"I see."

"And how have you fared, my king?"

"I am no king. You must never call me that!"

"And how has your life gone, my emperor?"

"I am no emperor. You must never say it!"

"As you wish, brother. It shall be as you wish. But tell me about yourself . . ."

"There is nothing to tell. Life has buffeted me, life has beaten me, life has tried to force me out of its pastures. I have suffered, I have fainted, I have bled. But I have endured."

"And what is it that you seek, brother?"

"I seek peace."

"And what more?"

"Nothing more."

"Not money . . . nor land . . . nor women . . . nor domination: not any of these?"

"None of them."

My brother put his lips close to my ear. "Not even the kingdoms you have lost?"

"Not the kingdoms I have—abandoned."

"Then you truly seek peace?"

"Yes, I truly seek peace."

My brother was silent. I could hear the lapping of the waves. Then he said, "I seek peace as well."

"I know. I heard you discourse on the steps of the synagogue."

"Did you hear my words?"

"I did."

"Did you comprehend their meaning?"

"Yes! Oh, yes, I did!"

"That is excellent," said my brother. "Excellent. As men seek some- one they can understand . . . so I seek those who will understand me." His long fingers lighted like moths on my shoulder. "Would you . . . will you . . . can you consider—?" Like some insect blown off by a wind, his voice sailed away, though his hand continued to rest on me.

"Consider what?" I said.

"Consider joining me. Consider following me where I go. Consider serving me . . . and God who sends me to men on earth."

"What does it mean to follow you?"

"It means to seek peace, as you said you wanted."

"But how?"

"I don't know. I cannot tell the end of things because . . . because the road curves, brother, and I cannot see around the bend yet." And here the "master" lapsed into a monologue concerning the destiny of man and authority of God, a swamp from which I believed he would not be able to extricate himself. Then suddenly, as mysteriously as he had begun, he stopped—almost in midsentence. "Will you join me, brother, will you join with me even if you do not know the end?"

"Yes," I said quietly. "Yes, I will."

My brother sighed. "God be praised! The name of God be praised!"

"God be praised," I echoed.

"You will complete the circle," said my brother.

"Complete the circle?"

"Twelve," said my brother.

"Twelve?"

"Twelve men with souls," said my brother. "With you, the circle is closed—as I dreamed it."

"What did you dream?"

"Six and six," said my brother in a singsong voice: "Six and six." He clasped his knees with his hands and began to rock as an infant rocks in the crib. "Six and six," he sang. "Two arcs of the circle . . . two arcs that converge." His voice took on a strange quality, almost the quality of an animal bereft of its young: "I dreamed there were six angels in one arc around the Throne of Glory and six about the other— except that one place was empty, one link was missing. And God, who sat upon the Throne of Glory spoke to me, saying: 'Wherefore is the circle not closed? Where is the twelfth?' And I said, 'Do not worry, Father, for the twelfth will come.' And God said, 'When?' And I replied, 'Soon, Father, for he is on the way.' And God smiled and all the heavens shone and God said, 'That is good, the circle will be closed.' And that was my dream not more than a night ago, brother, and I dreamed it before we quit Capernum." He left off singing and said, "You have come along and made the dream come true. And God is pleased—pleased that at last the circle will be closed." And he knelt on the earth and said, "Pray with me, brother."

"But I know not how."

"You would never pray with me when I asked you in the prison; you said you would not—do you remember?"

"I remember. But I have changed. I will pray with you now if you but show me how."

"You walk about as a priest and you cannot pray? How is that?"

"Oh, I can pray conventionally. That is not what I mean. Show me how it is that you pray—master." The word "master" was strange to my tongue—I had never before used it. It was strange to me, utterly foreign—and yet it was good. It was good to say "master": I knew now why so many sought only to use it, to yield up their souls as lambs to a slaughter, to surrender themselves completely. It gave them the perverse pleasure of denying existence, of avoiding life. "Show me . . . show me, my master."

And so my brother prayed, babbling and mumbling every sort of drivel. And I knelt beside him and faithfully, almost like an echo, repeated the inanities and the absurdities. And when we had finished, my brother clasped my head in his sweating palms and kissed my cheeks and said, "So, my servant, has your heart attained to peace?"

And I said, "My heart is washed clean of sin. I have peace."

And we wept together and were silent together, and in the stillness I heard the waves lapping ceaselessly on the shore, ceaselessly on the shore—as if they truly knew the secret of peace but would never reveal it.

And so my new life began, my life as a "disciple" of the "master." Wherever he chose to lead me, there—together with the other eleven of his followers, and of course, the woman—I went. And the woman was swollen with child and it was difficult for her to walk as we did so I gave her my mare that she might ride and I walked behind, and the "master" said that my heart was as a "goblet of gold that brimmed over with the rarest of wines— compassion" and in my humility I bowed my head and said that I was "unworthy" of such praise, that I crawled over the earth as an infant and had "a long way to go" before I could rise up and walk like a man.

And we were in Samaria when the woman's time came and she lay in a field by the road and was in heavy labor. And all that day, in the heat of the sun, on the dust of the earth that was mother to us all, she labored and when evening came she had not yet given birth. And the "master" cried out to God to ease her pain and let her child come forth and be a part of the world, and we knelt and prayed with him, but when the night had passed and the dawn came again and the roosters crowed—still she was not delivered of her burden. And the "master" beat his breast and cried out, "Bitter! Bitter! Let the child come forth, Lord, for it is bitter to me that the woman labors so and suffers so!" But his cries and our prayers availed not and the woman grew weaker and thrashed about in the weeds and in the dung of the earth. At noon the woman gasped and vomited up the water we gave to her and fainted, and the "master," when he saw what had happened, frothed at the mouth like a mad dog and struck himself and lashed out at others and had to be restrained forcibly until at length he too fell into a stupor. But then the farmer came and asked us what we were doing in his field, and the others were silent and abashed but I spoke up and told him that the woman would surely die if he did not help. And he sent for a midwife, and the midwife came and sponged the woman's forehead and breasts and the woman revived; then the midwife used her art, and toward the evening of that day the woman labored mightily and gave birth. But the child was a monster, such as no one—not even the midwife herself—had seen in all his days; and it was dead. The "master" was awake, and we showed him the stillborn child and he cried out, "The devil!" and foamed again at his mouth and lapsed into a coma. And the midwife went away and we buried the child in the field and the farmer said, "Pay me for the field and so that I can pay the midwife." So I gave him of the coins I had. When the "master" came to once again, the woman told him what I had done and how I had paid the farmer, and the master said to me, "You are the dearest of all to me, you are as of my own flesh." And I said once more, "I am not worthy of such words, but one day I will be." Then the "master" said that he would flagellate himself to "purge from his flesh the evil" that had produced the monster, and he stripped himself in a nearby woods and cut a sapling for a rod and beat himself until he was bloody—and we did the same and the woman, though she was weak, did it also. Then the "master," who was "not satisfied at all" at the punishment he had decided upon for himself, took up the knife with which the woman cut the bread and the meat, such as we had, and said he would cleanse himself of "the devil who produced the monster," that he would "purge himself of sex!" Had I not prevented him by force, he would have done to his body what Nahum had done in the sheepfold so many years ago. But all of it passed, as an episode, a dream—and the child, whom the "master" had called "*Mar-mareh*," or bitter-of-appearance, was never mentioned again by him or by the woman or by any of the other disciples.

So our life of wandering continued. In one of the cities which we visited in our journeying, I secured for myself writing materials and began once more, after an interruption of so long a time and so many events, to keep my journals. I observed my brother constantly, watched his every movement, knew each of his habits, kept track of his ruminations and visions, which seemed to me to be daydreams, recorded his sermons and preachments, and set down the conversations we had together. The "master" was pleased that I did so and said that it was a blessed day "when the circle was closed" with my presence and a "blessed act" when I took up the pen "to describe for all men and for posterity" the "wonders and miracles" that unfolded to him, "day by sun-haunted day . . . and night by star-teeming night." I kept my records carefully and guarded them jealously, for I knew they would be of indispensable use to me in my plan. For as we wandered, the plan was taking shape within me, and I was certain that one day I would put it into effect with undiluted and unhampered success. My brother—the "master"— was the key element in the plan: about him and his life all the rest would turn. I had realized—at first instinctively, and as time went on, more and more consciously—that my brother was the symbol and the vehicle I needed. In order that he would serve my needs, I pretended to serve him.

My brother, I had decided, would be the flesh in which I enclosed my word, and when his flesh perished, the Word would go forth. It was perfect: my brother had infected the spirits of his followers with his own, and I would use him as my agent with which to infect others, others beyond count and beyond number. As the days passed by, as the weeks flew and then the months, as our band wandered from village to village, town to town, farm to farm, as we traveled the highways and the back roads, speaking to peasants and sleeping in fields and ditches, I worked on the details of my plan. I thought everything out carefully, meticulously, thoroughly—yet always objectively, always disinterestedly, as if I were working out an abstract chess problem—and came to the conclusion that I had been working on such a scheme all the days of my life. The spirit was as prone to disease as was the body; all I had needed was a disease virulent enough and an infecting agent effective enough. Now I reckoned that I had both. I had a religious disease that could infect the world and a man through whom I could infect it.

There came a night when all the rest of them slept, and I alone was awake. As a brand that is lit by feverish fingers, I burned with the ideas that stirred within me. I left our little camp by the shore, left the "master" locked in his woman's hot, fatty arms, left the disciples in their soiled, tattered clothes and went barefoot down to where the Sea of Galilee bit into the land. Above me, the stars seemed to flit about like fireflies; to the east, the shapes of the mountains were like the giant black hulks of ships; under my feet the mud oozed as I walked; and in front of me the waves greeted my arrival with shimmering points of reflected starlight.

The Jewish God, I thought, was invisible, intangible. He was far too removed, far too remote from the suffering of men. He demanded a certain form in men's lives—and yet He Himself was formless; He demanded from men that they have a certain inner substance, and yet of what substance was He? He demanded too much and gave too little; His punishments were many and His rewards few. He was finicky, harassing, inflexible in His commands, exhausting in His statutes. Though He was purported to be everywhere, one could neither see nor feel nor hear Him: a man could not shed hot tears on Him in grief nor kiss Him ecstatically in joy. It seemed to me that His Everywhere turned into Nowhere. On the other hand, though the Roman gods were visible, they were too obviously lifeless, too patently without connection to life. It was quite evident that Roman gods were no more than playthings, fantasies made real by the imagination of writers and poets and by the skill of artists and artisans: they were fraudulent, pretentious, willful, capricious—too much the mirror of man's appetites and insanities. While the Jewish God was modeled on a strength men felt that they could never attain, the Roman gods were patterned on weaknesses that men resented as their own.

What I proposed to do was to invent a new god who would combine the merits of the Jewish God and the Roman gods, while eliminating the flaws of each. That men needed a god desperately, I knew: each day I lived verified that conclusion anew. For a god was the chief of all chiefs, the monarch of all monarchs, the master of all masters: a god was the ultimate opportunity for a man to yield up his self in unquestioning sacrifice. It mattered not why, nor what, nor to which end—the sacrifice was itself the act of importance! Yes, a god was the lord of all creation, the supreme excuse for the abandonment of the self, the power that relieved men of the responsibility for handling actions and coping with events they could not explain. What I wanted was a god who was nearer men, a god men could see and feel, a god who was close to their fear and their lust and their pride, a god who was a god—and was yet human! It was a revolutionary concept—and yet it was the right one, the perfect one, the one I had been searching for all along. I wanted a god who bled, who gasped, who cried, who caressed, who ate and drank and slept, a god who lived as men lived and died as men died—and yet was immortal. I wanted a god who would be at once direct and simple and esoteric and mysterious, a god who would be pursued hotly by superstitious hearts and scheming minds, a god who would stimulate and condone the worst in man—without his knowing it. I wanted a god who would be subtle enough to dupe men and wise enough to let them know they had been duped, a god who could play games with men and allow them to win every once in a while. I wanted a god who would conquer through humility, terrify through sorrow, command through passivity: a god who would spill his blood for man so that he could rise over man, a god who would die on earth so that he could live in heaven. I wanted a god-man who had the power of the word, *my* word; more than that, I wanted a man-god who would *be* the power of the Word. I wanted a god who would be willing to merge with man in order to subjugate man—much in the same way that I had joined with my brother in order to subjugate him. The Jewish God, though He kept a watchful eye, left far too much to man; the Roman gods, in their perversity and arrogance, turned their backs on man altogether. I wanted a god who would slowly, slowly creep into men's bones and cause them to ache and to rot, a god who would seethe like an asp in the depths of men's hearts, a god who would twist men's minds so that they would devour others and themselves without reason, a god who would clothe himself in men's basest fears and desires. I wanted a god who knew and understood and would thrive and wax mighty on guilt, as the buzzard gorges himself on rotting flesh. Of the two kingdoms —man's sanity and man's insanity—I chose the latter on which to build my empire, the latter as the fertile soil for my seed: my god would have to rise from it as the mist of the morning. I had decided that my real conquest, my real power lay in man's weakness, not in his strength, and that there was no weakness greater than that within him. If there were constants that I could rely on in man, they were his fear, his dread, his lust, his superstition, his vanity, his greed, his brutality, his boundless hypocrisy. My god must be suited to these traits. Man did not need a god who walked upright: he deserved one who bent his back and crawled on his belly through the swamps. His god must not revel in the joy of life and exult: he must wallow in life's sorrow and weep eternally. Men were awaiting a god who was created in their own image, and I would supply him: a suffering, sorrowful, tortured god—a god who in his own abject self-immolation would seduce the will of man into seducing itself, and by doing so vanquish all. My brother's life—or to be more accurate, my brother's death—would provide the myth from which my god would be born. For as man is born of woman, so I believed gods to be born of myth. As the "master's" woman had labored in the field and brought forth a monster, so would I labor and bring forth one as well—but mine would live!

I was with my brother and his followers for a little more than a year, during which time we traveled through a good part of the country, especially in the Galilee, which my brother loved and was wont to call his "pasture," or sometimes smilingly, "God's meadow." The year had passed swiftly—sometimes it seemed to me but a day. I had just observed my fortieth birthday, and my brother was thirty-three. I had worked out every facet of my plan and was ready to put it into practice. But in order to live, the plan required my brother's death. A living man could be a living god only when he was dead, only when the legends about him could take hold in men's turbulent imaginations and troubled hearts.

At this time we were just outside of Bethlehem, where we had been encamped for more than week, primarily because the woman was unwell and could not go on. Unfortunately, the mare had been lamed several months back; I had wanted to kill her but my brother had forbidden it, instructing me instead to let her go free. I told him that she would die anyway, but my brother said it "was none of our affair, but belonged only to the horse and God." He said that when God wanted the mare, "He would beckon her to Him." We had been in a little forest outside the city, but a group of farmers had come and threatened us. We told them that the woman was ill, but they would not hear and said that they would "come at us themselves with pitchforks and scythes" or else summon the men of Herod's constabulary, who would "soon make the woman well" and the rest of us very uncomfortable.

We moved onward and found ourselves in a small valley that was familiar to me: it was the very same valley which lay at the foot of mountain where our village was located—the village in which my brother and I had been born. When evening came and all was still, I could hear the dogs barking from the houses furtherest down the slope. I rose and went alone across the valley and to the road that led upwards. A jackass brayed, I thought I heard the voices of children, and then there was silence; I stood for a time, recalling the past as if it were a dream, and then returned to our camp. All were asleep, worn out with our endless journeying, except my brother. I could sense that he was awake and went over to him.

"Do you know this valley?" I asked.

"I've passed through it several times before, yes."

"But is it an intimate place for you? After all, you were born in this area, were you not?"

"I was. In Bethlehem. But I never came to this valley as a child. Or to the neighboring village on the mountain. For some strange reason, my father never allowed it—I don't really know why."

"Your parents—they are dead, are they not?"

My brother nodded. "Yes, my parents have left this sinkhole of a world for the kingdom of heaven. My mother, Mara, went first, and my father, Yosef, followed, not more than a few months after her. I went to Nazareth to seek them out after I was released from prison and learned of their deaths at the time. I mourned bitterly for them until the Lord visited me in a dream and gave me assurance that they were well among His host, secure and peaceful in His holy bosom."

"I see."

My brother leaned his head back against the cypress tree—the last one in a long windrow separating the meadow we were in from a citrus grove. Beside him, his woman was asleep—the breath coming hoarsely from her chest. My brother coughed, and weak from the spasm, held his head in his hands.

"Have you considered my proposal?" I asked.

If my brother heard me at all, he did not answer. He looked haggard, weary, almost as ill as his woman. Things had been going badly with us during the past few months. Few listened with interest to my brother's sermons, fewer still gave us food or clothing or shelter. If anything, the political climate had worsened. The harassment we had always been subject to, off and on, had intensified. New edicts restricting movement, speech, currency, dress and the like were issued almost on a daily basis by Herod or by Pilate or even at times by the priesthood, which I understood from conversations as we wandered had greatly increased its influence on the government since my departure as minister of war. Several times in the last two months or so, when my brother had preached of the "Kingdom of God not of this earth" and the "absolute salvation of the immortal soul"—ideas which I had knowingly and methodically injected him with in our discussions—we came very close to arrest. Only my soft looks, my well-modulated, ingratiating voice, and the words I carefully chose to mollify, flatter, and placate the soldiers saved us from imprisonment and corporal punishment. And there were several occasions when the utmost of my efforts proved to no avail, and I was compelled to draw the police officials aside and in secret press silver coins into their sweaty palms. The strain of the constant interference by the authorities, the rigors of our itinerant life, and the woman's illness were telling on my brother. Of late, I found him steadily more incoherent, more irritable and more than ever prey to the lapses of memory, spasms and seizures to which he was subject. I therefore considered the time ripe for a major step forward in the execution of my plan, and had in this connection suggested to the "master" that we go to Jerusalem—where he had never dared go—and that he preach openly there from the steps of the Holy Temple. It was this proposal to which I now referred. My brother heard what I said and smiled wearily.

"Yes," he said. "I have given your proposal thought."

"Do you find it has merit?"

"It has merit."

"Then why, master, do you wait? Why do you postpone what must be? Master, forgive me for my directness, but what are we now but empty wind blowing in the wilderness? Our voices are lost . . . Our message is lost . . . Our holy mission goes unheralded, unrecognized, unknown. God, in His infinite goodness and mercy, has sent you to earth that you may announce the coming of His holy kingdom . . . that you may redeem the erring sons of man who are blindly lost in their iniquity. But who hears you? Who understands your word? Who pays heed to what you have to tell? How can you expect your heavenly doctrine to take root on earth if it does not reach the sinners it was meant for?"

My brother sighed and held up his hand. "Patience," he said. "Those who follow me must have patience."

"Patience?" I cried out. "What patience? Has not patience turned itself into lethargy, into paralysis? If the fruit be ripe and a man's hand not reach out to pluck it from the bough, will not the fruit drop to the ground and decay? You yourself, master, have said many times over that 'the hour missed . . . is an affront to God!' You yourself have commanded that men not turn their faces and their hands from the hour

479

for action that calls to them. Why do you then delay? Why do you procrastinate? Why do you—as you yourself have phrased it—'stand upon the shore and yet not enter the sea'? I urge you, master, I implore you. As your faithful and loyal servant, I cast myself and my service—as unworthy and insignificant as they are—at your feet! I urge you to harken unto my voice. Jerusalem is the capital. Jerusalem is the jewel. Jerusalem is the holy nest. From Jerusalem 'goeth forth the Law.' The word from Jerusalem reaches to the ends of the empire . . . to the corners of the earth! The sacred Temple of Solomon is as the highest mountaintop from whose exalted crest all men will be able to hear you! Well do you know, my master, that the world writhes in an agony of evildoing, that the shadows of disease and dark death lie upon the land, that sin is rampant in every place a man may set his foot, that the end of days is in view. You are wanted, master, you are needed sorely! Your holy word will come as food to the starving, as clear water to those who die of thirst in the sun of noonday! Master, the world is waiting for you to save it from destruction, from perdition: it waits for you and none other! 'The table has been set and the food is placed out.' Master, why do you refuse the invitation?"

My brother coughed and struggled to recover from the fit. He tried to speak but could not. At last, gasping for breath, he said in a whisper, "I understand you, brother. Believe me when I say that I understand you fully. I know that you wish me to stand before the world . . . to open my embrace to all mankind. I know . . . I fathom . . . I comprehend. But I cannot heed your words . . . I cannot, do you hear? Much as I sympathize with your desire that I bear witness to the truth— openly, unabashedly, nakedly, before man and God—in the holy city, on the steps of the sacred sanctuary itself . . . I cannot accede to your wish . . . until—until—" The "master" began to cough and choke once again.

"Until what?" I said.

"Until God gives me—a sign . . ."

"What sign, master, what sign? What sign do you await that God has not already given you? He—in His infinite wisdom—has blessed you with vision and with voice, with dream and with inspiration! What more do you want? What else do you need?"

My brother put up his hands. "Enough," he said hoarsely. "You mean well, my loyal servant, but I am weary . . . very weary . . ."

"You are weary," I said. "Yes, most assuredly you are weary. You are worn out because you are muzzled, master, because your way is hedged about . . . because your speech is strangled in your throat! You are tired because the sons of man do not know who and what you are! That is precisely why I beg you—I beseech you to go to Jerusalem and to the Temple and there receive the homage and the acclaim that are rightfully yours! Master, listen to me—for I know whereof I speak."

My brother shook his head. "Enough," he said, with the annoyance that had become all too prevalent of late. "I can bear no more! Leave me in peace!"

I was silent. "As you wish, master," I said after a time. I rose. There was nothing more to say. My brother curled up on the ground. Beside him lay the woman, groaning in her sleep. Ranged along the windrow were the disciples, dreaming of the fruit of heaven or the wine of earth—it was hard to say which. Like dogs, they found comfort in slumber. But I was no dog . . .

I remembered the hut—it was lowest on the mountain slope. Without knocking, I pushed the lopsided door in. The crone was deaf—she must have been a hundred—and I had to go up to her and tap her shoulder before she noticed me. One eye stared at me; the other had gone to join Quaestoris. She had been eating by the oil lamp and her face was smeared with fat. Little bones and stringlike tails littered the floor about her bare, filth-encrusted feet—they must have been rats she had roasted.

"What is it?" she croaked.

"The paste," I said. "The paste that glows."

She shrugged. "I have none."

"I want some, Granny."

She sucked her fingers and spat a tiny, curved nail to the earthen floor. "There's no more left. No more."

I held up a gold coin. She reached up for it, but I drew it back.

"The paste, Granny—the paste that shines in the night."

"One moment, noble priest."

"Hurry! I haven't time."

Muttering, she burrowed in a pile of rags in the corner. She brought me a small vial which I opened and put to my nose. A terrible stench came forth: it was the paste—just as I remembered it from the days of my childhood.

"The coin . . . Give me the coin."

"Do you really want it?"

"You have the paste . . . Give me the coin."

"Beg for it, Granny!"

"The coin, you stinking priest: give me the coin—"

"Beg!"

"The coin! Have mercy!"

"I said beg!"

Groaning, the old woman imitated a dog on its hind legs. I laughed and tossed a copper coin into the dung of the floor. As she scratched for it with her bonelike fingers, I spat on her matted gray hair and left. Over the mountain of my childhood and youth, the stars flickered and flashed. If my brother wanted a sign from God, I thought as I descended the path that my feet knew perfectly after all the years, then he should have a sign from God. And who would be a better messenger than I?

Once outside of the village, I bedaubed myself with the phosphorescent paste—my hands, my arms, my face—and wrapped my cloak about my head like a cowl. As my brother slept beside his woman, I approached him silently through the citrus grove. Stretched out flat on my belly, I called his name repeatedly through a hollow log until I heard him stir.

"Who calls me?" he muttered.

"It is I."

"Who are you?"

"An angel of the Lord. Can you hear me plainly?"

"I hear you . . . I hear your voice. But I cannot see you . . . How do I know you are not the devil's agent? Let me look upon your face, if the Lord God has indeed sent you."

I had expected as much and was prepared. I stood up—at a good distance from him and half obscured by the cypresses—and let him see my glowing, cowled face and my hands.

At once he uttered a cry and said, "Lord God, you have heard the prayer of my heart! You have sent a sign unto me that I might know

Thy awful presence! God of Israel, Thy will be done! Command me and I shall obey."

I answered him in three words: "Go to Jerusalem!

In the morning, when first the sun's scarlet foam washed over the flank of the mountain on which I had been born, I heard my brother's footsteps approach me. I closed my eyes and pretended to sleep. He grasped me and shook me. "Wake up, wake up!" he cried.

"What is it, brother? What's wrong?"

"Nothing is wrong, brother. All is right. I have had a sign from God. It came to me during the night. Brother, the hour of the Lord is at hand. We must gather together our band of believers and together ascend to the holy city. There is no time to spare. God must not be kept waiting. As I have said many times over: the man for whom God must wait . . . will himself be kept waiting by God."

I sat bolt upright and said, "Brother, you have heard what I told you!"

And he said in reply, "No. I have heard what the Holy One, blessed be His name, has told me!"

So we rose up, the lot of us, the "master" and his woman and the number of his disciples, and we quitted the valley of my birth and of my childhood and we made our way to Bethlehem, where my brother claimed to have been born and raised, and even unto Bethany and thence unto the mountains in whose bosom Jerusalem nestles as in the mystic splendor of the ages. The sky above us was as clear as is the water of a river at its very source—not the print of a single cloud was upon its skin; the sun shone from it as a fountain of delight that splashes merrily upon fair, paved stones; the pines girded about the city's walls and climbing her approaches sparkled with the dew of morning as we arrived; the branches of the firs glistened with the dew of the creation: and I spoke all of this into my brother's ears as we walked, but if he heard or understood without hearing I did not know, for he was silent and withdrawn into the secret recesses of himself. We journeyed together, all of us as a band, walking single file at the side of the road of ascent, hugging the flank of the mountain as we went. My brother went first, wearing about his head the crown of almond blossoms I had woven for him that morning; after him plodded the woman, going with great difficulty and wearing the fear of death in her face; then I walked, near enough to my brother that I might speak to him when I chose, though he gave not a sign of hearing me, and with my heart rejoicing as I beheld the venerable City of David from whose shining-stoned ramparts a new power would now be given me —a power than none could take away from me though the race of man endure ten thousand years; and behind me, bringing up the rear as befitted them, were the disciples—dim, sold men, grim-visaged men. a herd of self-made sheep, self-decreed marionettes; a troop of self-willed pawns. When we neared the fringes of the capital, which washed like lava into the crevices of the rocks and splashed down upon the slopes of rock, a squad of the city's own guard force, Herod's elite corps, in burnished armor of silver and with shields of copper that were embossed with lions of gold, rode down to meet our caravan. And their young officer, whose horse pranced proudly out ahead of them, called out unto us: "Halt in the name of Herod the king and in the name of Pontius Pilate the governor! Answer wherefore you seek to pass through the gates of the holy city of Jerusalem."

I drew near to my brother and whispered, "Let me speak to him, master, for this is work cut out for my tongue and for no other! Let me talk to him and state our case—or else we shall suffer arrest, torture and imprisonment. Let me have my say, brother, or the word of God shall be silenced and ground into the dust."

My brother nodded, and I went forward directly and spoke out to the lieutenant of the guards, saying, "Come aside with me, sir, that I may converse with you in private."

And his lip curled and he said, "What foolishness is this, that you ask for a private audience? Do you mock me then?"

And I replied, "No, sir, I do not mock you—God forbid that I should mock an officer of the elite guard! Nor is it whim or foolishness on my part, sir, but a matter of the gravest importance which requires that we converse alone, out of the earshot of the others. With your permission, sir, I request that you come with me to the other side of the road. And if what I have to say still seems mockery or folly to you, you may cast me into the valley below that I may be dashed upon the rocks and die!"

And the lieutenant was amazed at the words I spoke and at the

484

earnestness of my tone, so he turned his horse to the farther side of the road that hangs over the deep ravine marking the western approach to the city.

And I wasted not a moment but looked up at him and said, "Sir, I have summoned you here to inform you that the man who leads this company, the man who wears the crown of almond blossoms like a king, is a dangerous man—a threat to the government and the people of Judea!"

Sitting straight in his saddle, the lieutenant frowned, obviously disturbed. "Then why—why do you travel with this man?"

I smiled. "To betray him, of course. What other reason would I have?"

"I see," said the officer. "Then I must place him under arrest—and his company as well. If what you say is true, they will all get their just deserts."

I shook my head. "No," I said. "You must not arrest him."

The officer was puzzled. "And why not?"

"Because, sir, arresting him now would accomplish nothing. What weight could my miserable testimony carry with the authorities? Who would possibly believe me when I told my story? What evidence could I marshal that would convict this evil man, this devilish traitor? What would be the outcome except that he might spend a little time in detention and then be released for new treason? No, you must wait."

"Wait? How is that possible? What are you driving at?"

"With your permission, only listen to me. This man plans to go to the Holy Temple. He will be there tomorrow at noon, when the holiday crowds are gathering. He will mount the steps and he will speak. What he has to say will incriminate him beyond the shadow of all doubt! When he opens his vile mouth, he will convict himself! Be certain that the proper officials are there to hear and to record. Then you may take him, and with the evidence he himself has given you mete out the fitting punishment—and believe me, good lieutenant, it can only be the most severe . . . when the full story is known it can only be death." I touched the flank of the officer's mount. "As for his followers" —I snapped my fingers—"they are fly-dirt, no more. They are less than nothing. It isn't worth bothering with them. He alone is the man the government must concern itself with: he alone is the enemy of the State. I must entreat you, sir, to inform the authorities at once of what

485

you have heard from me. Once in the city, we can never leave it without the government's knowledge. Tell the officials that tomorrow—at noon—they will have their man."

"I accept your words in good faith," said the lieutenant. "But if you do not speak the truth—beware! You and your fellow travelers will be under our watchful eye all of the time. Remember."

"Tomorrow my words will be proven!"

The lieutenant nodded, rode back to his men, and gave my brother permission to lead the caravan onward into the city. As we trudged along the final stretch of road leading to the gate, my brother turned his head and asked, "Why did you snap your fingers at the officer of the guards when you talked to him?"

"To show him, master," I replied, "how easy it would be for him to enter into the kingdom of heaven if he but believed on you."

My brother's smile was full and radiant. "There is no man closer to my heart than you," he said.

And I bowed my head humbly and was silent.

We slept that night in the Street of the Beggars, a cul-de-sac in the most run-down part of the city. The next morning, a Thursday, I rose before the sun came up, before all the rest, and made whatever preparations were necessary. When I returned to the gutter where the others were, the sun was already up; I wakened each one with the words "Blessed is he who riseth to the service of the Lord!" Many months ago, when things were not as bad as they were at present, the woman had sewn a new robe for the "master" out of cloth given to him by a merchant who had been moved to tears by one of his sermons; she had kept it hidden on her person all this time, and now she brought it forth, saying as she held it up for everyone to view, "Behold the raiment of our master, who has come to earth to save us all!" And we disciples said, "Amen!" And the "master" was pleased and commanded that water from the cistern down at the end of the street be brought; and I went with a bowl and there was indeed rainwater in the cistern and I brought it in the bowl back to the woman. When the others had stripped his old clothes from him and cast them aside into the street, the woman washed my brother's limbs until, as I commented, his skin "glowed with the freshness of the stars." Then did the woman dress him in his robe of the purest white, which fell to his feet "like the fall of virgin snow." And then I gave her of the oil I said I had begged for the purpose from a kind Samaritan, but had in reality purchased with my jewel money—and she did anoint my brother with it as I intoned in a whisper that brought tears to the eyes of all assembled: "Blessed art thou in thy anointment, O Master, O Savior, O King of the Jews and of all Mankind!" To which the others said, "Amen!" And then I took a wreath of almond blossoms that I had woven that morning before any of them were up and placed it as a crown upon my brother's head. And lo, my brother stood before us, every inch a king, every inch a savior, every inch a messenger of God; and he smiled—and the beauty of his smile did pierce us so that we went down upon our knees before his person and wept aloud. And all of the poor from the Street of the Beggars and the other streets around it, who had heard the tidings, came to see my brother and to "bask in the majesty of his presence," as many put it. And my brother stretched forth his arms to the crowd and called them his "flock" and his "lambs" and he did bless them and then turned, as I signaled him, to walk in the direction of the Holy Temple.

And so he went, and so the crowd that followed him grew larger every step of the way, for the people were curious to know what manner of man he was and what he would do and what he would say. And when his procession came to the first intersection of the streets, a man burst through the press of the people, and weeping, gave him the reins of a white mule and then fell upon his knees and called out blessing to my brother. And I drove the crowd back, with the aid of the other disciples, and helped my brother to mount the mule, which was as white as the skin of the lily, and to ride triumphantly ahead; and the "master" and all who were witness to the scene thought that the mule was a gift of love and acclaim, and their hearts were glad: but I knew that I had bought the mule that very morning and paid the owner to give it over so. Riding the mule, in his white robe and with his crown, my brother was a magnificent sight, and the people shouted at him from the rooftops and from windows and even from the branches of trees: "Hail, the king! Hail, the King of the Jews who comes from the throne of God the Father to save our souls; Hail to him who is crown king of our souls in Jerusalem!" And the chant pursued him and was taken up wherever he passed, for there were those I had paid in good coin to shout the refrain, to start it going and to repeat it until it caught the fancy of all who heard it, and they shouted it as well, scarcely knowing what they said or whom they welcomed in such a fashion. But my brother was pleased, was drunk with the pleasure, and—I could see—believed with all his heart that it was as the people cried out. And thus we came even unto the Temple of Solomon, whose marble pillars stood a hundred feet and more in height and were so great in girth that ten men joining hands could not reach around their span; whose roof of golden tiles was like a water-fall into which the burning sun itself had plunged; and whose orna-mental lions were bigger than any elephants I had ever seen and were carved entire of ivory, with manes of jade a dozen feet in length. And while I held the mule steady, my brother dismounted and with head held high and a look that was dark and fierce, even commanding, walked through the mob, which fell back in awe and fear of him, and then mounted the Temple's steps of pink Jerusalem stone—each of which was as wide as a river between its banks—until he stood at their head. And then he faced the throng before him and put up his hands and—wonder of wonders!—the multitude was silent and amazed at its silence; and again, as I knew, it was the men whom I hired that helped make the silence.

And when my brother opened his mouth to speak, I saw from his face that the trance would come upon him soon and I shouted up to him that he should begin and he heard my voice and said to the vast assembly: "Citizens of Jerusalem . . . Children of Israel . . . Sons of Man . . . I come to you on this day . . . as God's own messenger to you . . . as God's—own son."

And the crowd murmured and then was silent.

"I come to you . . . as the only begotten Son of God . . . born not of the loins of man but of immaculate conception . . . and nurtured by the glory of God on high. I am here before you . . . that I may bring to you the word of my Father in heaven, whose Holy Ghost fills the universe entire even from one end until the other." And here, in a strange, high-pitched voice, he began to chant the psalm "The heavens declare the glory of God" but left off abruptly and began to speak again, saying, "Sons of Man . . . hear me when I tell you that there is no cause for the evil that afflicts us, as blight does the crop in the field, but that there is evil . . . within ourselves. Judea . . . Judea is steeped in sin: she wallows in the mud of iniquity as does the ox in the mud of a river that has overflowed its banks. And the hand of Rome . . . the hand of Rome which holds her in an iron grip by her collar as does a master his mastiff . . . that hand is a bloody hand, a diseased hand—the hand of a thief and a tyrant! Brothers, brothers . . . Rome is an asp and Judea a worm; and the despots who made them so lepers of the soul!" My brother's arms opened wide: "Think on it, brothers . . . only think on it! How does the grapevine wither . . . How is the pomegranate consumed by rot . . . How are the wine casks smashed open and the wine spilled into dung . . . How does the granary burn! This is Judea, brothers . . . and this will be Rome! For I ask you, where is the care of the child and the concern for the old man? Why does the beggar wander without succor and why are the homeless scorned? Why is the widow mocked and the orphan abused in his loneliness? Who stops to bind the wounds of the sick man? And who assists the lame man on the road? And who will give the blind a hand and lead him away from the precipice? For I ask you, what does it profit that a man dwells in a palace of ivory and gold and his own inner house is empty? What is it that nothing can enjoy . . . but nothing? How does a man build up a fortress to stop his enemies from outside and death . . . will claim him from within? Verily, I say unto you: Rome is a savage wolf and Judea a jackal . . . and the men who are their citizens smeared over with sin! Their spirits are withered as is the grass in the drought: their bodies are as good casks, but the wine of the spirit leaks through nevertheless and is lost in the dust . . . The dust soaks it up and it is gone forever. For I ask you, wherefore has metal become more precious to you than flesh? How is stone more dear to you than a man's soul? Where is the mercy without which you are as clay of the pit? Where is the compassion without which you are rock?"

My brother's face was gray as ash; his cheeks twitched without surcease; sweat rolled down his forehead and face, splashing onto his white robe. He looked up at the sky and at that moment a great flock of white doves rose up into its flawless blue vaults as if on his signal— I had paid for that too. And my brother saw and cried out in a shrill voice, "A sign! A sign from my Father in heaven whose Holy Ghost fills the whole world like a mighty wind in the sail of a ship! People of Jerusalem! Children of Israel! Sons of Man! Heed the signs and cast off the yoke of Rome! Strike away the fetters of Judea! My children . . . my flock . . . my people! Turn your backs on the Princes of the earth, who would enslave you, and open your arms and hearts of the salvation of the Lord! Of what use are earthly kings except to oppress and destroy the people? Of what purpose are the lords of the land except to grind their subjects into the dust? It is time . . . high time, oh sons of man . . . to hurl the mighty down from their seats of vanity, the powerful from their thrones of arrogance! The reign of the haughty must end . . . It must end—must—" My brother's voice faltered. His eyes rolled wildly; his fingers clutched at empty air. The spell was coming on him. He would not last long. But it was fine. He had said enough—quite enough. "My children . . . " he began. "Listen to me . . . my flock . . . my dearly beloved . . . my lambs—lambs—" He staggered down a step or two, waving his arms and fighting for balance. "My people—banish tyrants—my God—my—" He spun around and reeled down several steps and then pitched full forward into the arms of two disciples who had rushed headlong up the stairs to catch him as he fell.

A great sigh of relief went up from the multitude when he was caught.

How touching! The man of God struck by God on the stone of God! How very moving! The crowd surged forward to see him better as the disciples bore him down. I, too, struggled to move forward until a strong hand clutched my shoulder so tightly that I winced. A fat, heavy-jowled face with a chin overgrown with fiery scar tissue thrust itself at me.

"Don't be alarmed," said the man's voice. "I know all about you."

"What—do you know about me?"

The man laughed. "Don't worry . . . I shan't hurt you, my friend. The lieutenant of the city guard. Remember him? Well, he talked to my superiors yesterday. They sent me to find you—and to hear your 'leader.' My name is Nachash Ben Arsi. I work for—internal security."

"You will arrest him?"

"Of course."

"Now?"

"No, not now."

"But why not now?"

Nachash Ben Arsi's face became even surlier, even uglier when he smiled. "Because," he said, pressing his lips to my ear, "because of the crowd. They're sorry for him . . . They may even sympathize with him. If we moved against him now . . . there would be trouble. It would spoil the Holy Days. Do you understand?"

"Yes . . . of course. But when?"

"Tonight. Late. When the populace is at Seder table." Nachash Ben Arsi grinned. "They will disperse now . . . They will melt away in peace, for they must prepare for Passover. And then tonight . . . in silence . . . we will take your friend. It's better that way, much better."

I nodded.

"Tell me, dear friend, do you have influence over him?"

"I do."

"Can you get him to Gethsemane tonight?"

"I can."

"Good. We'll arrest him there."

"So be it."

Nachash Ben Arsi squeezed my arm. "Tell me, my friend," he said, "why do you do it? Why do you betray him?" He began to wheeze as he spoke. "Can you tell me why?"

I was silent. Then I said, "Because if I did not hate him . . . I would love him."

I hired a loft above a carpenter's shop—I told them all the carpenter had offered it as a sign of his faith and devotion—for the "master" made it known that he wanted to mark the Passover. I thought it a good idea—I felt it would be an interesting note to the myth I was creating about him. Actually the service was dull, for the "master" seemed ill and had withdrawn into the illness: it was my belief that the trance was still upon him, that he had never emerged from it. The woman was deeply concerned; she hovered about him constantly, and when he upset his cup of wine, spilling it over the cloth of his table and over his new white robe— as if it were a great splash of blood—she wept aloud.

"Why are you weeping?"

"It's the master."

"What about him?"

"He does not look well. I—I see—" Her voice broke.

"What do you see?"

"I see the mark of death on his face. Violent death. Not death by his own hand, nor death by the hand of God: but death at the hands of man." She shuddered. "I see the gallows—or the cross."

I patted her shoulder. "All will be well," I said.

The disciples, reclining at the rude table which the carpenter had set up for us that afternoon as a part of the bargain—he had insisted on an additional fee for it and I had refused and won out—looked on sullenly as the "master" attempted to lead the service after his fashion. Some of them were drunk, others morose—the exultant mood of the Temple speech had deserted them completely. I looked them over and found little to redeem them in my sight. They were a mean lot, a pack of sluggards actually, who could be led about by their noses without much effort on the leader's part. Only one of them showed the least promise. His name was Simon, though he had been renamed Peter by the "master" one day when the whim seized my brother to do so. I thought to make a fascinating point about the new name in my myth, for the name Peter had its root in the Latin *petros*, or rock. Simon Peter was lean, with wiry black hair, a large sharply tapered nose and a chin that —as I said—"fell away from the world." He was cunning, falsely abject, skilled at winning people over, and had inside him more venom and blind hatred than any man I had ever encountered—except for myself. Though I had always treated the other disciples with disdain, I had reserved a measure of respect for Simon Peter. I had always felt that one day he would prove useful. And that day had almost arrived.

It was no trouble at all to get the "master" to go to Gethsemane—he was as docile as a lamb—and the disciples followed readily enough. My brother babbled all the way there—he was almost completely incoherent—and I pretended to listen, though actually I was reviewing my plans. The night was beautiful—a magic April night that breathed of the beginning of time. We left the city behind us and the sound of human voices. Over our heads the stars shone like silver foam on the crest of a black ocean. A faint breeze blew down from the west, gently stirring the silvery leaves of the olive trees. The garden itself was exquisite—it had a lush, haunted look about it and brought Eden inescapably to mind. We sat among the almond and magnolia trees, with the Mount of Olives rising over us darkly like a giant hand bent on plucking the moon from its nest like an egg. The "master" rambled on. Beside him, the woman stroked his cheek or forehead. The disciples sprawled on the grass, half attending or staring listlessly into space or snoozing. I heard a noise and slipped away. Nachash Ben Arsi stepped out from behind a tree.

"Is everything set?" he said.

"Everything is ready," I said.

"Then we'll take him."

"Wait one moment," I said.

"What is it?"

"Do you know who he is?" I said.

"Of course I know. I heard him this afternoon." Nachash Ben Arsi uttered a coarse little laugh: "There'll be quite a case against him. Sedition. Incitement to riot. Slandering the government. Preaching open revolution. What more do you want?"

"But do you know who—he is?" I said.

"What are you talking about?"

I took his arm. "Do you remember the prison episode—the 'raid' on Herod's fortress prison?"

"Of course. But what—?"

"There was a prisoner among them who—who . . . "

"Out with it!"

"—who was close to the—to the infamous minister of war."

Nachash Ben Arsi waved a hand. "But he was harmless. They decided as much and let him go."

"This is the man."

Nachash Ben Arsi shrugged. "So what? He was cleared. What does it matter?"

"They were wrong," I said.

"Wrong? How were they wrong?"

"I have heard him talk. I have overheard him plan. It became clear that he wanted to carry out the war minister's coup . . . to reestablish *Patish* . . . "

Nachash Ben Arsi turned pale. "Are you—certain of this?"

"It is my business to be certain."

"Then I must inform the Romans of this."

"Yes."

"Then surely he will die."

"Yes."

493

"Without delay."

"Yes." I dropped Nachash Ben Arsi's arm. "Give me a moment. I want to bid him—farewell."

"As you wish . . ."

My brother looked up at me, his face serene and trusting—he reminded me of Elazar. I bent over him and kissed his cheek: the skin was dry like parchment and thin—almost insubstantial.

"Are you going away?" he asked.

"No."

"Then why did you kiss me so?"

"You are."

Tears sparkled in his eyes. "Am I going far?"

"Very far," I said.

When they had taken my brother, I drew Simon Peter aside and told him what had to be done. He had heavy lidded eyes, and he stared at me as I talked as if he were not entirely awake, but I knew he both heard and recorded every word I spoke in his calculating mind. I saw at once that I had recruited a schemer who had only been waiting for his chance to emerge. Once, when I paused for a moment, he said, "Did the master instruct you so? Or was it God?"

I smiled. "Do I question you about your motivation?"

"No."

"Then do not ask me about mine."

Simon Peter proved effective in dealing with the other disciples, who relied on him and feared him. He also managed to quiet the woman, who had been weeping sorely. She was inconsolable, but he persuaded her to keep her grief to herself. By midnight, when my brother had been gone several hours, all were asleep except the woman, who shivered against a tree where she had curled herself, Simon Peter and me. We talked for a number of hours and understood each other well. I offered nothing I felt he could not accept; he did not ask for what I could not offer. In short, we struck a bargain.

Then he turned away and slept.

I lay on my back and looked at the sky. The stars were pale, weak: they fluttered blindly like moths. I dropped off to sleep. But I did not dream—I did not dare.

The cocks crowed. Wildly, exultantly, it seemed to me. I had never heard cocks crow so. Perhaps they celebrated the Passover with their human owners. Perhaps they heralded the death of a man and the birth of a new god. Pilate's men did their work efficiently and well. Simon Peter and I stood on the slope of Golgotha and watched from a respectful distance. Nachash Ben Arsi was there, but he stayed apart and did not speak to us. His arms were folded across his chest and he looked very official. The Roman soldiers were unconcerned. They worked unhurriedly and even had time for a bit of sport: they sliced an ear from each of the two criminals crucified alongside my brother—much as Ichavod had liked to do. For some strange reason they did not touch my brother. The strokes of the hammer on the heads of the spikes rolled out from the hill of skulls, dropped into the valley, and drifted toward the sleeping city. Each blow struck was a blow against Rome, a blow against Jerusalem: they would be at each other's throats for centuries over this event when I completed my work. I smiled. Each blow struck was a blow for me—a blow for the power that was beyond the power I, or any man, had ever known or would know. Poor soul—my brother! He went up on the cross easily. He expired quickly, the flies sticking to the paste of sweat and grime that covered his wan face. So little of his blood came out. He babbled for a time—like an infant, I thought —the froth collected at the corners of his mouth, and then he was gone. Like that! Like the snap of my fingers on the ascent to Jerusalem! The captain of the Roman detail certified his death, spitting as he climbed down the ladder propped against the crucifix. Then Nachash Ben Arsi went up and certified that he was dead. The Roman and the Jew exchanged death certificates.

My brother's life history was ended.

His myth began.

That same afternoon we were allowed to take the corpse down. Simon Peter chose four disciples, and they bore the body to a cave not far away. We took the woman along to show her that her lover was dead. The sun was on its way to hell as we trudged along the dusty road; the flies were thick. Overhead, the cheated kites circled soundlessly. On the way, the woman wept bitterly, and we had to stop once for a disciple to throw up and several times for his comrades to urinate. The body had swelled enormously, even in the short time it was dead, and it had turned yellow and black and it stank. We were all relieved to shut it into the cave and seal the tomb with a rock.

That night, Simon Peter and I came back, and with a large branch that we employed as a lever pried the rock away from the mouth of the crypt. We removed my brother's hideous, oozing corpse and bore it a distance into the wilderness. Of dry wood we built a fire, kindled it and thrust the remains of my brother into it. As the flames raged in their own secret fury, we gathered more fuel and fed the conflagration until the body was burned to ash. We scattered the ash, and whatever bones were left we buried in the earth. Then we heaped earth upon the embers of the fire until it was out, and we scattered its ashes and we were through. Then we left.

And I said to Simon Peter as we walked, "Now the Truth is dead. And the Lie will live."

And Simon Peter was silent.

And in his silence was his confirmation.

And on Monday morning we brought the woman and the four disciples who had carried the dead body of my brother to the cave, which Simon Peter and I had shut up again with the boulder after the fire was dispersed. Straining together, we shoved the rock aside and peered within; and lo, the cave was empty.

And I cried out, "God the Father has taken His only begotten Son to heaven: He has gathered His Son to His Bosom, and verily, His Son will live with God forever!"

And all fell upon their knees before the mouth of the cave and wept aloud and cried out, "Amen!"

And the woman, together with six disciples, I sent away to Jerusalem to wait until they were needed. And Simon Peter, together with the others, I took with me to the desert wilderness of Judah. And I took with us mules and supplies and writing materials. And I gathered my crew together in our retreat and spoke unto them, saying, "Each of you will now put down the words I say for him to write, for verily will this story live and gather life to it, as does a fistful of snow when it is rolled down a slope; and from this story will come power as it has never been experienced before by man on the earth."

And I thought: I will tell you words that will slide out like snakes from beneath the stones; and they will go forth and poison the wells of men. And this will be my revenge: on Rome, on Jerusalem, on mankind, on my brother who was sacrificed on the altar of my hate . . . and on myself. And verily I say unto you that I will be measure of the world . . .

And I turned to the first disciple of the four and commanded him to take up his writing materials, and he did as I bade him and when he was ready, I spoke unto him, saying, "In the beginning was the Word . . ."

About the Author

CHAYYM ZELDIS was born in Buffalo, New York, in 1927. He attended the University of Michigan on a creative writing scholarship for two years. While there, he won an Avery Hopwood Award in poetry. In 1948, during the War of Independence, he settled in Israel. He lived on various agricultural settlements, including five years on a *kibbutz,* and worked in many branches of farming. He served in the Israeli armed forces in the Sinai campaign of 1956.

Back in the United States in 1958, he graduated from the New School for Social Research, winning the John Day Novel Award there. He is the author of a previous novel, *Golgotha,* and a volume of verse, *Seek Haven.* His fiction and poetry have appeared in *Commentary, Accent, Midstream* and other publications.

He is married and has four children.